NIGHT AND DAY

NIGHT AND DAY

JULY 1, 1937   6d.

NIGHT AND DAY

EDITED

AND WITH AN INTRODUCTION BY

CHRISTOPHER HAWTREE

PREFACE BY

GRAHAM GREENE

CHATTO & WINDUS

LONDON

Published in 1985 by
Chatto & Windus
40 William IV Street, London WC2N 4DF

British Library Cataloguing in Publication Data

Night and day.
1. English literature—20th century
I. Hawtree, Christopher
820.8'00912   PR1148

ISBN 0–7011–2996–4

Printed by
Redwood Burn Limited
Trowbridge, Wiltshire

CONTENTS

Drawing by John Nash

ACKNOWLEDGEMENTS

I am very grateful to Graham Greene and Selwyn Powell for their memories of those extraordinary months in 1937, and to Mrs Joyce Marks for talking about her husband: I am saddened that he and Ian Parsons did not see this version of the magazine which they brought into existence.

The work of Jan Dalley at Chatto & Windus has been invaluable: I am considerably indebted to her for both editorial guidance and the way in which she prepared a book which presented complications at every turn.

I am also grateful to Dr Barnardo's, Dr J. A. Edwards (Keeper of Archives and Manuscripts at the University of Reading Library), Dr Desmond Flower, Walter Goetz, Ian Jeffrey, Peter Probyn, Alan Ross, Dr Michael Tilby, Derek Weber, and Dr Susan Wharton. The staff at the London Library and Battersea Park Library were as helpful as ever; those at the British Museum Reading Room put me to some inconvenience by going on strike at that time of the day when I find it easiest to visit.

We are, of course, grateful indeed for the willingness and enthusiasm with which authors and illustrators allowed their work to be reprinted. Although assiduous efforts have been made to trace every contributor, a few have been impossible to locate. The editor and publishers would be delighted to hear from any of these.

C.H.

PREFACE

'Under the shadow of a war
What can we do that matters?'

On 1 July 1937, when *Night And Day* appeared on the bookstalls for the first time, the shadow was very dark and perhaps that accounts for the rather strenuous determination of the editors, John Marks and myself, to make the weekly light and amusing at all costs. The Minutes of the Week were written by Peter Fleming and the influence of the *New Yorker* was very evident during the first months. That influence was fading, we were becoming ourselves, at the moment when death struck on 23 December 1937.

It was for all four of us who made up the staff a happy experience. I cannot believe that any paper has been so completely free from personal antagonisms – something I could not say later when for a while I was literary editor of the *Spectator*. John Marks, who when he invited me to join him I knew only as the excellent translator of Céline's *Voyage au Bout de la Nuit*, and I were co-editors rather than editor and literary editor: a younger man, Selwyn Powell, the fine art editor, and perhaps the best features of the paper were the drawings, especially those by Paul Crum who was killed a few years later at Dunkirk.

Once a week the four of us met to look at Selwyn Powell's selection. There was seldom any difference of opinion, and I don't believe that any paper – even the *New Yorker* at its best – has obtained the level reached by *Night and Day* in its comic drawings. Sometimes John Marks appeared a little jaded – this was when Céline was on one of his frequent visits to London; he always insisted on a late night with John at the Windmill Theatre where (a strange quirk of taste) he enjoyed the very modest English strip-tease far more than the extreme forms he could see in Paris.

The role of Patrick Ransome was undefined. He had a room to himself, a wheel-chair (for he was a cripple), he owned shares in the paper, and he was half-believed to be a watch-dog for the publishers. The sound of wheels approaching one's room as one talked to a contributor was not always welcome, but in fact he never interfered and his handicap never damaged his sense of humour. I remember after a rather alcoholic lunch running him at top speed in his chair down Cecil Court while he shrieked at the astonished shoppers with laughter and fear.

I was very proud of my regular team of critics – Evelyn Waugh (books), Elizabeth Bowen (theatre), Herbert Read (detective stories), Osbert Lancaster (art), Hugh Casson (architecture), and A. J. A. Symons, the biographer of Corvo (restaurants), and it amused me to include certain rather neglected sports – swimming, croquet, all-in wrestling, snooker.

It's sad to think how few of our regular contributors are left to remember *Night and Day* – Anthony Powell, V. S. Pritchett, Feliks Topolski, Malcolm Muggeridge, Osbert Lancaster, Hugh Casson – but is there any paper which can rival our roll of honour? It reads like the death of a whole literary generation: Evelyn Waugh, Elizabeth Bowen, Herbert Read, William Empson, Nicolas Bentley, John Betjeman, Cyril Connolly, Stevie Smith, A. J. A. Symons, John Hayward, Hugh Kingsmill, William Plomer.

Graham Greene

INTRODUCTION

'All the gossip was that Lydia [Keynes] thinks the *New Statesman* hopeless; much prefers *Night and Day*.'
Virginia Woolf, December 1937

In his celebrated review of Stephen Spender's autobiography Evelyn Waugh remarked that during the Thirties 'certain young men ganged up and captured the decade'. The notion of an Auden generation has since faded, and other contemporary writers, each of whom 'worked alone in quiet self-sufficiency', have assumed greater prominence. For the six months from July to December 1937 a number of them, sometimes in strange guises, did come together, in a remarkable weekly magazine. Although *Night and Day* has not yet found a place in the more orthodox literary histories, its contributors possessed a rare wit and humour which makes it perhaps the most entertaining periodical of the decade.

Chatto and Windus were already the publishers of two magazines in the Thirties, *World Review* and the *Geographical Magazine*. Both were regularly advertised in the third, *Night and Day*, which, as various publicity circulars said, was modelled to some extent on the *New Yorker* which had a fashionable English circulation at that time. With this it was hoped to find a lucrative market for the intelligent and witty entertainment which *Punch*, the *Bystander*, the *Humorist* and *Passing Show* failed to provide.

A need for such a magazine had long been felt in England. 'The world may be divided into those who enjoy *Punch* and those who enjoy the *New Yorker*,' observed Graham Greene in his contribution to the 1934 anthology *The Old School*. In 1936 Hugh Kingsmill wrote, after he and Malcolm Muggeridge had taken out an advertisement in *The Times* in the hope of encouraging a new paper, 'the critical press of England is in a poor state ... There is no critically humorous paper in England today. Nor is there any serious paper which has much, or any individuality. We live in an age which has kept the conventions without the convictions of the Victorians.'

Such hopes were viewed pessimistically by Harold Nicolson when he wrote to his friend Peter Fleming at *Night and Day* and bemoaned the amount of work which rendered 'it quite impossible for me to take on anything else. In any case I am not sure whether I approve of our trying to be witty instead of funny. I think England should face the fact that the best she can do in the way of jokes is *Punch* and Gilbert and Sullivan. This is a humil-iating thought but I like to face facts.' Waugh recalled an earlier, 1929 attempt to start such a paper 'that never materialised. Is yours soundly backed?'

Night and Day Magazines Limited, a company distinct from Chatto and Windus itself, was officially incorporated, 'somewhat fittingly perhaps, on April 1st 1937', as its Secretary, a barrister called Patrick Ransome, remarked to several of the shareholders. Among the first to express an interest was the local Inspector of Taxes, who wrote to discover 'the date to which the first accounts will be prepared'. Even if they did not envisage the Treasury's gaining much immediate benefit from their enterprise most shareholders must have been more optimistic than Peter Fleming. With characteristic aplomb, he bought 100 shares, and on 18 June wrote to Ian Parsons, the magazine's Managing Director and a partner of Chatto, and belatedly enclosed 'a cheque for £100 towards your well known swindle'. *Night and Day* owed its inception to the efforts of Ian Parsons, a publisher and scholar whose sympathies also embraced both Leavis and Bloomsbury.

This is hardly the place for lengthy financial analyses, but some details from the various unpublished archives will show the energy that went to make this long-cherished idea a reality.[1] Of the 19,000 shares issued about half were taken by the partners of Chatto and Windus, their relatives, or such associates as their printers, Raymond Hazell and Colonel Viney and William Maxwell at R. and R. Clark. Captain V. A. Cazalet M.P., of the Fairlawne Trust Ltd., which, with 3,500 shares, had the largest stake in the magazine, was Chairman until the pressure of his other work led him to resign.

It was decided to allow £3,000 for advertising, £2,500 of which would be devoted to the first three issues: £1,260 was to be spent on press advertising, £312 on posters in the Underground, £130 on bus fronts and £480 on sending out 100,000 circulars in the hope of stimulating annual subscriptions. £52.10s was spent on insurance by Lloyds' for libel costs up to £4,000. The advertisement manager, the 'excellent and indefatigable' W. G. Houghton who had been on *Vogue* and *Leisure*, reported that the situation was as 'good as could be expected at the time of the year' and it was decided to keep to the original plan of publishing in July. A leaflet, entitled *Snaring the Sophisticate*, outlined the desirability of advertising in the new magazine. 'Some are born sophisticated ... others acquire sophistication ... the vast majority have sophistication thrust upon them . . . By influencing the minority you reach the mass. By appealing to the ear of the born sophisticate – the man or woman who sponsors movements, invents fashions, coins the innumerable catchwords of modern society – you impose yourself upon the attention of that almost mythical being, the Average Consumer – you arouse the acquisitive, imitative instincts of the Ordinary Man.'

With such ideas in mind, there were long discussions about a name for the magazine. *Night and Day* was eventually chosen because it sounded well and had echoes of the sophisticated Cole Porter song. Before the first issue was published a complaint arrived from an unexpected quarter. Dr Barnardo's were annoyed by the inadvertent use of the name of their house journal, which thrives to this day, for the new magazine. 'After some discussion Mr Parsons was asked to write to the secretary in a firm yet tactful manner indicating the intention of the Company to proceed with their previous intention of using the title *Night and Day*.' Nothing more than a formal acknowledgement was received after that.

The magazine was launched with a cocktail party for 800 guests at the Dorchester on 30 June at six o'clock. A. P. Herbert made a christening speech. Each guest was given a numbered copy of the first issue, and a lottery was then drawn, the first prize being a copy signed by the contributors. The second prize was a year's subscription, the third prize was a subscription for six months: by sad irony these two prizes proved identical since the new venture was only to last for six months. Money troubles determined that the issue of 23 December was to be the last.

While the others were coping with administrative and business matters Graham Greene, the literary editor, John Marks, the features editor, and the art editor Selwyn Powell had assembled 'a strange mélange', as Anthony Powell has written, which 'synthesised pretty well'. Peter Fleming compiled the weekly pages of 'Minutes' under the name – a fairly well-kept secret – of Slingsby. (Slingsby Place, off Long Acre, was close to the magazine's offices in St Martin's Lane.) Although Peter Fleming, a distinct influence on the magazine, was famous as the best-selling author of such travel books as *Brazilian Adventure*, many of the contributors were not as well known as they were to become in post-war years. Now, when a run of the magazine fetches many hundreds of pounds, the discovery of the prize signed copy would doubtless excite transatlantic collectors to a fever.

A year before *Brighton Rock* eased his continuing debt to Heinemann, Graham Greene, then perhaps best known for *Stamboul Train* and *A Gun For Sale*, was extremely glad to have this regular job. Of the nine novels he had completed by 1937 two remain unpublished and he has chosen to suppress another two. His months on *Night and Day* were but a small part of one of the most diversely energetic literary lives: his work hardly needs further introduction here. His judicious editorial hand can be seen shaping the varied and unexpected material that he commissioned.

Like Greene's, the lives and works of many of the contributors – Osbert Lancaster, Herbert Read, Stevie Smith, Elizabeth Bowen, Christopher Isherwood, Anthony Powell, V. S. Pritchett among many others – have become so well known and documented elsewhere that they need no further explanation in this introduction.

A lesser-known figure, but none the less important in the day-to-day running of the magazine, was Selwyn Powell. He was already well known to many of the people involved in the planning of the magazine and was asked to be art editor while he was working in a similar capacity at Faber and Faber, having decided against a career as an architect. Circumstances became such that he later found himself trying for a job on *Punch*, and was told that *Night and Day* had 'scared them stiff'. During the Forties, after serving in the Navy and then a time on *Picture Post*, he joined the rather different territory of the *Geographical Magazine*, of which he became editor for a number of years at the end of the Fifties. He replaced 'Supercharger' as *Night and Day*'s motoring correspondent. 'But I know nothing of the technicalities,' he told Greene. 'No matter. You can drive, can't you? And write?' Each weekend dealers delivered motor cars, from sports models to Opels: a welcome change from review copies of books.

John Marks, 'a fervent hispanophile' as he remarked to one reader, was brought up in Borneo and Spain. He went up to Magdalene, Cambridge, in the later Twenties, where he edited a humorous incarnation of *Granta* and met some of the people, such as Ian Parsons and Alistair Cooke, later connected with *Night and Day*. After a year in Madrid, he returned to England and was employed as a reader by Chatto and then Cassell, as well as making translations from French and Spanish novels and having a stint as the *New Statesman*'s film critic. During the war he was one of many to find himself in the Ministry of Information. Later seconded to the BBC, he pioneered broadcasts to the Iberian peninsula and joined the press office of the Embassy in Lisbon. In 1943 he became *The Times*'s correspondent in Madrid, a post which he held for ten years until he was sacked by the newspaper's austere-minded new editor, Sir William Haley. He became Night Editor at United Press International in Lisbon for some years and then worked as a freelance until his death from cancer at the age of 58 in 1967.

Desmond Flower has recalled the Spanish Foreign Minister's remark that John Marks spoke the language as Cervantes wrote it, 'and although he spoke lightly this carried the mark of truth, and it expressed admirably the real sense of Spain which lay behind such superb speech'. Although so much of his life was concerned with news, 'John was truly a writer. . . . He had deep wisdom, of which he gave so liberally to others that in some ways he almost had too little left for himself.' Of his one book, *To the Bullfight*, Ernest Hemingway said that it was 'the best book on the subject – after mine'. At the same time as editing *Night and Day*, Marks, to the exasperation of publishers on both sides of the Atlantic, was struggling to keep to schedule with his translation of Céline's *Mort à*

Crédit.[2] 'Always in a hurry, always slightly behind,' continued Desmond Flower, 'he changed completely in the presence of people he knew, with whom he was both relaxed and relaxing.' 'We worked in an ideal partnership,' recalled Graham Greene in 1983, 'and I don't remember any differences between us.'

John Marks's letters from the *Night and Day* period reveal a man of extraordinary fortitude, good humour and kindness. 'I look forward to further tussles with you over submitted MSS and sincerely hope that you may turn out victorious,' he wrote to one lady, who, although never accepted, was moved to send a telegram to wish the magazine well in 1938. It arrived 'with rather sad appropriateness, at literally the very moment when, after we had tried by every means to keep the paper alive, defeat had to be admitted'.

Such readers of the magazine can have been little aware of its editors leaving the office each day to return to Clapham Common and Fitzroy Street and the very different worlds of *Brighton Rock* and Céline's *Death on the Instalment Plan*.

Instructions are not needed here on how to read the magazine, for they are printed on its opening page. The Marx of *Animal Crackers* provides the epigraph for these Thirties writers: '*All* the jokes can't be good.' From the start the editors were determined to make a stand against solemnity. Months before the first issue appeared, John Marks wrote to Jan Struther, who had been an early discovery of Peter Fleming's and later became famous as the author of *Mrs Miniver*, and said that the magazine would have to be confined to 'humorous and satirical stuff . . . until we have become known as mainly a comic paper, when we can print less ribald pieces.' He returned a poem to William Douglas Home and commented, 'I feel that if it appeared with the rest of the magazine – which is essentially flippant – it might run the risk of being misunderstood by our readers.' Pleased that John Hayward had agreed to write for them, Graham Greene told him, 'I think there are great possibilities in really frank criticism of BBC programmes, as there is no critic of any standing writing about radio at present.' Although Evelyn Waugh declined the job because he could not bind himself to be in London each week, Greene was able to point out, in a comment which is almost as true today, that 'our appointment of Miss Elizabeth Bowen as dramatic critic is of particular interest. Miss Bowen will be one of the very few women writers practising dramatic criticism.' Evelyn Waugh did, however, produce a book review for each issue, Greene being keen to have one regular reviewer so that readers would discover his enthusiasms and aversions. Waugh sometimes chose the most unexpected subjects: one week he wrote on *Men of Mathematics*, while the *New Statesman*, more predictably, sent it to Bertrand Russell.

As the magazine continued, John Marks's hope that it would be able to contain more serious items was realized. Christopher Hollis and George Martelli provided regular political columns which, however they might appear with hindsight, were frequently more pertinent than those to be found in sober-minded journals. *The Times*, for example, was still urging appeasement with Hitler. Patrick Ransome's early remarks to the motoring correspondent, 'Supercharger' (a man from Sheffield called Derek Senior), remained true. 'The policy of the paper is a strictly non-Party one, and any political article must depend entirely on its wit to secure inclusion, it does not matter in the least whether it inclines to the Right or to the Left.' A. J. A. Symons studied the Spanish Civil War from the interesting angle of how to maintain one's sherry supplies for the duration. For all its sense of fun, Muggeridge and Kingsmill's 'Next Year's News' proved uncannily accurate: the book version predicted a Nazi-Soviet pact.

The editors' attitude, and the results that it could bring, were recalled by Graham Greene in 1973. 'I had the temerity . . . to ask the author of *Art Now* to write for me regular reviews of detective stories and he promptly accepted . . . I would one day like to see those reviews republished, so different are they from the stock image of Herbert Read, the intellectual . . . I really believe he enjoyed writing these reviews more than that long series of art books which hid from so many eyes his real genius as a poet, literary critic and biographer . . . His reviews in *Night and Day*, I like to think, were a holiday to him, and his humour streamed suddenly and volcanically out. He quoted hilariously from second-rate authors who had certainly not learnt the lessons of *English Prose Style* . . . Alas that *Night and Day* died at the end of 1937, for on 4 November of that year, in an essay called "Life Without A Shoehorn", Herbert Read made his debut as a comic writer under the name of James Murgatroyd . . . He was planning a series. If he had completed it, we might have had a worthy successor to *The Diary of a Nobody*.'

William Empson, too, appears in a manner far removed from *Seven Types of Ambiguity* and his poetry. Almost as unlikely are William Plomer on all-in wrestling and Louis MacNeice at the Kennel Club. There has surely never been more enjoyable art criticism than the pieces contributed by Osbert Lancaster.

In compiling this anthology it was thought important to keep the original format: the chronological arrangement shows the magazine's development, its various series, a distinct French emphasis, running jokes about Godfrey Winn and the way in which it covered topical matters from the Paris Exhibition to Christmas. (Fun can be had in watching the changing weekly list of events, in which the Zoological Gardens Restaurant remains a constant. 'Excellent *table d'hôte*, 4s.6d. and 7s.6d. Floodlit animals. Band of His Majesty's Guards, but kept well under control.') Some juggling has been necessary: cartoons and verses have sometimes strayed from their original position. Deciding which pieces to omit for reasons of space and balance has been a painful task.

The letters and manuscripts in the magazine's archives give a picture of its day-to-day existence. There was much passing round of submitted material, which gathered comments as it went from desk to desk. A man from Pump Court sent in some 'topical humorous verse' under such pseudonyms as Algol and Hamadryal. '*No. E.S.P.* [Selwyn Powell] *Like the Algol – too tripping and Punchy? J.M.*' '*Don't like it. G.G.*' Such comments recur. '*No. Tripe. G.G.*' '*Very dim. G.G.*' Someone from the P.E.N. Club sent in verse which was '*TOO FRIGHTFUL FOR WORDS. E.S.P.*' Patrick Ransome scrawled a vigorous '*No*' over Jocelyn Brooke's 'Du Côté de Chez Prufrock'. Somebody put a question mark over verses by Giles Cooper – '*No! G.G.*' Marghanita Laski's 'Ode to Retribution' went back without comment.

A man in the King's Road offered a 'short descriptive commentary on the adaptation and commensalism of the hermit crab' – '*absolutely unsuitable. G.G.*' Inaccurate advice was forthcoming from St John's Wood. 'If any of your readers suffer from insomnia they may be interested to hear of the following infallible cure. Prop yourself up in bed with a profusion of pillows, and balance an ordinary rubber hot water bottle on your head. I do not know whether it is the pleasant warmth from the bottle or the effect involved keeping it balanced, but I have never known this method to fail.'

'Mrs Peter Rodd (Nancy Mitford) wonders whether the Editor of *Night and Day* could make use of the enclosed article ["I Am a Sailing Widow"]' '*I don't think this is our stuff at all. P.R. My God, no. And why be so worried about Peter Rodd? G.G.*' From Paris, where he was an associate editor of Alfred Perlès's *Booster*, Henry Miller pressed upon them a 'little skit on Gertrude Stein and Mr. Mortimer...' '*I think this is fine. But Raymond Mortimer won't. E.S.P.*' '*Won't do, alas, I feel. J.M.*' '*Fine – but Mortimer's not quite big enough game for an article of this length, is he? I'd say No, but please send us more. G.G.*' He offered pieces on war munitions, drugs and pharmaceutical supplies but none of them arrived in time. H. E. Bates offered a couple of stories, and said to Greene, 'I was disappointed you didn't like *Something Short and Sweet* [1937] – but no hard feelings, of course.' The eighteenth-century scholar R. W. Ketton-Cremer said to Greene that he did not 'think, though, that I could do this house [Felbrigg] in your "Stately Homes" series. Architecturally it really isn't important enough: it's interesting and I think beautiful, but has no claim to a place in a series dealing with genuinely important houses. And nothing of the slightest historical importance has ever happened here!' Twenty-five years later, however, his classic book *Felbrigg* appeared.

Marks's friend T. H. White was willing to appear but slow to produce his article. 'I was *delighted* to find in the Christmas number of N & D that writers were able to take things seriously when they wanted to, and it was this awful horror of always having to be funny even when you were interested in the thing that had sort of held me up.' He suggested a year's supply of blood-sports pieces, but nothing appeared. In the course of several long letters he explained that he was reluctant to put his name to sharp pieces at only four guineas a time. 'I have three novels

coming out this year, and they are all of a simple or sincere or warm-hearted (I can't get the word) nature.' A little later he concluded, 'on the whole I think you had better publish the sketch and then drop me. I feel dangerous.'

Night and Day also carried the work of some of the best illustrators and cartoonists of the time, and in this it was directly in competition with its main rival, *Punch*. Some came in through agencies; some, such as Botterill, appeared out of the blue; others were known to the editors: *Night and Day* was instrumental in launching, among others, Topolski and 'Paul Crum'. All relished the space and freedom of its pages. For all the jibes at *Punch*, it is as well to remember that efforts were made to win over their great cartoonist 'Pont', with the result, happy for him, that *Punch* immediately increased his pay. The deaths, in differing circumstances, of both 'Pont' and 'Paul Crum' ('so good he signs with a squiggle') during the war are something always to be regretted. The endless details of one and the economical lines of the other both reflect an England that so often escapes weightier commentators. Roger Pettiward, as Crum was really called, had accompanied Peter Fleming on the Brazilian expedition and was particularly thanked in the resulting book's preface for always being able to see the joke. Cartoons can easily date, but those in *Night and Day*, from the sophistication of Topolski's foreign perspective to the easier lines of Brian Robb and Nicolas Bentley, have a draughtsmanship, since vanished from the English cartoon, which so often makes them beautiful simply to look at. The cartoon on page 156 has been attributed to Cyril Connolly, of all people; certainly he was the model for the large lady on the sofa. Anthony West, son of Rebecca West and H. G. Wells, began his career as an artist, and an example of his work will be found among the cartoons. Eric Fraser designed the masthead and illustrated Slingsby's column, except for the final issue when the author, late with his copy, did so himself – the oddest contribution of all.

The tone of *Night and Day* was provided as much by its more obscure contributors as by the famous. The lively journalist Christopher Saltmarshe had a career typical of many. After a successful time at St. Paul's he went up to Magdalene in 1926, where he quickly became noted for his wit. During the Thirties he worked as John Summerson's assistant on the *Architect*. During the war he joined the BBC's monitoring service and remained with the Corporation, as John Davenport wrote, 'in a sadly subterranean way' until his death in 1966. P. Y. Betts's one novel, *French Polish* (1933), which concerns a group of malevolent, clever and lusty schoolgirls, should be sought out by all those who relish her satirical pieces here. (Similarly enjoyable is Yvonne Cloud's *Mediterranean Blues*, which was highly praised by Greene in the *Spectator*; perhaps that prompted her agent to submit a piece to *Night and Day*, but '*alas! this is sentimental and pretentious*'.) T. O. Beachcroft wrote on other subjects here, but Greene had the year before praised him as 'likely to become, after Mr H. E. Bates, the most distinguished short-story writer in this country.'

Many of the authors came from Chatto's list, which is more an indication of their quality than of any pressure to publicize them. Many are well known; two – Aldous Huxley and David Garnett – were announced but never produced anything. It is a pity that Rodney Hobson collected little more than his 1937 *Caustic Carols*; Dennis Kincaid, who had written a number of novels, died before his pieces appeared; George Martelli, best known for his 1960 *Agent Extraordinary*, published two political studies with the firm during the Thirties; the excellent Edward Bunyard, older than most of the contributors, should be far better known for his *Anatomy of Dessert*, which has lately been urged on readers by Jane Grigson in her *Fruit Book*. The splendidly named American correspondent Leona Rake will not be found in the publisher's catalogue, but in fact she was Mrs Greenough Townsend, who, as 'Esther Forbes', wrote historical novels and romances. Harold Raymond of Chatto wrote regretfully to the agent of one author, Iain Anderson, 'As regards reviewing in the *Geographical Magazine* and *Night and Day*, I will do what I can, but Chatto's have no editorial control over either of these periodicals. All I can do is to lead the horse to the water.' On one such occasion Evelyn Waugh did not at all care for the flavour of Frederic Prokosch's interminable *The Seven Who Fled*. The outraged author complained to his publisher. 'Yes,' replied Raymond, 'I feel very strongly too about the *Night and Day* review, but I am afraid nothing can be done. I wish it could.' Frederic Prokosch was another of the listed contributors not to appear.

Edwin Lutyens wrote to say how pleased he was by the profile in the 'Lion's Den' series; in his reply, Selwyn Powell regretted that 'the anonymity of Daniel's various identities is strictly enforced so that I cannot tell you who did write it, but it was not myself.' That author remains unknown, but it is now safe to reveal that Hamish Miles wrote the one about Victor Gollancz. The biography of St. Nicholas ('exactly what we wanted and will greatly improve the Christmas number') was the most unusual of Hugh Kingsmill's 'lives'. In the issue of 9 September, Lawrence Durrell appeared under his early, little-known pseudonym of Charles Norden. Rarely can shorter notices, traditionally the province of the hack, have been written with such trenchancy and authority. The anonymous authors, as they sat in their pink-walled office, did not always choose the obvious titles: Greene is as perceptive about *A Book of Birds* as he is about *Sally Bowles*, the latter in particular showing that brevity need not exclude prescience.

Despite the hopes with which the magazine was launched the readers of all this excellent, diverse material were soon proving to be rather too select a company. 30,000 sales – a quarter of *Punch*'s – would have been needed to make a decent profit. In August the advertisement rates had to be cut in order to counter the seasonal fall, and it was beginning to look rash to have rejected Morny's offer to take a series in December at the introductory rate. (The consistent support shown by Shell, the full-page advertisements illustrated by Robb, can doubtless be explained by John Betjeman's position in their publicity department.) None the less the Board held out hopes for the autumn, when it was planned to have a further sales campaign, with advertisements in the *Daily Express* and *Sunday Times*. On 30 August it was decided that 50,000 extra copies should be distributed to sales outlets; 75,000 leaflets were prepared which offered a trial three-month subscription at 5s.; local drives were to be held in Manchester and Birmingham, with the organisation of street sales to show that it was more than the London paper it might have seemed on the surface.

Six weeks later, the final call having been made on the shareholders during September, 'the present financial position was then examined. It was considered that the company's resources would probably last until about Christmas, upon the assumption that the present loss of £200 a week persisted.' The shareholders were to be informed of this position, and the first of several efforts to attract fresh capital was made.

This rocky state of affairs notwithstanding, *Night and Day* has become popularly known as the victim of a libel action. In fact there were two.

In the issue of 14 October Alison Haig described Rose Taylor's new fashions: 'Rose Taylor's collection was not an all-time high, but she is always good on sports clothes and travel outfits.... Besides exclusive models, she showed some ready-made clothes – possibly as a foil, certainly they left no doubt in your mind as to the worthwhileness of paying the extra guineas for a model. There was also a small collection of American ready-to-wears, for which we are told Miss Taylor personally crossed the ocean. My private suspicion is that she missed the boat and, not to be thwarted, took a bus to Margaret Street instead. They all seemed to have a tinselly guinea touch.' Despite an apology in the issue of December 2nd, the matter rumbled on, Jaeger loyally threatening to withdraw their advertisements, and it was finally settled in the High Court the following March.

On the same day the second and more famous case was heard, during which the notoriously severe Lord Chief Justice described an item in the issue of 28 October as 'a gross outrage'.

'I had not seen Miss Temple before,' wrote Graham Greene of *The Littlest Rebel* in the *Spectator* in May 1936. 'As I expected there was the usual sentimental exploitation of childhood, but I had not expected the tremendous energy which her rivals certainly lack.' Children grow up quickly, and three months later he was able to describe those energies in a way that anticipates the *Night and Day* piece. '*Captain January* ... is sentimental, a little depraved, with an appeal interestingly decadent ... Shirley Temple acts and dances with immense vigour and assurance, but some of her popularity seems to rest on a coquetry quite as mature as Miss Colbert's and an oddly precocious body as voluptuous in grey flannel trousers as

Miss Dietrich's.' Of the rumpus that his *Wee Willie Winkie* review in the issue of 28 October (see p. 204) provoked, Anthony Powell has commented, 'even at that distant period, the notion that children neither had nor could express sexual instincts was, to say the least, an uninstructed one.'

W. H. Smith immediately refused to touch the issue, and the magazine sought counsel's opinion. Mr D. N. Pritt, K.C. 'unequivocally stated that in his opinion the article contained no defamatory statement and could be published without risk. In these circumstances the Board decided to take no steps to withdraw the issue.' The other side was not given such enlightened advice, and the matter hung over the magazine for the rest of its short life, while the case was pending. The editors became somewhat cautious. John Marks sent a proof to Stevie Smith and drew her 'attention to the fact that we have discovered that there is a Mr Montague Cohen living in Golders Green. This unfortunate coincidence would make it highly dangerous to publish the poem as it stands.' 'I'm so sorry about Mr Montague Cohen,' she replied, 'and agree, from a quick glance at the telephone directory, that what you say is probably an understatement. I have therefore altered his suburb to Bottle Green.'

Despite these jocular exchanges, the *Wee Willie Winkie* review remained a serious problem. 'I kept on my bathroom wall, until a bomb removed the wall, the statement of claim – that I had accused Twentieth Century Fox of "procuring" Miss Temple "for immoral purposes",' Greene recalled in 1972. (The charges might have been even worse if he had not deleted from the typescript a comparison with Lady Macbeth.)

The case was resolved – at a cost to *Night and Day* of over £3,500 – in March 1938, three months after the demise of the magazine. It was heard in Greene's absence: he was by that time in Mexico where he was preparing *The Lawless Roads* and correcting proofs of *Brighton Rock*. He wrote to Elizabeth Bowen: 'I found a cable waiting for me in Mexico City asking me to apologise to that little bitch Shirley Temple.' Twentieth Century Fox insisted on his contributing £500 himself. As the Lord Chief Justice referred the matter to the DPP there was also a danger of prosecution for criminal libel, and Greene's publisher volunteered to send money so that he need not return. Gallantly, however, he took the next cargo boat back. Nothing happened, but the matter was raised when he joined SIS during the war. '"C" considered it was not sufficient reason not to employ me.' Having been put to similar trouble with *Stamboul Train* and *Journey without Maps*, it is understandable, as Julian Maclaren-Ross has recorded, that he did not find the matter altogether hilarious. None the less he came to accept it 'with ironical detachment'.

'Shirley's prank', as T. H. White called it, was a glorious symbol of the magazine's troubles rather than their cause. At a General Meeting on 1 November Ian Parsons announced that the Board thought 'that publication could not be effectively continued unless a large amount of fresh capital were procured.' The shareholders were asked for their views and 'a general feeling emerged' that this had to be attempted. About three weeks was thought sufficient 'to prosecute these inquiries'. In his diary for 18 November Evelyn Waugh wrote, 'Greene rang up to say that *Night and Day* is on its last legs; would I put them into touch with Evan Tredegar [2nd Viscount Tredegar], whom I barely know, to help them raise capital. They must indeed be in a bad way.' At a Board meeting on 24 November, 'a failure to attract a further sum of capital was announced.' A General Meeting was called for 1 December 'to ask for the views of shareholders as to an immediate cessation of publication.'

At the meeting Cazalet outlined the position and mentioned that a scheme had been put forward by the Editorial Board, which was then explained by Lord Hinchingbrooke and Graham Greene. Discussion ensued. Colonel Viney and Mr Maxwell, printers both, proposed to 'cease publication of the magazine forthwith.' Patrick Ransome and Greene then suggested that a committee of shareholders be appointed to consider the scheme in detail and report back in a fortnight's time. This was narrowly carried. Meanwhile a strict economy campaign was underway. 'What could be handsomer and nicer than your letter,' wrote Theodora Benson to John Marks. 'I accept 3 guineas for "Rise and Fall" as I daresay it is shorter and lousier than the things you gave me 4 guineas for.' Selwyn Powell has recalled a visit which Cazalet, the magazine's main backer, made at this time. He was dressed 'in an immaculate outfit of black jacket and striped trousers. We gave him tea and I very clumsily spilt some over the trousers. I apologised profusely and said, "But do send the cleaner's bill to us." It went down rather poorly, though I don't think it was the last straw!'

The committee concluded that up to £8,000 would be sufficient to continue publication for another six months. At a Board meeting on 13 December it was revealed that only £3,000 of conditional offers had been received. It was decided to ask the next Extraordinary General Meeting, to be held in two days' time, for authority to continue until the issue of 23 December 'with power to discontinue thereafter'. The shareholders agreed, short of the capital's appearing, that this should be done. Although the Company nominally existed for another eighteen months before it was liquidated, at the final Board meeting held during the magazine's run it was reluctantly concluded that the capital could not be raised. A possible merger with *Lilliput* was discussed. This would have been the worst sort of lingering death – who can now tell that over the years the *New Statesman* has absorbed the *Nation*, *Week-End Review* and *Athenaeum*? – and the final issue, which contained another hopeful invitation for subscriptions, was published on 23 December.

A few days before, Evelyn Waugh had written to Greene, 'I received your telegram this morning after the enclosed article had been written. As it had been definitely commissioned, and as it is unsaleable elsewhere, I am afraid that I must hold you to your offer, whether you print it or not.' Although forty-eight years late, his articles, previously unknown, for the two following issues are here published as an Appendix, together with one by Osbert Lancaster, which was scheduled for the 30 December issue, and the review of *Eyeless in Gaza* which Waugh wrote for the dummy publicity issue.

Many readers wrote to say how disappointed they were by the magazine's closure. In January 1938 John Marks said to Sir Stephen Bull that 'anyone thinking of starting a weekly critical-political magazine could of course buy the goodwill of *Night and Day* for next to nothing and resurrect it under any different form that might be desired. This is not quite as pointless a remark as it may seem at first glance because, from the point of view of circulation, organization etc., we have after all spent 20 thousand pounds opening up a favourable field and have at least quite a decent little following. I was most determined, when looking for further capital during the last few weeks, that a completely re-arranged magazine was essential – possibly with the addition of photographs, certainly with fewer humorous drawings, so that one could select only the best and with enlarged topical, political and review sections . . . What I do feel very strongly is that more good can be done, in the way of disseminating information and instructing public opinion on political topics under cover of . . . editorial stuff of general interest with no obvious message.'

Any magazine expects to develop and change, as *Night and Day* did during its brief existence. Marks was looking at it unduly harshly. Now, Lydia Keynes vindicated, one turns from its pages to find the racks full of stale periodicals which, lacking any original ideas and impetus, are a mere branch of the public-relations industry. One is left to wonder why nobody, despite the risk of an objection from Dr Barnardo's, has taken up John Marks's suggestion. A reader should have the last word. Mr E. G. Morris from Sheffield wrote after his submission had been returned and said, 'may I say how sincerely sorry I am that your excellent magazine has not been successful. A *Night and Day* was badly needed. You will at least have the consolation that its failure was only due to being too good.'

Christopher Hawtree

1 It is only right that the philanthropic shareholders should be recorded (some of the enlightened advertisers will be found later on in these pages). In order of investment they were: the Fairlawne Trust; Mr Ian Parsons; Mr Harold Raymond; Mrs Vera Raymond; Mr J. H. Barrett; Mr Patrick Ransome; the Cushion Trust; The Hon. John Hare; Lady Dawson of Penn; Lord Pentland; Viscount Hinchingbrooke; Mr G. Mercer Nairne; Mr Cuthbert Raymond; Mr Nigel Birch; Mr Raymond Hazell; Colonel Oscar Viney; Mr Peter Harris; Major Basil Bebb; Mrs M. A. Cooke; Mr John Musker; Mr William Maxwell; Mr Douglas Foulis; Sir Roger Chance; Mr Robert Morss; Mr Oliver Warner; Mrs Jasper Blunt; The Hon. Reginald Winn; Mrs Mabel Parsons; Mr J. Donaldson; Mr K. Macrae Moir; Mr Alfred Greenshields; Mr George Grundy; Mr Basil Hill-Wood; Mr Peter Fleming; Mr Ian Fleming; Mr Henry Hemming; Miss Marjorie Ritchie; Sir Jocelyn Lucas. A nominal five shares were taken by Mr Norman Crump, of *The Economist*, who joined the Board of Directors. Five shares were transferred to Mr Graham Greene on November 2nd so that he could attend shareholders' meetings.

2 In an article published in *The Times Literary Supplement* of 2 April 1982 M. J. Tilby gave an account of Céline's unpublished letters to John Marks. The sharp-eyed will notice a contribution from L.F.C. in Paris among the readers' comments printed in the December 9th issue of *Night and Day*: 'un triomphe, je crois.'

NIGHT and DAY

"The Old Order Changeth"

so does *SHELL*

The molecular structure of Shell has been altered in such a way as to make Shell still more suitable for use in the modern car. It means that whereas ordinary petrol "pinks" under the severe conditions existing in high-compression engines, Shell does not, because the atoms of hydrogen and carbon are "re-formed" into compact groups instead of the straight chains in which they normally exist. It means that Shell can offer you smoother running, better pick up, and freedom from "pinking."

YOU CAN BE SURE OF SHELL

HOW TO READ THIS MAGAZINE

NIGHT AND DAY is published on Thursdays. It can be bought (or stolen if you have the nerve) from all newsagents worthy of the name. Here are some simple rules to bear in mind :

1. Read from left to right. If you follow our advice and do this, the first thing you come up against is *London By Night and Day.* This section is brought to you, as they say, by our espionage department, and gives you the lowdown on what we call, rightly or wrongly, London's Pleasure Zone. Drama, films, sport, and the lights-and-wine racket—to all this and to a good deal more you will find NIGHT AND DAY a terse (advt.) and illuminating (advt.) guide.

2. Passing on, you come to Slingsby's *Minutes of the Week,* which are what used to be termed a *causerie,* but funny for all that.

3. By this time you are right down in the body of the paper, where—as Jonah discovered in vaguely analogous circumstances—you may find pretty well anything : fiction, satire, nonsense — pretty well anything, as we said.

4. It will not have escaped your notice that NIGHT AND DAY is illustrated. In this connection we would draw your attention to *Fe-Fo-Fi-Fum,* our weekly page of drawings by Feliks Topolski, a talented anthropologist who is conducting a little regular field-work in these islands and who lays bare, as with a scalpel, the essential whatever-it-is of Britain's most cherished institu-tions. We have a lot of other artists too, all darned good. One's so good he signs with a squiggle.

5. Have you ever wondered what it feels like to be a Mortuary Por-ter, a Three-Card-Trick Practi-tioner, or (see p. 16) a Tattooist ? *A Job in a Million* will tell you.

6. Flaxman. See p. 17 and, if that doesn't work, have a look at this feature in the next issue, and so on for quite a time. You'll catch on. We did. It's fun when you're used to it.

7. By reading from cover to cover (which, we think, is the best way) you'll eventually reach our up-to-date critical section, which will tell you, as man to man, what's what about what's on. (See by cross, but not too cross, reference *London By Night and Day* : go back where you started from, in fact, and lose three turns.) Here you will find Miss Elizabeth Bowen reviewing the theatre, while Mr. Evelyn Waugh does books, Mr. Graham Greene looks at the films, and other critics purr or wince at the offerings of Fashion, Art, Sport, etc.

8. For the rest, a wealth of talent, some of it anonymous, some of it not, invigilates over a mad world, annotating its absurdities as they come to light. Discriminating people who subscribe to NIGHT AND DAY as from the first number will have something to boast to their grandchildren about—assuming, of course, that discriminating people *have* grandchildren. We're not sure about this.

"ALL THE JOKES CAN'T BE GOOD"—Groucho Marx

MINUTES OF THE WEEK

Gently There, Reader!

We have seen, in our time, the birth of a good many new periodicals ; some grave, some gay. All, so far as we recall, kicked off in their first number with a short explanation of what they were for, what they meant to do, why you should read them. The grave ones took a forthright, an almost intimidating line. " Fearless . . . swayed by no factional bias . . . all whose common cause it is to preserve those standards which . . . a high purpose

. . . prove ourselves worthy of that fine heritage. . . ." This line was impressive. It made us look yellow if we didn't buy the paper.

Of the other kinds of manifesto, the arrogant always struck us as the easiest to write, because it concentrated less on what the editor's policy was than on what it wasn't. " Readers will scan these pages in vain for the bourgeois thought-forms of a moribund society." Hardhitting stuff, that was ; we always liked it.

Take Us or Leave Us

But now the time has come for us to do the trick, frankly we don't care for the assignment. We find ourselves suffering from indecision ; if proof is needed of this, we have drawn eight

goblins and part of a horse on our blotting paper. With us, this spells maladjustment. Things have been particularly bad since we went to a party the other night, there meeting an earnest, right-thinking man who had heard about NIGHT AND DAY and who asked us what we stood for. We laughed the question off, of course, and soon had him telling us about the sufferings of the middle class in Croatia, where it seems a thin time is had by many. Behind, nevertheless, our façade of *savoir faire* we were in something of a turmoil. What *do* we stand for ? Our colleagues, asked, seemed not to know. " Something *different,*" said a man who had come in to borrow our car, currying favour madly.

Feast of Fun

Are we different ? And, if so, what from ? It is not for us to say. Our aim is to amuse. We shall try to do it intelligently ; and without, if possible, being smart, fatuous, Bloomsbury or it-seems-there-were-two-Irishmen. But what we actually *stand* for, we still don't know.

Nor is it, in the last analysis, important. The question is : Can you stand for us ? We hope you can. If you can't, we shall go down smiling. But we should prefer not to have to do this. Tasmanian papers, please copy.

College Days

We shudder to think how much water (we shudder whenever we think

of water, as a matter of fact) has passed under the bridge since we last danced at Commem. Those adolescent bacchanalia took place again the other day and, as we read about them in a gossip column, we sighed for our vanished youth—moonlight on the quad and lipstick on the ear ; a couple of chaps from Brasenose throwing a poet in the fountain ; breakfast at the Trout, in a Bullingdon coat and dreadfully cold sunshine. Those were the days.

We were bored stiff at the time, of course. Commem., though you may not believe it, is not an abbreviation of Commemoration. It is a corruption of the Norman *quand même,* meaning, as the dictionary puts it, " all the same, notwithstanding, nevertheless, in spite of all." That was how we used to take our Commems : fatalistically, with a shrug of the shoulders.

R.L.S. into U.S.S.R.

The Detskii Kino is the studio in Moscow where they make films for children. A friend of ours who was out there recently heard they'd been shooting *Treasure Island* and went round hoping to wangle a preview. The film had been sent away to be cut, but they very amiably

handed him over to the director of the studio. Had the director, asked our friend, found it necessary to make any changes in the original story to bring it into line with current Soviet ideology ? Far from it, said the director ; the whole picture had stuck faithfully to the old Tsarist translation of Comrade Stevenson's romance.

Stevenson's hero is called Jim Hawkins ; the Russians haven't got an H and call Hamlet Gamlet. " What," asked our friend, hoping for a cheap guffaw at Gawkins, " is the hero's name in your version ? " The director raised his eyebrows and said that there was no hero ; Jim Hawkins had become Jenny Gawkins. " A girl ? " asked our friend, raising *his* eyebrows. Not so much one girl, explained the director, as a posse or squad of girls, led by Jenny. " But I thought," objected our friend, " that you had changed nothing in the original story ? " Neither they had, said the director ; nothing fundamental.

Then why replace one boy by a dozen girls ? The director, replying at length, was understood to say that mass-feeling will out.

" And the treasure ? " Oh, the treasure, regretted by none, had been cut ; the children were interested only in the social regeneration of the island.

" Island ! " cried our friend, entering into it at last. " *Island !* Why do you stick to such an outworn bourgeois concept ? "

The director, blushing, changed the subject.

★

Horses Are Thicker Than Water

" Sanchia Marsdyke had horses in her blood "—(*From a serial.*)

There is practically nothing a girl can do about this sort of thing. Horses in the blood are the very devil, keeping you awake at night, inducing hay-fever and causing the feet to swell. A dash of petrol in the morning tea will sometimes bring relief, however.

A cousin of ours had music in his blood and that wasn't so bad, except that every time he cut himself shaving a military band seemed to play *Roses of Picardy.*

Marriage Market Echo

We were intrigued (it's a long time ago now, but the memory has haunted us all through the Season) by one of the abstruser events listed in the programme of the Royal Military Tournament at Olympia. It figured, without a word of explanation, as " Dummy-Thrusting Championships ". Who took part in this cryptic competition, we asked an acquaintance of ours in the Brigade. " God knows," he said. " Unless," he added after a moment's thought, " it's the mothers of débutantes."

★

Soliloquy

Do people talk to themselves more than they used to ? We have an idea

'—*and Gay Crusader, a pound each way* '

that they do. In the course of last week, while prowling the streets of London, we tuned in to no less than four soliloquies. One, which was probably the most interesting, came— in his own vernacular—from an Indian student as he hurried down Gower Street ; we couldn't understand a word of it, worse luck. Two others were delivered by oldish ladies, one in Oxford Street and one in Sloane Square. The first, stationary, was rummaging in her bag : " I can't make it out. I can't make it out *at all,*" she was saying. The second was walking fast and talking faster ;

" It's going to be a lesson to us all " was the only remark that came through clearly. The fourth soliloquist was (to our mind) a retired colonel, taking the air in Chelsea and punishing the pavement severely with a malacca cane. As we overhauled him he exclaimed : " He may call himself Henry if he *chooses* ! " and thereupon broke into a tolerably melodramatic chuckle.

Pursued and inspired by the echoes of his mirth, we thought of having a word with ourself. Others enjoyed this sort of thing, why shouldn't we ? But somehow we couldn't get around to it. We decided upon a topic ; we cleared our throat ; nothing happened. It wasn't exactly that we were shy. We just didn't want to listen to ourself. We had a number of things which we felt were well worth saying, but nothing at all which seemed to us worth hearing. The shipwreck of this whim threw us into a state of depression and perplexity. When you hear another person talking to himself, there is something intriguing and almost formidable about the process ; when you hear yourself talking to yourself, it sounds ridiculous. It is perhaps the only kind of activity, from getting married to having a cold bath, which you find more interesting when done by others than when done by yourself.

All of which gives rise to any amount of disquieting reflections. Rather than let them spoil our sleep, we have decided to learn to talk to ourself. " Have you been to any plays lately ? " is as far as we have got up to the time of going to press. But the ice, definitely, is broken.

★

Casualty Monger

They tell us that Mr. Hore-Belisha coined a slogan when he was lately transferred from the Ministry of Transport to the War Office : JOIN THE ARMY ! IT'S SAFER THAN THE ROADS.

SLINGSBY

IN DEFENCE OF THE HOME

Rose Macaulay

WE have already so many periodicals that one often asks oneself, is a new one required ? And one always answers oneself, yes, it is. That is why new periodicals begin. For there is always some little thing in this imperfect world not yet done, some little function that remains to be performed, something to be stood for that no journal stands for yet. What many of us are hoping (and, I was told when I rang up the office, hoping with justification) is that *Night and Day* will stand for the Sanctities (by day and night) of the Home. The importance of this can scarcely be over-estimated, in a world where the home and its sanctities have always been in constant peril, threatened from all sides with destruction. For one hears daily of the grave dangers which attack it, and them.

A member of parliament not long since asked the Postmaster-General about a broadcast he had heard, which, he feared, would destroy, had already probably destroyed, the home. Apart from this aerial menace, many other insidious anti-domestic forces are perpetually at work, attempting to entice us from our homes. There are (to name only a few) the cinema, the coronation, the churches, and the dog. The churches, which should know better, peal continual bells, summoning men, women, and even little children to desert their homes, and more particularly on that day of rest which should, above all others, be spent at home. They have been of late endeavouring to recall us to religion (I always forget at what period of history it was that we had much religion, and the churches have so far omitted to tell us that ; rather oddly, they speak of a back-to-God, not an on-to-God, campaign) : and this will mean

a fresh threat to the home, even if we confine our religious services to those which come to us over the air. Of the cinema, the coronation, and the dog, the less said in these pages the better.

The home, frail and brittle institution, is by these massed attacks for ever being assaulted, disintegrated and destroyed. " If home life is destroyed," someone was saying on the air the other day when I turned on my wireless by mistake, " then the life of the nation is destroyed." What he meant, of course, was that the life of the nation would have to be lived in the open air, which would in this climate be very unwholesome and even dangerous. By all means let us retain our homes, their comforts, their sweet lethargy, their sanctity. My own flat is full of sanctity and lethargy, and I will not have it undermined. The home, where selfishness begins and charity ends, where we recline in one commodious chair and place the feet on another, moving not at the call of telephone or door-bell—we will admit no violation of this exquisite convenience. The little flats of England, how beautiful they stand ! Why not stay in them ? Against all the embattled forces of the anti-domestic, domicidal foe, let us, led by the sober and responsible journal, *Night and Day*, make our stand.

' 60927 *wants to stay another two months to finish* " Gone With The Wind ", *sir.*'

SOME LITTLE=KNOWN FACTS ABOUT MY LOVE=LIFE

Rodney Hobson

MULLING through a package of old love letters that had just come back from the laundry, I came across one faded, yellow missive that brought the tears into these rheumy old eyes of mine.

As I read the well-remembered writing, the years rolled back and I was once again an upright young ensign in Lady Astor's Light Horse, my breast aglitter with medals and my trousers too darned tight for comfort. Those were the days when chivalry was in flower, and there was hardly a house in the Bloomsbury square in which we lived that did not boast its little bowl of chivalry, bravely flowering in the front window.

But I digress. The letter I hold in my hands evokes memories too poignant for me to bear. It distils a nostalgic fragrance, and there is a stain that looks like plum-and-apple jam just below my dear Dulcie's signature. I would often tease her about her weakness for this delicacy and she would reply by tapping me on the wrist with her fan or turning, half grave, half gay, to catch me a sharp thwack on the ear with her parasol.

But let me read you her letter. That will give you a clearer insight into her sweet disposition than these stumbling words of mine. It runs thus:

Dear Mr. Fosdick,
Can you fix me a couple of tickets for the Brewers' Exhibition, Friday ?
Yours affctly.,
DULCIE

P.S.—Pappa says next time you drop fruitcake into the spinet, he'll tan the pants off you.

To understand to the full the old-world charm of this letter, it is necessary to know something of the leisured, spacious days in which we lived. The mechanical age was only in its infancy ; the pencil-sharpener, the pile-driver and the semi-stiff collar mere figments of the inventor's imagination. In a corner house in Oxford Street a young man was experimenting with the first gas-filled éclair ; Negretti and Zambra had been burned as witches at the Crystal Palace, and the first horse-drawn bathing-van had confirmed the expectations of the sceptics by sinking in three feet of water at Brighton.

That, then, was the age in which we lived and loved. Oh, yes, we loved all right. Oh, yes, indeed ! Any of you "enlightened" modern young people who believe that love in those days was a thing of long silences, quivering sighs, and glances that told all that lips did not dare to utter, should have been present at one of our Badminton Club dances.

Here was jollity run riot, an unbridled bacchanal that made the pulse beat faster and brought my Dulcie out in a rash that only served to heighten her fragile beauty. At the end of the hall was set up a long table groaning under the weight of ham sandwiches, meat pies and (delicious dissipation !) a plump flagon of Empire burgundy ; to which, needless to say, we revellers did ample justice.

As I swung my lovely Dulcie into the rhythm of the polka, I was aware that all eyes were upon us, except for one or two eyes that were on the burgundy. Dancing, I would bend down and whisper into her hair : " I love you, Miss Mahoney." And she would look up at me with her heart in her eyes and a macaroon in her mouth and answer : " I bet you tell that to all the girls ! "

Coquettish ? Perhaps. But she was young and impulsive and it only needed a playful wallop from me to stop any more nonsense of that sort.

Later, when the dance was over, we would rattle home over the cobbles in a hansom, her tiny hand in mine, the moon a silver fish in the net spread by the branches of the trees in Russell Square. The fare, I remember, was exorbitant.

Happy, halcyon days ! I have only to close my eyes to see a little church on the hill and a lot of yellow spots that I can't quite place. It is our wedding day. Dulcie is hanging on my arm like a wet sock, and outside the church door her friends of the Penge Wheelers are making a triumphal arch with their bicycles. " You're riding tandem now ! " shouts one strapping young Amazon as we pass out into our new life.

Even as I write, Dulcie is thrashing about in the kitchen like a mad thing, busy with my supper. Through the door I can see her stooping over the hot stove, and occasionally there comes a muffled oath as she stubs her toe against one of the twins. She is fixing me a dish of *bouillabaisse* such as her mother used to throw together, and soon, with the steaming dish in her hands, she will come across to the rocking-chair where I am sitting, and murmur with infinite tenderness : " Wrap yourself around this, you old buzzard, and I hope it chokes you."

Then she will shuffle back on her flat old feet to the kitchen, and leave me crouched over the dying fire, alone with my thoughts and about eight gibbering children. Heigh-ho ! Heigh-ho !

★

You never heard of a girl who wasn't proud to be seen out with a clever man, no matter whether he was poor or rich.
—*Dorothy Dix in the* DAILY MIRROR

Madam, when you say that, you insult the woman we love.

UPSTAIRS, DOWNSTAIRS

A Story by V. S. Pritchett

FROM years of habit the mare stopped a minute or two at the right houses in all the streets waiting for the milkman's voice to call : " Good day, ma'am, thank you, ma'am " in the alleys. Then she gave a slouching heave, the cans and bottles would start jingling, and, with the man following, she was off to the next stop. But when eleven o'clock came she stopped dead. She knew the house they were at now. She knew it well. An ungainly, warty and piebald creature, she loosened her shoulders, her head and neck hung to the ground, her forelegs splayed out, and she looked old, rakish and cynical.

For here was no stop of a minute or two. Down the passage strode the milkman, his lips whistling. Five minutes passed into ten, ten into twenty. Some mornings it was half an hour, three-quarters or the full hour. And when the milkman came back he was not whistling.

He was a short, ruddy man in a brown dustcoat with the firm's name on it and a hat like a police inspector's. But there is nothing like a uniform for concealing the soul. He was bald and battered under his hat and his eyebrows were thick and inky. If he took his hat off in the middle of a sentence, that sentence would become suddenly very easy and rather free ; if he wiped his bald head with his handkerchief, *that* was a sign he might get freer.

The first time the milkman went to the house a woman came across the kitchen towards him. The fire was murmuring in the range and a pot of coffee was standing on it. A tray of cakes had just been taken out of the oven and was standing on the table. The milkman's nostrils had small sensitive black hairs in them, and they quivered.

" Oh, I do like a snice mincepie," said the milkman.

She was a kind woman. "The early bird catches the worm," she said. " Have one."

She was a big creature, lazy and soft in the arms and shoulders. She had several chins. The small chin shook like a cup in its saucer on the second chin that was under it, and she had freckles on her neck. She was warm and untidy with cooking, and her yellow hair was coming undone at the back. Her mouth was short and surly, but now it softened in harmony with the rest of her into an

easy placid smile ; the rest of her body seemed to be laughing at her fatness, and the smile broadened from her lips to her neck and so on downwards, until the milkman put his foot on the doorstep, took off his hat and wiped his bald head with pleasure.

" I'm a rollin' stone, ma'am," said the milkman. " I don't mind if I do."

She turned round and walked slowly to the table and the cakes. They were small cherry cakes. When she turned, the crease in the back of her neck seemed to be a smile and even her shoes seemed to be making smiles of pleasure on the floor.

" Come in," she said. " I'm Yorkshire. I'm not like the people round here. I'm neighbourly."

" I'm Yorkshire. I'm neighbourly too," said the milkman, rubbing his hands, and he stepped in. It was warm and cosy in the kitchen, warm with the smell of the cakes and the coffee, and warm with the good-natured woman.

" Take a seat," said the woman. " I'm sitting down myself. I've been on my feet all morning. I come from Leeds and this is my bake."

" I come from Hull," said the milkman. " We never say ' no ' and we never say die. I've been on my feet too. What I mean to say—in my job, you can't ride because you're always stopping and you can't stop because you've got to keep moving, if you get me." The milkman sat down opposite to her.

" I could tell you were from the north," said the hospitable woman. She pushed the cakes towards him. "Go on," she said. " Take one. Take two. They're a mean lot of people down here. There's nothing mean about me."

" After you, ma'am," he said.

"No," she said, "I dassn't." She laughed.

" Slimming ? " said the milkman.

" Oh, ha ha," laughed the woman. "That's a good one. Look at me. I've got the spread. I don't get any exercise." She went into a new peal of laughter. " And I don't want it."

" We're as God made us," said the milkman. " All sizes."

" And all shapes," said the woman, recovering. " It wouldn't do for all of us to be thin."

" You want some heavyweights," said the man.

" They're all thin round here, and mean," said the woman.

The woman laughed until tears came into the small grey eyes which were sunk like oyster pearls between her plump, fire-reddened cheeks and her almost hairless brows. She laughed and laughed, and her laughter was like her smile. She laughed not only with her mouth, but her cheeks gave a jump and her chins jumped together and her big breasts shook, and she spread her legs with laughter, too, under the table.

" Oh dear ! Oh dear ! " she said. " When I was a girl I was in the catering business and they starved me.

One house I was in the boss used to follow me into the kitchen when I was putting away the snacks to see I didn't pinch anything. And I can tell you it was a work of art slipping a bit of cheese down the neck of me blouse to eat when I got up to bed, it was."

The milkman looked at her blouse. The milkman widened one eye and winked with the other.

" Oh, don't ! " cried the woman, going off again. " Don't ! Stop it ! Don't start me off."

" Don't mind me," said the woman wiping her eyes. " I've been here seven weeks and this is the first laugh I've had. My husband's a cripple. He's a watchmaker. Tick-tock, tick-tock, tick-tock, all day long. He hangs up the watches on the wall and that's all I've heard for seven weeks. Tick-tock, tick-tock, tick-tock."

She wiped the tears from her eyes with her apron and waved an arm to the wall.

There were four clocks on the kitchen wall and three on the mantelpiece, and there were watches hanging on nails. The big brown clock with the pendulum gave a slow grating " Tock " ; the blue alarum on the mantelpiece went at a run ; the big wooden clock next to it made a sweet sound like a man sucking a pipe, and the rest croaked, scratched, ticked and chattered. Carved in fretwork was a small cuckoo-clock beside the door.

" Who winds them ? " asked the milkman with his mouth full of cake.

" Who winds them ? " said the woman. " He winds them. He comes home and spends all night winding them. Have some coffee. You ought to see what I've got inside and upstairs."

" I bet," said the milkman, gazing at her from his still wide eyes. " If there's a drop of coffee, I'll have it."

" Laugh," said the woman. " You can't tell night from day in this house. They all say something different. I've been seven weeks here, but it might be seven years. It's a good thing I can laugh."

" It's slimming," he said.

" It's spreading," she said.

" Well, I like a bit of spread myself," said the milkman.

The milkman watched her go to the range. He watched her bring the coffee-pot over and bring a couple of white cups from the dresser. He got up and went to the door.

" My Jenny," he said. " My mare. Whoa ! Listen to her. She's kicking up the pavement."

The mare was kicking the kerb. She was standing with both feet on it, gazing down the alley and striking a hoof on the pavement.

" She knows I'm in here," he said, coming back. " I bet she knows I'm having a cup of coffee. I bet she's wondering what's happening. I bet she's thinking it out. Wonderful

things horses are. Jealous, you know, too," he said. " If she knew you was in here, I'd never hear the last of it."

" Eating's her trouble. She's old," said the milkman. " She's terrible. I've never seen an animal eat what she does. I bet she knows there's something going on."

The milkman sipped his coffee. His lips made bubbling sounds as he drank. Soon there were no sounds in the room but the ticking of the clocks and the bubbling noise of the woman's lips and the man's lips at their cups, and a click of the cups and a murmur of laughter from the woman.

Then the little fretwork clock which hung by the door gave a small sneezing buzz, a door clipped open, a tiny hammer rang and out bobbed the bird. " Cuckoo ! Cuckoo !" it called, and " Clap " went the door.

The milkman put down his cup with a start and gaped.

" They're all wrong," said the woman " Sit down. Have another cake, just a little one. Have a tart ? That cuckoo's never right. ' Oh, shut up,' I tell it. ' Keep quiet.' "

" I used to do fretwork myself," said the milkman.

" Sit down," she pressed him. "Another cup will warm you up."

" You're warm in here," said the milkman.

" I'm warm anywhere," the woman said.

" Don't want winding up, I bet," said the milkman with a wink. He was short beside her and he took a long easy look at her. He wiped his bald head and put on his hat.

" Well," he said. " Talking of time, one thing leads to another."

She looked at him sadly, and with a lazy yawn raised her big arms above her head.

" Come and see those clocks."

The milkman had his pencil in his ear, a small red stump of pencil. He took it out and, quickly, he gave her a soft poke in the waist with it and went off.

" Good day, ma'am, thank you, ma'am," he called, and went off whistling.

The next day the milk-cart stopped again at the house. Behind the cart the milkman walked, humming to himself. He looked up at the house. There was the short brick wall and the iron rail on top of it. There was the green hedge coming into leaf. He took his basket, he swung open the gate and he went down the alley. There was a smell of pastry just out of the oven. For a long time while he was gone the mare stood, then she stepped on to the kerb and began knocking her hoof upon it. The sound could be heard down the deserted road. " Whoa ! " shouted the milkman down the alley. The mare stretched her neck and sniffed the ground and then began pawing again. She got both forefeet on the pavement and kept stretching and shaking her smooth white neck. "Whoa!" shouted the milkman's voice. She pricked her ears. He was shouting from the front room window.

Half an hour passed. The mare had now stepped farther on to the pavement. Her neck was stretched out to its full length. She was sniffing the wall, the iron rail, and behind it the juicy green shoots of the hedge. She strained, her nostrils trembling, her soft mouth opening to seize a shoot in her old yellow teeth. She paused and made a greater effort, pulling the cart, and now her nose was over the top of the railing. Grunting, chewing, slopping, crunching sounds came from her mouth. She had bitten off her first piece. And, once on it, appetite leapt. She gave a wilder tug and now she could get at the hedge. Her teeth dragged at the hedge and crunched. She raised her neck, looked with discrimination at the shoots, then went on quietly browsing.

No sounds came from the house, no sound from the road but the chewing of the horse, the bit chinking like marbles in her slobber. Hearing him come at last, she backed on to the road. He came out very thoughtful and not whistling.

And some mornings there was the smell of cake in the alley, sometimes it was pie and sometimes it was coffee. Again a quarter of an hour passed, or maybe twenty minutes or half an hour, and often enough a full hour, and a shout of "Whoa!" came from an upstairs window. He had his coat off. "That clock's wrong," said the woman. "They're all wrong." The mare's neck was right over the railings and this was necessary because, as she chewed, the hedge got lower and lower.

"Eh, whoa there!" the milkman shouted down from the top floor of the house one morning and, looking in amazement at the torn and broken green hedge and the mare still tearing at it, he came down to the street.

"What's the idea? Come off it," he said, taking the mare by the bridle and jerking her head off the hedge.

He drew her off the pavement and went back and looked over the railings at the hedge, ruined by weeks of eating.

"Been getting your greens, haven't you?" he said. He stared at the mare and, bright under their blinkers, he saw the eyes of that cynical animal, secretive and glistening, gazing back at him.

★   ★   ★

THE BOTTLE=PARTY BELT

Maurice Richardson

DURING the last few months I have been making a fairly extensive tour of contemporary Night-Town, collecting fierce hangovers and an overdraft. Here are some rather gloomy little notes on the way downhill—fragments from the noctambulant travel-diary of an amateur sociologist.

Out after midnight I tend to go one better than Freud's theory of the death instinct and believe that life is only a disease of matter, a raging condition.

Higher walks of night-life conserve the masochistic traditions of British pleasure-seeking. In ten years nothing seems to have changed, except women's clothes and the names of tunes. Three quarters of the floor space is often taken up by unattached females so terrifyingly ugly that they ought only to be allowed out on Walpurgisnacht. Dance-music itself is lukewarm and would give Bojangles of Harlem pneumonia. Snooty boredom is still the correct facial expression; on sighting a familiar face a faint cry such as "There's Pamela with Duncan" or "There's Pamela without Duncan" is permissible. But in even the dreamiest, most swelegant places—where the 'smart' ones move slow like chameleons in air or schizophrenes emerging from a catatonic stupor—there are sure to be some lobster-pink old men and half-tight old women in funny dresses to provide a livelier, more agitated form of grotesque spectacle.

Another amusement for the savage misanthrope is watching the appalling, ill-concealed discomfort of the self-consciously unsmart out to make a night of it. For example, the following overheard dialogue in *Punch* style, well up to the standard of Swift's

Polite Conversation, between He, She, and the Head-waiter:

Head-waiter: "Is Madame cold?"

She (a languid yet somehow kittenish upper-middle-class ash-blonde): "Oh, I don't know. Yes, perhaps . . ."

He (a really classic bounder tortured by deep conviction of social inferiority and—actually rather handsome—Jewish appearance, but bursting with pride that She has allowed herself to be seen dead with him): "Madam's always cold. That's my trouble."

Visitors to the Bottle-Party Belt, which stretches from midnight to the milkman's round, should not expect too much in the way of excitement. Injections of negroes and swing have hotted up some of the night boxes (how repulsively knowing that sounds!) but plenty are still indistinguishable from their glorious ancestors of the Goddard-Merrick régime: same chlorotic ricketty dance "hostesses" reeking of scent as pungent as 'Flit'; same exasperated drunk banging the fruit machine against the wall. Purveyor of night-life is still a popular profession among ex-army officers of the chronically unsuccessful type. You know the sort : " Poor old Jacko never has any luck. First there was the tobacco plantation in Rhodesia, then the Riding School, then the garage and the flooded chicken-farm. And now he's in a nasty little spot of bother over his bottle-party place."

Describe a night-club. This is a very difficult literary exercise. Frisco's and The Nest, for instance, are both shaped like railway carriages, otherwise as different as the Athenæum and the R.A.C.

When only half full, Frisco's has a distinct melancholico-nostalgic effect, so that you sit quiet and think about the past. It is half dark and greyish-brown fog in colour. Matting and palm grass on the walls try to introduce a jungle motif. There are some livid red globes which may remind you of what your eyeballs will be like next morning. All sorts of people go there—smarties, tired business, films, press, higher bohemians. Their attitude toward Frisco and Frisco's varies from weary resignation to wild enthusiasm. Frisco is a large, astonishingly well preserved West Indian negro. His liveliness is extreme ; sometimes a little forced. I suspect that his laugh is automatic, worked by pressing his lower shirtstud. Rudy, Frisco's lieutenant, is jet black, but has European features. He is very proud of knowing French, and if he gets the chance—as he does when Frisco goes to Bath for his health and he is left in command— Rudy sings, without stopping, several thousand words of it, including *Parlez-moi d'amour*. There are two schools of thought about the cabaret : the naives say it's marvellous ; the sophisticates sigh deeply for Harlem. The band is good, better than anywhere else. There used to be a very clever little creature from Trinidad in it. He was called Cyril Blake and played the trumpet and sang. Even the most Harlem-blasé sophisticate would admit that his version of the *St. James Infirmary Blues* was nearly if not quite classic.

The Nest is tougher and much noisier. It is full of minor curiosities, like a provincial museum. A sleepy Barbadan negro looks after the hats and coats. To pass the time from midnight to breakfast he chews a policeman's truncheon. It was given him two years ago when the greyhound-racing boys were suffering from weltschmerz and he has since chewed it into a long greyish-white spike.

Downstairs the band blows the roof off in a little pen at one end, and at the other handsome suave greyhaired Mr. Cohen, distinguished-looking as a Pall Mall antique-dealer, stands behind a little bar which is stuck all

over with photographs of coloured stars. But he is only the husband of Mrs. Cohen, the finest specimen of a night-club queen in London.

Thin Mrs. Cohen has brilliant hair, wears aquamarine dresses, and is very good-natured. In the language of the guide-books, she would certainly rate four stars.

All colours, sexes and professions. Plenty of negroes—bandsmen, music-hall performers, students, West Indians, Americans, Africans. But very few coloured girls, and those few are nearly all London-born or from Cardiff. If you can forget your conventional agony in the night-club attitude you will find the atmosphere, for a little while at any rate, very friendly, quite democratic, very international. Left-wing poets can be guaranteed a dusty puff of afflatus here.

Most places shut on Sundays but the Nest stays open. You might think that the staffs of Frisco's and the Shim-Sham (rather like The Nest, only larger and less intimate) would be glad

of a rest. But these people have become completely nocturnal and batlike in their habits ; on Sunday nights they flock to the Nest and stay there till five, six and seven.

The number of "clubs" in the Belt must run into hundreds. There are six or seven in Kingly Street alone. They range from the high-class Four Hundred, where you have to be dressed, to little cellars where poor old tarts with sore feet stamp about to the noise of one accordion. I have only been to about twenty, but the sociological department of the London School of Economics will, I hope, conduct an intensive expedition throughout the remainder in search of the zeitgeist. Many of these clubs may be shut down at any moment, but each will figure in somebody's individual history as a landmark of the middle thirties. For many people some club or other in the Belt will be so closely connected with love affairs and sexual adventures that its image will linger in the mind, however blurred with drink.

Outside in the street, alley cats are raking over the muck in the gutters with their expert paws. You buy the *Daily Express* for twopence and try to read it with hot eyes in the taxi. Meanwhile that very silly fat woman who had been mixing gin with brandy has slipped off her chair onto the floor. The two good-timers with her are tugging frantically at her arms, giggling a little. Always end on a moral note.

*

Can you say "yes" in a way to express (a) Conviction, (b) Tenderness, (c) Uncertainty, (d) Contempt, (e) Indignation ?
—*Questionnaire in the* DAILY MIRROR
Yes.

CULTURE AT CARMELITE HOUSE

A crowded audience witnessing a performance of *Macbeth* at a theatre in Debosha, South Poland, tonight sat in complete quiet at the tense moment in the play at which Lady Macbeth kills her husband.—*Daily Mail*.

Kind of took them by surprise, we shouldn't wonder.

Felix Topolski

F^E·F^O·F_I·FUM

*

SHALL WE GATHER
BY THE RIVER?

Felix Topolski

NOTICE THIS GATE

William Empson

WE had stolen a noticeboard saying This Way to the Fairy Glen, which my hostess wanted for the door of her bathroom, and as the car sped away into the night with its secret burden we began discussing noticeboards we had known. Caution, Concealed Entrance, as we passed it, seemed an interesting model, though not a good enough joke to help furnish a house. A good notice gets its peculiar tone of futility from telling you something useless if not obvious, or something that contradicts its own purpose by being said at all. The Fairy notice, I suppose, comes under this head because if any of the Wee Folk were there they certainly trampled each other down as soon as the notice went up, in a mad stampede to get away. Whereas the Entrance was not concealed intentionally, so that the joke, if any, hangs on a misunderstanding. But it suggests a series of really good noticeboards, such as Beware—Police Trap, Warning —Hidden Treasure, and Do Not Step on the International Spy. There used to be a notice on the steps of London buses saying Do not Smoke where the Notice says No Smoking ; this in a way contradicts itself because it admits that people don't obey notices (like the international pacts to observe the previous pacts already broken). But perhaps it comes more under the head of the self-important notice, or notice that talks only to please itself.

I remember walking round one of the reservoirs that supply Tokyo, a very pretty place with wild duck on it but kept feverishly closed because an enemy might come and scatter plague-germs in it, for example. As you went round you met continual notices saying No Road, but if you turned back there were more notices facing the other way and still saying No Road. As trespassing off the paths on Government property is quite unthinkable, you are thus neatly trapped and have to stay where you

are, waiting for a police examination. One cannot say there is anything contradictory about these notices, which indeed carry out a rather ingenious plan, but one might regard them as hopeful to the point of self-importance. No less thoughtful, and more likely to succeed, was a notice somewhere in Wales over a small wooden bridge, which said No Accommodation for Locomotives. As it had no rails, I could more sensibly write on my front door No Admission to Kings, Emperors, or Archbishops, since these moving bodies could at least possibly *try* to come in. But perhaps this is only a Correct Language Joke, always the dullest form of humour ; I do not know why we should limit " locomotive " to railway engines.

A high place among contradictory notices must be taken by the legendary Irish one on a cliff, which said It is Dangerous to Come near Enough to Read this Notice, and may be

regarded as a kind of bait. On one of the fashionable jumps for suicides in Japan there is a notice vaguely like this, though less easy to think funny, which says Think Again—The Country Needs Soldiers, and it is a true but not an uproarious reflection that many visitors are more likely to jump after reading this than before. Perhaps the most simply contradictory notice is Please Ring : Do not Ring Unless an Answer is Required, which the collector can sometimes find combined on one doorway. As to part one, anybody can see the bell is meant to ring and that not everybody is meant to ring it ; as to part two, a boy wanting to ring a bell and run would be rather encouraged to choose this one than not. You would soon get involved in Hegel, trying to explain such a notice ; the thesis and antithesis, by their very incompleteness, are enough to adumbrate the synthesis which this house-

holder has not yet conceived. Or, like the founders of religions, it states a profound paradox merely to give you energy for your own choice of the truth. Also it counts as a self-important funny notice, because presumably what is meant is Use the Bell, Not the Knocker, but Do not Disturb when leaving Letters or Circulars, and the only reason for not saying this outright must be pomposity. And yet again the reason why the contradiction should satisfy a desire for pomp opens a wide field for speculation.

Perhaps the prettiest case of the purely self-important notice was one on a gate which said Notice This Gate. Admittedly it used to say more before it was broken, but the notices you see from the train which say This Is The Famous Jam Factory are not considered funny precisely because they are *not* broken, and mean to say only that. I grant you that one or other of these cases may be unfunny, but they can't both be. And on the whole notices are not funny if they realize what they imply. Thus the variously reported notices to the effect that Natives and Dogs are not Allowed in this Park are not simply funny, whatever else they may be, because they were meant. However, there was a good notice which had nothing whatever on it except Do Not Throw Stones At This Notice, By Order. I think this a valuable specimen of the purely self-regarding, as apart from the pompous, notice. No doubt it would have had other notices pinned onto it from time to time, but this only makes it a better image of the official mind which it unconsciously displays.

The merely unnecessary notice is almost always endearing, but only one grand specimen of it has stuck in my mind. On one of the main motor-roads to Winchester the down suddenly opens to show the whole place lying at your feet, and though the direction and the mileage have long been elaborately marked, and though there is no fork in the road, you find a small demure signpost saying The City of Winchester—and hoping to be included in the photograph.

NEW BOOKS

A Mystic in the Trenches

PAINTERS write well. They do most things, except choosing clothes, better than other people ; they can sail boats and prune fruit trees and bandage cut fingers and work out sums in their heads. The truth is that far higher gifts are needed to paint even a bad picture than to write a good book. Mr. David Jones's pictures are by no means bad and his first book, *In Parenthesis*, is admirable.

It is not easy to describe. It is certainly not a novel, for it lacks the two essentials of story and character ; it is not, what the publishers take it for, an epic poem, for it presents no complete human destiny. It is a piece of reporting interrupted by choruses. It reports a battle on the western front in the middle of the last European war ; a private soldier leaves camp in England, crosses with his regiment to France, goes up the line, is hit in the leg and drags himself off leaving his rifle on the field. It is a book about battle rather than war ; it is completely unsentimental and untendencious ; it is not like *All Quiet* ; it is not like *A Farewell to Arms*, though it might well have usurped that title ; it is not the least like any other war book I have read. I can best describe it by saying that it is as though Mr. T. S. Eliot had written *The Better 'Ole*.

The similarity to Mr. Eliot's work is everywhere apparent, but it is by allusion rather than imitation. The sentry's password is " Prickly Pear". There are the same defects of style— the statement in ponderous detail of simple physical facts—more common in the work of Mr. Eliot's followers than in his own ; the sentry setting his sights " slid up the exact steel, the graduated leaf precisely angled to its bed " ; on the officer's wrist " the phosphorescent dial describes the equal seconds." That way lie the extravagances of the Augustan tradition in decadence. There are also the too facile contrasts by juxtaposition of scholarly tags and modern slang—the standard fare of the parodist. There are whole passages which, out of the context, one might take for extracts from *The Waste Land*. " You sensed him near you just now but that's more like a nettle to the touch ; or on your left Joe Donkin walked, where only weeds stir to the night-gusts if you feel with your hands." But there is an essential difference between *The Waste Land* and *In Parenthesis*. Mr. Eliot in his great passage of the unknown intangible companion is writing metaphorically ; he is seeking concrete images to express a psychological state. Mr. Jones is describing an objective physical experience—the loss of contact with neighbouring files in a night attack. It is this painter's realism

---

In Parenthesis. David Jones. Faber & Faber. 10s. 6d.
Tunbridge Wells. Margaret Barton. Faber & Faber. 15s.

---

which lifts his work above any of Mr. Eliot's followers and, in many places, above Mr. Eliot himself. Moreover, he has a painter's *communicativeness*. The literary mind is a rat on a treadwheel ; too many modern poetic writers employ a language which can be intelligible only to themselves ; they relate experiences one to another inside themselves. Mr. Jones is seldom obscure and never esoteric ; he must be read with the attention of a surgeon, but there is not a sentence which on analysis lacks a precise meaning. Indeed he is at too great pains to explain himself. He would not, I think, like to pin an explanation to the frames of his pictures, and his writing is too lucid to need such adventitious contributions. For he writes with the respect of a stranger. He knows that he is practising an unfamiliar art, which has its own potentialities and limitations. As a painter he studies his subject for its visual qualities ; now he is dealing with words, and his aim is to make a book about the verbal aspect of battle. For twenty years the rich components have been seeking their proper arrangement in his mind— the liturgical repetitions and variations of the drill sergeant's commands, the luminous phrases of Cockney and Welshman, the songs and trench-jokes —and he has at last got them into order, with remarkable felicity. That is his *rapportage;* in his choruses—as for want of a better word one can call the metaphysical reflexions, often only a line in length—the reader is allowed the luxury of deducing his own conclusions.

It is always temerarious to attempt an explanation of a living writer's meaning. It seems to me that Mr. Jones sees man in a dual rôle—as the individual soul, the exiled child of Eve, living, in a parenthesis, a Platonic shadow-life, two dimensional, the Hollow Man ; and man as the heir of his ancestors, the link in the continuous life-chain, the race-unit. Perhaps it is presumptuous to go further and suggest that the final, exquisitely written passages in which the hero abandons his weapons on the field—the ultimate reproach of the heroic age—are meant to show that the race-myth has been sloughed off, leaving only the stark alternatives of Heaven and Hell. That anyway is how I understand it.

After reading *In Parenthesis* it is quite impossible to turn immediately to another book. The soft clay of ordinary workaday literary language gives no foothold after the rocks ; the lowland air is suffocating. But it is a matter of acclimatization. In a very different degree *Tunbridge Wells*, by Miss Margaret Barton, is a charming book, agreeably produced, full of flavour and readable discussion. It is a leisurely well-bred history, appropriate to its subject, of England's second Spa ; a work of culture and industry ; a flattering gift worth keeping permanently on one's shelves, providing for the reader a vicarious intimacy with his superiors.

EVELYN WAUGH

*

If you happen to use the wrong fork at dinner, can you be nonchalant ?
—*Questionnaire in the* DAILY MIRROR
Nonchalant ? We're positively truculent.

IN THE COUNTRY

The Artists Arrive

THERE is the swallow, of course ; but we never really feel that summer is here till the artists arrive. But for that derelict cottage down the lane we might never have had them. We get expectant about Whitsun. Then one day smoke is seen rising from the old chimney.

The tenancy of the cottage is vague ; rent has ceased to pass. There is a sort of implicit agreement that as long as they can keep the old thing habitable they can live in it. The cottage itself had come to look less like a habitation than a heap of straw left over from some bygone threshing. Or an old nest.

It has been uninhabited since Mrs. Cotts brought up a family of thirteen there. That was fifteen years ago. Its furnishing is disproportionate, being a residue from the house of a Victorian great-aunt deceased. There is a collection of wine glasses sufficient in size and number for a banquet, but only a few blankets ; specialized cutlery—a lobster pick, asparagus tongs—but not enough teaspoons.

These people positively enjoy what we endure : mud, draughts, winter. Yes, sometimes they come in the winter. I remember a particularly watery twilight in December The cattle were standing knee-deep in soupy mud, the only piece of ground left unflooded by the river. " My God—how lovely ! " cried the artist to his wife. " What's lovely ? " I ventured to ask. " Why, those cattle standing there, the mud, and the floods behind."

They sleep soundly on camp beds about as wide and as comfortable as planks, while farmers lie rolled in the ancestral feather mattress. Early in the morning the herdsman is entertained to see them standing waist-high in the river, cake of soap in one hand, loofah in the other. And the shepherd comes

later with the news that one of them's acting wholly queer up on Nine Acres. " Reckon he's a cloudy." Sure enough he is bent low, prowling along as though in pain or fear. " Every foot makes a difference," he says. He is hunting perspectives. He pulls up short. " What a wonderful colour that wire is ! "—in a tone of rapture. It is a line of crumply sheep netting, rusty and derelict. Not until one gets it out of one's head that it is old and useless and ought to have been taken up months ago does one see that it exists in its own right in a brittle luminous way.

Hay and corn harvest are feverish times for farmers : but for painters even more so. A field left for the night half cut : tomorrow it will be different ; tonight it is a composition. And what a race there is in the hay harvest. Captain, the grey, is trace-horse ; Boxer, the Suffolk, is in the shafts. The artist sits himself down right in front of them and begins painting for dear life, while the men unload at the stack. Every time they finish a load and want to shift, he has to move, canvas, paints, camp stool and all. They can't get by him, and it would spoil his picture if he sat anywhere else. But back he comes again and goes on titivating his picture till they return. Then he really gets down to it once more, as Captain and Boxer stand there and the men sweat unloading. They have a look at what

he is doing. From wispy bits of white and brown Captain and Boxer begin to emerge ; then—" Look, that's George. Hi George, here y'are, bor ! " The stack, the buildings beyond. It becomes quite exciting, wondering how much more of them there'll be by next time. The stack is finished first though, and Captain has to go cutting on another field. The picture is finished under difficulties : it is all in bits. The artist comes and hangs around wistfully, noting little bits of Boxer here, of Captain away over there, and the wagon laid up in the cart shed.

Things get behind during harvest : there's no time to put things tidily away. The farm buildings are all in a muddle. One day the farmer is shocked to find his farmyard being painted in its most shamefully muddy condition. " If you'd only ha' told me," he cries in vexation, " I'd have had the place cleared up a bit—not them barn doors left open, and all that litter of straw and hurdles about."

The painter begs him earnestly to alter nothing ; tells him it is beautiful, seemly, perfectly in keeping.

" That's all very well, but what'll people think when you show that there picture up in London ? ' Ho,' they'll say, ' so that's the sort of muck Farmer Brown keeps his place in, is it ? ' "

ADRIAN BELL

'What, fish again!'

THE THEATRE

Victoria Regina

VICTORIA REGINA has a frontispiece: the ordinary Lyric curtain rolls up to show the prettiest wreath of painted cochineal roses encircling an album dream-view—Windsor, glassy blue towers and blue swans. Everyone claps violently and goes on clapping till the frontispiece, too, rolls up and the play starts. This pink wreath might well be cut out and left stuck in position, for it is the note of the play. It is the polite (and very stylish) solution of all sorts of delicate points: it sets the nine scenes back in a *genre*, smiling, tearful distance, as it sets Windsor towers. It makes everything perfectly all right, and only shows what good taste and Mr. Rex Whistler can do. After all this fuss, we had naturally rather wondered. . . . But what we get served to us is a tasty little *khebab*, infinitesimal pieces of the royal vitals skewered between rose-leaves on a Cupid's arrow. The plot is about the Queen as a married woman.

As the play was first written, it need not have been shocking to the most loyal susceptibilities. But the result of the fuss is a sort of strip-tease effect, and that sort of thing makes you nervous and unsettled. The lights keep going out; in the (too many) intervals there is a bothered tension: you know you can't hope to begin where you left off. It is quite a miracle that the play as it is now has got *any* continuity at all—but it has. This is a grim play which, however mutilated, however much stylized, still keeps its hold on the nerves—a play about more than frustration, a play about the indecent human heart. Something crops up in every scene. But how the whole thing is obstructed—the first five minutes of each scene is stolen by the *décor*—so stupendously "amusing", stylized, scrolled, buttoned, gilded and coloured

that the eye just wanders round and you don't want anyone there. Then, from half way through, every scene is tensed up by a sort of overhead rustle—the curtain ready to drop. So that this is the sort of play you really only begin to see the point of on the way home.

The fact is, they have made this into a play about marriage; you can't have a play about marriage without some false position, and the false position, for drama, has got to be stressed. In this case the false position is being royal—that is really the only part being royal plays in the play. There has to be a predicament—the predicament here is Albert's, which makes him the big figure. He has to *se laisser aimer*—and how he could have courted! He has to make a business of what was meant for a pleasure. And there is public life too: one way or another he is never off duty. First of all, he stands looking out at the rain at Windsor: how much more rain he will see if Victoria marries him. He is a German, all soul and yet knowing the drill. The lot for which he is chosen holds no ecstacies; he is bothered by Victoria on the honeymoon running round while he shaves. This scene is called Morning Glory: they hear the band in the park. All their years he is making for her a gothic world of emotion in which she is as much out of place as one of her little buttoned Buckingham Palace armchairs. What a man he is! This play goes to show that cads have not all the glamour: here (alive inside that wreath of artificial roses) is the great tragic prig—he makes drama, he steals the heart. He is quite likely to start a new vogue in men. He gets the better of her in two sublimated rough house scenes that will leave no woman cold—her tears, his inexorable sad smile, her vain gestures in the tight little gloves. The way this play is played, it is not even satirical—and there is no doubt whatever that Albert steals it: it really ought to be called *Albert the Good*. As Albert Mr. Carl Esmond could not be better. He has such long legs, he is all deportment and soul.

This play looks like a compromise:

it may not really be what anyone meant at all. Most people are likely to go and see it, because it will make a topic, because it is once or twice so agreeably upsetting, because, what with Rex Whistler and one thing and another, it really is a first rate *tour de force*. If you have seen it in New York or Paris, come and see how London jumps its special difficulties. All honour is due to Miss Pamela Stanley, a spirited doughty moving little Victoria. She plays finely in a part that gives not much room to move in—she gives the effect of a temperament bumping about inside. This is finished acting, with a quite big imagination behind it; it comes from her head and her heart; she either uses her features or makes them for the occasion—eyelids, sharp nose, chin-line, tight little hands. She shows Victoria filling out from an unglamourous girl, with a certain amount of sharp charm and that rather dreary attribute "character", into a woman like a cardinal under her widow's cap, sentimental, but all control and astuteness. She shows that old baffled emotion keeps driving in. She shows flesh, grief, and the years acting on a mentality. I could swear her hands are plumper by the end of the play.

Mr. Ernest Milton as Lord Beaconsfield, sipping the situation in the marquee at Balmoral, is not played off by the wasp or eclipsed by Whistler geraniums. In fact, all the actors are up over this play.

The Great Romancer was another period play, about Alexandre Dumas *père*, which is now historical (it came off last Saturday). Mr. Robert Morley did Dumas proud: a rather grand incorrigible old buck rabbit, throwing about the money, grinding out the romances and making love. The play should have been either more pointed or more *risqué*: it was the sort of play we never do very well—but everybody showed verve and they deserved a pat on the back. There were three women, all in distracting dresses. Miss Coral Browne has an excellent Ingres face. Only I somehow feel we have had enough circumspect plays about great lovers.

ELIZABETH BOWEN.

THE CINEMA

Lenin and Lavender

NO need to stop and think about which is the best film to be seen in London. It's undoubtedly *We From Kronstadt*. Russian, full of absurd heroics, noble deaths, last minute rescues, wounded men played up to the trenches by a scarecrow band, it is no more propagandist than Henty. In a sense all writing for schoolboys is propaganda for the established order, and in this film, just as much as in *Tom Brown's Schooldays*, the people who don't stick to the old school code end by having a thin time. What makes the film immeasurably superior to its rivals is the strain of adult poetry, the sense of human beings longing for peace, grasping moments out of the turmoil for ordinary human relations, and the most cynical Conservative will cheer at the defiant closing line : "Who else wants Petrograd ?"

The best line to cheer on in *The Frog*, an English thriller, is " I must get John Bennett's gramophone record if I am to save his son's life." The dialogue otherwise goes rather like this: " My name is Bennett—Stella Bennett." " No, not really ? Stella Bennett ? What a charming name ! I very much hope we shall meet again one day soon." " Must you really go ? Goodbye then." " What, Stella ! Are these gentlemen still here ? " " We were on the point of leaving, sir." " This is my father, inspector. May I introduce Inspector Elk of Scotland Yard ? " " Goodbye, Miss Bennett. Please don't trouble to see us out. Goodbye, sir. Haven't we met somewhere before ? " " No. Goodbye." While the well-mannered dialogue drones on, a bomb is touched off in Scotland Yard, the voice of the master criminal is trapped on a gramophone disc by a bird watcher, the factory containing the matrix is burnt to the ground, an innocent man is sentenced to death, and the public executioner entering the condemned cell finds his own son there. Badly directed, badly acted, it is like one of those plays produced in country towns by stranded actors : it has an old world charm : Scotland Yard is laid up in lavender.

Make Way For Tomorrow is a depressing picture about an old couple driven by hard times to live on their children. No one wants them, no one can put them both up at the same time. After months of separation they meet for a few hours in New York before the old man goes off to a daughter in California and the old woman into a home, with no hope of seeing each other again. The Pullman slides out, the aged tortoise face turns away, the tight thin bun of hair drearily fades out, and a sense of misery and inhumanity is left vibrating in the nerves. Anyhow that was how the story appeared to me, though Paramount describe it in these terms : " One of the Three Smart Girls goes a lot faster. She wants to taste the Thrills of Life itself. WHAT HAPPENS ?"

Der Herrscher, except for a pleasantly savage opening, a funeral frieze of dripping umbrellas and heartless faces, is a wordy picture about an elderly ironmaster who wants to marry his secretary and is almost driven insane by his children's opposition. Herr Jannings has the meaningless gaze of a sea lion with huge sloping shoulders and watery whiskers, to whose emotions we apply, for want of anything better, such human terms as pity, anger, terror, though we cannot tell, on the evidence of those small marine eyes, whether he is really registering anything more than a dim expectation of fish.

GRAHAM GREENE

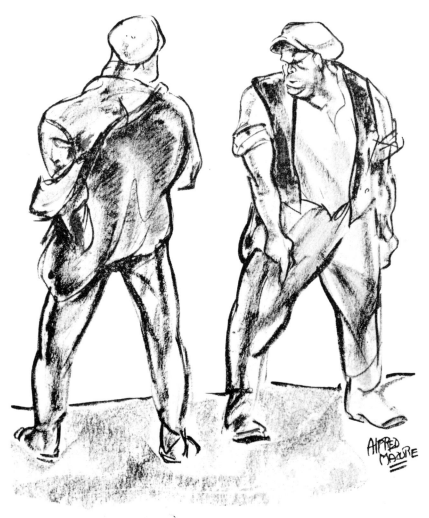

'*I tell you it was Beethoven.*'

LONDON BY NIGHT AND DAY

BALLET

A Selection of Pleasures and Places

ROYAL OPERA HOUSE, Covent Garden, W.C.2 (Tem. 7961).—Col. de Basil's Ballets Russes. Thur. July 8, 8.45 : *Les Cents Baisers, Cleopatra, Le Beau Danube.* Fri. July 9, 8.45 : *Cimarosiana, Choreartium, Le Spectre de la Rose, Prince Igor.* Sat. July 10, 2.30 : *Les Femmes de Bonne Humeur, Symphonie Fantastique, Danses Slaves et Tziganes.* 8.45 : *Le Pavillon, Cleopatra, Le Beau Danube.* Mon. July 12, 8.45 : *Scuola di Ballo, Le Tricorne, Cimarosiana.* Tues. July 13, 8.45 : *Le Lac des Cygnes, Symphonie Fantastique, Cleopatra.* Wed. July 14, 2.30 : *Scuola di Ballo, Symphonie Fantastique, Prince Igor.* 8.45 : *Les Cents Baisers, Choreartium, Cimarosiana.*
UDAY SHAN-KAR.—Unique troupe of Indian dancers and musicians. *GAIETY*, Strand (Tem. 6991), 8.45. Thur., Sat., 2.45.

PLAYS

BLACK LIMELIGHT. — Well-constructed thriller about homicidal maniac who kills when the moon is full. Margaret Rawlings in a double part and a bathing-suit gives a versatile performance. *DUKE OF YORK'S*, St. Martin's Lane (Tem. 5122), 8.30. Wed., Sat., 2.30.
FRENCH WITHOUT TEARS. — English adolescents having high jinks in French family. Good laughs and very good acting. Kay Hammond, Guy Middleton, Rex Harrison. *CRITERION*, Piccadilly Circus, W.1 (Whi. 3844), 8.40. Tues., Sat., 2.30.
GEORGE AND MARGARET.—Comedy of English middle-class life. Extremely funny and just the thing for the Great British Public. Joyce Barbour, Ronald Ward and Jane Baxter. *WYNDHAM'S*, Charing Cross Road, W.C.2 (Tem. 3028), 8.30. Wed., Thur., 2.30.
JUDGMENT DAY.—Strong drama of political trial in totalitarian state with underlined moral. By Elmer Rice. Catherine Lacey, Dan Tobin. *PHŒNIX*, Charing Cross Road, W.C.2 (Tem. 8611), 8.30. Thur., Sat., 2.30.
JULIUS CÆSAR.—Neil Porter, Phyllis Neilson-Terry, Fay Compton, Ion Swinley. Sylvan setting, perfect open-air technique, bearing no relation to vicarage-fête theatricals. *OPEN AIR THEATRE*, Regent's Park (Wel. 8162), 8.15. Tues., Thur., Sat., 2.30.
SARAH SIMPLE.—Comedy by A. A. Milne, well acted. Nice gentlemanly humour about divorce. Leonora Corbett. *GARRICK*, Charing X Rd.(Tem. 4601), 8.40. Mon., Thur., 2.30.
SATYR.—Psychological study of a diseased mind. Morbid theme conscientiously treated. Flora Robson, Marius Goring. *SHAFTESBURY*, Shaftesbury Ave. (Ger. 6666), 8.30. Tues., Thur., 2.30.
THEY CAME BY NIGHT.—Owen Nares in thriller about international jewel thieves. Ursula Jeans as the girl he loves. *GLOBE*, Shaftesbury Ave., W.1 (Ger. 1592), 8.30. Wed., Thur., 2.30.
UP THE GARDEN PATH.—Comedy of family life by Ireland Wood. Cast headed by Muriel Aked, Beatrix Lehmann. *EMBASSY*, 64 Eton Ave., Hampstead, N.W.3 (Pri. 2211), 8.15. Sat., 2.30.
VICTORIA REGINA.—Interesting characterization of Victoria the Good and Albert the Wise. Moving moments and good production. *LYRIC*, Shaftesbury Ave., W.1 (Ger. 3686), 8.30. Wed., Thur., 2.30.
YES, MY DARLING DAUGHTER.—The moral of this comedy is that mothers prefer their daughters not to be like themselves—at any rate in the matter of pre-marital chastity. Sybil Thorndike, Leon Quartermaine, Jessica Tandy. *ST. JAMES'S*, King Street, S.W.1 (Whi. 3903), 8.30. Wed., Thur., Sat., 2.30.

FIRST NIGHTS

WOMEN OF PROPERTY.—Strong, realistic drama of three women struggling for one man. Translated from the Finnish. May Morris, Griffiths Jones. *QUEEN'S*, Shaftesbury Ave., W.1 (Ger. 4517). July 8 at 8 p.m. Subsequently at 8.30. Wed., Sat., 2.30.

LIST OF CONTENTS

★

VOLUME I   NUMBER 2

Registered at the G.P.O. as second-class matter

NIGHT AND DAY MAGAZINES LTD.

97 St. Martin's Lane, London, W.C.2

Telephone : Temple Bar 9878/9.

★

PRINTED BY HAZELL, WATSON & VINEY, LTD., AND PUBLISHED FOR NIGHT AND DAY MAGAZINES, LTD. BY CHATTO & WINDUS, 40-42, CHANDOS STREET, STRAND, W.C.2.

MUSICAL AND VARIETY

BALALAIKA.—Pre-revolutionary Russia and what fun it was for dashing Cossack captains and beautiful ballerinas. *HIS MAJESTY'S*, Haymarket, S.W.1 (Whi. 6606), 8.15. Wed., Sat., 2.30.
FLOODLIGHT.—Revue by Beverley Nichols. Pretty décor, lively caste and chorus, less lively satire. Frances Day, John Mills, Hermione Baddeley. *SAVILLE*, Shaftesbury Ave., W.1 (Tem. 4011), 8.30. Wed., 2.30. [*See p.* 29.]
REVUDEVILLE.—Continuous revue, 1.30 to 11.30, last performance 9.30. *WINDMILL*, Great Windmill Street, W.1 (Ger. 7413).
VARIETY.—Harry Richman, Mills Brothers, Max Miller. *PALLADIUM*, Oxford Circus (Ger. 7373), 6.20, 9.

FILMS

WE FROM KRONSTADT.—Exciting Soviet film of the rout of White forces by Red sailors defending Petrograd in 1919. Ran for 9 months in Paris. *ACADEMY*, 105 Oxford Street, W.1 (Ger. 2981).
DER HERRSCHER.—Emil Jannings as elderly man who discovers that respectability and prosperity are dust and ashes. *BERKELEY*, Berkeley Street, W.1 (May. 5768).
I MET HIM IN PARIS.—Witty comedy of sexual rivalry. Claudette Colbert, Melvyn Douglas, Robert Young. *CARLTON*, Haymarket, W.1 (Whi. 3711).
BARBARY COAST (revival).—San Francisco in the roaring pioneering days. Edward Robinson. (Until July 11.) THINGS TO COME (revival).—Bastard vision of the future by Wells out of Korda. (From July 12.) *CHELSEA CLASSIC*, King's Road, S.W.3 (Fla. 4388).
THE COURT WALTZES.—Rivalry of waltz-king Lanner and young Johann Strauss at court of Queen Victoria and in Vienna. Fernand Gravey, Jeanine Crispin. *CURZON*, Curzon Street, W.1 (Gro. 4100).
THE MAN IN POSSESSION (revival).—Jean Harlow and Robert Taylor. (Until July 10.) *DOMINION*, Tottenham Court Road, W.C.2 (Mus. 2176).
NIGHT MUST FALL.—From Emlyn Williams's murder play. Robert Montgomery, Rosalind Russell. *EMPIRE*, Leicester Square, W.C.2 (Ger. 1234).
MEN AND JOBS (revival).—Russia laughs at itself. Not documentary. Also PETRIFIED FOREST. *FORUM*, Villiers Street, W.C.2 (Tem. 3931).
KID GALAHAD.—Edward G. Robinson and Bette Davis in boxing film. *GAUMONT*, Haymarket, S.W.1 (Whi. 6655).
ST. QUENTIN.—Prison picture on lines of " Big House." Revolt of convicts in American goal and complication created by the chief warder's sister. Pat O'Brien, Ann Sheridan, Humphrey Bogart. *LONDON PAVILION*, Piccadilly Circus, W.1 (Ger. 2982).
THE ROAD BACK.—Grimly sincere story of the soldier's return to civilian life from the novel by Erich Maria Remarque. John King, Louise Fazenda. *LEICESTER SQUARE*, Leicester Square, W.C.2 (Whi. 5252).
BLACK LEGION.—Best tough film since *Fury* and more ruthless. Humphrey Bogart. *NEW GALLERY*, Regent Street, W.1 (Reg. 8080).
REMOUS (revival).—French film with English sub-titles of crippled husband, wife and lover finely acted. Jean Galland. (Until July 10.) THE BRIDE COMES HOME, with Claudette Colbert. (From July 11.) *NOTTING HILL EMBASSY*, Notting Hill, W.8 (Par. 5750).
THE LAST TRAIN FROM MADRID.—Refugees escape from Spanish civil war. Public escapes from theatre. (Until July 8.) THE HIGH COMMAND.—More civil war, this time in Ireland in 1921. Lucie Mannheim, Lionel Atwill. (From July 9.) *PLAZA*, Lower Regent Street, S.W.1 (Whi. 8944).
LOST HORIZON.—Spectacular Hollywood adaptation of James Hilton's novel about a group of people who forget time in a Tibetan monastery. Ronald Colman, Jane Wyatt. *TIVOLI*, Strand, W.C.1 (Tem. 5625).

LONDON BY NIGHT AND DAY (continued)

ART GALLERIES

[Admission is free unless otherwise stated.]

ADAMS, 2 Pall Mall Place, S.W.1.—19th and 20th century French drawings, including works of Sisley, Constantin Guys, Boudin, Pissaro, Forain, Picasso and Utrillo.

AGNEW, 43 Old Bond Street, W.1.—Exhibition of contemporary paintings and sculpture chosen by the artists and including works by Sickert, John, Duncan Grant, Keith Baynes, Vanessa Bell, Henry Moore, Dobson.

COLNAGHI, 144 New Bond Street, W.1.—Old masters, English, French and Dutch of the 17th and 18th centuries; including the largest Gainsborough in the world.

LEFEVRE, 1A King Street, St. James's S.W.1.—19th century French masters from Corot to Cézanne. Also gouaches and oil paintings by Jean Hugo.

LEICESTER GALLERIES, Green Street, Leicester Square, W.C.1.—Pictures of Victorian life by artists of the period 1837-1901. *Admission* 1s. 2d.

MAYOR, 19 Cork Street, W.1.—Works by Georges Roualt and other modern masters.

REDFERN, 20 Cork Street, W.1.—Lithographs in colour by Bonnard, Vuillard, Marie Laurencin, Toulouse-Lautrec. Also recent water colours by Rowland Suddaby.

TOOTH, 155 New Bond Street, W.1.—Water colours and drawings for the Diaghileff Ballet by Alexandre Benois.

WILDENSTEIN, 147 New Bond Street, W.1.—Old and modern masters.

ZWEMMER, 26 Litchfield Street, Charing Cross Road, W.C.1.—Exhibition of Nigerian sculptures and paintings, from July 6.

SPORT

CRICKET.—Lord's. Eton v. Harrow, July 9-10. Gentlemen v. Players, July 14-16. Oval. Women's Cricket. England v. Australia, July 10-13.

CROQUET.—Hurlingham. England v. Australia, July 12-13.

GOLF.—British Open Championship, Carnoustie. Finishing July 9.

HORSE SHOWS.—Imber Court show, Thames Ditton, July 7-8.

LAWN TENNIS.—Army Championships, Aldershot, July 12-17.

POLO.—Hurlingham. The Tyro Cup, July 5-10; Cicero Cup, July 12-17. Roehampton. Shaw Cup, July 5-10; Military Handicap Challenge Cup, July 12-17; Ladies' Nomination Challenge Cup, July 12-17.

RACING.—Newmarket, July 13-15.

SPEEDWAY RACING.—Harringay, Saturdays, 8.15 p.m. Hackney Wick, Fridays, 8.15 p.m. New Cross, Wednesdays, 8.15 p.m. Wimbledon, Mondays, 8.15 p.m. West Ham, Tuesdays, 8.15 p.m. Wembley, Thursdays, 8.15 p.m.

RESTAURANTS

A L'ECU DE FRANCE, 109 Jermyn Street, S.W.1 (Whi. 2549).—For the connoisseur of food and wine who takes his pleasure gaily. French cuisine of the highest order, different regional dishes every day and many other eating adventures. Pleasant room, very full.

ANTOINE'S, 40 Charlotte Street, W.1 (Mus. 2817).—Good inexpensive French cooking in pungently Latin atmosphere.

AU PETIT COIN DE FRANCE, 7 Carnaby Street, W.1 (Ger. 5010).—French cooking with an Alsatian bias. *Pâté de Strasbourg* and Frankfürter sausages. Very inexpensive.

BERKELEY BUTTERY, Berkeley Street, W.1 (Reg. 8282).—Cool salads and light snacks for the Smart and would-be-Slim. Gay and always full.

BOULESTIN, 25 Southampton Street, W.C.2 (Tem. 7061).—Sacred temple of the culinary arts. Open on Sundays when a prix-fixe dinner is served for 8s. 6d.

CAFE ROYAL, 68 Regent Street, W.1 (Reg. 8240).—Bohemia, distinguished and undistinguished. The best 3s. 6d. lunch in Town.

CHEZ VICTOR, 45 Wardour Street (Ger. 6523).—Victor, ex-headwaiter of the Escargot, knows how to mix a French salad and many other essentials of the kind. Moderate prices.

CUMBERLAND, Marble Arch, W.1 (Amb. 1234).—Gives the biggest feed in London for 5s., eight courses with a *sorbet* halfway through to egg you on. The Grill is even cheaper, but there's usually a queue.

KEMPINSKI, 99 Regent Street, W.1 (Reg. 2939).—Specializes in Teutonic fare in a strongly Norddeutscher Lloyd setting. Excellent Rhine wines and solid comfort.

L'APERITIF, 102 Jermyn Street, S.W.1. (Whi. 1571).—Small, elegant, convivial. The agreeable cocktail bar upstairs is a favourite rendezvous.

LE COQ D'OR, Stratton Street, Piccadilly, W1. (May. 7807-9).—French auberge style, *poulet à la broche*, wine served *en pichet*.

LE PERROQUET, 43 Leicester Square, W.C.2 (Whi. 2996).—Small and soothing. Deep personal interest in all you eat taken by proprietor and entire staff. Prawn cocktail and *suprême de volaille sous la cloche* among specialities. Lunch 5s. 6d., dinner 7s. 6d.

L'ESCARGOT BIENVENU, 48 Greek Street, W.1 (Ger. 4460).—First-rate *cuisine bourgeoise*, very French and reasonable prices.

LE TRIANON, 89 Jermyn Street, S.W.1 (Whi. 1471).—New, spacious and well conceived. Lavish floral decorations and heavily guardée clientèle, but you can dine well, nevertheless. Theatre dinner 8s. 6d.

MAJORCA, 15 Brewer Street, W.1 (Ger. 6776).—Spanish, as its name implies. Good, moderately priced Spanish food and wines. Attractive décor.

MONSEIGNEUR, 16 Jermyn Street, S.W.1 (Reg. 6957).—Admirable for lunch or quick theatre dinner. Snack bar with delicious *plats du jour* and wine on draught.

OVERTON'S, 4 Victoria Buildings, S.W.1 (Vic. 3774).—Good English cooking in Victorian wagon-lit atmosphere. Fish excellent.

PRUNIER'S, 72 St. James's Street, S.W.1 (Reg. 1373).—Every variety of sea food from clams to caviare. Wine on draught, and oysters at any time of the year.

QUAGLINO'S, 16 Bury Street, S.W.1 (Whi. 7151).—The brave, the young, the fair have been coming here for ten years, and also the discerning if they're very rich. Evening dress except in the Grill. Theatre dinner, 10s. 6d.

QUINTO'S, Arlington House, Arlington Street, S.W.1 (Reg. 2874).—Of Monte Carlo fame. Excellent chef, highly priced wines.

SALZBURG GRILL (Austria Restaurant), Piccadilly Circus (Whi. 7361).—Austrian cuisine in Tyrolese décor. Light white Austrian wines.

SAVOY GRILL, Strand, W.C.2 (Tem. 4343).—Lunch with Press Barons, Film Magnates, Heavyweight Champions, Egyptian Pashas.

SIMPSON'S - IN - THE - STRAND, W.C.2 (Tem. 7131).—British to the bone and the best of its kind. Don't forget to tip the carver when you have a cut off the joint.

SOVRANI, 163 Knightsbridge, S.W.7 (Ken. 1400).—Late of Jermyn Street and now in wider, more open spaces, to which he is a useful addition. And his prices are lower.

ZOOLOGICAL GARDENS RESTAURANT, Regent's Park, N.W.1 (Pri. 6622).—Dinner on Wednesdays and Thursdays when Zoo remains open until 11.30. Excellent *table d'hôte*, 4s. 6d. and 7s. 6d. Floodlit animals. Band of His Majesty's Guards, but kept well under control.

SUPPER DANCE AND CABARET

BERKELEY, Piccadilly, W.1 (Reg. 8282).—Goes down with everybody from a débutante to a maiden aunt. Chick Endor and Charlie Farrell entertain with American songs until July 10. Extension Wednesday. (Dress.)

CAFE ANGLAIS, Leicester Square, W.1 (Whi. 7941).—Informal. Stage people. Eileen Stanley, American record and radio Baby until July 10. Extension Friday. (Dress optional.)

CAFE DE PARIS, 3 Coventry Street, W.1 (Ger. 2462).—Sophisticated atmosphere, good supper. Harry Richman, American singer, and Florence Desmond, well-known impersonator, in team work. Extension Wednesday. (Dress to dance.)

DORCHESTER, Park Lane, W.1 (May. 8888).—"Just For Fun," an elaborate cabaret show, including Maurice and Cordoba, ballroom dancers; Joe Jackson, clown; Senor Wences, ventriloquist; and the Albertina Rasch Girls. Naunton Wayne is compère. Jack Jackson's band. Extension Thursday. (Dress.)

GROSVENOR HOUSE, Park Lane, W.1 (Gro. 6363).—Home from home for millionaires and maharajahs. All-star Comedy Cabaret, with Harris and Shaw, American dancers; Keene twins; Paul Remos and his Wonder Boys; to say nothing of acrobatic dancers and stunt banjoists. Extension Thursday. (Dress.)

HUNGARIA, 16 Lower Regent Street, S.W.1 (Whi. 4222).—Local colour, exotic food, Zigani orchestra conducted by Bela Bizony. Also two Russian guitarist singers. Dim Dremo and Georges Gladyrevsky. Extension Tuesday. (Dress for restaurant.)

LONDON CASINO, Old Compton Street, W.1 (Ger. 4693).—Full size revue, "Folie d'Amour" on the stage, food in the stalls, conversation superfluous. (Must dress to dance after 11 p.m.)

MAYFAIR, Berkeley Street, W.1 (May. 7777).—Transatlantic crowd. Billy Bissett and his Royal Canadians. Edward Cooper with songs at the piano until July 10. From July 12, Fred Brazin, illusionist. Loper and Hayes, dancers. Extension Friday. (Dress.)

QUAGLINO, Bury Street, W.1 (Whi. 7151).—Very fashionable. Cabaret at midnight. Warner and Darnell, entertainers at the piano. Extension Wednesday. (Dress.)

RITZ, Piccadilly, W.1 (Reg. 8181).—Crowded with the fearfully smart. Reine Paulette, singer of French songs; Howard Brooks, conjuror; Stetson, juggler—until July 12. Extension Wednesday. (Dress.)

SAN MARCO, Devonshire House, Piccadilly, W.1 (May. 4811).—Striking Venetian décor by Oliver Messel. Dancing to Ben Oakley and his Barnstormers. Cabaret changes weekly. (Dress to dance.)

SAVOY, Strand, W.C.2 (Tem. 4343).—Gay and very smart, particularly during Ballet Season. Cabaret twice nightly. Cardini, the Suave Deceiver (card manipulator); Dario and Diane, high speed dancers. Extension Thursday. (Dress.)

TRIANON, 85-6-7 Jermyn Street, W.1 (Whi. 1471).—Large and airy. Bar within easy reach. Charlie Wright accompanies his songs with an accordion. (Dress.)

BOTTLE PARTIES

[The Private Party system operates at the undermentioned. Order drinks 24 hours before first visit.]

COCOANUT GROVE, 177 Regent Street, W.1 (Reg. 7675).—English and Hungarian bands alternate in a South Sea Island setting. Cabaret, supper. (Dress optional.)

FOUR HUNDRED, 28 Leicester Square, W.C.2 (Whi. 1813).—Favourite haunt of the rich after 2 a.m. Very subdued lighting, supper menu includes Chinese food. (Dress.)

FRISCO, 17 Frith Street, W.1 (Ger. 1446).—The genuine pulse of Africa, migrating via Harlem and Paris, now throbs in this Soho "boîte." This is the real thing. (Dress optional.)

HAVANA, 6 New Compton Street, W.C.2 (Tem. 7594).—Cuban band, rumbas, cabaret with Edward Cooper. Air cooled. Breakfast. (Dress optional.)

PARADISE, 189 Regent Street, W.1 (Reg. 1514).—Makes a feature of cabaret. Len Hayes' band. (Dress optional.)

THE OLD FLORIDA, South Bruton Mews, W.1 (Reg. 3016).—Eminently respectable. Supper menu and cabaret. (Dress.)

MINUTES OF THE WEEK

Over the Top

Looking back on it, the publication of the first number of *Night and Day* was a pretty hectic business. Chaos reigned in the office for several days ; our colleagues, haggard and unshaved, were for ever slumping forward on their desks with a groan, and we didn't feel too good ourself. The strain was awful. Some kind person with touching and persistent solicitude sent us four anonymous telegrams, one after another, saying "Call it Piccadilly ". It was a bit late to adopt this suggestion ; but the cumulative effect of the telegrams was such that the paper will always be *Piccadilly* in our hearts.

Somebody else kept on ringing us solely in order, when the telephone girl said " Night and Day ", to reply " You are the one " and ring off.

But in a way our most abiding memory of those desperate days was a

glimpse of a colleague's engagement pad. This recorded a long list of appointments, beginning " 9.30 : See D. about make-up. 10.0 : Ring printers *re* back page ", and so on.

It ended : " 6.15. See E. Jones about everything."

★

The Carriage Only Waits Once

What with Dumas, Raleigh, and the Great White Queen, there's been a lot of historical drama in London lately. We have only one thing against it, and that is this. When, going home in the taxi, we look at our programme, we *always* notice, in the long and distinguished cast, several characters who to the best of our knowledge never appeared on the stage. We remember George Eliot ; we remember A Portuguese Sailor ; but in between them on the list comes Sir Harry Pawnceby, and a little lower down is Mlle Eulalie Crâchepartout, and we are damned if we saw either of them. It's a small thing. They were probably very subsidiary characters, who chipped in with " Here's confusion to Boney ! " or " De Engleesh cooking—ah, mon Dieu ! " and then vanished among the bustles and cuirasses before we'd noticed them. It irks us all the same, and we shan't feel really happy about historical dramas until all the actors with speaking parts are numbered, like Rugby players.

★

Feuilleton Fixation

God knows why, but we've been reading a lot of inferior fiction lately : admittedly inferior fiction. Partly perhaps as a result of this we found ourselves compiling a list of small, almost diurnal experiences which other people seem to have all the time but we—much as we should like to— don't. Before we die we want, passionately, to have (a) heard a Frenchman call his wife " my little cabbage", (b) induced a girl to bite her lip till the blood came, (c) told our man to pack us an automatic, (d) vaulted into the saddle, (e) been at school with the Foreign Secretary, the Home Secretary, and the Chief Commissioner of Police.

It must be a great life, that. " Olga was waiting for him, looking lovelier than ever. ' Have you any news ? ' she queried immediately." Hardly anybody has ever waited for us.

The few who did queried like a shot ; but not along those lines.

Once, too, we tried vaulting into the saddle.

★

Introspection

A friend of ours swears that he heard an interpolation during a broadcast of a Glyndebourne opera. One of the singers, roaring away at the top of his voice, came to the sentence " Wer bin ich ? " which he had to repeat several times. " Wer bin ich ? " he yelled. " *Wer bin ich ?* WER BIN I-I-I-ICH ? " then added, in a quieter, rather puzzled tone : " What a dam fool question ! "

SLINGSBY

I WAS A TERRITORIAL

Anthony Powell

CAPTAIN BLOODWORTH'S face stands out from a number of other faces that have become blurred by the lapse of time. Captain Bloodworth was the adjutant and therefore a regular soldier. He had a penetrating voice and the appearance of a good-natured vulture. I liked him. He wore rather loud suits and belonged very much to the post-war army.

" Blow into the hospital sometime," he said. " Don't bother to make an appointment."

He leant back in his chair and pulled hard at the knees of his check trousers, showing in this way a lot of pale silk sock.

" I'll just strip and walk in, sir ? "

" Cough twice," Captain Bloodworth said, laughing balefully himself. The subject under discussion was medical examination. I was attached to the battery, pending a vacancy. Captain Bloodworth drummed on the table with his fists. I said good night and prepared to beat a retreat.

Captain Bloodworth stood up and stepped over a broken chair that penned him to the wall. He said " I'll give you a lift if you're going back to the West End."

I followed him down the narrow stairs and across a barrack square that recalled pictures of the military degradation of Dreyfus. Captain Bloodworth's sports model was parked on the far side of the square. We set off North in the direction of the river. As we drove through mysterious South London by-ways, Captain Bloodworth gave some of his views. His voice rose deafeningly above the clatter of the trams :

" . . . trouble about the army . . . have to spend so much of your time with such palsied . . . want to meet J. B. Priestley . . . some of the people who really count. . . ."

We reached Piccadilly and I climbed out.

" Good night," Captain Bloodworth positively yelled. He added something I could not catch about giving the girls in Half Moon Street a treat.

He drove off at a great pace. I made my way towards Shepherd's Market, where I inhabited the ground floor of a ruin. The house was haunted and my sitting-room had two wooden stanchions rising from the middle of the floor to prevent the upper part of the building from collapsing and overwhelming me ; but I liked living there because at this remote period of history the neighbourhood still hinted of Green Hats and deaths-for-purity. I was twenty and had just come down from Oxford.

It was partly a reaction from life at that university and partly an ingrained curiosity about military matters that had led me in the direction of the Territorials. Those qualified to know best advised the artillery, and I felt that if the gunners were good enough for Tolstoy they were good enough for me. I used to go down to the Headquarters about twice a week. The journey was made by means of a chain of buses. After various changes I was within ten minutes' walk of my destination. Fortunately for most of the officers of the battery, they had cars, and often there was someone to drive me home. These evenings, after a sandwich and a glass of beer in mess, were spent for the most part in the riding school. As many people have at one time or another undergone the humiliating experience of impelling a horse round a dusty shed under glaring electric light, it is unnecessary to say more than that these peregrinations were no worse than usual and that the sergeant in charge was an exceptionally

agreeable man. Goethe remarks somewhere how an air of brutality seems inevitably attached to indoor riding schools ; but so far as possible this was absent. Later one drank lager to wash away some of the tan.

More esoteric mysteries were performed in another outhouse, the upper storeys of which were reached by an external iron staircase like a fire-escape. At the top of this staircase was a low doorway. Crouching like a troll, one entered a long and gloomy attic at the near end of which were several benches and telephones. The benches faced a stage and at first suggested the prelude to some miniature dramatic performance. On the stage lay a brightly lighted panorama of the English Scene. Downs and fields, rivers and woods, railway lines, villages and churches spread out like those in Mr. Housman's poems :

> " Into my heart an air that kills
> From yon far country blows :
> What are those blue remembered hills,
> What spires, what farms are those ? "

Looking at this prospect prompted comparison with the two-dimensional landscape of some conservative member of the London Group.

The assembled officers would sit on the benches and Captain Bloodworth or the Colonel would then say : " A detachment of cavalry are advancing through the trees by that gully on the left " or " Such-and-such a gun has opened fire from behind the church on the right." One of our number then gave orders into a telephone with a view to dropping a stated quantity of H.E.106 (which I subsequently discovered to stand for High Explosive) on the invisible enemy. The range was estimated by holding the clenched fist at arm's length—the precise method escapes me. Some hidden agency behind the scenes, noting the details of the order, manipulated wires in such a way that a projectile was caused to fall on the exact place indicated by the calculations, often a long way from the target.

These exercises in gunnery were

BENTLEY
The Silent Sports Car

BENTLEY MOTORS (1931) LTD. 16. CONDUIT ST. LONDON. W.I. *TEL* MAYFAIR 4412.

BUY A CAR ·MADE IN THE UNITED KINGDOM

distinctly enjoyable. Apart from calling into play faculties of sight and hearing, as the telephone lines were far from clear, quick and accurate thinking was also necessary if Captain Bloodworth's scorching comments were to be avoided. It was impossible not to be impressed by the inadequacy of such an instrument as a rifle or shotgun for providing sport or pastime when compared with even medium artillery.

As a certain process of de-Oxfordization was one of my aims, I talked as little as possible when at the Headquarters, and in fact limited all conversation to those simple words expressing simple needs which provide a sort of burden or refrain that accompanies all army life. Silence seemed to work in mess, but I observed that sooner or later, if I were ever gazetted, I should be compelled to join in the highly organized social life of the battery outside barracks. This consisted primarily of small dances which gave everyone an opportunity to wear mess-kit. I was

cunning enough to realize that if I were ever entrapped into one of these, it would soon be discovered that I did not care for golf and bridge ; and for that matter could extend only a qualified approval to Mr. Chesterton's work. I knew that these limitations on my part would raise just the kind of barrier I wanted to avoid, as my only wish was to learn in peace how to kill people without being bothered with games or literary opinions.

I had been attached to the unit for about two months when one night an officer appeared whom I had not yet met. I think he had been absent for some time owing to illness. We were introduced. Someone said :

" Oh, Huxtable, this is Powell. He's a Senior Wrangler or something."

My little world lay shattered all round me. This was the reward of concentrated monosyllabicism. It was disappointing, to say the least. However, as I was already getting more than a little tired of the enormous

amount of my leisure that I found myself spending in buses, and as a *force majeure* caused me at about this date to begin a course of typography at a polytechnic where the classes were so arranged that it was impossible for me to have my evening meal within an hour of either the earliest or the latest extremity to which I had been accustomed, I felt that my lot had become too hard to bear. I hadn't any papers to send in, but I wrote to the Colonel and told him that I couldn't go through with it. I was sorry. As it happened, typography proved for various reasons as difficult to master as the art of war, but the scene of action was nearer home and the institution gave one the exciting sensation of being a foreign student.

I often read about the Territorial Army in the papers. Sometimes I see them galloping like Buffalo Bill through the streets on the way to some military exercise. My withdrawal seems to have made little or no difference to their activities.

EIFFEL TOUR DE FORCE

A VISIT TO THE PARIS EXHIBITION

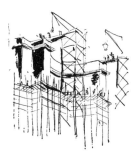

PARISIANS, resentful of the way their normal routine has been dislocated by the Exhibition, are now loudly proclaiming it is a first-class fiasco. Those who venture to pay the entrance-fee and examine it for themselves wander round chanting with a triumphant pessimism " Pas fini . . . pas fini . . . pas fini " before every pavilion. The fact that the three dictators, with the three largest pavilions, were ready on the opening day is an aggravation, as in each case punctuality was achieved without the help of the French workmen whose tactics have delayed the rest of the Exhibition, and in defiance of the international agreement not to import labour, which the other countries have continued to observe in the face of every provocation.

But, in spite of anything Paris may say, this Exhibition is, or rather is going to be, a terrific piece of showmanship. No other city could provide an area of nearly 250 acres in the middle of the town without pulling down a single building and with hardly a tree disturbed. And if many of the foreign pavilions have been built over roads (like the German and Russian) or railways (like the British and Italian) the additional expense has not been borne by the French, who will find themselves at the close of the Exhibition with a number of permanent structures admirably suited for occupation by Government departments.

The main entrance is through the reconstructed Trocadero and the view from the terrace alone is worth the money. The French genius for planning for effect is as alive as ever. There are fountains—hundreds of them, in the best vulgar colours—and towering above everything across the river is the Eiffel Tower, due unfortunately to come down as soon as the Exhibition is over (if it doesn't fall down first).

All the details aren't good, of course. A large and unimaginative column dedicated to Peace (tactfully, thanks to Norway, out of sight of the Spanish pavilion) need not be looked at very closely, but the two peasants on the Russian building hurling a hammer and sickle across the road at Germany are good fun.

Architecturally, as is usually the case, the small countries come out of it very much better than the big ones. Holland, Austria, Spain, and the Scandinavian countries all have charming and unpretentious buildings. The Great Powers have, with two exceptions, produced pompous and domineering horrors. The two exceptions are Great Britain, which is a great deal better, and the United States, which is a great deal worse. Thanks to the dignity and lightness of Mr. Oliver Hill's pavilion, we move at one bound from our usual last place to a position very near the top. First prize in the category of the quaint is awarded this time to Siam for a Royal Palace in miniature which admirably fills the gap left by the absence of an Elizabethan farmhouse.

The United States will, it seems, be the last finished and, judging by the pictures, a very good thing too. It will consist—believe it or not—of a large central tower and two square wings painted dark blue with gold stars at the top and white with red lines below. The same principle applied throughout the Exhibition would have made the floodlighting of the Eiffel Tower quite superfluous.

Hidden behind an insufferable Roumania and a depressing Hungary, and therefore very easy to miss, is an enchanting Japanese house. Completely contemporary in feeling, it yet remains unmistakably Japanese. The architect, whose name is Sakakura, deserves our thanks for showing that buildings need not be painted with stars and stripes and such to be recognizably national.

There are 42 foreign countries exhibiting, but there are also over a hundred pavilions built by the French. Many of these are devoted to Savon Cadum, Larousse and such firms, but others are worth seeing. An 8-franc trip down the river on a launch is probably the best way of seeing them. The yachting pavilion, Mallet-Stevens's Palace of Hygiene and the building of the Union des Artistes Modernes are the best of those on the bank, while on an island in the middle of the river are the French Colonies, where genuine native women conscientiously wave to every passing boatload.

Inside the buildings the success is of the display, not of the things displayed. Russia is almost entirely propagandist and therefore dull, except for a large map made of semi-precious stones with all the towns picked out in precious stones. None of the capitalist countries has quite equalled that, but Italy has a barge with a marble deck moored to the quay. The whole of the Italian pavilion, in fact, is a triumph of display once you're inside it. It's true that the cost must have been enormous, but the result justifies it. Here, as everywhere else, the goods (a too well-known face and the " pacification " of Abyssinia, for example) may not be worthy of the care given to them, but at least there is some lovely glass and pottery. Anyone who remembers a display from the Bauhaus for which Professor Gropius was responsible in the Salon des Artistes Décorateurs seven years ago will weep for Germany. It is better, perhaps, not to go in. The pictures in the main hall must certainly have been

18

painted by impeccable Nazis.

Outside the Exhibition grounds is the new Museum of Modern Arts, into which the collection from the Luxembourg is to be moved. It was built, after a competition, by four young architects, and is the only pavilion of which Paris approves, probably because it is a mild and inoffensive piece of neo-classicism. The internal courtyard, however, suffers from a surfeit of nymphs. Nearby, in a part of the Grand Palais, is the Palais des Découvertes, a beautiful display of popular science made as mysterious as possible. There are dread warnings of flames, explosions and sparks, against the danger of which every precaution has been taken, and a thoroughly bogey atmosphere has been arranged. There are also some mathematical models and diagrams that are quite the best abstract art in Paris. A chart made at the University of London tells you how high your son should be, if you can understand it.

One remembers the Ruritanian uniforms of the officials in the Ruritanian pavilion of the Principality of Monaco; the crowns, all different and all charming, designed by various firms appointed to the Court of Denmark; the back of the Austrian pavilion seen from the Restaurant of the Grand Duchy of Luxemburg, and a white flower-vase (the loveliest object in the whole Exhibition) in the Italian pavilion; the candelabras (the ugliest objects in the whole Exhibition) in the German pavilion; the inscription inside the doorway to Portugal: "Celui qui passe peut regarder et voir sans être obligé d'admirer"; the display by the Viking Pencil Co. in the Danish Pavilion; the two groups on each side of the German building representing Stages 1 and 2 of the Spirit of Germany pushing two presumably non-Aryans over a cliff; the Belgian cactus-garden; the Swiss mountain with all the products of the country on it, and a little blue paper sky above; a Belgian photo-mural of the Congo; a tiny brown cow from Palestine with a white leather udder, and a vast photograph of Mr. Neville Chamberlain fishing.

"Oh, how vulgar!" somebody said. "Isn't it lovely?"   J. D. M.

A JOB IN A MILLION—2
PRACTICALLY A JOKE

THE type of mind which conceives the rubber-pointed pencil, the squeaking nut or biscuit, and the clockwork mouse, is apt in inventing edible razor-blades and vanishing walking-sticks. In other words, the practical-joke trade goes hand in hand with the conjuring-trick trade, and firms that produce the one usually deal also in the other.

For nearly forty years the family of Davenport have been dealing, wholesale and retail, in jokes and magic; and their experience goes to show that this is a conservative industry. Naturally the latest joke—this year it is a box of wooden chocolates which emits a long spark when opened—is most in demand. But the old-fashioned plate-lifter and artificial ink-blot are still sold in large quantities, and the explosive cigar has never lost its popularity. Similarly with magic: while Belisha beacons may be made to appear and disappear one year and models of the Queen Mary another, the underlying ideas remain the same, and all tricks continue to be based on one of four principles—Production, Disappearance, Transposition and Change.

Yet variations on the old themes are always desirable. In their homes the three brothers and a sister who run the Davenport business invent jokes and tricks and try them out on each other. At their shop in New Oxford Street they give audiences to well-established magicians and aspiring free-lance conjurors with ideas to sell. And in the summer they go abroad in search of new material.

"The Japanese don't invent much in the way of jokes," said Mr. Lewis Davenport. "They chiefly copy other people's inventions. The Germans have a queer sense of humour. A German will put on a big nose or stick a funny face in his buttonhole and think he's a scream. But if you show him something really subtle, he won't see the point."

"The French," he went on, "like near-the-knuckle jokes, and jokes that hurt. These sugared almonds are a good example of a French joke of the second type—they've got Cayenne

'It says "Beat the eggs until stiff". I've been beating for two hours and I'm still as fresh as a daisy.'

pepper inside. The Americans like jokes that go bang, and the more noise the better. But we English like subtle jokes, like this "—he picked up a harmless-looking matchbox, and a many-legged animal rushed wildly down the counter—" and this "—he opened a pack of cards and a canvas snake shot across the shop. "Something really subtle, you know."

From humorous happenings in everyday life, on the stage and in films come ideas for something new in the practical-joke line. One of the Davenports saw Harpo Marx eat his zip-fastened banana in *Horsefeathers*, and at once put on the market a banana-like case which holds a real banana and fastens with a zipper.

" And so," the inventor said, " you can unzip your case, take a bite from your banana, and zip it up again. Very convenient."

Customers themselves often make suggestions for tricks and jokes, and practically anything that is asked for can be made. A chair that will turn into a table, an umbrella that will turn into a carrot—these may not have been done before, but such reasonable requests are easily satisfied.

A good deal of ingenuity is sometimes needed to meet the demands of the theatrical world. The producer of a pantomime in which children are supposed to turn into mice and mice back into children in full view of the audience may bring his problem to the Davenport firm, and the solution is by no means easy to find. On the other hand, a good deal of the film and theatrical work is fairly straightforward. A member of an amateur dramatic society writes to inquire how Mephistopheles can be made to appear in a burst of flame and smoke. A theatrical producer asks to have his chorus-girls taught conjuring tricks for a new revue. A film-director wants an actor to be able to produce coins from the air or invariably to turn up the ace of spades in a pack. These matters are all in the day's work in the magic trade.

Professional magicians buy their equipment from the Davenports, and strange dark men with dexterous hands are often to be seen in the shop exa-

mining wands and top hats and thimbles. From October to January, when the practical joke fever is at its height, the business is much patronized by schoolboys. But the most regular and enthusiastic customers are the amateur conjurors.

The supply of conjuring tricks to amateurs has increased immensely in the last forty years. Magic is not a popular hobby with women, but it is a favourite occupation for men of all ages, incomes and professions. Rich young men who can afford to buy the most expensive tricks, small shopkeepers who make a few shillings extra by giving conjuring performances, Harley Street doctors and barristers from the Temple are all among the regular clients.

Tricks can be ordered from a catalogue, wherein are described such equipment as the " Transparent Production Cabinet " and the " Demon Improved Vanishing Wand " and such magic feats as the " Demon Comic Egg Production " :

" During his performance the Magician requires an egg or two but finds that he has none. He calls his assistant across and taps him on the head, when to everybody's surprise and amusement an egg appears in the assistant's mouth. This is removed and the performer again taps him on the head, when another egg appears. In this way a dozen or more eggs may be produced, causing screams of laughter."

But it is much more satisfactory to sell magic by demonstration than by post, and the Davenports' shop is arranged with this fact in mind. Black velvet curtains adorned with demons' heads surround a small platform, and impromptu performances often take place.

" Here's a good opening trick," says the proprietor, putting a five-foot

walking-stick into his pocket without visible inconvenience.

" Seen this one ? " he goes on, pouring out a glass of milk and then holding the bottle upside down with the cap off.

" Have a cigarette ? " he invites, and a string of cardboard cigarettes shoots out of a packet.

A customer down from the provinces spends an hour seeing all the latest tricks, a messenger-boy runs in for an explosive cigar or a lump of sugar with a fly on it, and an amateur conjuror calls to discuss his last performance and suggest improvements for his equipment. Fires flash, handkerchiefs and flags appear and disappear, clockwork mice and spiders run about, and the shop becomes full of tangled paper streamers produced, apparently, from nowhere.

Along the counter mysterious conversations are carried on between those who belong to the inner circle of magic and possess all its secrets. The uninitiate, who has merely come to buy a celluloid broken-egg trick, presses eagerly forward to learn what he can, and is put off with long scientific explanations. Mr. Davenport, in his shirtsleeves, changes a bunch of red feathers into a bunch of green feathers and that again into a bunch of blue feathers. An absorbed magician tries out different sizes and colours of silks, to see which will go most easily into, and come most spectacularly out of, a wooden canary. Meanwhile, as often as not, somebody's wife is waiting outside, patiently or impatiently—for the devotees of illusion are apt to ignore the dull and unimaginative truth expressed by the hands of a clock.

MARGARET J. MILLER

Take a half breath and immerse the face. Open the eyes wide, turn the eyeballs upwards and wink the eyes rapidly. Repeat by winking the eyelids rapidly while the eyeballs are turned down, right, and left.

The foregoing exercise may be practised whilst sea-bathing.
—*Physical Culture for Beginners*.

But it's damned hard luck on the fish.

'*Listen, Fred, I don't think we shall be able to get over tonight,
Connie's not feeling at all the thing.*'

NEW BOOKS

For Schoolboys Only

IT is not surprising to find that of the twelve socialists who have compiled *The Mind in Chains* the leading four are schoolmasters and ex-schoolmasters, and two others lecturers. There is a natural connection between the teaching profession and a taste for totalitarian government ; prolonged association with the immature—fanatical urchins competing for caps and blazers of distinguishing colours—the dangerous pleasures of over-simple exposition, the scars of the endless losing battle for order and uniformity which rages in every class-room dispose even the most independent minds to shirt-dipping and saluting.

The twelve contributors, with perhaps one exception, are orthodox Marxists, but they are by no means of equal capacity—the editor, Mr. Day-Lewis, is lengths ahead ; Mr. Calder-Marshall and Mr. Upward run neck-and-neck for second place ; the rest are bunched on the rails, nowhere, an indistinguishable confusion of pounding hoofs and steaming horseflesh. Their aim is to state the benefits which they expect in certain representative human activities from the establishment of a Marxian state ; each treats of his own topic in a single aspect—the economic ; they do it concisely and competently. " Works of Art are produced by artists," Mr. Blunt begins his essay ; "artists are men ; men live in society and are in a large measure formed by the society in which they live. Therefore works of art cannot be considered historically except in human and ultimately in social terms." By " social " Mr. Blunt, as all his colleagues, means "economic". It would be equally true and equally fair to say " Men live on the earth, etc. Therefore works of art cannot be considered historically except in geographical and ultimately in meteorological terms." A metaphysician would

have little difficulty in demolishing Mr. Upward's elementary statement of the origin of life in a material universe. He jauntily skips every difficulty in his theory of automatic evolution. His essay is of value, not as stating a theory of æsthetics that can possibly interest an æsthetician, but as offering a rough and ready system of class-room marking by which a certain number of capable writers do in fact at the moment judge their own and other people's books. His thesis, if I do not misunderstand him, is that the class struggle is the only topic worth a writer's attention ; his difficulty that this means relegating to insignificance almost the whole of the world's literature. He avoids but does not

---

The Mind in Chains. Edited by C. Day-Lewis. *Muller.* 5s.

Swastika Night. Murray Constantine. *Gollancz.* 7s. 6d.

Sir Richard Grenville of the Revenge. A. L. Rowse. *Cape.* 12s. 6d.

The Pope in Politics. William Teeling. *Lovat Dickson.* 7s. 6d.

The Savage Hits Back. Julius Lips. *Lovat Dickson.* 21s.

---

solve the difficulty by assuming the social revolution to be so immediately imminent that the writer's task is *now*, for the first time, radically different from what it was in any other age. He cannot believe that there has ever been a time in history when economic problems seemed as serious or that great writers were willing to stand aloof. He contrasts Shakespeare's world with our own of " class struggle and crime and war " as though he really believed that *A Midsummer Night's Dream* was the product of an age of arcadian innocence instead of an escape from a world far more savage, far more unjust than ours, perplexed by a loss of belief far wider and by social disturbance far more bitter than anything we know.

It is interesting to see what books pass Mr. Upward's austere and rather capricious tests. *Swastika Night*

certainly does not. Mr. Murray Constantine hates Hitler every bit as well as anyone in *The Mind in Chains*, but he lacks their optimism. Like the revivalists, whose descendants they are, Marxians are inflated with apocalyptic confidence. They believe, more firmly than any Rotarian, that prosperity is round the corner. It is only a few years now before the trumpets blow and the portents appear and the reign of peace and justice and virtue is ushered in. Mr. Constantine, on the other hand, foresees several centuries of Nazi triumph. His novel deals with Europe some hundred years hence when civilization, religion, and domestic affection are dead ; it is a ghastly world, logically conceived ; we see Hitlerism failing not from heroic resistance of the workers—which at the best is patriotic melodrama—but from its innate weakness (and this is real criticism) that it can only exist as a negation. As soon as war and expansion are no longer possible, the body atrophies ; and the truth has still survived, hidden and indestructible. It is better as social criticism than as fiction, but it is a very readable book.

Sir Richard Grenville of the Revenge will not do for Mr. Upward either. It is totally wrong. Grenville, apostle of piratical private enterprise, colonial expansion, national patriotism, is presented as a hero. My own quarrel with the book lies on other grounds. I cannot enjoy the way Mr. Rowse writes. He has been at work on Grenville's life for years, with all the industry and enthusiasm of an American woman thesis-writer. But there is more to making a book than assembling the facts, and Mr. Rowse seems to me to have missed his opportunity. It is not that his writing is actually illiterate ; it is shapeless and characterless. I do not know how anyone can have read so much pointed and melodious prose as Mr. Rowse must have done in searching his authorities and have learned so little.

Nor do I think that Mr. Teeling's *The Pope in Politics* will do. No one is more conscious than the author of the economic discontents and distresses which Mr. Upward regards as the sole realities ; he has made a study of them and, I should hazard, has travelled more widely, shared the conditions of more unfortunates, conversed more humbly with working men and learnt more from and of them at first hand than Mr. Upward has done. But he accepts a more ancient ideology and I am afraid that puts him out of the running for the Left Wing Biscuit. His book on modern papal policy makes no pretensions to being a work of literature. It is first-class topical journalism, well-informed and critical, dealing with a topic that has not so far been treated at length and in a single book.

The one book which I think might prove acceptable is *The Savage Hits Back*. It is not absolutely clear that Mr. Julius Lips is a communist ; indeed, he shows a painful respect for parliamentary institutions and religious missions, but he has suffered abominably at the hands of Hitler, and his book is so entertaining that I think even Mr. Upward must enjoy it. (Even monks are permitted a few hours of innocuous recreation.) It is primarily the catalogue of a collection. Mr. Lips, in the days before Hitler, was head anthropologist at Cologne University and Curator of the Museum. He specialized in collecting photographs of savage art : a hobby which proved fatal to his career under the new race-conscious regime. After a great deal of petty persecution he escaped, with his specimens.

The Savage Hits Back is a collection of native representations of the white invaders. The letterpress is a commentary full of gentle irony. The illustrations are a joy, some very beautiful, many comic, a few extremely witty. I think it is a mistake to include the Chinese among savages—even as in this case with conscious satire. As a reference book it suffers from being too inclusive (I think it would have been better to have confined it to African art) and from a few typographical errors. It was a pity, too, to use the ugly impermanent clay-faced paper that the publishers have chosen. But these are niggardly complaints. It is a delightful and desirable book.

EVELYN WAUGH

PURSUITS AND VERDICTS
Answer to Lord Peter's Prayer

WINTERTON was my maths. tutor at one of the colleges so well known to Miss Sayers. Something of an amateur geologist and an expert climber. His brain fits neatly into a square box and that gives him a healthy contempt for literature, but like many of his kind he has an insatiable appetite for detective fiction. I consult him about mysteries and thrillers as other men consult Boulestin about food or Sir Herbert Barker about feet. I have my own views, but they are merely literary—questions of split infinitives and gerundive nouns. These, I realize, have nothing to do with a world of sustained suspense, baffled suspicion, frustrated clues, clean exits.

" Mr. Gollancz," I observed on my

Busman's Honeymoon. Dorothy L. Sayers. Gollancz. 8s. 6d.
Hamlet, Revenge ! Michael Innes. Gollancz. 7s. 6d.
The Theft of the Crown Jewels. Edgar Jepson. Jenkins. 7s. 6d.
Murder in Hospital. Josephine Bell. Longmans. 7s. 6d.
I'll be Judge, I'll be Jury. Milward Kennedy. Gollancz. 7s. 6d.

---

last visit to his rooms, " says the new Sayers is ' running away'."

"Miss Sayers," he grimly retorted, " is running away from me."

" You mean . . . "

" I mean that all this love interest is so much padding. I am prepared to admit that women make admirable writers of crime stories—something to do with their repressed sadism, I suppose. But they should leave the serious business of love to men. Good God, do you remember what that essentially bourgeois duke's son of hers calls his long-limbed, honey-skinned and bone-shaking wife ? "

" I seem to recollect ' Heart's desire'."

" Worse ! ' Domina ' ! The book is 446 pages long. Somewhere embedded in its pulpy thickness is the material for a short. And not a very good short at that. She kills her man with a ridiculous contraption worthy of Heath Robinson, and even then there is a screw loose."

" You mean Mrs. Ruddle ? "

" Exactly. It is not credible that a garrulous old magpie like that would forget to mention that she found a fishing-line fastened to a suspended cactus-plant when she came to tidy up the room where the murder had been committed."

" It is hardly in character."

" Neither in character nor in reason. But I distrust this itch for introducing characterization into detective fiction."

" You must find much to object to then in *Busman's Honeymoon*. The oh-so-determined-to-be-passionate lovers, the dear old Dickensian Bunter, the poetic Superintendent, the country cottage by Beverley Nichols. . . ."

But he would not let me finish. He fixed me from behind his steel-rimmed spectacles and uttered his final judgment : " I can stand most things for the sake of a teasing problem ; I have endured an incredible dose of the facetious Whimsey and the bland Bunter ; but that there should be added to these a general atmosphere of lubricious coyness. . . ."

" But there are some pretty quotations to give it a face," I interrupted.

" The last depravity ! " he cried. " Why should my corpse be garnished with parsley from the Young Maiden's Garden of Verses ? "

There was no more to be said, so I picked up another volume, *Hamlet, Revenge !* by Mr. Innes, and flicked through the pages. Shakespeare, Proust, Dr. Johnson, the Russian Ballet. . . . " More parsley, I see."

" Yes ; but I suspect it may be literature. I couldn't get on with it myself, but I would recommend you to read it. The plot seems to be ingenious, but it is so wrapped up in highbrow patter that I simply can't understand half of it."

" You prefer Edgar Jepson ? " I suggested.

" I used to," he replied. " But even Jepson has become infected with highbrow fever. His hero reads Montaigne and Burton, and as for his heroine— listen." He found the book and read this surprising paragraph :

" With an easy mind she settled down to a volume of Nietzsche, on whose works she was spending much of the time she had proposed to devote to vacation reading for the Schools ; but Nietzsche was a discovery. None of her tutors knew that she was reading Nietzsche ; they would not have liked it : he had never been regarded with great favour by official Oxford, and none of the lady tutors at St. Margaret's Hall believed it to be a good thing for a young girl to know too much, except about matters purely psycho-analytic and of those he did not bother to treat."

" This charming ' creature of the purely pragmatic imagination ', as Mr. Jepson calls all his characters, is the offspring of a Chinese mother and an Irish father and can, when the occasion offers, kick a fallen man hard on the right ear."

" I can see I shall fall for such a girl. You must lend me this one."

" And if you want what I would allow to be in the right tradition, take *Murder in Hospital*. The atmosphere is too clinical, perhaps, but Shakespeare and Aldous Huxley are never once mentioned. It is the best of the bunch."

In exchange I left him Milward Kennedy's *I'll be Judge, I'll be Jury*, which I had read on the way down. " It is hot from the press," I said, " and I dare say you will like it well enough. At least it is not highbrow. The opening is dramatic, and the end is cynical ; the characters arouse no sentiment except a slight disgust. If Mr. Kennedy had more sense of style and would not hop disconcertingly from the inside to the outside of people's minds. . . ."

But from the look in Winterton's eyes I knew that once again I had dropped into the habits of literary criticism.   HERBERT READ

GENERAL

THE GOLDEN SOVEREIGN. Laurence Housman. (*Cape*, 10s. 6d.) Little plays, each a little Sugar Calvary—Wilde, out of prison and talking about the Artist in a Paris café, is cut by a sometime friend ; Mill comes to tell Carlyle that the manuscript of *The French Revolution* has been burnt and Carlyle and Mrs. C. talk it over ; Parnell and Mrs. O'Shea (he calls her " Wifie " and she calls him " King ") find solace—and of course there are some Palace Plays. Any one, given a convenient Censor, might make a fortune and is in any case the Little Theatre Movement's meat.

THE LAST ROMANTIC. William Orton. (*Cassell*, 7s. 6d.) A characteristic up-to-the-War autobiography—from small grocer's shop with living-quarters upstairs and elementary school, to larger grocer's shop and University College School and Orage and the *New Age*, to grocer's shop with branches and a house with a drive and Cambridge ; from Emerson and Carlyle to Pater and Shaw and Ibsen (much Spiritual Travail over Ibsen), and hosts of girls—Rosa, Dorothy, Brenda, Lais, Monica—any number of girls, culminating in Katherine Mansfield, then Katharina. " Do you believe in Pan ? " Katharina asked Michael (the Last Romantic) in the Underground. That set them going. There was no stopping them after that. Michael was succeeded as far as Katharina was concerned by— you know who. He went to the War and there it ends, and perhaps it's as well.

THE FIFTH DECAD OF CANTOS. Ezra Pound. (*Faber*, 6s.) Mr. Pound's huge surrealist *collage* continues rather monstrously to unroll : the general subject of this section usury : scraps of Latin, Greek, Italian, Chinese ; Renaissance documents on the subject of interest ; scrap of private letter about a Cairn puppy ; how to make a fly for March fishing ; in corners, among the busts of Rothschild, Marx and Mr. Kolschitsky, lines of what sound like poetry :

Lalage's shadow moves in the
    fresco's knees
She is blotted with Dirce's shadow
dawn stands there fixed and unmoving
    only we two have moved.

Lord Bountiful

THE debt which art in this country owes to private benefactors is, as we are so constantly reminded, considerable, and last week it was further increased by the opening of the new sculpture rooms at the Tate : a princely gift from that generous and enlightened patron of the arts, Lord Duveen. It is sad to admit that we have as yet neither a very large nor a very distinguished amount of sculpture with which to fill them, but it is nevertheless comforting to reflect that, if we do by any chance acquire a masterpiece in the future, we have now a worthy shrine in which to put it. The gallery itself is an impressive achievement in the neoclassic style, and at a time when so few architects are courageous enough to build in the grand manner, the effect of vastness and dignity has all the charm of novelty. Mr. Russell Pope, who is largely responsible for the present gallery, is one of the few remaining architects who still work in that great neo-classic tradition which produced so many remarkable buildings in the last century, particularly in this country and in Russia, and which still retains a certain vitality in the United States. Some of the greatest masterpieces of this style have been railway stations, and Mr. Pope's own *magnum opus* is the Pennsylvania Railroad Station in New York : an achievement which is worthy to be compared, if not altogether to its advantage, with Hittorf's Gare du Nord and Hardwick's Euston.

However, in this instance it must be admitted that the ample scale so suitable in backgrounds for locomotives is perhaps a trifle overwhelming ; few pieces of sculpture are calculated to appear to the best advantage in the surroundings of the Pennsylvania Railroad Station. Were there an ample supply of Egyptian colossi and Michael Angelesque monoliths, all would be well, but, as it is, works of the size and inspiration of Rodin's John the Baptist possess about as much significance in their new home as a row of tin-soldiers in a wardrobe-trunk. Moreover it is a little unfortunate that sculpture should be a three-dimensional art and that a statue, to be fully appreciated, should be visible from all sides, as here it has been found impossible to arrange the exhibits in any other way than in rows against the walls ; for, as Lord Duveen has so aptly pointed out, were the statues to be placed in the middle of the room the splendid architectural vista from one end of the new galleries to the other would be irretrievably ruined, which would, of course, be an unthinkable outrage. In the cause of art it is frequently necessary to make sacrifices, and although it is certainly a trifle unlucky that the colour of the stone is such that a statue in any material other than bronze, when placed against the wall, tends to merge gracefully into the background, one must always bear in mind that one has at least been granted the compensation of a noble unbroken vista. Whether posterity, when confronted with this gallery which has an almost terrifying air of permanence, will consider that the present generation possessed any real understanding and appreciation of sculpture is a little doubtful ; what they will be forced to realize, however, is how splendid and opulent a man was Lord Duveen.

If the visitor to the Tate can bear to tear himself away from the noble unbroken vista of the new galleries, he would be well advised to inspect certain of the impressionist and post-impressionist paintings in the adjoining rooms, for the chances are that he will not have so many more opportunities for doing so, as many of them, particularly the Van Goghs, are showing ominous signs of deterioration. Alas, such is the financial position that the funds available for restoration and scientific preservation are woefully inadequate. What is needed here is a benefactor whose generosity is a trifle less spectacular than Lord Duveen's, who would provide a sum of which the interest would be sufficient satisfactorily to augment the annual allowance for repairs ; architectural vistas, how-

ever impressive, will provide but cold comfort in the event of the disappearance of many of the finest examples of nineteenth-century painting in the country.

What with new sculpture galleries, a staggering collection of Cézannes at the Lefèvre and another stimulating Epstein row in the offing, a gala time has recently been had by all. In case anyone amidst all these excitements should have missed it, I would like to draw attention to the Sisley exhibition at Tooth's. Here is a painter whose reputation steadily increases as time goes on. At the outset of his career he was rather overshadowed by his friend and more spectacular contemporary Monet, and then, when we all discovered Cézanne, he suffered from the general neglect which overtook the Impressionists. Now that Cézanne has himself become a long accepted figure and such quantities of brilliant paint have since flowed down the Rue de la Boétie, we are in a position to reconsider our judgment of the Impressionists. As a result Sisley now emerges with first-class honours. With all Monet's skill in the rendering of atmosphere and light, he never made the

former's mistake of assuming that light was the beginning and the end of painting, and consequently his best pictures have a solidity which is lacking in many of Monet's later canvases. Above all he was, like Boudin, a painter first, last, all the time, and he never compromised the directness of his vision by acquiring a larger dose of theory than he could digest with comfort ; with him Impressionism was the natural way of painting and not something imposed upon his eye by an intellectual effort. The result is that his best work has retained all its original vitality, while much of his contemporaries' now gives the impression of being nothing more than an incredibly skilful series of exercises—mere curiosities of art-history without any genuine æsthetic value at all.

May I point out that the Country Life Exhibition has been extended to July 15 and urge all who have not done so to rush round to 33 Grosvenor Square, if for no other reason than the fact that it contains the picture which many consider to be the all-time high mark in English painting—Gainsborough's Mr. and Mrs. Andrews ?

OSBERT LANCASTER

'Many happy returns, Edith, and when this you see remember me.'

THE THEATRE

No Sleep for the Wicked

NO Sleep for the Wicked at Daly's is a good-hearted, rattling, all-anyhow sort of an English comedy-thriller—just the thing for a Coronation summer. What a pity it was not on in May. Any Empire visitors left in London certainly ought to see it : I am afraid Americans might not like it so much. It is very lightly boiled. It shows you the way we have in the public schools, and to some extent accounts for the Empire. This is a play about gun-running in Tangier, arms-dumps, hotel bars, dungeons underneath kasbas and Englishmen who are not such bloody fools as they look. Only one incident makes it unsuitable for the children : a nice man (the gang have got him) doubles up and dies of poison in the hotel bar. But this could be got past by upsetting a box of chocolates at the critical moment—which occurs at the end of Scene 2, Act I. Because apart from this there are many things they would relish : the wisecracks, the quick shooting, the grinding-open secret doors in the kasba, the drunks. And Mr. Peter Haddon.

John Sixsmith (Mr. Peter Haddon) quite likely had Sir Percy Blakeney in his pedigree, and must be some sort of cousin of the Whimseys. He is a Secret Agent, sent out to stop the gun-running ; his wife has come with him as a hotel visitor. They are a nice county couple, full of married backchat ; by the end she has shown she is really a great girl. The grim game must be played out, and she is no handicap. It seems to me that he needs every bit of her loyalty : he is a bit deaf and not too competent—or so it looked to me, as I watched him poking about the eerie court of the kasba, waving his torch all ways, with a crook (and he had been warned, mind you) creeping perfectly audibly up behind. As the secret door swung open, the crook nabbed him—and deserved to, I thought. John plans

to seem dumb, but there are moments when he does seem about as dumb as he plans to seem. However, his asset turns out to be sex-appeal, that sex-appeal that only the Englishman can exercise, while going on looking all the time like a fish. For the Achilles' heel of the gang is a woman, a blonde Russian with the most lovely white outfit, the right thing for every occasion, who is also staying at the hotel. She and John exchange badinage, but are implacable enemies—all the same, you can see he has got her heart quite early on. Miss Claire Luce is a lovely ; her Beautiful Spy has a great gloss. Her one breakdown is a pity : she was never meant to jitter ; she hasn't got the inside for it.

This is the sort of play there will always be an opening for in London. It made a good start, and looks likely to stay the course. Myself, I liked it because it *was* so traditional. As a thrill, of course, it suffers every possible disadvantage from being a play—and not a movie, I mean. It's a dear old-fashioned play, at once homely and artificial. It does one good to see that sort of thing once or twice. People (of whom there still seem to be quite a number) who prefer plays to movies

say that this is because they like the human element. By which I take them to mean that at plays there's always the chance that something may cause a diversion by going wrong. There is also the hope that actors may show nervousness, pass out and have to be carried off, or twist their ankles backstage, which makes them more human than on the screen. The first night of this play nothing went wrong, except that someone forgot to switch on the Morocco moonlight in one act, then put this right with a sort of unheard bang. Without a hitch, we greeted all the comedy old friends— natives, Americans, dagoes, old maids,

hotel bores. Perhaps, if plays are to survive, they should be a bit amateurish : this one certainly was, and it rather warmed the heart. I see this is the last show we shall see at Daly's : sad !

Floodlight

Floodlight at the Saville is nothing so nice as amateurish ; it simply does not come off. I found this a gloomy evening. There is *nothing* wrong with the caste, who are all quite delightful people, all guts and twinkle. How they do it I can't think, but they, disguised their depression. Miss Frances Day, Miss Hermione Baddeley and Mr. Lyle Evans, all save a number or two by putting themselves across. Miss Frances Day and her smile are both perfectly ravishing. She floats all her numbers in blonde light ; she reads out her piece of Wordsworth, then Dances with Daffodils that take some time showing up ; she kittens about the White Room ; she sings a song, *I Will Pray*. But all the same, *what* an evening ! *Floodlight* gives one a Rip Van Winkle feeling, as though one had gone to sleep at it ten years ago and now woke to find it had civilly waited for one before finishing up. In 1927 a lot of the numbers would have been up to date : it seems too bad *Floodlight* did not get written in time for them.

Of course, possibly Mr. Beverley Nichols wrote this review out of well-known kindness of heart. I mean, with his understanding of human nature he may know how daunting it is to see anything going on that you feel in any way out of, especially if you have paid to see it. If, in writing *Floodlight*, he had in mind old ladies who are his friends, I honour him. For those leaving the fragrant cottage to visit London, there is nothing here to cause distress or mystification. Even his naughtiness has an evangelical bias, and we all know, alas, how wicked the world was in 1927. There seems no reason why intelligent study of A. P. Herbert and Noel Coward should not teach any moral person how to be quite a satirist. We are told that all satirists are moralists, so why not take heart and begin the other way round ? By 1929 the world might be quite a clean place.   ELIZABETH BOWEN

THE CINEMA

Horror for Adults

BLACK LEGION, an intelligent and exciting, if rather earnest film, is intended to expose the secret society of that name and the financial racket behind it. The Black Legion, with its policy of America for Americans, its melodramatic black hoods, must have had an appeal as wide as humanity : to the natural bully, to the envious and the unsuccessful, the man with a grievance, the romantic. Frank Taylor (admirably acted by Humphrey Bogart), a factory hand who finds himself passed over for the post of foreman in favour of a Pole, attends a meeting at the local chemist's, a little rabbity man with defective eyesight who resents the cut-price drugstore further down the street. We hear the long pompous literary oath full of words too difficult for Taylor to pronounce ; then the playboy hoods are raised to disclose the familiar faces, the chemist's, the bully's from the works, the organiser's, who informs the new recruit that he can now get " a regular thirty dollar revolver for fourteen dollars fifty cents", and afterwards the drinks all round, the hearty good fellowship.

It is an intelligent film because the director and script-writer know where the real horror lies : the real horror is not in the black robes and skull emblems, but in the knowledge that these hide the weak and commonplace faces you have met over the counter and minding the next machine. The horror is not in the climax when Taylor shoots his friend dead, but in the earlier moment before the glass when he poses romantically with his first gun ; not in the floggings and burnings but in the immature question at the inaugural meeting, " If we join up don't we get a uniform or something ? ", in the secret accounts read to the managing director, so much from the sale of uniforms and regalia, so much from officers' commissions, so much from revolvers at wholesale rates : total profits for the month, $221,049. 15 cents.

Comparisons can obviously be made with *Fury* and at least one to the advantage of *Black Legion* : no factitious happy ending is tacked on (though the producer probably has one up his sleeve in case of need). But *Fury* with all its faults was the work of a very great director, *Black Legion* only of an intelligent one. The immediate impact of the horror has seeped away somewhere—perhaps in the camera positions—between the script and the " take ".

There never was any genuine horror in *Night Must Fall*, and Emlyn Williams' pretentious little murder play has made a long dim film. Like an early talkie, it is no more than a photographed stage play and its psychological absurdities are mercilessly exposed. But there are worse pictures in town than this. *Top of the World* may appeal to readers of *London Life* (the heroine wears very high heels, a kind of long Cossack coat and carries a little cane), but it is one of those distressingly carefree musicals (elderly people in evening dress romping up and down a restaurant for ten whole minutes at a stretch) when the only ungay faces are among the audience.

As for *The Last Train from Madrid*, it is probably the worst film of the decade and should have been the funniest. Emotional and uplifting dialogue (" I don't want to die, Señorita. I'm young, I want to live. My father kept a farm . . .") : Mr. Lionel Atwill (" a grand old trooper," as Miss Lejeune would say) playing the Madrid Commandant, full of sternness and duty and tenderness (" You will be tried by court-martial tomorrow ", and his warm encouraging paw falls like a headmaster's on the prisoner's shoulder) : all we still need for a really good laugh are the presence of the Dean of Canterbury and the absence of actual war. For there is something a little shocking about these noble self-sacrifices and heroic deaths —the eyes close always of their own accord—in front of a back-projection of ruined Madrid itself, about the facetiousness of the screen journalist in a screen air-raid mingled with news-shots of the genuine terror.

GRAHAM GREENE

' This is hardly the time for jokes of that sort.'

MINUTES OF THE WEEK

Putting It Across

An advertising copywriter we know was running off a masterpiece about an excellent preparation for putting on gravel drives and such. Wanting to know whether there was anything in particular he should mention about the stuff, he called a minor executive into his room and asked him. The minor executive pondered for a moment and then said : " You know of course, sir, that the preparation is wholly non-injurious to fish ? "

Carry On, Empire

We had always wondered just how fond the British Empire was of this sceptred isle, which owns it. Do diggers down under wax sentimental about England? Or is it all propaganda, that stuff about the Dominions wistfully revering the Old Country ? Do

they indeed, except in books, refer to it as the Old Country ?

Our scepticism on the last point, formerly considerable, has been dissipated by a letter just to hand from a Mr. H. E. Latham-Collins, who writes from the Elks Club, Calgary, Canada. Mr. Latham-Collins uses, throughout, the term " O.C'y " when he means England. (" Do you know

of a sect called The Free Thinkers, and is there a periodical of that name in the O.C'y ? ") There is something most reassuring about this abbreviation. Though unpronounceable, it has an affectionate air ; and it shows that the Old Country is an habitual usage, because you don't abbreviate words unless they crop up pretty often.

Nor must it be supposed that Mr. Latham-Collins is a conventional, diehard sort of person. " I have," he writes, " nearly decided, with several others, to found a society to be called ' The Truth Vigilants'. We are not orthodox, many of us far from it."

So there.

Deathless Prose

We always read the captions under the photographs in the *Tatler* with the eye of a connoisseur. Unlike the *Bystander* and (to a lesser degree) the *Sketch*, which have gone all slick, the *Tatler* is loyal to its traditions of elephantine fatuity, calling French actresses " little ladies " and freely using the old " who is of course " gag. The last copy we saw finished up one of its captions with a sentence which epitomizes the subtle, elusive charm of the *Tatler* style : " The list of Mrs. Alec Tweedie's publications is a very long one indeed—far too much so to refer to in such space as is at the present disposal." That gets our Femina Vie Dégoûtante Prize for the Sentence of the Week.

Spacious Days

The traffic bustles tirelessly past our window. " 𝔐errie 𝔈ngland CANNED FRUITS LTD.," we read as a maroon van flashes by. What feasts they must have had at the Mermaid Tavern ! What dogs they were, those bards of passion and of mirth !

Futility Corner

Plumb opposite us, as we write, a notice on a building urges, in man-high letters : " Thousands of Pounds Wasted Daily—Save Your Waste Paper." It would be presumptuous, we obscurely feel, to short-circuit the natural processes of metropolitan life ; otherwise we should send these random notes straight across, with our compliments. It might not save a thousand pounds, but it would save an awful lot of time and trouble. They'll get there in the end, of course ; even the weariest river winds *somewhere* safe to sea. " See you in the pulp-mill ! " as the limited edition of *Sparkenbroke* said to the Coronation number of *Horse and Hound*.

Ration

Near the Elephant and Castle there was lately to be seen a poster advertising a film. From across the street, whence it was possible to read only the heavy type, it came out like this :

ONE HOUR OF LIFE

TWICE DAILY

IN THREE PARTS

Slingsby

A*

DIARY OF PERCY PROGRESS—I

By John Betjeman

With drawings by Christopher Sykes

THE CAG BAG AND THE MAGS

HERE'S cheers that we'll be real pals before you've finished reading this story. Allow me to jolly well introduce my jolly old self.

Name, Progress, Percy. *Born*, Anno Domini 1906. *Educated*, Carshalton. *Occupation*, Back Numbers Limited. *Recreation*, platinum blondes. *Favourite Author*, Dornford Yates. *Address*, Olde Chimneys, 142, Maconochie Way, Iver, Bucks. *'Phone*, Dial IVE any old time, ask the girls there for " P.P." and they'll put you straight through—I've whispered words of love to the whole lot of 'em in my time.

Well, that's about all, in black and white. I'm a breezy fellow, said to be handsome by the female element in our population, possessor of a couple of smart lounge suits, decent tweeds, and grey bags, a honking little sports car that'll rev up to fifty, overhead exhaust, all spring valves, seating accommodation—one blonde and yours aforesaid.

It might interest you to know how

I came to start Back Numbers Ltd. and what sort of a business it is. Well, it all started through my old school. If you were to look up in some list of old school clubs you would find us down as Old Carshaltonians. But we call one another, in old public schoolboy slang, Old Cag Bags, or sometimes just Old Cags.

I wear the Old Harrovian tie for business purposes, of course. However, let us *revenons* to our muttons. I was walking home pretty sozzled one night from the palatial dining establishment of one of our better-known North West London hotels and was singing a snatch of the Old Cag Song :

"What tho' in age we forget we
   were youngsters ?
   What tho' in youth we omit to
   grow old ?
Still let us never be shirkers or
   bungsters,[1]
   But clean-living Cags in the Carshalton mould."

A fellow tapped me on the shoulder. " Cag Bag ? "

" Ashur," I assented.

" *Ditto ici*, which, being interpreted, is ' Same here'. Let us make the welkin ring, ole man, with our jo-holli-olli-ficashuns." The lad seemed a bit one over the eight, but he was quite decently dressed, had an Old Eton boy tie, and spoke with quite a decent accent, so we galumphed off together. I was in whimsical mood, ready to do anything for a joke. I paid for a double Scotch and polly for us both, then it was his turn. He said he didn't want to change a note just yet, so we both toddled off on down the Edgware Road. I 'phoned up a doctor by way of a lark and gave him a wrong address. That kept us chuckling all the way to Marble Arch.

Under a street-lamp in Oxford Street there was an old fellow selling newspapers and film magazines, waiting for the people to come out of the flicks. It was too late to get my pal to make it even over the double Scotch and polly I gave him, so we were looking about for something to do. Then I had a wizard wheeze. The newspaper-seller had one of those wire arrangements full of spicy magazines displayed cover foremost. It was duly propped up against a wall. " Let's pinch that," I said ; " the old

---

[1] *Public-school slang.*

feller won't half swear." " Who's going to do it ? " said my pal. " Bet you that double Scotch and polly, ole man, you daren't do it yourself," I returned. " I'll wait here and keep cave."

Well, my pal pinched it, though he didn't seem keen to go, and the feller roared something at him. I didn't have time to hear what, because I yelled out : " Skidaddle— he may fetch a bobby!" He hared down a side-turning. When he came back, it was with a bobby holding onto each of his arms and the blasted magazines, stand and all, being carried by the old fool of a newspaper-seller himself.

Now, I'm not a fool. If I had been, I'd have hooked it and been caught pretty soon. Besides, I didn't want to let him down, even though I had only just met him. Now, I've got a code of morals,

though I'm not one of your religious chaps. There's some things you can do and some things you can't do, and one of them is to try to get another man into a row with whom you've been pretending to be friendly. And that's just what this Old Cag Bag did to me. He said I'd suggested his taking the mags and the bobby had charged him with intent to steal.

Of course my suggestion had only been a joke. But when they charged me point-blank I naturally said I didn't know anything about it. Then the newspaper feller said he'd seen me with this cad in Oxford Street. I saw no point in our both getting into a row, so I said : " Well, constable, it's this newspaper tike's word or mine. I'm an old Carshaltonian. Here's my card. And if you want to know any more about me, 'phone up my Governor, Sir Cattlebag Progress, chairman of Amalgamated Spare Parts, Ltd." I then bethought me of the note our friend didn't want to change. " If this feller's a gentleman," I added, " he'll pay up for any damage he's done in a friendly way."

It then transpired that he hadn't got a bean on him, let alone a note. Bang goes a double Scotch and polly, I mused. However, I could afford to be philosophical and thank my stars I wasn't saddled with him for the evening.

They took us all off to the Station and 'phoned the Governor. He was damned annoyed to have to get up and come and identify me. But, of course, I got off. I learned afterwards that the two of them got run in for "conspiring with intent to defraud". They dropped the blackmail charge. The newspaper tike got off with a fine —he *would* in these days when even magistrates seem to be bolshevists —and the Cag Bag couldn't pay his fine and went to jug, silly fool. But that's not the important part of the story. Point is, those out-of-date mags gave me a notion for a business venture. I now buy old periodicals at waste-paper rates and hire them, by a weekly exchange service, to doctors and dentists and others of that ilk. I make 150 per cent. profit on every copy I buy. If it is of any interest to you, last week's *Tatler* does well in Harley Street, the week before last's in Welbeck Street. In outer London they don't mind them two or three months old.

I got a letter from some sort of Delinquents' Aid Society or something, asking if I would find jobs for these two. That was going a bit far, I do think. Of course there

A**

was probably no doubt that the Old Cag Bag was an Old Cag Bag, but I noticed that when he was flurried during the arrest, his accent wasn't out of the top drawer, if you know what I mean. I mean, I'm not snobbish. But you've got to have complete gentlemen in my business. Some of the doctors among my clients come from the very highest families — Dr. Grosvenor Westminster, Dr. Cavendish Portman, Dr. H. Cameron-Douglas Fitzpassionfruit, Dr. Sutherland Argyle, and many more. Naturally I couldn't have a fellow who was not quite a gentleman and a gaolbird to interview these clients, if you know what I mean. I mean, I'm not snobbish.

'*Get ready to run.*'

THE POET AND THE SAGE

Jan Struther

"NEXT applicant, please," said the Clerk of Careers. A young man, small, fair and eager, was ushered into the cubicle, and the sound-proof steel door closed behind him.

"Morning," said the Clerk.

"Good morning."

"Siddown. Name ? "

"John Smith."

"Real name," said the Clerk.

"John Smith."

"Oh, very well," said the Clerk. "Age ? "

"Nineteen."

"Proposed career ? "

"Just a moment," said the young man. "This place hasn't been going very long and I'm not quite clear how it works. Am I bound to ask for your advice ? And if I do, am I bound to take it ? "

"The Ministry of Careers," the Clerk rattled off, "is a new Government Department instituted to prevent needless waste of human energy, to lessen disappointment and to eliminate occupational misfits. It has, of course, been made compulsory to ask our advice before embarking on any career. You are not, however, obliged to take it ; but refusal to do so disqualifies you from receiving any unemployment benefit or other State assistance in the event of your own choice of a career proving, as so often happens, a failure."

"I see," said the young man thoughtfully. "That must save the country a lot of money."

The Clerk shrugged his shoulders. "People will learn in time, no doubt, that an ounce of expert advice from trained psychologists, supported by up-to-date statistics, is worth a ton of untutored instinct. Especially as the advice is free. And now, as I am pressed for time, suppose we get on. Proposed career ? "

"I want to be a poet," said the young man. His eyes lit up as he said it, but the Clerk did not see them ; he wrote the word "Poet" very neatly in column two and then pressed a small electric buzzer.

"Take this gentleman in to Mr. Sage," he said to the messenger.

John Smith followed the messenger down a long corridor and was shown into another sound-proof cubicle, where an old man was seated at a chromium-plated desk drawing triangles on the blotting-paper.

"Mr. Sage ? " said the young man.

"No," replied the other wearily, "but that's what they always call me in this place. You see, when I applied for a job here they asked me what my profession was and I said : 'Sage.' Ignorant devils, never heard of the word, I suppose ; put it down as my surname instead. Never bothered to correct them. No good arguing with fools."

"And what *is* your name ? " asked the young man, suddenly interested.

"Oh well, never mind. You'd know it, I dare say, if you heard it. Times are hard. But now, about yourself. I see from this form that you have set your heart on becoming a poet."

"Yes."

"What kind of poet ? "

"A—a great poet," said the young man, absurdly enough ; but the Sage was very patient with him.

"Naturally. But do you mean by

H. Botterill.

that a successful one ? Famous in your own lifetime ? "

" I suppose so."

" Ah! That makes it more difficult. Have you studied modern poetry at all ? "

" Not specially," said the young man. " But poetry is poetry, isn't it ? "

" No," said the Sage gently. " Any more than beauty is beauty. There are fashions in both of them. Now tell me, what are the subjects that inspire you ? "

" Oh . . . Nature, for one."

" Nature ? You mean roses and nightingales and so on ? "

" Roughly speaking, yes. And a thousand other beautiful things. Oh God, sometimes I could die of beauty ! "

The Sage looked gloomy.

" I must tell you," he said, " since you do not appear to know it, that these somewhat jejune phenomena have no place whatever in the modern poet's property chest. The mention of them has long ago ceased to evoke any response in the reader's mind. To put it crudely, he has had his bellyful of nightingales."

" There are worse surfeits," said the young man, smiling. " But of what then does the poetical landscape now consist ? "

" In the foreground," said the Sage, " there is a railway track, on one side of it a coal-mine (disused), on the other a football ground. In the middle distance is a power-station, and stretching away to the horizon a row of pylons."

" I see," said the young man. " But why ? "

" Because these things, nowadays, are the cogent evocative symbols. You must remember that the population is no longer a rural one, but predominantly urban. People who live in industrial surroundings respond to industrial images."

" Forgive me," said the young man, " but do the people who live in industrial surroundings read modern poetry ? "

" Very few people," replied the Sage, " read modern poetry at all. Except, of course, critics, and other literary men."

" And do the critics and other literary men live in these stark industrial surroundings ? "

" No," said the Sage. " They mostly live in Bloomsbury, Hampstead and Sussex."

" Well, then ! " said the young man.

" I am not here to argue," said the Sage. " I am merely telling you what's what. Are there no other topics that fire you ? "

" Social injustice," said the young man eagerly. " When I see great wealth existing side by side with utter poverty and wretchedness—— "

" Ah ! This sounds more hopeful. I see you are a Communist."

" No. I'm a Socialist. But that's all right, isn't it ? "

" Worse than useless," said the Sage, shaking his head. " It would have been almost better if you'd said you were a Conservative. In that case your work might at least have

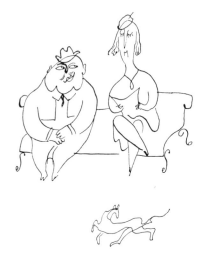

had a kind of period interest. But Socialism—that is merely dingy and boring, like the fashions of the year before last."

" What has fashion to do with it ? " cried the young man. " We are talking of the equality of mankind. I tell you I would willingly die for it."

" But would you kill for it ? "

" Certainly not. For to use violence would be to create further injustice."

The Sage shook his head again.

" I am becoming less and less hopeful about your chances. Tell me,

have you no other source of inspiration ? "

" There is love," said John Smith.

" Certainly there is," agreed the Sage. " You have experienced it already, and so young ? "

" Oh God, I am ready to die of it ! "

" That makes three things you are ready to die of, or for : beauty, justice, and love. Let us hope that the third will prove of greater use to you than the other two. Tell me more."

" I am fortunate enough to love one who loves me in return."

" Good—good," said the Sage, with an approving nod. " Unrequited passion, like nostalgia, is at a discount. Nowadays there must be no frustrations, no regrets."

But the young man was not listening to him.

" If you could only see my beloved," he cried, his face illumined. " She—— "

" She ? " said the Sage.

" She is as lovely as—— "

The Sage stood up and held out his hand.

" You are wasting your time," he said simply. " If I granted you a poet's licence, I should merely be disqualifying you for the dole. There isn't the faintest hope that you would be a success."

" I don't understand," said the young man miserably.

" Read the moderns," said the Sage, " and perhaps you will. I'm afraid I must bid you good-bye," he added, as the other made no attempt to go. " I am sincerely sorry that I cannot help you, for I have taken quite a liking to you."

" Good-bye," said the young man, and moved away like a sleepwalker. At the door he turned round.

" You don't think," he suggested wistfully, " that all this will pass ? That posterity—— "

" Posterity," said the Sage, " is not in this Department. Consult Uplift and General Purposes—nineteenth floor."

But there was a prim twinkle in his eye.

ARCHITECTURE

The Demolition of Oxford

SOME weeks ago a letter appeared in *The Times* protesting against the proposed demolition of some seventeenth-century houses in Merton Street, one of the few cobbled streets left in Oxford. As a result the scheme has been dropped for a year in the hope that an alternative site be found, but the case is important as a typical example of the furtive way in which our cities are being destroyed.

The University claim that a library is required for the use of lecturers working in the Examination Schools. In view of the vast new Bodleian soon to be completed, it is doubtful if this claim is justified. Assuming, however, that the need is there, is this, as they also claim, the only possible site? Just beyond the houses in question there is a nondescript huddle of buildings comprising a bath-house and a garage. These are of no architectural merit, are conveniently placed for access from the Examination Schools and are the property of University College. Another site equally convenient is the property of the University. Round the corner from No. 17 Merton Street is a screen pierced with an ornamental gateway, closing the three-sided quad of the Examination Schools. The destruction of this screen and gate, a conscientious bit of bijou-tijou work by T. G. Jackson, would be no loss and would leave vacant a fine site for a library building to form the fourth side of the quad. It is difficult to understand why the claims of these two sites have not been officially put forward.

The houses it is proposed to destroy admittedly are not particularly beautiful nor in very good condition. Their beauty, however, is of secondary interest to what has been termed their "continuity value". They are of a type and style now rare in Oxford, and should thus be preserved, not in a spirit of sentimental fetishism, but in order to keep an unbroken line of old work along which modern ideas can inevitably develop.

The visitor will find that this is not the only architectural scandal in the city, existent or proposed. The chaotic layout of the Plain, the sham-Tudor rebuilding of Carfax, the new Christchurch boathouse, the shoddy ill-lit railway station with its confused approaches and, most of all, Gloucester Green, a truly horrible mess of drainpipes, kiosks, enamel signs, scaffold-poles and hoardings, are a disgrace to a university city. Opposite the Clarendon gapes a yawning hole soon to be filled with the new Bodleian and disclosing all manner of curious objects. One of the most puzzling is a small half-finished cottage in Colonial-Cotswold style, which turns out to be a garage and chauffeur's quarters. It is impossible to discover why it was allowed to sit there, or what purpose it serves, except the convenience of the Master of Trinity, whose property it is. More comical still is a curious little building, disclosed by surrounding demolition, which looks like a laundry or a squash court. It is, in fact, the backside of the Trinity College War Memorial Library, which is revealed as one of the most blatant examples of "window-dressing" architecture in existence.

As to the new Bodleian, it is a conscientious compromise between new and old. The external massing has a certain charm, but the windows and para-

'Come, come, Sotheby—up ladders and down snakes.'

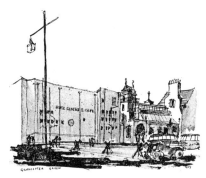

pets disturb the eye with their arbitrary variety of placing and design. " Ornament," says the architect, " has only been used where it serves a definite æsthetic purpose." It is difficult to see what purpose is served by the indiscriminate use of urns and swags.

Opposite is a large slice of property between Ship Street and Broad Street, scheduled for destruction in two years' time. Here admittedly the owners, the city of Oxford, have little alternative, for in the centre of the site is a huddle of shacks and tottering fences, reminiscent of an early René Clair film, and constituting in parts a slum. It is hoped that the Ship Street houses will be preserved and also the large bastions of the old city wall, which still stand in comparatively good repair among the cabbage stalks and clothes lines of back yards.

There is a widespread complacency in these matters arising from the erroneous belief that there is some law or authority which can prevent the destruction of ancient buildings. The fact is that in English law there is no sure defence against architectural vandalism. Such Acts as exist are permissive, not compelling, and call for compensation which local authorities are usually unable or unwilling to pay. The Ancient Monuments Act is able to protect a building only when it is uninhabited, and thus often ruinous, or one not the property of the Church. The natural assumption is that the Church can be trusted to look after its heritage. The Ecclesiastical Commissioners are notorious, however, for their concentration on financial matters. The post-war proposal of the Bishop of London to demolish nineteen of the city churches, the more recent destruction of the gateway to St. James's, Piccadilly, and

of All Hallows, Lombard Street, and the scheme conceived by the Archbishop of Canterbury to pull down the lovely stone houses in Palace Yard, Westminster, to clear the way for a memorial to King George V, bear sad witness to the æsthetic taste and discretion of the Church.

The list of non-Church property scheduled for preservation under this Act makes interesting reading. The majority of names are those of earthworks, heaps of prehistoric stones, tracks, Tudor barns and Saxon walls. Any building in a good enough state of repair to be worthy of preservation seems deliberately omitted. More extraordinary still is the fact that the Royal Commission on Historical Monuments is empowered to notice only buildings erected up till 1714. This eliminates with one arbitrary blow the work of Vanbrugh, Kent and Adam. Thus the responsibility of preserving our heritage has passed into the hands of voluntary societies, who can only be effective in a limited way. The Oxford Preservation Society have prepared a valuable list of interesting buildings which, they hope, will not be destroyed without good reason. But the fact that these buildings are for the most part individual units takes away half the usefulness of the list. The character of a city lies more in the vistas of streets and terraces, in the groups of squares and crescents, than in individual monuments

however excellent. A perfect Queen Anne house preserved in a street of towering flats looks merely ridiculous. The solution for Oxford and, for that matter, for the whole of England is to make a complete survey, scheduling

for preservation groups and collections of buildings as well as isolated monuments like churches or tithe halls. There is a common belief that a " green belt " is the climax of town planning ; but this is not an end in itself. A " green belt " is only a protective framework within whose limits a city can then proceed with the more diffused, but more important, process of area planning. In the rush to preserve the countryside the needs of the city seem forgotten, though they are equally urgent. The Oxford Preservation Society continue to buy up fields in which the citizen can exercise his dogs, while the city is being destroyed under their noses. The National Trust purchases Foxcombe on Boars Hill to preserve the magnificent view over Oxford, but all to be seen is an ugly manufacturing city in which the colleges emerge as anachronisms. HUGH CASSON

*

The building was typically Spanish, from the ornate clock tower topped by a red flag, to the barred windows in sharp relief against the white walls.—*Single to Spain*, by K. SCOTT WATSON.

But perhaps the second floor was neutral-coloured.

*

It is time somebody wrote a great play not based upon a famous novel or life, but original in its conception of plot and characters.—*Daily Mirror*.

Do you mean something really *natty* ?

*

THE POOR MAN IN HIS CASTLE

As I glance at the great bundle of these begging letters I wonder whether I should really enjoy being made the target of all this wheedling duplicity. Perhaps after all it is more comfortable to keep our Irish sweepstakes in the realms of the day-dream, and in actual life to remain respectably, gaily, energetically, and quite undramatically poor.——*The Hon. Harold Nicolson in* THE LISTENER.

For us both the journey entailed certain sacrifices : I had to forgo my tiger-lilies and my peaches, my car its weekly wash and overhaul.—*The Hon. Mrs. Harold Nicolson in* HARPER'S BAZAAR.

THE THEATRE

Hamlet

THIS latest *Hamlet*, at the Westminster, ought on no account to be missed. Its excellent plainness makes it remarkable. Too many producers have, I take it, baulked at what seemed an intellectual coldness in the frame of the play. So they have cooked and coloured the plot up, to make a stage " situation " out of what is in fact an *impasse*, domestic drama out of a tragedy in the mind. Successive players of *Hamlet* have been either all mannerism, like Mr. Gielgud, or all *fugue*, like the irresistible Mr. Olivier. So for seasons the play-goer has come out of *Hamlet* feeling battered to bits, but without any clear feeling of the play's motivation or any enduring view of the issues raised. Has anyone really wanted to know what the play is *about* ? Going to *Hamlet*, one found oneself in a world of surrealist behaviour, in which magnificent words described parabolas. Apart from the facts that Hamlet has seen a ghost and heard his father was murdered, and that his mother and uncle present figures of sin, the hero might seem to be in the throes of a self-spun crisis. His infuriated inaction, his maltreatment of Ophelia never explain themselves. Put on as it often has been, over-produced and thundered across the footlights in a colossal mixture of tears and blood, *Hamlet* might well have seemed, if it were not *Hamlet*, fine theatre but a quite incompetent play.

None of this applies to the *Hamlet* at the Westminster. Produced by Mr. MacOwan " according to the ideas of Professor Dover Wilson," this is, above all, a *Hamlet* that offers a key. The tragedy becomes lucid, therefore inevitable : you see the figures move in almost deadly-clear air instead of in great rolling fulvous clouds of smoke. This production has

been called (and is in fact) scholarly : do not let this be forbidding. What does above all inform the production is a high, a sublime kind of common-sense. Upon two points of Dover Wilson's, both perfectly simple, a good deal is made to hinge. First, Hamlet makes an early unheard entrance during the conversation between the King and Polonius ; he overhears what they say and is thus, from then on, in possession of all details of their plot —including the fact that Ophelia is, or is to become, their tool. Second— ghosts at that time had not a good moral colour ; to the stern mind they were as much suspect as spiritualistic manifestations today. Hamlet's is a stern mind ; he is fastidious and sceptical. So, though the Ghost's appearance affects him strongly, emotionally, he cannot fully accept the Ghost as his father or act on its revelations as being valid, till he has applied the cunning test of the Play Scene. Point one explains his agonised cruelty to Ophelia (who had been up to then his one refuge, outside thought); point two, his reluctance to act in the early part of the play. If his uncle is to die, it must be execution, not murder. After the Play Scene, Hamlet is only waiting to strike. . . . So here we are given a *Hamlet* with all those time-honoured mystifications lopped away. What is left is frightful, but never incomprehensible. The play is not less majestic for being in human terms.

The cast show a calm grasp of the parts Shakespeare wrote for them. They act plainly and ably, without frills or hysteria. Mr. Christopher Oldham's unstressed Hamlet has very great distinction : he shows the height of unegotistic acting. His technique is certain : he gives the effect of tension, of a man almost paralysed by a held-in frenzy. Do not miss this *Hamlet* (only here for a short time) and then go trooping in hundreds to swoon and mystify at the next dressy attempt.

Women of Property

Women of Property, at the Queen's, is a good Finnish play—yes, we are

much luckier this week. It is not at all stark or oppressively Nordic—in fact, it is not in any way exclusively Finnish : what happens in it might happen in any country that keeps a tough and obstructive integrity. It shows the battle between the new will and old tradition. The manor of Niskavuori, snow-bound in winter, matriarchally governed, is the scene. The young squire, Arne, makes a desperate break for manhood by falling in love with the new schoolmistress, a young creature of the New World—gallant, fearless, with more than a flaming touch of the Hilda Wangel about her, and an engaging sophistication too. But Arne is married, in the Niskavuori tradition, to a vulgar young woman who has brought in money. This wife of his, Marta, seemed to me, though her rôle is unsympathetic, the outstandingly tragic figure of the play. Partly perhaps because of the range and depth Miss Dorice Fordred gives her—but also because she, too, is a creature of the transition, expecting in her own way what we heard denounced last winter as a " private happiness ". Her mother-in-law's contempt for her is unbounded ; the old lady made early her own sacrifice to tradition. " The women of Niskavuori," she tells the unhappy Marta, " do not run after their men." Marta does run after her man, to the extent of mobilising the village and searching the schoolmistress's bedroom for him. They get there just too late. Back home at Niskavuori, that evening ends in hysterics, contempt and gloom. One point brought home by this play is the difficulties of conducting an illicit love affair in a snow-bound neighbourhood —Arne's ski-tracks are traced from his mistress's window back to the manor door. This makes a situation he would gladly brazen out, but that his family are anxious to smother. The Niskavuori men have always loved in the village, but Ilona is a quite new kind of menace. Mr. Griffith Jones as Arne and Miss Nancy Hornsby as Ilona are excellent. The love scenes have an authenticity and dignity that do much to keep the play on its pretty high level.   ELIZABETH BOWEN

THE CINEMA

What Man Has Made of Man

THE technicolor expert, like Wordsworth, is most at home with Nature. In *God's Country and the Woman*, a tale of the timber forests, we see some pretty shots of trees cutting huge arcs against the sky as they fall, but no technical advance since *The Trail of the Lonesome Pine*. In the city sequences the lounge suits don't come out too badly, but there's an appalling orange taxi and the headlights of cars are curiously ugly. An attempt at fast cutting and quick dissolves confirms our belief that colour will put the film back technically twelve years.

The plot may roughly be described as a combination of *Romeo and Juliet* and *The Taming of the Shrew* : Katharina has become a Capulet, the Montagues and Capulets run rival timber companies, and Romeo has to do some taming as well as loving. But it is his loving which fascinated me. A wealthy young man fresh from Paris and the Riviera, he has earned a reputation as a wonderful quick worker with women, a breaker of hearts, an American Juan. His technique is interesting and perhaps national : we see a few flashes of it in a Paris lift and on the quayside at Cherbourg : he treads hard on a woman's foot and then apologises or else he takes a crack at her ankle and catches her as she falls. The method never fails. When he meets Juliet-Katharina for the first time he remarks " O boy, what a fuselage ! " with his eye on her bust, and when he kisses her he says " That went right down to the soles of my goloshes." Irresistible in strong-toed shoes, he hacks his way to happiness.

It isn't a very good film, and Mr. George Brent is hardly improved by blue-black technicolor hair and a little Parisian moustache (next to the orange taxi he's the worst bit of colour in the picture). Far more interesting is the effect it has had on a veteran film critic. "The thought of so much beauty of forest and mountain being ruthlessly destroyed," Mr. Sydney Carroll writes, " almost broke my heart. These trees were treated so savagely. Their sufferings made me feel the need for a Society for the Prevention of Cruelty to Trees." And Mr. Carroll concludes his outburst, written on woodpulp which ought to account for a fairsized sapling : " I could not see this picture again. It would for this reason alone give me a heartache."

" Captain Strogoff, the fate of Siberia is in your hands. Go for God, for Russia and for the Tsar." The words echo down the years from the caption of the early Mosjoukine film. Mosjoukine will be remembered as the player Pudovkin cites as an example to prove that acting was a matter of montage. Intercut Mosjoukine's face with a child's coffin and you got tragic acting. Intercut the same white turnip of a countenance with charging cavalry and you had the heroic. Mr. Anton Walbrook does a lot better than Mosjoukine in this new *Michael Strogoff*. As dashing and open-air as a good Western, this Jules Verne tale of a Tartar rising is motivated in the grand manner. A Grand Mission to save the Russian empire ; a Grand Sacrifice when the hero denies his mother ; a Grand Courtesan who repents and dies grandly for love (" Do you not want to be a Quin ? " the renegade colonel—Mr. Akim Tamiroff—whispers into her jewelled ear) ; even the Sensualities are Grand in a torture scene which begins with dancing girls and ends with a white-hot sword. Simple, passionate and certainly sensuous, the whole thing is like a poem for boys, and not a bad poem either. If we cannot treat it quite seriously, it's because Russia, whether under Tsar or Stalin, remains incurably comic even in tragedy. " To Omsk ! " the renegade leader cries to his Tartars ; " I must get to Omsk," the heroine piteously murmurs, and the hero, wounded and feverish in a peasant's hut, can find no better syllables to murmur than " Irkutsk, Irkutsk." How wise the Soviet policy of renaming their cities—and how pathetically useless when " Gorki " is the only substitute.

GRAHAM GREENE

' I'm the husband—and I carry a gun.'

'Oh, Cézanne! He's mad about Cézanne.'

* * *

Mr. U

Paul Morand

"EXCUSE me, sir. Is this actually No. 489 Fifth Avenue?"

"Yes—can't you read?"

"No, sir."

"Good God! After all that the Government has done for education!"

At three o'clock in the morning Mr. Doolittle had emerged from the Palermo and was trying to get home. It was raining. Putting behind him the low ceiling of the night club, the pleasant coloured lights and a troublesome concoction of fruit-juice, dynamite and eau-de-Cologne, he had just turned into Fifth Avenue—in order to avail himself of the whole width of that vast sleeping street in which to drive his car—when a man on the sidewalk signalled to him to stop. Mr. Doolittle braked, turned a circle and, as you might say, almost dived through the backcloth. He got out of the car and cursed, delighted at this last excuse for not going home to bed. Before him stood a tall Chinaman, thin and dusty, covered with cobwebs, inadequately protected from the rain by a couple of old mats in the form of a chasuble tied on with one piece of string, and leading a white cock at the end of another. Mr. Doolittle imagined that he had chanced upon the cleaner from an opium den, and started to move on, when the other continued:

"Excuse me, sir; I am in a bad way—indeed I am in a very bad way. I have asked you a small service which costs you nothing. My name is U. I belong neither to New York nor to 1936; I come from Kansou and the IXth century."

Mr. Doolittle had drunk so much that it seemed quite natural for him to be stopped on Fifth Avenue by a man a thousand years his senior.

"You're a ghost?" he asked.

" I am," the Chinaman replied ; " and a ghost in need."

" Well, I come from Ireland, as you can see for yourself," said Mr. Doolittle, heeling slightly, " and I'm just crazy about banshees. What can I do for you ? "

" This," replied the spectre. " No doubt you are aware that in the time of the Tangs—I lived under that dynasty and died in the year 837 of your reckoning—the dead were buried with little figurines of baked clay which, once in the tomb, came to life and took their place in the service of the defunct. Following the usual custom, my own grave included servants with their hands folded, dancers, grimacing warriors, dromedaries with bridles of green enamel, wild boars, and a magnificent cavalcade of terra-cotta horses equal to that which I had left on earth, where I was a member of the Academy and honorary Viceroy of Kansou. These figurines watched over my rest and waited upon my repasts according to the proper rites. Unfortunately, they were very beautiful. For their beauty they were coveted. Two months ago, about the time of the eighth moon, a merchant from New York, who was gathering up antiques wholesale from Kansou, took advantage of the lamentable state of civil war into which that province had fallen to break open my tomb. His attention was attracted by the large number of allegorical inscriptions and the richness of the mausoleum. (I designed it myself during my life-time ; eighteen astrologers consulted on the choice and orientation of the site, and they selected its position, with the aid of mirrors and magic compasses, from among a hundred others : no star above and no dragon below should trouble my rest.) But one morning I heard the sound of blows ; there came a blinding light and I beheld, leaning over me, a little dark man clad in a grey jacket, with small white leggings, and a rose in his buttonhole ; his hair was as the head of a new-born lamb. Behind him stood a carriage with four wheels and without horses, like that which you are driving, but filled with sacks of money. This man, who dared thus to unite the world of light with the region of shadows, offered the local sub-prefect a bribe, in return for which he was permitted to remove the statuettes which were both the decoration and defence of my tomb. Like the foxes which, in our legends, enter houses and bear away what they will, this person, having violated my sepulchre, incontinently crossed the ocean with his spoil in a large junk propelled by fire.

" Since when, sir, I have known no repose. The dead around me, knowing me now to be defenceless, stole the food, the castor oil, the ginger wine, the incense and the candles with which my descendants still paid pious homage to my shade . . . I was forced to come forth in search of food. I became one of those vagrant spirits of which every honourable Chinaman lives in horror. I was forced to consume the offal of chicken, dead cats, and even my own fleas. I descended to waiting outside slaughter-houses and on my stomach—I, a Viceroy—had to lick the rivulets of pigs' blood which flowed thence in the gutter. I cannot bring myself to tell you of the mixed company of homeless spirits with which I was forced to join in my struggle for existence—not only sailors drowned in foreign seas but, what is far worse, soldiers killed on the field of battle. . . Now, you can see for yourself, I am as thin as a lath. . . My soul has no strength left with which to attain reincarnation. It is a tragedy. I cannot be promoted to higher rank and I remain a ghost deprived of all posthumous advancement."

The Chinaman opened the matting ; his empty stomach was diaphanous ; within, Mr. Doolittle beheld a skeleton and, in a greenish circle scarcely encompassing that skeleton, the astral body ; and through the astral body he could see the lights of the Plaza.

" After searching for a long time," continued Mr. U, " I have discovered that the thief is called Willy Judesheim and that he lives in New York. My hunt was particularly arduous because by day I was held fast in my tomb and it was only at night that I could

'*Now who says Wellington was a greater general than Lord Roberts ?*'

roam. Now the hardest part is over, for I have found his house. But with whom should I lodge my complaint? In China a gong hangs at the gateway of each mandarin's abode and, when a plaintiff strikes the gong, the official is bound to hear the suit and give immediate judgment. Where is your justice?"

"I've no idea," replied Mr. Doolittle. "I told you I am an Irishman. As a politician I get things done without justice."

"Mark moreover, sir, that I have not even the customary means of revenging myself on Mr. Judesheim by killing myself before his door, since I am already dead. Otherwise I should naturally choose to die in the most unpleasant way, by hanging, in order to make myself disagreeable to him. To make him publicly responsible, I should slip my indictment of him into my shoe, or, as an ultimate refinement which would completely discredit him, I might write on my own skin the exact motive for my suicide . . . But we cannot achieve the impossible. The only thing that remains for me is to settle the matter in my own way, with your help. As I asked when I first addressed you, is this in fact No. 489?"

With his fleshless finger Mr. U pointed to a large Renaissance palace in Tudor style, built of stone and brick, which showed no outward sign of commerce except, flanked by two clipped yews, a charming plaque of marble, as discreet as a visiting-card, on which was engraved:

WILLY JUDESHEIM
EXPERT AND DEALER IN CHINESE
ANTIQUES AND WORKS OF ART

"Here we are then," the spectre resumed, after Mr. Doolittle had read the inscription out to him. "We must be quick . . . I feel quite lost in your distant country where the houses grow up more than one storey high, the women have large flat feet, and one never comes by either a yellow llama or a camel . . . This is what I require of you, O living man: that you cry out in Chinese this phrase:

YU-TCHE LI-K'O CHANG KAN-SOU K'IU K'INN TSE—

which, being roughly interpreted, means: 'It is ordered by Imperial Command that this rabble shall return immediately to Kansou.' At the words 'Imperial Command' my servants and my guards of terra-cotta, since they belong to an age in which inferiors still respected their masters, will obey immediately and repair to my tomb. But it is essential that you should say the words, and not I; for, as perhaps you know, terrestrial authority still has power over infernal beings, and in that place where a ghost retains but the shadow of his strength the prestige of a living being remains untouched, especially when he gives orders by Imperial Command."

Mr. Doolittle observed that it would be impossible for him to get into Mr. Judesheim's house, since the door was guarded by detectives and burglar alarms.

"You need only go close to the wall," the ghost replied. "My servants are just on the other side of it —I can see them. They are grouped round the marble hall on the ground floor, tier above tier in glass cases; they will hear you. Since you have no sword, so useful for intimidating spirits, brandish your umbrella, and turn to the four points of the compass while you repeat the incantation. Now take a deep breath, like the astrologers, and shout as loud as you can."

"YU-TCHE LI-K'O CHANG KAN-SOU K'IU K'INN TSE!" shouted Mr. Doolittle twice, with all the pleasure that a drunken man gets from hearing his own voice.

A frightful racket ensued. The night porter at the Plaza ran out. Whistles blew. Cops dashed up on motor-cycles, followed by a group of newspaper-sellers and one or two prostitutes. Then there was a deathly silence . . .

"I thank you, sir," said the gentleman in the mat. "Already, as you see, this white cock, which I have on a leash and which is the constant companion of all ghosts, begins to show signs of restlessness. His first crow is not far distant. It is necessary that I should reinstate my body in my desecrated tomb. For

you, still living, it is more than three weeks distant from here; but I shall take a short cut through the nether regions and be there in a matter of seconds. . . Meanwhile, please accept this little token of my esteem and thanks."

As he said these words, Mr. U placed in Mr. Doolittle's Ford a heavy bag of money which, he remarked, contained a thousand strings of coin. He then drew his old mat closer around his shoulders, pulled at the cock's leash, walked across to Central Park and disappeared beneath the grass.

Mr. Doolittle went home. After several times arriving at the wrong floor, he at last found his own apartment, and in his own apartment the door, and in his door the keyhole. He threw the sack of money and himself on the bed, and went to sleep.

The next morning he woke up still fully dressed. He was brought the *New York Times,* and there he read in large type that the house of Mr. Judesheim, the well-known connoisseur, had been entered during the night, and that a unique collection of Chinese *objets d'art,* for which the Boston Museum had recently offered a million dollars, had been found in pieces on the floor—while the rarest among them, the funeral statuettes recently brought from China, had disappeared.

Mr. Doolittle remembered then that, when he lay down, he had thrown his reward on the bed. He felt around. He dragged the sheets half off as he braced himself to lift the heavy sack, but, to his surprise, it now weighed no more than his morning paper. He fetched his nail-scissors and opened up the treasure. The sack was filled with little gilded slips. After a moment's thought he concluded that these must be confetti brought home by mistake from the Palermo; but in reality they were that imitation money made of paper which is distributed at Chinese funerals.

(Translated from the French by Desmond Flower.)

Sponge and Press

LIGHT READING FOR SPECIALISTS

Antony Coxe

"SAVAGE three-a-breast for sale. Superb condition. What offers?" That notice, read in a weekly paper called the *World's Fair*, got me. I drew mental pictures of what I imagined her to be like. She (I was sure it was a She) haunted my dreams. I thought of buying her, but I had no idea what she would fetch. I might offer £50 and find myself the owner of a very ferocious ant, or for five shillings become the possessor of some dark and disturbing Diana.

The next week I opened the paper eagerly to see if it had been sold. The advertisement wasn't there ; but I received some enlightenment. Another offer was printed :

FOUR-A-BREAST BY SAVAGE FOR SALE.

ONE OF THE BEST RIDES IN THE BUSINESS.

So that's what it was . not a freak but a " ride ", the technical term for those lovely gilt and white horses, gaudy dragons and gay pigs that go bobbing up and down round the steam organ of a roundabout—a merry-go-round designed by Mr. Savage.

It is to my savage little three-a-breast, as I affectionately called her, that I owe three months' amusement. Lured on by her, I read not only " Circusdom " and " Round the London Halls " (the weekly notes which led me to become a subscriber to *World's Fair*) but all the advertisements and a good deal of the Showman's Editorial. I found that the person who said that half the world doesn't know what the other half is up to had put a much too over-generous estimate on the knowledge of mankind. Any ninety-five per cent. of the Earth's population have no conception of the affairs of the remaining five per cent.

" On the tober I found a few of the boys having a gallop," wrote a weekly contributor, " all surrounded by a decent-sized hedges . . . they were ring pitching . . . one only was all on his tod . . . In the half-hour I was there three had a gallop and copped for a bit of greens and scarpered. Going from one pitch to another, I found sniftems, chits, slums, the broads, cornflakes spread . . . the hat varied from a clod to a tusheroon. Oh yes, a couple of grafters had the courage of their convictions to bat for a straight tush and I was glad to see they had a hand out for a few ! One finger, batting for deuces, came to his bat to a bit ring edge and copped for a suzy (three drops) and that was about as much as his fanny was worth."

This is not an excerpt from a stunt column, but a weekly feature that reports " News from and about the Grafters ".

In the next column an advertisement ran : " Coronation Tins of Toffee, size 3 in. by 4 in. by 2 in., very attractively labelled and marked 6d. each, 2s. per doz. tins." This appeared in early February.

And just above : " 500 Gross of Genuine Wonder Safety Razor Blades, British made, obtainable in Half-dozens or 1 dozen packets, a guaranteed shaver marked 2d., 2s. 2d. per gross."

Wherever my glance fell I saw such advertisements as :

VACANT NOW.
Great Wizard with two Beauties.
Own Spieler. Also Driver.
Cabinets of mysteries. All first-class.

I noticed, too that " Coloured girls " were " urgently sought for a walk up ", "a Spieler required for a Lion Show " and " A Giant Rat " was selling for £5.

WANTED.
Three men for a Swirl.
Beer merchants need not apply.

WANTED ALSO
Young ladies for games for the season.

Apart from these ads. and the grafters' column, " Automatic Gossip ", " Border Bits ", " Northern Notes ", " Pithy Pars " and many other features proved of great interest. The " In Memory " at the end once contained a very sad little poem, which went as follows :

The loss was great, our hearts were sad,
Since the day we lost our dear old Mam.

How long the bereaved had expected Mother to outlive Father I do not know, but clearly this reversal of their prognostication left them quite incapable of rewriting their verse.

Having gained much knowledge of the show folk, I broadened my outlook by reading other trade papers, from the *Baker's Record*, which "stands for Integrity of Thought, Independence of Action, and Individuality in every phase of Baking ", to the *Pawnbroker's Gazette*, where in a column of offers and ' wants ' someone was advertising " Fancy Box 6 pairs of O.E. Fisheaters ".

The former had a feature called " It Is Whispered . . ." from which I learned tactfully, and of course *sotto voce*, that " rock bottom has been reached for almonds ".

The titles of newspapers may sometimes prove more interesting than their contents, but naturally one has high hopes of the *Haltwhistle Echo* and the *Ramsbottom Observer*. The sonority of the name *O'Connell's Coal and Iron News, Wagon Owner and Transport Gazette* must have a great snob appeal. If only it could be amalgamated with *The Confectioners' Union and Ice Cream and Soda Fountain Journal* I should certainly become a life subscriber. The simple charm of functionalism may also be found represented on the bookstalls by *Jute, Bottling,* and *Cheap Steam*.

I used to wonder if keen rivalry existed between the *Bartender* and the *Abstainer*, but I came to the conclusion that it did not when I found that the advertising rates were considerably higher in the *Bartender*—although the *Abstainer*, I dare say, charged a lot for the space on the front page which implored you to get your fireplaces and baths at D. M—rg—n & S—ns. The *Cab Trade News* and the *Cigarette Card News* appear to have a clear field, and there can be little doubt as to their contents. *Seed Thoughts*, however, is not concerned with the arable side of agriculture, except in connection with the Bible ; its subtitle runs : "The Sunday School Magazine". I have gained a complete understanding of Douglas Byng's song " The Sunday School has Done a Lot for Me " since reading *Seed Thoughts*. For it impresses on teachers that "when describing (as realistically as possible) an Eastern marriage, without elaborating or giving the meaning of every detail to the children, the Boy Scouts' motto might well be stressed with regard to the preparation for the greatest of all events. If we are prepared, it means happiness ; if unprepared, grief or sorrow. It is a serious question . . . more attendance at Sunday School is not sufficient . . . Go on to speak of what is really neces-sary. The importance of being prepared in time should be emphasised."

Flame does not principally cater for the leisure moments of the fire-brigade, but provides its readers with delightful stories bearing such titles as " Up to No Good—Like Her Mother " and " Spare My Children ". Unfortunately *Flame* has no adoptable Auntie or Kind Friend to write letters of encouragement and advice to its readers, as *Good Taste* has. *Good Taste* maintains a great prestige in the *comme-il-faut* world. In answer to Worried Wife's complaint that " my husband says I am like a block of ice if he comes near me ; this is perfectly true ; I would do anything for him but we have three babies already, and only a small income, can you help me ? " the kindly adviser replies : " There is no need at all for you to be unhappy. Send me a stamped addressed envelope and I will tell you how to live a happy married life without any more risks."

Picking up *Cats and Kittens*, I found what surely must be the only social register for the feline race. Births, Deaths, and " Visits " are recorded, and although there were no deaths or births in the copy I bought, there should be a number of the latter quite soon now, because I noticed that the visits are many :

'Remember—Harris tweed and no gewgaws.'

The advertisement only costs 3s. 6d. per single column inch for twelve insertions.

"Round the Southern Shows" is obviously written by a gossip-writer: "Mrs. Stow was attractive as usual in a naughty little green felt hat . . . Miss Wilson looked somewhat disgruntled and not her usual cheery self . . . can do a killingly funny turn, including male impersonations. . . . Elderly lady of somewhat stern and commanding aspect, she affected a three-quarter-length coat and skirt of coarse grey tweed ; a man's white collar peeped coyly above a blue knitted jumper, a camera was slung over her shoulder, and, somewhat surprisingly, a large, very bright enamel blue-bird brooch was stuck into her uncompromising black felt hat . . . the wrinkled-stocking brigade was there in full force . . . The ladies' retiring room is a positive disgrace . . . one can see hardly anything to speak of . . ." Yes, indeed: *Cats and Kittens* is the title.

But the list is limitless, and if you get any pleasure out of seeing the other side of life think kindly of all those editors, sub-editors, office boys and printer's devils of the 4,200 daily, weekly, fortnightly, and monthly publications (not forgetting the one quadrimestral) that are published in Great Britain. To the staffs of these papers, which instruct those who know, and amuse me who do not—from the *Abercorn and Risca Weekly Argus* to *Zenana*—I take off my hat.

'Tough, huh?'

PETER THOMAS

Jan. 9th : Mrs. Cloake's cream Queen to Mrs. Yates's Son's Fleck.

Jan. 9th : Capt. St. Barbe's Mittens of Hanley to Mrs. Sampson's Golden Arrow.

Feb. 4th : Miss Heywood's Beauty of Porchester to Mr. Howe's Beatrice of Topography.

Feb. 11th : Mrs. Leonard's Alice and Mrs. Hesketh's Margried to Mrs. Sargent-Stowe's Mathew of Green Gables.

And I expect Mathew made a pretty penny into the bargain, for it seems that the usual stud fee is about two guineas and their railway-fare home. The ads. run something like this :

"Ch. Patrick of Allington, lovely pale son of Irish Boy, gorgeous eyes, snub face, wonderful width between ears. To a few Queens £2 2s."— and probably well worth it, at that.

★

TO THE PURE . . . .

"It is not a question of censorship. It is a question of decency. Some modern books are quite all right, those about travel and those about Sussex, but others ought not to be available."—Interview in the *Evening Standard*.

A JOB IN A MILLION—4

PIGEON-TRAINER FRED

WHY the racing or carrier pigeon has the instincts of a boomerang, no one has ever learned. Not even Fred, and he knows more about pigeons than most. Holding one of his favourite blue chequer cocks in the most unexpected of lofts (the attic of an early Georgian house in Highgate), after all his seasoned years of intimate experience he just says, sincerely and in all amazement : " Pigeons are bloody marvellous."

Which, of course, they are. Send a pigeon almost anywhere in the country and she will be back in four hours or so. After some characteristic obstruction on the part of the War Office their merits were recognized during the Great War, and every decent columbophil quite properly ranks the famous V.C. pigeon, Captain Crisp, whose eye was shot out, as a feathered Nurse Cavell. And we hear, very privily, that pigeons are the least expensive but by no means the least important part of the present re-armament campaign.

The——marvellous instincts of the racing pigeon, have, as hinted, baffled intimate research. Books have been written about them, charts drawn to explain them. Of the latter there is one which we have seen, some eight times life-size and very anatomical, showing the " *Columba Domestica,* Disposition of Intestines : Body cut open on the left side and turned a little upwards". But no one would dare to turn a little upwards to a pigeon.

Then there is the awkward question of deciding their sex ; if kittens are hard enough for the layman, let them try an adult pigeon. Easy enough for Fred, who has to make certain of such little technicalities when he crosses strains as pure as that of any racehorse. The cock, he suggests, is more literally highbrow than the hen ; the ladies are just a lot of flat-heads.

In Fred's model columbarium a kind of ante-natal clinic adjoins the general racing stable, and after August he separates the cocks from the hens and pairs them according to a cunningly conceived plan, which entails for them a ten-day stay-at-home honeymoon. After the happy event the cocks sit on the eggs during the day, while their wives go out on what Fred calls a " toss ". This means a short training flight. About five or six o'clock of the evening the cocks come off the eggs and the hens do the night shift. If a cock should show an over-developed maternal instinct and sit beyond his time, the hen is said to " coo " him off, which, of course, is just nagging.

And then with the pattering of little pink claws Fred's work really begins. When the birds are six days old he puts the aluminium rings of that exclusive body, the National Union of Racing Pigeons, on their legs— rings that are passports throughout the world. NURP, with year, initial and

THE PATIENT   Trying to take a linked puzzle apart.

number, will tell any pigeon-fancier (if he looks up his elaborate files) the bird's address and most of its family history. If the owner sells it, he must pay a transfer fee of 3d. to another august body, the National Homing Union, otherwise its birth certificate and training are ignored and negatived. The pigeons' Debrett makes pretty formidable reading. Their aristocracy is truly exclusive and the strains are purer than anything Hitler could achieve. No pure Wegges would dream of marrying below their loft, and are justly proud of being "the old original Janssens-Wegges—the cream of the World's Wegges". And that goes for Grooters too.

These blueblooded youngsters, hatched, as it were, with a silver ring round their leg, are known as "squeakers" and are quite happy if you throw them a small gallipot of tares. But Fred has to watch them closely, for squeakers are apt to fall ill or "go crooked in the keel" and not feather properly. In fact, as another old hand so succinctly puts it, "if young squabs make a bad start in life, they never do throw off that weakness". And that goes for Grooters too.

Apart from such complex and usually unpleasant maladies, food presents a rather difficult problem to the incipient pigeon-fancier. The menu can be astonishingly varied, truly cosmopolitan. There are, for instance, Giant Goa Tares, Old Tasmanian Maples, Special Hand-picked Tic Beans, Red Danubian Maize (or, should you prefer it, from the Argentine), Brazilian Lentils, and, as a savoury perhaps, DRABBLE'S GRIT. An army cannot march on an empty stomach, but pigeons, for some reason, fly better with an empty crop. Perhaps it is because they prefer travelling light, or, more likely, because they are looking forward to their Giant Goa Tares. At any rate Fred keeps them on the lightest of diets before the big race, unlike some folk who give them near-aphrodisiacs like "speed cake". And after the race, a cold bath, sir, and some watercress.

When the young 'uns, "squeakers" or "squabs", are twenty-four days old Fred takes them from their parents and their education starts. He takes them out with an older bird on a "toss". At first it will only be a few miles away, say Alexandra Park, if they are being trained for the Northern race. The distances will be increased week by week; soon it will be Huntingdon, Newark, and, in six months, Berwick. By that time the squeaker's voice has broken, and he knows all the answers and more than a lot of hikers. He is ready next year for the big race from Thurso, which is just about 500 miles. The southern race was from San Sebastian—before the "throubles"—which made rather an agreeable trip for the pigeons. They were liberated at 12 noon, reached one of those pleasant little places on the French coast just in time to roost (perhaps a quick apéritif and a flutter at the tables before turning in) and across the Channel to England, home and Fred, in time for lunch the next day.

Fred isn't usually worried about his pigeons finding their way back; pigeons almost always do that. The test is the time they take to get into their loft and be properly clocked-in by the Toulet automatic timing-clock. If they make too many circles they lose the race. It all depends on fatigue and their personal relations with the trainer, and as Fred knows them all by name and has handled them since they were squeakers they usually drop out of the sky almost into his hands. This brings us to the question of handling pigeons, which obviously needs tact and experience. Fred says that mostly they don't peck, with the warning that "old 'uns will, on the nest".

But Fred knows everything: how many tail-feathers they should have, whether they are "red chequers" or "blue chequers" or "dark chequers pied" or "mealies". He scrutinizes their droppings as a Tiffany would quiz pearls. He knows that they can fly a mile a minute with a tail wind and do the 260-mile race from Morpeth in six hours, or be slowed down to a mere built-up area pace by haze or a head wind. He cares for them as one would a wife—after all, a 1681 definition describes a "pigeon" as "a young woman, a girl, a sweetheart". His columbarium is therefore almost a sublimated harem, scrupulously clean and, very rightly, the envy of the Federation Nationale des Colombophiles de France.

In a certain obscure but well-patronized hostel in Camden Town we once saw our Fred showing his pigeons for prizes along with many others. Some were in Coronation panniers, and no doubt heavy with Coronation Mixture—"in popular use since the crowning of King Edward VII. No better recommendation necessary". It was enough to listen to the learned conversation generally, and in particular to Fred trying to buy a promising squeaker for a couple of guineas, to realize that, as Darwin wrote in *The Origin of Species*, "it takes years to make a pigeon fancier".

CHRISTOPHER SALTMARSHE

★

Do you always sound the "g" on the end of words without making it sound like "k"?——*Questionnaire in the* DAILY MIRROR.

Except when out of breath, playin' pinkponk.

"*My God, my pocket's been picked!*"

Pins and Needles

COMMENT ON CLOTHES

The Magnetic North

THE Expedition usually consists of much the same little band of heroes and heroines, and there would be no need to issue clothes warnings for the Twelfth were it not that every time a train steams out of King's Cross it bears with it a few novices, who may be harbouring in their trunks some darling crazy purchases that Scotland will not take to its bosom.

It is difficult for them as they toil and moil about the London shops these July days to keep their minds on tweeds and shooting-sticks and burberrys and woolly underwear, surrounded as they are by distracting playsuits and sun-tan oil and dark glasses and sea pelts. Difficult to grasp the fact that in a few weeks' time they will be sitting in butts

as soldiers sit in trenches—passing the time away as best they can, and thinking it might be a welcome break in the monotony if a stray shot should come their way.

Lurgan's of Old Bond Street is where many of the well initiated go. It is famous in the Stately Homes of England, and is one of the first places American women ask to be led to when they disembark from the *Queen Mary*. Yet it is a house that has never advertised nor breathed its own name above a whisper. Homespun Shetland tweeds —soft in texture, soft in colour—are likely to be the most popular this year, as the King is particularly fond of them. You will find beautiful examples at Lurgan's, and the Duchess of Norfolk has recently ordered a suit in one of them. They have, too, the famous Hardilam tweeds, and the hand-made Irish ones . . . all masculine tweeds as distinct from dressmaker tweeds. Checks are not popular with their clientèle, that is, not big checks. For they like their tweeds to be unobtrusive. They're not buying them just for one season, they expect to wear them for ten years and love them all the more. And in the face of all this, it is interesting to note that Lurgan suits are from 10 gns. made to measure, readymade from 8½ gns. Compare that with the prices of many houses of lesser merit. . . .

At Lurgan's, too, you will find the Brook style sweaters that every American woman wants, and therefore sooner or later gets. They are hand-knit in Shetland wool with small round neck, no collar, and corded-ribbon edging to take the buttons and buttonholes. You wear a long-sleeved cardigan over a matching sweater. The colours are soft and turfy. Only Standen's in Jermyn Street, specialists in Shetland jerseys, have anything like such a collection of Brook style sweaters to choose from. Lurgan's also have an exclusive and famous scarf in thick tie silk with two or three stripes of different coloured silk running down the length of it. This scarf is so well-known that policemen in Bond Street are sometimes asked which is the shop that sells it.

For shoes worthy of good tweeds you might go to Tricker's in Jermyn Street, where four generations of Trickers have spent long and highly-to-be-commended lives making boots and shoes by hand. It seems a tradition with the Trickers to live to a grand old age, and they all begin young. One of the treasures of the shop is a shoe made by the father of the present principal at the age of seven. Your shoes will probably cost you round about 3 gns., and you will have the satisfaction of knowing that they are made by some of the finest craftsmen left in the country.

The theme of Jaeger's collection of shooting clothes is " family tweeds "; that is, tweeds of the same dye and texture, but woven to a different pattern. Thus you get a checked skirt worn with a striped coat which exactly matches it in texture and colouring. Or you get a checked tweed combined with a herringbone tweed of the same family. Most of their suits have a narrow belt with a wide basque and little " bullet " pockets rather more than breast-high. Fullness in their skirts this season is arrived at either by gores or wrapovers, not by pleats. They have the nerve to produce female plus-fours, though I should think few females would have the nerve to wear them. But you never know what the tall, striding woman will do. The pair I saw were in a subdued green tweed ; the coat was longish and had a leather belt and buttons. You wear them with thick socks and stout shooting shoes.

Frockcoats based on men's old-fashioned frockcoats are another feature of the collection. Most of them have velvet lapels and buttons and they are very waisted with considerable fullness at the small of the back. They are worn with matching tweed waistcoats and skirts. Jaeger's are using sealskin to finish some of their long coats, and introduce a tight narrow sealskin cuff to keep out the wind. Otherwise their overcoats were not notable. Except one. A loose splashy affair with the biggest and brightest check it has ever been my horror to see—calculated to flush up the grouse, and the dogs and beaters too. But maybe it's not meant for shooting but just for loose splashy travel.   ALISON HAIG

Felix Topolski AT THE BALLET

F^E=F^O=FI=FU_M

NEW BOOKS

Bonhomie in the Saloon Bar

I HAD not seen Mr. Chamberlain's *What the Sweet Hell* (good title), so his second book *Sing Holiday* came as a surprise to me—a delightful one. It is a thoroughly enjoyable story. The theme is far from unfamiliar—a prosaic hero sets out for a brief holiday, falls accidentally into strange company and finds himself transported far beyond his normal horizons and translated into a new character ; finally he returns to his humdrum habits. It is one of the basic stories of the world ; in recent times it was the plot of *The Wheels of Chance, Faraway* and a thousand others ; it has been treated romantically, farcically, sentimentally, satirically, melodramatically ; it never fails if it is well treated. Mr. Chamberlain has quite unusual gusto, virtuosity and discrimination, and his book is one to be grateful for.

The (perhaps over-long) prelude describes the home life of the hero, Mr. Matthews, a slovenly footling idle old widower who inhabits a decaying villa in the suburbs of Birmingham. Himself and his household are examined with Proust-like acuteness ; most of his idiosyncracies are repellent, but he emerges anything but a repellent character—and he *is* a character, three-dimensional and fully coloured, never once degenerating into a type. Mr. Matthews takes an annual holiday " for the sake of the servants ". As it turns out, the event is just as unwelcome to them as to him, but it is one of his habits and he observes it conscientiously and reluctantly. He goes this year to the Isle of Man, where, though he does not know it, the motor races are about to begin ; the island is overrun and possessed by the drivers, mechanics, agents, officials, spectators, reporters and nondescript hangers-on

of the motoring world ; Mr. Matthews finds himself their boon companion ; he is nicknamed " the Professor ", appointed an official of the course, and swept up in a cyclone of drinking, flirtation and chaff ; mostly drinking—Mr. Chamberlain presents a great gift to the amateur of philology in the most complete anthology I have yet seen of the *facetiæ* of the saloon bar ; he knows every turn of phrase and inflexion of voice of the motorman's drinking bout, from the first rather strained bonhomie to the final crapulous lamentation, but it is not a mere glossary, for Mr. Chamberlain has a fine selective *flair*, so that the dialogue, here and there, approaches within measurable distance of poetry. He also has a remarkable gift for rapportage ; the descriptions of the two races are fit to rank with the memorable passages of sporting literature. Occasionally he spoils the integrity of the narrative with explicit comment—that is a beginner's fault ; where he leaves his characters to do their own speaking he is first-rate. He knows not only the speech but the minds of his world, their generosity, flamboyance, ruthlessness, occasional acuteness ; he has enough sympathy with them to save his account from parody ; he knows their curious canons of etiquette—" It's all wrong to drink in one's own pub at this time of day "— " No drinking at meal times at this table," etc. He has done for this particular stratum of society what other writers have done for Wessex yokels and Connemara peasants—and done it a good deal more surely. One incident, for me, upset the artistic rhythm—the attempted seduction of Mr. Matthews by Rose, the barmaid. I felt it was a false climax, introduced adventitiously and unhappily ; but the excellent last pages of homecoming restore the sense of decency and probability and leave one with unaffected gratitude to the author.

EVELYN WAUGH

CONSIDERATIONS INSPIRED BY THE REPORT ON THE OCCUPATIONAL INCIDENCE OF FEMALE IMMORALITY

A girl may be a good all-round
    soprano,
and yet become the Plaything of a Day,
a girl may be proficient at piano,
yet be compelled to take the Easiest
    Way ;
a girl may be a prodigy at college,
yet have to barter honour for a price,
a girl may be a snip at general know-
    ledge,
yet driven to shelve her mother's
    good advice.

But a girl who can break records in a
    stadium
no economic shortage need perplex,
she's practically worth her weight in
    radium
even before she makes a change of sex ;
and a girl can be self-supporting in a
    manner perfectly proper,
gaining respectful applause in all civi-
    lized lands,
if she knows how to use her feet to
    put on a topper
while walking on the palms of her
    hands.

THIS YEAR OF GRACE

This year won't go down to history as
    the year of rearmament revelry,
Or the record year for Bright Old
    Things' Memoirs of Edwardian
    devilry,
Or the year when Mr. Baldwin retired
    in his own time, *odium cum dig-
    nitate*,
Or the year when the Bishops stepped
    out, becoming the life of the party,
Or the year when the Lord Chamber-
    lain finally put his foot down on the
    divorcée,
Or the year when the beautiful vamp
    cited the oldest inhabitant of the
    Quai d'Orsay,
Or even the year when an Imperial
    statesman's offspring married into
    Variety,
But simply as the year when the
    Dirndl, as worn at Kitzbühl and St.
    Wolfgang, appeared in Society.

GUY FFOULKES

THE THEATRE

St. Moritz

A SHOW on ice, all space, with a mountainy back-drop and the breath of a frigidaire, was just the thing, this week, for the left-in-London. The speed of the show at the Coliseum is a little less than ice hockey: instead of those visored eagles we get flights of lovelies, tensely but imperturbably smiling through. The ice, through which a ghostly board floor appears, does cut : now and then a skate sends up powdery white ice-dust ; now and then sparks fly. Spotlights go swooping after the figures, or spokes of violet limelight cross in the air. There is a chalk-blue moon, and last of all a snowstorm. The last number but one, Cossacks' Dance, is made still more complex by the tentative entrance of scene-shifters in mufti, crawling on all fours. These, keeping as much in the shade as possible, poke and prise cautiously round the rim of the ice-stage. At the same time a châlet, stuck with blondes along its two balconies, descends with equal caution into a chasm. You soon see the reason for this, for the stage, unhooked from its moorings, starts to revolve and soon gets up terrific speed. The entire cast —for this is a slap-up finale—hang on to the whirling ice by their skates and the grace of Heaven.

But I anticipate. There are three acts to *St. Moritz* : two on the rink and a middle one in the hotel lounge. In the middle act no one skates. The ballroom dancers at the opening of this act clearly feel a bit wet and anti-climatic : they foxtrot all in a huddle, away from Bob Campbell's band. In the interests of St. Moritz as a resort, this ballroom number wants glamorizing. If evenings there are like that, I should go to bed after skating. The non-skating girls are nice girls, who ought to get better dresses. Well into the cabaret in this second act, the audience, missing their ice, behaved like the old-time Coliseum lions with the supply of Christians suddenly cut off. And the frigidaire draught was missed. The Max Rivers Girls, in gold Waterloo helmets, did their best by tripping up and down silver ladders. I take it the scene was shifted to the hotel lounge to allow the ice to re-freeze and to rest the skaters. The cabaret brightened with the entrance of the St. Moritz kiddies, two little Swiss boys in charge of a taciturn relation, who yodelled to an accordion very obligingly. They share their turn with adult Miss Gritli Wengen, who has a good stern face below a coquettish hat, and yodels to the accordion more surprisingly. What a subversive noise it really is. Other bright spots were Hibbert, Bird and La Rue—a mixture of abandon and propriety—and the two Gaudsmith Brothers with their Canine Comics. This fine pair of attenuated poodles, with manes like prophets, are worth seeing. They are not dog-lovers' dogs ; they are perverse, anti-human and sardonic, not to say satanic.

But the skating was the thing. What is this kick we get out of seeing other people do things ? Vicarious pride perhaps ? Fine skating is above all things noble and un-silly. The skater is the human at his most heroic. He is more exciting than would be a man with wings, for he maintains a precarious, mystical, infinitely mathematical relation with the earth. There is a fierceness about skating that even its most composed blonde mistress, dressed as a powder-puff like Miss Pamela Prior was, cannot abate. The sound of the heated blade on cold ice is a deep satisfaction to the nerves. Complete virtuosity sheds a peace of its own : there is no vulgar tension, no feeling of " *Can* he do it ? " The skater (at least, at the Coliseum) is not winning anything, not getting *at* anything, not expressing anything—he is simply skating. I keep on saying " he ", because Mr. Hermann Steinschaden is, to my mind, the axis of this fine show. He puts you back into such a primitive state of bliss that all I can find to say is : " My, you should see him ! " Of course, I know nothing about the abstract side of skating. Maybe Mr. Steinschaden is over-dramatic. But look how you have to skate before you can be dramatic. He comes on only twice—first in a number called Sensational Speed, in which, in glittery black, he flies over a mounting-up number of barrels, over the faces of rows of prone girls on chairs, through arcades of hoops held high, straight through a papered hoop. The second time he is got up as a car mascot, gilt all over his skin, and with horns. In this number he Skates on Stilts. This really is the climax, and is in a way appalling.

Miss Pamela Prior stays unruffled the whole time. She looks the Home Girl. I feel this is as it should be : a champion skateress ought not to look sinister. Naturally her skating is the goods. I could have wished her not got up as a powder-puff, but perhaps this is all in the picture too. She is at her most effective skating with a long chiffon handkerchief. Ladies get only half the value out of their chiffon handkerchiefs if they have not yet taken them on to ice and skated with them like Miss Pamela Prior. These accessories need a swooping high speed, and light.

The chorus deserves all praise ; it whizzes round and round, forms fours looking pretty in upright cellophane coffins, and does one very pretty ballet called *Clair de Lune*. This is poetic with only one hitch : skating-boots look all wrong under angel draperies. But the superhuman hypnotic melting *smoothness* of the ballet, in which the girls slide together like pats of blue butter on hot plates, mass in wedges and then advance in fatal beauty, like icebergs, is worth any number of tight little white boots. The perilous dash of the finale, on the revolving ice struck by savage darting lights, was frightening : it had the air of a *débâcle*. Half the cast were masked for this as Mickey Mice, pussies or what-not, so it was like a Bosch picture I once saw, in which animal-headed creatures fly from a burning town.

ELIZABETH BOWEN

THE CINEMA

Without Beard or Bed

THE fictional screen has never really got beyond wish-fulfilment dreams, and the only interest this week is in seeing the kind of wish-fulfilment the big film executives enjoy. In that light *Parnell* becomes almost interesting. At any rate it isn't shocking like *Call It a Day*, the close adaptation of Miss Dodie Smith's popular play, the day-dream of a good woman.

Of course the first thing one notices about the Metro - Goldwyn - Mayer dream of how history should have happened is the absence of Parnell's beard. Pigott is allowed a beard (a magnificent spade-shaped affair in which there is ample room for two owls and a wren, five larks and a hen), but he's a villain. How exactly this beard-neurosis has arisen one cannot say : I think it may have something to do with the astrakhan coats film financiers wear : a kind of whisker weariness.

Then, too, anything secretive, anything middle-aged, anything a little bit lecherous in the story has been eliminated. No illegitimate children, no assignations in seaside hotels under assumed names, no furtive vigils at Waterloo Station. In the divorce suit O'Shea hasn't a leg to stand on (it's just his dirty mind) : the suit is followed immediately by Parnell's political overthrow and his death the same night. Far from any adulterous meetings the lovers are not even allowed to marry, and never in this film hang the engraving of Lord Leighton's " Wedding " above the legalised bed. But poor though the picture may be, it is pleasing to think how clean a film magnate's wish-fulfilments are, how virginal and high-minded the tawdry pathetic human past becomes when the Mayers and Goldwyns turn the magic ring.

I'm a lot less happy about *Call It a Day*. A picture of one Spring day in the life of an ordinary prosperous English family, full of characteristic touches about bathrooms and the cat kittening and how women can't be trusted to read *The Times* tidily, crowded with dreadfully recognizable details " My dear, that's just how Henry behaves "), it might have been compiled from the sly diaries of members of the P.E.N. Club. Good aunts or wives all, we know, whatever we may think at literary parties of their long incisors and prominent shoulder-blades, but who would imagine, before seeing this film, of what *their* wish-fulfilments consist ?

In this picture the middle-aged husband, a chartered accountant, is " tempted " by an actress with whose income-tax he is dealing. She is the sort of vicious woman only a really unsullied female could invent, and sets to work on the traditional pair of steps as soon as she is alone with her man. Then it's no time at all before she's playing hot music to him after a little dinner in her flat. Follows the dirty look, the well-known phrase, " Do you mind if I slip into something more comfortable ? ", the strategic retirement. But at this point the authoress's imagination wavered, or perhaps fear of being blackballed for the P.E.N. checked her exuberant fancy, for to our astonishment the temptress reappeared in just another evening dress. Meanwhile the wife, middle-aged but handsome in an aunt-like way, understanding and healthy-minded, is ardently beseiged at home by a man she only met at tea-time. Nobody, of course, gives way : but what agreeable titillations and temptations : what a Dodie dream of a world where all the heavy labour and the missed cues of infidelity are eliminated and the two-backed beast is trotted out quaintly, gaily and whimsically like a character in *Winnie the Pooh*.

GRAHAM GREENE

' Ah, that hat is made for a slightly taller man, sir.'

AMATEUR ATHLETICS

We Run Better Than We Jump

THE English, we are often told, make good losers. Perhaps the nice way we lose explains why it is that our national athletic championships are sometimes turned into a kind of sack of England. The visitors like it and we don't really mind. It takes an English runner to say courteously, as he is passed ten yards from the tape in an important race, " Well run, you've got me nicely "; then to catch his victor as he falls all anyhow and help carry him away. That is the fine art of losing as only Englishmen can do it.

A glance at the results of our championships this year—seven of our titles spread round the map of Europe—might make people think we'd been losing at our very best. But actually the championships themselves did not leave that impression. Visitors come over (and we should take it as a compliment) to win the things they know they can win—jumping and throwing; and they leave us to get on with the things they know we can win—which means the races.

It was very obliging of three Germans, Hein and Blask, who were first and second in the Olympic games, and Lutz, who is almost as good, to come and show us how it is done, and walk off with the first three places in the hammer throw. Heil Hitler. Alongside the prize table there's a forest of Nazi handraising as Lord Burleigh and the prizes and Ribbentrop and the three splendid Germans are all presented to each other. The crowd certainly did not get a good enough view of this.

In the discus-throw Schroeder, the German big shot and world's record holder, is also going great guns; but on the day Syllas, the Greek, is just too good for him. One likes to see a Hel‑lene winning anything so classic as a discus-throw. (Was it not a German professor after all who reconstructed Discobolos with the head the wrong way round ?)

The most exciting thing an Englishman has done yet is to break a hurdle with a neat throw to cover point. The idea of using the discus as a missile reminds one that the Metropolitan Police are even now making a really intensive study of this business of field events. Good luck to them. In a year or two's time we may regularly see a police officer get his man with a javelin throw of seventy yards, or pole-vault gracefully over a fourteen-foot wall after a miscreant.

In the meantime a third German, Woellke (also an Olympic champion), has won the weight-putt with one of his milder efforts. Howland, our veteran putter, is well up. And a fourth German called Long has won the long jump with a very hot jump of 24 feet 10 inches. He does not appear to defy the laws of gravity as Jesse Owens did last year. Jesse Owens and Nijinsky alone among humans have been able to wait about in the air before descending. Two Englishmen, Beattie and Breach, have both cleared 23 feet : good jumping.

The hop, step and jump is a remarkable form of progress, not much affected as yet in England : it goes to Peters, a Flying Dutchman, who has won it here twice before, and is now perhaps doomed to go on winning it for ever, or until somebody loves him.

In the javelin, the high jump and the pole-vault we are left to ourselves.

Let us turn to the running. Speaking as an unregenerate runner, I claim that the races are better to win and to watch than the field events. What is more, at the middle distances English runners are always in the first class, and at any English championships you may see a genuine world-beater doing his stuff. Why is it that running is in this country comparatively neglected ? Possibly it is because education runs so strongly on team-games. However, putting aside the many moral disadvantages of allowing a man to win a race, it is a big thrill to see him do it.

On Saturday Wooderson's mile was an impressive and splendidly craftsman-like affair. He ran it the perfect way— an even speed throughout. He finished perfectly under control, and did not go mad up the straight. The time 4 min. 12·2 was a championship best ; he made it look almost effortless. Schaumberg, the German champion, was fourth.

The half-mile was as nice a dust-up as you can want to see. Ever since Tom Hampson retired, the half-mile situation has been very interesting. There has been no one to follow in his and Lowe's footsteps : to dominate English half-miles and bring back Olympic crowns for us.

On Saturday it was said that Stothard was right back in his 1935 form : meanwhile Powell and MacCabe, last year's Olympic pair, were also in the final, and so was Collyer, who recently put up a new native record.

Collyer led the field round the first lap smoothly and fast. But up the back straight he let Stothard and MacCabe go by and the others bunch up all round him. In the finishing straight there was an extraordinary scene. Stothard and MacCabe struggled along on equal terms—then all the others came again : and fifty yards from the tape there were six men in a bunch. Then at last Collyer picked his way through with a strong spurt to win by a yard from Handley in 1 min. 53·3 —and everyone did very good time.

In the Marathon a phalanx of fifty or sixty brave hearts with one Greek among them left the stadium for their twenty-six mile tour of some of London's least attractive suburbs. It was a keen race all the way, and McNab Robertson, the Scot, could not shake off Kyriakides, the Greek, till the last four miles. After Robertson had finished very strongly, he still kept trotting round the stadium. Kyriakides didn't, like his Greek prototype, run twenty-six miles back again.

Now for the future : On August 14 we entertain the Germans in a straight match, and this all-Nordic contest (cock house match so to speak) should be for sheer win-or-lose excitement the peach meeting of this year.

T. O. BEACHCROFT

A JOB IN A MILLION—5

QUEER FISH

HE has one up on Izaak Walton: he is "The Compleat Aquarist". You probably saw some of his work when you last visited the Zoo. It was he who supplied the vivaria for the Eastern Corridor of the New Reptile House, as well as aquaria and many fish for the Tropical Fish House in the Aquarium.

Not only does he deal in strange fish from strange places, but he designs their living-places, where through glass we see them darting or curving silkily among coral bastions or the waving fronds of tropical water-plants. He is the architect of that curious underworld.

You may also have noticed his shop in the Pentonville Road, a narrow-fronted inconspicuous place, with a few varicoloured fish and some water plants, and over the windows the sign, " B. T. Child, The Compleat Aquarist ".

Inside the shop the tanks range along the walls of the long, narrow rooms—tanks maintained at a tropical temperature. Snaking lines of piping aerate those tanks which are not occupied by " air-breathers "—those fish which must periodically rise to the surface for a breath of our kind of fresh air. There are seamen or engineers or stewards on many ships who know this curious setting, and men on the Amazon or in Siam are today sliding jewelled fish into glass jars destined to travel a few thousand miles before they reach the Pentonville Road.

Mr. Child, one of the oldest practitioners of this rare trade in tropical fish, in which perhaps not more than half-a-dozen persons are occupied in the whole country, is delighted to show one round. And this is no mere form of words, for here is a man who truly loves his job.

The rarest and most expensive fish on the premises, at the moment, seems to be the electric cat-fish, which costs £3 ; it comes from West Africa and its habits are literally shocking. But this is by no means the dearest fish Mr. Child has ever handled. The trade of the tropical fish dealer is rather like that of the dealer in rare books. His greatest acquisitions depend greatly upon chance. Just as the bookseller tells his customers that some rare volume has come into his hands, so Mr. Child circularizes amateur aquarists throughout the country when a particularly distinguished visitor has arrived in his cosmopolitan tanks.

" There is no end to the new species of fish which arrive," said Mr. Child, who is fifty-six and tall and burly and ruddy and looks more than anything else like an English squire, or at least what an English squire ought to look like.

"We know of the fish," he said, " but getting them here to London is another thing. For instance, it's reckoned that there are over eight hundred different species in the Amazon alone, but the majority of them have never reached this country alive. You have them preserved in the museums, but that's all. Why ? Well, say you want a fish from Manaos— that's a thousand miles from the Brazilian coast. Some job getting it down the river and then to England ! "

He stopped for a moment to show me an Indian climbing perch, which by way of variation was walking on its fins along the bottom of the tank. Then some " mouth-breeders " which come from around Cairo. Rather than wear their hearts on their sleeves, these eccentric creatures carry their eggs in their mouths. But Mr. Child's " Black Mollies " go one better: they bear their young alive, poor fish—a most unorthodox thing to do. We were then dazzled by the (pre-Belisha) beacon fish who carry iridescent lights on their tails and over their eyes, and the Neon fish with their glittering horizontal strips of metallic golden green.

This business of keeping tropical fish—and the hobby is growing in popularity, Mr. Child claims—means something more than just buying a few fish and dumping them into a tank and showing them off to your friends.

First, there is the question of temperature. From 75° to 85° Fahrenheit suits most tropical fish. Then, food : some are as vegetarian as G.B.S., others fiercely carnivorous. And within these two main classifications various species have all kinds of dietetic whims. Water-fleas are much appreciated by some, and there are London urchins who earn their regular pence by collecting these from ponds and bringing them to Mr. Child. Lighting and aeration are also problems the aquarist must face. The choice of plants to put in the tanks is most important, as some fish will breed among one kind of plant and not another. In all these things Mr. Child is expert. He will supply you with your fish, will erect your tank, furnish it with the proper kinds of plants and rocks or coral, and see that your pets get the right diet. And if you don't let him have his way, they won't last long.

"Remember, tropical fish are the ideal pets," he will tell you. " They never wake you up at night, barking or mewing, and you can safely leave them at home over the week-end."

Apart from a few of the more common species, which are now bred in Europe, tropical fish sold to the dealers by seafaring people on their return from tropical ports must form one of our largest " invisible imports ".

The usual thing is for the collector to write to Mr. Child by airmail from his last port, before sailing for Europe, telling him just what he has. The ship is not always bound for a British port, and Mr. Child often has to journey to Antwerp, Rotterdam, or some other harbour town, to close a deal when some exceptionally fine specimen is due to arrive.

As a youth he worked for a famous firm of scale-makers, which may have given him the idea, for he used to spend his evenings " pond-dipping". The young naturalist would go out of an evening with his tin can to gather tadpoles, water-boatmen, water scorpions and other pond denizens, as well as water weeds. Later, he found it profitable to sell his gleanings to schools for use in the natural history classes. And so, in 1904, he went into business, at that time dealing only in pond fish.

Interest in tropical fish was nothing

'He's fine, but all he keeps saying is "Get a horse!"'

*   *   *

then to what it is now. There are thousands of collectors (the designation " fish-fan " is apparently already an accepted term) and two monthly publications are devoted to their hobby. They form their local aquarium societies and have annual shows. Frequently Mr. Child must act as judge at these contests. " I judge as many as twenty or thirty classes at one show," he said.

If you are interested in reptiles, by the way, Mr. Child can do you some very neat Californian Red Tritons—a kind of salamander, I gather—at six shillings each and Fire Frogs at half-a-crown. Stump-tailed Lizards come dearer at seventeen-and-six apiece. Snails, too, may be bought from the Compleat Aquarist ; they are sometimes used as scavengers in fish-tanks.

But the tropical fish form Mr. Child's chief interest and main stock—he always has from thirty to a hundred varieties on hand to choose from : for instance, the Siamese Fighting Fish, which shows all its finest colouring when angry ; or the Croaking Gourami from Singapore, that croaks like a frog at breeding time ; or the Chanchitos who kiss when courting. . . . They have Mr. Child to lead them.

CHARLES ASHLEIGH

*

" . . . the day is not far distant when all readers of daily newspapers will also take the *Daily Express.*"—DAILY EXPRESS.

Now, let's think, what *is* the Daily Express ? An after-breakfast indigestion powder ?

ENDPIECE

These have I hated most : the rumps
   that bump.
The human form's divine, the body
   beautiful,
but not the elbows and the rumps that
   bump
in crowded places.
I don't so much mind faces,
though oftentimes they're little more
   than mugs
with all the base torpidity of slugs
crawling about amongst the roses.
I don't mind eyes or ears or noses
or arms or legs, or even an occasional
   torso,
but for rumps I do not care un
   morceau.
O rampant rumps !   K. K. BUSVINE

ZEBROLOGY

By
H. A. REY

PARIS LETTER

FRANCE seems to be in for one of those spells of political unrest which daily fill the more sedate French press with envious appreciations of " British phlegm " and the *bon sens* of " our friends across the Channel ". The political leaders, in brief, seem to have recommenced that typically French *divertissement* : Hold the baby. The baby in question has grown considerably fatter and naughtier since the days of Poincaré and Doumergue, and the strain of holding it proportionately severer. But the French statesman is nothing if not an artist and, when he hands on the burden to his successor, always contrives the suitably pathetic gesture of renunciation and an appropriate break in his voice. M. Blum, with a year's leadership to his credit, is, as they say here, almost a " recordsman " in the baby-holding competition. It's hard to see how anyone except an autocrat could cope with the enormous legacy of debt that has come broadening down from President to President. And, very definitely, we do not like dictators. Even *pleins pouvoirs* can only be tolerated as a tragically last resort. Things have indeed come to a pass and, though M. Chautemps may set his Bonnet at the deficit, the future looks pretty black or (if you prefer it) red. Hopes have been expressed that M. Chautemps will live up to his name, in its sense of " warm weather ", and last out the summer ; but it might equally mean " hot time " —a less favourable omen. A symptom of the times is that the French seem to have lost confidence in French methods ; the *bas de laine* is empty (often its contents have fled abroad) and is now used for polishing a radio bought on the glad-and-sorry system. The late

government, too, we are sometimes told, set out to emulate American methods. But there is some marvellous resilience in the American constitution that enables it to digest the most amazing remedies (we know in Paris an American who cures recurrent bouts of malaria with a tumblerful of monkey-gland cocktails) ; to the French temperament such methods seem inapt : despite repeated doses of the Blum cocktail the Treasury showed no signs of convalescence.

Rising prices are amongst the principal causes of the present *malaise*. Throughout the past year the cost of living has been steadily increasing ; the *lois sociales* gave the profiteers their first pretext and, when it looked as if prices had touched the ceiling, devaluation pushed them through it. One of those little French legs of mutton—so succulent with just a soupçon of garlic —weighing four pounds at most, now costs 60 francs (over half a guinea) ; the tiny *poulet du dimanche* for a family of three costs 35–40 francs as against 22 francs last year. Sugar has gone up 25 per cent. In fact the worker has gained nothing by his rise in wages and the *petit rentier*, who is legion in France, has had to draw in his belt. Why M. Blum, to whom even his enemies do not deny acumen, didn't include in his social experiments a decree fixing retail prices is one of those

' I used to have a partner for this act.'

mysteries to which the only answer seems to be that threadbare tag, *Quem deus vult*, etc. Profiteers and middlemen would, of course, have raged furiously together, but why should the sound and fury of their least popular *concitoyens* have troubled a Front Populaire ? One thing seems certain, either the *grande pénitence* preconized by elder statesmen some years ago is close at hand, or one of these days the lid will blow off.

Often in Paris *la femme de quarante ans* scores off the younger women, and Her Eminence La Tour Eiffel in her new "lightdress", pink one night and green another, more than holds her own amongst the upstarts of the Exhibition. We may suspect that she regrets (as many of us do, despite the beauty of the new buildings) her opposite number, the defunct Trocadero, with its rococo airs and graces. Had it survived, it would have found one day an Osbert Sitwell to write up its superb absurdity. In La Ville Lumière—the City of Dreadful Light, as (unjustly) it has been called —the Tower stands for discretion in the use of electricity. Jean Cocteau in his recent and delightful travel book, *Mon Premier Voyage*, describes the moon as " the sun of ruins " and, oddly enough, the new pavilions at the Exhibition look their best by night, when the lights are dimmed for fireworks on the Seine. Seen by moonlight, even the rubble on the quays and the skeletons of unfinished buildings —ruins *à rebours*—acquire a Gothic picturesqueness that would have rejoiced Horace Walpole or " Monk " Lewis.

As a triumph of picturesque disorder the recent Nuit du Directoire, a *fête costumée* at the Palais Royal, certainly stands out. Nothing could have better recalled the spendthrift splendours of the years between the Reign of Terror and Napoleon's Consulate. And if the staff-work " left to desire", so much the better for the period atmosphere. The night was unseasonably cold. In revolutionary days,

when the Palais Royal Garden was a popular Lovers' Walk, the doctors are said to have done well out of its revelries by night. This year they did as well, but with a difference ; the maladies they had to treat next day were mentionable : common colds and 'flu. The scene at the opening banquet was in the best Directoire manner. The noble Marquis receiving the guests was literally mobbed by 800 would-be diners clamouring to be shown their places. The Lord Mayor of London was the guest of honour, but when he arrived no one was there to receive him. In the general scrimmage he passed unnoticed. After several vain attempts to find his place at table he retreated to his carriage and drove back to his hotel —reflecting, we may suppose, that they order these things better at the Guildhall. . . . Still, it was a great night as such nights go, the costumes were beautiful beyond description and, if Paris once was worth a Mass, the proximity of Mistinguett, Marguerite

Moreno, Moussia and Suzy Solidor may have been worth a *grippe*. And, of course, there was a tombola, the first prize of which was 24 hours of the company of a certain very charming actress—a day and a night, no more, no less !

Not all Parisians rejoice to see their city made over to the "exhibitionists" ; but they have a consolation in the reopening of the Champs-Elysées The-

atre, which had remained more or less permanently closed during the depression years. As in the great days of the Russian and Swedish ballets, an international elegantzia throngs its splendid staircases and fine proportioned auditorium. The season of British ballet at this theatre has been a vast success. The Vic-Wells announcements came as a surprise to Parisian balletomanes. They knew, of course, that a few English dancers had made their name —Russianized, of course—under the Diaghilev régime. But few suspected the existence of a permanent English ballet. (It was, perhaps, a pity that this admirable ensemble did not style itself the " London Ballet " for the occasion. " *Vicvells*," with its faint suggestion of Vichy *plus* Vittel, struck our French friends as a *drôle de nom*.) The Parisian balletgoer is terribly sophisticated : even the Russians face a season here with fear and trembling ; some years they prefer not to face it at all. Nevertheless, the English ballet came, danced, and conquered. A chorus of praises greeted the perfect training, beauty and (as one critic described it) *le physique printanier des jeunes anglais*.

The success of *Candida*, the play selected for the British Season, came as a surprise. Needless to say, the French public was ready to take to its heart the lovely and lovable heroine of *Cavalcade*, Diana Wynyard. But the play was forty years old —wouldn't it date, wouldn't its problems and declamations bore the public ? It was another triumph for the forty-year-old ; as things turned out, no better choice could have been made. The French public loves its glimpse of English interiors and home life—hence the great vogue here of such writers as Maurice Baring and Rosamund Lehmann. *Candida* was exactly to their taste. The central figure is a clergyman, dog-collar and all, with a wife and family—and to the Frenchman there's always something a shade improper in the notion of a married priest. So typically English ! STUART GILBERT

Music Notes

In the London Parks

THE L.C.C. are not only concerned with refuse-collection, sanitary inspection and welfare clinics. They have their human and æsthetic side and the music and entertainment they provide in the London parks deserve a music critic's notice as much as many a pompous orgy in the Albert Hall. Sixty bands are engaged and play in different parks throughout the summer. Nearly every park has a band on Sunday evenings, from 7 to 9. On Mondays, Tuesdays and Fridays Victoria Embankment Gardens revels alone, but on Wednesdays Bethnal Green Gardens and Deptford Park join in, and on Saturdays, Highbury Fields, Islington, and Clissold Park. But on Thursdays there is music from Kilburn Grange in the north to Mountsfield Park, Lewisham, in the south, and from Horniman Pleasance, Kensal Road, in the west to the Recreation Ground, Wapping, in the east. Then Hyde Park daily and Green Park, Regent's Park and Kensington Gardens on Sundays form a sort of blackleg group not subject to the L.C.C.

Everybody loves a military band. It has a tang of sincerity, a lack of affectation, a straightforwardness, which appeals to the musician as much as to the nursemaid. When a brass band plays " good " music it does not desecrate it. It broadens the nuances and lessens the contrasts, but it gives an honest-to-God brass-band rendering.

In July there are no concerts to go to. If you are fond of music, of the open air and of your fellow Londoners, why not go to the parks for your music ?

I did. I went first to Victoria Embankment Gardens. A different band plays there every night from 8 to 10. Sitting down costs 2*d*., and you can buy a programme for a penny. There are a few of the usual green wooden park seats free, but these are crammed like a Southern Electric compartment some time before the music begins. People (the general tone is very respectable) walk round or stand and listen. The acoustics of the covered bandstand are remarkable. You can hear every note from 300 yards away without difficulty. The band the night I went was first-class. We had Schubert, Gounod, Messager, and Sibelius, apart from *Colonel Bogey*, *Forget-me-not* and *The Uhlan's Call*. A delightful evening.

On Thursday I tried going further afield. Mountsfield Park, Lewisham, had a band, so I went there. I was surprised to find it one of the finest flower gardens in London. On the top of a hill, with a fine South London view, it is an ideal place to walk in on a summer evening. And when you've walked, you have the band to hear, and there is even a restaurant close to the bandstand for your refreshment. The crowd was a more drifting one than at the Victoria Embankment, wandering round past tennis-courts and cricket-pitch and children's playground and back to the music. Not quite so comfortable a crowd, perhaps, but still not badly off.

To see the poorer and, to me, more attractive audience, you must go to Myatt's Fields, Camberwell, also on a Thursday. This is a pretty little park which not long ago was a market garden, " with cabbages growing instead of flowers ", as I was informed. The band plays in a circular railed bandstand, with a wider circle of railings shutting off a space from the tennis and cricket. I arrived punctually at 7.30, but there was no sign of room on the seats and I couldn't squeeze onto the railings. So I selected a tree to lean against, which I shared with a thin elderly workman.

The band wasn't up to Victoria Embankment Gardens standard, but the children made so much noise that this wasn't important. You could only collect the broad trend of the music, and it was good enough to please us all. The children danced to it, played ball to it, sang to it and ignored it. The grown-ups, all elderly, all listening, sat round on their wooden seats or leant against their green railings and were happy.

One bald and fierce man, clutching two Bibles under his arm, walked round the garden twice, violently looking for converts or sinners. Then a little child of two, dancing a *pas seul* to selections from Tchaikowsky's *Eugène Onègin*, caught his eye. Would he even try to convert this child, I thought, bristling ? But I misjudged him. He broke into a smile of phoney happiness and joined in the dance, making a *pas de deux* with the child.

My neighbour at the tree told me he was very fond of music. Especially opera. He used to go to the Old Victoria Hall, he said, about forty years ago, when Miss Bayliss first took it over. (Can it really be as long ago as that ?) " They were a rare tough lot in the gallery in those days," he said. " At least they looked tough. But once the music was on you could hear a pin drop. I believe they'd of thrown out anybody who made a noise, but nobody did." It used to cost him 3*d*. for a seat in the gallery, 1*d*. fare there, 1*d*. fare back, and 1*d*. for a packet of Woodbines (they used to give away a box of matches with it)—6*d*. for the evening. *The Daughter of the Regiment* and *Faust* were his favourites.

I think Myatt's Fields provided the best evening of all. Tchaikowsky was the only classic, but there was an Overture by Bilton (" My old Stable Jacket ") which, with the noise of the crowd, and one's eyes shut, sounded like a scene from a Rossini opera.

JACK DONALDSON

★

Yesterday in this column we discussed the quality called foresight. This newspaper has it.—*Leader in the* DAILY EXPRESS.

Why didn't you say so at the time ? Too shy ?

NEW BOOKS

The Soldiers Speak

IT is the natural inclination of any trade to provide the public with what it wants rather than what it needs ; in the sphere of economics this produces a recurrent disastrous succession of slumps and booms. In matters of the mind exactly the same process is at work. It should be the proper function of an intelligentsia to correct popular sentiments and give the call to order in times of hysteria. Instead the editors and publishers, whose job it is to exploit the intelligence of others, see it as their interest to indulge and inflame popular emotion, so that the mind moves in feverish vacillation from one extreme to another instead of in calm and classical progress. People now use the phrase " without contemporary significance " to express just those works which are of most immediate importance, works which eschew barbaric extremes and attempt to right the balance of civilization.

Mr. Chapman's preface to *Vain Glory* raised the hope that he had produced one of those books ; there are many sharp disappointments awaiting the reader and one moment at least of disgust, but in the end he is left with the belief that, in the present neurotic state of the general mind, this is as sane and valuable a book as could have been expected. I am sure it will have a wide popularity ; it is a book that is badly needed almost everywhere but in England. Germans will not be allowed to read it, and I think the editor has made a great mistake and severely impaired the usefulness of his own work by yielding to the temptation to score points against the Nazi régime. We have no need in England to be reminded of the intolerable injustices of that régime ; or have very little need to be reminded of the tedium and futility of war. There is,

thank God, no considerable party in England which attempts to glorify war. Mr. Chapman admirably states the traditional English attitude. The Englishman, he says, " is the most serious fighter. He does not believe in war. In 1914 all the other combatants did. And the decline in their morale is the measure of their fallibility. The Englishman looked on it without enthusiasm as a dirty job to be carried out." The danger in England today is that people will come to look on it as a dirty job to be evaded at all costs. But in Germany, and to a far less degree in all European countries, there is again the appalling danger of a generation growing up who look upon it as a glorious vocation to be followed for its own sake. Mr. Chapman has made it absolutely impossible for his book to reach these wretched youths. Perhaps it

Vain Glory. Edited by Guy Chapman. Cassell, 8s. 6d.

could not have done so in any form, but it would have been better, surely, to leave the terrible responsibility of withholding the truth to the rulers themselves. So far as the abominable case of persecution with which he closes his narrative has any application to the history he is trying to relate, it is this : that by being defeated in battle one loses more than lives and land. I do not believe that the worst features of the Nazi régime could have appeared in a victorious nation. It is part of Mr. Chapman's thesis that no one gains anything in war. This of course is true, absolutely. War is an absolute loss, but it admits of degrees ; it is very bad to fight, but it is worse to lose. That was the realistic attitude of the British soldier which brought him to victory. Mr. Chapman admits this important principle in his preface, but he seems to lose sight of it in the subsequent, often painfully pert, comments ; it is a principle which, in general, Englishmen today are in grave danger of forgetting. *Vain Glory* would have been a more valuable book if it had been better emphasized.

But it is, nevertheless, a valuable book. It is almost entirely the work

of soldiers, and, when soldiers speak, it is better for those of us who were too young to fight to keep silent. We are at liberty to quarrel with our contemporaries when they declare that nothing is worth defending, but we must avoid the vile impertinence of assuring our elders that fighting is on the whole rather fun. Mr. Chapman has followed the course of the war in a series of extracts from the vast accumulation of documents at his disposal, with a preference for untendencious, unliterary, personal, transparently sincere narrative. He has chosen them, admittedly, to illustrate a theme—the effect of war upon the survivors. He is prepared to write off the obvious losses—the death and physical suffering—as irrelevant to his purpose. He has, generally speaking, avoided the temptation, ignobly exploited in a hundred war-books, to make the flesh creep. He is occupied primarily with the spiritual consequences, the pollution of truth, the deterioration of human character in prolonged unnatural stress, the emergence of the bully and cad, the obliteration of chivalry. In his selection he has admitted occasional records of courage and adventure (among the flying-men for instance), but he has preferred those in which the temper is one of muddle and futility. Thus of the number of highly exciting successful escapes from German prison camps which he had at his disposal, he has chosen one in which the fugitives were recaptured. Zeebrugge and Jutland are the only naval engagements described ; the first battle of Gaza is chosen to typify the Palestine campaign ; a vulgar little incident outside Jerusalem is recorded instead of Allenby's noble entry ; when Mr. Chapman wishes to give an instance of the heroic tenacity of the French he chooses one which was magnificent but ineffectual—the defence of Fort Vaux. Almost every big battle is seen from the eyes of the defeated or of those units which muddled their objective. Each narrative is clearly truthful, but in combination they seem ill-proportioned ; there are equally truthful accounts of the exultation of success, of neat ambushes and triumphant dashing raids ; of endurance which was relieved in time, of self-sacrifice which bore fruit. Reading simply for information, as one who was not in the war asking those who were for a true account, one feels that one is not getting quite a straight deal.

From the literary point of view there are few complaints. The cross-headings are pointed enough ; often too pointed ; they smack of the " This England " column in the *New States-man*. One is foul : " Gott mit uns " above Haig's sober and reverent statement of his sense of responsibility. " Must not occur again ", too, is shoddy ; but one is given reason to

hope that these are not from Mr. Chapman's pen. There is a nasty atmosphere of *Cavalcade* in places—the extract from *The Times* for instance on page 8. But, taken altogether, the book has more sound unfamiliar narrative in it than I have met for a long time. And that is because it is not for the most part the work of professional writers.

EVELYN WAUGH

FICTION

THE METAMORPHOSIS. Franz Kafka. Translated by A. L. Lloyd. (*Parton Press*, 3s. 6d.) A grim little story, this, which begins " As Gregor Samsa awoke one morning from a troubled dream, he found himself

changed in his bed to some monstrous kind of vermin." With admirable and revolting detail the idea is worked out ; the brutality of Gregor's father, his sister's hate ; Gregor crawling over the walls, the apple his father had flung stuck in his flesh and rotting ; Gregor dying of the want of will to live, and the charwoman disposing of the corpse (" You old cockroach," she used play-fully to call him as she did his room. " Come out, you old cockroach.") In its small horrifying way this story is unmistakably stamped with the genius of *The Castle*.

*   *   *

FLAXMAN 1937 :
Feeling that rather less than justice has been done to the distinguished artist who gave his name to a London telephone exchange, and wishing also in our modest way to celebrate the Constable Centenary, we have decided to reissue a weekly series of John Flaxman's ingenious drawings. As this, after all, is Coronation Year, we have substituted good plain captions in the mother tongue for the unpatriotic quotations from Dante which accompanied the original designs ; but in all other respects these illustrations are exactly as published in 1807. The first of the series appears below.

' *Been to any good dances this season ?* '

THE THEATRE

Comus

THERE is something chancy and romantic about acting out of doors—any acting, from the playlet out on the lawn at the Rectory fête to these fine floodlit performances in the grass theatre inside the Inner Circle of Regent's Park. In acting outdoors the elements are an element—the wind's frivolity, the threat of the sky. Draperies blow all ways; leaves distractingly glitter; voices meet competition in the hum of the trees. The actors' shadows fall on the bumpy contours of nature, not the planes of the stage. The height of the sky is, for some reason, kinder to drama than the proscenium arch. There is not so much illusion, but more vigour. Acted out of doors, the squalidest little play inherits dignity.

As for great plays—the words go towering up, and the movement has room to deploy itself. Roar the wind as it may, there is no difficulty about hearing in Regent's Park, thanks to the amplifiers fixed round in the trees. Gusts of Shakespeare or Milton out of the heart of a beech are odd till you get used to it. Indeed, to the uphill seats it is the trees that are speaking: you wonder at the actors synchronising their gestures so well. The deck-chair rows, however, get their Shakespeare or Milton straight from the so-to-speak horse's mouth. The comfort of these front rows is very great: deck-chairs, with decent spaces between row and row, are much more sympathetic than sticky velvet tip-ups. The audience in these deck-chairs may now and then sneeze, or scratch their ankles where a midge has got in under a rug, but they do not fidget anything like so despairingly as the audiences in most West End stalls, and things they drop fall silently on the grass. I may say that the half-crowns do not do badly either; I have tried most prices, in the course of experience.

The grass stage, with its flat-topped mound and its fine extent, must have been built as artfully as a tennis court, but manages to look as natural as a glade. Another mound goes uphill behind the trees, so that characters enter at any height and wind down. The trees behind the stage suggest immense depth, a primitive hinterland—when actors go off, they go off into *somewhere*. And after dark, brought out in planes of lighting, how magnificently theatrical trees are!

Comus is the first break in a Shakespeare programme, and I do not think myself that it is a happy one. This is no possible place to discuss Milton. I can only say that, theatrically, his words do not *rise*. Perhaps they are for the eye. But heard, acted, they lack clearness and passion. Shakespeare's plays have taken off to any height from this Regent's Park airport, but *Comus* is like a plane taxi-ing round in circles, never leaving the ground. Of course, *Comus* is a mask, and a mask written for young people to act. Milton was twenty-six when he wrote it—but for Milton twenty-six was quite old. I think that in this present (the Regent's Park) *Comus* the casting is wrong. I should like to see *Comus* acted by children—ceremonially, flatly, with a touch of bewilderment. The naturalistic high-relief grown-up acting of Miss Fay Compton as the Lady, and Messrs. David King Wood and Peter Osborn as her brothers, destroys the mask character and makes their spoken lines sound fatally long-winded and spurious. All this grandiose agitation about virginity. . . . No, I am sure *Comus* is only possible stylized. The effect, as it is, is an alternation of long speeches and ballet—the grouping is certainly very pretty. Comus himself is most alluringly played by Mr. Jack Hawkins—though I doubt whether Milton meant this to be a sheik part—and Mr. Leslie French does his vital best with the consequential Spirit. Throughout, lovely lines, lovely images and the Sabrina lyric rise like bubbles out of the ferment of morality, and like bubbles sail away through the mind. The entrance of Sabrina with six watery nymphs, with a water-quiver of light over their faces, could not have been more exquisitely done.

Comus was preceded by a really very pleasing scarlet-and-white ballet, *Pyramide*. This wanted more light.

Revudeville

Revudeville—ninety-fourth edition—is great fun. From 1.30 to 11.30 it goes on, just off Piccadilly Circus, at full blast, and is a thing to pop into when you feel in the mood. The small light bright hustling stage positively darts out energy. The Windmill is very anti-agoraphobic. Everything hits its mark; nothing evaporates. " Britain for the Britisher " is Mr. Van Damms motto. And something here—perhaps partly the cosiness of Mrs. Laura Henderson's name—makes you feel rather warmly towards the British, however matey you naturally are not.

The revue has to be intimate, because the cast are practically in your lap. But nobody is attempting to get intimate with you on the mental plane—which is what I like so much. There is not a snobbery in it—not even sex-snobbery. Which is not to say there is no sex. But as a comment on *mœurs* it is not classy or esoteric. These are *mœurs* that we all ought to know about—as, for instance, the three good ways to say goodnight to your girl.

The cast are very resourceful The Windmill Girls are piquant and " different " rather than straight pretty: they bounce themselves like ping-pong balls in a small area. The *Tableau*, which I hear is quite a feature, is very pretty, against a Dali sky; it is much less inexplicit than a Dali. My favourite man in the show was Mr. Johnnie McGregor, and Miss Paddy Browne was my favourite woman. The whole thing is ingenious, and some numbers are physically witty. What puts the show on a finally moral footing are the Metroland homes advertised on the drop-curtain. Taken all together, this *is* Britain, no doubt.

ELIZABETH BOWEN

[65]

'*Tell him we shall be happy for him to be our guest until there's an " r " in the month.*'

SWIMMING

England in Deep Waters

NO man revels more wholeheartedly than I in chalking rude things on walls about Hitler, Mussolini, and Mosley. I am as intolerably anti-fascist as anyone, but I do rather wish that we could have a Reichssportfuehrer in this country. I saw the English swimming team happily whipped by Germany in the blue waters of Wembley's Empire Pool last week. And I knew the reason why.

The Poet Laureate holds that there is no more beautiful sight in the world than a meet. I wish he could have been at Wembley to see the diving contests between Mr. F. G. Hodges and Herr Erhardt Weiss and between Miss Jean Gilbert and Fräulein Anni Kapp. They might have altered his opinion. He would have enjoyed also the march-past of the swimmers at the start. I enjoyed that—but I wondered at the strange English passion for the sloppy. The Germans knew how to march. So did our men in the straight, but they did not know how to turn a corner, found themselves hopelessly mussed up and lost their step and everything. Each German wore a neat brown suiting. Would it have been regarded as the use of an illegal uniform if our people had agreed at all about their clothes? Some chose white pants, some dark blue, some light blue. Some had "Great Britain" ornamenting their chests, others a Union Jack.

We proceeded to lose six-and-a-half events to two-and-a-half and also a water-polo match on Friday and eight events to two on Saturday. Now, I don't care a couple of flicks of a duck's tail how often Great Britain loses football matches, cricket matches, bowls matches, and croquet marathons. But it would disturb me to learn that there were more analphabetics here than in Siam. And it seems to me as important that every human being should be able to swim as that he should be able to read and write. The ability to swim is not a dilettante attainment like the ability to shoot down clay pigeons. It is almost as necessary as the ability to walk.

It appears that there are vast and moderately expensive schemes by which Great Britain is to become physically fit. This means, I suppose, that school-children will be dragooned into dressing up in shorts and doing a quantity of hips-firm-knees-bend nonsense, with or without some tossing around of dummy rifles. This will be good fun for those that like it. To me it seems as pleasant as a poke in the eye with a blunt stick. But I do think it utterly necessary that all children should be *forced* to learn to swim and given a chance to learn to swim well.

The real reason why we were so badly beaten by Germany I learnt a day or two before the Wembley match. The St. Pancras Federation of Boys' Clubs held its annual swimming gala. I was invited. I attended. I watched. I saw prizes presented by a Knight. I saw a number of enthusiastic infants, none of whom will ever join the Bath Club, all of whom must have been eager to swim as well and as fast as possible, swimming badly because they had not been taught to swim well. They could keep themselves from drowning. Probably they could save others from drowning. But, however much they might desire to, they could not swim with real speed.

The elementary-school child in London is, I believe, taught to swim by the elementary-school teacher. Would it not be an equally sane idea for the L.C.C. to hire swimming professionals to teach the children to read and write?

To return to Wembley—and a most charming place to return to it is. I doubt if you would have enjoyed the water-polo on Friday. I unfortunately missed Saturday's game in which the unbeaten "Empire Swimming Club" team became the beaten ditto to the tune of ten goals to two. I merely saw England's team whipped by Germany by nine goals to one.

I have played enough water-polo to believe that it provides a more gruelling 14 minutes of play than any other game. (Personal conceit parenthesis: I once won a pleasing and useful pewter tankard for playing in a team which beat a team led by Reggie Sutton, England's captain on Friday last.) I believe that a good game of water-polo is the best game in the world—and Friday showed me that a poor game of water-polo is about the poorest game in the world.

Polo demands good marking and good throwing of the ball. Only Sutton seemed capable of either. Marking demands speed and the Germans always had the edge on those of our men who were not Sutton. The result of our inefficiency was raggedness and (with the aid of indifferent refereeing) some rough play. If water-polo is worth playing at all, it's worth playing seriously—simply because it's more fun that way for players and spectators. But we prefer to be sloppy. So what?

Let observers note: If the band plays, in succession, full versions of *Deutschland über Alles*, the *Horst Wessel Lied* and *God Save the King*, it seems to be the duty of all *Echtdeutschen* present to extend the right arm all the time. Fun: but, to my way of thinking, horribly tiring and a great strain on a prospective swimmer of fifteen hundred metres.

JOHN CROW

SINK OR SWIM

The Jesus style and the super-Jesus style of the Germans did not suit the day, and never have two more exhausted crews passed the finishing post. Either might have cracked at any moment.—THE TIMES *Rowing Correspondent.*

I have rarely seen a crew less distressed after the race than the German Wikings. Jesus College started magnificently, but could not stay; they shortened perceptibly in the last 200 yards, and the Germans, rowing like a machine, wore them down, finishing with hair unruffled and faces serene.—CLUBMAN *in the* STAR.

MINUTES OF THE WEEK

Outlook

We live in stirring times and relish it but little. We met the other day a journalist of note who epitomized the current situation neatly enough. " None of us," he said, " will live to see another Silly Season." We asked him if there were any compensations to look forward to. He said no, unless you counted the Palestinian Ambassador presenting his credentials in Berlin.

We decided that we counted that.

Crisis

As crises go, the Far Eastern crisis suits most of us pretty well. It's a long way off. Nobody expects us even to pronounce the proper names involved : far less to have met the people who bear them (" In Salzburg, dear. He was at the next table. Don't you remember ? "). There's none of that tiresome business of hav-

ing to differentiate between the Little Entente, the Secession States, the Danubian economic bloc, and what Stoyadinovitch said in June. The woes of China are an even easier wicket for us than they are for Japan.

We were once in Peking on a highly critical occasion. Martial law had been proclaimed, riots were expected, and extra troops had been called out. Nothing happened, of course. We remember it because we then saw, for the first and probably the last time, two Chinese soldiers patrolling the streets with fixed bayonets and holding each other by the hand. We've had a weakness for China ever since.

Rough Island Story

As if we weren't acutely conscious that modern life is all too synthetic, we've just heard two young men in a club talking about an island. It's a very, very small island off the Dorset coast ; it has a house on it ; and we deduced on internal evidence that it's for sale. One of the young men—a potential purchaser—had flown over it. " It's all right," he said, " in a way. I mean, you have the sea lapping on your front doorstep and all that ; but they haven't got a swimming-bath and, what's more, there's no room for one."

Thwarting and Foiling

A motorist, who's had trouble with gongs, evolved and passed on to us the following scheme for hoodwinking the Law. When gonged, accelerate sharply. Then turn down a side road and change places with your companion. When the police arrive hotfoot to take particulars, your companion shows his licence and gives his name and address, but otherwise says nothing, creating the impression of a chap pretty well overcome by terror and remorse.

In due course he gets a summons and attends the court. When the magistrate asks him if he has anything to say, he drops his bombshell and says he wasn't driving the car. What

happens then our friend doesn't quite know. But there's a chance that the police, having sworn that the wrong man was driving at 37·4 m.p.h., may find themselves in a bit of a hole.

Book Choice

What with Foyle's to the right of us and Gollancz to the left of us, there's not much room in the field for Slingsby's Own. But we thought we'd better put up a fight while we could. So we went round to the bookseller the day before yesterday and chose our own book. It's called *A Handbook of Modern Croquet* (just published by Longmans at 2s.) and the only tendentious thing about it that we can see is that it has a preface by a viscount. Unless, of course, you think there's something subversive in the epithet " modern ". Anyhow we bought it in the belief that croquet, ancient and modern, will remain ideologically neutral unless Herbert Read takes it up.

Slingsby

DIARY OF PERCY PROGRESS—II

By John Betjeman

(Illustrated by Christopher Sykes)

MY TALK WITH AN EARL

THE little bus was ticking over nicely, her pistons greased, mag. super-charged, all spring sprocket detonated, fuel in tank, oil in sump, platinum cutie in front and Asper Invoice and a rather fascinating little brunette in the rumble seat. It was a fine morning. I was wearing my plus-fours (as I always do on Saturdays and Sundays) and all of us were ready to make whoopee in the balmy country as per arrangement. Asper Invoice is a pal of mine in the Accounts Department at the office. Not absolutely a gent, but a good old sport—a rough diamond, if you know what I mean. As a matter of fact, he's got a public-school accent when he cares to use it. He took a course in salesmanship and of course he wears an Old Harrovian tie like I do, and we kidded the birds we picked up that we were old college pals.

It all happened like this. I said to Asper on the Monday : " Doing anything Saturday ? "

" Nerts," says Asper. (He's a bit of a wit in his way and comes out with funny remarks ; he can always be counted on to make a party go.) So we fixed it up. I got my bit of platinum goods from—well, that's another story.

" Where shall we go ? " says yours truly, when we were all outside Asper's house out Colindale way. " Drive like Helen B. Merry to where you like," says Asper. " If Mrs. Invoice looks out of the drawing-room and sees this bit of goods in the back with me, there'll be the devil to pay." The birds chirruped a bit and we tootled off straight for the Watford By-Pass.

" Is yon an hostelrye I see before me ? " quoth Asper as we approached a go-ahead looking roadhouse called " Ye Queen Elizabeth's Tankarde". " What say you, messmates, to pausing for a said tankard of ye goodly beverage wherewith to wet our erstwhile whistles ? "

" Oh, you men," said my bit of goods.

" Righty-ho," said Asper's.

So we alighted.

We met some really good sports while we were imbibing—a Mr. and Mrs. Wainwright and a friend of theirs called " Mac", who was exploitation chief of " Jazzolol". We all decided to join up. This Mac was

full of ideas—for his job, of course, is to popularize " Jazzolol " with the public in every possible way. " Let us foregather where the crowds foregather. Isn't there some of this here National Trust property about ? " (Mac was not quite top-drawer—but then the Scotch can't be expected to be.) The barman told us of some downs or something. I had arranged with Invoice that he should stand the drink, as I was providing the car ; so we brought a couple of bottles for each of us and one for the girls, and the Wainwrights led the way. I must say there's nothing like spinning down a by-pass when you've got a drop of drink in you and a couple of cuties to wile away the irksome while. I must have overtaken twenty cars, and the Wainwrights ahead of us overtook as many, though if I had let her full out she could easily have overtaken the Wainwrights. We shoved one old geyser right into the ditch for not letting us get by soon enough, and I held up a Frazer-Nash the whole way, thanks to a clever bit of driving. I wasn't going to let anything get past the little bus—and I can always make the excuse that my choke prevents me hearing anything, if somebody turns nasty.

Well, we got to a godforsaken bit of country that had been " preserved for the nation "—high up it was, and so damned quiet, when we had pulled up on the grass some way off from the statutory car-park, that it made the birds feel nervous. So I put the car radio set on ; the Wainwrights hadn't got a radio fitted, but they had brought a gram, so they put on Bing Crosby and when both things were going we felt we were back in civilization. Then the birds and Mrs. Wainwright spread out the culinary repast.

Asper and I felt pretty sozzled after the eats and Mac had had one or two from a bottle of Scotch he took with him. Mac proposed a picnic paperchase. It's rather a novelty game and I daresay you might like to know how it's done.

Instead of leaving the paper and bottles from your picnic where you had your meal, like you would normally, you put them all into the back of one of the cars—the more cars and the more picnic refuse the merrier. The car with the refuse in it is the " hare " and is given five minutes' start, somebody sitting in the back to chuck out the paper and bottles which leave a track as in an ordinary paperchase, only easier to see. Obviously you don't want to stick to the main roads for this sort of thing ; grass shows up the litter best, so you try to drive on grass as much as possible—crashing across fields when the springs will stand it and through any open gates and along bridle roads. Mac had several packets of throw-away leaflets advertising " Jazzolol " which he was going to use when the waste paper and bottles had run out. " Exploitation stunt combining business with pleasure," as he put it, which I must say was rather neat.

I suppose we must have been following about five miles when we came across a sprinkling of "Jazzolol" pamphlets by a gate that went into a sort of park place. "Beshrew me if we are not now entering the sacred precincts of my lord's domain," carolled Asper. "Odsbodikins if we are not," I returned. After a time we came to a sort of water-garden place with rockeries all round and plants and whatnot. The bits of fluff were screaming to be let out to pick some of the lilies and things which were making blithe the lissom scene.

Just at that moment I noticed an under-gardener fellow, careering along towards us waving his arms. "Cave," I warned, "and keep your mouths shut." "Excuse me, sir," said the under-gardener wight, "but have you seen the motorist who has been scattering bits of paper all over my water-garden?" Then he held up some of Mac's "Jazzolol" pamphlets. "Why, the devils have actually driven over a couple of flower-beds! This is what comes of opening one's park to the public."

"More fool you," said Asper, and the birds twittered.

Now there's one thing about being a public-school man—I'm an Old Cag-Bag (Carshaltonian) myself—and that is that it makes you recognize another. I realized at once what Asper Invoice couldn't do, since he hadn't the—well, you know what I mean. I realized this old josser was probably a gent, despite his clothes, and certainly rich. If you're in business you can't afford to be rude to rich people. So I had a brain-wave. The old boy was a bit deaf or he might have been put out by Asper's joke—so I raised my voice and said, in my Old Harrovian voice:

"Yes, sir. We've been following the car. It has

been creating a nuisance by scattering litter all over the countryside. We saw it turn into your park and proceeded with the object of obviating it."

"Thank you very much, sir. Very good of you to take so much trouble. I think I'll catch it all right. I've had all the lodge gates shut. But please look round yourselves . . . Oh, and this'll let you out." He scribbled a missive to present to the lodge-keeper.

"This is where we buzz off pronto," declared Asper.

"Steady, me lads," I interjected. "The old geyser—he signs himself Portisherwood without any initials (must be a Lord or something)—said we could look round."

"Goody, goody, goody!" chirrupped Asper's little brunette. "Dulcie

wants lovely daisy-waisies." So we stopped while the birds rooted up some decent-looking flowers, and then we spun merrily back to the gay metropolis.

Asper and I chuckled a good bit more when Asper produced a bit out of the *Daily Mirror* front page some days later. ANGRY EARL AND PAPER-CHASE : THEY STOLE HIS FLOWERS.

There was the story in full. Mac, whose name turned out to be Sparke —not Scotch after all (I suspected him all along)—was fined £5 and so were the Wainwrights. Well, it served them right. People should respect decent people's property. Lord, how we chortled about those flowers! Asper says one of them is doing quite well in his garden at Colindale.

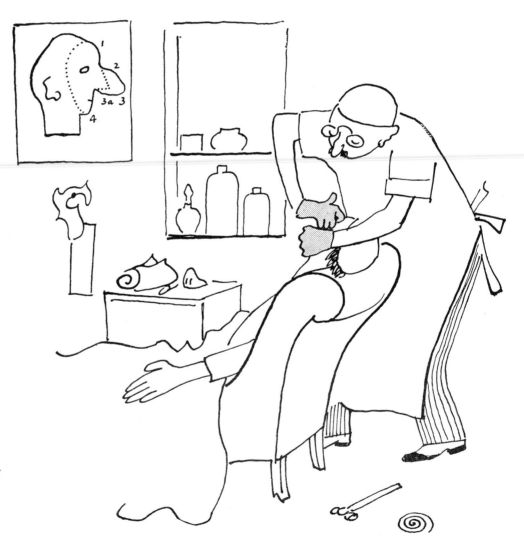

'Well, we've broken the back of it now.'

A JOB IN A MILLION—6

ALPHABETIC ALCHEMIST

THE average person who picks up a magazine or Sunday newspaper, covets the First Prize offered in some literary or cross-word competition, and enters a coupon with high hopes of success, has very little appreciation of the technical knowledge and experience which lie behind the prize announcements and printed results. Yet the compilation and solution of modern newspaper competitions has apparently become a specialized profession, in which the evolutionary law, " the survival of the fittest", has peculiar significance.

Mr. J. R. Constance, of Edgware, has always appreciated the strenuous, almost merciless nature of the battle in which he is engaged, and has equipped himself accordingly. To begin with, his library at Edgware comprises over seven thousand volumes. He has collected, over a period of twenty years, every conceivable kind of reference work directly or indirectly connected with the analytical study of words. The reason for this, he says, should be obvious : in the final analysis all newspaper competitions are based upon the twenty-six letters of the alphabet and the ten numerical signs. Mr. Constance may have the world's knowledge at his finger-tips, but he is not even content with this—the peculiar exigencies of his unique profession demand that he penetrate deep into the uttermost recesses of human language. In his library are over two hundred English dictionaries, almost every encyclopædia published in this country, numerous dictionaries of synonyms, dictionaries of ideas, rhyming dictionaries, acrostic dictionaries, thesauruses, and vocabularies of every description. His reference works are not restricted to the English language—he has French, German, Spanish, Italian, Russian, Japanese, Chinese, Burmese and, of course, Hindustani dictionaries.

Mr. Constance's achievements in the realm of newspaper competitions certainly seem to justify his claim of supremacy as " a general knowledge expert ". His exploits may be roughly divided into two distinct classes—the compilation of skill contests, and the solution of them. Naturally he does not enter for, or supply solutions to anyone in connection with, those skill contests which he devises or organizes, for this would not merely be unprofessional, but unfair and dishonest. For this reason his activities are divided into " watertight compartments". Some of the competitions, the names of which have been "household words" with competitors in recent years, were invented by Mr. Constance. One of the most interesting of these was a series of knowledge contests which ran for four months in the *Strand Magazine* at the beginning of 1930. Of this "Yes or No" contest Mr. Constance is especially proud. In each

part of the contest a number of questions were asked, and entrants had merely (like Beachcomber's Mr. Stummock) to answer " Yes " or " No " in the spaces provided. Had not the questions been devised almost diabolically, the result would have been the sharing of the prizes offered between thousands of competitors, which would have been less fun for Mr. Constance. Yet the results of those four contests showed that no person in any contest succeeded in answering all the questions correctly —despite the fact that they were answerable from standard reference works, readily available to the public. Only fifteen questions were given in

each contest, and the fact that the prizes were usually won with two or three errors shows the sort of thing one is up against. Mr. Constance says, referring to the compilation of this contest as if it were a commonplace occurrence : " I went through the *Encyclopædia Britannica*, from beginning to end, once a month when compiling that contest, to get the questions." The evolution of this contest is a fair example of Mr. Constance's activities in this connection—he concentrates always on the original, the unique, the intensely difficult and the bizarre. At the present moment he has a competition in hand designed to promote greater safety on the roads. You have been warned.

Turning to the solution of modern competitions, Mr. Constance's records are no less extraordinary. For many years he was a private competitor, before he took up his present professional activities. One of his more sensational successes as a layman was won in a " Missing Words " contest promoted by *Answers* some twelve years ago. In this contest, which ran for fifteen weeks, an extract from a speech by a well-known politician was given each week, and from each extract two or three words were omitted. These missing words were really unguessable, for the contexts were, of course, very carefully chosen. When this competition started Mr. Constance was inspired by the idea that many of the extracts could actually be found. He commenced the task by searching the files of newspapers in a public library, but quickly realized that this field of research would be too limited, and extended his activities throughout the country —searching files of newspapers and magazines in various districts, which he thought might prove fruitful. Altogether he reckons that he searched a quarter of a million pages of *The Times*. As you have already guessed, he found the majority of the speeches and won over £2,700.

In the solution of general knowledge contests, Mr. Constance's records are again terrifying to the casual competitor. Seven general knowledge contests have been promoted in this country in the last ten years, and in each of these Mr. Constance's entries have been in the first positions, though not necessarily in his own name. As a typical instance, he entered four separate papers, each consisting of answers to sixty questions set by the world's leading knowledge experts, in a big national competition organized by the proprietors of *The Universal Encyclopædia*. One of those four papers gained maximum marks and appeared at the top—winning Mr. Constance £500 ; and his three other papers also gained positions immediately below this in the contest.

Mr. Constance is also something of a sportsman, and follows the football game with such keen interest that he has been known to forecast twenty-five out of twenty-five matches correctly. In the last few years Mr. Constance has confined his activities, as a solver of competitions, to a limited and lucky clientèle, to whom he regularly supplies solutions for the " literary " competitions promoted by *John Bull* and other journals. He has captured forty-two first prizes in such "literary" competitions in forty-three months. Among these first prizes—which bring him commissions from the fortunate winners—he secured the biggest first prize ever awarded in any literary competition. A casually-employed seaman living in a Liverpool slum district sent Mr. Constance a small postal order for solutions which he entered in *John Bull's* " Bullets ". Mr. Constance evolved and supplied him with the line that won him £4,000 and £2 a week for life.

He is but one of the many competitors in the various contests who owe success to Mr. Constance's extraordinarily fertile mind. There is no false modesty about Mr. Constance : his notepaper is almost a signature tune. It carries a list of his achievements and it also carries conviction. When one reads " 50 questions by the Rt. Hon. J. H. Thomas : 100 per cent. accuracy", one hardly dares to try the weekly crossword without paying a pilgrimage to Edgware.

CYRIL BENHAM

BABE IN THE HOLLYWOOD
A Lament for the Father of a Child Film Star

O, where is baby Joan to-night ?
She's busy filming, honey.
Then we'll be all alone to-night ?
Alone—but in the money.
It is detestable to rest
Upon one's daughter's laurels—
On alien knees I see her rocked,
In mock-maternal clutches locked
And not, it seems, the least bit shocked
By movie parents' morals.

*O, it is very little cop
To be a baby film-star's Pop. . .*

*O, it is really rather dire
To be an Infant Marvel's sire. . .*

O, where is Poppa's little pet ?
She's working on location.
But if it rains and she gets wet ?
Aw, we'll get compensation.
Through baby years I dried her tears
As well as I was able—
But now where those hot tears have
    been
I see great blobs of glycerine
As used in the divorce-court scene
(Paternal knee by Gable).

*O, on the soul it leaves a scar
To be a Prodigy's Papa. . .*

O, where's our curly-headed tot ?
She's had to do a re-take.
She must be earning quite a lot ?
Well—look how little WE *take.*
I miss the beat of tiny feet
My homeward trek rewarding.
But then, I only have to go
And spend my eighteenpence or so
To hear it at a talkie show
By true-to-life recording.

*O, it is very, very sad
To be a Baby Wonder's Dad. . .*

O, where's our precious little one ?
She's gone uptown, first-nighting.
Ah well, she'd better have her fun—
And THEN *we'll teach her writing.*
Once on my knee she'd lisp to me
Some artless infant ditty,
But now she chooses to rehearse
Her lyrics, which disgust the nurse
And (this, I think, is rather worse)
Are very far from witty.

RODNEY HOBSON

In assuming the Presidency of the National Book Association Earl Baldwin declared his intention of devoting himself to the cause of political education. He will take a very active part in the work of the National Book Association. . . . The Association's first book, *Coal-Miner* by G. A. W. Tomlinson, has been issued to members and is available to new members. . . . With their copies of *Coal-Miner* members receive a *FREE COPY* of Arthur Bryant's new book, *Stanley Baldwin, A Tribute.* The second choice of the Association is *Service of our Lives*—the last Speeches as Prime Minister of The Rt. Hon. The Earl Baldwin of Bewdley.—*Messrs. Hutchinson's Autumn List.*

Well, well, if it isn't our old friend Sealed Lips !

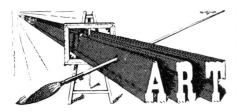

Kultur-Bolshevismus

AFTER the Fuehrer's recent epoch-making pronunciamiento on Modern Art one feels that the whole subject has been exhausted and any further remarks are a superfluous impertinence. However, on the assumption that there remain a few aspects of this question which the genius of the Leader has left unresolved, we return to the consideration of a painter whose work, while it is unlikely any longer to grace the walls of the temples of Nordic culture, still fetches gratifying prices in the sale-rooms, even in Munich.

Herr Hitler, you will remember, stated that those artists who persisted in painting the sky green and the grass blue were either mentally deficient, in which case they should be sterilized lest they transmitted their unfortunate affliction to future generations, or else they were wilfully perverse and should be prosecuted for false pretences. Now, misguided as this attitude undoubtedly is, one must point out, at the risk of being dubbed a cultural fascist and a traitor to the United Artists Front, etc., that it is no more so than that of the opposite school which holds that those who give us green grass and blue skies are either the bourgeois slaves of an outworn representational æsthetic or artistic prostitutes pandering to the degraded tastes of capitalist wreckers. All of which only goes to prove that while you may paint grass red, green or tartan, the result will only be a work of art if you have a legitimate reason for doing so. But alas ! while green grass and red grass both stand equally in need of artistic justification, for the man in the street (and the man in the Brown House) it is far more difficult to appreciate the reason for the former than for the latter. For green grass has at least a natural justification, which is not, however, the same thing

as an artistic one. Thus when confronted with red grass he will either, like Herr Hitler, take refuge in the traditional bull-like reactions or else will reveal himself a culture-snob and assume the picture to be a work of art solely because the grass is not the usual colour. Anyone who wished to find out whether he fell into either of these two categories should have visited the Matisse Exhibition held recently at the Rosenberg Galleries.

That Henri Matisse is a very great artist few critics would dispute : that he never exhibits anything but his best work is a proposition which I for one would not be prepared to defend. He is therefore a useful touchstone by which to assess the genuineness of one's reactions to art ; for in some of his pictures there is a justifiable motive for his distortions and apparently arbitrary use of colour ; in others, such a justification seems lacking and the whole amounts to no more than an incredibly skilful but unnecessary tour-de-force. In the recent show there are two pictures of a woman in a purple dress which seem to illustrate this point admirably ; while one is as exciting as only the best work of a great master can be exciting, the other, I submit, is nothing but an inspired piece of *rive-gauche* window-dressing.

To turn to equally great but less controversial masters, there is at the moment at the Lefevre Galleries a most admirable collection of nineteenth century French paintings. While there have been dozens of similar shows in the last few years, few have had a similar interest ; for here we have several examples of great painters working for once rather outside their usual easily recognizable styles. There is a head of a woman by Renoir in which there is no trace of that glowing raspberry pink, there is a Boudin that might well be the work of Jongkind, an early and very lovely Monet with no Impressionist nonsense about it, and, above all, a quite staggering Corot. This last picture, *Les vieux quais à Rouen*, is not only unusually large for a Corot but is painted with all that solidity which characterized his early paintings in Provence and

which was subsequently absent in his landscapes and reserved for his figure studies. The colour—a most subtle combination of browns—is something that, as far as I know, he never again either attempted or achieved. The general impression is that of a Van de Velde endowed with an almost supernatural feeling for form. Observe particularly the drawing of the horses in the foreground, for they are an achievement of which even Stubbs might well have been proud.

Apart from these excursions from the normal, there are many equally admirable, though less surprising, works : a splendid head by Cézanne which reveals his gifts as a portrait painter far better than many of his paintings that have been shown recently ; a quantity of brilliant Lautrecs, of which the portrait of M. Manuel is perhaps the finest, as well as a lifesize young lady in a Japanese dress by Monet which I cannot bring myself to believe will add anything to that artist's reputation.

As this is probably the last important exhibition in the private galleries until the autumn, it is not out of place to consider a recent show which may have been overlooked in the rush but which had nevertheless a permanent significance. The exhibition of the designs for stage settings by Alexandre Benois at Tooths' revealed an artist of the front rank—a worthy successor to the glorious Bibbiena family. When the ballet first demonstrated to western Europe the skill of Russian stage-designers, the glow and shock which the products of Léon Bakst's opulent Hebraic imagination then produced tended rather to eclipse the less showy but far subtler nature of Benois' genius. Now he stands fully revealed as the greatest scenic artist of our time. OSBERT LANCASTER

★

O BRAVE NEW WORLD
The lonely woman continues to multiply.—*Sunday Dispatch.*

[73]

BROADCASTING

Music on the Air

LISTENERS to the National pro-gramme at 8 o'clock next Saturday evening will hear a noise like a tropical hailstorm, followed by the B.B.C.'s richly over-orchestrated version of *God Save the King*. This, as the prisoner in London during August knows, is the traditional prelude to another season of Promenade Concerts at Queen's Hall. Thenceforward any-one dwelling in towns or small islands —*domus* or *rus*—who wants to polish up his classics in comfort and privacy can do so every evening except Sunday for eight weeks on end. These nightly programmes may not be the high-brow's idea of musical education and entertainment—an orchestra will not respond night after night to Sir Henry Wood as it does on two or three splendidly isolated occasions to Tos-canini—but they are the biggest musical treat of the year for the un-pretentious music-lover.

If you take your listening seriously, you'd better ask the B.B.C. to send you a free copy of the complete pro-gramme of the season. If you ask for it once, the B.B.C., which is not as Olympian as people pretend, will go on sending it for ever. With a marked programme lying around, you are less likely to find you had arranged to play bowls in Hyde Park on the very evening that you would have preferred to stay at home and listen to the Emperor Concerto. This year the B.B.C. has made it easier for listeners to plan ahead by extending the policy of reserving certain nights for indivi-dual composers. As usual, if you want to wallow in Wagner or soak yourself in Beethoven, you will have to stay in on Monday and Friday evenings respectively. But there are more opportunities than ever during the present season for making a night

of it with your favourite composer. This month, for example, you may take your choice of Elgar on August 10—that's next Tuesday—Bach on August 11, Tchaikovski on the 12th, Brahms on August 18 and September 1, Haydn and Mozart on August 19, Sibelius on the 26th and Liszt and Busoni on the last day of the month. My own experience of listening-in to the "Proms" is that it is unprofitable and tiring to attempt to sit out a whole concert. It is far more enjoyable to choose a single item, or possibly two, and then switch off. In this way, incidentally, you may get in your game of bowls after all.

With so much music on the air this month in contrast with July's rare and vapid programmes, it is worth while trying to settle in advance what one wants to listen to. You're probably already booked up tonight, but if you happen to be free the B.B.C. are relay-ing from the Salzburg festival the second Act of *Die Meistersinger* under Toscanini, and you will never hear a finer performance. And in case you're thinking of going to the theatre today week—August 12—the B.B.C., be-sides offering a Tchaikovski Promen-ade, has engaged the Lener Quartet to play Haydn, Kodaly and Bridge, and, as if this were not enough, has called in the Dean of the Faculty of Music in the University of Saskatchewan to con-duct what remains of the B.B.C. Symphony Orchestra.

All this must be infuriating for the brass-band lovers, musical potpourri pundits and croon-as-croon-cans, even if much of their indignation has recently been spent against the B.B.C's salutory decision to curb the crooner's activities and so disinfect the air from the horrible whinneying and neighing affected by some of the dance-band vocalists. Actually, when one comes to examine the programmes during the Promenade season, one finds that there is no reduction in the number of hours devoted to the type of music these people prefer. There is even a new delight in store for them in the person of Mr. James Gilroy, who will begin a series of programmes on August 18 with a description of the dance-music played in the Rainbow Room in Rocke-

feller Centre, New York City. Thus Nation speaks unto Nation on Wednes-day afternoons all the live summer long.

I'm afraid it's unlikely that anyone, least of all the B.B.C., would notice my taking off my hat ; but I raise it in the hope that the existence of one grateful listener may be an encourage-ment to Victor Silvester and his Band to continue to play without the help of vocalists, and to the B.B.C. to go on employing Silvester or any other man who has the sense not to ruin excellent tunes with the puerilities of the so-called lyric-writer. I find it difficult to believe that anyone, even the most hopelessly love-sick motorcyclist or languishing girl-friend, would lose anything or miss very much if they were banned altogether. And such a ban would be effective enough if it amounted to no more than forbidding the broadcast of certain rhymes, e.g. Baby : Maybe ; Moon : Soon ; Remember : December ; Blew : Yew; and so on.

I protest in my helpless way against crooners ; and I want to protest against something much worse than the neighbour's loud-speaker—against those who leave their cars unattended, as somebody did the other day outside my window, with the radio full on,

the engine half-drowned by the boom of *The Londonderry Air* per-formed on the Würlitzer. All the Promenade Concerts in the world would not drown such a horror as this.

After these protests, a final word of congratulation to the television engi-neers at Wimbledon. My first experience of television was watching a tennis match on the centre court and I found it an absorbing and fascinating experience. If it is not too late and if you know where you can get a look-in, do not miss the opportunity.

JOHN HAYWARD

TRAVEL NOTE

ONE of the things you go to see in Ceylon seems to point a moral in a pleasantly resounding way. The story goes that a son of a concubine of a king of Ceylon, somewhere about the sixth century, drove his brother who was the rightful heir out of the country, captured and imprisoned his father, and finally walled him up alive. From then on he perpetually built walls. After some years his terrors had reduced him to fortifying an enormous lump of sheer rock called Sigiriya, overhanging on three sides, far back in the jungle, and without water ; he stayed permanently at the top and must have given up all serious attempt at running the country.

The exciting thing about these bare rock hills in Ceylon is that you see a long way over a flat plain which is nothing but one ordinary wood right to the horizon ; it makes you see something startling and different in a lot of views from English hills. A moderately wooded plain easily looks messy from a height, not a thing that would paint well. But if a man sees it as a plain that has not quite stopped being jungle, even after some millenia of cultivation, and if he remembers the fright you would have got when it was a sheer flat sea of trees, then the thing becomes dramatic and might even be paintable. You can climb Sigiriya by a rather alarming walk up the remains of a lightly hacked stairway, now equipped with chains, that slips and twists over the smooth curve of the rock on the side that doesn't overhang ; it is certainly no place for an invading army. There is nothing at the top but some unfruitful excavations and the view. Similar rocks that were used as sites for Buddhist monasteries often have wonderful seven-headed snakes, or what not, in low relief on the rock overhanging a well-head, so that they still seem a natural product of the scenery ; you get the same effect from the ruins of the buildings, sensible and tidy outlines ; they were arranged to have running water under them, used for sanitation at the end of the house ;

and always you find the floor of the watercourse (a thing that seems beautiful though perhaps it was only lazy) left as the unsmoothed and natural-seeming rock.

You feel that Sigiriya, placed where it is, must always have been pretty useless, and when the usurper's brother at last came back from India with an army, what you suspect was admitted. The king was killed on an elephant in a swamp trying to escape and the palace on the ledge was razed wholly to the ground.

So far the only merit of the story is the magnificence of its futility. But halfway up the rock there is a long raw crack about as high as a man, and this was used as a lookout post, reached presumably by ropes from the top. It was so inaccessible that the destroyers ignored it (and one must remember that practically every work

of art in Ceylon has at one time or another been destroyed). During the enormous work of decoration that must have gone on at the palace one artist was let down to this crack, and he painted on its unsmoothed rock face some no doubt second-rate angels for the guards. These nobly delicious female figures have all the holy sensuality of the monastic frescoes on the caves of Ajanta ; and yet they add a kind of hieratic simplicity, a quality that implies that you have fitted the sensuality into a clear and tidy view of life. That was, after all, a puzzle at Ajanta, and a puzzle in the great Italians. The Ajanta stuff is much more glorious, but any visitor can despise dates and see that it had to be brief : he has only to turn from the Venetian splendour of its applauding crowds and subtle richness of its flesh painting, and, walking to the door, see that uniquely romantic and ascetic **V** of the river and the monkish rocks that hem it in. It is interesting to remember that D. H. Lawrence refused to go

nearer India than Ceylon, on the ground, so he said, that the Indians have too many babies ; and though this remark goes deep into the troubles of India, it was hardly a thing he was in a position to say. Whether or not he went to Sigiriya the copies in the Columbo Museum are extremely good, and it seems likely that these copies were the first to convince him that the kind of thing Ajanta stood for was what he really admired. In any case it is true to say that they stand for a very special and valuable state of feeling.

Of course one must not force the point, because some of the monastery stuff on hilltops might have survived. The particular form that madness took in this king was not the only possible means that might have preserved some of this painting. But, granting that, and seeing how the thing turned out, and seeing how much weight our most respected advisers put on the arts and their survival, it seems difficult to be sure that any disaster may not prove useful. The most tragic or most ludicrous king of Ceylon was the only one to leave us a witness to a great epoch in the painting of the world.

WILLIAM EMPSON

Nur wer der Zeitgeist kennt
Weiss was wir leiden.

"The Life of Emile Zola", changed to "Life of Zola", will now be called "Life of Emile Zola", says Warner.—*Daily Film Renter*.

That's a relief !

MINUTES OF THE WEEK

The Crack of the Rifle

By the time these words appear in print we shall be banging away at the little brown birds, agreeing that lunch is the best part of the day, and trying to remember what a greyhen looks like. What with class-warfare and humanitarianism, grouse-shooting isn't what it was. Even in its last strongholds, the ladies tend to bring an interior decorator with them when they join the guns at lunch, and the pretty creature quite puts the Colonel off his port.

With very few exceptions, women ought never to be allowed on the moors. When a débutante gets into our butt and asks " Shall I be in the way here ? " we always answer " Yes, you will." If that doesn't work, we ignore her entirely, except for saying " Get out and go home, get out and go home," in a small, faraway voice, without stopping and without moving

our lips. Ten minutes of this usually breaks her nerve. The idea is that she doesn't know it was us speaking and blames it on the pixies. Sometimes it works out like this ; more often not.

★

A Long Way After Lenin

We see no reason to disbelieve the following story from Spain. At the beginning of the Civil War government forces took possession of a small village and the local worthies met to consider the situation. The general consensus of opinion was that they were now all communists and ought, as such, to lose no time in burning down the church. The grocer, however, objected. " Next week," he pointed out, " we hold the fiesta of our patron Saint. People come from all over the countryside and that is good for business. To burn down the church would be economically unsound."

The others saw the sense of this, and it was decided to put off burning down the church until after the fiesta. But would the Red authorities approve of the religious processions which were traditionally an important part of the fiesta ? Grave doubts were expressed on this point, but in the end they held the fiesta and it was a great success.

What distinguished it from previous ceremonies of the same kind was the fact that the images of St. Peter and the Virgin Mary, which were carried in procession, wore red arm-bands for the occasion and were afterwards shut up for the night in the village lock-up.

★

Sahibheit

Bengal Lancer, somebody told us yesterday, is still packing the cinemas in Germany. It's been doing this for months, the Germans being as partial as anybody else to wish-fulfilment and liking nothing better than to see what it feels like to have colonies. Hitler was swept off his feet by it and made attendance (followed by a lecture) compulsory for all SS troopers. Being lately in Berlin, we found ourselves discussing the film—which

if you remember was a tolerably laughable affair—with two orthodox but intelligent Nazis. They took it plumb seriously and thought it fine. The only bit they couldn't stand at any price was a bit in the sequence where the three British officers are facing unspeakable tortures in a noisome cell ; Franchot Tone declaims a fairly Rupert Brooke-ish patriotic poem and then laughs off his lapse into heroics by some such crack as " If I'd known I was going to make a speech I'd have brought my ukelele".

This got the Germans on the raw. " How could you," they said (they thought it was a British film), " how *could* you introduce cheap comedy into a moment of such high and glorious emotion ? It shocked us deeply."

We couldn't think out an answer to this, but rather unfairly took the chance of telling them that the film had been made in America by Jews. This explained a good deal, but we left them still writhing.

Slingsby

THE HOUSE OF ARQUEBUS—1

Cyril Connolly

DOODLES is our Cairn, with lovely crinkly ears. " So young and so untender," Dad says sometimes as he prods him with his evening slipper, and I'm sure if he could answer back he would say " So young, my lord, and true." He is the smallest but not the least important member of the House of Arquebus, so I have begun with him. Dads is the head. He is Philip Arquebus and I expect not unknown to you. He calls himself a " blurbie " but he is a good deal more than that—author, essayist, talker, quoter, no mean cricketer and philosopher, an earl's great great nephew through Granny, and literary adviser to some publishers, and " the famous critic", too, of course. And he wields no mean skittle either. And then there's Mums whom we all adore— a very special person. And Uncle Pat—Mum's brother, who's been " staying " with us for the last two years, who's been a judge or something in Jamaica or somewhere, and Granny — Dad's mother — a real old Edwardian, and Baby —my young sister who goes to a psycho-school—and my brother Chris who's at Cambridge and terribly Left. All his friends are communist and one of them is C.P.! And myself, "the girl Felicity " as Dad calls me—but better known as Fellow. I've often tried to describe myself. Chris is much easier, he's square and solid, but also rather tortured and always running his fingers through his hair. I'm rather elusive and faunlike, a Slade-school Primavera Uncle Pat described me as, but we don't listen to him very much. Love in the Valley, according to Granny. Mariella in *Dusty Answer,* I think, but with a good deal of Roddie too. But it's silly to think about oneself. I realize that as a family we are rather special— happier, cleverer and better-looking than most—good heavens, I've forgotten my elder sister, Jan, who's

married to Jeff Crace ! He's something the wrong side of Temple Bar. A stockbroker, in fact, but they don't live with us. Since I do, though, I've decided to keep a diary, or rather Journal, because I think the doings and sayings of a family like ours, with Dads a public figure etc. and Granny a link with the past, and Mums so special, will be worth remembering some day and incidentally be worth a hundred down and twelve per cent. if anything should happen to him.

Best-looking boy friend, Hugo.

Most interesting b.f., Lambert.

Hugo is a Young Conservative and very necessary to any Berkeley Buttery

'*It all started at Pisa.*'

side. Lambert was very well-known at Oxford. My girl friend is called Cecily.

Family politics—The Ruling Caste: Granny ; Dads ; Me ; ? Baby. The Ruled : Uncle Pat ; Doodles ; Chris ; the Craces. The Administration : Mums.

Also—four servants and Nurse.

Of course the governed kick against the traces quite a bit. Uncle Pat is an escapist and Chris tries to be cold and rebellious and writes furious letters to Lackstrop, who's a don. And Doodles gets lost on the Heath. But we're essentially a happy family, and all thoroughly binworthy—which is something in these standardized times. Like all happy families, we don't talk at meals unless there are visitors, but

I took down some conversation at dinner last night. The dining-room is rose, with a shiny mahogany table and lots of silver and candles. It looks out on the garden. The only house in Hampstead Leigh-Hunt didn't live in, according to Dads. There is just the faintest suspicion of spring, a premonition of green on the privet. The bulbs look rather impertinent, and everything seems to say " Just you wait ! "

Dads : " Well, Chris, not gone to Madrid yet ? "

Chris : " If that's a joke, I don't think it's very funny."

Mums : " Chris ! "

Dads : " And if it's not a joke ? "

Chris : " Then I'll try and oblige you by going now."

Dads : " Master Chris doesn't feel very well, Fawcett, you can take his place away."

Mums : " Chris ! Come back ! "

Miss Saint-Gothard to Uncle Pat : " And who do you think are going to win ? "

Dads : " I only hope Cambridge's loss will prove Madrid's gain."

The B.F. : " No business of mine of course, but I shouldn't think they'd let your brother past the frontier."

Me (oil on troubled waters): " All one can say is that everything one likes is going to go, whatever happens."

Miss Saint-Gothard : " How I agree ! "

Jeff Crace : " Depends on how much one likes Rio Tinto."

Miss Saint-Gothard : " And Rioja. And Valdepeñas ! "

The B.F. : "And Lalanda and Belmonte."

Humble Self: " And Goya and Greco."

Dads (finding his form) : " There used to be a posada, the inn of the beekeepers, in a certain hidden valley near a small town which I'm not going to mention because, if the fascists don't spoil it, I know one of you would, where they sold me a brandy from Queen Isabel's reign that was paradise to young limbs that had crossed the arrête and walked through the chestnut woods from Roncesvalles. Wines of Navarre ! Woods of the Val d'Arasas ! What do they care about isms and ologies—what do ists and ologists care about them ? "

Miss Saint-Gothard and Mums : " Bravo ? "

B.F. : " What, politically, is your father ? "

Dads : " I usually describe myself as a liberal rather liable to pink deviations."

Miss Saint-Gothard : " I'm a socialist."

Humble Self : " I'm just frightfully Left, I'm afraid."

B.F. and Jeff C. : " Come, come !"

Humble Self : " But I think the most wonderful people are people like Mums, who still manages not to be anything."

Sister : " And it gets harder every day."

Mums : " Well, somebody has got to look after you all, and happy families have large appetites."

B.F. : " An army marches on its stomach."

Dads : " Well, here's to our quarter-master-general."

Miss Saint-Gothard : " I think it's much more likely to march on mine."

General merriment. Miss Saint-Gothard is finding her form. She's so crisp. That's what I want to be like when I'm fifty, a nice clean stick of celery. Though she's not really one of the family, not in the know. Uncle Pat, for instance, doesn't get a second glass of wine ever—Fawcett sees to that—and, when you know, it makes his dinner manners much more comical. And there's Chris stealing down the stairs with a suitcase, silly boy ; he puts his finger to his lips as he goes by. I feel so much older than him tonight. It doesn't seem fair to let him go. " Why, there's Chris ! " I cry. He looks quite odious for a moment. " Oh, do come in," says the male parent. " Have some dinner, won't you ? And bring your luggage." " We've all missed you," from Miss Saint-G. " Is your headache better ? " (Mums). " I don't want any dinner, thank you, and I don't enjoy sitting for hours over a meal in any case." " Perhaps you'd like a soap-box."

* * *

When Dads gets in a shrewd blow like that there's not much to say. Uncle Pat makes one of his Eyeless in Gaza noises. Chris goes out and is tiresomely careful *not* to slam the door. " Supposing he does go ? " says the B.F. " How's the exchequer, Mrs. Arquebus ? " says Dads. " He had nine and elevenpence when Nurse turned out his suit this morning." " And I've locked his passport up—he won't get farther than Cook's. I think somehow before the night is out we shall be a united family again." Dads *can* be sweet.

*

Within six hours of the wreck of the Dutch K.L.M. £20,000 all-metal Douglas air-liner Flamengo yesterday, Belgian Air Ministry officials, who had rushed to the scene of the crash, gave their verdict.

" Lightning caused the crash," they declared.—DAILY EXPRESS, *front page.*

How did she break up ? Was it fire ? Structural fault ? The visibility was good, the 'plane in good flying order. The pilot was excellent.

It was the machine, not the man, that failed. But WHY ?—DAILY EXPRESS, *leading article, same day.*

If you want to know the answer, read the *Daily Express.*

COTTAGE HOMES

The cottage homes of England
once teemed with simple life,
and wholesome rustic nonsense there
was absolutely rife ;
when winds the daub and wattle shook
the cotters had no match
for tickling in the ingle-nook
and tumbling under thatch.

The cottage homes of England,
all moss-bound still they stand,
though Rural District Councils house
the workers on the land ;
no longer sunk in squalor deep
'mid the ancestral scene,
they learn through broadcast talks to
keep the messuage sweet and clean.

The cottage homes of England,
how glorified they are,
with Heal and Fortnum furnishing,
and chromium cocktail-bar !
What modern comforts we contrive
among the old oak beams,
as down the wild week-enders drive
in loud rejoicing streams !

Ex-cottage homes of England
see parties strange and odd
who do not heed the church-bell's chime
athwart the churchyard sod,
but keep one rustic custom which
the past and present spans—
viz., tickling in the buttery niche
and tumbling on divans.

FELLOW = FEELING

R. K. Narayan

THE Madras-Bangalore Express was due to start in a few minutes. Trolleys and barrows piled with trunks and beds rattled their way through the bustle. Fruit-sellers and beedi-and-betel sellers cried themselves hoarse. Late-comers pushed, shouted, and perspired. The engine added to the general noise with the low monotonous hum of its boiler; the first bell rang, the guard looked at his watch. Mr. Rajam Iyer arrived on the platform at a terrific pace, with a small roll of bedding under one arm and an absurd yellow trunk under the other. He ran to the first third-class compartment that caught his eye, peeped in and, since the door could not be opened on account of the con-gestion inside, flung himself in through the window.

Fifteen minutes later Madras flashed past the train in window-framed patches of sun-scorched roofs and fields. At the next halt, Mandhakam, most of the passengers got down. The compartment, built to " Seat 8 Passengers, 4 British Troops, or 6 Indian Troops", now carried only nine. Rajam Iyer found a seat and made himself comfortable opposite a sallow meek passenger, who suddenly removed his coat, folded it and placed it under his head, and lay down, shrinking himself to the area he had occupied while he was sitting. With his knees drawn up almost to his chin, he rolled himself into a ball. Rajam Iyer threw him an indulgent compassionate look. He then fumbled for his glasses and pulled out of his pocket a small book, which set forth in clear Tamil the signifi-cance of the obscure *Sandhi* rites that every Brahmin worth the name performs thrice daily.

He was startled out of his pleasant langour by a series of growls coming from a passenger who had got in at Katpadi. The newcomer, looking for a seat, had been irritated by the spectacle of the meek passenger asleep and had enforced the law of the Third Class. He then encroached on most of the meek passenger's legitimate space and began to deliver home-truths which passed by easy stages from impudence to impertinence and finally to ribaldry.

Rajam Iyer peered over his spectacles. There was a dangerous look in his eyes. He tried to return to the book, but could not. The bully's speech was gathering momentum.

" What is all this ? " Rajam Iyer asked suddenly, in a hard tone.

" What is what ? " growled back the newcomer, turning sharply on Rajam Iyer.

" Moderate your style a bit," Rajam Iyer said firmly.

" You moderate yours first," replied the other.

A pause.

" My man," Rajam Iyer began endearingly, " this sort of thing will never do."

The newcomer received this in silence. Rajam Iyer felt encouraged and drove home his moral : " Just try and be more courteous, it is your duty."

" You mind your business," replied the newcomer.

Rajam Iyer shook his head disapprovingly and drawled out a " No." The newcomer stood looking out for some time and, as if expressing a brilliant truth that had just dawned on him, said " You are a Brahmin, I see. Learn, sir, that your days are over. Don't think you can bully us as you have been bullying us all these years."

Rajam Iyer gave a short laugh and said " What has it to do with your beastly conduct to this gentleman ? "

The newcomer assumed a tone of mock humility and said " Shall I take the dust from your feet, O Holy Brahmin ? Oh, Brahmin, Brahmin." He continued in a sing-song fashion : " Your days are over, my dear sir,

'Do go away—you only confuse me.'

learn that. I should like to see you trying a bit of bossing on us."

"Whose master is who?" asked Rajam Iyer philosophically.

The newcomer went on with no obvious relevance: "The cost of mutton has gone up out of all proportion. It is nearly double what it used to be."

"Is it?" asked Rajam Iyer.

"Yes, and why?" continued the other. "Because Brahmins have begun to eat meat and they pay high prices to get it secretly." He then turned to the other passengers and added: "And we non-Brahmins have to pay the same price, though we don't care for secrecy."

Rajam Iyer leaned back in his seat, reminding himself of a proverb which said that if you threw a stone into a gutter it would only spurt filth in your face.

"And," said the newcomer, "the price of meat used to be five annas per pound. I remember the days quite well. It is nearly twelve annas now. Why? Because the Brahmin is prepared to pay so much, if only he can have it in secret. I have with my own eyes seen Brahmins, pucca Brahmins with Sacred Threads on their bodies, carrying fish under their arms, of course all wrapped up in a towel. Ask them what it is, and they will tell you that it is plantain. Plantain that has life, I suppose! I once tickled a fellow under the arm and out came the biggest fish in the market. Hey, Brahmin," he said, turning to Rajam Iyer, "what did you have for your meal this morning?"

"Who? I?" asked Rajam Iyer. "Why do you want to know?"

"Look, sirs," said the newcomer to the other passengers, "why is he afraid to tell us what he ate this morning?" And turning to Rajam Iyer, "Mayn't a man ask another what he had for his morning meal?"

"Oh, by all means. I had rice, ghee, curds, brinjol soup, fried beans."

"Oh, is that all?" asked the newcomer with an innocent look.

"Yes," replied Rajam Iyer.

"Is that all?"

"Yes, how many times do you want me to repeat it?"

"No offence, no offence," replied the newcomer.

"Do you mean to say I am lying?" asked Rajam Iyer.

"Yes," replied the other, "you have omitted from your list a few things. Didn't I see you this morning going home from the market with a banana, a water banana, wrapped up in a towel, under your arm? Possibly it was somebody very much like you. Possibly I mistook the person. My wife prepares excellent soup with fish. You won't be able to find the difference between dholl soup and fish soup. Send your wife, or the wife of the person that was exactly like you, to my wife, to learn soup-making. Hundreds of Brahmins have smacked their lips over the dholl soup prepared in my house. I am a leper if there is a lie in anything I say."

"You are," replied Rajam Iyer, grinding his teeth. "You are a rabid leper."

"Whom do you call a leper?"

"You!"

"I? You call me a leper?"

"No. I call you a rabid leper."

"You call me rabid?" the newcomer asked, striking his chest to emphasize "me".

"You are a filthy brute," said Rajam Iyer. "You must be handed over to the police."

"Bah!" exclaimed the newcomer. "As if I didn't know what these police were."

"Yes, you must have had countless occasions to know the police. And you will see more of them yet in your miserable life, if you don't get beaten to death like the street mongrel you are," said Rajam Iyer in great passion. "With your foul mouth you are bound to come to that end."

"What do you say?" shouted the newcomer menacingly. "What do you say, you vile humbug?"

"Shut up," Rajam Iyer cried.

"You shut up."

"Do you know to whom you are talking?"

"What do I care who the son of a mongrel is?"

"I will thrash you with my slippers," said Rajam Iyer.

"I will pulp you down with an old rotten sandal," came the reply.

"I will kick you," said Rajam Iyer.

"Will you?" howled the newcomer. "Come on, let us see."

Both rose to their feet simultaneously.

There they stood facing each other on the floor of the compartment. Rajam Iyer was seized by a sense of inferiority. The newcomer stood nine clean inches over him. He began to feel ridiculous, short and fat, wearing a loose dhoti and a green coat, while the newcomer towered above him in his grease-spotted khaki suit. Out of the corner of his eye he noted that the other passengers were waiting eagerly to see how the issue would be settled and were not in the least disposed to intervene.

"Why do you stand as if your mouth was stopped with mud?" asked the newcomer.

"Shut up," Rajam Iyer snapped, trying not to be impressed by the size of his adversary.

"Your honour said that you would kick me," said the newcomer, pretending to offer himself.

" Won't I kick you ? " asked Rajam Iyer.

" Try."

" No," said Rajam Iyer, " I will do something worse."

" Do it," said the other, throwing forward his chest and pushing up the sleeves of his coat.

Rajam Iyer removed his coat and rolled up his sleeves. He rubbed his hands and commanded suddenly " Stand still ! " The newcomer was taken aback. He stood for a second baffled. Rajam Iyer gave him no time to think. With great force he swung his right arm and brought it near the other's cheek, but stopped it short without hitting him.

" Wait a minute, I think I had better give you a chance," said Rajam Iyer.

" What chance ? " asked the newcomer.

" It would be unfair if I did it without giving you a chance."

" Did what ? "

" You stand there and it will be over in a fraction of a second."

" Fraction of a second ? What will you do ? "

" Oh, nothing very complicated," replied Rajam Iyer nonchalantly, " nothing very complicated. I will slap your right cheek and at the same time tug your left ear ; and your mouth, which is now under your nose, will suddenly find itself under your left ear and, what is more, stay there. I assure you, you won't feel any pain."

" What do you say ? "

" And it will all be over before you say ' Sri Rama '."

" I don't believe it," said the newcomer.

" Well and good. Don't believe it," said Rajam Iyer carelessly ; " I never do it except under extreme provocation."

" Do you think I am an infant ? "

" I implore you, my man, not to believe me. Have you heard of a thing called ju-jutsu ? Well, this is a simple trick in ju-jutsu, perhaps known to half a dozen persons in the whole of South India."

" You said you would kick me," said the newcomer.

" Well, isn't this worse ? " asked Rajam Iyer. He drew a line on the newcomer's face between his left ear and mouth, muttering " I must admit you have a tolerably good face and round figure. But imagine yourself going about the streets with your mouth under your left ear . . ." He chuckled at the vision. " I expect at Jalarpet station there will be a huge crowd outside our compartment to see you." The newcomer stroked his chin thoughtfully. Rajam Iyer continued : " I felt it my duty to explain the whole thing to you beforehand. I am not as hotheaded as you are. I have some consideration for your wife and children. It will take some time for the kids to recognize papa when he returns home with his mouth under . . . . How many children have you ? "

" Four."

" And then think of it," said Rajam Iyer : " you will have to take your food under your left ear, and you will need the assistance of your wife to drink water. She will have to pour it in."

" I will go to a doctor," said the newcomer.

" Do go," replied Rajam Iyer, " and I will give you a thousand rupees if you find a doctor. You may try even European doctors."

The newcomer stood ruminating with knitted brow.

" Now prepare," shouted Rajam Iyer, " one blow on the right cheek. I will jerk your left ear, and your mouth . . ."

The newcomer suddenly ran to the window and leaned far out of it. Rajam Iyer decided to leave the compartment at Jalarpet.

But the moment the train stopped at Jalarpet station, the newcomer grabbed his bag and jumped out. He moved away at a furious pace and almost knocked down a coconut-seller and a person carrying a trayload of coloured toys. Rajam Iyer felt it would not be necessary for him to get out now. He leaned through the window and cried " Look here ! " The newcomer turned.

" Shall I keep a seat for you ? " asked Rajam Iyer.

" No. My ticket is for Jalarpet," the newcomer answered and quickened his pace.

The train had left Jalarpet at least a mile behind. The meek passenger still sat shrunk in a corner of the seat. Rajam Iyer looked over his spectacles and said " Lie down if you like."

The meek passenger proceeded to roll himself into a ball.

Rajam Iyer added : " Did you hear that bully say that his ticket was for Jalarpet ? "

" Yes."

" Well, he lied. He is in the fourth compartment from here. I saw him get into it just as the train started."

Though the meek passenger was too grateful to doubt this statement, one or two other passengers looked at Rajam Iyer sceptically.

*   *   *

SONG OF THE CITY

Oh, brighter than the starry firmament,
   And fairer than my well-beloved's charms :
A block of Cumulative 5%
   Preferred Participating Shares in Arms.

A. S. J. TESSIMOND

★

" The fact that I have taken an independent line in nearly all my undertakings," he says, " may be due to the accident of my birth. I was born on July 4th. It may be due to my solitariness. It may be due to my energy."— *S. P. B. Mais quoted in a publishers' circular.*

It was more likely due to your parents.

★

A girl with April in her eyes and music on her tongue told me this morning that God made Ireland when the moon was at its brightest. " That is why this country is so mad and beautiful," said the girl who had April in her eyes and music on her tongue.—' *Souvenirs from Erin' by Idris Davies in the Eistedafod Number of* WALES.

C'mon, mad and beautiful, what's your *name* ?

NEW BOOKS

Bloomsbury's Farthest North

TWO qualities are needed in the writer of a travel book, an aptitude for writing and an aptitude for travel. This simple principle should be too obvious to state, but it is one which seems in great danger of neglect by the publishers who now cater for a growing taste in the semiliterate public for vicarious locomotion. A large number of writers of this generation—Mr. Robert Byron, Mr. Peter Fleming, Mr. Patrick Balfour, etc. — possess these two qualities ; it is not surprising, because one feeds upon the other ; writers tend to be restless and travellers tend to be garrulous ; as a result the legend has grown up that it is only necessary to send an author abroad to compel him automatically to composition ; writers in need of a holiday find that it can always be obtained in exchange for a contract. How burdensome these contracts can become is evident in *Letters from Iceland*. " I haven't the slightest idea how to begin to write the book," says Mr. Auden, and presumably he also speaks for the less self-explanatory, almost enigmatic Mr. MacNeice. " Gollancz told me before I left that it couldn't be done, and he's probably right. Still the contracts are signed and my expenses paid, so I suppose it will get done." Wise Mr. Gollancz ! Unhappy Mr. Auden ! No professional writer can fail to suffer with him in his predicament, but his professional sense will be outraged at the clumsiness of the solution. No aid of typography has been eschewed ; the pages are divided into sections and subsections, " cut " like a film, but they never for one moment look remotely like a book. Iceland is a country which gives the visitor no opportunity for heroic feats or æsthetic discoveries ; it has no significance in

world politics to excite the propagandist. Its only point is that it is a cheap clean holiday resort. I suppose there is no subject in the world about which it is impossible to make a good book, but Iceland is a tough job. Mr. Auden and Mr. MacNeice never seem to tackle it at all ; they took some photographs of some good-looking youths ; they wrote some rough Byronic verses of the kind that are turned out in paper games at old-fashioned house-parties ; they compiled a dozen pages of hints for fellow tourists—and that is their most valuable contribution. Finally to make weight they added the letters with which they had wiled away the time during their tedious little holiday.

It is a common complaint that editors do a disservice to the illustrious dead by publishing jottings and trivial correspondence that the authors never intended to preserve. Mr. Auden and

---

Letters from Iceland. W. H. Auden and Louis MacNeice. Faber. 12s. 6d.

Mr. MacNeice have conspired to perpetuate what even the most assiduous editor would have rejected. Occasionally very conceited people are worried by the fear that one day a woman undergraduate, toiling for the B.Litt., may take it under her mortarboard to write their lives. They think, in those heady moments, of all the trivial notes they have scribbled and pray to see them destroyed. It seems scarcely credible that two quite young trippers should take pains to make the collection themselves and publish them within a few months of writing. Yet here they are, fresh from the stylo pen, with all their personal trimmings. " By the way, I've finished that sketch with the goose for Thérèse. I haven't a copy, as it is appearing in the next volume of *New Writing*, but I'll send you a proof copy as soon as it arrives." What sketch ? Who, pray, is Thérèse ? " The best poem I have written this year " (!) " was written immediately after having a wisdom tooth out."

The book, if book it can be called, is flabby, pretentious and humourless, but it is only fair to say that, after

reading it, one does get some idea of what Iceland is like—and Mr. Auden. Not so Mr. MacNeice, who remains a shadowy figure and stimulates speculation. He appears to wear a kind of beard and to have a taste for bilberry soup. His collaboration is claimed in a gossip column named *Last Will and Testament*, but I suspect that his name was inserted to give a rhyme for 'peace' (Mr. Auden everywhere has difficulty with his rhymes. How lucky that he did not take his former collaborator, Mr. Isherwood, on the jaunt). He makes an intriguing contrast to the elaborately over-self-explanatory personality of Mr. Auden. I like to think that, all the time, he was keeping a little journal of his own, for he has a sly look in his photograph.

EVELYN WAUGH

*

GENERAL

CIRCLE. Edited by J. L. Martin, Ben Nicholson, N. Garbo. (*Faber*, 21s.) This " international survey of constructive art " is ambitious and difficult to assimilate. Its three editors have attempted to proclaim a new cultural unity. At best they have shown what many of us have realized for some time that (in the words of their own contributor Mr. Herbert Read) we are " at a stage of experimentalism, trying in various ways to find a new law of identification." *Circle* proves nothing more than that the quest has so far been in vain. Quite the best section is devoted to architecture. The clear and constructive articles of practising architects—le Corbusier, Neutra, Gropius, Breuer—provide an overwhelming counterblast to the jargon and muddled theorising of Mumford and Richards. Of these le Corbusier really gives the most effective retort to the artificial conception of the book. " Architecture", he says, " is an event in itself. It can exist independently. It has no need either of sculpture or of painting . . . I fear this immense artistic production which is quite indifferent to the advent of contemporary architecture." Which might well serve as an epitaph to this pompous, confused, depressing, but very nicely illustrated volume.

PURSUITS AND VERDICTS

The G-Man and the Dames

MR. PETER CHENEY is the berries. He is London-Irish, and boasts of controlling (as part of his journalistic organization, and what organization!) a "Special Investigation Department " working on specific crimes under the direction of Ex-Detective Inspector Harold Brust, late of the Special Branch, Scotland Yard. He must also control a Dictionary of American Slang, or words to that effect.

His hero is Lemmy Caution, G-man, the toughest guy in the fiction racket, who, as this new book shows, don't at all disdain the dames. " There's something fascinatin' about 'em. They got rhythm. They got technique—and how ! " There are two janes in this little story— Henrietta and Paulette. They've both got what it takes—and then a bundle ! Henrietta is tall and slim, and she's got all the right curves. " She's as pretty as a picture an' she has got her nose stuck up in the air like she was a queen. She is a brunette an' the way she has her hair done is aces. It was swell. An' she looks tough. Her mouth is set in a hard line an' she has got a jaw." Before meeting her Lemmy has taken a look round her bedroom, and it's a dame's room all right. " There is a wrap lyin' over the back of a rest chair, an' there is a long line of the swellest shoes you ever saw. Oh boy, was they good ? There is little shiny patents with French heels an' there is dress shoes in satin an' crêpe-de-chine. There is polished brown walkin' shoes, ridin' boots an' a pair of pink quilted satin mules that woulda knocked a bachelor for the home run. I tell you these shoes was swell. They sorta told you that the dame who owned 'em

knew her way about, an' I reckon that if the rest of her kit was on the same level, well, she was an eyeful any time."

Now for Paulette : " She has got curves that woulda made King Solomon sign off the roster an' turn into a one-woman man, an' she has got the sorta style that woulda made that Roman baby they called Juno look lika case of gallopin' consumption. If Henry the Eighth coulda taken one peek at her ankles he woulda figured to have got himself born about six centuries later just so he coulda given Anne Boleyn a quick bum's rush an' made this Paulette top sergeant in the royal runaround squad." Dames like that

---

Dames Don't Care. Peter Cheney. Collins. 7s. 6d.
Dumb Witness. Agatha Christie. Collins. 7s. 6d.
Verdict Without Jury. Anthony Webb. Harrap. 7s. 6d.
The Murderers of Monty. Richard Hull. Faber. 7s. 6d.
Murder Most Artistic. William Gore. Harrap. 7s. 6d.
These Names Make Clues. E. C. R. Lorac. Collins. 7s. 6d.
Secret Sceptre. Francis Gerard. Rich & Cowan. 7s. 6d.

---

may be afraid of spiders, but Lemmy knows they'd as soon stick a stiletto into their boy-friend as call for a chocolate sundae. We leave you guessing which of these dames is phoney— perhaps you can tell from the shoes.

But we can't all be tough all the time, and if you want a nice quiet story written in English, then you can rely on Agatha Christie. It is a neat little mystery with a sweet little doggie in it, and though we may be getting rather tired of Poirot and his Watson, he is less tiresome than usual. We wonder why everybody is so willing to talk to him, but if you are the tender type of detective you must have the conversational technique. Lemmy Caution makes 'em talk at the end of a gun ; they just talk to Poirot for the sake of passing the time and filling the

pages and solving the mystery. But it is pleasant talk, skilfully drawn out.

Mr. Webb must also have his Poirot, but he calls him Pendlebury. He is rather too Dickensian and suburban for my taste, and really too much of an old fool to be credibly tolerated by a busy Detective-Inspector. But the plot is ingenious and pleasantly unfolded. Mr. Hull, too, has a pleasant way of writing, but his plot is rather too facetiously ingenious ; you can't go into this business with even a millimetre of tongue in your cheek. It is better like Mr. Cheney to set up a Special Investigation Department.

Mr. Gore's book at first threatens to be depressingly highbrow, if not fatuously comic ; but the plot stiffens and the author threads his way through the contemporary art world without once slipping up. I felt uneasy when the suspicion fell on an art-critic (" A man who will become a critic ", says one of the characters, " is just the kind of man who would stab anybody ") ; indignant when the surrealists were dragged in ; and very grateful when finally the murderer turned out to be exactly the kind of painter I would suspect myself. Altogether a witty and agreeable book.

With Mr. Lorac we pass from art to literature, anagrams and sports cars : the world of Torquemada and *The Times* cross-word puzzle ; if you like that sort of thing you will like Mr. Lorac. Mr. Gerard is more in the Buchan style—hooded monks in ruined abbeys, animated suits of armour and sinister international crooks plotting against England's glory, and bright-eyed English giants to foil 'em. The *roman noir* crossed by the *roman policier*. The dialogue is amusing, sometimes intentionally, sometimes in this way :

" ' So perish all traitors,' repeated the Duke, and his voice was gravity itself.

" There was a moment or two's silence, and then John glanced at the other and said, ' And the Grail was destined for ? '

" ' For the Anti-God Museum in Moscow,' said the Duke, his eyes glinting dangerously."

HERBERT READ

A Reporter in Los Angeles—I.

ALL GOD'S CHILLUN GOT KILTS

A TROPICAL forest. It is night time and a storm is raging. Giant cactuses spread their spikes, making the luxuriant way almost impassable. Far off there is the throb of drumming and the echo of shrill laughter. The trembling foliage parts. Two big negroes in ostrich-plumed headdresses, carrying swords and wicker shields, step through into a clearing in the undergrowth. They seem knights of Benin, Ethiopian nobles, or perhaps chieftains from south of the Sudan. The first of them pauses and speaks :

" So foul and fair a day I have not seen."

" How far is't call'd to Forres ? " says the other.

A green glare above them lights up three witches, perched in a neighbouring eucalyptus tree. They cackle horribly. The second speaker adds :

" What are these so withered and so wild in their attire ? "

You will have guessed that the travellers are Macbeth and Banquo. The witches have come to the jungle to practise voodoo. The scene is Africa.

The Mayan Theatre in Los Angeles, where this performance is being given, is decorated to suggest a temple in Yucatan. Low and terracotta-coloured, it stands near the corner where South Hill Street cuts West Eleventh. Clumps of twelve-storey buildings rise up round it on all sides. Trams clatter by through a wilderness of car-parks and mean shops in which trusses, panama hats and second-hand typewriters are exposed for sale. The Mayan is one of the Federal Theatres, run by the WPA, a government organization for dealing with unemployment. The show tonight had a coloured cast of over a hundred.

Most of the action of the play had the Palace for a background. This set showed the interior of a West African fort built of mud. In the centre of the stage a deep archway led to a gate and above this stood a turret. It was in this turret that Duncan, a short negro, white-bearded and crowned with a high cylinder hooped with gold, slept and was murdered with his grooms. On either side staircases led up to the ramparts. The heavy wooden door was the one upon which Macduff and Lennox knock. This incident was one of the best moments in the play, as the porter himself was a splendid actor although his lines had been shamefully bowdlerized. He was the only one of the cast who allowed himself any of the traditional dialect of the South :

" . . . Knock, knock, knock. Who's dere in de name ob Beelzebub ? . . . Knock, knock. Who's dere in de oder debil's name ? . . . Knock, knock. Neber at quiet. What are you ? But dis place is too cold for hell. . . . Anon, anon. I pray you, remember de porter." The rest of the actors spoke well and with quite unusual clearness, and when the stage was dimly lighted there was nothing except their moves to indicate their race.

Lady Macbeth was small and a good actress. Here, however, something seemed a little wrong, perhaps because Macbeth and his wife are such an essentially British couple. Her lines are so clearly not intended for the favourite of the harem. In the torrid zone weak husbands and strong-minded wives behave differently from the Macbeths, so Nordic in their moods.

The banquet on the other hand had been turned with considerable success into a wild party, a shake-those-feet hot number, in which first dancers and then guests themselves, the thanes of Scotland and their ladies, palpitated madly backwards and forwards in a cakewalk, which but for its grace might well have been a reel. When the dancing had subsided Macbeth and his queen mingled with the guests and drinks were handed round. " Now good digestion wait on appetite," says Macbeth, " and health on both." At that moment there was a blinding flash of fire and Banquo's head some twenty times larger than life appeared in the form of a mask, peering over the wall. This happened several times and it was no wonder that the party was wrecked.

In the scene where the three witches (with their voodoo men and voodoo women) preside over their burning cauldron certain lines from the spell had been omitted :

" . . . Liver of blaspheming Jew,
Gall of goat and slips of yew
Sliver'd in the moon's eclipse,
Nose of Turk, and Tartar's lips..."
This was done no doubt in deference to the proximity of Hollywood, where these particular ingredients are more familiar as the backbone of some swell motion-pictures than as the hors d'œuvres of Black Magic. Another concession to local usage was that, with the exception of Duncan's, all the murders in the play were committed with firearms. Even when young Seward fights with Macbeth and cannot slay him because he is " born of woman ", his failure is due to missing his adversary with his pistol.

On the whole it was an enjoyable entertainment and it suggested a number of interesting possibilities as to future productions. What would this cast do with *The Merry Wives of Windsor* or *The Taming of the Shrew* ? For some reason negroes in tragedy always get the better press. *Macbeth* has few lighter moments, but even here it was impossible not to feel that these were the best things in the show. They should try *Love for Love, The School for Scandal,* or *The Importance of Being Ernest.* The scene could be laid in Haiti and I believe the acting would be superb.

At the Mayan Theatre there was a small item that made a perfect footnote to the play. It came at the end of the programme : " The Federal Theatre project is part of the WPA program. However, the viewpoint expressed in the play is not necessarily that of the WPA, or any other agency of the government."

So that if anyone thinks he can get away with putting Roosevelt on the spot when he is asleep in the White House and blaming it on a couple of bell-hops, he makes a big mistake.

ANTHONY POWELL

THE CINEMA

Tribute to Harpo

OF course the long vulpine stride of Groucho is still there, *ventre à terre* with a suitcase and an umbrella, Chico's piano-playing and Harpo's dumb pagan beauty—but there is so much else these days as well. The money is fairly splashed about : the capitalists have recognized the Marx brothers : ballet sequences, sentimental songs (" Your eyes will tell me secrets your lips cannot say "), amber fountains, young lovers. *A Day at the Races* is a lot better than *A Night at the Opera*, it is easily the best film to be seen in London, but all the same I feel a nostalgia for the old cheap rickety sets, those titles as meaningless and undifferentiated as Kipling's: *Duck Soup* and *Horsefeathers*. I confess to a kind of perverse passion for Miss Maureen O'Sullivan (she satisfies a primeval instinct for a really nice girl), but what business has she in a wild Lear world where a veterinary doctor is in charge of a sanatorium, with Chico as handyman and Harpo—no room to tell why —as a jockey ? Miss O'Sullivan is a *real* person—at least I have a dim idea that one met girls like her when one was adolescent ; she is the archetype of " a friend's sister " ; but real people do more than retard, they smash the Marx fantasy. When Groucho lopes into the

inane, they smile at him incredulously (being real people they cannot take him for granted), and there was one dreadful moment when Miss O'Sullivan murmured the word " Silly ". Silly—good God, we cannot help exclaiming since we are real people too, have we been deceived all along ? Are Groucho and Chico just silly and not poets of Edward Lear's stature ?

" Sun-Up's the worst horse on the course."

" I've noticed he wins every race."

" That's only because he comes in first."

Silly ? How horribly possible it sounds when we watch Miss O'Sullivan, and how thankful I felt that I was not in her company at the Surrealist Exhibition. Those charming, dewy and hygienic eyes would have taken all amusement out of an exhibit like the " Virginal Slipper "—the white dance shoe, the piece of fungus and the contraceptive.

No, these revellers of the higher idiocy should not mingle with real people nor play before lavish scenery

' I shall monkey around with the face for another couple of days and if it still looks like a boot I shall most likely scrap the whole thing.'

and an arty camera. Like the Elizabethans, they need only a chair, a painted tree. There *are* moments in this picture as good as there have ever been, and it is Harpo who shines the brightest, with his carved curls, his lunatic goodness, his air of having strayed out of Greek woods in his battered topper. I shall remember the short miming scene at night in the hedged garden where Harpo tries to convey to Chico that Groucho (Dr. Hackenbush) has fallen for a woman and is about to be framed (it takes Chico a long time to understand the ritual of whistle and gesture—" Dr. Hackenbush has got an apple-dumpling ? "), a scene oddly young and Shakespearian in its lunacy. And the scene when Harpo takes his pipe and leads a rabble of negro children from hut to hut, interrupting this black beau tying his best tie, that black woman at her cooking, to the musical refrain, as the faun face peers in, " Who dat man ? " has an emotional effect he has never previously secured.

King Solomon's Mines must be a disappointment to anyone who like myself values Haggard's book a good deal higher than *Treasure Island*. Many of the famous characters are sadly translated. It remains a period tale, but where is Sir Henry Curtis's great golden beard (into which, it will be remembered, he muttered mysteriously " fortunate " when he first met Allan Quartermain) ? Mr. Loder's desert stubble is a poor substitute. Umbopa has become a stout professional singer (Mr. Robeson in fact) with a repertoire of sentimental lyrics, as un-African as his figure, written by Mr. Eric Maschwitz. Worst crime of all to those who remember Quartermain's boast—" I can safely say there is not a petticoat in the whole history " —is the introduction of an Irish blonde who has somehow become the cause of the whole expedition and will finish as Lady Curtis (poor Ayesha). Miss Anna Lee's performance is rather like one of Miss Carroll's seen through the wrong end of a telescope, with the large tortuous mouth, the intense whispers and the weighty coquetry.

Yet it is a " seeable " picture. Sir Cedric Hardwicke gives us the genuine Quartermain, and Mr. Roland Young, as far as the monocle and the white legs are concerned, is Captain Good to the life, though I missed the false teeth, " of which he had two beautiful sets that, my own being none of the best, have often caused me to break the tenth commandment " (what a good writer Haggard was). The one-eyed black king Twala is admirable, the direction by Robert Stevenson well above the English average, the dove-tailing of Mr. Barkas's African exteriors with the studio sets better than usual, but I look back with regret to the old silent picture which was faithful to Haggard's story : I even seem to remember the golden beard.

GRAHAM GREENE

"*Veil of Youth*" . . .
by "*Le Gant*"

"*Veil of Youth*" *Model*

Featherweight Belt of fine net with back and front panels of good satin, incorporating "**Lastex Yarn**." This charming little garment weighs only 3 ounces, but it does a "four square" job of control for slender figures.

Yo596.   Sizes 24-28 . . . . . 39/6

The Bra (*illustrated*)

Is one of the famous "Alphabet" Bra's. Made of lace and satin incorporating "**Lastex Yarn**."

1049A.   Sizes 32-38 . . . . . 28/6

These delightful Garments are obtainable at all the best Stores and the leading Corsetieres.

Write for Booklet "N & D"—
"the corset that's different."

MINUTES OF THE WEEK

Nichevo

A young French couple we heard of the other day arrived in Moscow in the course of a protracted honeymoon, the bride bringing with her a fairly large trousseau. The Russians, who had Schiaparelli over recently to give them a few wrinkles, are chasing after elegance for all they're worth, and the girl's clothes were much admired. One morning the happy pair broke down very early in the course of a sightseeing tour (this is a tremendously easy thing to do in Moscow) and came back to their hotel. The husband, going upstairs to fetch some cigarettes, heard a hum of activity going on inside their room. Entering, he found it full of bustle. Seamstresses, draughtsmen, photographers, and fashion-experts were feverishly at work copying his wife's clothes. The noise was deafening, as it always is in Russia, and no-

body noticed the new arrival. A little piqued, he tried to call attention to himself, but couldn't get them interested. At last he found a photographer who spoke French and explained who he was. " What ! " cried the photographer. " All these clothes belong to your wife ? But I really must congratulate you ! Sit down, comrade, sit down, we'll get you a cup of tea."

And the good work went on.

Fit

Recently we were looking at a poster put out by the Central Council for Health, whatever that may be. It seemed fairly straightforward, clean-limbed stuff—a lot of little pictures, each with its hygienic message. MAKE THE TAP YOUR FILLING STATION, with a hapless Garden City child standing brightly by a sink : that sort of thing. But we were puzzled and disturbed by one of the exhortations : DO YOUR SLEEPING AT HOME. It struck us as un-Utopian, somehow.

Robert !

A friend of ours, who lives in the cosiest neo-Etruscan building in South Kensington, took us aside the other day to tell us about his telephone. Not so long ago, it seems, he dialled a Mayfair number and, instead of obtaining it, found himself overhearing a conversation between two of his acquaintances on a Regent line, in the course of which he learnt to his satisfaction that he had been the success of a dinner-party the night before. Dismissing this as a coincidence, he went on to describe three calls which, as he said, seemed to him to have more in them than met the ear. On three occasions, separated by some months, he attempted to attract the attention of the operator at a private

switchboard, who had apparently forgotten his connection, by jigging his receiver-rest up and down. At first nothing happened, but after a few seconds a mysterious ringing-tone was heard and then a gruff voice announcing : " Police Station." The first time this happened, he says, was when he was waiting to be connected with a department at Fortnum & Mason ; it happened again with the B.B.C., and a third time with a newspaper office—either the *Daily Mirror* or *The Times*, he can't remember which. He thinks the whole business sinister in the extreme and proposes to call for papers the next time it occurs.

★

A wistful little suicide story, vouched for as genuine by the friend who sent it to us from France, concerns a man who walked up to the fifth floor of a large house to throw himself out. Climbing on to the window-sill, he decided it was too big a drop, so went down again to the third floor. A fussy fellow.

TROTSKY OR NOTSKY
Nigel Balchin

SOMEBODY has been pointing out that the Soviet history books must be getting a little sketchy. Apparently when some member of the Old Guard is liquidated, all mention of his services to the revolution is expunged from the history books. The name of Trotsky has disappeared long ago. The next generation of Russians will presumably be taught that the Red Army " just growed ". And with the latest liquidations it begins to look as though the October Revolution was carried out by Lenin and Stalin aided (with that subtlety and snakiness which seems to characterize enemies of the U.S.S.R.) by a number of Fascists and Capitalist Tools, who helped in the setting up of the Communist State for the fun of having something to wreck and sabotage.

For my own part, however, I am less interested in the historical side of the matter than in its psychology. And during the last couple of years, I have become more and more fascinated by the psychology of the man Trotsky. He seems to me a supreme example of the lengths to which your real dyed-in-the-wool Fascist will go to gain its own tyrannous ends. Consider :

(1) For many years prior to the Russian Revolution Trotsky was in exile, posing as a Communist. We now know that he wasn't a Communist at all. He was, and always has been, a Fascist. In fact he may almost be said to have invented Fascism. For there he was subtly working for Fascism years and years before anybody else, Mussolini and Hitler included, realized that there was such a thing. The reasonable assumption is that Trotsky hated Communism so much that he went abroad and plotted to bring Communism about in Russia, so that when Communism *had* been brought about in Russia, he would have something nice and big to overthrow. Few of us, I suspect, would have thought as far ahead as that.

(2) Returning to Russia (still disguised as a Communist) he created the Red Army. This, clearly, was a mas-

terstroke. For he must have seen, with his uncanny foresight, that a strong Red Army would frighten the life out of Germany, bring about Fascism there, and so provide him with somebody to plot with and somebody to offer the Ukraine to.

(3) In order to strengthen his disguise, he got himself kicked out of Russia, *not*, mark you, as a Fascist but because he pretended to want to carry on the principle of World Revolution against the wishes of the eminently conservative Stalin. That, I think everyone will agree, was rich.

(4) Since then of course he has surpassed himself. Living in apparent innocence in Norway, he even succeeded, by the

simple device of leaving a repeating gramophone playing the works of Marx in his bedroom, in persuading the childish Norwegians that he was in their homes, at times when he has been proved to have been in Berlin, New York, Rome, Tokio and Tooting. To avoid suspicion he has organized (*vide* Press) an attempt to overthrow the government of Belgium and replace it by Communism ; and has attempted to cover his guilty relations with Germany by persuading Hitler to express great dislike of all Jews, and Russian Jews in particular. Few have realized that all this Jew stuff in Germany was just Trotsky being subtle again.

(5) In the meantime he has been corresponding with almost everybody in Russia in complicated codes. I have seen one of these dastardly code epistles. It ran " Ywha etha ellha ontda ouya urderma Alinsta ? Etga noa ithitwa. Uchma ovla. Rotskita." After hours of patient effort the G.P.U. succeeded in decoding the

message—a plain incitement to murder Stalin and establish Fascism. In return for this Judas-like betrayal he is understood to have been promised the first pick of all General Goering's cast-off uniforms.

Yet even now I doubt if the simple and trusting Russians have plumbed the full depths of this man's subtle villainy. Consider. As we have already said, we have now reached a point where the Russian Revolution is seen to have been brought about by Lenin, Stalin, and a lot of Fascist hirelings. *Suppose Trotsky is plotting with Stalin ?* You see the implication ? In a little while there will be another big trial, Stalin will be proved to be a disguised Trotskyist Fascist, and the people of Russia will wake up one morning to find themselves faced with the possible alternatives : (*a*) that what they had always supposed was a Communist Revolution wasn't a Communist Revolution at all, but a Fascist Revolution (in which case they are clearly all Fascists, which would be a disconcerting discovery) or (*b*) that historically speaking there hasn't been a revolution at all—which is silly.

But this is to anticipate. For the moment I will content myself, for the benefit of those who find Trotsky a fascinating character, with throwing out a broad hint which may send a flood of light over the whole matter.

In recent years *comparatively* little has been heard of Mr. Winston Churchill. Many of us have smiled quietly at the way in which the public has been gulled into accepting the Conservative Member for Epping, in an ordinary trilby, as the Winston Churchill we once knew, and have been wondering where he would turn up next. I would suggest that in their ability to turn up in the oddest places, in the knack of being right in the thick of positively every funny business, and above all in their slightly bewildering political evolutions, the resemblance between Trotsky and the earlier Mr. Churchill is, to put it mildly, suspicious. I suggest that Trotsky and Winston are two of the four best known disguises of this mysterious Arch Conspirator. The others, of course, are Sir Basil Zaharoff and Mrs. Harris.

FE=FO=FI=FUM

★

Felix Topolski

AT THE

LIDO

(SERPENTINE)

LEARNING CHINESE

William Empson

I HAVE been trying to pick up a little Chinese, a most entertaining thing if you take it as casually as the insolent Britisher does take foreign languages, and are not anxious for quick results. They say that in the old days a resident English lady would be firmly discouraged from learning to speak, because she would be sure to get the wrong tones, and when she got the wrong tones she would be sure to say something improper, owing to the wealth of the language in that direction, and this would be bad for prestige. I fancy they were too nervous here, but it's true that the sounds for God and Pig differ only by a tone, and the poster of the pig on the cross is still used for anti-Christian demonstrations. It is more reassuring to find how many colloquial phrases go word for word into English with our own effect of being casual but evasive—" a bit busy ", for instance, and " a good few ", where you rely on the tact of the listener. However, my Chinese teacher tells me that spoken English is much more polite than Chinese on the more fantastic tricks of vagueness : " I daresay that . . ." " I won't be certain it isn't . . ." " Wouldn't you say that . . . ? " " Of course a lot of people think—" Whereas in good spoken Chinese it is assumed a man knows his own mind. I made a curious discovery in turning over Giles's dictionary, by the way, that the character for the male organ is a combination of signs meaning the Imploring Corpse, or the Corpse in Pain, a fancy that would suit John Donne better than the China we have been told about. But most characters won't analyse into the meanings of their roots, anyway.

All teachers are liable to get interested in the difficult parts of what they teach, and make the most of them ; and it is difficult not to suspect your Chinese teacher of this fault particu-larly sharply. I wanted to get a Chinese student in London to come and make the noises at me and tell me I was wrong, and after careful and friendly inquiry, through a long list very kindly provided, I was told that no Chinese student in London could speak correct Pekingese at all. I know what this means because I've met Japanese who were brought up at Eton, and these unfortunate men talk the most terrific Eton accent ever heard, a thing almost unintelligible to most Englishmen, and painful even to Old Etonians. On the other hand there have been occasional revolts from Chinamen teaching Chinese in England,

who say that, though they have pains-takingly learned what the foreigners call the four tones of Mandarin Chinese, there aren't really any more than two, if that, and they don't feel that all students need take the same trouble. The revolts are tactfully suppressed, and I have no doubt that certain grave errors are avoided by the curious machine of teaching Chinese that the West has invented, but still the official tone continually changes when the word is actually used in sentences, and the main thing is to talk and not be afraid of being wrong.

This background of doubt adds a good deal to the puzzle of trying to get the right sound. One does not know what range of variation from the sound is supposed to be all right (of course no-body can copy a sound *exactly*) and, then again, what range of sound would actually get across. " That is Ping," my learned teacher will say chattily ; " some people in Peiping pronounce it Ping, but that is thought rather affected. You had better just say Ping." The sounds are exactly alike, but after all I am not likely to hit on the affected one. " Ping," I reply firmly. (I can well hear what a beautiful voice he has; it sounds more like the breaking of a lutestring than any performance of the human chords. But we haven't all got to talk English exactly like the Archbishop of Canterbury.) " What a curious thing ! Have you any friends from central China ? I should know just where you came from, if you were a Chinaman who said Ping like that. The Pekingese form is Ping." " Ping," I go on, a bit dashed. " Ping, ping, ping." " *Ping*. You are forgetting your tones now ; that is the third tone —it could mean eczema, for instance. *Ping*." " Sorry . . . *Ping*." " Now look at my mouth : ping. *P i n g*. You keep your teeth together and put the tip of the tongue just behind the upper teeth. And perhaps you had better *aim* the sound rather at the *back* of the roof of the mouth. Now say Ping."

" Ping."

" Oh, but that is how the *women* say Ping in Peiping. You will be laughed at if you say Ping ; you must say Ping." I become rather talkative about how I don't in the least mind being laughed at, and only want to be understood. "But it is not Ping, it is Ping." " Won't I be understood if I just say Ping, like the women ? " " I am afraid you are getting tired. That would not be heard as Ping at all ; it would be taken for Bing. Of course the distinction there is different from the English one. You must just practise at it, and we will try again next time. Now in the next sentence the sounds are quite easy. Start reading here."

" Ping, ping, ping . . ."

A Reporter in Los Angeles—2.

HEMINGWAY'S SPANISH FILM

THE film was billed for 8.15. We called up that morning to reserve seats but were told that this would not be necessary. However, brisk booking was in progress when we arrived in Los Angeles at about seven o'clock in the evening. After what turned out to be an indiscreet dinner of clam chowder, sea-food à la Bernstein, and Sonoma Valley chablis, we crossed Pershing Square, where bums cluster in the twilight under sub-tropical vegetation, and began forcing our way into the Philharmonic Auditorium. There was a large crowd trying to get in. Outside the neon lights said :

HEMINGWAY AUTHOR
SPANISH EARTH

Inside there were 3,000 or more people. A disbelief in private property had induced a number of old-fashioned socialists, and one gentleman who announced himself as a Cuban fascist, to sit in seats which had in fact been reserved by other people. By the time these wreckers had been liquidated it was nearly nine o'clock. Many of the audience had to find accommodation on the stairs of the gangway.

Two kinds of pamphlet lay about on the seats. After reading the one in red advertising *We From Krondstadt* the man next door handed me the yellow one and said : " This should be good too." It advertised a meeting of protest on the anniversary of the outbreak of the Spanish Civil War. " Did you come last time ? " " No, what was it ? " " Well, they had a loyalist flying ace." He returned to the *Western Worker*. Over his shoulder I read the headline : STOOGES OUTGAG UNIONS IN SACRAMENTO.

The audience were getting restive and occasional outbursts of clapping settled down to a regular tattoo. A sort of compère came on to the stage and begged for a little patience. It appeared that there were still people who wanted to get in. The man next door said : " Are you Canadian or English ? " " English." " I like the English," he said ; " I've been to London several times. I saw Sir Oswald Mosley. Woolwich was the part that appealed to me. I've been in the East too. To your face—to your face, mark you—the Japanese are the politest race in the world. And after them the English. A Camel ? " " Thanks." We just had time to light them before the compère appeared again and requested everyone to stop smoking. My friend threw his cigarette away. The reputation of the Old Country was in my hands and I followed his example. The lights went out and the show began.

Spanish Earth was directed by Ernest Hemingway and Joris Ivens. Precisely who did what was not stated, but presumably Mr. Ivens, who is a professional movie man, was responsible for the actual shooting and Mr. Hemingway wrote the treatment and the commentary. The film opened with a sequence of shots showing Spain in time of peace, through which the commentator was accompanied with bursts of Spanish music. Now, no voice but a Spanish voice can be heard above Spanish music ; but on the other hand no music can entirely drown a determined commentator. The ensemble was not successful. Later on, however, victory went to the commentator, who held his own throughout the greater part of the film, with occasional lapses, as when *Giovanezza* ushered in some Italian prisoners.

There followed scenes in the line, in besieged Madrid, or at the Left's headquarters at Valencia. *Spanish Earth* is frankly propaganda, but not up to the Russian standard. It is true the Russians made theirs after the fighting was over ; but I suspect that with the Spanish material at hand one of the big-shot Soviet directors would make something distinctly more effective.

Mr. Hemingway's film was either too ham or not nearly ham enough. There were good shots of air-raids and troops training or on the march ; but we continually cut back to one of those impassive peasant faces, the backbone of propaganda films all the world over. This particular old-timer was engaged in making a gully to bring water to Madrid. Like all his kind, he just got it fixed in time. Then there was the boy writing home. We were shown Juan's letter, the lorry on which Juan goes on leave, Juan drilling the village boys, etc. Later there was a close-up of some art treasures—an eighteenth-century edition of *Don Quixote* and an oil painting attributable to a disciple of Carlo Dolce—being rescued from a bombardment.

At the close of the film Mr. Hemingway himself came on the stage and read an account of the war and made an appeal for ambulances. He wore a dark-blue suit and leant on the lectern, straddling out his left leg awkwardly. What he read had no very personal touch about it, except perhaps when he referred to a shell's direct hit on a tram : " Two persons were taken to hospital, the rest removed with shovels." He spoke with dignity, but it was evident that he was in a highly nervous state. The audience received him with loud applause. When he had finished, and Mr. Ivens had said a few words, the compère appeared again and took a collection. The compère's manner and methods would have cleared any hall in England in ninety seconds, but I believe they were the traditional ones of American preachers beginning " Is there anyone here who will give one hundred dollars ? " and working down to dimes and nickels.

Spanish Earth is said to have been run off for Twentieth Century Fox, and it seems likely that if they do not take it on one or other of the big companies will mother it. But the Spanish war will be a picnic compared with Mr. Hemingway's battle with the Hollywood bosses to keep the film as he likes it. There are rumours that he has already had one brush in the Green Hills of Beverly with a director best known for his comic - opera fantasias, whose criticisms were too astringent.

The fact is, *Spanish Earth* has the

documentary interest attached to any good newsreel of contemporary danger. As a film, it will not make movie history. It asks to be judged by severe standards because its pretensions are considerable. Mr. Hemingway has an immense talent and it is no doubt remarkable to get a shot of men going into action ; but should the commentator say : " These men's faces are something a little different from anything you have ever seen before ; they are men going into action " when the shot is too blurred to distinguish the faces of the men at all ? Why make a claim to which the photography shouts a denial ?

The American Press has strange habits. The showing of this film was obviously an important event in local life. When Jean Harlow died some weeks before, half-a-dozen pages were devoted to her biography. The crowd standing in awed reverence in front of her former " gorgeous residence " was described as vast. Quite by chance I happened to pass the house on the day of her funeral. The street was empty as far as the eye could see. On the lawn a bored policeman, looking like one of Mr. Wyndham Lewis's self-portraits, sat on a kitchen chair.

Yet the newspapers scarcely mentioned *Spanish Earth* or Mr. Ernest Hemingway.

ANTHONY POWELL

★

Insurgent territory lies south of the dotted line. Arrows show converging attacks.—*Daily Express.*

And a third arrow shows the road to " Seville and Corunna ". We knew the country had been turned upside down, but didn't realize it was as bad as that.

ON AND OFF THE ROAD

Less Vile Bodies

IN 1900 to be a superior person you had to know a man who had been in a motor-car. In 1910 you were all right if you knew a man that owned one. In 1920 you had to own several. Today the only way to be superior is to say that you do not own a car and that you consider self-propelled vehicles suitable only for the masses.

In forty years motoring has changed from exhilarating lunacy to domestic service. Internal combustion is now a political issue. A chicken in every pot was once a winning election slogan in the United States. In more prosperous times two motor-cars in every garage was the watchword. In 1930, when the depression came, some one suggested a chicken in every garage. The development has been remarkable— particularly in body-work.

The first cars were called horseless carriages. But they were really carriageless too. They were made for pioneers and pioneers didn't want protection or beauty. All they wanted was coachwork from which they could depart instantaneously in all directions. You took out the horse and substituted what was, at any rate for the first few miles, an engine and a tank. You sat up high. Instead of reins you had a bar or wheel. And of course a great deal of fun.

About 1903 the women got restive. They said that if they were expected to go banging about in these contraptions there must be more luxury. They asked for windscreens and wheels that didn't come off and plug-holes to let the water out of the body after rainstorms and a lot of similar knick-knacks.

Then came the first Ford car— with three pedals. One for stopping, one for changing gear, and one for going backwards. They were quite namby-pamby—with glass in front and

a hood. But it still required a tremendously tough man to swing the engine and a nimble one to get out of the way. The first Fords had a way of creeping at you.

The closed car as we know it today began to clatter about after the war, dropping panes of glass here and there. Then the Americans, who had been canning meat for years, decided to deal with motorists in a big way and the all-steel saloon arrived with a clang. At first it looked dreadful, but unlike the early saloons it did need a crash to jam the doors and windows. Then some-one said something about streamlining and the fat was in the gear-box.

For a couple of years bodies slimmed madly. Until the sunshine roof was invented fat men could not enter their cars without taking their clothes off.

Today we're off again. Quite suddenly people have said *on ne passe pas*. The new idea is the fabric convertible saloon. The doors and windows are not draughty and don't rattle. The top is heavy waterproof fabric that can be rolled back almost as easily as the hood on the old touring car. On fine days you have a graceful open car. In winter you have a handsome saloon, on doubtful days you have a handy compromise. The new convertible body is not so good in a smash, but it's better in a fire. It is not so simple to make as a steel saloon. It may take as long as ten minutes to make a car with one of these new bodies, but that is all in favour of British makers. In this country we're good at productions that require care and time and we like to have our little differences here and there. The new convertible body is a most ingenious solution to a difficult problem and—if he is still alive—we congratulate the inventor heartily.

SUPERCHARGER

★

MATHEMATICS FOR THE MILLION

In a four-engined flying-boat the fuel and oil for such a journey weigh nearly 20,000 lb., or nearly as much as a 40,000 lb. flying-boat.—*Evening Standard.*

THE CINEMA

Pawn's Move and Knight's Move.

THIS is the season of slow-motion emotions : Warner Baxter in *Slave-Ship* staring from his boat at back-cloth Africa (we still read in little books on the cinema : " The film as compared with the play has the advantage of real backgrounds ") registers his conscience coming on, and come on it does, reel after reel of it, as he flaps his heavy insomniac eyelids—at Elizabeth Allen, saying, " I tried to tell you, but I couldn't.... Will you ever find it possible to forgive ? " ; at the cabin-boy, remembering he slapped his face ; at his friend and first officer whom he has just shot in the stomach : " I didn't want to do it, Thomson . . ." ; flapping them stubbornly at the English court-martial.

It isn't a bad film, it has excellent moments — seamen flinging knives from top-gallants and Wallace Beery as the soapy and mutinous mate, less soft-hearted than he has been for years, giving his finest performance since *Treasure Island*. The film story is by William Faulkner, the direction by Tay Garnett, the course seems set for distinction, but it remains a hot-weather picture : human relationships converge with the slowness and inevitability of pawns, though a film should consist of knight's moves only : the oblique jump, the unexpected encounter.

In *Stradivarius*, the worst film to be seen in London, we are so much ahead of the picture that we can come out, thank God, halfway through. A violin, which brings bad luck to all who own it, is left to a young Austrian army officer who takes it for valuation to a professor. In his house he meets an Italian pupil-teacher (the year, of course, is 1914), and we watch in infinitely slow-motion love registering on Pierre Richard Willm's foxy features. The violin is an unsigned Stradivarius (dreadful harkback to seventeenth-century Cremona and Stradivarius, in a little white sailor's cap, lifting a pointed nose and remarking pansily " What does the reward matter ? My dream is to liberate the voice that dwells within "). Then the Great War breaks out, and the rest of the picture is just hearsay to me. *Stradivarius* is full of sublimated sexuality and artistic abandon. " I adore it ", the heroine says, stroking the violin. " It has such a tender note . . ." People are always hearing violins played on the other side of doors and going into rapt attitudes in passages. It is packed with the awful gusto of the balletomane : the sweet Haskell-trained tooth, nourished on nougat and Njinski, moistening at the sound of music.

Woman Chases Man is a blessed relief. Sex isn't sublimated, and the knights do move, jumping obliquely, landing the rich man and the out-of-work female architect drunk in a tree at midnight, and instead of gipsy orchestras, classical music, back projections of Budapest, Miriam Hopkins's sad volubility and her predatory and rewarding eyes. This picture is what *Easy Living* sets out to be, though *Easy Living* has the better subject : the huge importance in a money-eyed world of the rich man's eccentric act. But *Easy Living* is too strenuously gay : people drop plates and fall cheerily downstairs on every foot of film. And it is the cheeriness which is wrong. As Chaplin learnt long ago, the man who falls downstairs must suffer if we are to laugh ; the waiter who breaks a plate must be in danger of dismissal. Human nature demands humiliation, the ignoble pain and the grotesque tear : the madhouse for Malvolio.

GRAHAM GREENE

' It looks like an inside job to me, sir.'

DIARY OF PERCY PROGRESS

By John Betjeman

III—BUSINESS

With drawings by Christopher Sykes

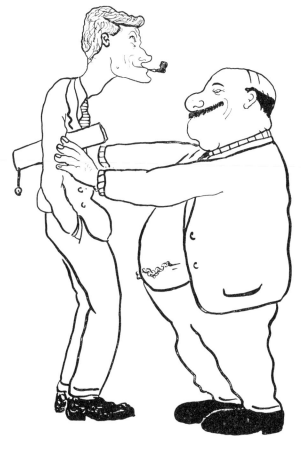

I WAS having a pi-jaw with a padre the other day. " Padre," I said, " I've never been to church in my life. My governor says to me ' Going to church won't get you on in the world, Percy my boy.' And my God, Padre, the old guv's right. Of course, I hold with doing the right thing. But I can get all the religion I want out in the open air—down in the garden at Skindles on a summer evening, that gets you into contact with nature and you don't need to be cooped up in a stuffy old church to learn about God. In fact, Padre," I said, " you'd be making a hell of a lot more dough if you just put your collar on the other way round and set to in my office addressing envelopes." I've no time for these clergymen. Of course he hadn't anything to say to that.

I write all this, folks, by way of intro., because some chaps have been accusing me of sharp practice. Well, that's a bit more than I can stand. When you're in business, you do business. Religion doesn't come into it. Why, if I had bothered my head about religion I shouldn't be where I am now —Chairman of Back Numbers Ltd., managing director of Tudor Bungalettes Ltd., on the board of the Art Stone (Condensed Milk) Products Co.,

director of the Tinned Carrots Co., Hoots Waha ! Synthetic Whisky, Chemical Fruits Ltd., Beautisite Billposting Co., The Take It And Leave It Building Society and subsidiary companies.

I aim to give the public service. By means of a skilful combination of the activities of my companies I am able to work for the public to their mutual advantage (and that of my own concerns, of course), thus combining at a reasonable rate of profit to myself the activities of firms that might otherwise be in regrettable competition or, worse still, be nothing to do with one another.

Allow me to give you an outline of my methods. I choose a suitable undeveloped stretch of country near a town. I stake my claim with one of our Art Hoardings of the Beautisite Billposting Co. These hoardings, though I say it myself, are artistic productions, artist-designed with bevelled edges and a trellis frame in the Louis Seize style —in fact, an asset to any amenity. Of course some cranks make objections. But trust Percy, he's one too clever for that sort of thing.

I have already naturally made pals unto myself of the members of ye town-planning committee of the local council concerned. If it costs me a saloon car or two to cement the friendships, where's the money thrown away ? I get it back again several times over by the time I'm finished. A business man must take a long view if he wants to get on. That's why I always say a business man must worship God in the open air—on tops of hills and places like that : they give him breadth of outlook.

Well, the local council agrees that no " amenity " is spoiled by our Beautisite Hoarding. Here's where the Governor comes in. He's chairman of the Take It And Leave It Building Society. He then finances your ole chum Percy to the tune of a few hundred for the purchase of the said field on which the hoarding is situate. The owner may jib a bit. " But it's not an amenity," says me ; " you won't be able to get a top price from one of these crank trusts, you know." I end up by giving the man a decent price for his land ; one must be fair and I don't reckon on making more than three or four hundred per cent. I mean, there are limits.

Next a local surveyor has to be squared. Saloon cars for councillors, whisky for surveyors. That's my motto. Happening to be a director of Hoots Waha ! Synthetic Whisky, I find that a case sent to the right quarter produces the right result. No questions asked, and I can start building immediately. Then if there's any little difficulty, faulty foundations, bad concrete —you know—well, another case of the aforesaid puts things right.

Now I don't want you to think I'm not giving the public what it wants. Tudor Bungalettes are distinctive with old-world charm. Each has a gable on the roof and a stained-glass window in the front door and for a trifling extra payment stained glass may be set in the upper lights of the windows. Furthermore, I am able materially to assist in the good appearance of the bungalettes, by embellishing the garden with Art Stone (Condensed Milk) Products, since I am a director of the A.M. (C.M.)P. I can supply dwarfs, rabbits, sundials, squirrels, cats, wendy-houses and witches' kitchens executed in lifelike manner from the designs of our own Polytechnic-trained artists at a reasonable profit to myself.

Now I have one great advantage I offer gratis to every purchaser of one of our bungalettes. Half a dozen tins of Artificial Canned Carrots (price 9*d.*, cost price 1½*d.*) and one tin of Chemical Fruits (price 2*s.*, cost price 1*s.*) will be found in the kitchen cupboard, or in the smaller-type houses, where there is no kitchen cupboard, under the stairs. The tins I can supply at cost price in my capacity as director of the companies concerned. I am thus able to advertise that the builder provides free meals to each householder.

Tudor Bungalettes, being in the black-and-white design with pink roofs and blue ridge, or vice versa, are naturally in keeping with any district in which they may be set up.

The Take It And Leave It Building Society lends money for the purchase of Tudor Bungalettes on very reasonable terms. Naturally it does not extend its loan beyond a period of ten years, as the bungalettes themselves are not designed to last longer than that term and one must be businesslike. I mean, the guv'nor and I are not running charitable institutions. But I think you will all agree that there is no

sharp practice in my dealings. I have been perfectly frank. There is, as there should be in all business, a little co-operation between myself and outside bodies—some of that give-and-take which is the essence of good business.

I hope my readers will accept my regret in not producing a story for them this time. But I have felt it necessary for me to under the circumstances clarify my position by so far as is reasonably possible removing those obstacles to a true appreciation of the real facts as they stand which have tended to give the impression that it is not my object to give the best service to

the public I can, at a reasonable profit to myself. I must express here my thanks to the Editor of NIGHT AND DAY for allowing me to show you in its true light the essentials of good business and, of course, I have done that in my usual style. But I do appreciate, I really do appreciate, the opportunity afforded me of addressing a really high-class clientèle, such as this, a sixpenny journal, enjoys. The guv'nor can square the advertising managers of the penny dailies, but this is where a public-school man like myself has to use his powers of personality and salesmanship. Thank you very much.

'*That's the third lion that damned goat has killed.*'

Pins and Needles

COMMENT ON CLOTHES

Peepshow :

For Men Only

SOME of the most boring people outside Cheltenham Spa are the wives who tell you that their husbands can't bear wearing new clothes. Cyril, so it goes, has an old jacket which he adores. It's been patched at the elbows and bound at the cuffs, but nothing, no, nothing will induce Cyril to part with it. The inference is that Cyril looks like a Duke in anything. Actually, of course, the miserable Cyril hasn't been able to afford a good tailor since he married the woman, and he's clinging on to his old jacket as a last remaining proof of happier days. Men adore clothes, especially new ones. Once started, they'll talk of them for hours at a stretch. Not even the subject of their babies is more enthralling.

In a Simpson catalogue it says "One of the pleasures of attending any social function is to feel you are sortorically (*sic*) beyond reproach". How right they are. They know their men. And if men aren't interested in clothes, why do they allow them to become so much a part of their careers ? I am told that you can tell a man's politics by his hat. Fascists apparently affect green pork-pies ; Communists bare heads. And without doubt you can tell a man's profession by his hat. A barrister—yes. A doctor—yes. A fireman—most certainly, it flashes in the sunshine. Looking back, a man could visualize his whole career by the clothes he has worn. I once knew a man who came down from the North to take a job in an advertising firm. He started off in dark suits and stiff collars. Very soon he was wearing the less formal lounge suits, soft collars, and often no waist-coats, of his colleagues. Later he left

advertising and went in for film producing. Need I say that almost directly he was to be met—or cut—in suède shoes, navy-blue hat, and loathsome navy-blue shirt?

Sometimes it is the clothes which come before the careers and direct the choosing of them. Many a young man, vaguely wondering what to make his life work, has been taken for a novelist because he wears corduroy trousers and an emerald-green jacket. To be taken for a novelist is only one step short of being taken up by Gollancz. Personally I feel this obviousness is degrading. No respectable woman wants to look like a Member of Parliament, or a secretary, or a hospital almoner, or whatever her profession may be. She wants to look like the Duchess of Kent, and that's that.

I have taken a fairly methodical look in the haberdashers' to see what seems newest and latest in men's wear. Naturally I have only looked in the windows—it would take a Jeanne d'Arc to go further than that. And even the window-gazing had to be fairly swift, since you are apt to be asked to move on if a policeman sees you loitering in Jermyn Street. But I had time to make a few notes of the things which interested, surprised, or disgusted me.

(1) I had thought that maroons (i.e., wines, plums, puces, crimsons, and air-raid warnings) had gone right down to the provincial proletariat. But evidently they are in the ascension again. Several shops, including Gieves and L. Victor, had special window displays of maroon ties, scarves, shirts, socks, braces, suspenders, etc.

(2) In Jermyn Street I came across an establishment called Delf & Co. with a " modern " shopfront. This must have given its neighbours a turn at first. It is featuring Florida Silk ties, Jaquard Batiste for town shirts, and uncrushable materials for sports. There is a little notice in the window saying that their shirts are cut by F. M. Tracey, for many years head cutter of Messrs.

Hawes and Curtis, and by J. C. D'Ahetze of Paris. Paris ? So Parisian cut is a thing to be desired, is it ?

(3) Owen and Newman offer pure-silk pyjamas made to measure *including monogram* for 75s. That monogram opened my eyes.

(4) Chas. A. Hodgkinson show a new cotton fabric which is so fine and light that a shirt made up in it weighs only 4 oz., a dress shirt 6 oz. Yet it has remarkable strength, because it has 192 threads to the square inch. They suggest it is ideal for sport or summer shirts, and equally good for underwear, collars, and handkerchiefs. It seemed to me a really beautiful material, with the appearance of the finest Irish linen. They had it in white and in colours.

(5) Turnbull and Asser, and also Noble Jones, are showing Indian Print silk squares in hot Eastern colours and designs for prices between 7s. 6d. and 12s. 6d. These seemed a turn for the brighter after the long years of heavily masculine tie-silk squares.

(6) In Lincoln Bennett's window there is the discreetest little notice announcing that APPEARANCES DO COUNT NOWADAYS. They are showing hats in a new colour—granite. This, you will be happy to hear, is not the Aberdeen granite which looks like brawn, but the plain grey granite. They also show " Our new M.X.H.

'*I'd sooner have written Gray's Elegy any day.*'

Bowler, 30s. Made in medium and light-weight, with material under the brim. The ideal hat for professional wear". I like their square leather hat-box for travelling. This takes an opera hat in the lid, and has arrangements for holding a bowler, a silk hat, an Anthony Eden and a tweed cap round the four sides. It is 63s., and they have a smaller and less expensive version without Anthony Eden.

(7) Dressing gowns, of course, have for a long time been man's proudest trappings. Apart from the gorgeous foulards you expect, Hawes and Curtis are doing a line in grey jersey fabric, with navy-blue revers, piped with yellow, and yellow tassels to the belt. Peal's in the Burlington Arcade have bath wraps with huge lobsters on them. The Duchess of Windsor, you will remember, had an evening dress in her trousseau with a giant lobster on it. Perhaps Peal's remembered too.

(8) I like the thick tartan socks that are in most shops, the lisle sports shirts, and the reversible alpaca pullovers. Austin Reed seem to be on to a good thing with their Bermuda lightweight suits—I wondered if you could get the same thing in bespoke tailoring. The Tenova self-supporting sock looked pathetically gadgety on the plaster legs in the window, but for men who have a sufficiently protuberant calf it seems a very good method of getting rid of suspenders. I suppose it keeps its self-supportment in the wash.

(9) I don't know what prestige the Burlington Arcade has nowadays. I love it myself. Rose and Co. still go on with their old school braces, Noble Jones with their nymphs and hunting scenes. But the old tradition is the most strongly upheld by Brown and Co. who have suspenders done up in boxes and labelled PARIS. The city or the person ? Not that it matters—it's the same thought. ALISON HAIG

IN THE COUNTRY

Regatta

A straight mile of river beside the town meadows, a level sward, a background of poplars. When the tumult and the shouting dies, or diminishes to backchat, you can hear the poplar leaves like the sound of rain. When I arrive the first race is just over, and the loudspeaker is playing with brilliant inconsequence a Spanish dance. It is a blazing afternoon. Both banks are strewn with a confetti of people. The farther side is somehow the more classy : there are set the two lines of bunting on blue poles (first acquired for the Jubilee and variously useful ever since) ; there the mayor ; there most of the pretty girls. On our side (a hayfield) are those who are too large or too old or too young or too timid to trust themselves to the ferry. It is a hulk low on the water, with an enormous rusty engine which does not work. In addition to the pay-load, this ton or two of iron is heaved cheerfully to and fro all day long. The speed of the ferry is in marked contrast to the speed of the racing crews. Mostly it drifts across crab-wise, or rotating slowly. People meet on it, converse, exhaust the possibilities of conversation, and sit waiting silently for arrival at the other bank to release them from each other's company. Last year the ferry boat sank as the brass band were crossing over. They were left hanging in a row to the rope overhead, still holding on to their instruments. The spectators thought it a merry sight ; the band did not. This year there is a loud-speaker.

There are numbers of little rivers in the county ; and all of them have their rowing clubs. Hence the regatta. The blue and silver colours of the local club fly from the boathouse. The young fellow who spends his days hooking down kettles and water-cans from the ceiling of the ironmonger's now comes knifing through the water in his narrow craft, rufous and god-like, wildly cheered. Another victory for the home town.

As the river is just not wide enough for crews to row abreast, there are two starting and finishing posts at intervals of about twenty yards. Two men sit on chairs behind the noticeboards with sporting guns, looking as though they were waiting for the grouse to come over. The gun which goes off first marks the winners. As there is no means of knowing who is ahead, except by judging the interval between the crews, the excitement, mounting all the while, is turned finally on the gunmen. They aren't at all happy under it: especially one, who seems to have difficulty with his gun. We see him heaving madly at the trigger. Nothing happens till the boat is half a length past him ; then a terrific explosion which makes the gun recoil like a piece of artillery. After this has happened twice, the unhappy man is the object of withering indignation from those opposite. One spectator, venting perhaps the discomfort of a high stiff collar, cries " Are these races being rowed under National Association rules or aren't they ? " His forefinger looks more menacing than the gun. " These gentlemen could object to you, and have the race rowed over again." These gentlemen, being the losing crew, look as though the last thing they want is to row the race over again.

He is interrupted by a woman sitting near his feet, who asks irrelevantly ' Why do you men always wear them black striped trousers, getting yourselves up to look so lah-di-dah ? "

He looks down sharply to find she is addressing a person of less respectability at her side.

"Ma'am," this man cries, "I bought these trousers for a shilling two years ago, and they're the only ones I got."

Next from the loudspeaker comes that noise which in the cinema we recognize as the pouring of refreshing liquor into glasses; a noise as of icebergs clashing in mid-ocean. Instinctively we perk up. Necks are craned. Are they really starting the next event? We are suspicious. Sure enough, after the icebergs have subsided, the voice comes again, suave, refreshed, a little apologetic. "There has been a slight delay over one of the signal guns."

The unhappy man opposite who can't make his gun go off in time is seen to be the centre of a mayoral group. The question seems to be, a new gun or a new man? A new gun is seen approaching under the arm of an official. Lest we should doubt the evidence of our eyes, the announcer tells us that a new gun is on the way.

The man in the tight collar is only partially appeased. "You watch him closely," he warns.

They're off! The announcer, copiously refreshed, loses all inhibitions. Long has he listened to wireless commentators on sporting events; and now a secret ambition is realised.

"'A' crew" (that's us) "have made a beautiful start. They're rowing like one man. In—Out—In—Out. Ah! number three has caught a crab. It's all right; they're still continuing. They're coming to the bend. They're doing a beautiful bend . . ."

Interest with us is centred on a boat laden to the waterline; a family party propelled by a fat woman in black. They are in the middle of the river and execrated from both banks.

"Get out of the way! Get off the course!"

The woman paddles wildly with the one paddle, the passengers bob about looking for the other, and the boat goes round and round like a wounded duck. The more the people shout the hotter she gets, and the less able to do anything but go round and round.

Here comes our winning crew; the policeman, the house-agent, the window-cleaner, the builder's man, com-

bined in a classic rhythm. How far away at this moment the raucous little 20th-century town. The spirit of ancient Greece is on them; athletes, beautiful in body . . .

There's that dratted woman still going round and round. They'll cut her in half. Let them. Go on, cut her in half, drown her. Thumbs up.

Three mothers sit, as they have sat all afternoon, on the bank, their backs to the river, sunning their newest-born and watching their other children playing in the hay. They make a stir. "Time to be getting home." They congratulate one another on the success of the afternoon. "Never thought they'd a-been so good, hot as it is. Ernie! Harry! Sylvie! Come you home to tea."

Sylvie, who has been made to wear gloves, has turned even that to account by picking nettle leaves and placing a handful in the dent of every trilby hat in the line of seated onlookers.

The loudspeaker plays *God Save The King*. Hands go up to remove hats, fingers couch themselves among nettles.

ADRIAN BELL

MERVYN WILSON

THE CINEMA

What's Left is Celluloid . . .

THERE is more than curiosity value in *Saratoga*, Miss Jean Harlow's last film which she didn't live to finish. A comedy of the race tracks with Mr. Clark Gable as a bookie, it has points of odd documentary interest : a yearling sale attended by Miss Harlow in a silver lamé evening dress, an amusement car in the Racing Special noisy with the innocent songs of men who in this country would be busy in the third-class carriages with packs of cards. At first one may be a little repelled by the unlikelihood of such enormous good fellowship. The broad poster smile of " The Old Firm " on a racing card doesn't seem quite plausible in private life. But wait awhile and you'll find it's only the Rotarian smile after all. The bookie at the start may refuse payment of a fifty thousand dollar debt because it means foreclosing on a stud farm which is the sole joy of somebody else's " grandpop " (Mr. Lionel Barrymore makes his usual blot on a not so virgin film), but his morality isn't as strict as that for long ; he's quite crooked enough before the film's through to satisfy our passion for probability, wringing the dollars out of Miss Harlow's rich and unoffending fiancé, helped by Miss Harlow who double-crosses her fiancé by tipping the wrong horses. Later she has a quarrel with the bookie and double-crosses him, but that cross doesn't come off, the millionaire retires baffled by these bewildering moralities, and Mr. Gable and Miss Harlow are left together in the happy expectation of a lifetime of false tips and bought jockeys. Tough and conscienceless, containing one admirable scene of carnal comedy with a nerve specialist, *Saratoga* is one of Miss Harlow's better films, though there is no sign that her acting would ever have progressed beyond the scope of the rest-less shoulders and the protuberant breasts : her technique was the gangster's technique— she toted a breast like a man totes a gun. The film has been skilfully sewn-up, and the missing scenes and shots lend it an air of originality which the correctly canned product mightn't have had : the story proceeds faster, less obviously : the heroine is less unduly plugged. The psychological transitions have a surface obscurity similar to those of living people, and not the steady movie progression from love to jealousy to reconciliation.

The old Irene Dunne, not the new groomed Dunne of *Theodora Goes Wild*, appears in *High, Wide and Handsome*. She plays a showgirl, oh so generous and unspoilt, in the 1850's who loves and marries a Pennsylvanian farmer. He discovers oil, gets too busy fighting the wicked railroad trusts, neglects her ; so she goes back to the road and returns only in the nick of time with the elephants and trick riders of her circus to defeat the hired toughs who are breaking up his pipe-lines. There are two hours of this long, dumb and dreary picture (" so good that it might have been inspired "— Mr. Carroll) ; the story doesn't really get under way for an hour ; and one is left with a few dim distressing memories : Miss Dunne splashing and kerning away in her bathtub while Mr. Mamoulian's camera pans coyly round the kitchen, carefully avoiding her till it fetches up for climax on the glossy face and the shiny knees and the dis-creet soapsuds : Miss Dunne singing beside the farm horse (Miss Dunne is the one without the white patch on her forehead) : a song by Mr. Kern about " Darby and Joan who used to be Jack and Jill ", and masses of irrelevant Mamoulian blooms flowering at the right, the sentimental, time : nature panting to keep abreast with studio passions, flowering for first love and falling for separation.

His Affair, on the other hand, is exactly what a melodrama should be : the best American melodrama of the year, a tough story of bank robbers set in Edwardian times to give it a light and spurious romance. The boater and the belted waist take the too-sweetness off the love, and we don't mind suspending the disbelief we should normally feel when the President of the United States personally sets a young naval officer to track down men his whole Secret Service has failed to catch, because we get so much in return : admirable acting by Mr. Robert Taylor and Mr. Victor MacLaglen and quick and cunning direction which gives us from the first shot an expectation of the worst, so that this shocker does — however fallaciously — carry about it a sense of doom, of almost classic suspense in the skittle alley and the music-hall.   GRAHAM GREENE

'What's the meaning of this, man—are you stark, staring mad ?'

CROQUET

"There's a Breathless Hush.."

REMEMBERING nothing much of croquet beyond (aged eight) back-heeling the ball through a hoop on a lawn stodgy with daisies and wormcasts, and afterwards glancing down with sneaky pride at my mallet, I was exercised as to what one wore to the England *v.* Australia match at Roehampton last Friday and Saturday ; for it is almost a truth that the apparel of the spectators is the barometer of the status of a game. Should I wear a bustle and tittup along like a jolly little centaur ? Should I wear leather in rust reds and Imperial yellows like the young women in the Lucky Strike advertisements ? To my mind, croquet was a music-hall joke, a game comparable with the self-conscious cricket played in top-hats by humorous colonels in aid of hospital charities.

A murrain on my cattle if I seem to sneer. Croquet is a serious and scientific business, as I have discovered by reading two books. One is *Croquet* by Arthur Lillie, a champion of the '80's, and the other is *A Handbook of Modern Croquet*, published by Longman's and helpfully recommended by Slingsby a week or so ago in NIGHT AND DAY.

Just in case one or two readers know as little about croquet as I did a few days previously, let me tell them a thing or two. Croquet derives from the old game of pele-mele, played by Charles II in St. James's Park. It was a becoming pastime for the gentry, as Waller testifies :

" Here a well-polished Mall gives us the joy
　To see our prince his matchless force employ.
　His manly posture and his graceful mien,
　Vigour and youth in all his members seen,

No sooner has he touched the flying ball
　But 'tis already more than half the Mall ;
　And such a fury from his arm has got
　As from a smoking culverin 'twere shot."

Croquet, as such, was introduced into England in 1847 by a Miss Macnaghten. It was still an average sissy game, but it got tougher. The first great tournament, inaugurated by the game's first titan, a Mr. Walter Jones Whitmore, was played at Moreton-in-Marsh in 1868. After a period of boom and a following period of trance, croquet was revived once again in 1894 by a Mrs. Hill, of Cheltenham. From that time onwards it has held favour with a fierce and scientific minority.

Bustle and dundreary jokes haven't killed it. The game itself has evolved considerably during the course of its history, and now laugh at your peril.

Last weekend's play was the fourth in a series of five Test Matches, the fifth to be played at Brighton on September 4 and 6. Up to now England has been victorious. Roehampton, with its faintly Monet topography, saw good weather on both days, though a nasty little wind whipped up on Saturday. A small but reverent gallery followed the game, which is just as jolly to watch as chess. The linesmen—if I am not calling them out of their names—present a touch of dreariness in their black coats ; they look a little like undertakers who have somehow mislaid the body.

Now I am well aware that to all the contemplative sports a good-mannered silence should be accorded, but somehow I had subconsciously connected croquet with a pretty light-hearted chitterchatter under the elms and a little flirtatious badinage between opponents. Seing one solitary player upon each court grimly driving the ball about with no opponent in sight, I thought he was just practising ; and it was not until a perfectly strange lady, whom I had taken to be somewhat of a friend of mine, gave me a viciously dirty look, that I realized I must preserve breathless decorum. Later I noticed this note in the programme : " Spectators are requested to abstain from audible comments while the game is in progress, to remain silent during the playing of any stroke, and not to move after the stance of a player has been taken." I apologize. But I only said " When do they start ? " and my friend said " Why doesn't he let someone else have a go ?"

After the merited rebuke, I settled down to watch the match and was surprised to see what an exact and thoughtful business croquet is. It is necessary to bring to it an extreme foresight, exactitude and coolness of nerve, because a single unwary or a single brilliant shot can reverse the tenor of a whole game. There seemed to be no opportunity for *bravura* playing ; though Mr. Colman, of England, and Mr. Miller, captain of the Australian team, both did a smoking culverin occasionally. At a croquet match you don't applaud very much, no matter how exciting it all is. Happily I didn't try to.

The game ended in a fourth victory for England. In the singles Mr. Miller (Australia) beat Lieut.-Col. W. B. Du Pre (England), Miss Steel (England) beat Mr. Windsor (Australia). In the doubles Mr. C. F. Colman and Mr. R. Tingey (England) beat Mr. E. M. Hunt and Mr. A. B. Morrison (Australia). In this game, incidentally, neither sex nor muscles matter, though in the '80's there was a certain lady who, hampered by her clothing, would bend her knees as she struck the ball, so adding a push " neither graceful nor fair ". No lady croquet player, even today, plays in trousers. On the other hand, her dress is not long enough, nor voluminous enough, to get all tangled up in her mallet.

PAMELA HANSFORD JOHNSON

Beauty re-born

Elizabeth Arden maintains that there is no face so lost to beauty that it cannot be transformed, revivified, remodelled. To this end, she has now created, with the aid of a Continental specialist in electro-therapy, the **INTRA-CELLULAR MASK.** It is designed to promote the health of the actual cells which comprise the tissues of the face by means of a new method of adapting micro-waves to this particular purpose, and is an outstanding achievement. For women over thirty, for women whose tissues have become depleted through illness or worry whatever their age, the Intra-Cellular Mask treatments are invaluable. The Intra-Cellular Mask, itself, is a simple, perfectly co-ordinated electrical device, conforming in every detail to the rigid tests imposed by Miss Arden and the scientist who designed it with her. The treatment is always given by a graduate nurse, trained especially in electro-therapy work. It is followed by Miss Arden's Muscle Strapping treatment and proper make-up, which are included in the price of the complete course. *Course of Six Intra-Cellular Treatments — 10 guineas.*

Elizabeth Arden Ltd.

ELIZABETH ARDEN 25 OLD BOND STREET, LONDON W.1

MEDITATION IN THE BELLY OF A WHALE

P. Y. Betts

PRICES have gone up in France. You have to pay 4d. for a private bathroom now, at least in Dijon.

" For thirty francs," said Madame (thirty francs is now about five shillings), " for thirty francs I can let you have a handsome room with a large bed and a private bathroom adjoining. A newly-sprung bed," she added, " immensely comfortable and big enough to accommodate three full-grown persons at their ease."

" But I have no wish to have three full-grown persons at ease in my bed," I objected, " and I don't especially want a bath either."

I'd come straight off the Domodossola-Paris train, in a compartment where a Milanese family with three atrabilious children of the early-Mussolini type, having hung up the bambino's diapers to dry on the heating pipes under my seat, had invited me to share their meal of salami, goat cheese and oranges. The hotel proprietress gave me just a look.

" At least a private bath," I yielded, as her nostrils began to twitch. " Have you no cheaper room than that ? "

She made a gesture as if to wash her hands of the whole affair.

" Eh bien, there remains one other room. A small, dark room, immediately above the kitchens, looking out upon a courtyard belonging to a butcher who occasionally slaughters a pig or two out there. . . . At other times the courtyard is comparatively tranquil. There is, of course, no bathroom. The bed is narrow. The price of this room is twenty-eight francs," she said, eyeing me malevolently.

I gave in. The bathroom seemed worth the extra fourpence—if the worst came to the worst I could sublet two-thirds of my immense bed and take in washing. So I filled in the usual form and followed the chambermaid upstairs to my room.

It was a great big room, done all in shiny dark grey paint, with deep red curtains and bedcover, and a frilly red silk lampshade by the bed and red drugget on the floor. With all that arterial red and glossy elephant-grey there was something faintly anatomical about the look of the place, as if somebody at the Natural History Museum had had the idea of fitting up the belly of a whale as a bedroom. Out of it led the bathroom, shiny, gurgling, windowless—the whale's appendix. The bath itself was fullsize but designed in the hip-bath manner, excessively deep for its length and tailored to fit the figure, if one had a figure ; if not, not.

Hanging on a hook on the wall there was a long white cloak of Turkish towelling, complete with hood, evidently intended to enfold the steaming body as it stepped out of its tailored bathtub. I had never seen its like before. I tried it on. It was quite becoming in a macabre way, like a piece of Klu Klux Klan regalia. I mopped and mowed about in it in front of the looking-glass for a while, until a straggly spider of the sort that frequents waste pipes dropped out of the hood into the bath and bolted down the drain. After that I laid the cloak aside.

There was a printed notice by the door, setting forth in French and English the regulations of the house :

It is recommended to the customers nevers to use electric light for the branching of heating or other apparatus.

It is forbidden to the customers to wash linen in the washhand-stands and to trow in them any objets, hairs, fruits, etc. KEEP THE COCKS CLOSED.

This piqued me to defiance. As there were no fruits handy, nor any apparatus which lent itself to branching, and as I judged hair-trowing to be a finicking, un-English kind of sport, I contented myself with opening the cocks, both of which were marked Chaud. Both ran cold. After about ten minutes, just as the right-hand cock was beginning to yield a lukewarm flow, I wearied of my daredevilry and closed the cocks again. The bath by this time was full of cold water, which during the next three-quarters of an hour continued to seep slowly away, impeded no doubt by the macédoine of fruits, hairs and objets thrown down the plug-hole by former customers.

This fruit-and-hair-throwing business is plainly quite a problem in France, for you may see in almost any hotel notices asking visitors to abstain from it. I am broadminded enough to see that it takes all kinds to make a world, if you must make a world, but the sport, as a sport, leaves me cold. It is possible that for people who find themselves in the situation of Greta Garbo in *Queen Christina*, snowbound in an hotel bedroom for the inside of a week with nothing to help pass the time except a foreign ambassador and unlimited supplies of black grapes, there may be a certain recreative value in throwing the grapes, at least, down the plug-hole—indeed it will be remembered that towards the end of her visit, when the thaw set in, the Queen was pleased to signify her satisfaction with the entertainment provided by crawling round the room embracing the furniture—but for the ordinary tourist, who has to pay for his own fruit anyway, it seems a pretty dim sort of sport. Presumably there is a close season for fruit-throwing, though you can chuck your hair and objects about all the year round ; but I don't really know; in fact I dissociate myself utterly from this niggling game, which lacks even the madcap thrill of cock opening.

I spent four nights in my whale-belly suite. What with the stopped-up drain and the vagaries of the hot-water system, I was never actually able to take a hot bath during that time, so except for the social cachet which the occupation of a room with a private bath gave me in the eyes of the hotel servants I might have saved myself that extra fourpence a night ; especially as on the morning of the fifth day I discovered that the courtyard my room looked out on happened also, by a coincidence, to belong to a butcher who occasionally slaughtered a pig or two out there.

At other times the courtyard was comparatively tranquil.

Pins and Needles

COMMENT ON FASHIONS

Lido Beach

THE disappointing thing about clothes is the people who wear them. The Venice Lido is called one of the most fashionable bathing resorts in Europe, and it is probably the most cosmopolitan. Yet even at the height of the season the beach outfits, on which thousands of pounds have been spent, for the most part fail to ring the bell. The reason being, I suppose, that so many of them are worn by those who have grown fat as they waxed rich. All those darling playsuits and little sea-pelts and swaggering beach-coats which were—in the London, Paris, New York, and Vienna shops—so full of hope and promise . . . *tu Marcellus eris.*

The Lido is some three miles long, hidden behind solid rows of bathing boxes and *stabilimentos.* Only about three-quarters of a mile is fashionable, and if you happen to turn in the wrong direction on landing from Venice you are quite likely to find yourself in the Municipal Baths with a bar of Primrose Soap. Even of the fashionable three-quarters of a mile, a certain 300 yards is considered more desirable than the rest. This is the beach of the Excelsior Palace Hotel, and the people who are not within the 300 yards spend most of their time yearning through the wire fence at those who are. Not that there is any difference in the beach or the sun or the sea. But it is the fate of the fashionable, as well as of prize cattle, to spend their time in enclosures, and if you have elected to go on show at all, you naturally want to be in the very best pen. The beach is on the level of the garden and is lined with two rows of *capanne.* These *capanne* with their awnings,

cushioned chairs, and camp-beds for sunbathing, are all in vivid colours, so that the general effect is very gay. The beach is raked over every morning and, contrary to what the blasé lead you to expect, the Lido sand is really good sand, and the Adriatic does have a slight tide, and it is a very nice blue with no cigarette-ends or cabbage-leaves floating about. The temperature of the water feels as if the hot and cold taps had been turned on about equally. This means that bathers can wander about in full make-up and coiffure without being forced by cold to swim or splash vigorously and thus risk disaster. Apart from this warmth, the chief differences between bathing at the Lido and at Weymouth is that the floating millionaires you bump into are less likely to hit back than Weymouth's squealing children, and that when you are idly

swimming along in a doze you know you are coming up upon somebody else by a waft of some perfume such as Lanvin's Arpège.

As for clothes, the first, last, and really the only essential, is an even sun-tan all over. Without this, it is impossible to look smart on a beach. This is interesting to note after the beauty specialists' efforts at the beginning of the summer to make sunburn unfashionable. Those who have only lately arrived and have omitted to get themselves done in the garden or on the roof at home creep away into corners and get busy in solitude with bottles and tubes. No well-dressed

man nowadays wears a bathing dress. Shorts only—and it is amazing what waist measurements can be had in shorts. Men are disappointingly timid about beach-coats. The majority of them at the Lido wear their dressing-gowns, or what appear to be their dressing-gowns. The women's sandals all had high heels. When worn with shorts, this gives a peculiar farmyard strut, and nobody loves a hen. Shorts should *never* be worn with high heels. But they seem to be more becoming than long trousers or culottes. One of the worst things I noted was a buttoning-up skirt unbuttoned down the centre back. Very queer effect. And there was one woman, who couldn't be expected to know better, in a striped dress like a nightmare neapolitan ice. Not only a dress—but also a bandeau headdress tied in a fly-away bow centre-front, and a playsuit under the dress, and a parasol, and a bag, all in the nightmare neapolitan ice. It's foolish to stake your beach success on a thundering clash of colour. Lie low on the Lido is the motto of the wise. Plain navy-blue wool suits were worn more than any others by the French and the Italians, and white, as ever, proved best for shorts and for lunching dresses. Venetian reds and oranges looked good on some of the younger and browner. Handkerchiefs were tied round most heads instead of bathing caps, which shows to what depths the bathing went. A few wore dress-maker suits in the sea, but they were not a success. The United States was responsible for some of the worst horrors in strolling-about get-ups. But most of the. Kings and Queens of Industry seemed to be over without their charming daughters, so that it is hardly fair to judge the taste of this generation of Americans by the specimens on exhibit.

Vulgarity is appetizing in small portions at well-spaced intervals, and in any case the fashionable Venice Lido is not altogether a case of give a dog a good name. In fact it is an excellent place to spend a day or two. One might even stay three days if one had an interesting book to read.

ALISON HAIG

Those Stately Homes—1

Osborne House

IN a memorable passage of his great work Proust described how, on meeting Mme de Guermantes at last, Swann realized at once the significance of a variety of little social tricks and verbal inflexions he had encountered and speculated about during his life in Society—they were all based on the behaviour of the aristocratic prototype whom he saw before him. Much the same sensation is experienced by the architecturally-minded visitor to the Isle of Wight on first seeing Osborne : all those round-headed Italianate windows, those square flat-topped watch-towers with which Ryde and Ventnor are so lavishly supplied are now explained—their origin is undoubtedly, if indirectly, royal.

In 1845 the newly-married Royal Pair paid a visit to the Island and, being much struck with its possibilities as a royal holiday resort, straightway purchased the Osborne estate. In Queen Victoria's eyes its greatest advantage lay in its nearness to Spithead, which would be very gratifying to the Fleet " and so nice for our boys ". For Albert its chief charm was the view, which reminded him very forcibly of Naples—a resemblance which strikes one to-day as being a trifle elusive. The actual house, a plain eighteenth-century building of which nothing now remains but a rather fine portico incorporated in the royal kitchen-garden, struck them both as being quite unsuitable, and Albert at once set about designing an imposing residence worthy both of its occupants and of the Bay of Naples. The architect employed, Mr.

Thomas Cubitt, President of the Royal Institute of Engineers, worked under the constant supervision of the Prince Consort, which possibly explains the merit of much of the detail and the extreme inconvenience of the plan. So rapidly was their joint task accomplished that the foundation-stone was laid in the same year.

" Osborne House," the official guide informs us, " was built more for comfort than for architectural effect." It is all the stranger, therefore, that whereas comfort strikes one as being conspicuously absent, much of the interior is not without architectural merit. It is probably the last large country-house to be built in the direct classical tradition of English architecture, and though that tradition might have produced something a great deal better in the hands of Barry or Cockerell, Osborne has its own lowly place in " the architecture of humanism ".

However, it is not for its architectural beauties but for the sake of the artistic treasures it contains that one makes the pilgrimage to Osborne— and how rich is one's reward ! Fully to appreciate the value of the collection one must always bear in mind that " Art for memory's sake " was the chief tenet of Queen Victoria's æsthetic faith. This charming marble statue of a chubby lad clasping a quantity of grapes, labelled " Autumn ", is obviously a work of art of a high order ; but how much deeper is one's appreciation when one realizes that it is H.R.H. the Duke of Edinburgh at a tender age. That mournful marble collie opposite, which one recognized at once as being a masterpiece of canine portraiture, is raised to a higher plane by the knowledge that it represents Noble, " for many years a favourite companion of Queen Victoria. Died at the age of 14 years ".

While all the statuary, with the possible exception of a bust of Caligula which makes so inexplicable a pendant to that of Princess Alice in one of the corridors, has this satisfying emotional justification, one or two of the pictures

have certain merits of their own. There is a portrait of a Rajah by Winterhalter that shows what he could achieve in portraiture when confronted with an unfamiliar subject, and which might profitably have been included in the recent Winterhalter exhibition in London. There are two delightful portraits of children by Lauchert, in which the charm is quite independent of the fact that the sitters are English princesses.

This royal treasure-house also contains a large number of objects whose value is neither directly sentimental nor, in most cases, artistic, but which are nevertheless of absorbing interest. These are the gifts to the Queen from her fellow-sovereigns and from various bodies of her loyal subjects. In the former class the presents of the Emperor of Germany are conspicuous for their number and for their exceptional nature ; so numerous and so costly are they that it is difficult to choose the best. Personally I incline towards a porcelain plate " painted in the centre in imitation of an onyx cameo with a portrait of King William III of Prussia on a gold ground in a border of flowers ", with, as runner-up, a fine trio of enormous vases—the two smaller decorated with dashing battle scenes from Prussian history, the largest bearing a truly colossal *backfisch* clad in classical draperies, emblematic, so the catalogue informs us, of Peace. In the latter class the Archbishop of Malta's

offering of a bouquet of tinsel flowers twined round a gold paper mitre is undoubtedly the prettiest ; the model of a half-timbered house in ebony and mother-of-pearl, presented by the women of Stockport, the most ingenious ; the twisted elephant's tusk cleverly converted into the likeness of a giant cobra by the addition of a silver snake's-head, the gift of the Arab community of Mombasa, the most inconvenient.

Curiously enough, of all the sights of Osborne, it is not the great Durbar Room (decorated in the most approved styles of Indian art by local workmen under the expert direction of Bhai Ram Singh) ; nor the tulipwood piano enriched with enamel plaques reproducing the most celebrated works of Raphael ; nor the ivory back-scratcher (Dutch work, late 19th century), the daring and improbable gift of some Eastern potentate ; nor even the Swiss châlet in the garden, filled with a fascinating collection of natural objects made by the Royal children themselves, that linger longest in the memory—but an indifferent portrait of one whose connection with the house and its inhabitants was of the slightest. On the table in the drawing-room there stands a water-colour of Elizabeth of Austria. She is looking out from a large black frame heavily encrusted with Imperial emblems, cutting dead the late Duke of Cambridge, whose bovine whiskered features stare from a coloured photograph on the same table. One has encountered that lovely face, far more faithfully rendered, on the walls of a dozen continental palaces, but here the very incongruity of the setting underlines the charm. It is presumably a memento of that day when Elizabeth came over from Freshwater for luncheon : the only occasion on which the two Empresses met. What, one wonders, did they, who had nothing but their rank and their loneliness in common, talk about in that cosy dining-room with all those dear familiar faces smiling down from the canvases of Von Angeli and Winterhalter ? But that, thank Heaven, is something which even Mr. Housman will never know.

OSBERT LANCASTER

NEW BOOKS

Companion to Fleming

"AS a matter of fact, I'm going back to Europe by that route. You can come with me if you like."

" I beg your pardon, it's my route and it's I who'll take you, if I can think of some way in which you might be useful to me."

With this exchange of civilities began an association which has already provided the material for one highly enjoyable travel book. The route was from Peking to India by way of North-West China, the Kokonor and Kashgar. Owen Lattimore had made the

---

Forbidden Journey. Ella K. Maillart. Heinemann. 12s. 6d.

99 *Wimpole Street.* Dr. *Johnston Abraham.* Chapman and Hall. 5s.

---

journey in 1927. Since then there had been a complete and rather sinister silence from the large province of Sinkiang ; the Chinese were unwilling to let Europeans discover how much they had lost control ; the Russians still more unwilling to reveal how much they had assumed it. Both newspapers and governments had an interest in obtaining authentic information and thus, at the beginning of January 1935, two journalists who had both made themselves prominent in their own countries for their enterprise found one another simultaneously in Peking, Miss Maillart for the *Petit Parisien* and Mr. Fleming for *The Times,* both fired with precisely the same ambition. It is interesting to speculate what would have happened if they had decided not to travel together. I like to think of them plodding across the desert, aloof and watchful, pitching their tents on opposite slopes.

" Miss Maillart, I presume ? "

" Sir, I am not aware that I have the honour of your acquaintance."

" Miss Maillart's compliments to Mr. Fleming and will he kindly refrain from shooting over her camp ? "

And of their meeting later in London or Paris. " I believe you know my friend Ma. . . ."

But they decided to join up. When one thinks of the dark suspicions with which one regards a fellow-passenger in the opposite corner of a railway carriage, of the savage hostility with which one discovers an alien suitcase in a second-class sleeper, of the infinite heart-searchings with which a week-end party to Le Touquet is arranged, one is left gasping at the heroism of Miss Maillart's decision. The subsequent perils and endurances of the journey can add little to our wondering esteem. She counted up the advantages and disadvantages. She appreciated " Peter's brilliant intelligence and his faculty of being able to eat anything and sleep anywhere "—qualities rarely found in conjunction, qualities, in fact, that for any other journey than the one projected would render him supremely incompanionable. She " appreciated still more his horror of any distortion of facts and the native objectivity with which he recounted them ". Well, there's no accounting for tastes. Personally if I were choosing a companion for a journey I can think of no one who would commend himself less to me than an inveterate debunker. There was a major in Brazil ; there was a peer in China . . . one would have to be very sure of one's stamina, dignity, freedom from laughable idiosyncrasies before one chose Mr. Fleming. Also one would have to be pretty sure of one's literary ability before inviting a successful fellow-writer to accompany one, whose avowed intention was to write a rival account of every incident. Last, and to my mind worst, Mr. Fleming had " opinions on dramatic art ". That would have been the end, as far as I was concerned.

A further radical difference of temperament was revealed later. Miss Maillart travelled because she liked being abroad, Mr. Fleming because he liked covering ground. He wanted to be in Scotland for the grouse ; she was quite prepared to spend the rest of her life in the desert. " Peter was furious,

I was enchanted " when the caravan was dishonestly held up at Sian. " Every night Peter would repeat his refrain : ' Sixty *lis* nearer to London.' He did it to annoy me ". They were travelling, too, towards an immediate destination where Mr. Fleming would be at home and rather famous, and Miss Maillart would be strange and unknown, where she would be known as " the French girl who travelled with Peter Fleming ". There was every human cause for disagreement, but the association was a brilliant success. The reading public are the gainers by two excellent books. One may be perfectly sure that either writer would have ruthlessly exposed any failing of the other, and the lightness of their banter gives testimony to the mutual esteem with which the journey ended. This is not the place to retrace the various stages of the march. It is enough to say that, however much one enjoyed *News From Tartary*, one can still read every word of *Forbidden Journey* with delight— with greater delight, in fact, from being able to correlate the two descriptions of each incident. Miss Maillart is less consciously literary than Mr. Fleming and less verbally witty, but she allows herself the luxury of an occasional touch of romance and of those Latin suspicions of British policy that are always a treat to English readers. A thoroughly respectable book.

99 *Wimpole Street* is a book of essays by Dr. Johnston Abraham, whose *Surgeon's Log* was a popular travel book in the gentle days when readers demanded less strenuous feats than those of Miss Maillart and Mr. Fleming. It is easy reading and should form a mild palliative to the corrosive action of Dr. Cronin. In a mellow, ruminative, rather trite manner Dr. Abraham discusses why women dress, what doctors think about novelists, the romance of medicine and other semi-professional topics. He gives some advice about holiday resorts for invalids and some popular sketches of the history of medicine. A nice bedside book.

EVELYN WAUGH

*

And some of us, myself included, if we found ourselves sitting at a switchboard of the telephone exchange for a few hours, would not only learn how wrong numbers happen so frequently but also what it is like to have one's ear drums blasted by an irate subscriber.—*Godfrey Winn in the* DAILY MIRROR.

We're sure you would, Godfrey— in almost no time.

Paul Crum

'*Ah, Percy! Perhaps* you *can think of a good reference number.*'

THE THEATRE

Time and the Conways

IN *Time and the Conways* (excellently produced by Miss Irene Hentschel at the Duchess Theatre) Mr. Priestley has written a play of brilliant dramatic quality ; the construction is economical and subtle ; its power to hold and at times to move an audience is beyond question ; its characters are presented in the round. As " theatre " it gets full marks. Its philosophic content seems to me jejune, arbitrary, and unoriginal ; but you can't, after all, have everything.

The first act shows us the Conways celebrating Kay's 21st birthday in 1919. The war is over ; hopes are high. Kay means to write, and cherishes immortal longings for an Ivory Tower. The pretty Hazel aspires to a handsome husband. Robin, just demobilized, looks on the world of commerce as his oyster. Madge is afire to put a battered world to rights in countless committees. Mrs. Conway, vaguely optimistic, looks forward to the half-forgotten compensations of family life in peace-time ; and Carol, her youngest, asks no more than to be allowed to live, a process to which she brings a lyrical and disarming spontaneity.

Having presented us to this agreeable and auspiciously situated family, Mr. Priestley borrows (without, rather surprisingly, acknowledgment) Mr. Dunne's *Experiment With Time*, and assumes that time is like a piece of string, so that two points in time may, by virtue of loops and twists in the string, find themselves in juxtaposition. Kay is one of the rare beings who possess the kind of second sight necessary for a manœuvre roughly analogous to cutting in at the fifteenth after playing eight holes ; and from the first-act *feu de joie* of high hopes we switch, in the second, to the disillusionment of the present day. The present day is hell, as far as the Conways are concerned. They've lost their money, their looks, and their charm. Kay's Ivory Tower has shared the fate of other castles in contemporary Spain ; she works as a sob-sister in Fleet Street, interviewing film stars and feeling pretty bad about it. Robin drinks. His wife is a misery. Madge's ideals, roughly handled by the post-war world, have turned sour and so has she. Nothing has happened to Carol (who wanted only to live) except that she has died. The romantic Hazel is married to a common little bully (brilliantly played by Mr. Mervyn Johns). Silly, likeable Mrs. Conway groans under the twin burdens of an overdraft and filial ingratitude. Only Alan, the quiet, dim son, is—in a quiet, dim way—content with his insignificant and shabby destiny. Him Mr. Priestley endows with a great air of understanding, and he enunciates the rudiments of a philosophy which appeared to me to be that of a Chinese peasant, greatly simplified. This part was very finely played by Mr. Raymond Huntley.

And so back to 1919 in the third act. Charades and chatter have now a facile but effective poignancy, for we know the drab doom in store for these bright creatures ; and Miss Jean Forbes-Robertson, whose performance as Kay is throughout sure and sensitive, intimates most skilfully the extent to which she shares our knowledge. But in the third act—though as entertainment and in technical merit it is not below the very high level reached and maintained elsewhere—doubts which we began to have in the second act are at least half-confirmed. Mr. Priestley has given these Conways too raw a deal. The law of averages does not exist ; and it is quite possible that eight out of the nine members of a

---

During Miss Elizabeth Bowen's absence on holiday, plays will be reviewed this month by Mr. Peter Fleming, Mr. Malcolm Muggeridge, Miss Antonia White and Mr. Richard Jennings.

given family circle—normal, healthy, intelligent, and rather charming people—will reap in 20 years nothing but the bitter fruits of despair. It is possible ; but oughtn't Mr. Priestley to tell us why—apart from having been born into the twentieth century—*all* the Conways had to have such a perfectly beastly time ? The curse that Mr. Priestley puts on his characters is as arbitrary and as comprehensive as if Kay had been given the eye of an Eastern idol on her 21st birthday. In the absence of any funny business of this sort, I can't help feeling that the Conways, in Acts I and III, might have done something to deserve what they got in Act II. *Time and the Conways* is an admirable play, which everybody ought to see ; but the *very* best playwrights—of whom Mr. Priestley is potentially one—usually get their tragic characters to load the dice against themselves, to cross their own stars. It is surely neither true nor truly dramatic to regard Time—even our own sad sector of it—as an inexorable sausage-machine, converting every gay piglet into sequent sausages of sorrow. Mr. Priestley, for one, has somehow weathered the post-war years.

Wanted for Murder

There is a lot to be said for *Wanted For Murder*, the melodrama with which the Lyceum is now reverting to tradition. It features the homicidal pervert, today an established favourite on the English stage ; and it infuses into the story of his downfall a proper and portentous urgency. And yet this melodrama is like most veal and ham pies ; there isn't enough ham. When Miss Louise Hampton (the accused's mother, rather arbitrarily inset) brings down the house, we are reminded of what is missing. At the Lyceum you've got to lay on tears and laughter with a trowel ; psychology and sociology—both featured in this play—are out of place. More suspense, more heroics, more black, more white : that's what this melodrama needs. Still, it's a good evening's entertainment as it stands.

PETER FLEMING

ALL=IN WRESTLING

Actors at Blackfriars

THE Ring, formerly a church, is sometimes used for performances of Shakespeare. But not tonight.

It may amuse you to consult your programme and (such are the refinements of " sporting " prose) to try to distinguish if you can between a Star International Heavyweight Match, a Stupendous Heavyweight Clash, a Classic Heavyweight Contest, a Supreme Heavyweight Match, a Stupendous Heavyweight Attraction, and an Ultra Star Heavyweight Battle of Battles. Presently two large men will be taking off their dressing-gowns in opposite corners of the ring, and it will become clear at once that for many in the crowd one is a hero and one a villain. The wrestlers, aware of this, will play their parts properly. The hero will smile at awkward moments, the villain will scowl continuously ; the hero will draw attention to the cleanness of his tactics, the villain will kick out behind like a two-legged mule.

Here is some of the best acting in London. Like Miss Lilian Braithwaite or Miss Marie Tempest, handsome George Pencheff (" the Golden Idol ") and well-known Jack Pye (" the Doncaster Panther ") have an audience to consider, and their audience is all round them. The acting is a sort of stylized realism. The equivalent of a " good line " is a particularly undignified position, and like a good line it deserves, and gets, a good laugh.

Even a drawing-room comedy should be as far as possible a good spectacle, and a good spectacle the Ring can certainly offer. Those two large bodies so curiously entangled, what do they resemble so much as a gigantic *netsuké*, some freakish ivory produced by a craftsman with a distinctly Asiatic

imagination ? And this big-bellied person who has just stepped into the ring, no wonder his figure provokes from the gallery a loud rhetorical question, " 'Ere, 'oo's the farver ? "

Your attention, I notice, is confused by the shrill female behind us. Take a look at her : one of nature's viragoes or tricoteuses. Her hair is coppery, but dark near the parting, having grown since it was last tinted. Her nails are smudged with scarlet and not too clean at the extremities. There is hair on her forearms and dandruff on her royal-blue satin shoulders. The diamonds on her fingers are real and were not cheap ; her lipstick has come off on her cigarette ; her voice is exacerbating ; and next to her is the mate she deserves and has got, a flashily dressed man with a moist mouth and an ignoble forehead. She has vitality, he has life, but—" *dites, Monsieur Vollard, c'est effrayante, la vie !* " Half her pleasure is in heckling ; the other half below the belt. Directly a pair of wrestlers steps into the ring, she picks her favourite and encourages him against his opponent : " Knee him, Johnny ! " " Sling him out here ! " " Go on, rough-house him ! " " Break it off ! " " Kick him in the guts ! "

Would this audience demur if the rules were relaxed, if tempers were irrevocably lost, if the Greek Goliath suddenly began to tear the Glasgow Torpedo limb from limb, to gouge out his eyes, to rend his mouth to right and left with inserted thumbs ? I think not. It would have gained what is called a thrill ; it would have something to write home about.

Here, potentially, is a scene of ferocity from late Roman times, a gladiatorial show ; but the British Empire is evidently not decaying from self-indulgence and excess, it is rather thriving on its legacy of puritanism and " playing the game". This wrestling is a game, an exercise, that may teach a man how to fall, but teaches him less well than ju-jutsu, and is a less impressive proceeding than wrestling in Japan, where wrestlers are caught young and fattened like geese and learn to play a game

more ritualistic than cricket.

A black man and a white man have entered the ring. The " Black Butcher " has an amiable and mischievous expression, and it presently becomes clear that he is a bit of a comedian. The white man looks equally good-natured. We are a long way from the world where lynchings happen. The black man is down. " Rabbit ! " urges a voice from the crowd, and " Scissors ! " These are technical terms.

The rabbit punch : a smart blow on the top of the spine.

The scissors : to compress one's opponent's belly between one's thighs.

The aeroplane scissors : to raise one's opponent, while thus gripped, from the ground and twirl him in the air and bump him sharply floorwards again.

Often it is the referee who has the roughest time. While he is crouching to see whether A's shoulders are flat on the floor, A and B roll over suddenly on top of him and flatten him on his face ; or A, reaching blindly for a hold on B, grasps and firmly twists a limb of the referee instead ; or the referee, reproving A for pulling B's hair, is attacked by A and perhaps pitched out of the ring into the second row of spectators—which may hurt them more than it hurts him.

To go back to the point that the ring is also a stage. The limelight that brings into bright focus a pair of antagonists is obviously illuminating a *drama*. The actors, like any other actors, live to score over a rival, to get the quick effect, the immediate response, the final frenzy (if possible) of approval, but how much oftener here than in " theatreland " is one able to see a genuine drama of *character*. The comic puzzled face, the look of righteous indignation, the laughing torso, the brains in the biceps, the mean or playful gesture, the spontaneous and unexpected reaction, the occasionally lost temper and its unrehearsed consequences, the sudden geranium glow of blood that makes a face more luminous than grease-paint can—really all this takes us deeper into character than the comedies of Messrs. Ian Hay and A. A. Milne.   WILLIAM PLOMER

MINUTES OF THE WEEK

High Priestess

Wondering what the Valentino fans thought of the boom in Robert Taylor, more particularly as the annual revival of *The Son of the Sheik* was taking place, we had a talk with Miss Marie Elliot, secretary to the Valentino Association. Miss Elliot, a pleasant, voluble lady who looked too young to have the record as a war nurse which she claimed, almost spiked our guns at the outset by saying : " Now do be original and take it seriously." We hadn't the heart to explain that our assignment was to take nothing seriously, so we let her rip, and she finally did have us taking it seriously. Apparently the Valentino Association in this country has nothing to do with the sexy hysteria of the American fans (the chairman and vice-chairman are men, anyway), but was founded to commemorate its hero with dignity. " Not," the prospectus says, " as the ' Matinee Idol ', an angle he disliked, but as the artist who gladly made considerable personal sacrifices

to maintain his ideals and to improve screen conditions." The commemoration is practical : it includes a Valentino Roof-Garden for the Italian Hospital in London, a Valentino Ward for children, Valentino cadets (seven of them) in the Dulwich Naval Brigade, and a lively interest, plus endowed

room, in the Embankment Fellowship Centre for unemployed men over 45 : all very remote from our red-hot memories of the playboy of *The Four Horsemen*.

Miss Elliot first came into contact with Valentino after seeing him in *Blood and Sand*. She watched him die in that film, gored in the stomach by a bull, with flaccid limbs, a sagging jaw, and an upward twist of one corner of the mouth. As that was the way Nurse Elliot had seen men die of abdominal wounds on the Western Front, she wrote to congratulate him, and Valentino wrote back, thanking her, and adding that he had never seen a man die that way : just did it intuitively. Thereafter, though they never met, Miss Elliot used to send him as critical a review of every film as she could, always getting a personal answer back. She believes he was a great artist because he achieved so much with such poor material, in days when the actor didn't have good dialogue or brilliant directors and cameramen to cover up his faults. Only three of his films were any good, she thinks —*The Four Horsemen*, *Blood and Sand* and *Monsieur Beaucaire*. She has her own lively explanation of his notorious sex-appeal, says it was something wider that appealed to animals and children as much as women : human appeal, she would call it.

★

Tea for Two

A girl we know, a rather shy girl, is going to have a baby. The other day she summoned up her courage, marched into a big London store (which shall be, as they so strangely say of vices, nameless), and asked for maternity wear. Third floor : first left, second right. Up she went. But first left, second right, yielded only a section labelled " Tea Gowns." Our friend drifted disconsolately about for a bit, in the way shy people do, and at

last had another shot at getting, so to speak, her bearings from an assistant. Second left, first right, and back she found herself among the tea-gowns. Once more she shied off, took hounds back to the lift-shaft, and made another cast. Things might have gone on like this for ever if she hadn't stubbed her toe on a mowing machine, lost her temper, and raised hell with the nearest sales-girl, who was presiding over clock-golf, hammocks, and papier-mâché gnomes. The sales-girl grasped her point at once and said that Tea-Gowns was what she wanted. They called them that, she explained, to avoid embarrassing prospective mothers. " You tell them," said our friend, " that next time I'd sooner be embarrassed."

★

Slingsby

NEW YORK BOOK=HUNT

Leona Rake

WHEN in a mad moment I undertook to scout for American books suitable for British publication I started with the preconceived idea that publishers and literary agents had books to place and wished to place them, and that I should spend every evening reading manuscripts of genius. This proved to be a laughable delusion.

The first publisher I saw had nothing to offer but a little gloomy advice. Give it all up, he said in effect, it's a dog's life. No, he had no books to show me. No, he was not expecting to have any books to show me, at any time, ever. But he was pleased (he said) to have met me.

A little dashed, for I had brought my Ford to cart home the masterworks, I proceeded to the next office. Here I was told that there existed somewhere, only they couldn't remember where, the first two chapters of a book about Icelandic peasants which when translated might or might not be worth looking at. This was their sole suggestion, so again the Ford and I were sent empty away.

My third interview was with a disgruntled man who seized delightedly on the opportunity of criticizing foreign publishers, and spent a satisfying half-hour scolding me for their narrowness of vision, want of co-operation, and unwillingness to collaborate (only he called it colloberate) with their American colleagues. He succeeded in getting a lot of peevishness out of his system, while I affected a meekness learned at my German governess's knee and never used since; we both enjoyed ourselves very much. But he had no books available, and I began to see that I must either renew my library subscription or take to reading other people's private letters.

As the days went on I became convinced that each publisher, on being warned of my approach, hurried to lock away all his books, proofs and manuscripts in a safe, but after weeks of nagging and imploring, and the free use of pathos, false cordiality, and feminine wiles, I was at last offered three works of literature.

One was a novel about Japan, said to be brimming with local colour, although written by a Rumanian living in Kansas City; one was a poetical fantasy about parents seen through the eyes of two tots aged six and four (not really a case of the patter of little pens, since the writer was adult, or as adult as such writers ever are); while the third was a comprehensive study of snakes. These common objects of the countryside have a life of their own, it appears, and this was recorded in a handsome volume lavishly illustrated.

I rejected all three, rightly, as I still think, but reluctantly, for by this time I would have accepted almost anything, even the widely advertised reprint of the Bible recently issued by an enterprising firm, complete with publishers' blurbs and recommendations by the intelligentsia. (This scheme greatly took my fancy. I do hope the book did well.) I also toyed with a vast anthology of Jewish prose and verse, arguing to myself that some of it must be good, as it covered twenty-five centuries, and surely in that time they must have produced *something* besides annoyance in Hitler.

But, before committing myself, I decided to abandon publishers for the moment in favour of literary agents.

My scientific knowledge is slight, but I have always understood that before Man existed, the earth was inhabited by jelly-like substances called amœbas. These were continually splitting into pieces which in their turn became new and perfect amœbas. It has been well said that so it is with New York literary agents, except that they are not in the least like jelly. Just as I had got to know the personnel of an office, it began splitting up and reforming into new agencies, so that I was constantly meeting the old amœbas at new addresses. This happened about three times a week and was very muddling and difficult. But, old or new, I usually found the same regretful inability to show me any books at all, or the familiar offer of a whimsical juvenile about teddy-bears or a long novel about politics in North Dakota. Most amœbas had excellent books on their lists, but someone else always had the first refusal. This immutable law also applied to publishers' lists.

I had a good deal of trouble with professional competition. Representatives of rival firms came swooping across the Atlantic and conducted in-

'He'll be a riot at the Queen's Hall.'

tensive whirlwind campaigns which left us New Yorkers panting in the rear, full of resentful respect for British hustle. They had a maddening talent for being on the spot, and were always just coming down in the elevator, laden with best-sellers, as I was waiting to go up. When at last they departed they left not a wrack behind except farm novels, sheaves of inferior verse, and immense biographies of obscure New England clergymen.

Unfortunately most books which shriek to heaven of the American scene have very little chance of wide sales in England. The very word Bronx appears to daunt the average Britisher, except of course at a bar, and I had to train myself to read everything with one ear cocked in the direction of the popular English lending-libraries. " Boots, Boots, Boots," said Rudyard Kipling. I found this a useful reminder.

For a time I stopped going to offices and frequented literary teas instead. There never was any tea, only the most vigorous Martinis, but I always found plenty of publishers. Some of them, in a genial haze, offered me great future masterpieces, all unwritten as yet, " but when he gets around to writing it, it's going to be a big book," they assured me earnestly. England is still waiting for these treasures.

Incidentally, at one such gathering I met an author. If I have not mentioned these before, it is because they play so small and insignificant a part in the New York world of letters, but they do exist, and I saw at least two during my career as a book scout.

On the whole it was, as the first publisher said, a dog's life, but oddly enough I rather enjoyed my short and unproductive excursion into the literary racket. I am not sure whether my employers enjoyed it quite so much. Anyway they have a new scout now. I wonder if the poor dear ever gets anything to read.

Literary Notes.—Most New York publishers and amœbas are just as vague, dilatory, talkative, procrastinating and unbusinesslike as other American business men, but they are uniformly friendly and charming, with one or two exceptions who are definitely Not Quite The Clean Potato.

American books are often well-written, have character, and tell a good story, but in the main they lack quality, and the exceptions are on option to another firm. Worse, nearly all of them have the grave fault of being about America.

★　　　★　　　★

Our Continental Correspondent

Salzburg in the Distance

BY now the Festival will be over and everyone who was at it will be going away. Pressure will subside in the town crowded between two rocks and strung along the unnaturally quick river. A loud hum and a routine of excitement has been imposed by the visitors. I take the norm of Salzburg to be a perpetual Sunday afternoon. Lush fresh uncut grass grows in the gardens of the silent villas, and weeds lodge in the cracks in the steps of the municipal buildings. The stucco residential streets, and the shady faubourgs at the other side of the tunnel through the rock, kept right on through August their dusty hush, disturbed only by the occasional tinkling of a piano by some unmusical child. Already the metal of autumn was on the lime-trees, and down alleys and up the wooded height the powerful quiet of autumn seemed to be waiting to come out when everybody should go.

The Salzburgers, relaxing, may fritter away on each other what is left of their tired spontaneous charm. Pulling up square to their desks, they unlock the tills and tot up the final accounts. At the banks, no longer busy with changing foreigners' money, an involuntary understanding smile will communicate itself even to the cashiers. It has been a successful season.

A highly successful season. Everywhere was booked up. There was a great last-minute trade in tickets ; the tout was in power ; the late-comer paid through the nose. There was not even standing-room in the Café Bazar, where everybody felt bound to show up at least once, so that this place became a sort of social register. At the height

of a day at the height of the season there was almost nowhere you could sit down, and certainly nowhere you could sit down without sitting by someone else, which made you feel what a gathering you were at. It was impossible not to share your café table, but less oppressive to do so with a complete foreigner. Those who secured standing-room in the Café Bazar could remain for hours craning their necks round, obliged to pay nothing, as drinks could not be served to them. The only place where it was forbidden to stand was the main bridge with the scarlet-and-white banners. If you stopped here to look at the blue-glassy panorama of mountains, a policeman coaxed you to move on. This was the only point at which Austrians interfered. Otherwise they behaved like a nice school that has had a lecture on good manners to a visiting team. Their shops were crowded with special objects that could be of little interest to them.

Articles of native dress are chiefly sold to the visitors. A good deal of excitement goes on before hotel mirrors during the first phases of dressing up. Few visitors, thus got up, look conspicuously ridiculous, though men conscious of hairless pink knees communicate their distress. The effect of the bunchy dress with the searching diaphragm-line on women is pretty neutral. It makes Englishwomen look like helpers at an English garden fête. It shows off well the American exotic make-up, jewellery and curled heads. It divides ex-débutantes sharply into two classes, the self-conciously depraved and the merely self-concious. The French only seem to buy such garments as seem to them to have an intrinsic chic, such as off-white circular belted frieze capes. These capes can only be worn by the unsloppy. The dressing-up shows the visitors to be diligently merry ; it shows that they have money to throw about, which is good for their morale and the morale of the town.

In Salzburg in August it is either very hot or very wet. In September perhaps there is a nip in the air. The August weather makes for a sort of gay lassitude : in the rain, which is dark brown and torrential, you cannot go anywhere ; in the heat you do not want to. The river protests against this feeling of lassitude with its neurotic speed. Livid, opaque as milk of magnesia, not reflecting even the bluest sky, it tears between the weed-studded embankments, split angrily by the piers of the main bridge. The social dynamo is on its right bank. On its left bank, the grand and silent part of the town is packed in under the towering bare rock. Two funiculars play up and down this rock from sources almost impossible to discover. One goes up to the fortress, the other up to a restaurant. The heights between these two salients are crowned by a forest-park, sylvan in character, full of glades and dells, in which a sort of ghostly June persists. Peasants were busy saving a second crop of hay there. Round the edge of the plateau a chipped bench faces every extensive view. Hand in hand, sentimental moral lovers in shorts and aprons make the place look like a nineteenth-century print.

After dark an inept searchlight wavers from this height, directs itself on the fortress, skids off it, picks out the façade of the cathedral, skids off

that, fumbles with innocent slyness about the roofs of the city, catches now a dome, now a pavilion lodged up among the trees on the opposite height. From near the stance of the searchlight, when you are not at the Opera, you look down dizzily over a railing and see the Festspielhaus entrance throw out its mat of hard theatrical glare. There is the nerve of Salzburg.

Almost everyone admits to hunger during the Opera. To smoke in the intervals, you go out into the open-air theatre quarried by Rheinhardt for the production of *Faust*, and stand looking

up the rock in the dark. But out here you can purchase nothing to eat. Hunger is so exalting that during a last act you practically levitate. . . . I met nobody who had been lucky enough to see Toscanini or even Bruno Walther drive away from the Festspielhaus at the end. . . . The interior of the present Festspielhaus is arty-crafty (peasant style) and stuffy : none of the proposed changes can be for the worse. The dark wood beams ruled across the heavy ceiling give you an uneasy feeling in the scalp if you are claustrophobic in any way. But the Mozarteum is elegant inside, and the little Stadttheater is a gem.

The linked empty pale-coloured squares under the rock, round and behind the cathedral, have peculiar

acoustics that make bells' echoes echo a long time and draw out the splash of the baroque fountain between weeping willows into a sigh. The façades and stretches of gravel are dazzling here. You are commanded by the grandness of the Prince Bishop. Tucked between the rock and another baroque church is a sunless cemetery of immense charnel elegance, with stone helmets on the tombs, and arcades of family vaults.

Favoured hours in Salzburg were at the Café Glockenspiel, whose flank adjoins the Cathedral square. It is from this café's veranda that you can most pleasantly watch dusk fall. The Glockenspiel tables are imperfectly screened from the square by exotic plants with long, ribbed leaves. At 6 p.m. the real Glockenspiel, or carillon, sweetly strikes out overhead the serenade from *Don Giovanni*. After dark they will floodlight the fountain with the cavorting stone horses. There is a smell of dust, awaiting tomorrow's watercart. In the last light, humble figures slant across the square from the humble streets. Chaste chilly mountain night begins to possess Salzburg. This place and hour focuses my nostalgia, now I have gone away like everyone else. Salzburg, pale with social tension, awaited silence and autumn, and I suppose those are both flowing in now.

ELIZABETH BOWEN

★

VIA MEDIA VIA DOLOROSA

There's so much to be said on either
   side,
I'll be dumb.
There's so much to be said on either
   side,
I'll hold my tongue.
For years and years I never said a word,
Now I have lost the art : my voice is
   never heard,
For my apprehension
Snaps beneath the tension
Of what is to be said on either side.

STEVIE SMITH

'*So, you see, we never had the other half cleaned.*'

NEW BOOKS

Peter Pan in Politics

 SOME weeks ago on this page I reviewed a book called, appropriately enough, *The Mind in Chains*. It consisted of a series of articles by writers who were able to claim some specialized acquaintance with their subjects, examining the defects of the present economic system and their possible improvement under Communism. It was of topical interest or, as the authors would no doubt prefer to phrase it, " contemporary significance ". Now one of the contributors, Mr. Calder-Marshall, has aspired to rewrite the book in slightly more ponderous form. He seems happily unaware of the great disadvantage at which he is working, for his colleagues, however prejudiced and in many cases half-baked, had this qualification: that they had given a fair amount of time to the study of the particular problems with which they were dealing. Mr. Calder-Marshall is still in his twenties, but this does not prevent him from describing in the most cocksure manner the social conditions of the pre-war era ; he was educated at a London day school, but he is ready to lay down the law about both public-school and state education. Broadcasting and daily journalism, two trades full of professional secrets, are treated with easy familiarity. It is thus not surprising that he sometimes makes himself rather foolish. He gives a list of important independent newspapers which does not contain the *Manchester Guardian* ; he seems unaware that English state education excludes religious instruction. " The Church," he says, speaking of elementary education and presumably of the Church of England, " lends all its power to fix its masochistic imprint on the souls of the poor." He talks of proletarian fiction as though it were the very recent discovery of a few of his friends. He does not seem to have learned that all the great stories of the world are prole-

tarian ; has he ever heard of *Piers Plowman* or the *Pilgrim's Progress*, or of the enormous, various and opulent folk-lore of his own country ? Of those he mentions as the significant novelists of today, there is only one to whom I can give any real respect and that is to the author of *Mr. Norris Changes Trains*, a book which seems to me to epitomize all that Mr. Calder-Marshall abuses as bourgeois.

He touches on one very interesting topic but fails to exploit it. That is the effect in propaganda of visual impression. We are all accustomed to verbal lies and are on our guard against them. But a photograph, and still more a cinema film, carries an almost hypnotic force of conviction. He gives a good instance of fraudulent photo-

---

The Changing Scene. Arthur Calder-Marshall. Chapman & Hall. 10s. 6d.

Coming, Sir! Dave Marlowe. Harrap. 8s. 6d.

---

graphy from the Spanish civil war. I could give dozens from the only war I saw anything of at first-hand. With the regrettable fixed idea that determines all he thinks, he takes this propaganda to be capitalist. Newspapers and cinemas are owned by rich lords ; rich lords are bloodthirsty parasites ; therefore newspapers and cinemas are the tools of exploitation. The truth, I think, is sadder and more sordid. Reports are written, photographs are taken, by people who have to earn a living. Their living is dependent on success in a scramble to get in first with the story. The editors and sub-editors are far too hurried and far too simpleminded to have any ideological preconceptions. All they want is noise and speed, so that the reading public and the audience are supplied with a dizzy succession of distortions, some wildly maligning one political side, some the other ; all figures are liable to indefinite magnification and the public, living in a comparatively tranquil world, are made crisis-minded, set a state of neurotic apprehension in which crises may very well occur. One other thought I would commend to Mr. Calder-Marshall. He must not despair

of growing up. He looks about among his very young friends and observes that they are most of them hysterically disposed to one political extreme or the other. He therefore assumes that, intellect leading, the world in ten years' time will be a scene of irreconcilable class war. But the opinions of the young are not necessarily the opinions of the future. There are always a number of political Peter Pans drifting wistfully through the woods, but it is to be hoped that Mr. Calder-Marshall, who elsewhere has shown a robust narrative talent, and even here, in this very unworthy book, some gusto in invective, will not be one of them.

Coming, Sir ! gives a more realistic and far more depressing picture of the struggle of life than *The Changing Scene*. There seems some doubt as to who is responsible for this painful document. In his preface Mr. Desmond MacCarthy claims to have suggested the work ; in *his* preface, the author, Marlowe, gives the credit to an anonymous American lady of " slightly artistic appearance ". Anyway here is the book—eminently readable. It is written with little talent and no taste. This is the author's description of an American night club—the only place of employment for which he had any real esteem: " Money had been no obstacle to the outfitters and decorators ; good taste and imagination had worked hand in hand to produce a place that attracted the élite of Gotham's Society. The ceiling was covered with black velvet and star-shaped holes gave the effect of a tropical sky. Scenes from the gardens of Versailles cunningly lighted from within, little balconies . . . all combined with a system of concealed coloured lighting to produce a wonderful effect. The lighting, controlled by the electrician, was slowly varied as the people danced to the rhythmic harmony of the Vallee orchestra ; colours were subtly blended, changing imperceptibly from purple to red, on to a soft shade of green ; then the room would be flooded with glowing amber . . . it had that rare quality of glamour." But this, and other disagreeable passages, should not discourage one. There is plenty of exciting anecdote and almost indecent self-revelation. Marlowe makes no pretensions to heroism or high-mindedness. I do not think anyone could find him a likeable character, but some queer things happened to him. He was a ship's steward, bootlegger, barman and waiter. He saw many sides of life from an odd angle. Reading it one is struck by one thing—how far more decently one behaves towards waiters than they deserve. Their attitude towards us, apparently, is one of hostility tempered by avarice, towards one another they are competitive and disloyal, resentful of discipline. There is one very significant feature. Marlowe constantly complains of the captiousness of those whom he has to serve. He never once seems to ask himself whether he is serving them with anything that is good. The idea that food and wine can be good and bad never seems to occur to him ; it is merely cheap or expensive. If his customers do not like what is brought he assumes that they are actuated by spite or arrogance. No wonder so few waiters are English. This book would make a very good text for the Colonel Blimps who delight to denounce the proletariat. But perhaps it is because Marlowe is half literary man.   EVELYN WAUGH

FICTION

THE RISING TIDE.   M. J. Farrell. (*Collins*, 7s. 6d.) A novel of the Ancestral-Mansion-March-of-Time *genre*. The ancestral mansion is Garonlea and the March of Time from Lady Charlotte McGarth, who talks to her daughter like this, " Well, but, my dear child, surely if mother says she wishes the doctor to see you, you must know she has her reasons," to Cynthia McGarth who talks to her children, Simon and Susan, like this, " Hullo, Angels ! You know Captain and Mrs. Church, don't you ? Simon, darling, you must see that Sue goes to bed at one and don't let her get drunk." A lot of hunting and talk, and two parties. The scene is Ireland.

★

FLAXMAN 1937: No. 10

'*But, darling, we were in the same house at Eton.*'

FAÇADE

A View of Architecture

Good Building and Bad Theatre

IN matters of design it has always been difficult to distinguish between passing fashion and significant trend. Mannerisms creep in so quickly, and are nourished by the dramatic publicity of architectural journals, until they become clichés as ridiculous as they are boring. The time lag in these matters is pretty constant. The speculative builder today is only trying to do (perhaps more cheaply) what the average architect was doing thirty years ago. Another thirty years and we may see the suburbs of London laid out as half-hearted " Villes Radieuses ". The indifference and occasional antagonism of public opinion to true modern architecture is largely caused by the fact that few people have ever seen a really modern building. To the press the exotic-Baroque-Romanticism of the interior decorator, the brutal forms of the functionalists, and the copyist fripperies of the traditionalists are all modern architecture, and only good for a story when the adorning sculpture is by Epstein. But architecture depends for its existence on the interest of the ordinary man, and it is therefore important to lose no opportunity of calling public attention to any example of sound vernacular design.

Such an example is the new office block for Messrs. Gilbey, in James Street, Camden Town, designed by Serge Chermayeff. A city building is primarily an element of the street, not an individual unit independent of its neighbours. A street is a channel for traffic and a street building should be capable of being appreciated by the passer-by. The architect has recognized this by curving the façade to the line of the roadway and treating it as a mobile composition. There is no necessity to stand centrally opposite it to enjoy it. It is finished white, with a tiled dado to prevent dirt and scribblings. The windows are trimly and logically spaced, the entrance well-defined and inviting. The board-room and directors' club-room, both excellently designed, are placed on the top floor, connected by sliding doors to a wide terrace overlooking Primrose Hill. The most remarkable thing about this building is that it is one of the first in England to be entirely air-conditioned. It is literally sealed, for the windows open only for cleaning purposes. The site is particularly noisy, both the streets outside being cobbled, but no air-borne sound penetrates. Vibration from a neighbouring railway-line is prevented by resting the whole building on cork blocks. The large raking letters spelling out the firm's name are not a success. Their theatrical note is out of keeping with the reticence and urbanity of the main design. Curiously enough, another excellent modern building, Peter Jones' store in Sloane Square, has this same fault. The name " Peter Jones " is scribbled weakly across the King's Road façade as though it were a box of confectionery.

A bulkier, less successful building is the new Earl's Court Exhibition Centre, completed fifty years after the opening of the original Exhibition. It is one of the largest in the world, covers nine acres of space, straddles six railway-lines, and contains four exhibition halls, three conference halls, a large swimming-pool and numerous restaurants and offices. No building of such size could fail to be impressive. At the same time no effort has been made to dispel the deadening effect of such massive scale. The amateurish little plaques over the entrance (representing industry, music, Earl's Court, games and horticulture) only serve to intensify the repellent vacancy of the walls to which they are fixed. There is no attempt to lighten the design by using flagpoles, flower-boxes or gay colouring. An exhibition centre needs more light-hearted treatment than this if it is to attract the public.

The main hall, despite its colossal scale, is not overwhelming. The effect of height is largely lessened by the strong horizontal lines of the surrounding balconies and a coarsely coffered ceiling. In the centre of the hall is the swimming-pool, its bottom formed of three movable sections, which can be raised, lowered or tilted to meet special requirements. The water is normally never emptied, as the floor rises and sinks through it. The construction of the surrounding fabric is completely exposed. Here are the bones of a vast modern building laid bare. Ducts and ventilation trunks writhe in all directions, beams of all sizes cross and interlace at varying angles and levels, different materials obtrude on the eye with bewildering effect. The mezzanine floors, containing restaurants and offices, on the other hand, contain an attempt at " decoration ". Walls are plastered with horizontal strips of wood, floors are covered with horrible modernistic patterns, and vents concealed behind arty little grilles. There is even some spidery steel furniture and a bar decorated to represent the hall of a *gasthaus*.

Undoubtedly a remarkable example of engineering and planning, this building is almost devoid of architectural merit. In no place does it rise above the level of a boiler-house. It is merely construction. Construction, Chambers Dictionary tells us, is " anything piled together ".

HUGH CASSON

THE CINEMA

A Flicker from the Flames

"IT'S feudal," a character remarks with resignation in *Marked Woman*, and there are moments of creative imagination (vivid enough to have suffered British censorship) in this picture of the night-club racket and the night-club baron which do convey some of the horror and pathos the Anglo-Saxon chronicler recorded of Stephen's reign : the exactions, the beatings and murders, and above all the hopelessness. We remember Faustus' questions and Mephistopheles' replies.

" Where are you damned ? "

" In Hell."

" How comes it then that thou art out of Hell ? "

" Why, this is Hell, nor am I out of it."

3.30 in the morning and the cars drawn up outside the Club Intime ; the new boss with the lined scorched face of Eduardo Ciannelli taking a look round while his henchman gives his pekinese an airing (the air's too stale inside for a dog), issuing his orders to the dancing partners (he owns every club in town : there's no escape) ; the trailing of the long evening gowns down the pavement to the shabby digs as the milkman goes his rounds ; the routine murder of a young man who has paid with a phoney cheque ; the impregnability of the baron in his tenth-floor flat with his seedy lawyers. It's been done before, of course, this picture of the feudal hell, but it has never been done better than in some of these scenes : the awful contrast between the Rotarians' liquored cheer-fulness in the early hours with the bad champagne and the sentimental songs, and the next morning, when one of them has been found dead in the river, and the little sober shamefaced group drifts into the police station to identify their dance companions ; the spirituous poetics of the middle-aged lecher in the roof garden—" Those stars . . . they remind me . . . that moon, you've only to ask me for that. . . ." between the nuzzlings of the big grey moustache. Ciannelli lends distinction to any film : he can convey not only corruption but the sadness of corruption : the mind in—unpolitical—chains. But it is unfortunate so many of us said once that Miss Bette Davis was potentially a great actress, for now she plugs the emotions with dreadful abandonment. Only once does she really get across : in the horrifying scene of her beating up by the pervert henchman Charlie (her sister has been murdered and the worm tries to turn).

GRAHAM GREENE

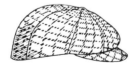

MINUTES OF THE WEEK

Heroine

It's a long time, a horribly long time, since we made *The Rainbow* our weekly paper and indeed read no other periodical. We lately found ourselves discussing with a contemporary those dear but distant days, when Tiger Tim meant as much to our nursery as Godfrey Winn means to any modern servants' hall. Reminiscence led, as it so often does, to controversy, and we waxed as fretful as a Shakespearian pedant over a minor point in connection with " Bluebell in Fairyland ", which in our day was the principal serial and most eagerly looked forward to. (Never end a sentence with *one* preposition.) We for our part maintained that the formula invariably used to introduce Bluebell read as follows : " Bluebell, as you know, is a fairy and wears magic gloves. With these she has only to wish for a thing and her wish at once comes about." Our contemporary held that it ended " her wish at once comes *true*".

Textual polemics ended in a pointless draw, so we went out and bought *The Rainbow*, with a view to checking up. Alas for whimsy ! The bottom is out of the goblin market ; Bluebell's magic gloves are gone, or more probably have been handed over to a finger-prints expert. Bluebell herself still carries on ; but she isn't a fairy any more, she's a girl-detective. Some of the old tradition still survives (" Ha ha ! " laughed our little favourite. " I can guess *that* one.") But there's no disguising the fact that Bluebell has lost her glamour ; she's now merely No. 1 in a team known as " Bonnie Bluebell and Frank, the detective chums". For us, this is like Ellen Terry playing the hind legs of a horse ; and we feel particularly bitter about Frank. We decided long ago that if Bluebell really needed a helpmate, there was only one man for the job ; unless we're greatly mistaken, we wrote and told her so.

Chums, indeed !

Advt.

Nowadays the camera seldom tells the truth, and this story is just another proof of it. It is the story of a photograph taken in the works of one of those manufacturers who advertise their foodstuffs as being " untouched by human hand ". It was the original of an illustration used in an advertisement, and had the title " Baker carving fresh dairy butter ". It had been rather heavily re-touched, and our friend who saw it happened to notice the directions for the re-touching which had been pencilled on the back of the photograph. " Take the man's fingers out of the butter," it read ; " don't let either of his hands touch it." And again, in different, larger, more imperious writing : " Take out upstanding knife, and take fingers of *both* hands right off the butter."

Left

NIGHT AND DAY's Tokyo correspondent called on the spokesman of the Japanese Foreign Office to ask why they'd massacred several hundred Chinese refugees in a Shanghai railway station.

" But don't you understand that we're fighting Bolshevism ?" cried the spokesman.

" I don't see what that's got to do with it," said our correspondent.

" They had a Left Luggage Office in the station," said the spokesman. " We had to teach them a lesson."

Pantechnicography

Driving daily up and down the Great West Road keeps you in touch with a stimulating form of publicity. The independent van and the hobo lorry nearly always carry some slogan, cherished brain-children of their owners. WE MOVE ANY WARE ANYWHERE has the mark of a midnight inspiration, and the man who has written KEEP MOVING ! on his furniture pantechnicon must be a proud and happy fellow. We know them all by now. THE STORE WITH AN IDEAL is the Reading Co-op ; the lorry with CROSS HERE ! and two Belisha Beacons on its tail board belongs to George Cross, Contractor, of Southall ; LET THE BIRDS BUILD YOUR HOUSE belongs to Bird and Sons, Builders, of Sherborne. But we have a favourite —the blithe, self-confident HUXLEY'S AGAIN ! Amidst a welter of professional advertising, these slogans have an amateur, an almost dewy touch.

PEN-PRICKS AND PRAISE
For NIGHT AND DAY

Dear Sir :

I read your paper " night and day " this evening and was so disgusted with the " tripe " it contained that I returned it to the newsvender I bought it from.

If your paper is an example of modern journalism to be found in 6d. books I am afraid your firm will be " on the rocks " in the near future. L. G. G., London, W.11.

If I may say so, I think Night and Day is swell.   K. B., London, N.W.3.

May I congratulate you on your efforts ? (Purely rhetorical, because obviously you can't stop me.) The announcement of your first appearance belongs in the " It's about time " department ; I'm glad you have at last materialised and want to thank you for something rather more astringent in the way of humour and criticism than we have had before.   D. M. C., London, W.6.

I have often wished, whilst thumbing thru the pages of that periodical, that there was an English magazine of the same kind as the NEW YORKER, & am extremely pleased that you have filled the void.
             F. K. P., Manchester.

Congratulations on getting off with something that this country sorely needs. A light you're-the-topical weekly that isn't crammed with press-agentry for this year's crop of debs and debits. *Anonymous.*

I honestly do wish you every success in establishing what has promise of being a first class magazine. K., London, S.W.

It strikes me as being exquisitely produced, & the substance also is so lively & what one does not expect in a journal which sets out to amuse its readers, *informative* as well.
             J. E., London, S.W.1.

I think the first three numbers have been admirable—in fact, it appals me to think of the difficulty of keeping it up to that standard.   J. M. G., Sussex.

Congratulations on Night & Day : best paper out.   K. F., London, S.W.3.

I have been reading N & D from cover to cover and have laughed a lot. The Minutes of Week made me burst out in front of a railway carriage full of people. C. H., Kent.

I have ordered it until further notice, but I thought it a poor show, old boy. I might say frightfully weak, old chap. Cheer up, it may catch on, God knows queerer things have happened.   S. G. J., Cheshire.

Nice work ! Keep it up and lots of luck.
             G. W., Surrey.

Jokes *very* poor, illustrations *rotten*. Nobody will *ever* get used to " Fe-fo-fi-fum." Give us *real* humour in both letterpress and illustrated jokes, or in my opinion—*early demise.*   Yours regretfully, 6d. ?

I do think " Night and Day " is so *very* good, that I must write and say so. I read it from cover to cover in the train today, and was really hit by it. It's *my* form of humour anyway ! V. R., London, N.W.8.

I have just purchased a copy of the " Night and Day Magazine " and have read some of the articles and looked at the pictures, and as a journalist myself I think that the magazine is a very low form of literiture. Please do not tear this letter up yet ! It is also crude, if you had decent pictures on the front page or even if they were well drawn they would then be at least artistic. The pictures contained inside the covers are really revolting.

I am not just trying to be narrow minded— far from it—I am just kicking against such an unclean article to be sold in Fleet-street. After all why print such a thing when you can get better value for your money with a *clean* magazine.   J. B., London, E.7.

" Night and Day " is badly needed in Great Britain. It is very intelligent.
             A. L., London, E.6.

I have just picked up one of your papers, not knowing anything of the contents—by the title—I must say I am amazed and thoroughly disgusted & shall at once inform the authorities of its infamous immoral illustrations and reading. *Anonymous.*

Just look at your third number (you can get one from a chap who stands outside the London Pavilion) and look at all the long words in it. Lots of them. Words like ' parabolas ' and ' congenial ' and ' scrutinize.' If you nose them out in the dictionary as I have, you'll see that they have nothing to do with sex.

Now I'm a great book-lover and I know just how a really modern writer writes. He uses all short words. And as there arent many and a book has to have a great many pages, he puts them down again and again and again. And here and there, he shoves in as long a word as he can find. And it ALWAYS has something to do with sex. Otherwise, there's no sense in reading anything.

So, why dont you go out and pick up some good writers like Evelyn Waugh and Rose Macaulay and Elizabeth Bowen and Theodora Goes Wild Benson and Graham Greene and David Garnett and Peter Fleming. Well, why dont you ?

             B. K., A Deck-chair, Hyde Park.

I was surprised and delighted, though a bit hurt to be told " How to Read this Magazine." Of *course* I read it the way I read the NEW YORKER, in the same order, and with just the same kind of expectation. I'd got so afraid you'd all be struggling to find ways of being different from the N.Y. that I was immensely relieved to find you'd had the courage to adopt its lay-out and methods pretty faithfully. It lays you open to a lot of taunts, maybe. But what of that ? What we've been wanting for years is *something like the New Yorker*, and the better the likeness, the better I, for one, am pleased.

             A. F. R. C., Sussex.

When your paper first appeared, I thought how nice to get " The New Yorker " for sixpence, and very nearly worth it. Since then, however, " Night and Day " has consistently risen in my estimation.

             P. M. H. S., London, E.C.1.

THE FIRST JOURNEY

(From an autobiographical work in progress, " The North West Passage ")

Christopher Isherwood

ON August 3rd, 1922, I woke up on board a cross-channel steamer from Southampton, to find that Le Havre was already in sight. It was my first unforgettable view of anywhere abroad. The coast rose solemn behind the town. Tall houses were like shabby wings of stage scenery which had been left out of doors all night, propped against the cliffs. As we approached the quay, we heard the faint vigorous shouting of the inhabitants, the crowing of cocks, and the clanging of the bells of trams. Bolsters were hung out from the windows to air in the pale sunshine.

Mr. Holmes—the history master—was beside me at the rail, and Queensbridge, another member of the History Sixth, a freckled jolly boy with a bright red nose. Mr. Holmes had arranged this trip : we were on our way to a walking-tour in the French Alps. He wore a cloth cap which made him look more than ever like a Renaissance cardinal on holiday, and a surprisingly loud suit of pepper-and-salt tweeds.

We crossed Le Havre in a tram, and found ourselves in the great gloomy shabby platformless station, where grass grew between the rails and the grimy locomotives looked so rusty and ancient that one expected them at any moment to blow themselves to bits. Le Havre had not yet been tidied up after the War. I was duly shocked and remarked on all this to Mr. Holmes, who retorted that every European country looked like that just now, except England, where a lot of money was wasted on coats of paint, most uneconomically, since we were every bit as much in debt as the others. We sat down in the waiting-room and ordered coffee and brioches. Mr. Holmes was enthusiastic about the prospect of eating brioches again. I thought they tasted of cardboard and cheese ; and the coffee was dirty water full of floating wisps of skin. But I was not disappointed, for I had never for a moment expected that I should like French food. I was very pink and young and English, and quite prepared for a Continent complete with poisonous drains, roast frogs, bedbugs and vice.

Our train stopped at Rouen, where Chalmers, it had been arranged, would join us. It was strange to see him standing there, puffing at his pipe, placid and vague as usual, and seeming perfectly at home amidst these alien porters and advertisements. He had grown a small moustache and looked exactly my idea of a young Montmartre poet, more French than the French. Now he caught sight of us, and greeted me with a slight wave of the hand—so very typical of him, tentative, diffident, semi-ironical, like a parody of itself. Chalmers expressed himself habitually in fragments of gestures, abortive movements, half-spoken sentences ; and if he did occasionally do something decisive—take off his hat to a lady, buy a tin of tobacco, tell a stranger the correct time—he would immediately have to cover it with a sarcasm or a little joke. Getting into the carriage, he was received by Queensbridge and Mr. Holmes with congratulations and witticisms on the moustache. Mr. Holmes was, of course, delighted, and only sorry, I

' Pretty paper, isn't it, Sergeant ? '

think, that Chalmers wasn't also wearing a velvet jacket, corduroy trousers and a floppy tie.

In Paris it was terrifically hot. We visited Les Invalides ; I was secretly very much impressed by the coloured lighting, but I wasn't going to show it. Chalmers had denounced the building in advance—a shrine to War ! And of course one couldn't admit that a shrine to War was anything but vulgar and ugly. As we leaned on the parapet looking down at Napoleon's shiny tomb, we reminded each other of H. G. Wells's verdict in the *Outline of History* : " Against this  stormy and tremendous dawn appears this dark little archaic personage, hard, compact, unscrupulous, imitative, and neatly vulgar." Chalmers suggested that the only adequate comment was to spit. Mentally, we spat.

The Sainte-Chapelle I privately thought hideous ; Mr. Holmes told us that it is one of the wonders of Europe, so I dutifully noted in my diary (needless to say, I was keeping a diary of our tour ; how I wish I had put down in it one interesting, one sincere, one genuinely spiteful remark!) "a marvellous example of the colouring of mediæval cathedrals ". Finally, after a glance at Nôtre-Dame and a brisk trot through the Louvre, we sat down at a café on the Place de l'Opéra and watched the people. They were amazing—never had we seen such costumes, such make-up, such wigs ; and, strangest of all, the wearers didn't seem in the least conscious of how funny they looked. Many of them even stared at us and smiled, as though we had been the oddities and not they.

We were to travel all night, third class, on wood. Mr. Holmes hired a pillow for each of us. People were settling into the compartments as though they meant to inhabit them for a month : fathers of families were heating up food on stoves, a baby had been slung in a miniature hammock, everybody had changed into shirtsleeves and bedroom slippers. We got

a carriage to ourselves and dozed uneasily while the train dashed screaming through the darkness, towards the Alps. As its speed increased, the jolts lengthened out into jumps, until we seemed to leave the rails altogether for seconds at a time. Chalmers murmured sleepily that they had told him at his Rouen pension that P.L.M. stood for " Pour les Morts".

But in the morning we were still alive ; we changed at Aix-les-Bains and by breakfast-time we were in Annecy. The sun was shining on the lake. The mountains rose, steep and wooded, sheer out of the bluish-green water ; high above, they were black and veined with snow. It was the most beautiful place I had seen in my whole life. I wrote in my diary : " There is an impressive château and a clerical school, with a long stone staircase approaching it, where Rousseau was educated for a time".

Next morning the walking-tour started. We took the steam-tram, with its enormous funnel, to Thônes ; and then set off on foot, up the road which led to the Col des Aravis. Mr. Holmes and Queensbridge stopped frequently to take photographs : they were both experts. Presently the mountains disappeared into the clouds ; it began to drizzle. We stopped at a chalet where drinks were sold. Queensbridge tried to order beer and was given Byrrh instead : an opportunity for Mr. Holmes to read us a little lecture on the correct pronunciation of the two words. We were learning all the time.

From the Col des Aravis, in fine weather, the tourist gets his first view of Mont-Blanc. But now, as we climbed the last loop of the road to the summit, we were enveloped suddenly in a clammy mist, there was nothing to be seen—not even the cows, whose clanging bells were moving invisibly all around us. This, as far as I remember, was the only one of Mr. Holmes's effects which failed to come off. He was endlessly considerate and sly. However, we were glad of our supper. Mr. Holmes, I read in my diary, " was very gay at the expense of Queensbridge, who stared too hard at the waitress ".

After breakfast we started off down the pass. The cows were being driven out to pasture ; their bells made a continuous jangle, pretty and metallic, like a musical-box. Peasants were cutting hay in the steep upland meadows. Here and there, on the gigantic mountain-side, clearings had been made in the forest ; the felled trees lay scattered like a box of matches. The gorge grew narrower and deeper. Waterfalls sprayed the ruins of the precipice ; we remembered how Tennyson had described them as " downward smoke ". Charabancs came tearing round the corkscrew corners, missing death by inches, and girls waved their handkerchiefs to us and screamed. Mr. Holmes waved back, encouraging us to do likewise. Throughout the trip, he lost no opportunity for facetiousness, even skittishness, where the opposite sex was concerned. This naughtiness seemed rather forced ; it didn't suit him. No doubt he was trying to continue our education in yet another direction. If so, his problem was certainly a difficult one : he couldn't, as a respectable-master in an English public school, have taken us to a brothel. Yet how I wish he had ! His introduction to sexual experience would, I feel sure, have been a masterpiece of tact ; it might well have speeded up our development by a good five years. As it was, he merely joked and giggled, unsure of his ground, and we, reflecting that Mr. Holmes belonged, after all, to an older and more innocent generation, felt superior and amused and slightly pained. For Chalmers, thanks to Baudelaire, knew all about *l'affreuse Juive*, opium,  absinthe, negresses, Lesbos and the metamorphoses of the vampire. Sexual love was the torture-chamber, the loathsome charnel-house, the bottomless abyss. The one valid sexual pleasure was to be found in the consciousness of doing evil. Its natural and honourable conclusion was in general paralysis of the insane. Needless to say, Chalmers and myself were both virgins, in every possible meaning of the word.

FLAXMAN 1937 : No. 12

Dante Up-to-date : a series of John Flaxman's illustrations to the Divine Comedy, as published in 1807, with new captions.

' No, no—it was nothing really.'

FILM LUNCH

Graham Greene

" **I**F ever there was a Christ-like man in human form it was Marcus Lowe."

Under the huge Union Jack, the Stars and Stripes, the massed chandeliers of the Savoy, the little level Jewish voice softly intones. It is Mr. Louis B. Mayer, head of Metro-Goldwyn-Mayer, and the lunch is being held to celebrate the American company's decision to produce films in this country. Money, one can't help seeing it written on the literary faces, money for jam ; but Mr. Mayer's words fall on the mercenary gathering with apostolic seriousness.

At the high table Sir Hugh Walpole leans back, a great bald forehead, a rather softened and popular Henry James, like a bishop before the laying-on of hands—but oddly with a long cigar. Miss Maureen O'Sullivan waits under her halo hat . . . and Mr. Robert Taylor—is there, one wonders, a woman underneath the table ? Certainly there are few sitting anywhere else ; not many, at any rate, you would recognize as women among the tough massed faces of the film-reviewers. As the voice drones remorselessly on, these escape at intervals to catch early editions, bulging with shorthand (Mr. Mayer's voice lifts : " I must be honest to myself if I'm to be honest to you . . . a 200,000,000-dollar corporation like the Rock of Gibraltar . . . untimely death . . . tragedy ") ; they stoop low, slipping between the tables, like soldiers making their way down the communication trenches to the rest billets in the rear, while a voice mourns for Thalberg, untimely slain. The bright Very lights of Mr. Mayer's eloquence soar up : " Thank God, I say to you, that it's the greatest year of net results and that's because I have men like Eddy Sankatz " (can that have been the name ? It sounded like it after the Chablis Supérieur, 1929, the Château Pontet Canet (Pauillac) 1933, G. H. Mumm, Cordon Rouge, 1928, and the Gautier Frères Fine Champagne 20 ans).

" No one falls in the service of M.G.M. but I hope and pray that someone else will take his place and carry on the battle. Man proposes and God in his time disposes. . . ." All the speakers have been confined to five minutes—Mr. Alexander Korda, Lord Sempill, Lord Lee of Fareham and the rest, but of course that doesn't apply to the big shot. The rather small eyes of Mr. Frank Swinnerton seem to be watching something on his beard, Mr. Ivor Novello has his hand laid across his stomach—or is it his heart ?

One can't help missing things, and when the mind comes back to the small dapper man under the massed banners Mr. Mayer is talking about his family, and God again. " I've got another daughter and I hope to God . . ." But the hope fumes out of sight in the cigar smoke of the key-men. " She thought she'd like a poet or a painter, but I held on until I landed Selznick. ' No, Ireen,' I'd say, ' I'm watching and waiting.' So David Selznick, he's performing independent now."

The waiters stand at attention by the great glass doors. The air is full of aphorisms. " I love to give flowers to the living before they pass on . . . We must have entertainment like the flowers need sunshine. . . . A Boston bulldog hangs on till death. Like Jimmy Squires." (Jimmy Squires means something to these tough men. They applaud wildly. The magic name is repeated—" Jimmy Squires".) " I understand Britishers," Mr. Mayer continues, " I understand what's required of a man they respect and get under their hearts."

There is more than a religious element in this odd, smoky and spirituous gathering ; at moments it is rather like a boxing match. " Miss O'Sullivan "—and Miss O'Sullivan bobs up to her feet and down again : a brown hat ; a flower ; one misses the rest. " Robert Taylor "—and the world's darling is on his feet, not far

from Sir Hugh Walpole, beyond the brandy glasses and Ivor Novello, a black triangle of hair, a modest smile.

" He comes of a lovely family," Mr. Mayer says. " If ever there was an American young man who could logically by culture and breeding be called a Britisher it's Robert Taylor."

But already we are off and away, Robert Taylor abandoned to the flashlight men. It's exactly 3.30 and Mr. Mayer is working up for his peroration : " It's midday. It's getting late. I shall pray silently that I shall be guided in the right channels. . . I want to say what's in my heart. In all these years of production, callous of adulation and praise . . . I hope the Lord will be kind to you. We are sending over a lovely cast."

He has spoken for forty minutes : for forty minutes we have listened with fascination to the voice of American capital itself : a touch of religion, a touch of the family, the mixture goes smoothly down. Let the literary men sneer . . . the whip cracks . . . past the glass doors and the sentries, past the ashen-blonde sitting in the lounge out of earshot (only the word " God " reached her ears three times), the great muted chromium studios wait . . . the novelist's Irish sweep : money for no thought, for the banal situation and the inhuman romance : money for forgetting how people live : money for " Siddown, won't yer " and " I love, I love, I love," endlessly repeated. Inside the voice goes on—" God . . . I pray . . ." and the writers, a little stuffed and a little boozed, lean back and dream of the hundred pounds a week—and all that's asked in return the dried imagination and the dead pen.

'And you can go and tell your old Dr. Cronin to put that in his pipe and smoke it.'

★

" Sympathy is two hearts tugging at one load," says our calendar. How much will the big firms offer us for this delicate piece of verbal bric-à-brac ?

NEW YORK LETTER

From Alistair Cooke

Fights and Fidgets

HALF a dozen New York sports-writers were sitting around in a favourite bar trying hard to remember the peak moments of the year's sporting events which they had themselves at the time called " unforgettable ". They bunched over steins of beer in mumbling trances, then somebody would shout aloud a name or a descriptive phrase and, if the image was allowed by the others, another toothpick would be propped against the winner's beer. So it went, cheerfully enough, until somebody cried : "Louis knocking away Braddock's left." And then they all leaned back in what is perhaps the nearest any of them come to silent prayer ; they looked in their laps and thought again of the reproving pat on Braddock's left wrist, the split-second's pause which let in Joe's final thunderbolt to the jaw. When they were back again to the tempo of more routine memories, one of them looked at his watch and mentioned the third race for the America's Cup. " Oh, for Chris' sake," somebody said, and gulped down his beer. The meeting thereupon agreed to abandon in disgust and the man who gave the last one went off to his appointment.

It's sad that, no matter how friendly the protagonists appear in the news-reels, no matter how guarded their pronouncements before the races are on, each series always manages to add another glum chapter to an eighty years' record of petulance, misunderstanding, and a particularly queasy brand of sportsmanship. You think of the Wightman Cup and recall Alice Marble's brown thighs being whisked away from her control by her own racquet, the resounding flomp on her fanny, her cheerful grin while her opponent took time out for convulsions. And there was that amiable day at Wimbledon when Budge and Austin swapped racquets and drank tea on the sidelines. But you think of Newport and it's the 1934 squabble all over again. On the first day Ted Husing, Columbia's top sports commentator, was handling the broadcast in his usually alert and friendly way, describing rapidly the weather, the look of the boats, recalling the previous records, staking out the course, introducing the British and American experts to each other. At the end of the first leg Sopwith held the wind after he was passed and the American tactlessly remarked " Yes, I guess he learned his lesson in 1934." Swiftly on the breeze came the high, trembling voice of the English announcer : " I don't know that I'd say that was quite an *acc*-urate account of what happened in. . . . " Husing saw ahead the shuddering gulf of gentlemanly disagreement and discreetly wafted the radio audience on to the state of the race itself. Somehow it's that sort of detail that sticks.

The series, however, was safe from calumny until the end of the third day, when Mr. Sopwith unfortunately said aloud what might easily be a real private worry ; he thought that probably his hull had been fouled by a lobster-pot or two. Overnight both boats were put in dry-dock and " upon examination," wrote H. I. Phillips of *The Sun*, " Mr. Sopwith could discover no lobster-pot, but what they did find was sixteen lobsters, all swimming backwards." Thus the 1937 contest was brought handsomely into line with all the others, except those few civilized by the rude grace of the late Sir Thomas Lipton. The League of Nations has still one good and urgent office to perform before it goes out of business. It would bring international peace just that much nearer if it could decide to abolish the Olympic Games and the races off Rhode Island.

As a build-up to the Louis-Farr fight, Max Eastman lately went in to see his publisher. It may have been, of course, that he really had an interview. But by the time he left Scribner's, an hour later, the newspapers were already carrying two-column headlines about his brawl with Hemingway. Their separate versions differed so substantially that perhaps it may help to straighten out the fight of the cen-

tury if we add the evidence of an eye-witness (I was under the carpet at the time).

Eastman came in and shook hands with Mr. Scribner. They started talking and then Hemingway appeared in the doorway. " Hullo, Max," he said and " Hullo, Ernest," came back at him. The business conversation trailed away into agreeable generalities until Hemingway suddenly blushed hard at Eastman, pulled open his (Hemingway's) shirt and bellowed " Have I got hair on my chest, or haven't I ? " Eastman, who was as overcome as the rest of us, said " Why, sure, Ernest, you have hair on your chest." Hemingway strode across the room, pulled open Eastman's shirt, and visibly sneered. Then Hemingway was back in his corner again crying aloud " If only I had your goddam book here ! " This must be counted as rhetoric or dramatic irony, for the book he had in mind was right under his nose. He picked it up and turned to an essay insultingly called *Bull in the Afternoon*. In it Eastman had said there must be some circumstance that made Hemingway protest so about his virility. Hemingway leaned hard over Eastman and crinkled up his right eye. " What do you mean, *some* circumstance ? " he leered. Eastman sat there tapping the telephone, thinking hard, then rang up Information, it had been so long since he wrote that piece. " Hey, what did I mean when I said *some* circumstance to Ernest Hemingway about three—maybe two—years

ago ? " They couldn't tell him that, but the girl said " How about asking Mr. Hemingway ? " By this time we were getting nowhere, and I was pretty nearly suffocated. So Hemingway gave a great whinny and backed up against a wall. He threw the book on the desk and papers crackled through the air. Then Eastman said " Are you interviewing me or Hemingway ? " Mr. Scribner said he'd like to have Ernest play too, but of course it was Max's interview. So Ernest stood in the doorway, sulking and buttoning up his shirt (after taking a peek just to reassure himself) and he said " Well, anyway, I hit him with his own book." Then he left and I crawled away to record it accurately, as you see it here.

This little affair was written up with great glee (the *Post* turning over the job to its Boxing Correspondent), but it wasn't completely done with until Robert Taylor sailed for England —and Oxford. Mr. Taylor checked in modestly from the Coast on a Thursday and lay around the Waldorf waiting to be interviewed. He was interviewed. The *Telegram* man, who had done an uproarious job on the Eastman-Hemingway bout, leaned up against the door and struck a nonchalant pose which the poor interviewed celebrities have come or know as a mild challenge to be outsmarted. " Well, gentlemen, what do you want to know ? " grinned Apollo. " Do you think you're beautiful ? " drawled the *Telegram* man. " That's a question I always resent," Mr. Taylor re-

plied with some heat. " Stick to the question, do you think you're beautiful ? " Mr. Taylor shrugged defeat and said all right, he was beautiful. " Have you got hair on your chest ? " the reporter continued, writing tiredly the while. Mr. Taylor pouted and finally said he had. " What," asked the *Telegram* man, folding his notebook, " would you say are the constituents of a good marriage ? " Taylor was slowly festering but he was surrounded by the cleverest crowd of interviewers in the world, who once made Bernard Shaw sound like a blundering shepherd. So Taylor gritted his teeth and said " Well, I think marriage should be a mixture of good companionship, and mutual consideration, and——" " Yeah, and how about sex ? " asked the *Telegram* man.

It was a very hot day and Taylor was dripping with moisture as well as anger. So he smiled through the rest of his third-degree and the next day that same reporter stood guard at Taylor's stateroom, keeping overcurious people out of Taylor's way. Which only proves that, with the temperature in the middle nineties and the humidity a little higher, even spite is a conditional mood. As witness, most pathetically, that curse inscribed on a wall just near the East River. Some furious moppet had written out carefully the following blast : " Nuts to all the boys on 53rd Street "——then a thin, trailing line of chalk and she had added " between Second and Third Avenues."

THE THEATRE

Richard II

AT the Queen's Theatre Mr. Gielgud presents Mr. Gielgud's production of *Richard II*, with Mr. Gielgud in the title-rôle. Critics enthuse, dowagers are melted, highbrows seek in vain for foot-faults, and even the poor little smarties will have to go if they get back to London in time (the run ends on Oct. 30). The production deserves all the nice things that have been said about it ; I find myself writing more as a fan than as a critic, and propose therefore to lodge the only available complaint before it is trampled to death by wild superlatives. This complaint is against Motley's scenery. The sets are very greatly helped by excellent lighting (a department in which the London theatre is apt to be either under- or over-inspired) ; but for all that the sets are bad, being liable to violent attacks of arty-and-crafty castellation. The chief symptom of these attacks is an embryo form of real estate, something like a cuckoo-clock, which breaks out over fireplaces, on the canopies of thrones, and elsewhere. There is also a windswept tree, very nice in its own way but too ubiquitous. They really are not good sets, and they don't help the actors.

Not that even the least distinguished of the actors needs any help. It might almost be a Russian company, so compact and smooth is the texture of a large cast, most of whom have bad parts. After the second act I gave up waiting for the man with bow legs, a cleft palate, and no make-up south of his ears who always (in London) comes loping on in the middle of a purple passage and makes us all sob with laughter by saying in a tone of disillusion : " My lord, the Duke of Bagshot and the Earl of Bude lie, with ten thousand horse, at Finsbury."

This chap just wasn't in the cast ; God knows what he does for a living now. As a matter of fact, it is the excellence of the small-part players—and, still more, the skill with which the producer has shown them their chance and how to take it —that is the special virtue of this production. Mr. Anthony Quayle, for instance, makes two very minor rôles contribute something of significance to the play. And it's the same with the others. Instead of being one of the chorus to whom Shakespeare has arbitrarily given a couple of lines, they are real people, of importance to themselves and—in a minor, rather abstruse degree—of importance to the audience. Aumerle we remember, though we cannot quite remember why. Bushey, Bagot, and Green are no longer, like so many Trotskyists, the perfunctory symbols of half-comprehended conspiracy, but three dangerous and individual men whose doomed postures stand out fleetingly indeed, but clear-cut and different from each other.

Most of the credit for this must go to the man who cast the play and produced it. Mr. Gielgud has shrewdly discerned and conquered an idiosyncrasy, amounting to a fault, in his technique of production ; his younger, less experienced actors no longer disconcert us, as they used to, by catching and reproducing the cadences and intonations of their coach. This negative (though possibly difficult) achievement is, however, eclipsed by a wealth of more positive brilliance. " Was I as good as all that ? " Shakespeare would say if he visited the Queen's, kicking himself in a resigned way for not taking the theatre more seriously. The curtain goes up on a court, as it does in every second production of a play by Shakespeare ; but for once we are not assisting at a kind of threadbare tattoo, a blazoned concourse of wax-

During Miss Elizabeth Bowen's absence on holiday, plays will be reviewed this month by Mr. Peter Fleming, Miss Antonia White and Mr. Richard Jennings.

works briskly rattling off obscure allusions, slapping each other on the back, waiting for somebody important to come and say something that the audience knows by heart. Mr. Gielgud shows us a court, but a real court, belonging to an inadequate king in the Middle Ages. For perhaps a minute nobody speaks ; but there before us, true and suggestive, is the court : an anteroom, darkly splendid but above all a place for waiting about in, shot with fears and ambitions and jealousies, heavy and violent with glances and encounters and withdrawals and the things these things portend. That opening was superb, making its point so deftly yet without any unwarrantable improvisation. Another characteristic bit—the sort of bit which only a man who thoroughly understands Shakespeare and the theatre *and* who is also a very good actor could have managed so well—was the scene where Green breaks in on Bushey, Bagot, and the queen to tell them that Bolingbroke is back in England and has already a powerful following. How aptly Mr. Gielgud here makes his actors intimate the shifting, treacherous quality of the age and their awareness of it ! How rightly he insists that each name in the list of newly-risen rebels is important to the people on the stage, giving an intimate, stop-press quality to what is usually gabbled as out-of-date Debrett.

But all this leaves little space to praise the acting. Mr. Gielgud, beginning very quietly, shows us with a kind of disdainful integrity the anomaly between Richard's soul and Richard's station. Mr. Michael Redgrave is a very fine Bolingbroke indeed, and Mr. George Howe's Duke of York is a brilliant study of an Englishman. So, in a different way, is Mr. Frederick Lloyd's Northumberland, though voice, uniform and manner incongruously recall any White Russian officer in any Moscow play. Miss Peggy Ashcroft's queen has much more than the pathos of irrelevance, and indeed if there was room I would praise the whole cast, some of them twice. Motley's costumes, by the way, are in a different class from their scenery.

PETER FLEMING

NEW BOOKS

Art from Anarchy

HOW hard it is, in literary critic- ism, to find words of praise. There are infinite gradations of blame, a thousand fresh and pungent meta- phors for detraction, the epithets of dissatisfaction seem never to stale (per- haps that is why contemporary writ- ings, and particularly contemporary essays, are usually noticeable only when they are abusive), but the moment one finds a work which genuinely im- presses and delights, there seems no article of expression other than the clichés that grin at one from every publisher's advertisement. " Promis- ing ", " powerful ", " establishes his claim to a prominent place among the younger writers ", " authentic artist ", " meticulous craftsman ", " breadth of vision ", " variety of theme " . . . what is there left to say ? *A Date With a Duchess* is a collection of short stories. The publication of such a book is a sticky business and one which publish- ers for the most part are reluctant to tackle. A single short story by a new (as, for that matter, by a very old) writer will often startle one when it is met in a magazine sandwiched between poli- tical lies and warnings against bad breath (according to the price of the magazine). There are attempts to read half a dozen by the same writer and one finds how mechanical or jejune and bogus he really is. In the case of Mr. Calder-Marshall the cumulative effect of the whole book is greater than of any part of it. It shows him as a thoroughly good writer with an ad- mirably wide range of interests. The difficulty about praising a work justly is that any qualification appears con- demnatory or patronizing. Mr. Cal- der-Marshall is not within measurable distance of being a great writer, but I think that there are discernible ele- ments of greatness in him. Whether

they will ever mature is another mat- ter. Mr. William Gerhardi showed similar symptoms ; so did the author of *The Young Visiters.* Mr. Calder-Mar- shall's avowed aims, which he expanded at too great length in a book recently reviewed on this page, strike at the whole integrity and decency of art. I approached this book prepared to see signs of deterioration, eager perhaps to point a moral against doctrinaire stu- dents. I find instead a book of fresh and vivid narratives, full of humour, penetration and acute observation. If this is Marxist fiction, I have no quarrel with it.

The eponymous story deals with re- pressed romance in the life of an hotel manageress. It is not the most import- ant story and I suspect it has been given primacy simply because of its ex- cellent title. Mr. Calder-Marshall is so particularly attentive to vernacular propriety that I am surprised to find him using the abbreviation " Guins ". Surely there is no precedent for this ? *One of the Leaders* is altogether ad-

~~~~~~~~~~~~~~~~~~~~~~~

A Date With a Duchess. Arthur Calder-Marshall. Cape. 7s. 6d.

~~~~~~~~~~~~~~~~~~~~~~~

mirable. I suppose it might be called proletarian in so far as it deals with a clash between strikers and police, but it is a thousand miles from the sancti- monious abstractions of Mr. Calder- Marshall's colleagues in English poli- tics. The mood of rebellion is bril- liantly treated—the background of five weeks' boredom, of a nagging wife, of the camaraderie found only among fellow unfortunates, of the physical itch to hit something in an idle body accustomed to hewing coal. The whis- pered agitation before the outbreak of violence, the sudden sense of liberation in finding that bosses can be knocked about, that policemen's skulls can be cracked, the symbolism and futility of pushing the safe down the mine shaft, the exultance of manslaughter—all excellent. *The Swan* shows another side of proletarian activity: the wanton destruction of something beautiful be- cause it is felt to be alien and superior. *Mr. Thompson* is a delicious piece of satire on a hackneyed subject—the af- fection shown by old ladies and the

sycophancy of the fortune-hunter. Nothing new there, but it is treated with an acidity that gives it a fine quality. *Bulls* is enchanting: the story of a nightmare: Mr. Wyndham Lewis tried something of the kind years ago in *Childermass.* In *Bulls* there is no at- tempt to make the narrative anything but what it is—a straightforward docu- ment from the psycho-analyst ; its madness is so prosaically and tersely stated that it is as pleasing as a painting by Dali.

The Cat is a little slice of life. Raw material but funny. *Rosie* is almost whimsical, almost a *tour de force,* as though to show that the author can perform all the tricks if he cares to. But it has inimitable characteristics of its own.

My Brother and I Were Walking is the story of a scuffle in which a younger brother asserts his physical equality with his elder. It might give a slightly lubricious thrill to some spinsters ; it left me cold.

Bulge is not much good and need not have been there. It doesn't make weight. The theme is old and for once Mr. Calder-Marshall has been unable to infuse any new life into it. *Sugar From the Air,* which I reviewed some months ago, did the same thing better.

Pickle My Bones is bound to be the most popular story in the book. It is about two youths who drink wood- alcohol. One dies and the other goes blind. The climax is skilfully man- aged. This isn't the first time a blind man in fiction or drama has called to have the light turned on, but it is al- ways good for a few shivers and Mr. Calder-Marshall does it as well as most of his predecessors. What I valued and admired the story for was the first seven pages which give one of the best drunk conversations I have ever read.

A Pink Doll is an echo of Katherine Mansfield with a hint of something rather vulgar out of *Good Housekeep- ing*; *A Rich Man* another slice of raw material. *The Password* is by far my favourite. A really memorable, irre- sistibly funny piece of rapportage about a polite lunatic. I don't see how an in- cident could be funnier or how it could have been better recounted. Really first-class. *L'Enfant Posthume* is very grim and a little priggish : an anecdote of a barmaid who has seen better days, who has aspirations to liberty and taste and fecundity which all end in a little pet dog. Very horrible ; a real shocker in no pleasurable sense. *Terminus* gives a little touch of decorated Hemingway. In addition to these there are two stories showing the superiority of gypsies over refined Europeans, and two which I could not read, *A Crime Against Cania* and *The Smuggler's Wife.* Taken as a whole, the book justifies my sanguine judgments. It is the work of an anarchist, not a Marxist—and anarchy is the nearer to right order, for something that has not developed may reach the right end, while something which has fully developed wrongly cannot. I do not think any artist, certainly no writer, can be a genuine Marxist, for a writer's material must be the individual soul (which is the preconception of Christendom), while the Marxist can only think in classes and categories, and even in classes abhors variety. The disillusioned Marxist becomes a Fascist ; the disillusioned anarchist, a Christian. A robust discontent, whether it be with joint stock banking or the World, Flesh and Devil, is good for a writer, and if that is all that Mr. Calder-Marshall meant by his " Left " politics, I am sorry I grumbled about them.

EVELYN WAUGH

GENERAL

ALL THE DAYS OF MY LIFE. S. P. B. Mais. (*Hutchinson, 10s. 6d.*) Mr. Mais's account of Mr. Mais and his diverse activities—teaching, journalism, broadcasting, ramble- and hike-conducting. He began as a schoolmaster of the new type ; the War missed him, or rather he missed the War—" I woke up to a World War and I missed it . . . I remained, against my own inclination, but by command of the War Office, an officer in the O.T.C." He dived into journalism as *Daily Express* book critic. From the *Daily Express* he migrated to the *Daily Graphic* and thence to the *Daily Telegraph.* On the *Daily Graphic* he was news-editor, and " worked indefatigably to get scoops, and got in point of fact a great amount of advance news, but

as it was usually supplied by friends in confidence I said nothing." In any case, the *Daily Graphic* soon ceased publication. After the *Daily Telegraph* Mr. Mais took to broadcasting, like a duck to water. He broadcasts still. The following episode gives some idea of the range of his contacts : " At Lords as I was walking round one year I smiled graciously at our present Queen, and said as I passed : ' You and I have met before somewhere, haven't we ? ' And she instantly smiled back and said, ' Yes, of course. How nice to see you again,' which was not only quick of her but characteristically kind." It was also quick of Mr. Mais. Of his " University life " his happiest memory is " the day on which we loosed thousands of rats and cartloads of pigs in the middle of the High ".

FICTION

FOURTEEN : A DIARY OF THE TEENS. By a Boy. (*The Fortune Press, 7s. 6d.*) The diary of a boy's first year at a public school, the year being 1915–16, though some of the slang used suggests a later period. The boy's name is Aubrey Fowkes. He is a timid little boy with long hair and a pretty face. At least he likes to think he has a pretty face. His hero is Pestie, a big boy. For Pestie's sake he makes himself good at boxing, and prays in chapel that Pestie may love him and be with him always. Pestie, however, only likes girls, to Aubrey's great grief. When Aubrey felt sad he " stayed an extra long time in the rears, thinking in the dark. Nobody came, and so was able to have one of my nicywicey thinks ". (Is it Miss Naomi Mitcheson having us on ?) The big boys go straight into the army, and this makes Aubrey cry. He has a non-athletic friend named Kes over whom he can lord it a bit. When he gets home for the holidays there is his doggie, Goggles— " My sweetling was waiting for me with waggy tail in the hall. I picked him up and kissed him. . . . Home was best." (Is it Mr. Beverley Nichols having us on ?) For breaking a bird's egg Ashford, a big boy, bummed him with a switch in a wood, " making some pretty little scratches on me." Aubrey did not mind much really, though, " because it was the first time I'd ever bled from a beating, and I've often dreamt of this ".

Salon d'Automne

One thousand and one naked ladies
With a naïveté
At once pedantic and unsympathetic
Deck the walls
Of the Salon d'Automne.
This is the Slap school of art,
It would be nice
To smack them
Slap, slap, slap,
That would be nice.
It is possible
One might tire of smacking them
In time
But not so soon
As one tires of seeing them.
We too
Have our pedantic and unsympathetic
School,
It used to show
A feeling for animals.
The English are splendid with animals,
There was The Stag at Bay
And Faithful unto Death,
And Man's Best Friend the horse this
    time
Usually under gunfire,
The English are splendid with animals.
That older school
Was perhaps
On an intellectual level
With the Salon d'Automne.
Nowadays, of course,
We are more advanced :
The bad modern painter
Has lost the naïveté
Of that earlier school
And in its place
Has developed a talent
For making the work of his betters
Seem stale
By unspirited
Imitation.
Really
This is more tiring
Than the thousand and one
Naked ladies.

*

Sigh No More

Sigh no more ladies nor gentlemen at
    all,
Whatever fate attend or woe befall ;
Sigh no more, shed no bitter tear,
Another hundred years you won't be
    here.

STEVIE SMITH

TOURISTS' GUIDE TO ART

The Secrets of the Schloss

THE mercury is way up, the walls of the galleries are furnished from stock and the great army of art-lovers is scattered over the face of Europe from Salzburg to Inverness. But whether we are disporting ourselves on the plages of Boudin, tramping those Highland glens so dear to Mr. Farquharson, R.A., or going all Dufy by the shores of the Mediterranean, culture will keep breaking in. There comes a day when some member of the party, more conscientious than the rest, announces firmly that a visit must be paid to Schloss Weissnicht or Castle Whatnot and off we go, clutching the Kodak and the Bædeker, for our annual orgy of self-improvement. Arrived at the Castle, Château, or Schloss, we are herded together by an elderly gentleman who appears to have slept in his clothes, and led through a series of apartments at breakneck speed while our guide drones " Queen Elizabeth's bedroom", " Ici on a assassiné le duc de Guise", " Schlafzimmer der Kaiserin Maria Theresa ". His attitude towards art is always one of strictly limited appreciation, but the limits vary in different countries. Thus while all the tribe know enough to halt us before the family Titian, or whatever the four-starred picture may be, in England—particularly if the house remains in private hands—the clou of the whole collection is usually considered to be either the late Duke's most celebrated race-horse or the Duchess at the time of her marriage by Sargent or McEvoy. In Germany the highest praise is generally lavished on one of those fearful pictures in which, when viewed from a particular angle, the subject appears to be walking out of the frame ; while the simple French reserve their greatest enthusiasm for some spanking nude by Corregio or Boucher. But it is universally certain that, in whatever country one may be, nine-tenths of the pictures will be passed by with neglect if not with scorn. This is a pity, for while it is unlikely that among them lurk many unrecognized masterpieces, one frequently finds admirable examples of minor masters whose work it is not easy to study elsewhere.

The pictures in the average royal or ducal collection may usually be divided into three categories : fine art, portraits and military-historical. Of these the first is almost always the dullest and most numerous. Whole rooms will be covered with seventeenth-century Dutch landscapes—a class of art which has to be very good indeed to be interesting—but there is quite a chance, particularly in Germany, that one will find, lurking among the less inspired products of the school of Hobbema, a Bellotto. This is a painter who, unlike Canaletto, is none too well represented in our national collections, and much of his best work consists of paintings of palaces and country houses executed for various eighteenth-century German princelings who liked to possess a pictorial record of all their residences. Hieronimos Bosch, the darling of the surrealists, is another painter whose work one may come across, hidden away in the corridors of princely castles. In the royal bedroom one is almost certain to discover a lachrymose Virgin by Guido Reni, while some of the gloomier monarchs had a taste for waking up opposite a Salvator Rosa. On the whole, it is unwise to expect too much of the fine art section, and one is well advised to concentrate on the portraits.

The majority of these are usually the works of minor eighteenth-century painters, and to realize how good they are one has only to glance across the room at the Crown Princess by Laszlo or the Dowager Duchess by Poynter. Even a vulgar second-rate painter such as Nattier never fails to produce something which is undoubtedly a picture— a power which seems to have vanished from academic circles in the nineteenth century. Moreover, there is always the possibility of finding a Liotard, a painter whose work, except for a roomful at Dresden, is confined almost entirely to private collections. And there is one nineteenth-century artist who retained much of the grand manner and splendid self-assurance of an earlier age and whose works dominate many a princely portrait gallery. Winterhalter was a name which until recently stood for all that a generation brought up on Lytton Strachey considered most laughable in art ; now there is a fashionable reaction which tends to place him on a pedestal alongside Mr. Beaton and other exponents of the neo-Victorian picturesque. Actually he was a superbly competent portrait-painter who at his best almost reaches the level of Lawrence. He is perhaps best known for his portraits of royal beauties of the Second Empire period, but much of his finest work consists of men's portraits, such as the one of Franz Josef in the Hofburg and of the Prince Consort in the National Portrait Gallery. Of these a plentiful supply is scattered through the castles and country-houses of Europe. Another nineteenth-century painter, a miniaturist, who retains the aristocratic charm of the previous century, and whose work is plentiful in palaces, particularly in Austria and Bavaria, is Stiegler.

The last category, the military-historical, is, I admit, an acquired and probably debased taste, but it is one which can seldom be studied elsewhere. Those vast canvases crowded with uniformed figures (each one a *real* portrait) congratulating some royal octogenarian on his jubilee ; those dashing Van der Meulens with Louis XIV and staff galloping across the foreground far removed from the fearful slaughter cleverly indicated at the back ; those glittering court balls with every order and every ribbon lovingly and correctly delineated by Herr Menzel—they may not constitute a very exalted department of art, but they possess much of the charm and interest of back copies of the *Illustrated London News*. And when one compares them with the galas of the proletariat as recorded by Diego Rivera or one of the ideologically sound painters of the U.S.S.R., one can almost believe that they have a certain æsthetic merit as well.   OSBERT LANCASTER

ROUND THE RESTAURANTS

There's an R in the Month

ONE of the most completely involuntary jokes I have ever heard was brought off by my waiter at Bentley's (Swallow Street, W.) when I complimented him on the first-of-the-season oysters I had just enjoyed, adding a qualification that they were not cold enough. "Well, sir," he answered, "the sea is very warm at this time of the year." This notable non-sequitur does less than justice, however, to the establishment in which it was made, for the oysters were, despite their unchilled state, the finest I found in London on September 1—Essex natives, surprisingly fat for such early days, not too salt, firm fleshed, served, as I prefer them, on the deep shell with their juices conserved. They were dredged from the Mersea and Paglesham beds ; the grandees from Colchester are not released until the end of the month. Bentley's wine-list includes an inexpensive Alsatian Riesling of Hugel's, which is an admirable background (or foreground) for oysters—provided it is served at the right temperature, and not that of the air "at this time of year".

Essex natives of the same fine quality were also to be had at the recently opened Ecu de France (111, Jermyn Street, W.) which, despite occasional confusion of service, has already taken a very high place among London restaurants. Here there is the advantage of a more ample cellar, which includes a number of carafe wines, charming and not costly, particularly a still champagne which sets off oysters as well as any wine I know. It would be a mistake, however, to visit the Ecu only for its oysters, good though they are ; the French regional dishes which are given as *plats du jour*

are a daily instruction in good living. I shall have something more to say about L'Ecu de France in these notes.

For those who prefer Whitstables (or Colchesters when they come in), a recommendation to Wilton's (King Street, St. James's Square, W.) is perhaps unnecessary. Here the largest natives cost 9*s.* a dozen and, much though one regrets the price, they are worth it. The wine list is meagre, the Graves unsuitable for oysters ; stick to champagne or stout. Wilton's have the distinction of opening the oysters at Buckingham Palace.

The best cheap oyster bar I know is Wheeler's (Old Compton Street, W.). Here the speciality is relaid American blue-points, from Kentish waters, sold at half-a-crown the dozen. Do not be put off by the price. They are not as good as the natives, naturally, but at their best they are very good. The proprietor and his manager are both enthusiastic ostreophiles, and

Paul Crum

very willing to share their knowledge (and their oysters). The bar is not confined to blue-points, and offers several grades of natives. Wheeler's also make a shell-fish soup of the *bisque* type, which, like the Stock Exchange, has unaccountable variations, and a fish pie which is not to my taste.

Other oyster resorts of merit are

Driver's (46 Glasshouse Street, W.), Gow's (357 Strand, W.C.), Overton's (4 Victoria Buildings, S.W.1) and White's (Chancery Lane, W.C.). And no survey of London's oyster-field would be complete without mention of Scott's (Coventry Street, W., at the top of the Haymarket), the Olympus of our fish restaurants, which specializes in the finest oysters, lobsters, crabs and soles, with equally good game and meat, and has a first-rate wine-list. I shall reserve further description, however, till the lordly Colchesters come in.

There is a reasonable variety of views as to how the oyster is best served, whether on the flat or deep shell, cut ready for the mouth, or, like a timid general, attached to his base. My own preference, but without bigotry, is for the deep shell and the cut, as at Bentley's. (These remarks do not apply to Portuguese oysters, which are not true oysters, and repay cooking.) Sauce, salt or pepper with oysters I do regard as a heresy, if the oysters be good ones ; indeed, I would go further, and condemn even the "touch of lemon" which makes all oysters kin—to the lemon. Once, when drinking a Grand Montrachet in wine-learned company, with H. A. Vachell as host, I observed that the only dissent in the consensus of admiration came from the one guest who had sprinkled his oysters with lemon-juice ; on a second consideration he joined the majority (in agreement, not the graveyard). Oyster cocktails may be a way of enjoying whatever liquid they are made with, but not of enjoying oysters.

My oyster quest ended, late in the evening, at Prunier's (St. James's Street, W.) where the French Belons were excellent, in every way better than the Whistables, which were rather small and salt. My real reason for visiting Prunier's that day, however, was less to compare oysters than to show three friends one of the most remarkable wines to be obtained in London, Château Suduiraut 1900. Suduiraut was rightly classed as a first growth of the Sauternes in the assessment of 1855 ; it adjoins Yquem, to which it is proximate in quality as well as geographically. 1900 was a noble vintage for red and white wines alike —nowhere better than Bordeaux. I have never seen any example of the Sauternes of that year save this Suduiraut, which has attained the tawny colour that Oscar Wilde, in the quest for the perfect phrase, compared to a lion's eye. Its flavour is that of etherealized marmalade, its bouquet a honeyed reminder of the golden age. But do not make the mistake of drinking this nectar during the meal, or with less than three companions. It is a dessert wine, demanding suitable fruit as its complement ; and to go beyond a second glass at a sitting invites satiety, the worst form of vinous irreverence.

A. J. A. SYMONS

★

Plain and Milk

THE Chocolate and Confectionery Exhibition, the first to be held in the gigantic new Earl's Court building, was primarily designed for the Trade. The people who went round popping liquorice All-Sorts in their mouths and drinking free cups of tea with the stand proprietors were all in the know where sweets were concerned. There was much talk of " good twopenny counter lines " and " sure-selling novelties ", and many of the visitors were stout little women in spectacles who could readily be visualized in a setting of barley-sugar sticks and peppermints.

The smell of the exhibition was heavily chocolate-flavoured, except in one corner, where an overpowering smell of cough-drop prevailed. The appearance of the exhibition was attractive but redundant. One tended to move in circles, like an explorer lost in the jungle, and to see the same stalls again and again. Only with a guide or a map could one have hoped to cover the whole vast acreage.

Every product in any way connected with the sweet trade was represented. Solid Centre Moulding Machines and Irregular Shape Wrapping Machines were on show. There was a display of adhesive tape for sealing, with the comforting slogan for the benefit of exporters to the more sinister countries, " Ants Abhor our Adhesive ". Patterned foils for wrapping were there—characterized, according to advertisement, by " glamour—dignity — modernity — persuasiveness ". There were Seasonal Fancy Boxes, Mechanical Advertising Models, and Fancy Packages with definite After-Use Values. There was a counter of trade literature, featuring such books as " All About Biscuits " and " Manna : a comprehensive treatise on bread manufacture ".

If you have only a consumer's knowledge of sweets you find yourself liking all the wrong things at an exhibition of this sort. While everybody else is crowding round some startling " newcomer to the penny market " you are standing fascinated and alone in front of an exhibit which has probably been a commonplace on counters for several years.

Bubble Gum, apparently an old line, is particularly intriguing if you have not met it before. When you have been chewing it for some time, it seems, you can work it onto the tip of your tongue and blow, thus producing the most astonishing bubbles. It was difficult to visualize the bubbles and one hoped for definite proof on the subject, but unfortunately there was no one there to perform a demonstration chew. But then everybody else had known about Bubble Gum long ago, and took it as a matter of course.

Although the nice distinctions of the trade are baffling to the novice, one can pick up a few of the more obvious sweet trends. It can be confidently stated, for instance, that American influence is remoulding the dialogue of the Conversation Sweet. It has become sceptical, tough, even belligerent. " Will you be mine ? " is dying out. " Oh yeah ? ", " Sez you ? " and " Sez me " are taking its place.

" We are a conservative firm, madam," said a salesman presiding over a tray of these, " but we had to give in in the end, and change our ' Fairy Whispers ' to ' Broadway Echoes.' "

Another salesman had a display of sweets with the old-fashioned messages—" I love you ", " May I hope ? " and " What will you give to know ? " " None of your ' Sez you's ' for us," he said. But no doubt he too will have to give in in the end and submit to the influence of the movies.

One's mind began to get confused after a couple of hours of looking at Milky Lunches, Midget Jap Desserts, High-Class Boilings, All-Milk Poppets, Rum Beans, Swizzles and Dewdrops. Even the Trade grew less enthusiastic, and watching crowds tended to melt away as saucers of free samples hacked from mountains of chocolate and toffee were handed round. People wandered about, rather angrily chewing gum—the one free sample that lasts, and lasts, and lasts. . .

I remembered something I had been told earlier in the afternoon : " Americans park their gum when they don't want it, and go back to the same piece again and again. The Englishman usually gets tired of his and throws it away after the flavour has gone out of it."

It wouldn't surprise me to hear that Earl's Court's very beautiful new exhibition building is, after its first exhibition, just a little sticky.

MARGARET J. MILLER

IN THE LIONS' DEN

1—Victor Gollancz

IN the early autumn of 1928 Warner Brothers Vitaphone, featuring Al Jolson and his Sonny Boy, were causing no end of agitation in Wardour Street and its dependencies. And just about the same time the name of Victor Gollancz, with plenty of bold claims in equally bold Fanfare type, began to flutter London's book-publishing dovecotes as they hadn't been fluttered for quite a time. A distinctly independent dynamo had started humming, hard by Covent Garden, and disturbances were felt as far away as Paternoster Row and Bloomsbury. The dynamo hasn't slowed up since :

and won't so long as Victor Gollancz is Victor Gollancz. In fact, he has doubled himself since then, being by now not only the General Publisher he began as, but also more and/or less the Political Force he had it at the back of his mind to become. For he is also the celebrated Left Book Club. And his right hand knows remarkably well what his left hand doeth.

All the time he has moved along a line quite clear to him, though it had bumps and détours. At the age of ten, before even reaching St. Paul's School, Gollancz's mind was fixed on being somehow or other a Reformer. In those days Liberalism was the way you went about this, and we have a clear

memory of V.G., Scholar of New College, going about it with decided zest at the Union. Soon the *Oxford Magazine* noted that he was " beginning to state a very extreme view with considerable moderation, but he must avoid wishing to do so too often". Two terms later this dangerous figure was deploring General Botha's " unjust treatment of Labour in South Africa".

But literature as well as reform was in his blood, and there was an essay-reading club at New College, styled The Midwives, which knew him well. The two strains were blended in 1913 when he was awarded the Chancellor's (Lord Curzon's) Prize for a Latin Essay, to which he gave the form of an elegant chat between certain polite disputants named Tanio, Cleanthes, Sosiades and Epiondes. Seated in pleasant weather in Tanio's " *hortuli pleni iucunditatis* ", these personages speculated on the practicability of Socialism : or, as they put it, "*meliorne opificum futura sit condicio si negotium cura nonnisi ab universo populo suscipiatur* ". Tanio said Yes, it was—in Latinity which we believe impeccable. And Yes, it is, Gollancz has said ever since, in no uncertain tones.

Then there was the War. His military career was brief, and little is told of it except that he acquired a distaste for horse exercise after taking a toss on (of all places) a ferry over the River Blyth. But where his personality made a sharp impact, even a dent, was at Repton School, where he became a master about the middle of the War. We can imagine Gollancz being a good schoolmaster, at the right school. The gown would suit his ample form and gestures ; his restrained joviality would go down well ; and he can always talk with enthusiasm. But the Repton adventure ended in a reverse. What happened was this. In gene-

' Ah doant give a dang if Ah do look loike Robert Taylor —you'm still trespassing.'

ral V.G.'s view was that "reconstruction" (a popular word with idealists at that time) had already begun with the outbreak of war, and that the public schools ought to do something about it. He argued that the O.T.C. trained some members of the school to fight "for the creation of a 'New World'" and that somebody should see that some at least should be trained "to think intelligently about that creation". So along with a sympathetic colleague he started a voluntary Politics Class, in the Easter term of 1917. Now, twenty years ago this was a really startling idea. Repton quivered a little, but quickened at the Gollancz touch. Before long about forty boys were voluntarily attending informal classes in a formal classroom, lending ears and energy to lectures on Parliamentary Reform, the Future of the Empire, the Position of Women, Trade Unions, Alsace-Lorraine, the League of Nations Idea, the Russian Revolution, and so on. What's more, Medici Prints appeared on the walls and Beethoven and Debussy records began to vie with Irving Berlin and Nat D. Ayer. And still more : this *élite* began the publication of a new school magazine of vanguard opinions and having the bodily shape of the *New Statesman*. The *School Observer* came out with notes on current affairs, thoughtful "middles" on "Sin" and "Voluntary Religion", leaders on "Armenia Irredenta", the Lansdowne peace proposals, psychology and politics, the progress of poesy, and land nationalization, and all complete with reviews, poems, and paid advertisements—all on quite a good business footing. But Repton is as Repton does. There were qualms in high places. The War Office didn't care so much for this collaborator in world-reconstruction. And with some flurry, and even a question in Parliament, the *School Observer*, the politics class, and their animator were jettisoned.

But not *spurlos versenkt*. Reformers go on. In two firmly persuasive books Gollancz and his collaborator, D. C. Somervell, told the story of their experiment and pointed a number of morals for the public schools—quite a

'*It isn't only the hat—it's the whole capitalistic system I'm aiming at.*'

'Curse that fellow laughing at me ; I was just going to laugh at him !

number of which are by now fairly current coin. And then, on the editorial staff of Benn Bros. who were then breaking out of technical into general publishing, V.G. gained his first experience as a publisher. But what with one thing and another he outgrew, almost violently, his discipleship, and started to publish on his own account in 1928. A signboard with his initials painted in the fashionable angularities of the moment (by now indecipherably begrimed) was hung up over the door of rather dingy premises in Henrietta Street ; and from that moment, though he may have looked Left, he never looked back. He laid his stakes for quick returns, and got most of them. He had mustered for his company the manly sum of £45,000, but has never used more than a comparatively small proportion of that. Not for him the classic long-term investments of the graver publishers : and these gentlemen shook their heads and thought it was all very questionable and sensational. In Paternoster Row the illustrious past turned in their graves, not at all appreciating the Covent Garden touch.

But Gollancz was not really playing the same game. Behind all this quick, noisy outpouring of standardized bright-yellow books lay a political consciousness and a political ambition. For some time he did not, in personal debate, disguise the fact that his motive in building a profitable publishing house was to make a direct entry into politics. But as time went on his angle of approach shifted. A spirited attempt to break the 7s. 6d. convention in the field of novels by issuing hand-picked new novels at 3s. didn't work out and was quietly shelved. But the Gollancz imprint consistently inclined, wherever it could, to the Left political wing, and alongside his dexterous successes with serious and less serious books he ran, as it were, a literary branch of Intourist. It was a bullish market, and it was intellectually congenial to V.G. The front door of public life opened on to the disheartening rough-and-tumble of Westminster with a National landlord in apparently permanent possession. Wasn't this other door equally good ?

Time marched on ; and the advent of Hitler drove Gollancz further, more doggedly, Leftward. In the spring of 1936 he seized a chance which others had fumbled : he organized the Left Book Club. By May it had 7,000 members subscribing for these half-crown books on politics, economics and sociology, selected by Laski, Strachey and Gollancz. Study groups sprang up spontaneously all over the country, and the Club's membership graph-line kept on the up-and-up : August, 20,000 ; November, 28,000; January '37, 35,000 ; March, 40,000. More and more the founder became conscious of a political force growing under his fingers. He lisp'd in thousands, for the thousands came. The *Left Book News* (monthly, free to members) reported Club news and became a monthly Left magazine ; there were film activities and dramatic activities and training classes for group discussion-leaders, and much else, all directed to lend intelligent power to the famous struggle-against-war-and-fascism. In February '37, the Albert Hall was filled with 7,000 cheering combatants, who heard loyal messages from France, Switzerland, Ceylon, South Africa, Mauritius, Australia, New Zealand, India, and Mr. Attlee. The first main objective of 50,000 members remains a little elusive : there seems to have been a slow-up somewhere. But the next big move is planned in a new series of sixpenny books to be subscribed for through factory organizations. And in June the Club was able to announce its " first victory ", in the form of improved conditions for convicts, a matter ventilated by W. F. R. Macartney's *Walls Have Mouths*, the Club's biggest general seller so far.

It is all a long way from Tanio and Repton : but a straight enough line. V.G. has his own *hortuli jocunditatis* agreeably situated in Berkshire, and gardens with zest, albeit by proxy : the delphiniums and dahlias are especially notable. During the Coronation period (or the " national preoccupation", as he archly termed it in advertisements) he paid his first visit to the U.S.S.R., and received the honours due to a friendly Power. Otherwise his recreations are officially listed as listening to music, sitting in the sun, and arguing. And indeed his figure is genially familiar at Queen's Hall and the ballet. As also at one or two decidedly good restaurants. We mentioned once to a couple of friends who devoutly study one and all of the L.B.C. publications that we'd lately seen their chief lunching at one of these. " Oh, nonsense ! " they protested incredulously. " Not at all," we said, and argued the case for getting the most out of things. Which is something that V.G. does all the time with the most likeable enthusiasm.

THE AUTUMN FAIRS

Zero Hour in Oxford

FAIRS are recurrent movable feasts and there is something like a Church Calendar for them. From Easter till November they travel up and down the country, but the bumper crop in the south is in the autumn. Some fairs are utterly memorable like Widdicombe Fair : some merely well-known like the Nottingham Goose Fair, or the Temperance Festival in Newcastle during the week the Pit-men's Derby is run. The September and October fairs belong to the south and the southern midlands : to Oxford and Stratford (Stratford Mop Fair, October 12), Banbury (October 13–15) and Salisbury (October 18–20).

The St. Giles Fair at Oxford starts the autumn season. It is held always on the first Monday and Tuesday in September and the school-children's holidays are extended two days for it. How long the fair has been going on nobody knows and it is indecent to inquire. " Donkey's years," said a roundabout man as a concession to historical accuracy. It is rumoured that the show-people will have to move to Port Meadow one of these days as Progress and Commerce demand the ever-open door on the Banbury Road. But the " populace", as a Guess-Your-Weight-Within-Two-Pounds specialist remarked, are against this surrender of privilege, and the coconut-shies, the Eskimo Midget (The Life of a Tiny Eskimo—told by the SMALLEST of his RACE), the hoopla stalls and the Headless Wonder, the Lady Stansteta, are openly scornful.

Early on the Monday morning the police close the strategic entries to Oxford " beyond Magdalen Bridge at the place called the Plain", at the Stations, Folly Bridge and Staverton Road. The caravans, the lorries, the heavy engines with trailers make a queue. At 4.40 a.m. the white-gloved hands go up simultaneously and the big outfits—the Giant Racers, Over The Falls, the Helter-Skelter, the Dodge 'Ems (Bright—Cheerful—Refined) are allowed to move into the town. 5 a.m. is zero-hour for the

lesser fry. Within twenty minutes the façade of St. John's is fast disappearing behind crudely painted three-ply displaying lions and tigers in their virgin jungle and ukulele girls in grass-skirts. Prestige accrues to the man who gets the music going first, also a prize and a blue ribbon to tie on his hurdy-gurdy. It costs a shilling for every stake driven into the ground. In the forecourt of St. John's the Ambulance Brigade in their natty uniforms soon start dealing with crushed fingers. Workmen on their way to housing-estates and factories dismount from their bicycles to add a

coconut to their luncheon menus. A fire starts in a sideshow and is extinguished with two buckets of water. Argument follows.

The keynote of the whole business is rugged individualism. All the barkers now make a cut-throat use of loud speakers and amplifiers, and an inarticulate babel results. There is a curious mixture of ancient and modern. The cake-walk is still popular, the painted nymphs would delight Renoir, the boxing booths display Jack Johnson, and the showmen talk of the great Hackenschmidt and the Terrible Turks. But the old roundabouts of horses and leopards and unicorns—except for the handworked 1d -for -the-

children kind, which operates on the principle of the mangle—are gone for ever and racing motor-bikes, Blue-birds, etc., have taken their place. To the music of the Duke or of Armstrong's swinging trumpet they serve equally well for casual amours.

Throughout the day thin men in open-necked cricket shirts wheeling prams and women in print frocks, carrying parcels and with children hanging on to their skirts, pack the alley-ways. The pubs do a roaring trade. At night the lamps shine on the trees, the Martyrs' Memorial and the workers from Cowley who have come with their young women to see the fun. The pubs still do a roaring trade. " But the drunks are worse at Abingdon," an oily mechanic on the racing cars said to me. There is some refinement at Oxford. Even so, in a time-honoured phrase, North Oxford was conspicuous by its absence. I looked in vain for a member of a Senior Common-room, who was not climbing in the Lake District or seeing Spain for himself, to descend from the helter-skelter on a mat or ring a spotted China dog with whoops of delight. The Christian Colportage Society with its tracts and banners and Bibles shines like a single good deed in this naughty world. Even the City Fathers have let themselves go. This appears on a lamp-standard :

Any Person who may be proved to have assaulted another with any of the following ARTICLES :—

Balloons (if charged with gas), Meal, Confetti, Flour, Rice, Sand or Water-Squirts . . .
is liable to be prosecuted and punished with two months' imprisonment or a fine of five pounds.

What vistas this opens up. Strings of sausages, mouth-organs, shark fins and candelabra, it seems, are not proscribed weapons of offence.

But by 9 a.m. on Wednesday morning this microcosm which sprang up as quickly as a Yukon mining town will have vanished : the mechanical amusements and the sideshows to Hinksey ; the stalls which sell fried fish or lemonade or overalls to Hinksey, or home to Banbury or Evesham or Northampton—they come from all

'*What the devil are we going to tell the Museum about this?*'

these places; the snapshot photographers, the sellers of favours and enamel brooches (" Is your name here ? ") to London and the Caledonian Market. The fair has a small nucleus of shows which travel together in the season—Easter till Christmas—from the South Coast as far north as Sheffield. Round this nucleus swarm the get-rich-quick merchants, the vendors of quack medicine, the tipsters,

the Bachelors of Science who will read your Fate in the Stars for sixpence. They join the fair and leave it as they like. But the patrons of the fair, the townspeople and the hundreds of folk from the neighbouring villages brought in by bus, car and charabanc, know very little about how their fair is organized. They are out to enjoy themselves and they do so, spending money freely and going home at night

laden with bars of rock, cheap clocks, tins of toffee, paper caps, comic noses, mascots, etc.

During the day I thought of looking into the Ashmolean Museum to see that piece of decorative gaiety " The Hunting Scene " by Uccello. It may be nobody's business, but even the Ashmolean closes for the St. Giles Fair.

KENNETH ALLOTT

One day cruise

THE idea G and I had of a one-day cruise was of people singing. We thought our fellow one-day cruisers would all start singing and we should join in and think : " This is wonderful — people singing unself-consciously, without Mind gnawing, gnawing." We saw ourselves attached, diffidently at first, but then easily, to a noisy party, arms linked, wearing paper hats, and hoped to make interesting discoveries about how one-day cruisers spent three continental hours.

None of this happened, of course. The *Royal Sovereign*, a most comfortable boat, carried us sedately down the Thames from Gravesend in the early morning. " Perhaps," we thought, " the ' real crowd ' comes aboard at Margate," and we sat quietly in our deck-chairs with our books, talking as people like ourselves talk continuously, throwing out words as slugs do slime to ease our way along. A trip to Margate on the *Royal Sovereign* was one of Samuel Butler's favourite diversions. He and Festing Jones would sit side by side, as G and I did with opened books in their laps, talking, and hoping that people would start singing. Sometimes Butler took Mr. Cathie, his confidential clerk, with him instead of Festing Jones. Mr. Cathie, elderly now, still occasionally makes the trip.

No " real crowd " came aboard at Margate, but only the same sort of people who had come aboard at Gravesend, mostly family parties and couples, and no unattached girls. They too sat about on chairs in the sun, and wrote postcards to post with foreign stamps, and ate picnic lunches, and listened to the loudspeaker recommending an excursion by motor-coach to places of interest in Ostend. The loudspeaker recommended this excur-

sion four times in identical words, the same joke four times repeated—" It won't be possible, I'm afraid, to stay long in the Casino ; but perhaps it's as well ! " It must be painful to have to make a joke of this calibre again and again through a loudspeaker.

We had a feeling we ought to do something documentary. We wandered about and looked at a girl sleeping in the sun, but there was nothing documentary about her ; and saw a man reading NIGHT AND DAY and thought we detected a faint smile. " How differently," I thought, " Mrs. Passfield and Lord Webb would have handled this situation ! They would have begun by finding out how many passengers there were ; then what proportion were on holiday with pay and what proportion belonged to the capitalist and landlord class." I saw them working through the ship from the bows to the stern questioning, noting down, preparing data, diving into the engine-room, climbing up on to the bridge, dauntless. Inspired by this idea, I went to change some money. That was documentary.

" What name ? " the officer asked.

I told him the name.

" Funny name," he said, not unkindly.

" I know," I said.

Wandering about, G remembered Mr. Whip. He had a letter saying that Mr. Whip would be at Ostend. He was Our Mr. Whip, and would tell us all we wanted to know about the *Royal Sovereign* and its clientèle. We fixed our documentary hopes on Mr. Whip and, secure in the prospect of meeting him, felt free to go back to our chairs. At Ostend, however, we faltered. There were two persons on the quay, either of whom might have been Mr. Whip. " Probably he's busy," I said. " It must be his busy time when the boat arrives. We can't bother him now." G agreed, and we never saw or shall see Mr. Whip. He passed out of our lives before coming into them.

Our fellow one-day cruisers dispersed, some into motor-coaches for the four times recommended excursion, some to sit on the beach and some to sit in cafés and restaurants. We watched them go helplessly. How were we to know their secret purposes, what propelled them here or there, what they hoped for in Ostend and what they found there ? " This documentary business," I said, " is absurd. What's the point of knowing about these people, what they do, how much money they spend and on what, who embraces whom ? The Mystery remains, each of us opening his eyes this morning, stretching, dressing, making for the boat, being carried over the sea's surface to this coast and in due course departing thence. Being all equally involved in this Mystery, the experience must be more or less the same for all of us, their day and ours the same." G suggested lunch.

The waiter who served us was a little florid excitable man with bright

FLAXMAN 1937: No. 13

Dante Up-to-date: a series of John Flaxman's illustrations to the Divine Comedy, as published in 1807, with new captions.

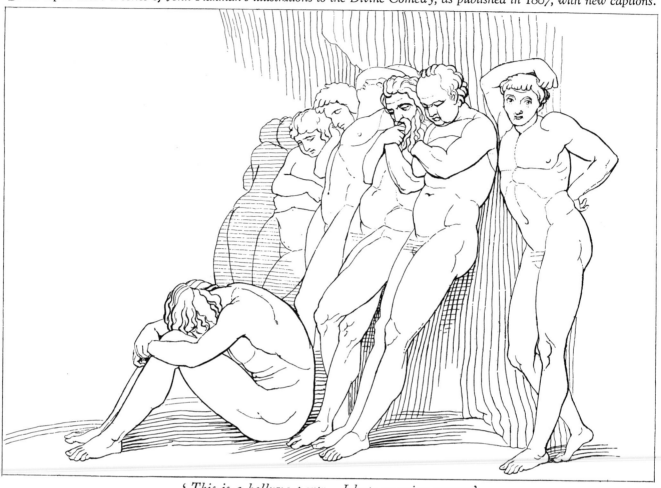

' This is a helluva party—I hate guessing games.'

eyes. I asked him what he thought of Degrelle and the Rexists. It is always foolish to talk in a foreign language. The mere delight of being able to do so at all lures one into foolishness, like making love on board ship. This is why the best foreign secretaries have known only their own language and detested going abroad. Talking to this waiter made me think apprehensively of Mr. Eden talking to, say, M. Daladier. As he served us with an inferior and expensive lunch he poured out vehement adulation of Degrelle, who, he said, was certain to come into power within a year; contemptuously dismissed parliamentary government as corrupt and irresponsible, and insisted that totalitarian States were necessary to prevent war. A washed-out-looking Swiss youth feebly protested that in Switzerland there was freedom. The little waiter laughed like Charles Laughton

playing Macbeth—" Freedom ! "

"Now we're on to something good," I thought : " Informed circles in Belgium take the view. . . . Feeling in favour of the Rex party is stronger than is commonly supposed among all sections of the population . . ." " C'est une crise morale, n'est-ce pas ? " I said. The little waiter beamed with savage enthusiasm. Even the Swiss youth smiled wanly. We got up to go, and I shook hands warmly with the little waiter. G more or less had to shake hands with him, too, but with understandable distaste. He managed to avoid the Swiss.

In a café in a sidestreet a woman sat with a man and moved her hand with quick sensual movements backwards and forwards across his waistcoat, but without touching it. He looked dazed and apprehensive. " Crise morale," I thought. Crowds of people lolled on the hot sand and

splashed in the sea and sat in coloured chairs listening to an orchestra. " Crise morale," I thought, angry with the little waiter lurking in his restaurant, shouting and gesticulating.

On the return journey we were both reconciled to being undocumentary. We did not even go through the pretence of looking for Mr. Whip, but sat in the saloon and had a drink or two and felt at ease. Night came on; no one sang or grew boisterous. It was all subdued and quiet. The little coloured lights on Margate pier appeared suddenly, and, behind them, a huge floodlit Dreamland, with a scenic railway and a solemn midget performing on a trapeze and a little phosphorescent lake in which boats bumped against each other, and an elderly bitter man grinding round a children's roundabout, and more people endlessly processing.

MALCOLM MUGGERIDGE

PURSUITS AND VERDICTS

Not So Tough

AMERICAN crime has a better sales value than our native kind. We still live in a world which has time to say " Criminal Investigation Department "—eleven syllables to the four (or is it three ?) of " Homicide Squad ". The two phrases express the difference between the two types of detective fiction. It does not follow, of course, that the squad stuff is written by tough guys on Broadway ; it is more likely to come from a Boston spinster or even an English highbrow. Have no illusions about the kind of people who write thrillers. There is Woosnam Mills, for example, " Mills for thrills". The publishers say that " he looks as if he came straight out of one of his own stories ; when he strolls into Nelson's office, looking leisured and carefree, we instantly begin to expect spies in the corridor, a lovely girl in distress ringing for the lift, and a high-powered Mercedes purring impatiently down in Paternoster Row ". But above this grim evocation they unfortunately print a photograph of his wistful intellectual face—the face of a poet, a mathematician, or the more ascetic kind of monk. Art, we are sometimes told, is a sublimation of our less reputable instincts ; but to the sublime all things are sublime, and in imagination they are free to lust and murder till the instincts are appeased.

The trouble, from my point of view, is that the sublime keeps creeping in. It is generally the lovely girl in distress who is responsible for its intrusion. To take the example of Mr. Mills again : " Proud as a fallen angel she might be, but such pride was good ; lovely as a morning sky and cool as the dew on meadow grass before it is touched by the sun—these also were her qualities by right. For these he loved her." Didn't I tell you he was a poet ! More-

over, " he vowed that no vultures should glut themselves because of her folly ; nor should she suffer the hell of remorse which must be hers if their schemes were successful ". So what then ? " So, with faith restored and a renewed zest for battle, he walked down into the hall to face madame." Still, the thrills are there, rather artificially contrived perhaps. The villains are scented, and have the right wispy kind of moustaches ; and the heroes have terrific punches. The aeroplanes perform incredible feats, and that high-powered car is always purring round the corner. It is grand fun for the younger members of the family, but I wish Mr. Mills would refrain from putting winter into

---

One Murdered—Two Dead. Milton M. Propper. Harrap. 7s. 6d.

Beginning with a Bash. Alice Tilton. Collins. 7s. 6d.

The Stairs Lead Nowhere. Howard Swiggett. Heinemann. 7s. 6d.

Stormy Night. Christopher Hale. Heinemann. 7s. 6d.

Grim Chancery. Woosnam Mills. Nelson. 7s. 6d.

The Blue Ridge Crime. Wyndham Martyn. Jenkins. 7s. 6d.

---

people's eyes ; Donne, we know, tried autumn with some success, but that is the limit.

The Blue Ridge Crime is written to recipe by an old hand who has more than twenty thrillers to his credit (financially speaking). Mechanical in construction, it moves like an old horse-cab, cluttered up with all the conventional properties, even the Voodoos. *The Stairs Lead Nowhere* does not live up to its good title ; it is a pretentious story in a setting of " exclusive Long Island society, dubious international financiers and New York racketeer intrigue "—the properties are more up to date, but they are properties all the same. The style is the best part of the intrigue. " Maynard poured some more coffee and broke the narcissistic shell of another egg." We

have always found our eggs distinctly indifferent to their own appearance. Christopher Hale (? male) is also betrayed by his/her style. On page 2 it puts us badly off the trail. " As she waited, stiff with dread, an enormous swallow forced its way down her throat." And there, from all the enlightenment we get from the story, the swallow still remains.

Beginning with a Bash has the mild and pleasant quality of an Agatha Christie, but either her sex or her nationality incapacitates the author when she brings her gangsters on the scene. They talk like last year's films and they act as if they had just been to Sunday School : " ' Say, maybe he's in the furnace, Bat ! ' ' He'll wish he was in the furnace if I lay my paws on him,' Bat promised darkly. ' Grabbing my sister, the ——— ' ' Well,' Biff said, ' you never give her no chance with none of the boys, why shouldn't she take up with him ? She had to take up with someone——— ' ' Shut up ! The mug ! ' " The detective is of the quaint eccentric type, visibly related to Poirot and Father Brown. The book is amusing rather than thrilling, which shows that the author ought to be doing another job.

One Murdered—Two Dead is by far the best story on the list—indeed, with the possible exception of Peter Cheney, Milton Propper is the best detective writer I have come across in my exploration of this underworld of literature. Though this story also has an American setting, it has nothing in common with the Cheney type ; that is to say, it is written in straight English, there are no gangsters in it, and the G-men are called detectives. Mr. Propper must be an American. The plot is dramatically effective ; the guilt is carefully concealed ; the clues are credibly baffling. Rankin is the ideal detective—sensible, serious and logical. There is no characterization nonsense ; the people are pawns ; the crime's the thing. There is also no poetic nonsense : the style is clear, colourless and effective. It is a dirty world, with no love and little laughter. It is the real world of murder and sudden death.

HERBERT READ

MINUTES OF THE WEEK

Autumnal

The season changes, in an aroma of moth-balls and to the tentative shuffle of dead leaves. Our unaccustomed sweaters fit snugger than they did in April. Bathing belles on posters have the awful, *passé* pertinence of yesterday morning's paper. Strange finds are made in fireplaces. Leggy, Leica'd squads of Central European and Middle Western youth no longer prowl before the outworks of Buckingham Palace. In smart night-clubs the faces of returned exiles are losing their mahogany, reverting to the good old brandy-beetroot. Along the top of Trafalgar Square, and in other places, you hear once more the starlings going to roost, making a fretful sibilant palimpsest of sound ; for months they have prepared for bed while you were at dinner. In the country young pigeons have learnt not to fly out on the

near side of a plantation, and already the partridges call at dusk with a slightly desolate note. Grass is green under white goal-posts. A prodigious number of mothers are wondering if it's really true that there is no bullying now. People smell different, and not so bad, in tubes and lifts and buses.

Only one major war has started

since we last drew the curtains after tea. Civilization is good to last till Christmas, in our view.

Feminists Under Fire

A good deal of brouhaha seems to have been caused by the references, in Mr. H. G. Wells's latest novel, to the weekly *Time and Tide*. Its presiding genius, Lady Rhondda, appears in the book as Lady Roundabout, and *Time and Tide* is rechristened *Wear and Tear*. The resultant stir prompted us to re-examine this earnest but sloppy publication, which we haven't been seeing for some time. *Wear and Tear*, we decided, wasn't a bad name for it ; only haggard, muggy good intentions could explain the sort of nonsense they were printing about (for instance) Russia and China. But one of the book reviews (some of which were quite good) had a sentence in it that we wouldn't have missed for worlds. Assessing Mr. John Lehmann's book about the Caucasus, an anonymous contributor wrote : " His book conveys better than any other I know the enthusiasm and tempo which is (*sic*) such a marked and exhilarating feature of Soviet life today." We'd imagined that the enthusiasm and tempo of Soviet life had gone, even in Bloomsbury, out of fashion, and we were delighted to see them reappear. We knew them both, at first hand. The vague, kindly, pregnant woman who takes two days to sell you a railway ticket ; the express due at midnight which interrupts your lunch next day ; the long and lapidary queues stamping mechanically against the post—we count ourselves

an expert on the Soviet tempo. Nor can you stump us on enthusiasm ; even the firing-squads, we hear, give three cheers for the other side before ejecting their spent cartridges.

All the same, we wish that *Wear and Tear* would set an example by indicating the real, not the imagined, delights of Russia under Stalin. Persuade people it's a kind of streamlined Rotarian Y.M.C.A., and they'll be sadly disappointed when they get there. Tell them it's a semi-Asiatic madhouse afflicted with European pretensions but endowed with considerable charm, and they may conceivably like it. And they can get a good reaction from the Russians, too, by calling them quaint and old-fashioned. But we doubt whether *Time and Tide*—proverbially accustomed to wait for no man—would ever get really broken in to Russia, where waiting for people is a national pastime.

Charity

The Chinese are having the hell of an awful time, and the public in this country is contributing to their relief. We had a sidelight on the motives behind a certain type of charity from a scribe we know. He had by him a list of names of donors to a fund and rang up the appropriate source to confirm the list. He was greeted by a squawk of dismay and a plea that he should keep his knowledge private until an official list was given. "You see," the voice said anxiously, "we've received several cheques from people on condition their names are published in the first list."

Slingsby

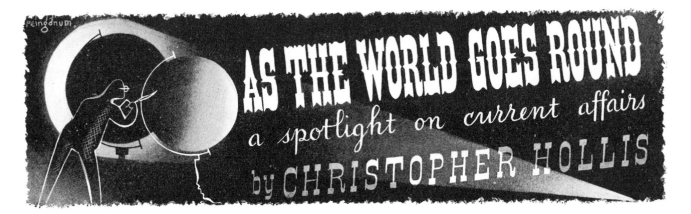

AS THE WORLD GOES ROUND
a spotlight on current affairs
by CHRISTOPHER HOLLIS

Stalin v. Trotsky

I DO not pretend to know—and I do not imagine that anybody else knows—the precise explanation of all the recent Russian executions, but at least it is possible to understand the broad issue of the controversy between Stalin and Trotsky. The Trotskyites say simply that Stalin has played traitor to the principles of Lenin. The Stalinites, less lucidly, evade definition by using Trotskyism as a term of abuse and accuse Trotskyites of wantonly sabotaging the magnificent Soviet effort. The truth is not quite so simple.

The personal antagonism between Stalin and Trotsky is easily explicable. Stalin is an old Bolshevik of no great philosophical capacity. Trotsky was a Communist who had consistently refused to ally himself to the Bolshevik party, and who was included by Lenin in the party at the last moment before successful revolution because Lenin despaired of the ability and courage of his regular Bolshevik subordinates. When the moment for revolution came, Trotsky stood by Lenin in his readiness to go through with it. Stalin —and Zinoviev and Kamanev— showed nerves and played for safety. As a result, when the Government came to be formed Trotsky was put over the heads of the old Bolsheviks, and it was beyond question Trotsky who saved the whole experiment in the critical years of civil war. Even Stalin admitted as much, though subsequently he wished that he hadn't.

On the other hand Trotsky lacks the gift of tact. He knew that he had been called in by Lenin because Lenin felt that he was indispensable. He did not forbear to show this. He is a Superior Person. He was, in great contrast to all his colleagues except Lunacharsky, a man of wide general culture, an intellectual, who had actually read the books which the others denounced as bourgeois. At meetings of the Cabinet, whenever any of the old Bolsheviks spoke Trotsky would ostentatiously take from his pocket a volume of Proust and read it until other opinions had been expressed. Then he would replace it and express his own. He disdained to play politics, thinking himself certain of the succession to Lenin, not because the others loved him but because they could not afford to lose him.

Stalin on the other hand is the supreme ward-boss. He is a man who can make others work for him. He established his position in the party by collecting funds for it—funds which he obtained through the organization of successful bank-robberies. He did not take part in these bank-robberies himself; he organized them. The agent of them was a certain Ter-Petrosian, an Armenian, who did the deeds and brought to Stalin the money which Stalin then distributed. When at last, after many hair-breadth adventures,

Ter-Petrosian was prosaically killed by being knocked off his bicycle by a motor-car, Stalin said "That only proves that nothing can stand in the way of mechanical progress." While Trotsky was away at the war, Stalin was busy filling up all the key-positions with friends of himself and enemies of Trotsky, and, as a result, when Lenin died, Stalin was able to seize power and to drive Trotsky into exile.

The issue between them is commonly stated to be whether, as the Trotskyites say, it is necessary to plot for a world revolution, or, as the Stalinites, Communism can maintain itself in Russia alone. Both appeal back to Lenin as infallible Pope, and both with a certain economy of honesty. For there is no doubt that Lenin thought that the Russian revolution must be followed *quite soon* by revolutions in the Western countries. He did not think that the developments that have in fact taken place were possible. His contention was not so much that Communism could not maintain itself in a capitalist world as that capitalism would not be able to maintain itself in a world in which the workers had before them the example of a working communist government. It is therefore a little absurd for either party to appeal back to Lenin as the judge of their present disputes.

Anyone who reads the works of Lenin which the Stalinites have selected for publication, or V. Sorin's Stalinite biography of him, must see that it is a mistake to imagine that the Stalinites have abandoned their desire for a world revolution. Both Stalinites and Trotskyites are Marxians, and

' You don't think they're awful, you know they're awful ? Why, that's what Gladstone used to say about oysters !'

★   ★   ★

Marxians are compelled to believe not so much that world revolution is desirable as that it is inevitable. The difference between the two groups is a difference concerning the method of working for it. The Trotskyites prefer direct communist propaganda in capitalist countries. The Stalinites are more subtle. They recall the teaching of Lenin between the Russo-Japanese and the Great War. Lenin thought that a capitalist government at peace would always be able to suppress a communist movement. War was communism's opportunity. And so the Stalinite policy has been to intervene in European politics in such a way as to foster enmity and to preserve division between the Western powers.

Whether Trotsky did plot with either the Germans or the Japanese to cede to them Russian territory I do not profess to know. Certainly the official story that was told against him was not wholly true. Some of the details of it were demonstrably refutable. At the same time it is only reasonable to understand that such a bargain would be in no way a violation of Trotsky's principles of honour. Trotsky is an internationalist. To him Russia is nothing. The world revolution is all that matters. National divisions are capitalist fictions to deceive the workers. At the Treaty of Brest-Litovsk he and Lenin made gigantic concessions to the Germans and justified themselves by the plea that both Germany and Russia would be communist soon and temporary national boundaries were therefore of no importance. What Trotsky did at Brest-Litovsk he may well have done again. If so, he does not think of himself as handing over Russian territory to Hitler or the Mikado. He is plotting a war—a war in which the anti-Communist Hitler and Mikado and the pseudo-Communist Stalin will infallibly go down and true Communism find its opportunity to establish itself in their places.

BLACKPOOL BELLE

WHATEVER way you come to Blackpool the first you see of it is the Tower, Eiffel's not so much smaller sister. That's where little Albert was eaten by the lion and his mother wept for the lost new cap. You can dance here for a shilling and choose any of Lancashire and Yorkshire's neat-fingered little mill-girls you see for a partner. She won't expect you to take her any farther than the edge of the floor after the dance, though if you are interested you can go and see the caged birds and the fishes free, and for an extra sixpence go up the Tower and look down on Blackpool's swarming sands and Prom.

After you have first seen the Tower you run through the newly built *umgebung* of camps. The biggest of these has just opened a new ballroom, a " Moorish Palace of the imagination, with a colour scheme in the traditional Spanish idea, bright orange, blue, gold and silver predominating ". Campers, though, live in Swiss chalets, for about a shilling a night each.

Then Blackpool proper begins, the Blackpool of the boarding-house and bed-and-breakfast lodger—trim little houses with rockeries in front, known by the landlady's name and a number. There is usually a tent in the back garden, where the family overflows to make room for the lodgers. You get a double bed for four shillings a night and bring your own food in. The landlady gives you a cupboard in the sideboard and cooks the food for you without charge. At the bigger lodging houses, the Bella Vistas, the Cliftons and Marinas, there is usually a choice of full board, and visitors are asked to state, before ten o'clock each day, whether they will take the lodgers' pudding for dinner. You must be punctual for meals, out of your bedrooms by ten, put the lights out by midnight ; and you must not empty your sandshoes onto the carpet. Visitors are particularly requested to prevent their children from playing the piano. Beyond these again lie the superior castellated hotels.

But social distinctions, neatly de-fined by the lodgings you take, break down once you get out of them. On the Pleasure Beach there is an " attraction " called the Social Mixer which hurls you about, separates you from your girl, batters your inhibitions down and puts you, for a mere shilling, into a new class. But on the Prom. and the sands, in the Tower and the Bathing Pool the mixing is as effective and less rough. There is no pretentiousness, and everybody takes it for granted that you are a normal being, who likes being splashed by a pretty girl, knows the words of *In September* and *Boo-Hoo*, and eats fish and chips when the pubs close. " Bathers are advised to remove spectacles and teeth before entering pool, to save losing same," reads the notice in the baths.

These millions who come to Blackpool work mostly fifty-one weeks in

the year and pay for their own holiday of one week. They work in small bleak manufacturing towns on each side of the Pennines. Once a week they go to the cinema, they meet few strangers, and on Sundays they go to tea with friends. Radio and newspapers have peopled their world with personalities whose activities seem remote enough from Keighley, Irlam-o'-th'-Heights, and Ramsbottom. And suddenly, at Blackpool, the Grand Transformation Scene—Gracie herself, eyes flashing specially at you, head flung back, her personality as infectious as La Argentina's. And on the sea, in sight from ten thousand boarding-house windows, what other possible ship than the Girl Pat ? " She looked at me, she looked up and smiled," said the young woman as she came from seeing Colonel Barker in pyjamas, corralled by Belisha beacons from the bed of " his or her bride ".

This policy of plugging the Real Presence, Blackpool puts it across every time. It wins all along the line over mechanical games. Real Abyssinians at Luna Park, Reginald Dixon zooming up out of the ballroom floor at the seat of his great white organ, to the greeting " Eh, Reggie " of ten thousand radio fans. Lobbie Lud, Gordon Harker, Bebe Daniels, they're all here and they all get their clothes torn off their backs if they are recognized. Outside the booth where he was exhibited last year stands the Rector of Stiffkey's tub. On it there is a white sheet, spread over a dummy figure. There is no notice, no explanation. But Blackpool files past and says, with reverence : " That's the tub 'e was in last year, and that's 'im, see ? "

Souvenirs are selling well this year. But rock is demodé, and more sophisticated shapes of sweetmeat are now to be bought : a tie modelled in sugar paste, with stripes ranging from the local cricket club to Old Marlburians ; May's Vest, a nicely modelled sugary torso ; and " 'er Thing-ume-Bobs ", another part of female attire.

A fortnight ago the lights went on, th' Illuminations. During four months it is the people who have made the picture, massing on the Prom. in routined rhythm. Now, in the autumn when other resorts are totting up their takings, Blackpool turns a hand to picture-making. This flowerless town is suddenly festooned with electric vegetation, in which electric parrots flap their wings.

A favourite hymn at Revivalist meetings this year runs :

I lost it on Calvary's Hill,
It tumbled and tumbled until
It rolled out of sight,
I was happy that night,
I lost it on Calvary's Hill."

That's the Blackpool spirit. Normality rolls out of sight. The factory chimney blossoms into a tower. Girls wear trousers and men wear women's straw-hats. Breakfast is late every day. You don't listen to the wireless because the stars are there, looking down at you with a smile. The pubs are open half an hour extra.

" Isn't it grand ? " " Love*lee*."

RALPH PARKER

[145]

Contentment Column

Reassuring and Inspiring Items from the Press, a Corrective to Scare Headlines and Private Worries.

SOLUTION

In the novel he has just published, Mr. H. G. Wells throws out an interesting suggestion as to how women might widen their intellectual interests. The heroine, Brynhild, decides to have " not one child, but *children*, and the best I can get. . . . When all that is under way, then surely at last I shall take an intelligent interest in—say—education. And politics."

SAFEGUARD

In the Thames Valley Bus Company's timetables we read :
Specials to Berkshire Mental Hospital First and third Thursdays of each month only.
Return Fare 2s. 6d.
Only Return Tickets Issued.

SEEING IS BELIEVING

The Rev. Leslie Weatherhead, of the City Temple, supports the movement for introducing films into religious services. In the Gospels, he says, religion was made thrilling, and God became " what journalists today call ' hot news '. We must do the same."

SYMPATHY

Anyone contemplating suicide will be relieved to learn that Mr. Godfrey Winn has passed through the same experience. There have been moments, he tells us, when he has had suicidal thoughts. " I am not, you see, lacking in sympathy, and understanding of the things of the spirit—of the conflicts that go on deep below the surface."

BENEVOLENCE

" Laicus Ignotus," of the *Church Times*, tells us that the Bishop of Liverpool has " with his characteristic kindliness " informed " Laicus Ignotus " that he misrepresented what the Bishop said about the Spanish war.

SUCCESS

A counsel defending a man charged with bigamy has disclosed that the fracture of his client's skull some years ago released a streak of genius which enabled the man, though without education, to become a successful journalist. Now all that remains to be discovered is what form of physical injury will enable an educated man to succeed in journalism. **H. K.**

Those Stately Homes—2

Where Starlings Nest

THERE is only one really terrific, really breath-taking house—Seaton Delaval. Nobody lives in the main part of it. It is full of starlings, and if you go in with your best hat on your head it won't be your best when you come out. Seaton is in Northumberland. If you have a car, you go there by car ; if you haven't, you go by bus from Newcastle. They put you down at the gates. Unless you are expected by the people who live in the low building along the forecourt you won't know what to do, because you can't go into the house and you can't stand in the road and gaze at it indefinitely. So either you cross the road and take the next bus back to Newcastle or you make shift to see the house from new points of view. I forget whether you have to trespass to do this, but with tact and forethought it can be done.

Seaton was designed by John Vanbrugh, an architect with an imagination like Shakespeare's, by which I mean that he wasn't just a professional person who tried very hard and came out top of the class—he found life too exciting for that. First soldiering, then writing plays, absorbed him. But he hadn't quite that kind of mind ; he needed something with more obvious, hearty difficulties than writing so he took to architecture. He had few themes and he worked them pretty hard. Perhaps you've seen them on parade at Castle Howard or Blenheim or Eastbury or King's Weston. But it was at Seaton, his last great house, that John Vanbrugh, in a manner of speaking, rang the bell.

I suppose anybody who has been in prison for something they're not expected to be ashamed of looks back on prison days with a certain horrid but pleasurable excitement. Vanbrugh

did. He'd been shut up in Vincennes and in the Bastille for running about France without a passport. He went to prison a soldier and a man of the world ; he came out ditto, but chastened by two years' compulsory introversion and haunted by Gothic ghosts. The older he got the more the shapes of Vincennes and the Bastille possessed him. . . .

Hence Seaton. From the distance it's a monstrous, craggy pile, humped in the middle like an angry cat. It has none of your South Kensington connoisseur's elegance, grace, charm, urbanity, nice distinction. It is grotesque, mordant, flaunting the dangerous crenels and murlons of an enchanted castle. It is a fragment of Claude come abruptly to life, with the painter's brush-strokes adjusted into a fantastic ordonnance.

And there is nothing soft or caressing in the landscape—raw Northumbrian low-land, dead level with the sea. East winds thunder across it, vibrating little stiff oaks, crimping the hedges and tiding the coarse grass into grey-green eddies. Underneath is coal. Coal threatens Seaton as it threatens every great house in east Northumbria. There are pitheads on the skyline and locomotives clank

across the park to Cullercoats and Tynemouth.

So Seaton Delaval, for all its bulk, may not last our time. It is certain that nobody will ever again live in its wrecked and fire-scorched towers. The Roman goddesses in the inaccessible niches will stand there till the frost cracks away their torsos. Limbs and faces are already gone.

Who built this house ? An old weather-beaten admiral, a bachelor, humorous, cynical, much decayed with the scurvy : George Delaval. He didn't expect to live long. He'd had his day. In Tangiers, Portugal, Morocco he'd paid court to Alcaids and Emperors—and come back the richer for it. He bought the Seaton estate from his cousin and to employ himself in some way that might be useful to posterity he started building. Vanbrugh came over from Castle Howard to see about it.

"The Admiral is very gallant in his operations," said Captain Van, when he had persuaded Delaval to leave the old house and start building from scratch. A capable clerk-of-works was got from York and the gigantic rustics of the basement storey heaved themselves out of the plain. Then, block over block, the walls and columns rose till the wind whistled through a stark yellow carcase of fresh masonry. One day, riding about the place, George Delaval fell off his horse and died.

But Vanbrugh went ahead, and Delaval's nephew, Francis, came and lived at Seaton. Glorious days followed. Francis had a wife called Rhoda, plenty of money and a huge family. Seaton glittered. There were parties all the time, with " Pantomin entertainments", tilts, tournaments, gamblings and bull-baitings. And dancing bears. After Francis came ambitious " Punch " Delaval who got himself made a lord. His son and heir was called John. Following the routine of his caste and station John, aged 19, assailed the modesty of one of the domestic staff, was kicked for his pains (never mind where) and died of it. He was the last of his line, so they built a huge mausoleum over him, but it was never consecrated, because the Bishop's fee was too high.

There are no Delavals at Seaton now. There are no Delavals anywhere that I can discover—none in Debrett, Who's Who, or even the London Telephone Directory.* The Delavals are

---

* Unless you count a de Laval, Walker Richard, Sydenham 6967.

extinct. And, come to think of it, it's not a bad thing, because to have that centre block at Seaton inhabited by anything but ghosts would be unbearable. Only imagine the loathsome conversational skirmishes of the Mrs. Delaval-Smythe the centuries might have thrown up. " Of course, if you're interested in old things you ought to see our place in the north. A Vanbrugh house, you know. Yes—Vanbrugh. The architect, you know." And at Seaton we should have purred and lapped whisky, listening to the Major's strictures on death duties and the price of coke. . . .

No, it can't happen. And if anybody tries it, the ghosts of infuriated Delavals will hurl them out on their necks.   JOHN SUMMERSON

*

Saturday's Football. Many Surprises Expected.—*News Chronicle.*

When is a surprise not a surprise ?

ON AND OFF THE ROAD

Ambling at 70

RIGHT up at the top of the motoring tree are two cars—modern representatives of makes that have been there since the start—the 4¼ litre Bentley and the 4·3 litre Alvis. Both cost a thousand pounds or more, they are nearly the same size, and split seconds divide their performances. Both more than fulfil the exacting requirements of a car in this class—and in case you don't know what those requirements are, here is a list : it should be able to travel at 90 miles an hour, to accelerate from rest to 50 m.p.h. through the gears in under 11 seconds, its brakes should be 100 per cent. efficient (which means stopping in 30 feet from 30 m.p.h.), it should be able to hold the road like a leech, to travel in the Mall easily and comfortably yet be able to corner at speed, it should be at least moderately silent and not wildly expensive to run. All this is a lot to ask of a car, but then twelve or fourteen hundred pounds is a lot to ask for a car.

Like a well-known brand of whisky, the 4¼ litre Bentley is an excellent example of good blending, although the Rolls Royce influence is the more noticeable—that is to say, its quietness and smooth running tend to make the terrific acceleration and high maximum speed (the old Bentley characteristics) seem less than they actually are. But the most interesting thing about the car, both when you first take control of it and after several hundred miles, is the extraordinary ease with which you can drive it. Everything is exactly where it should be, the pedals are all well placed and the right height (a great rarity) and the controls work simply and well. Under these conditions one could drive a much more sluggish car long distances without fatigue. And that I think should be the

first consideration of anyone buying a car.

Perhaps the least remarkable thing about it is its performance, which is excellent, but that is not surprising. What is surprising is the way it goes about its work, without fuss or effort, almost without appearing to try ; it is in fact a rather misleading car to drive at speeds between 40 and 65 miles an hour, as you get the impression that you are just ambling along and it isn't until you get beyond 70 that you feel you are going at all fast. A speed of 70 to 75 seems to be the pleasantest for cruising and I should like to emphasize that at that speed, with its really good steering and superb brakes, it is a very much safer vehicle than the average baby car travelling at 37 miles an hour.

This question of braking is rather an important one. I feel that too many manufacturers are fitting brakes that will pull the car up in the shortest possible space, without paying enough attention to their smoothness and the progressiveness of their action. It is tiring and dangerous if the passengers are flung forward every time the brakes are applied suddenly. The Bentley is a model of perfection in this respect. I have never driven a car that can be stopped so swiftly and smoothly.

Compared with its engine size, it is not a large car, but there is plenty of room and a great deal of comfort for four people, and on the Vanden Plas drop-head coupé which I tried there was a generous luggage locker. This particular body, which was tomato-coloured, with dark red wings, was able to wring praise from the least motor-minded of my acquaintances.

Finally there were two small points which indicate the tremendous amount of care that goes into the making of a car like this. The first concerned the tyres. As you can imagine, the unusual accelerating and braking qualities of the car on modern non-skid road surfaces soon wear out ordinary tyres, so Bentleys have theirs designed and built specially for them, and in order that the balance should be as accurate as possible the weight of the cover is

specially reduced at one point to counteract the extra weight of the valve.

The other point that I liked was a centrifugally controlled loader which automatically hardens the springs as the speed of the car increases. The ordinary hand control is superimposed on this in the same way that the hand ignition is superimposed on the automatic one, so that you are able to get the maximum benefit on varying road surfaces.

4¼ litre Bentley. 30 h p. Tax £22:10:0. Maximum speed over ¼ mile 90·91. Acceleration from rest to 50 m.p.h. through gears 10·3 seconds. Braking from 30 m.p.h. 30 feet. Petrol consumption 16 miles per gallon. Tank capacity 18 gallons. Price £1,550 with a Vanden Plas drop-head coupé body.

The 4·3 litre Alvis is the largest car that the firm has built, and although it costs three or four hundred pounds less than the Bentley it falls into the same category. I have not had an opportunity of taking it on a long trial run, but the impression it gave me in the short time that I did drive it was of a car with tremendous zest ; it actually seemed more lively than the Bentley, although the test figures show that it is slower. The engine was just a little rougher and the springing harder over the hand-controlled range, and with the slightly larger engine it costs just a little more to run. On the whole I should say it was more of an enthusiast's car—less docile at low speeds and less unobtrusive when being driven in the Park.

I understand that the Alvis company are shortly bringing out a short chassis model with a touring body which sounds even more exciting. They claim a top speed of 100 miles an hour, 50 m.p.h. from rest through the gears in 9·2 and 80 in 22·2 seconds ; it will stop in 25 feet or less from 30 m.p.h. These are amazing figures for a car that will sell at £995 and I am very much looking forward to trying it.

4·3 litre Alvis. 32 h.p. Tax £24:0:0. Maximum speed over ¼ mile 90·00. Acceleration from rest to 50 m.p.h. through the gears 10·9 seconds. Braking from 30 m.p.h. 33·5 feet. Petrol consumption 13·16 miles per gallon. Tank capacity 17 gallons. Price £1,185 with a Vanden Plas pillarless saloon body.

SELWYN POWELL

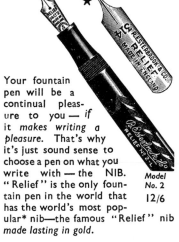
ROBOTS AT EARLS COURT
FASTER, FASTER !

THE busy captain of industry could see the Business Efficiency Exhibition which closed at Earls Court yesterday with amazing rapidity. " The first impression of the visitor is that of an immense executive office—the whole of which can be viewed immediately one enters the doors." Everything had been done to make the exhibition convenient for those who live by the second-hand of the clock.

Naturally time-saving exhibits predominated. " It is calculated that the average user of pencils wastes six hours every year trying to keep his pencils sharpened," said the proprietors of one stand, offering a pencil which needed no sharpening. A firm which manufactures dictaphones wrote : " If you count up the many minutes lost in waiting for your shorthand typist to appear, sharpen her pencil and find the place in her notebook, you will realize why many " Ediphone " users gain without effort fully sixty minutes a day—more than a whole month in a year."

All the precious moments which the business man probably enjoys wasting are swept away from him. He has no longer any excuse for a pleasant game of noughts and crosses against himself as he waits to put through a telephone call to someone in another part of the building. Winking lights and ringing bells will find the person he wants in a second.

The uncompromising faces of clocks were to be seen all over the exhibition. There was a clock which automatically records the time when employees arrive at work ; if an employee is late, it severely draws attention to the fact in red ink. There were time-stamps which print out the exact time at the touch of a finger, and devices which will ring bells and sound hooters at any given minute throughout the week.

The statistics given for the innumerable labour saving devices are overpowering. There were Lightning Letter Openers which open 500 letters per minute ; Sealing Machines which seal over 100 envelopes per minute ; Stamp Affixing Machines which affix 70 stamps per minute ; Copper Counting Machines which sort and count thirty shillings' worth of copper per minute ; Electrically-driven Silver Sorters which sort large quantities of mixed silver at the rate of £60 worth per minute ; Addressographs which print 60 names and addresses per minute.

All these machines could be seen busily working away with very little outside help. Outstanding among them was the Auto-Typist, who is already making her insidious way into offices. One girl can look after four of her, and she produces 180 to 200 full-length quarto-sheet letters in eight hours. Next in interest in the typewriter class came a baby portable, the smallest and lightest yet made, which is very little higher than an ordinary matchbox.

A large number of the typewriters were in use, and their clacking mingled with the ticking of various strange machines which continually disgorged yards and yards of paper from their entrails. Telephones—green, red, brown, black, and even gold and silver ones—buzzed or rang intermittently. Electric signs flashed off and on : " Engaged ", " Come In ", " Engaged ", " Come In ". People sat about raptly listening to their own voices coming back to them on Dictaphones or Ediphones.

A little business inefficiency would be nice for a change. One thinks yearningly of dusty offices in small provincial towns with improbable pictures of prize bulls round the walls. Where the clerk sits on a high stool at a desk on which he has carved his initials deep into the wood and inked them in—the work of long hours of laborious leisure. Where no one ever has an indiarubber, and pencils are sharpened with razor blades. But no doubt in a few years they too will have engaged an Auto-Typist.

MARGARET J. MILLER

RADIO

a commentary by JOHN HAYWARD

Public Relations

A RUMOUR seems to have got about in the last few months that the B.B.C. is hopelessly out of touch with its listeners. I suspect that this rumour is, in part, an off-shoot of the campaign to popularize all-wave sets, the implication being that no one wants to listen to the silly old B.B.C. now that China and Peru can be had (after a fashion) for the asking. I very much doubt, though, if the B.B.C.'s programmes are bombinating in a total vacuum, for, in spite of the roaring success the manufacturers had with their cheap all-wave sets at Radiolympia, it won't be long, I believe, before the public finds that short-wave listening is a cheat and a disappointment and is likely to remain so until a cure is found for fading, man-made static and other interference.

The B.B.C., it is true, would like to know more than it does about its listeners' views. Its mail-bag is not any smaller, though, than it used to be. 150,000 letters were popped into its letter-box in 1935; 10,000 more last year; and this year they've already started overflowing on to the mat. All, except the very rude ones, are answered. Or so I'm told. Yet I can't help remembering an experience I had some years ago when I attempted to make a helpful gesture.

I'd set an English Essay paper for candidates (both sexes; ages 18–20) for jobs in the public service. One of the essays was " Write a criticism of British Broadcasting ". A very large majority of the 500 candidates took this question and between them produced an extremely varied and interesting commentary on the B.B.C.'s work. Their criticisms were valuable for three reasons: (1) They were serious; you can't afford to play the fool in a competitive examination. (2) The candidates belonged to the class that provides the bulk of the B.B.C.'s licence holders. (3) The candidates fairly represented the listening public, for they came not only from London but from regional centres. I happened to know a high official at Broadcasting House just well enough to ask him if he would care to dine with me and hear what some of these young critics had to say. He accepted with what I took to be enthusiasm. But on the morning of the day in question, I was rung up by his secretary, informed with regret that pressure of business prevented him from coming, and told that he would ring me up the following week. I have heard nothing more from that day to this.

I quote this fragment of autobiography not as a warning but with the hope that this sort of thing no longer happens now that there are a Public Relations Department and a Listeners' Research Department eager and anxious to know what people think and what they want. They're particularly anxious, for example, to know what you think about the " Clear Thinking " series of talks that begins on October 5 and will send special question forms and reply-paid envelopes to anyone who thinks he'll be able to listen to all or at least some of the talks. (Every Tuesday evening 7.30–8.) Send in your name and address " and, if possible, occupation " (this, out of consideration, presumably, for spies and burglars). It's just part of the B.B.C. service.

THE BALLET

A Triumph for Lichine

COLONEL W. de Basil's Ballets Russes are back again at Covent Garden and so are all of us. There is one important change in the company, but with so much individual talent and the inestimable advantage of more than five years' work together—enabling them to reach a standard unapproached by any other ballet dancers since the death of Diaghilev—there is every reason to suppose that the September season will be as successful and satisfactory as the July season was. As a matter of fact (I hope the gallery will never unmask my incognito) Massine's absence in many ways adds to the interest of the performances. *Petrouchka* must have surprised all but the most penetrating balletomanes : I never thought Shabelevsky would be able to do the difficult title-rôle so well. His make-up was not good and, probably because he could not manage the very complicated timing of the solo scene, he was not sufficiently moving at the end, but he started extremely well and no doubt in time he will be able to sustain our sympathy right through the ballet. Fokine's direction is evident in the improvement shown in the crowd scenes (though they always did them well) and Lichine's lazy stupid Blackamoor is delightful. Danilova was the Dancer.

It is difficult to keep reviewing *Aurora's Wedding*, *La Boutique Fantasque* and *Prince Igor* without lapsing into technicalities. These ballets were well danced, *Aurora* not quite so well as the others, but the remarkable thing was Lichine's Can-Can dance. In July this was uncertain ; now it is brilliant. Surely this suggests that among so many talented dancers the rôles could be interchanged occasionally without waiting for necessity to compel.

Lichine's *Francesca da Rimini*, which continues to impress me, is taking an important place in the repertoire of the company. This dramatic version of Dante's story, adapted by Lichine and H. Clifford, is thrilling from the point of view of plot alone even when one is seeing it for the third time in six days. I have watched Lichine's progress as choreographer with excitement : *Nocturne* already gave promise of poetry and *Les Imaginaires* of intellect, unsatisfactory ballets though they were ; then came *Pavillon*, a charming success, and last *Francesca*, fully justifying one's hopes. Naturally the influence of Nijinska is apparent in *Pavillon* and that of Massine in certain crowd arrangements in *Francesca*, but they are the best possible teachers to develop Lichine's special gifts of vitality and original thinking.

How greatly I admire Mme. Tchernicheva, both when she is handing out poisoned cups and stabbing herself with well-tempered steel, according to the exigencies of the situation ! She portrays Francesca with a beauty beyond praise ; her first entry and her solo dance at the beginning of the second scene are the most moving moments in the ballet. Platof (he *is* a good actor) makes a dignified and sinister Malatesta and Petrof is a sympathetic Paolo, though I prefer Lichine himself in this romantic part. Riabouchinska leads the angelic visions and Danilova and Baronova alternate in the rôle of Guinevere, but, lovely as Guinevere's dance is, it is not altogether à propos in style and the costume seems more suitable for Lady Godiva, even if Francesca *did* consider the unfortunate Queen a barbarian. Lazovsky and Borovansky danced well and so did the corps de ballet in their difficult crowd scenes—even the duel did not appear ridiculous. The early Renaissance atmosphere is most convincing except that Chiara and her companions, dressed like nuns, are in the nun-conscious likely to produce a twentieth-century titter instead of a period horselaugh. Perhaps one may count on the audience not to be nun-conscious : even so the sight of the poor good woman worried by dwarfs fails as robust sacrilegious comedy ; it is somehow a little foolish and one feels one could get her removed more satisfactorily with a block and tackle. Mr. Messel's costumes are very handsome and parts of his setting admirable. Am I right in wishing him to have a little more courage and a little less fidelity to his sources ? Dishonourable mention must be given to the drop curtain. I like the Tchaikowsky music a great deal better than is fashionable.

In acclaiming *Francesca da Rimini* as a work of importance we must not forget that such a success is only possible now because of Fokine's revolt nearly twenty years ago. I was indeed disturbed that anyone should have put themselves out to revive *Cleopatra*, much better dead in my opinion (I believe she is dead again now), but it was all the same interesting to attend the resurrection last July of this work, one of Fokine's earliest attempts to show that ballet can be truly dramatic. The interest remained mildly archeological, however, as the ballet is composed largely of *longueurs* and languors, and it was difficult to imagine that the Queen's singular and no doubt authentic entry, or the " bee-keepers' veil " dance, the George Arliss Chief Priest and the missish Bacchantes were a courageous attempt to introduce real local colour and costume instead of the traditional travesties prescribed by usage. Still that was the beginning, and now we can add ten years to our lives by watching Francesca and Paolo die in genuine Renaissance agony.

PERDITA STANLEY

British Raj
by Patrick Balfour

THE new Governor was about to be sworn in. Nairobi had gathered before the building of the Legislature in coats and skirts and chiffon frocks, terais and topees, white suits and morning coats, white and khaki uniforms, with parking labels on the windscreens of its cars and tickets of admission in its hands : pink, white, or blue ones according to its various degrees of importance. A detachment of native troops in pale khaki uniforms, red fezes, red cummerbunds and blue puttees was drawn up behind a drummer in a leopard-skin. There were detachments of Wolf Cubs, Boy Scouts and Girl Guides (principally Indians), and some Indian girls in green and yellow saris. The Chief Justice, in red robes, the Mayor, in red robes, the Town Clerk and another legal official wearing a topee over his lawyer's wig were gathered under the portico of the Legislature, and a loudspeaker relayed their conversation to the crowd. Spectators craned from the windows of the building, which had been designed by Sir Herbert Baker in his apologetic imperialist style and resembled a smaller edition of the Secretariat at New Delhi. There was nothing to indicate what country we were in, save that we were under the British flag. But it would have been pardonable to guess India.

The ceremony was as apologetic as Sir Herbert Baker's building. The Governor and his wife, who wore pearls and a smart black fur, drove up in an open car while the band played *God Save the King*. The crowd hesitated whether to take its topees off and risk sunstroke or to keep them on and risk disloyalty. Most of it compromised and raised them two inches from the head. The Governor made an informal inspection of the Guard of Honour. The band played a deprecatory air from light opera, as though echoing the general feeling that all this ceremonial stuff was rather absurd, really, but one supposed it had to be gone through with.

The Governor proceeded to Sir Herbert Baker's portico. A black-robed official read the oath with not too many mistakes. The Governor repeated it. A red-robed official mumbled it again, self-consciously. The Governor repeated it and firmly kissed the book. The loudspeaker relayed the kiss and then broke down. In dumb show the mayor addressed the Governor and made him a presentation which he accepted with becoming embarrassment, as though it were a complete surprise. The loudspeaker recovered in time to relay his thank-you and the modest speech which followed.

The Governor said what a help it was to his wife and himself to have such a welcome. He had never had this sort of job before, and the audience had no idea what a difference it made to feel such an atmosphere of goodwill and friendship surrounding him and to have such a welcome. He could assure them that both he and his wife would do their best to live up to the characteristics, might he say ideals, of our most precious heritage, ideals which must always of course be tempered by a sense of balance and a sense of humour. " Sometimes (*sic*)," he said, " it is a good thing to think widely " ; and he modestly implied that he would endeavour to do so. " While we are here," he continued, " my wife and myself intend to make Kenya our home." This was a highly popular remark and occasioned loud applause. The last Governor had been accused of a violent antipathy to the settlers. When the applause subsided the Governor quoted General Wolfe. Then he quoted Solomon, to indicate that he had spoken quite long enough, said thank-you again, and sat down.

Tension relaxed and a buzz of conversation started on the dais.

" Well," shouted the loudspeaker, " *that's* over. Went off all right, didn't it ? "

" Excellent speech, I thought, very much to the point."

" I was wondering if you'd care to lunch with me on Thursday."

" That's very kind of you. I'd love to."

" Capital. One-fifteen. I'm off on leave on Friday, you know."

" Lucky fellow. Wish I was."

A procession of ladies and gentlemen shook hands with the Governor and his wife.

" *How* do you do ? " the loudspeaker asked, in a loud flat voice

" How *do* you do ? "

" Nice of you to write."

'Do you remember any of the jokes about this situation?'

★   ★   ★

" How do you *do* ? "

" Oh, not at all."

" *Howd*'youdo ? "

" Yes it was lovely flying over Entebbe."

" Howd'*do* ? "

" It *must* have been."

" How'do ?   How'do ?   H'do ? "

The party descended from the dais and shook hands with a few people in the crowd, the Diplomatic representatives were forgotten, the Girl Guides were inspected, the car drove off, Nairobi dispersed to buy plants at the florist's, the ceremony was over. From start to finish I had not detected a reference to the African. He could have been pardoned (perhaps wrongly) for thinking that the whole thing had very little to do with him. But then I didn't see many Africans present.

RAG GIRLS'

EVERYTHING is supposed to have its funny side, and generally it's the inside. " Get the inside story," people tell you ; " some jolly amusing things go on behind the scenes." When I asked Mr. Victor Stiebel if he would let me be inside his mannequins' room while his Press Show was going on, he very kindly let me, though he wasn't very keen. There were seven mannequins with their seven dressers, and two women from the workrooms with pins in their mouths and needles in their bosoms, and hundreds of dresses and hats, and gloves, and bags, and shoes. But although the room was very small, there wasn't any screaming or snatching. Everyone was very busy and extraordinarily quiet. Nothing funny. Nothing like back-stage in the *Good Companions.* And there was nothing that I could find amusing in the revealed perfections of the mannequins. I could only feel uncomfortably jealous. It was when I rejoined the audience, the Ladies of the Press, that I saw which was the funny side.

BY ALISON HAIG

Women of the Press who write about fashions are known as Rag Girls. But whether it is the clothes we write about that are the rags, or our papers, or the clothes we wear ourselves, isn't clear. But since it was the dress houses, I believe, who christened us, I have a feeling that we don't get the name from the clothes we write about. Anyway, just now are our glad rag days. The merry-go-round of the dress shows is on. Out we come from our crevices in Fetter Lane and Shoe Lane and Carmelite Street, and take buses to Piccadilly and taxis round the corner to Bruton Street, Grosvenor Street, Berkeley Square.

The disturbing thing about these Autumn Dress Shows is WHAT TO WEAR. Most of us haven't long come back from our holidays but, however warm the September sunshine, it wouldn't do to wear summer clothes to an Autumn Collection. There's the prestige of the paper to consider, and the competitive spirit. Some seem to think that the difficulty is solved by piling on furs. Nearly everybody purchases a new felt hat in haste, which everybody else prophesies will be repented at leisure. A few rush into a whole new outfit which all but bears the price-ticket—a pity not to have the courage to wait till after we've seen the new collections. But quite a number are of the perennial coat-and-skirt kind, so for them there is no problem. Their interest in clothes is purely professional. But how it was ever aroused, how they ever became Rag Girls, that is one of the sweet mysteries of life.

Press Shows would start on the tick if it weren't for the Press. The mannequins are waiting, made-up and on their toes, but still the Rag Girls come. Some arrive late in order to give the impression of being busy, important people. Others because they believe it isn't done to arrive in good time. Others because they are scared of being early. Others never seem to get there at all. It is disappointing to take the chair next the one reserved for the *Queen* and find she doesn't come. Disturbing to be put next to the *Lady* and find that after all there isn't one. But it makes up for everything to sit behind the editress of a leading fashion magazine and discover she hasn't brushed the shoulders of her jacket after combing her hair any more than anybody else has.

Refreshments vary according to the time of day and the house showing. It seems unnecessarily friendly of Hartnell to provide champagne at 11 o'clock in the morning : he'd get plenty of write-ups in the Press in any case. The big designers are the life-blood of the fashion writers— after all, they've got to have something to write about. And the result is that, as day after day starts with champagne and ends with cocktails, the poor Rag Girls get

merry-go-round

THE DRESS SHOW PRESS SHOW

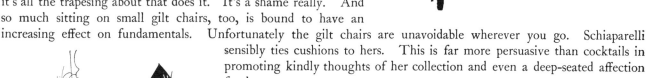

more and more dyspeptic. The more champagne you drink in the morning, the deeper the evening depression, the more necessary more and more cocktails. Towards the end of the merry-go-round you notice that the houses which serve morning coffee are becoming the most popular, and that increasing favour is shown for tomato-juice before lunch, tomato-juice in the evening, and no doubt Bisodol on reaching home.

About now I should explain that the Rag Girls are by no means all girls in the common sense of the word. Some are married women, some spinsters, some grandmothers—all with their portion of lipstick and fun. To think of a Rag Girl as exclusively a product of this generation, like neurasthenia, is unjust to this generation. Those who have grown up since the war have, on the whole, thanks to Cheltenham Ladies' College and Miss Prunella Stack, fairly straight legs. But amongst the Rag Girls there are a surprising number who go in for bow legs and flat feet. I suppose it's all the trapesing about that does it. It's a shame really. And so much sitting on small gilt chairs, too, is bound to have an increasing effect on fundamentals. Unfortunately the gilt chairs are unavoidable wherever you go. Schiaparelli sensibly ties cushions to hers. This is far more persuasive than cocktails in promoting kindly thoughts of her collection and even a deep-seated affection for her.

There is never any great show of taking notes, perhaps because that might suggest a faulty memory or inexperience, or insufficient boredom. Tongues work faster than pencils, and there seems to be no time to write down more than a jotting or two. Besides, about four women out of every ten are very shortsighted—so shortsighted that they can't see anything across a room ; and three out of the four won't put on their glasses because it upsets their looks. Stiebel and some other houses very wisely supply notes already written. This lessens the danger of the Rag Girls getting the main points of the collection wrong and writing about a single belt or ornament as if it were the one thing in the show. Provided with these sheets, they can happily gossip away without having to concentrate at all. For the Rag Girls don't come to form opinions of their own. You never find criticisms of a dress-designer's collection. A theatre-critic makes a show of forming his own opinion of a play, however famous the playwright ; and an art-critic doesn't hesitate to criticize a painting according to how much he can remember of what he was taught at the Slade and his personal opinion of Tonks. But not so the Rag Girl, which seems a pity really. The fact that she can't dress herself should not deter her. A theatre-critic can't write plays, nor an art-critic paint pictures, as any artist or playwright will gladly confirm. But still, they do have a certain advantage. They don't suffer from flat feet and gilt chairs.

WITH ILLUSTRATIONS BY TAGE WERNER

Our Continental Correspondent

Kultur and a Congress

NO visit to Munich is complete, whether you are an art fan or not, without looking in on the two art exhibitions—the Sacred and the Profane, so to speak. To study the onlookers alone is worth the trifling entrance-fee at the former. The drove of dutiful citizens mooching through the marble halls of the House of German Art seem apathetic, incurious, uncertain where to browse. The pictures are nice and hygienic-looking, but the sort of things you take for granted. Fan interest is attracted by a painting of the 1933 gathering of triumphant party leaders at Potsdam. Everyone speculates as to where Roehm originally appeared on the canvas, for, to bring his picture up-to-date, the artist subsequently painted out that Judas figure. Painters pause for a momentary scrutiny of Max Zaeper's verdant landscapes on technical grounds. This artist dared a critic of his acquaintance to write unfavourably of his work, declaring : " It's going to last anyway. First of all I have discovered a special process for making my paintings absolutely fireproof, and secondly I am a member of the Party."

Professor Ziegler, one of the Profane Art Purgers in Chief, dominates a whole room at the House of the German Art with a slim, wholesome-looking nude, archly brandishing in one hand a stick. Needless to say, Munich citizens profess to know on the best authority that " Highest Placed Quarters of all " asked the Professor to introduce him to the model. I doubt the story, but its moral is evident. Why worry about baldly representational art when there are such admirable originals?

This thought is borne out in other ways. The House of German Art presents a somewhat pompous temple façade to the street. But almost opposite is a highly respectable pension for girls, from which some dazzling lovelies emerged as I was driven past on duty bound for the temple portals. At the back of the temple is an excellent terrace restaurant. Sinking with a sigh of relief into a chair at last, you can let your eyes rest on a vision of real parkland and river. No glossy landscape here to tick off in your catalogue.

As for the Profane Art, ill-lit, badly hung, the exhibition of " Entartete Kunst " is a cunning bit of work. Opinions of Dadaists expressing mocking derision of all pompous sentiments about Art's high purpose are prominently reproduced. Modern art, lock, stock and barrel, refuted from the lips of the devil's advocate ! Out of Dada's canvas projects a whacking great nail, a few odd trouser-buttons and a bit of barbed wire, just dripping with oil. And that was a joke fifteen years ago. Now Dada, long since forsaken by his propagandists, enjoys a veritable resurrection at the hands of the bourgeois, over whom he has once more, positively, the last laugh.

The spectators at this show at least register some reaction to the exhibits, even if it is only to guffaw. Not all the pictures, however, can be relied upon to antagonize the ignorant. Franz Marc's *Tower of Blue Horses*, exhibited here at the outset, has since been removed. The fact that Marc was killed at Verdun, fighting for Germany in 1916, formerly quoted by Nazi art-critics in his favour, was evidently not the reason, for other specimens of his pneumatic-looking cattle, bathed in prisms of constructivist bliss, are still exposed for public obloquy. A charming seashell study by Max Ernst makes one wonder why they could not have raised some of his naughtier collages for this exhibition—O paranoiac shades of Salvador Dali ! But Otto Dix's *War Cripple*, that memberless torso, smoking a cigarette in silent derision at all patriotic whoopee, and some dreary studies of prostitutes in the school of Georg Grosz, are quite a help ; and probably the heedless juxtaposition of all this varied, often conflicting modernism seems to bring it under one confused heading of " art bolshevism " for the bewildered bourgeois. No examples of official Soviet art are available in the Reich, where nobody will be foolhardy enough to compare its innocuous orthodoxy with that of the House of German Art. Cubes and platforms by Kandinsky (not his best Russian period) and Lissitsky are on show here, but without any tactless reminder that their constructivism proved equally unpopular in the totalitarian U.S.S.R.

' *I'm sorry, my dear Countess, but I still feel pretty Left Wing.*'

Everyone is wondering just how far the Art Purge will go. Count Baudicini, of the Decadent Art Exhibition Committee, is all in favour of searching the houses of art-lovers and confiscating private collections as well. But what should be done with the pictures when seized ? A Kandinsky was sold abroad from the Essen Folkwang Museum, over which the Count now presides, for 9,000 marks. The Count's action was criticized by many, who held that Decadent Art should be preserved in Germany as a perpetual warning to the young. The Count took his stand on the ground that foreign *devisen* so realized could be used for the purchase of better art. Such realism recalls the good sense of General Bramwell Booth, who, when criticized for accepting for the Salvation Army a bequest from a Marquis suspected of living on the proceeds of prostitution, replied : " Never mind, I will wash this tainted money white in the Blood of the Lamb."

Weeks have sped by since the Nuremberg Congress, which, in the language of the trade, is dead from a news angle. But I do not see why, with Time the Great Healer on my side, I should not record a few mellowed impressions, remembered in tranquillity. A week at Nuremberg during the Party Congress, early risings, perpetual din, fighting for food in overcrowded hotels, can usually be relied upon to remove the tan of summer holidays and usher in the autumnal fall of leaves with a dripping cold. The 1937 Congress was, if hectic, better organized and better-tempered than its predecessors. Nuremberg was on its best behaviour, in view of the high-powered diplomatic guests present.

Critics say that Adolf was not too pleased with the quality of the other guests of honour invited. The Oracle does not frequent international society as a rule, but he has a certain peasant shrewdness, and if Ribbentrop's hand-picked selections hadn't quite the fragrance of last year's nosegay, that wouldn't get past the Führer. Parked as usual in the Guest House, the honoured guests (delivered to Nuremberg " f.o.b." and " all found ") were carefully segregated from the common

' And with a little cry I was in his arms again.'

ruck of " paying guests " at the Grand Hotel by black-uniformed S.S. cavaliers. Much the same bunch as usual, if not quite so classy : a well-wishing peer, an M.P. or two ; a couple of Seekers after the Truth ; and some Old School Ties, of various sexes, anxious, like Wardour Street, to achieve that " something different ".

Anglo-German rapprochement was fostered at 5 o'clock *thés dansants*. A young Reichswehr subaltern who had put in time on the dance floor confided to me pensively that too many of his English dance-partners had " that mouth that stretches from ear to ear ".

But you can't keep a good army down. Their mimic warfare was easily the best show of the week. Lowering clouds prompted an officer in the Press gallery to predict that the aerial exercises would be eliminated. An American colleague, who had chanced 'phoning an advance story to his paper before leaving his hotel, giving the airplane raids as the highspot of the day, provided a study in contemporary gloom. When the air squadrons finally appeared, his enthusiasm knew no bounds. " There's no stopping these guys!" he cried.

JOHN KINGCASTLE

High Hat Notes from Paris

REBOUX ET COMPAGNIE

Heads and Tails

REBOUX has shown her collection "pour la Parisienne". This means that the Paris season is officially open. Something like the private view at Burlington House, with a difference. It is a sight not to be missed. Reboux used to occupy palatial showrooms on the Place de l'Opéra over what was once a famous British bank. Her windows dominated the that-time fashion centre, the rue de la Paix. Now she has followed the general trend westwards. Her windows overlook the Rond-Point des Champs Elysées. One used to go up in a lift and walk along a circular stone gallery into the great room that was littered with tall stands like sunflower stalks. Now one goes up in a lift and walks along a circular gallery with rich red carpet, into a great room laid out in exactly the same manner, with

quantities of triple mirrors, but no sunflower stalks. The hats are all kept in an anteroom so that they shall be untouched by profane hands.

To the newcomer who strays in on opening day the scene is reminiscent of Bedlam. Scores of women sitting round the room. Everybody talking at once. Saleswomen rushing hither and thither, screaming orders. Nobody taking any notice of anybody else. An exquisite American demonstrating the pitch to which scientific slimming can be brought in New York. The representatives of the great New York stores, eager to dispatch by the *Queen Mary*, the *Normandie* or the *Europa*, the ultimatum of Lucien. Lucien of Reboux's is a famous Paris figure. To have your hats fitted by her means you are supremely chic. To be seen walking across the showroom with Lucien's arm lightly laid round your waist means that you almost amount to

royalty in the realm of fashion. Women have been known to wait for hours, just to get her opinion on the type of hat that will suit them.

To see the parisienne choosing hats is a lesson. An appointment is made. A table with triple mirror is reserved. Lucien, for the elect, a saleswoman for the world in general, arrives with a satellite who carries a basket of models. One after the other is tried on and borne away. Five, six or seven are chosen. For the parisienne orders for the season when she has chosen her frocks, and comes in for one or two more when a special occasion arises.

If you are very chic Lucien may design a hat specially for you on your own head. Nobody just buys a hat. Each order is built and modelled on the head of the woman who is to wear it. She comes back for at least two fittings, usually devoting three whole afternoons to the collection of her season's supply.

The whole method and principle is entirely different from that prevailing in an English showroom. The unknown stranger gets the impression that they don't want to sell hats. She sits and sits. Nobody bothers. Finally she may manage to persuade somebody that she really wishes to buy hats. If she shows discernment in her choice and wears hats well, it is another story. Something is brought out of the secret treasure house, fitted on her head, twisted and pinched and pulled until she looks and feels like a million dollars. Millinery is a great art.

The new Reboux line is still high hat, but without exaggeration. Everything is worn perched over one ear like a page boy's pill-box cap. Some are tilted forward. Most sweep upwards at the back. There are close-fitting skullcaps with lofty trimming in front. Paradise plumes are back again. Bonnets are shown with headbands of a contrasting colour : passing across the top of the forehead, under the brim, crossing at the back and coming round the neck, they are tied in demure bows under the chin.

A little black velvet cap fits close to the head at the back. On it is laid a black ostrich feather. This rises in front like a wave and curls over, sur-

*'My husband calls it
the flower pot !'*

mounting a curl of grey, and under that one of rich turquoise blue. It is bewitching. So is a high-pointed hat made of four triangles joined together, two of black astrachan and two of grosgrain.

Paris refuses to forget the Exhibition. Reboux makes a swathed turban and trims it with long shaded blue Paradise plumes that rise to a height of nearly a foot, curve round and flow down like the *fontaines lumineuses*.

Across the road Suzanne Talbot devises fascinating hats, gloves and fans. Everything she touches has character. A little round pill-box of black velvet is worn tilted down over the forehead. A tall spike juts out in front at an angle. It is made of one of those heavy skunk tails that used to fringe Grandmother's fur cape, mounted on wire, like the brushes used to clean bottles.

There is a lovely portrait by Manet at the Chefs-d'Œuvre de l'Art Français on view at the Palais National des Arts. It is of a woman in a riding habit such as was worn by Cora Pearl in the sixties. Inspired by this, Suzanne Talbot made a little tapering top hat of dark grey felt and draped it with a blue veil. (Rose Bertin has this.) Another with a tall, narrowing crown which might have come out of *Anthony Adverse* is stitched with rows and rows of gold thread that look like stripes. Qute a different type is a Welsh crowned black velvet hat with a wide brim turned up in front and draped with a black lace veil which sweeps across one side of the face and is draped round the neck. It was designed for Annabella in her latest film. (Santa of New Bond Street has this.)

Agnès, further up, at the corner of the street, makes lovely draped turbans, so high they will cause a complete black-out if women don't remove their hats at the play. They are made of soft pliable jersey in black intertwined with Pompeian red, or of felt swathed with various colours. For the evening there is a cap without a top to the crown. It looks like a fez and is made of scintillating sapphire sequins. Shaped like a Spanish comb is the fascinating black lace hat with an enormous mantilla edged with a flounce in which Madame Maggy Rouff made a sensation in London when she wore it with a black velvet evening gown.

A turban of draped blue jersey has a twisted loop at the top, through which is thrust a silver fox's tail that slants across the front.

One of my favourites in the Agnès collection is a black felt that fits snugly to the head behind, with a turquoise velvet crown like a pointed cap which is draped forward to pass through the wide upturned brim of black felt, showing a blue bow in front. (Harrods have this.) Another is a large black felt béret, pulled forward over the eyes, with a frivolous little butterfly bow of black dotted net posed on top, well to the front.

WINIFRED BOULTER

NEW BOOKS reviewed by Evelyn Waugh

Love Among The Underdogs

THERE is nothing apocalyptic about Miss Johnson's latest novel. The World's End of the title is the shabby district at the extremity of the King's Road, Chelsea, and the story deals with its denizens. Those who have a decent dread of books about artistic people need not flinch. The hero, it is true, once had some unrealized aspirations to " write ", but his meagre living comes mostly from the dole; when in luck he gets ill-paid office jobs. The secondary male character gives music lessons; the secondary female character gets an occasional part in touring theatrical companies—but all these characters are infinitely remote from the Bohemia which is associated with Chelsea. Their education is negligible, their understanding of events outside their immediate circle non-existent; they have " feelings " instead of opinions, they are economically, politically, socially, theologically in a mess; they are proletarian in all except the single determining character—they are sterile, and when, by mistake, the heroine conceives, she is extinguished as though the author realized that she had stepped beyond her limits. The hero, Brand, has all the marks of the underdog, shiftless and self-pitying, one in whom the universal reluctance to work under orders has become a neurotic dislike of his immediate superiors and a cosmic resentment against the world in general. It may be supposed from this that *World's End* is a depressing book; it is sad but not drab, a book of genuine human interest. The hero is not wholly despicable; he is capable of physical courage on two occasions and of moral courage on one. There is nothing doctrinaire about his final decision to join the Spanish war; it is part of his restlessness; he has never had any acquaintance with serious values and it is natural that he should accept the fifth-rate. The minor characters are all admirable, particularly the Hogben children; there is a delightful description of a drunk woman in a train—a true flavour of Hogarth in its sudden transition from truculence to woe. The mutual endearments of husband and wife made me sweat cold; for the very reason of their obvious truth, neither writer nor reader had any business there. It is a pity that, with her abundant gifts for narrative, Miss Johnson should have

---

World's End. Pamela Hansford Johnson. Chapman & Hall. 7s. 6d.

The Rhubarb Tree. Kenneth Allott & Stephen Tait. Cresset Press. 7s. 6d.

The Seven Who Fled. Frederic Prokosch. Chatto & Windus. 8s. 6d.

---

fallen into the prevalent trick of giving a topical background with extracts from the day's news.

The Rhubarb Tree is profoundly different, though it begins with a destitute hero. The authors—it always seems to take two people to write a book nowadays, how do they manage it?—are also conscious of " ideological " stirrings, but their work is refreshingly out of date. We are back among the whimsical loves and light villainy of an early Nancy Mitford. The characters and the chain of events—it can scarcely be called a story—which connects them vary greatly in reality. The heroine is straight from the 1920's—elusive, irresponsible, promiscuous, a little wistful, avaricious, delectable, ruthless—how often we have all read or written about such people. Well, the type wears well and I found Miss

Mormon highly agreeable. Miss Mormon? Yes, the characters have comic names—da Capo, the Nazi boss, Edward Tatham the deceased husband of an eccentric, M. Bordel, Dr. Rumble, Dr. Bluffheim, Mr. Death, etc. That is in the tradition of English humorous writing and a pleasant change from the austere abstractions of many contemporaries. Lady Sybil Tatham goes back to a still earlier epoch; she might very well have appeared in *Major Barbara*, and Dr. Rumble's Nursing Home has a pronounced **resemblance to** Beachcomber's Narkover. It would be irrelevant to give a résumé of the plot—and barely possible without transcribing the book, so frequent are the changes of scene and so terse the description.

Is the story funny? Well, I cannot say I ever laughed aloud, but I found it easy reading. Unpretentious, gay, enterprising. I wonder whether the appearance of two names on the title page made me unduly suspicious—or did I really discern the work of two hands in it, one of them writing a sober little love story about Sykes, Angela, Helga and Mountebank, the other acting as *animateur* constantly making Puck-like intrusions, spinning the actors into fantastic situations; did Mr. Allott employ Mr. Tait to hot up his story as, unwittingly, de Villiers employed Bunny?

The Seven Who Fled won a prize of $7,500 in U.S.A. It is very long and costs a shilling more than the others. The style is " Came-the-dawn " combined with " The-Home-Beautiful ". " Dry as a bone the earth was ", " The snow had now captured the rising sunlight. Beautiful it looked, pure, icy, incorruptible ". What a trio of epithets! The plot is philosophy of a kind plus tolerable bazaar-junk, local colour. Lots of philosophy. Mr. Prokosch must have been one of the multitude of Americans who are said to have read Mr. Charles Morgan's *Sparkenbroke.*

SNOOKER

Take my Cue

THAT Tom Webster should act as official framer of handicaps for a snooker tournament whose list of entries includes Melbourne Inman sounds too good to be true. Next to Tishy's legs, Inman's nose did more to popularize Webster than any single butt of his humour, and it is nice to see him paying an old debt of honour by allocating by far the longest handicap in the tournament to the old master with the lugubrious countenance; it would be even nicer to see Inman carry off the magnificent gold cup which the *Daily Mail* puts up for the winner. But that is looking ahead.

From a post of vantage just behind the cartoonist's reserved seat, I watch the lights go down on the opening of the professional season and the first heat of the *Daily Mail* Gold Cup Snooker Competition with all the excitement of renewing old acquaintances after a long interval. First to appear is Charles Chambers, marker and referee, as much part of the furniture at Thurston's as the faded red plush, the embossed gold walls and the somnolent veterans that line them. " No expression in the world like his, and certainly no wing collar like his" is how Tom Webster sums him up— and he should know. The embodiment of quiet but inflexible authority, he is the owner of a voice so absolutely non-committal that one wonders why the B.B.C. hasn't bribed him away.

Then the players themselves. On his right, Tom Newman (receives 27), stiff cuffs, square links, dark hair; on his left, Alec Brown (receives 23), soft cuffs, oval links. Tom, who has had to watch Lindrum compile more thousands against him than any living human being, is an old stager; Brown,

a mere youngster and a newcomer to the competition, has fair hair and a poker face, but he is conceding Newman three points and must be pretty useful. Both men, of course, are faultlessly waistcoated—for faultless waistcoats and that peculiar droop of the mouth which culminates in the sneer of Melbourne Inman are the hallmarks of the billiard professional.

Newman breaks the ice with a crashing excursion into the reds, and under the dazzling light the balls scatter across the green cloth like the beads in a kaleidoscope. Brown flukes a red off an improbable cushion, and Newman grins " You started well " at him. Brown smiles deprecatingly and warms quickly to his work. He pots very straight and knows all the tricks ; snooker is obviously his *métier*, whereas to Newman it is little more than an amusing sideline.

Meanwhile, Tom Webster slips into his seat and opens his notebook. He smokes a cigar, and has prominent wide-open eyes with the all-embracing stare of an inquisitive child. I peep over his shoulder and see him taking longhand notes in his beautiful handwriting. Newman has not yet found his touch and Brown is methodically polishing off the reds. Newman brings off a fancy double-the-blue to the accompaniment of discreet tapping of umbrellas and dudding of feet, but loses the first game 34-60. In between breaks the players chat with Webster, who, for reasons best known to himself, is sketching a detail of one of the pockets. Newman, on his home ground, is showing surprising lack of reserve. He chats to his friends and his Hulbertian chin wags lightheartedly. Referee Chambers eyes him with reproof, restores the red balls to their pyramid, and spots the colours sharply for the second game.

With Newman beginning to run into form in the second game, things become more lively. Challenged to get out of this one by Newman, Brown smiles enigmatically and obliges by steering his way through a mass of coloured balls to cut a red into the bottom pocket. The old gentlemen tap enthusiastically and we hear the first " Good shot, sir ! " of the season from

the white spats and a carnation in the front row. So far they have been keeping surprisingly wakeful; the rough and tumble of snooker has not quite the soporific effect of the monotonous click-click of Lindrum's close cannons, punctuated by the drone of Chambers's toneless voice.

The players indulge in a bout of vicious snookering, with Newman looking complacent every time he has left his young rival really awkward. Even the sardonic Chambers can see this sort of a joke, and his voice almost takes on a note of approbation as he rakes up Brown's forfeits to Newman's account with a rest. Newman collects all the coloured balls at his last visit, to win the second game, 54-42, and runs away in the third with a masterly break of 55 which draws a round of outright clapping, and an encouraging " Good old Tom " from a bowler-hatted back-bencher. Brown sits out while Tom is in play, and Webster sketches him with such concentration that his cigar goes out. Brown pretends not to notice that he is being recorded for future reference, but looks pink and self-conscious.

After a lot of finessing for a winning position, Brown equalizes by taking game number four, but number five drags on unaccountably, as the balls "run funny" and both players and public seem to lose their concentration. Someone in the row behind engages his neighbour in a throaty whisper, and the mention of John Roberts makes it plain that we are back in the good old days and that billiards is not what it was.

The white-spatted clubman with the carnation now has both eyes definitely shut. Once the rot sets in we go down like ninepins and I wake just in time to see an exciting finish in which Brown scrambles home on the black. With Tom Webster gone and only the table to watch, the last frame seems pretty dull. Still, it is a beautiful game—so restful and pretty. Out in the light of Leicester Square, it takes the shock of an evening paper bill to smash the feeling of false security into which one is lulled, quite inevitably, by this gentlest of all British sports.

SYLVAIN MANGEOT

[161]

MINUTES OF THE WEEK

Totalitarian Tots

We hope, we hope very much, that Hitler is really going to pay that return visit to Mussolini. Dictators may not be awfully attractive apart, but when they're together we find them obscurely endearing. It's partly, of course, their being so little. Mussolini, if we remember right, is about five-foot six ; Hitler is a half-size larger. One small man can always suggest a colossus, even against a background of towering S.S. troopers; but two small men, bustling about side by side in the middle of the stage—no: the illusion cracks, mass-hypnotism is illogically sabotaged, and we breathe again. We loved the newsreels from Berlin—the two chubby little fellows—ever so serious and just the teeniest bit sulky, like pages at a wedding—sticking out their chins and going sturdily through the ceremonial motions. Each, alone, may seem a menacing and enigmatic *enfant terrible*; but put them together and noth-

ing is terrible any more. We're right back in the nursery, smiling through our tears at a couple of spoilt, rumbustious little scallywags playing at Power. The newsreels won Slingsby's support for the Rome-Berlin axis; our only fear is that in their next picture those boys will get into a scrap over Shirley Temple.

Our Relations With Miss Ricks

The Fitter Britain campaign is in full swing and we, daunted, have made at last a tentative attempt to toe the line, nerving ourselves to buy two gramophone records whereon a Miss Elsie M. Ricks dispenses only too mellifluously the secrets of Eternal Youth. (We only meant to buy the

one for elderly women, but we got such a look from the sales-girl that we had to take the other too.)

Thus far we haven't got on any too well with Miss Ricks, who still, admittedly, believes us to be an elderly woman and may therefore have some excuse for treating us the way she does. She is bright, antiseptic and faintly contemptuous, like a night-nurse. "Stand up straight! Head up! Pull in the abdominal muscles! Pull in the seat muscles! Feet together!" All this is enunciated with a dreadful cheery crispness. Later she grows vaguer, merely adjuring us to "feel tall and slim". (But, lady, if we felt tall and slim we shouldn't be pulling in our seat muscles for you.)

Finally a piano plays, while Miss Ricks sings instructions at us and we—our spirit broken—mix a stiff whisky and soda. Her song begins:

"Knees springing—Ready!
Go and bounce and bounce!"

All this to a jaunty little melody that takes us right back to Pearl White strapped to a railway line until next Saturday. We're sorry, Miss Ricks, but under these conditions we can't play. Our physique is staying as it is—C.3 and horrible.

Specialist

"What is your occupation ? " " I am a chemist and cheese specialist." This rapier-like piece of dialogue occurred in the *Evening Standard* report of an inquest the other day and caused many a gourmet to choke over his Wensleydale. Of course there are cheese specialists and cheese specialists. We once called on one who dishonoured his tasty profession. His laboratory was an eerie place. A stuffed cow—symbol of outworn superstitions concerning cheese—hung over the crucibles. The specialist and his minions were experimenting with a new and necessarily secret formula. All that we are permitted to tell you about the muck they hope eventually to put on the market, wrapped up in filthy little cubes of silver paper, is that it will be called " Tudor Cheesettes ". You will be able either to eat it or to use it as shaving soap. It will be the first dual purpose cheese.

Slingsby

IN THE LIONS' DEN

BY DANIEL

4—Ambassador, New Style

HERR VON RIBBENTROP once controlled the German agency for Johnnie Walker. Like that famous whisky, he is still going strong. The fact is surprising. Apart from the Anglo-German Naval Treaty, in which others had a hand, there is no major diplomatic success to be reckoned to his credit. His greatest achievement was the final negotiation of the German-Japanese alliance against the Comintern; his most characteristic gesture the anti-Communist speech which he made the moment he landed in England as German Ambassador. The one move was so obvious that anyone might have made it; the other so tactless that it is difficult to understand how any Ambassador could have made it.

German diplomatists have long had a reputation for putting both feet in it whenever they touch upon Anglo-Saxon politics. The wartime activities of von Papen in the United States are sufficient illustration. Yet Herr Hitler might reasonably have expected that his own particular choice for the London Embassy would prove more practical. Both in himself and in his history Ribbentrop has many qualities which make him particularly acceptable to Englishmen.

Joachim Ribbentrop—the "von" is a post-war acquisition—was born forty-four years ago at Wesel, a small Rhineland town near the Dutch frontier. His family were well-to-do and not without distinction. They had been soldiers for generations. One of them had served as Quartermaster-General on Blücher's staff at Waterloo and, after Waterloo, had gone to Paris to recover German artistic treasures which Napoleon had collected on his campaigns. Young Joachim was sent first to school at Metz, then to live with a professor's family in England. The professor taught him an English purer in grammar and accent than that of most Englishmen. From England he went to Switzerland, to perfect his French. In 1910, when he was eighteen, the Ribbentrop family made a shooting trip to New Brunswick. The shooting trip over, Joachim stayed on. In Canada he earned his living in a number of ways, among them that of a labourer on the new railway bridge across the St. Lawrence at Quebec.

The Canadian sojourn ended abruptly with the outbreak of war in 1914. Ribbentrop smuggled himself out of Quebec in a Dutch steamer. When she called at Southampton he evaded the British agents who searched her by spending two very uncomfortable days in the coal-bunkers. His war record was comparatively quiet, but creditable. He served first as lieutenant in a regiment of Hussars on the Russian front; next, owing to his knowledge of French and English, in the War Ministry in Berlin; then on the staff in Constantinople; finally, as an assistant on the staff of the Peace Commission.

For fifteen years after the War, Ribbentrop's career was primarily commercial and cosmopolitan. He became an agent in Germany for British whisky and French champagne. The whisky required frequent trips to England; the champagne brought him into touch with what remains of French aristocracy. His position was improved when he married Fräulein Henkel, daughter of the head of a well-known German champagne firm. Their house in Dahlem became a centre for Republican Germany's cosmopolitan society.

Dahlem is a fashionable suburb of Berlin. Baron von Neurath, German Foreign Minister, lives there. Dr. Niemöller, a leader in the German Church's struggle against "German Christianity", is pastor of the Dahlem parish church. The Ribbentrop home has a secluded garden, with tennis-court and swimming-pool. The Ribbentrop family is agreeable. Herr von Ribbentrop himself is a sportsman, an accomplished amateur musician, and a brilliant linguist. It was natural that distinguished foreigners should meet distinguished Germans in that pleasant household. It was natural that the head of it should have become an intermediary between the powers of Germany that were and the powers of Germany that were to be.

Exactly what part Herr von Ribbentrop played in the Nazi approach to office is uncertain. It seems to have been through him that Hitler consolidated financial-industrial support for the Nazi movement; and rumour has

WYNDHAM
ROBINSON

' I'm from the Daily Mirror.'

it that Hitler and Papen often met in Ribbentrop's country house during the fateful negotiations of December, 1932. Whatever it may have been, Hitler is evidently grateful for this midwifery to revolution. Though a member of the Black Guards, Ribbentrop is not a Nazi of long standing. He has refrained from taking any violent part in the more absurd Nazi compaigns. It is even said that he was guilty of sending his daughter to a Jewish specialist for treatment when she fell ill. Yet his influence under the Nazi régime has steadily advanced.

Ribbentrop had been the advocate of an Anglo-Franco-German understanding before Hitler came to power.

'Ssh! Daddy has to get this doodle done before the post goes.'

His friendship with Hitler gave the advocacy a new meaning. He pursued it by a new method. His business trips to England had taken him into English society. His charming manners and attractive appearance—not unlike that of an overgrown English public schoolboy—had made him a welcome guest in some once famous English houses. As Hitler's unofficial ambassador, Ribbentrop set out to explain the Nazi Revolution not to Whitehall but, as he thought, to England.

In strict reason, there could be no objection to this method. Professional diplomats privately protested against it. Their alleged ground was the inability of anyone but a professional diplomat to understand anything that has ever happened abroad; their real ground the sound trade-union principle that a trade must be closed to anyone who has not served his apprenticeship. The alleged ground was a very thin crust: it is notorious that the professional diplomat has failed to understand every revolution from 1789 onwards. Because of its thinness, the real ground of professional objection could well have been ignored. Had Ribbentrop's method succeeded, it would have been lauded as much as any other success.

Unfortunately, or fortunately, the method did not succeed. The reason lay partly in the mixing of older methods with the new, partly in the deceptive nature of English society.

Herr von Ribbentrop's new diplomacy carried over two characteristic defects from the old. It was secretive when there was nothing to hide. It was verbose when there was nothing to talk about. I met Herr von Ribbentrop when he was in London as Herr Hitler's Disarmament Commissioner some years ago. He had just come from the Foreign Office when I called upon him. I happened to know that he had just come from the Foreign Office, and there was every reason, including courtesy, why he should have been to the Foreign Office. Yet when I mentioned the fact, he at once denied it. His charming smile gave way to that rather worried expression which has become more common with him of late; and what might have been a profitable conversation turned from cordiality to polite, but meaningless, formality.

It was on that same visit that Ribbentrop met Bernard Shaw. The meeting may or may not have been the reason for Shaw's later admiration of Nazi achievements. It could certainly not have been less profitable to the Nazi cause than some of the other English acquaintances Ribbentrop has formed. Except for its newer and tougher members, the peerage in England is of little consequence. Castlereaghs and Shaftesburys were important in the nineteenth century; in the twentieth century their aristocratic descendants have an influence limited (*pace* David Low and Colonel Blimp) to the comparatively uninfluential class they represent. Herr von Ribbentrop, however, seems to have had his eye on nineteenth-century England. He acquired some fashionable friends, and with them some fashionable influence. The acquisition would not have done the Nazi cause much good. It would not have done the Nazi cause much harm, had these friends been content to leave well alone. Whether wittingly or not, they won the reputation of interference in matters which were not their concern. Herr Thost, first unofficial Nazi representative in London, had attempted the same diplomacy. He was required to leave the country. Ribbentrop, contrariwise, came back here with all the dignity of German Ambassador. It was unfortunate that his coming should almost have coincided with the outbreak of the Spanish civil war and with a consequent intensification of political feeling in England. The task of Anglo-German rapprochement, which he had set himself, has thereby been rendered doubly difficult. But his will to accomplish it remains. If present European hatreds should cool, this charming amateur diplomat may yet succeed.

★

Milan Stoyadinovitch, Yugo-Slav premier . . . today has outmanœuvred his enemies by taking a large group of them bodily into his cabinet. They are MM. Stoshovitch, Madarasevitch, Kulunyitch, Miletitch, Chverkitch, Simonovitch and Novakovitch.—*News Item.*

All must Stoyadinovitch praise
  As combined opposition he ditches
And intense irritation allays
  By removing the itch from the
    itches.

Our Continental Correspondent

Death in the Pot

STOMACH-LOVERS meet to-day in Dijon, where until the end of the month they will be able to revel repletely at the justly famous Gastronomic Fair. After that comes the surfeit, and Toussaint, and thoughts of death. Meanwhile at Dijon man's mortal enemy, his stomach, is by gastronomes from far and wide loved, honoured and obeyed.

Dijon is a mellow and substantial town, lolling at ease in the middle of the fat lands of Burgundy. Wine flows like water there, and for about six shillings a day you can feed like a lord. Among the specialities of the place are chicken cooked in red Burgundy, suprême of pike, cassis— which is a liqueur made from black-currants—and a kind of gingerbread cake. Also the best French mustard in all France and, above all, escargots de Bourgogne.

The escargots are notable eating. Nourished on vine leaves in life and before death purified of slime and grossness by a weeks-long immersion in salt water, these edible snails are the least bestial of all cooked animals, the closest to the innocent company of the vegetables. They are served up to you by the half-dozen on a round dish and look very plump and pretty with their shells of clear fawn softly speckled with light brown, something like the eggs of the black grouse. Their compact, coal-black insides, seasoned with butter and parsley, are already detached from their shell before serving and have only to be yanked out with the slender two-pronged fork that is provided. Their flavour is salt, savoury; the texture not quite meat and not quite mushroom, of a unique succulence. Snails are a concentrated food and fill you up pretty quickly, in fact a dozen is a meal in itself; but not to your Dijonnais. A dozen of escargots is no more than an appetizer to him, he tosses them off in the grand manner with as little ado as if they were so many green peas.

For the most part, as might be expected, the faces of the people of Dijon are either purple with plethora or yellow with jaundice, their bodies pinched or paunchy. In spite of their rich feeding, or perhaps because of it, many of the children of Dijon have a stuffed, anæmic look and are not attractive. I have seen one child here that was, I think, the most unpleasing child anyone ever set eyes on.

It was a girl child, perhaps two or three years old, pale, podgy and buttoned so tightly into its saxe-blue coat that its arms stuck out slightly from its sides. Its waxy legs bulged over button-boots of white and black kid. It wore long white socks, gartered below the knee to the point of strangulation. Round and round the public gardens this etiolated little creature staggered aimlessly, with the tiny trotting Chinese steps that were all its deplorable boots permitted it to take. About the shoulders of its coat were sewn strips of dingy white fur, repeating the Michelin-tyre coiled-worm effect of the outrageous pom-pommed woollen cap it wore upon its head. It was an unspeakable child. I felt sorry for it, but all the same it was unspeakable—so pale and maggotty, for all the world as if it were the Larva crawled out of Capek's *Insect Play*. After looking at it for a little while, and at its mother, a normal-looking woman who seemed to be quite pleased with it, I left the public gardens and went to the museum to see not only what the catalogue described as " fine mirors and various artistic things " but " religious objetcs, pannels, waterpaintings, and gorgeous pictures of the Rhenan and Swiss primitive painters, unic in France ".

One thing that is unic about Dijon is the sharp contrasts it offers between the fleshly and the ascetic, the temporal and the spiritual. Though such contrasts are not uncommon in Catholic towns, they seem to strike you more strongly in Dijon than in most places —when you lurch out of your restaurant gorged with coq au Chambertin and mushrooms grilled in cream there is something peculiarly chilling and inevitable about that sixteenth-century skull and " Respice finem " scratched on the outer wall of Saint-Philibert. The glutted beast, once the first rosy glow of digestion begins to fade within him, is of all creatures the most susceptible to intimations of his mortality. Few of us have not at some time in our lives awakened to a rumbling belly just before dawn and thought penitently of death and the cold grave; at such times we are all, in our inarticulate way, John Donnes for a brief moment. Then we too know the anguish of the marrow, the ague of the skeleton, as our mortal stomach groans distressfully within the prison of our dry immortal ribs. For the men of Dijon, who overeat habitually, it must be often thus, and it must have been thus for the men of Dijon at every time, if the great cooking-pots in the ducal kitchens are anything to go by. They feasted, they caroused, they snored in drunken stupors ; and in the morning, spiritualized by the consequences of

' Welcome !'

'I like sucking-pig all right, but I'm afraid it doesn't like me.'

★   ★   ★

excess, they vowed themselves to God and in a ferment of repentance set about designing a tomb for their father, honorable homme, dead at forty of a surfeit. A multitude of unrecorded hangovers have left their mark upon the monuments of this town of Dijon.

Consider the dolorous figures in stone carved on the late fourteenth-century tombs of Philippe le Hardi and Jean sans Peur, in the town museum: a wailful choir of nightgowned old men, some hooded, all standing in postures of lamentation and despair, wringing their hands, desolated, their ancient faces made beautiful with grief. The very type and symbol of suffering bereavement, you would say. Yet look more closely, rid your mind of that churchy, tiptoe, hush-a-bye-bishop at-titude it instinctively assumed in the presence of a tomb, and you will be obliged to admit that these expressions of pain, touching as they are, might just as well have been induced by violent colic as by a passion of mourning for a noble prince gone to his death. Doubled up with grief or doubled up with indigestion, the outward and visible signs of distress are the same. From the point of view of an impartial observer there isn't two pins' choice between them, and either form of suffering may well serve as a model for the other; above all in Dijon, where the sentiment of the skeleton is ever present at the feast. It is easy to be pious when you have a pain. So yesterday's orgy becomes tomorrow's stained-glass window, and future generations call you holy.

Respice finem, indeed—a finis which, in this fat land of Burgundy, will almost certainly be an enlarged liver, if not an apoplexy. Here the funeral furnisher's is never far from the tavern. Knock upon the wall of the wine-cellar and you will hear a hollow echo from the vault below the church next door. Respice finem, for there is death in the pot.

But in the meantime are there not suave snails plumper than abbots, Burgundy smooth as silk, mushrooms of a flavour to bring the rare tears of perfection to your eyes: and all for six bob a day ? For though there may be death in the pot, it is, after all, only at the bottom of the pot ; and the pot is deep, in Dijon.   P. Y. BETTS

NEW YORK LETTER

From Alistair Cooke

The War on Times Square

THE American Legion parade is all over, and it now can be soberly reported by your correspondent, an understatement man from away back, that it topped anything of the sort since Nero and the Fall of Babylon. If Hitler ever gets a glimpse of Universal's magnificent newsreel, he will probably weep his way into a psychosis to think that all this singing and marching and rhythmical saluting should be wasted on a twenty-year-old memory.

It started at nine in the morning from Twenty-third Street and was scheduled to end at nine in the evening at Ninety-sixth. That allowed twelve hours for a hundred thousand men to walk eight miles. But it wasn't enough. By two-thirty the next morning the forty-five-year-olds who had started out smartly in the early morning sun were already tucked away in sodden sleep while a few thousand of their pals had still twenty or thirty blocks to tramp.

The legion was born nineteen years ago when a third of the three million men under arms returned to join it. It was committed to certain generous and fairly confused loyalties. It was pledged not to forget, to work against war, to inculcate law and order, to support the Constitution, etc. Fourteen years ago the Commander (who is elected annually by a majority vote on the last day of the convention) could say that "the Fascisti are to Italy what the Legion is to the U.S." This year's commander would have had to be drunk or insane to say anything like it. In 1923 the Fascisti looked, at three thousand miles, like a band of gallant vigilantes and the vigilante tradition is vivid enough in American history to get a cheer any time. In 1937 the Legion made a special point of declaring rhetorical war on all isms except Americanism. The actual expression of these sentiments always gets lost in the week's blind. What practical campaigning there may be is for quite

other causes, the legionaires from South Dakota, for instance, this time passing out fifty thousand handbills canvassing the purchase of farm lands. But the working excuse of the Legion is the annual jamboree, which is any political convention on a gargantuan scale. They have come chiefly to put back their age twenty years, to drink with their cronies in hotel bedrooms, to cheer indulgently enough the particular patriotic slogans that the Legion chairman or commander has happened to think up. And anyway the first day's political orating is the ostensible reason for so many respectable clerks, brokers, salesmen, lawyers and farmers to leave their questioning wives.

The parade itself was a sort of vaster Nuremberg punctuated by the Marx Brothers. If fascism happens here, somebody is going to have a herculean time suppressing the national humour. All day long soldiers came by in solid phalanx, the soldiers of five wars, symbolizing the American dream no doubt, but also—like the love scenes in a W. C. Fields film—providing a rest period in between the comic sequences. There was naturally a regiment of minute-men from Lexington, but they were followed by a disconsolate British

'*I see the doorman's pawned the clock again!*'

soldier leading a hot dog on a string. There was the usual Miss Legion of 1937 (stunning enough to set the Coast wires buzzing and have the lady bought by Paramount before she had moved a mile). But there was also a harridan carrying a Japanese umbrella bearing the label "Miss Pennsylvania". Every time the parade stopped to straighten itself out, the men from Wisconsin sat down on stools and milked imaginary teats into empty buckets. Outside Radio City a baby alligator which had panted so far expired, and the Legion carefully and comically performed a solemn mass.

So it went on and the day waned and the half-million lookers-on decided it was time to eat or see a movie. This was a crisis which most people had not anticipated. The *New York Times* published on its theatre page a footnote to the announcement of Henry Fonda opening in a new play. It said that playgoers having to come from the East side would be able to cross Fifth Avenue at Twenty-third Street or *alternatively* at One Hundred and Tenth Street, a mere detour of nine miles uptown and seven miles back to the theatre. It seems Mr. Fonda had some sort of an audience but it opened one's eyes to the prospect of New York in time of siege: hold Fifth Avenue and the war is yours.

By four o'clock Times Square looked like election night in Hell, except that everybody was well-mannered and the legionaires fought only with each other. When the uproar was wavering, a group of the boys decoyed the traffic cops by odd fake accidents and faintings. Then several of their pals took over the traffic control.

The cross-town traffic would be started, then jammed in mid-stream, and the buffoons would confidently signal the uptown buses and taxis to come on. Just when the place was beginning to look like a salmon stream in full whirl, there would be the distant screech of a siren. Somehow by titanic jostling the police would get back again to let the emergency through, and when a way was clear, there it was—a resurrected "voiture locale" with a legionaire atop the most intimate throne known to man.

The next day the Police Commissioner publicly announced that the police department had "capitulated" and that policemen who were also legionaires would have to police Times Square for themselves. The Astor Hotel was practically denuded of foyer

furniture. All the hotels ordered their chambermaids to make up beds without pillows, to prevent an epidemic of feathers. The second night somebody sprayed tear-gas and the police came bawling by telling everybody not to rub their eyes. For three nights this went on and the total cost must be a pretty figure. This, of course, had been al-

lowed for. The Americans are a practical people and they learned a lesson from their last convention, when fifty thousand dollars were set aside for accident liability and the total bill came to sixty-five thousand dollars. So this year they allowed a million dollars' damage: four dollars' worth of blissful sadism for every legionaire. Most of them were way ahead of their budget.

By the Thursday people were asking how long is this going on, thus reverting to the native psychology whereby a parade is welcomed the first day, tolerated the second and run out of town the third. By way of consolation, a paper published figures showing that the Legion—mostly men around forty-five—was now about in its peak year and its figure would begin to run parallel with the history of the Grand Army of the Republic. The Civil War veterans have already withered to a handful of bony elders and their last reunion is already in sight. A fantastic suggestion was started that the Confederate and the Union soldiers should now join together, an idea which twenty years ago would have been enough to start the Civil War over again. But rather than be denied their parade, the old veterans will merge. The Legion has had more foresight. They have already started organizations for the sons and grandsons of the Legion. So it looks after all as if the crack of doom will be practically any minute after the last Legion parade. Ideals may come and slogans may go, but the boys will insist, as all good Americans do, that a man in his early forties has a right to one single nostalgic burst before he gives in.

Next Year's News

A PREVIEW OF 1938

By Hugh Kingsmill and Malcolm Muggeridge

MR. EDEN'S QUESTIONNAIRE

Following upon the sinking yesterday in the Western Mediterranean of S.S. *Euterpe*, which was flying the British flag, lights were seen in the Foreign Office until early this morning. The whole Foreign Office staff under the personal supervision of Mr. Eden were engaged in drafting a questionnaire to be sent to the chief European Powers embodying the following queries:

(1) Are you in favour of peace or war?

(2) Are you in favour of limiting the operations of submarines to certain specified areas, and/or renouncing the use of torpedoes other than as a defensive measure?

(3) Would you be prepared, before having recourse to military measures, to participate in an international conference, at a place and date to be later specified, for a discussion of:

(*a*) Raw materials.

(*b*) Colonial trusteeship.

(*c*) Loans.

Dismissed Charge

Charged with being a public nuisance by persistently revolving in a swing-door and refusing to remove himself therefrom, an elderly man, who gave his name as W. Churchill, said that it was through no wish of his own that he always came out when he thought he was going in.

ANTARCTIC AS WAR THEATRE ?

At the League Assembly yesterday a proposal was put forward by M. Politis, the Greek delegate, for localizing future wars. "Would it not be possible," M. Politis said, "in view of what had been learnt from the Spanish experience, to set aside a specified area which should provide a terrain for international conflicts, if and when they arose?" M. Politis went on to say that Spain itself for various reasons did not provide an ideal area for this purpose. What was wanted was a territory which was on the one hand sufficiently extensive and on the other sufficiently remote from the European System. The Antarctic alone met both these requirements, and he contended that the obstacles in the way of transforming this at present somewhat forbidding region into a suitable theatre of war were by no means insurmountable. It was decided to set up a committee to investigate the practicability of this proposal.

New Book by Mr. Wells

The forthcoming publication is announced of a new book by Mr. H. G. Wells, entitled *Deliverance from the Deep*. It deals with a final collapse, in 1988, of the present world order, with its " mental tangles, egocentric preoccupations, obsessions, bad habits of thought, sub-conscious fears and dreads," and the gradual emergence, after a disappointing interregnum of Dictatorship from the Air, of a Submarine Aristocracy, who point the way to a larger and freer life.

Germany and Ban on Bombing

With reference to Lord Plymouth's appeal to both sides in Spain to abstain from air bombing, a spokesman of the Wilhelmstrasse said: "Germany is in principle in favour of the prohibition of inhuman warfare. But, if inhuman acts of warfare are to be suppressed, then all such acts must be suppressed. It will not do to pick out just one at will."

Japanese Bonds Rise

The remarkably steady tone of London stock markets was further illustrated yesterday. News of the gross outrage offered by a party of Japanese marines to the *Times* correspondent in Chang Tu was received with regret, but had little effect on prices. Gilt-edged stocks closed only slightly below opening figures, and the effect on Far Eastern securities was almost negligible. In fact, Japanese 5 per cent. of 1907 and 6 per cent. of 1924 closed slightly higher on the day.

TROTZKYISTS BLAME LENIN

An unexpected development in the latest Trotzkyist mass trial in Moscow is the confession by a number of the accused that in their betrayal of the Soviet Fatherland they have been following out the secret instructions of Lenin, issued shortly before his death. They allege that these instructions were to make contact with Japanese secret service agents, to sabotage all electrical developments in the U.S.S.R., and to foster the incipient National Socialist movements in Germany and Austria.

No Viking Galley at Henley

Relations between Herr Hitler and General Ludendorff have again become strained as the result of General Ludendorff's bitter attacks in his newspaper on the *Teuton Strength and Fecundity Association* for refusing to allow a Pagan Eight to row at Henley in a Viking galley.

Mr. Yeats-Brown and Spain

Interviewed on his return from Spain yesterday, Mr. Yeats-Brown said: "I want to make one thing absolutely clear. The Moors are not fighting in Spain for pay. They are not fighting for fighting's sake. They are fighting for Allah against atheism, for Mecca against Moscow."

MR. EDEN'S QUESTIONNAIRE

Replies have now been received to Mr. Eden's questionnaire from France, Portugal, Holland and Belgium. It is understood that these replies answer Question 1 ("Are you in favour of peace or war?") satisfactorily; France, Holland and Belgium with a categorical "Peace", and Portugal with certain reservations relating to Colonial trusteeship. A request has also been received from the Greek Government for further details respecting Question 3, Section (*c*) (Loans).

Prince Bernhard for Prague

At a farewell dinner at the Hague yesterday to celebrate the departure of Prince Bernhard-zur-Lippe-Biesterfeld on his visit to Prague, the Czecho-Slovakian Minister to the Netherlands said that Prince Bernhard-zur-Lippe-Biesterfeld was rapidly assuming the rôle of an unofficial ambassador for peace, and he was confident that this visit to Czecho-Slovakia was an important step towards the pacification of Europe.

Dismissed Charge

Charged with loitering with intent at Bow Street yesterday, a middle-aged man who gave his name as V. Bartlett, of no settled occupation, said that he was waiting for the rainy season in Abyssinia. The charge was dismissed.

NEW BOOKS *reviewed by Evelyn Waugh*

Strange Rites of the Islanders

"MASS-OBSERVATION", as its promoters claim with naive pride, has already attracted ample notice in the newspapers; in a leaflet which accompanies *May the Twelfth* the editors relate the number of columns and half-columns in their press-cutting book as eagerly as a débutante of the 1920's. Their pride is naive, for this publicity impairs at the outset the value of any results for which they may hope. There are some hundreds of Mass-observers regimented about the

May the Twelfth : Mass Observation Day-surveys. 1937. Faber and Faber. 12s. 6d.

country whose business—or rather re-creation—it is to jot down the doings of their neighbours. Some of them are Conservative, Anglican domestic nurses, some of them atheist vendors of Communist periodicals, most of them, in the matter of education, appear to belong to the middle forms of the Gollancz extension school, but all are animated by a primal curiosity. They differ from other keyhole-observers and envelope-steamers in the show they make of their work. I cannot help feeling that there must be countless provincial tea-tables at which it is whispered "She is so clever and so dangerous—a mass observer, you know." (In my youth it used to be a hobby to hoax the sex-psychologists with fantastic case-histories; no doubt we shall find fun in exhibiting Chestertonian eccentricities to the mass observers.)

Another characteristic, besides the zest for advertisement, of this first major work of the group is the persistent denial of individuality to individuals. It is the basic assumption of all traditional Christian art and philosophy that every human being is possessed of free will, reason and personal desires. Mass-observation is based on the rudest of classifications—upper class, middle class, lower class; old, middle-aged, young. No doubt one of the first developments of the school will be to multiply these distinctions; probably we shall see the evolution of a system of enumeration by which eventually a symbol may be found for any gradation of income and refinement; classes will have to be divided and subdivided until the permutations become so elaborate that it will be found convenient to resort to the original order of names, Christian names and prefixes, but meanwhile, in its early stage, the observers are touchingly reliant on the value of rudimentary abstractions.

These perhaps are merely tricks of presentation. A more modern characteristic is at the root of the whole movement: that is the distrust of democracy. In the brave days of John Stuart Mill the "Left Wing" radicals believed that a popular suffrage combined with popular education was all that was needed for good government; some years later when no sensational advantages were found to result it was thought that fuller education (which is a way of saying more prolonged adolescence) and more frequent general elections, with the right to promote professional instead of amateur politicians, would do the trick. Now it is found that all over the world hitherto respectable democrats will enthusiastically vote themselves out of their own political rights. From the position of divinely inspired oracle, the lout with the ballot-paper has suddenly been deposed and his place taken by an automaton for whom the key has got into the wrong hands and the manufacturer's book of instructions mislaid. Scientists have been too long abroad, strutting through the jungle with callipers, categorizing the love-rituals of remote islanders; there is work for them at home, to find out what buttons and switches animate the European voter; how he can be made to relish the institutions which reason prescribes for him. One thing was abundantly clear—the beast loved a show. The ceremonial of Nazi Germany and Marxist Russia, the rattling wheels of the tanks and the amplified platitudes of the broadcast orators stirred the people to irrational enthusiasm. Well, we were having a show of our own on May 12. It was not indeed got up for the occasion; it was an inherited piece of expensive ritual which had grown soberer and more modest with the centuries; but it got together a large assembly of people and it subjected them to a series of stimuli. Out crept the mass-observers with their stubs of pencil. After that there was office work to be done—a prodigious amount, I should imagine; and finally a collection has been published in a single substantial volume.

Let me say at once that it is well worth the price of 12s. 6d. As one would have expected, it varies greatly in artistic and human interest; there is a good deal of irritating pseudo-scientific showmanship, phraseology worthy of the efficiency advisors of American commerce; there are bits of narrative that are flat and dull, but it would be hard to find any recent work of the same length which had so little that was dull and so much that was highly amusing. In the first 80 pages, the press-cuttings might well have been omitted; they are inadequate if their object is to explain the nature of the Coronation to an uninitiated reader and they are not nearly fantastic enough to expose the kind of extravagance in which the popular press wallowed. Their object presumably was to be normal, but they seemed to me flat. The succeeding section on London's May 12 could scarcely be better. It provides a real documentary survey of the event as seen by the crowds. It is regrettable, but in the nature of things unavoidable, that there were no observers in the privileged parts within the Abbey. The anecdotes that were current at the time of the behaviour of various peeresses would have made delicious reading. There is only one record from inside the Abbey and that of a very unimportant officer. We should have welcomed a detailed description of the behaviour of the protagonists. But the descriptions of the crowd are incomparably better than anything that was published in the press. No doubt many novels are in preparation for the autumn season with Coronation scenes. I suspect they will seem pretty flat. The two sections of National and Individual Reactions are less of a piece artistically and sometimes pretty shoddy. Taken at random, the description of Leeds, pp. 287-288, and of Oxford, p. 313, seem to me quite worthless, but there are many very bright passages—particularly the scraps of dialogue. The Normal Day Survey smacks of parlour games—no harm in that. One further criticism: the observers ought to have kept to the job of objective rapportage. It is tiresome when they offer comments.

A BOOK OF BIRDS. Mary Priestley. (*Gollancz*, 7s. 6d.) On the surface an elegant Christmas present: an anthology beautifully printed and produced with admirable wood-engravings by C. F. Tunnicliffe. Then doubts arise. The compiler is a bird-watcher ("in the dark shade of the tree I found a spotted missel-thrush, whose bright eye I could vividly see"), one of those people with Zeiss glasses whose excitement over their small feathered discoveries is so embarrassingly persistent and literary. And surely even a bird-watcher's interest may flag before the end of an anthology of more than 360 pages devoted to nothing but birds. Another warning—there are a lot of passages like this:

> The bobolisks rallied them up
> from the dell,
> The orioles whistled them out of
> the wood;
> And all of their saying was,
> 'Earth, it is well!'
> And all of their dancing was,
> 'Life, thou art good!"

And so we pass on to the ruby-crowned kinglet.

'*Come on, Stanislaus, you never let me throw anything.*'

THE FILMS BY GRAHAM GREENE

Big City—Tales from the Vienna Woods—Children at School

IT has been a bad week in the commercial cinema—*Big City* and *Tales from the Vienna Woods*. I think it is just possible to sit through the first, thanks to Borzage, the sentimental but competent director who made *Seventh Heaven*. Spencer Tracy plays a taxi driver, Luise Rainer his foreign wife. In a war between a taxi combine and the independent owners a bomb is thrown, a man killed, the woman framed. Though she is the wife of an American, by United States law the woman can be deported because she hasn't been in the country three years. If the drivers can hide her another six weeks from the police she'll be safe. Pathos accumulates. She is going to have a baby, she gives herself up when her friends are arrested for sheltering her, harrowing farewell in a steerage cabin, last-minute release. Domesticity and tenderness are heavily laid on: people in this film are *too* happy before disaster: no one is as happy as all that, no one so little prepared for what life is bound to do sooner or later. One remembers with how few shots Lang in *Fury* established the deep affection between his characters: the shop-window gazing in the rain, the torn macintosh sewn up on the platform. This good-bye while the detectives wait in the corridor and the drabs watch from the other bunks is moving, of course, but one resents being moved by so exorbitant an agony—the eight-berth metal cabin, the imminent labour, the permanence of the separation—the woman bound for some Central European village, the husband without the money to follow her.

Tales from the Vienna Woods is an Austrian film and you know what that means: it means Magda Schreider's deep-sunk eyes and porcine coquetry; courtyards where everyone in turn picks up a song as they mend cars, clean windows, wash clothes; a festival in a beer-garden with old Viennese costumes, balloons, slides, laughter, and driving home at dawn in a fiacre; Magda Schreider's trim buttocks and battered girlishness; a musical tour of Vienna—no sign, of course, of the Karl Marx Hof, only palaces and big baroque dictatorial buildings; Magda Schreider's mouth wide open—rather too much gum like a set of false teeth hung up outside a cheap dentist's. Leo Slezak with his magnificent buffoonery tries to save the film, but Austrian films are born dead: horrible bright fakes from a ruined country, libellous laughter.

The Gas Light and Coke Company —uncompromising and gritty name— provide the only relief from these gay and gloomy fictions. They have followed up their excellent Nutrition film of last year with an even better documentary, *Children at School*, directed by Mr. Basil Wright with a commentary by the Editor of the *Spectator*. It begins a little untidily with the Parthenon (only because the commentary refers to Plato), it reverts too often to Mr. Wilson Harris's modulated and Liberal features, his discreet tie-pin, and Lady Astor tries to storm Hollywood with untimely histrionics, but these are the only serious criticisms to be made against a film with the exciting lyrical quality one admired in Mr. Wright's *Song of Ceylon*. The picture starts with a comparison between State education in England and that of the Dictatorship countries ("Drill the children, school them into believing that the Dictator is always right"). It presents first the new type of Infant and Nursery Schools—romantically in terms of sunlight, of absorbed and brooding infant faces, of a child by a blackboard telling an obscure surrealist tale to his class about a policeman, a man with a sword. . . . The romantic movement reaches a lovely and nostalgic climax as the camera sweeps a huge grass plain, children exercising, playing games, a sense of freedom in the bright wide air, while high immature voices are overlaid in a traditional hymn, overlaid across open windows, gymnasium, changing room. ("O les voix d'enfants chantant dans la coupole.") Then the realistic movement, the reminder that hell too lies about us in our infancy. A small child hurries down a dreary concrete passage, while from behind a door comes a voice reciting the rich false lines— "And softly through the silence beat the bells along the Golden Road . . ." Cracks in the ceilings and the beams, damp on the walls, hideous gothic exteriors of out-of-date schools, spiked railings, narrow windows, scarred cracked playgrounds of ancient concrete: A.D. 1875 in ecclesiastical numerals on a corner stone: the wire dustbin, the chipped basin, the hideous lavatory seat and the grinding of trains behind the school yard. Teachers with drawn neurotic faces flinching at the din: two classes to a room: conferences of despairing masters—the thin-lipped face, the malformed intellectual night-school skull, the shrewish voice of the cornered idealist as he reports progress to his colleagues—a new set of desks.

For the second time this commercial company has done the Health Ministry's work. It is just as well: a politician is professionally an optimist; he has the cheery complacency of the salesman (listen to Mr. Chamberlain in a week or two); and in spite of its romantic first movement this is not an optimistic or a complacent picture.

★

The crisis such a moratorium would produce would be so grave that . . . [next day] . . . it is unlikely to create a situation much different from that previously existing.—*From two successive issues of* THE TIMES.

That's grave enough, certainly.

Jaeger NOTES FOR *November*

For the COMPLETE TRAVELLER

The modern peregrinator, like his forebears, wants to do it in **comfort**, *and we are known all over the world to possess that idiosyncrasy; but consider these points :—*

1. The question of weight. The weight of this Jaeger dressing-gown is less than two pounds. Cashmere and wool give real content.

2. The lapels are in contrasting colours—royal blue, wine, black, or nigger.

3. The girdle is in self or contrasting shades

4. Note the patch pocket and initial.

5. Do the slippers complete the symphonic effect, or don't they?

6. The silk pyjamas are of the same colour as the lapels, or an equally effective complementary hue with darker piping.

★ *All have the hard-wearing qualities which Jaeger gives.*

Jaeger

JAEGER HOUSE. REGENT STREET, W.1.   GO TO YOUR NEAREST JAEGER SHOP.

ON AND OFF THE ROAD

Earls Court Exhibitionism

YEAR by year the Motor Show becomes a more wonderful tribute to the honesty of the motor trade. If anyone still feels like buying a new car after getting to Earls Court by road they must have wanted one very badly indeed. Once you're inside, of course, it's very pleasant. Earls Court is immense and glorious, rather like East Anglia with a roof on —but far more peaceful.

The show is beautifully staged. Looking like a vast and highly refined traffic jam, it allows visitors to examine cars in their natural surroundings. But of course it's really far nicer than an ordinary traffic jam, which is usually rather a rude affair. No engines are running, you can lean on radiators without getting charred and there are refreshments all over the place.

It is not easy to form an accurate opinion of business conditions. A famous manufacturer, asked for his views on the economic trend of internal combustion, said that he hadn't had a drink for nearly two hours. One of the heads of a great distributing organization, when asked his opinion of the consuming power of the market, said he hadn't touched a drop since breakfast time.

On the technical side great progress has naturally been made. Engines are becoming more incomprehensible than ever. This year all of them have to have air cleaners, which seems fussy in view of the fact that the owners and passengers have to use the air just as it comes.

Petrol consumption figures are better. There is one magnificent town car which used to use ten gallons an hour standing in traffic blocks. This year it only uses nine.

It's the same with bodywork. There is one remarkable family saloon that could only just hold a family of four last year in great discomfort. This year it can only just hold five in even greater discomfort, and it's the same on every side. Progress in all directions. Cars are all getting lighter—you can lift some of them quite easily. This is most promising. In a year or two we shall with luck be able to buy cars that we can put on our backs and carry past traffic jams rather like canoe owners when they come to locks.

Gear-boxes nowadays appear to be quite uncanny to tough old motorists who were brought up to put their feet on the dash and pull the gear lever till sparks came through the floor-boards. Even on cheap cars today it's like stirring treacle and some expensive gear-boxes seem to operate by witchcraft.

Tyres continue to improve. The makers make them so well nowadays that they say they can't make any profits. In the good old days if a man got to Brighton and back with a pair of tyres, his name would appear in the advertisements. Nowadays if a tyre ever shows any signs of wear at all, the owner writes a stiff letter to the manufacturer about shoddy workmanship. Still, the tyre manufacturers are very enterprising and continue to do everything they can to make things comfortable for pedestrians.

That seems to be one of the secrets of the success of the Motor Show. It is one time in the year when the pedestrian comes into his own. He can rush in front of the most expensive cars whenever he likes. He can walk over them and through them. The place is full of people pounding cushions and shaking headlights and kicking wings. They pretend, of course, that they are thinking of buying cars. But actually they are revelling in the fact that for one brief hour of glorious life they can lean into the window of any car they like and tell the driver that his bodywork is a disgrace and his face an outrage without waking up in hospital.

SUPERCHARGER

'Shall we go round again?'

With THE KENNEL CLUB

by Louis MacNeice

THE place where a dog show is held is called a venue. The Kennel Club's venue used to be the Crystal Palace where, when bored with the dogs, one could look at the goldfish. Their latest exhibition last week, their seventy-sixth, was held at Olympia. Both the dogs and their owners seemed to enjoy Olympia and there was comparatively little grumbling or migraine on the part of either. (If you want to see what difference a venue makes, go to the great winter dog show at the Bingley Hall, Birmingham.) As for the owners, I was sorry to notice better manners and less eccentricity. In the toy department I missed the customary six-foot Sapphos in breeches, while among the St. Bernards and Great Danes I missed the tiny sentimental old ladies with game legs who feed their pets upon bull's-eyes.

The dogs themselves remain as odd as ever. I have little sympathy with the people who complain that breeding for show purposes produces an artificial type of dog. Dogs lead such artificial lives that they may as well look artificial into the bargain. But the fancies should keep their breeds differentiated and this is counteracted by excess of trimming—witness the flashier terriers. Kerry Blues do not look themselves at all when they are pruned like Airedales. And there are many developments which I would criticize on æsthetic rather than functional grounds. The Sealyham, say the older breeders, is becoming a sissy—no good for badger. But what does that matter to the countless Sealyham owners in N.W.8 or S.W.1? What does matter is that when Sealyhams get too narrow in the head, they lose their expression of bonhomie.

On the whole I prefer big dogs to small and smooth-haired dogs to rough-haired. Among the bigger breeds I was sorry to notice that there was a very poor entry of mastiffs, the bitch certificate not being awarded, though the dog certificate went to a fine-looking fawn who is a son of that late prince among mastiffs, Champion Joseph of Hellingly. It was nice to see twenty-one Newfoundlands, walking about like sofas, but why so few Landseers? And I should have liked some more bull-mastiffs, for the bull-mastiff, in my opinion, has the greatest appeal of any dog on the bench, with his plodding feet, his thumpability, his piggy eyes, his casual ears and his fascinating manner of yawning. Great Danes, I think, have developed for the worse and are now too gawky. Bloodhounds had a very fair entry, several champions being defeated, and were slobbering less than usual. Being a Borzoi owner, I was disappointed that I could only look at the Borzois on the bench, for you cannot judge a borzoi unless he is standing up. Most of them seemed to be lacking in coat and their owners were less made-up than usual. I noticed several dogs with the famous Mythe profile—one of the triumphs of breeding for a special feature. (The Mythe profile is more convex than that of the most decadent human aristocrat.)

Among the native breeds which are less often shown, it was pleasing to see bassets, beagles, smooth collies, Irish water spaniels and Staffordshire bull-terriers—the last-named a very *natural*-looking dog. Among the more exotic novelties I have no use at all for anything which comes out of Tibet except the pleasingly grumpy Tibetan mastiff. The other Tibetan breeds are what you would expect from a country where people are holy and never undress. The two specimens of Chi-huahua, which got such a wonderful press, could beat the miniature black-and-tan terrier for any comic strip part as an insect. The Zoo lent a husky with a very falsetto voice. Shaggy Bernese mountain dogs and black-and-tan broad-headed Rottweilers both had appeal, but the prize for charm must go to the solitary specimen of a Chesapeake Bay retriever, a dog of a most unnatural fusty liver colour. And there were twenty-five Boston terriers, which are charming but not terriers.

Of toy breeds the best is the pug, inadequately represented at this show. I cannot understand why this classic little beast with its Quaker-like elegance and its marvellous dark popeyes full of *Sehnsucht*, should be so much less popular than the vulgarly pretentious Pekinese. Some pugs also are very good mousers. There was a good turn-out of Afghans and I revised my opinion that these are essentially ludicrous dogs—baboons dressed up in pyjamas. Some of these Afghans had the presence of sheiks. As for gundogs, I say nothing of them because they are useful. Their praises are printed in that eternity where stuffed trout swim in glass cases and it is always the Twelfth of August. Old English Sheepdogs might also be claimed to be useful but only by their breeders, for all dog-breeders have Faith. I should be sorry to be a sheep in the care of one of these boisterous hundred-pounders. Alsatians are to me an abomination and I was glad to see that they were just outnumbered by bull-terriers. Some regard the modern bull-terrier as a monstrosity, but except for someone I knew at Oxford I have never met anything to match their albino allure and their blend of indecency and pathos.

For the rest, dachshunds were many and well-polished, schnauzers were noisy, poodles wore coronation ribbons, Bedlingtons, those nasty little zanies, sat quivering in overcoats. Old ladies in all directions produced sandwiches from handbags, not to mention small but attractive bones. England is still herself, I thought, as I left this parade of dogs and drove away towards Knightsbridge.

The SNOB'S GUIDE to Good Form

by P. Y. Betts

FOOD.—In eating, perhaps more than in any other social activity, it is important to realize that the opposite pole to good form is not bad manners, but gentility. Bad manners, indeed, are often rather good form, as they show how completely you are at your ease. Nobody will think the worse of you for ignoring the handle of your tea-cup or audibly spitting out cherry stones or sucking your sticky fingers clean with loud smacking noises; but dabbling about in finger-bowls and a reluctance to pick bones with your teeth or your teeth with bones will soon stamp you as bourgeois. It is quite all right, therefore, to sop the bacon-fat up off your plate with a bit of bread, though it is rather better form to do this at two o'clock in the morning than at nine o'clock breakfast, when it is seemly not to be able to support the sight of food.

This brings us to the subject of certain foodstuffs that are good form or bad form according to the time of day at which they are eaten. Kippers are an example of this sliding scale—at breakfast they are decidedly poor form, at lunch impossible, laughable at tea, unthinkable at dinner, but for about six hours after midnight they become completely sophisticated and, as is the custom when sophistication sets in, their price rises steeply. The same law applies to eggs-and-bacon (preferably known as bacon-and-eggs), sausages, grilled ham, etc. Foods which are permanently bad form and unknown to the palates of wordly people are shepherd's pie, sardines (except isolated specimens, in hors d'œuvre), boiled bacon and beans, pig's trotters, suet pudding, tripe and onions, custard, and soused herrings, unless you call them rollmops. As for drinks, the first thing to bear in mind is that you must prefer them *dry*; if you don't, then you must pretend to. French Vermouth is better form than Italian, pale than brown sherry, and so on. Cider is a sweet, sissy and shameful drink, little better than cocoa in the estimation of people who really know what's what. *China* tea, please. Some good-form foods are toast, York ham, underdone cold beef, trout, oysters, and anything in a pot from Fortnum & Mason's. Savouries are better form than sweets. Smoked salmon is slightly better form than hors d'œuvre or grapefruit, and lemons are socially acceptable at any meal.

HEALTH.—The Snob may suffer from colitis, malaria, appendicitis, concussion, sinusitis, antrum trouble, fractures, neuralgia, or laceration in motor smashes. But there are some maladies which may not afflict the Snob—fallen arches, among others.

BABIES.—Thoroughly good form at the moment, though Snobs are advised that the boom may not last indefinitely. Boy babies continue to be slightly better form than girl babies, no doubt because it gives Mr. Hore-Belisha pleasure to see a nice long rank of new boy babies parked down the front page of his breakfast *Times*.

ART.—To enjoy the best of both worlds, the Snob should be who's-whoish enough to receive an invitation

' May I introduce Mr. Russell—Mr. Watson.'

to the Royal Academy private view, yet emancipated enough to be able to sneer at *all* the pictures when he gets there.

French painters who flourished towards the end of the last century should always be firmly admired. Among the near-moderns, Picasso and Braque are the names to toy with; among the moderns, Dali and Joan Miró and Balthus. (*N.B.*—Miró is a man. The name Joan is only a trap.) It will always be effective to hit upon some reasonably obscure foreign artist with a difficult name and profess great admiration for his rhythm. See Mr. Huxley's essay *Conxolus* for the proper technique.

If it is impossible to divine the subject of a work of art, or if the work of art is made from unfamiliar materials (a pink Australian wood, for instance, or hair-clippings from a saluki belonging to a Sitwell), the Snob will be safe in assuming that the work of art in question is an example of significant, or good, form.

DRESS.—Either very new clothes or very old ones.

TRAVEL.—The faster the better; thus—flying is fashionable, hiking is horrible. It is only getting to places that is important, and having been there. Nowhere in England counts, but Scotland will do if you've been abroad first.

PUBLIC SCHOOLS.—The Snob must sneer at these; but he should also have been to one of them.

NAVY, THE BRITISH.—Outmoded by the Air Arm, except as a career for our boys. (See also section on *Babies.*)

LITERATURE. — You need never actually be seen reading a book but it is a good thing to give the impression that you have read a few, by mugging up the reviews in the Sunday papers. If you must read, read American writers—these are all very good form just now, but don't enthuse too much over Hemingway, the critics are just beginning to criticize him.

HUMOUR.—A sense of humour is an indispensable part of the Snob's

equipment; but it must be the right kind of humour, and rather than be amused at the wrong things it is far better never to be amused at all. The present encyclopædist is collecting data on this difficult subject, but until these researches are complete Snobs who wish to be on the safe side are advised to laugh at nothing whatever except Anglo-Indians or Selfridge's decorations, both of which are definitely foolproof fun.

SERVANTS.—Though the Snob need not employ any servants at all himself, his manner towards the servants in the houses he frequents should make it plain that he was brought up in a household where the staff consisted of a minimum of three maids and a handyman. For Snobs who can afford only one servant, it is better to have a daily woman who comes in to do the chores than to have a general living in; if servants live in, there should be more than one of them. The reason for this is that so long as you employ only a daily woman you can pass off your tatty flat as simply a pied-à-terre; but a living-in maid-of-all-work sets upon any establishment a seal of bourgeois permanence which is highly undesirable.

POLITICS. — Communism and Fascism are both à la mode, but to be a Liberal is social suicide. It is good form to be extreme.

WORK.—The Snob can take up almost any kind of work which does not oblige him to attend an office daily as a black-coated worker. In addition to the regular professions, publishing, advertising, interior decorating and the B.B.C. are pretty well thought of. Lots of Snobs go into the catering trade (roadhouses, coffee-stalls, hotels of the rose-petal jam type) without losing a ha'porth of caste. As a rule, if he sticks to his accent and his old grey flannel bags and never forgets that to do a job of work is definitely amusing (see *Humour*), the Snob can't go far wrong, whatever job he chooses. But to take working for one's living as a matter of course is as drab as to send one's bags to the cleaners now and again.

'*He wants to paint like Van Gogh, and luckily he's only got one ear.*'

' It's very sweet of you, Fred, but what ever should I do with it ?'

★   ★   ★

MONEY.—It is permissible to be broke, provided you always have enough money in your pocket for drinks all round and your credit's holding out. It is quite good form to ask for money as a loan, but to ask to be given money or to repay loans is equally bourgeois. Having money tied up in foreign stocks that have slumped is very good form indeed; also to be crippled by death duties.

SPORT.—G.F.: Polo, golf, Rugger, racing (horse or motor), cricket, sailing, all-in wrestling, winter sports. Also shooting (grouse and the better-class animals).

B.F. : Soccer, racing (dog or motor-bike). These can be good form, though, provided you realize that by watching them you are temporarily declassing yourself and being democratic by associating yourself with the masses. Shooting at targets or rabbits is not good form, and cycling is unspeakable, but the Snob may play darts in pubs and skittles in riverside skittle-alleys, thanks to the splendid work of Mr. A. P. Herbert. Ambiguous sports include boxing, tennis, swimming, etc., depending on who the players are and where they play. Even rounders is good form when played at Frinton.

CINEMA, THE.—All Russian films are marvellous, even magnificent. You may enjoy Hitchcock films so long as you make it clear that of course you realize that it's popular stuff, though good enough of its kind. But Cecil B. de Mille productions should never be enjoyed. The only singing-and-dancing films that should be treated tolerantly by Snobs are the Rogers-Astaire collaborations; and Disney cartoons must be loudly adored.

Mention the montage of the Grierson documentaries from time to time.

UNCONVENTIONALITY.—It is a splendid thing to be unconventional, if only you are unconventional in the conventional way. For example, if you simply must cut down expenses on account of crippling death duties, slumps in foreign stocks, etc., you may do so by frying sausages over a gas-ring in a Chelsea attic, but certainly not by renting a villa in Tooting and taking to high tea at six instead of dinner. The same law applies to moral unconventionality — adultery, yes ; overlooking the bills of tradespeople, yes; cheating at cards, a thousand times no.

To sum up—break as many rules as you like, but be sure to find out first which rules it is good form to break. This is the whole art of being a Snob.

A JOB IN A MILLION

13—HE KEEPS DEAD

THE daily round of a mortuary keeper and pathologist's assistant, as described by Mr. Discord, sounds like the common task which it obviously is not. In the morning you call the roll of the dead—tidily housed in the huge refrigerators known to Mr. Discord as "the Chamber"—check over details of cases for postmortem examination with admission papers, and prepare the bodies for examination, having first made certain that the necessary permission of relatives has been obtained. Then the appropriate physician or surgeon is acquainted with the diagnosis and notices are posted in the pathology laboratory, the various surgical units, and the students' club, giving details of the day's programme. The post-mortems are carried out in the afternoon, and arrangements made for the funerals to proceed as soon as possible. Finally the post-mortem room is restored to the state of spotless order in which it started the day. A surgeon's operating theatre has nothing to teach Mr. Discord either in the matter of dazzling tiles and shining instruments or of well-kept operating tables ("You can eat off 'em, and no nonsense").

Dealing as he does with doctors, hospital officials, and students, relations of the deceased, undertakers, and often the police, Mr. Discord needs ready wits, besides plenty of tact and judgment, for his highly skilled and responsible task. The slightest hitch or error may lead to endless complications, for, as he says, nothing gives a hospital a bad name so quickly as a bad mortuary keeper. His watchwords are cleanliness, efficiency, and dispatch.

His attitude to his work is strictly logical: a corpse is a corpse. At the same time his duties involve a nice combination of a very real respect for the dead with devotion to science, of readiness to oblige a doctor anxious to preserve some pathological curiosity, with consideration for the feelings of relatives, who naturally like to bury a presentable corpse.

One of Mr. Discord's little boasts is of his uncanny skill in what he humorously calls "making good"—not always an easy task after a searching post-mortem. A bald man whose brain has been removed sets a pretty problem in invisible repair. A dummy hand that will not cause embarrassment needs a delicate touch in modelling and fixing.

These are some of Mr. Discord's minor triumphs. A slave to his art, he scorns the protection of the customary rubber gloves, and for the sake of precision invariably works with bare hands smeared in vaseline and repeatedly washed in disinfectant. In spite of this he has twice come very near to taking his place among his wards. The first accident was due to a clumsy piece of porterage ("You see, handling a corpse is more a knack than strength"). He was carrying a particularly stout party who had died of typhoid, when his assistant, a mere novice, suddenly doubled up the knees into the pit of the stomach, with the most unfortunate results for Mr. Discord, who was officiating at the head end. He waited philosophically for the period of incubation to elapse and retired to his own hospital for attention. After a close fight he was sent to the seaside to convalesce, still troubled with internal poisoning, which he succeeded in dispelling by an original process of kidney-flushing that astonished his medical advisers and would have provided sensational advertising copy for brewers and gin-distillers.

The second contretemps was the result of a splinter from the ossified cartilage of an old gentleman whose ribs Mr. Discord was engaged in "making good". This was a plain case of septic poisoning, and once again his robust constitution pulled him through. In neither case would gloves have helped him.

One of the most comforting things about Mr. Discord is his respect and admiration for the medical profession. With his unique opportunities for observing the seamy side of hospital life, he has nothing but praise for the medical and nursing staff, the students and the organization. Twenty-five years ago, however, things were very different. Medical exams were not so strictly supervised as they are today, and Mr. Discord has gruesome tales to tell of dead men buried alive. One Monday morning years ago he opened his ice-box to examine its contents, and, to his astonishment, saw an arm move. "I'd been out on Sunday evening and had a beer or two, so I took another look. That arm moved again, no nonsense about it. Out you come, my girl, I said. Mind you, sir, the young lady'd been there over the weekend, and her parents notified and everything. That didn't worry me; I applied artificial respiration and she came round and lived ten days."

Now all that is changed. After a death has been certified, the body must lie unmoved until unmistakable signs of death occur. In the bad old days cases were often removed to the post-mortem room still warm and, as Mr. Discord indignantly declared "*rigor mortis* never had a chance to set in".

This raises the whole question of the macabre side of the profession; here again Mr. Discord's attitude is one of sound common sense. As a young man, it seems, he used to think about his work with depressing effects; he noticed a tendency among his colleagues either towards drunkenness or lunacy. Neither alternative appealed to him, and he decided some sort of outside interest was needed. Printing and pisciculture gradually became whole-time relaxations, and doubtless the rearing of his own family later provided him with an additional distraction. Like any good doctor, he has accustomed himself to the sordidness inevitably connected with his work, without either allowing it to interfere with his efficiency or warp his feelings as a human being. "Some fellows," he says, "will pretend they're never upset. Don't you believe 'em. Everyone's liable to a turn sometimes—it's all according to what condition you're in. I've known a good dinner make a wonderful lot of difference."

Mr. Discord is as full of sympathy for students whose first post-mortem proves too much for them as he is full of help for the young police-man bringing in a messy accident. "When there's a leg off," he explained, "or bones sticking out, it naturally gets 'em groggy." At his work he realizes the importance of showing as little emotion as possible, but real callousness still shocks him, and he resents the occasional accusations of nurses or students who mistake his

professional manner for lack of feeling.

Asked if he'd ever been scared, he told of a crude joke played on him in his early days, involving a booby trap in a dark cellar. His revenge was satisfying, but nearly cost him his job. Disguised as a corpse, he lay in wait for the jokers as they were bringing in a body, and rose stiffly from the waist at the psychological moment. "Of course, they didn't wait to ask any questions ; just dropped the body— I had to clear it up myself. Twenty minutes later I look in at the porters' lodge and see them trying to play nap. You won't believe me, sir, but they couldn't: their hands trembled so."

Mr. Discord's sense of humour finds all sorts of outlets. Take his visiting-cards. He prints them himself and can afford to be fanciful. For random distribution to reckless pedestrians and careless drivers there are two nicely

graded warnings : the jocular, with a reverse that reads " Cats have nine lives ; you only have one. Take care of it ! " and the more sinister " W. Discord ———Hospital ", bearing a hearse (" My own design, sir "). The card I liked best is the one he reserves for the purpose of deflating bigwigs who try to impress him with an array of professional qualifications : W. Discord, K.D., M.P., C.P. " You see," he explained, " Keeper of the Dead, Mortuary Porter, and Commercial Printer. That takes the wind out of their sails, and they never care to display their ignorance by asking."

Though he talks prosaically enough about his job, Mr. Discord's life has never lacked adventure. Running away from home and the buckle end of his father's belt, he knocked about a good deal and educated himself at night schools before settling down in

'How's that for a stunt?'

' Yes, yes, but for the moment we need only discuss his replacement value.'

the job in a million which is undoubtedly his vocation. In his time he has been suspected of theft—a diamond solitaire from a corpse's finger turning up in the hospital drainage system in time to clear him—and even murder. He has been ostracized on account of his calling and cruelly misjudged by people who should have known better. His harmless custom of carrying a razor in his pocket, for the obvious reason that he likes to be well shaven at all hours of the day, has led to ridiculous misunderstandings, but he takes everything in good part and philosophically compares his lot with that of a public executioner, for whom he has a certain professional sympathy.

But, for all his association with the dead, Mr. Discord's real interest remains with the living. " I like to live," he admits; " and I like to see something else living, too." So, besides his cat and his South African Singing Finch, he keeps an aquarium. It contains goldfish, tench, trout, and newts. The newts were lying in a voluptuous pile, six or seven deep, and in the most abandoned attitudes. We were not surprised to learn that they bred in captivity. The yolk of Mr. Discord's hard-boiled egg goes every morning to the goldfish, which will give you some idea of his calibre as an animal-lover. He has no use for people who do not care for animals and has noticed that some of the finest doctors he has worked with share his enthusiasm as fish fanciers. One day he means to retire to the country to grow things and breed things to his heart's content. The dead will miss him. SYLVAIN MANGEOT

NEW BOOKS *reviewed by Evelyn Waugh*

Edith Sitwell's First Novel

SOME time ago I was privileged to hear a lady of modest private means and modest literary attainments talking about book-reviewing. She was describing how she had been sent a book for review by a weekly (of modest circulation). "I had to send it back," she said. "I do not see how it is possible to give one's opinion on a book until one has read it twice with at least a month's interval between. I suppose the other wretched people do it for money." At the time I felt unsympathetic; certainly we wretched people do it for money, but it has to be done quickly; there is just time to jot down a few points before the book fades from memory. The best we can hope to do is to give our readers some idea of a book's character so that they will know whether they are likely to want it. But now and then a book arrives which defies this cursory treatment. Miss Sitwell's novel is one of these. It is a book of delicacy and subtlety; but it is more than that; it is a book of deep shadows, obscure, almost impenetrable at first; one's eyes must adjust themselves to the gloom before it is found to be richly peopled; these dark places lie next to brilliant points of lyrical light. One meets this vivid chiaroscuro often enough in modern fiction, but it is usually the black and white of the lino-cut; the blacks are flat dabs of ink, the whites simple patches of plain paper. Miss Sitwell's book, or so it seems to me, is like a magnesium flame in a cavern, immediately and abundantly beautiful at first sight, provoking further boundless investigation. It is a book that must be read patiently,

more than once, and it must be read. I say this in apology, for it is impossible in the limits of weekly journalism to do more than suggest its unique character. To say that it is a novel about Dean Swift, Stella and Vanessa translated into modern life is nonsense, but it is the best that I can find in a single sentence to describe it.

The date of the story is of no importance. Elsewhere Miss Sitwell has shown herself a master of " period ". It is easy to imagine with what deft and significant touches she could, had she wished, have given us a historical background to the life of Swift ; perhaps it is not impertinent to think that she may have begun with some such idea—a historical novel, the main theme set against a rich and various scene of court and café and

---

I Live Under a Black Sun. Edith Sitwell. Gollancz. 8s. 6d.
To Have and Not to Have. Ernest Hemingway. Cape. 7s. 6d.
Tinpot Country. Terence Greenidge. Fortune Press. 7s. 6d.

---

lonely deanery. But the tragedy and the mystery of Swift were too potent for such treatment; she seems to have seen deep into his tortured soul, to horror lurking beneath horror, into a world where costume and décor become meaningless. It is a terrifying book.

Arrested development is the character of almost all American writers; too often they are living and working at the stage of growth of prurient schoolgirls; Mr. Hemingway is a clean, strapping lad, upper fifth (modern side), house colours for swimming, etc. He writes in an exuberant schoolboy slang and he deals with the topics which should—but too often don't—interest little chaps of his age: pirates, smugglers, dagos, Chinks, plenty of bloodshed and above all the topic dearest to the heart of the healthy boy—How does it work? He exults in the technical details of almost any trade or hobby, with the breathless interest with

which we used to watch a plumber putting a washer on a tap. Bull-fighting, man-fighting, fish-fighting, getting the best out of the little motor—anything with a knack to it absorbs his acute vision. He has, too, a proper contempt for swots—the uncouth, spectacled figures who shuffle about in the library when they might be at the nets or sprawling across the counter of the tuck-shop. He is greedy too, as any healthy boy should be. His grown-ups consume whisky and rum, but they do it with the gusto of little boys attacking ice-cream cornets—indeed with something of a swagger, like first-eleven colours calling for doughnuts over the heads of their inferiors.

Well, there is a lot to be said for not growing up. Mr. Hemingway's books are always a delight. The new one consists of three stories about a courageous but unfortunate waterman. He starts life taking tourists fishing, but he can't keep his temper with them and gets bilked. Then he murders Chinks instead; then he gets shot at by coastguards and loses an arm (and a nigger?), then he gets kidnapped by Cuban desperadoes and murders them and gets murdered himself and that's Harry that was. It would be idle to say that one's delight is as keen as when, unawares, one first picked up *The Sun Also Rises,* but most of the qualities are there which made that book memorable. Perhaps the holidays have gone on too long; there is too much noise about the house; how many days to the beginning of term? Well, give the boy a treat for his last day—a quart of Baccardi and a dago's spine to break.

There have been many books, mostly satirical, about the cinema world. They have been written from a superior position by writers who have, at one time or another, become temporarily involved. They have found the film magnates outrageous; they have lived dizzily for a few weeks in a world bereft of all logic and decency and have emerged immensely the wealthier.

[183]

Tinpot Country is written from the point of view of one of those unhappy figures whom the novelists pass unnoticed as they are ushered into the hideous offices of the bosses—those wistful, often hungry hangers-on who loiter about the studios in the hope of irregular, illpaid employment. We learn from it that there is an uglier side to the lunacy; that the buffoons can be bullies. Mr. Greenidge's hero goes into the business with a boyish zeal and faith; he believes in the cinema as an art and himself as a potential director. He learns from below what others have learned and expressed from above—that there is no place for an artist and a gentleman in the business. By some curious confusion of logic he regards this cosmopolitan madhouse as an epitome of British industrialism and, granted this single fallacy, it is natural that he should welcome the communist revolution with both hands.

★

Literary Snack-Bar

GENERAL

SALLY BOWLES. Christopher Isherwood. (*Hogarth Press*, 3s. 6d.) A long *conte* about a very young amateur whore in Berlin in pre-Hitler days—an English girl called Jackson-Bowles, who sings in a night-club and moves with rather factitious enthusiasm from bed to bed. For a few days she and Mr. Isherwood (who is teaching English and acts as her confidant) nearly get their break when she picks up a drunken American millionaire who proposes to take them both round the world, but such things don't really happen, the millionaire goes away to Budapest, leaving them 300 marks in an envelope. . . . Sally Jackson-Bowles becomes a little more whorish as time passes, has a grotesque night with a loony swindler in a hotel "of a certain kind", disappears from Berlin. Postcards arrive from Paris, from Rome . . . silence . . . Simple, amusing, with an unforced unsentimental pathos, saying no more than it means, it conveys an odd sense that we may be reading a classic.

PURSUITS & VERDICTS
Herbert Read

Here We Go Round the Prickly Pear

I MUST apologize for giving Mr. McCabe more than a mention. He has himself provided, by way of an Epilogue, sixty-five pages of self-criticism in which he anticipates everything the reviewer is likely to say about him. He does it, very cleverly, by quoting the very words of the reviewers, culled from their weekly columns. Torquemada, Milward Kennedy, Howard Spring, Francis Iles, Cyril Connolly and the anonymous minotaur of *The Times Literary Supplement* are in this manner very effectively flattered; coming late to this business, I feel cruelly detached. But Mr. McCabe is a very complicated case, the self-conscious cynic, the hollow man listening to his own reverberations. He describes himself, obliquely but none the less portentously, as "a typical twentieth-century big-city middle-class man, essentially post-war in his attitude towards that present-day structure of society which he himself helped to build", as "another typical member of those who got caught in the machinery of that society which they refuse to change", "like Hemingway, 'the prophet of the lost generation'". His thriller is cunningly constructed on the formula of the Hegelian triad—thesis, antithesis and synthesis, though you wouldn't know it unless you read the Epilogue. This Epilogue tells us much else—is, indeed, a complete philosophy of life—but on the whole it would be better not to read it if you wish to continue to enjoy your thrillers with an innocent mind. For this "dour Scotsman" (I wonder if he is quite so Scottish as his name) insinuates that the detective story is

merely a symptom of our social degeneration, and as such an art-form which the Wide Few can only use in utter disillusionment. In his desperation Mr. McCabe makes himself the villain of the piece, and commits his crime for the mere fun of showing how easy it is to evade and insult the social order he so much despises. He does it very well in the tough Hemingway-Hammett style.

It would not be worth while discussing this book so solemnly had not

---

The Face on the Cutting-room Floor. Cameron McCabe. Gollancz. 7s. 6d.

Rhapsody in Fear. John Newton Chance. Gollancz. 7s. 6d.

Death on the Borough Council. Josephine Bell. Longmans. 7s. 6d.

The Dusky Hour. E. R. Punshon. Gollancz. 7s. 6d.

The Ten Teacups. Carter Dickson. Heinemann. 7s. 6d.

The Body That Came by Post. George Worthing Yates. Lovat Dickson and Peter Davies. 7s. 6d.

Mr. McCabe come so near to what, on his own showing, is a possible justification of the detective story. You have only to give your villain a social conscience—pitting him against the smug values of the capitalist system—to make him a popular hero. Thus conceived, the criminal becomes the lineal descendant of those Robin Hoods and Dick Turpins who have always captivated the imagination of the poor and dispossessed. It is this slant on the criminal which gave more than usual significance to Edward Anderson's *Thieves Like Us,* and which makes *Rhapsody in Fear* a more than ordinary thriller, giving distinction in a literary sphere where distinction is rare.

Mr. McCabe, who can and dare write phrases like " the syncopic after-beat of the door-knocker", promises to try simplicity next time. He might consider the art of Josephine Bell. *Death on the Borough Council* follows *Murder in Hospital* at an interval of a few weeks, but the promise of her first book is amply fulfilled. She is presumably a doctor or a doctor's wife, and writes with an intimate knowledge of low life in London's purlieus. Her plot is not particularly exciting, and the motive of the murder, when it is revealed, is not convincingly adequate. But she can tell her story naturally and economically, without any fuss or facetiousness, with the result that she creates a completely realistic atmosphere. She is threatened by the faults of most female detective writers—wish-fulfilment heroes and sissified slang—but so far these faults are not at all obvious. If you are tired of Poirot and the whimsical Peter you will like Dr. Wintringham.

In the works of Mr. E. R. Punshon, we are told, Miss Dorothy Sayers salutes distinction every time. But judging from this specimen of his craftsmanship, distinction is just what Mr. Punshon does not possess. It is an unreal world of card-sharpers and share-pushers, of ex-convict butlers and suicides disguised as chauffeurs, of unreal wealth in the form of bearer-bonds and of unreal detectives known as Bobby and the Colonel, of literary clichés and arbitrary complications—the method and the materials of the average thriller. The libraries order them wholesale. *The Ten Teacups* is more ingenious, the writing occasionally vivid, the humour not too objectionable. *The Body That Came by Post* is more original in plot, and manages to weave into its romantic texture some topical descriptions of the present civil war in Spain. It has also more real sense of horror than any of the other books on the list. Horror is not essential to detective stories; the "thrill" we get from them is actually a form of intellectual suspense. But the thriller proper works on our obscurer instincts — fumblingly and nowadays feebly—and horror is the evocative medium. It is odd that surrealism, for all its admiration of the thrillers of a century ago, has not yet created a modern equivalent of *The Mysteries of Udolpho*.

FAÇADE
A View of Architecture

"horn carson."

Design for Sea-Faring

MOST people are tired enough of hearing modern architecture compared to the external appearance of ships. It is, however, unusual to find a ship designed with all the elegant and crisp qualities of a good modern building. The recent maiden voyage of the Orient liner *Orcades* is a sequel to the courageous experiment made two years ago by the same company, when they placed a new ship, the *Orion*, under the sole designing control of an architect, Mr. Brian O'Rorke. This ship was an immediate success. Her external appearance (she had only one funnel and one mast) was afterwards widely imitated, but not the simple and reticent design of her public rooms. It was argued that it may have been all right for Australians, but for the Atlantic route it simply wasn't good enough. Hence the ridiculous magnificence of the *Empress of Britain* and *Queen Mary*, the tawdry work of a bunch of academicians and fairy-book illustrators. The Orient line have, however, shown their faith in good contemporary design by entrusting another ship to the same architect, and for him and his team of collaborating artists it is a personal triumph.

In appearance *Orcades* resembles the *Orion*, though her funnel is nine feet higher, in order, we are told, "to fling the products of combustion still further from the ship". The internal decoration is everywhere restful, cool and shorn of extravagance. What may be termed O'Rorke's drift has always been in the direction of simplicity and an almost Scandinavian delicacy of detail. His work is never vulgar and the obvious is confidently avoided. There are none of the bulbous bogus-dynamic shapes beloved of American industrial designers like Beljeddes and Loewy, nor the fripperies of an interior decorator's ship, with white rope festoons, horizontal railings, sail-cloth curtains and life-buoy cocktail-tables. O'Rorke has realized that the dramatic shapes of the ship herself, of ventilator, bridge and spar, need contrast in plain surfaces and quiet colouring. The public rooms are higher than usual on board ship, very openly planned and threaded axially one beyond the other. The dancing space, decorated in perhaps the commonest of modern colour schemes, —white, blue and ochre red—is perhaps a bit poverty-stricken, but the library is a charming room, in soft tones of blue, grey and dusty yellow. One wall is gracefully curved to the form of the ship, completing the long vista through the café and lounge. The latter room has rugs, curtains and chair-covers designed by Marion Dorn in a scheme of coral, maroon and azure blue. Although clever and original, this room is not really a success. The patterns are too oppressive, the colouring too hot for the tropical conditions under which it will be used.

The main feature of the café is a heavily patterned green glass screen with a rather unpleasing gelatinous appearance. It is a pity also that the chairs are of the unfriendly tubular type. Another café, gaily blue and yellow, and roguishly known as the tavern, overlooks the swimming pool, which has a notice saying "It is dangerous to dive", a fact which we have long suspected. In the main dining saloon, a well-proportioned room in grey, white and canary yellow, is a large mural decoration by Ceri Richards constructed in various planes of glass, steel, wood and copper. This work is amusing enough, but it is doubtful if its lively quality will be so evident after the close acquaintanceship of a six-weeks' voyage.

The cabins are ingeniously planned with plenty of cupboards and are air-conditioned. Gone are the brass bedsteads, Aubusson carpets and Gainsborough reproductions of the Aquitania period. The only familiar object is the moustachioed face of the gentleman, closely resembling Sir Cedric Hardwicke, who has for the last fifty years been demonstrating in a series of photographs the etiquette of the life-belt. The rooms are well-shaped and charming, but there is no evidence of the same taste in the selection of the carpets. One of the nicest rooms in the ship is the playroom, equipped with miniature steering wheels and signal halyards which look great fun. There is an elegantly detailed shop selling that curious miscellany of scent-sprays, plush rabbits and heraldic spoons which seems to find so ready a market among seafaring folk. The standard of design and workmanship throughout the ship is remarkably high, but particularly so in one or two cases. There is a convex mirror in the hall, the work of Lynton Lamb, which is a brilliant piece of design and craftsmanship. Equally successful are

the murals in the first-class lounge by John Armstrong, and in the tourist café by John Hutton. Marion Dorn's rugs and fabrics are, of course, excellent, and outside the first-class saloon there are some delightful metal doors with trident handles, designed by Brian O'Rorke. There are also some clever floor inlays by H. W. Collins, and some charming bentwood chairs in the tourist saloon. Mr. O'Rorke and Mr. Colin Anderson are both to be congratulated on a second triumph. The *Orion* and the *Orcades* must

surely be followed by the *O'Rorke*.

We have seen what a shipping company has contributed to modern design. It is perhaps of interest to point out in passing an example of the Church's indifference to her architectural heritage. The charming little gateway to St. James's Church, Piccadilly, was recently demolished to make way for some seats on a Coronation stand. In its place has been erected some elaborate wrought-iron gates between two piers, crowned with the florid urns which are the unmistakable signature of Sir Reginald Blomfield's heavy hand. Few designers could have succeeded so well in the difficult task of making Piccadilly uglier than it already is.　　HUGH CASSON

*

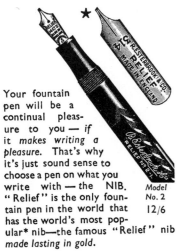

BEDROOMS can be planned in a number of ways according to the habits of the owners. Some people need very little sleep and look upon it as a waste of precious time. They drop off as soon as they get into bed and wake with a start next morning and jump straight out of bed. What such people need is a room where they can change their clothes in the most efficient manner with a bed put away in a corner where they are not constantly reminded of the need for sleep. But there are other people to whom a bed is the most important piece of furniture in the house. We agree with them. We have always wanted to build for ourselves a room which is all bed. On Sundays and feast days we would spend all day in bed and anybody who comes to see us would come to bed, too. Behind the bed a moving shelf would carry round drinks and cigarettes. Unfortunately we've never been able to afford it. But we'd like to build it for somebody else.

by Edward A. Bunyard

The Decay of Carving

IT is to be regretted that modern life has abolished the ancient and honourable art of the carver. England's most aristocratic sons were not ashamed to learn the art at the tables of their compeers so that when they, in their turn, found themselves at the heads of their own tables, the right solemnities and rituals would be preserved.

As in other arts, a complex terminology grew up as time went on; one did not merely " carve " a roast or a bird, each had its appointed word to describe the carver's act. A Heron was " dismembered ", a Cony " unlaced ", a Hen (as so often today) was " spoyled " and a Plover " minced ".

If the art of carving is to be renewed we must revive these ancient terms, and indeed it will be necessary to create a few new ones for our modern dishes. Thus a rice pudding should not be merely *served*; let us say " Disseminate that Rice Pudding ", " Untangle that Macaroni ", " Invalidate that Oyster "—such are a few terms that suggest themselves as likely additions to our table terminology

There are, however, more serious issues which have resulted from our lost interest in the carver's art, and one strikes at the very roots of family life. Who can doubt that parental authority suffered its gravest blow when father ceased to carve the duck ? As we of the older generation sat down before a noble joint, the head of the household, in those days often the father, took his seat with a solemn and purposeful air. Then

followed an awe-inspiring duel between the " steel " and the carving knife which showed you at once what Father could do if really put to it.

Peace having been proclaimed between the two opponents, the steel was laid down and the knife poised for a breathless moment over that portion of the joint where the meat attained its maximum development. It fell with the inexorable quality of fate, and after a bold and sliding stroke we were asked " Who will have the first cut ?" Warming to his work, slice followed slice and the observant eye would note how a favourite daughter would be rewarded by a dainty titbit and an erring son chastened by gristle.

This sacred office has now been abandoned to the cooks and parlourmaids. Does history record any like case of power so lightly thrown away ? Small wonder that parental authority is now in ruins; the youngest keeper at the Zoo could have told us that the power to give or withhold food is the greatest that man possesses.

Were not voices raised in protest at the secret and illicit carving of joints

in kitchens and sideboards ? Certainly. George Augustus Sala (would he were with us at this hour !) protested vehemently at the French innovation of leaving the carver's task to servants. He disapproved of having " the devil knows what handed over your shoulder

by the devil knows who". Like the immortal Shepherd of the *Noctes Ambrosianae* he liked to see his food " in its integrity ".

The influence of carving on diplomacy was known long before Talleyrand's day, but who touched it to finer issues ? Each guest had the portion to which his prestige entitled him and the favoured ones would be asked if it met with their approval; those at the lower end of the table were made also to realize their position.

How could the wily Wilkes have conquered Samuel Johnson's look of " surly virtue " as he did save for the lucky accident that Wilkes was opposite the veal and had therefore to carve it ? " Pray give me leave Sir; it is better here—a little of the brown— some fat, Sir—a little of the stuffing. Let me have the pleasure of giving you some butter. Allow me the pleasure to recommend a squeeze of this orange; or the lemon perhaps may have more zest."

" Rough Samuel " fell to the wheedling carver and soon they were laughing together. Now if Johnson had happened to find himself before the veal, can it be imagined that a like result would have followed ? Of course not.

The English joint, thank heaven, still retains its ancient power in families who do not trouble to be genteel on cutlets and sponge roll (the men are splendid) and if England is to regain her old supremacy it must return to the tables of the mighty.

Que messieurs les parents commencent!

★

Chicago stockyards boast that they can dispose of everything about a pig except the squeal.—*Daily Herald, London Edition.*

The Chicago stockyards boast that they can dispose of everything about a pig except the grunts.—*Scotch Edition.*

You can't get round us, we still hate the whole idea.

On July 18, 1936, the army hissed the banner of nationalism in Morocco, and I immediately left by air to join the movement.—*Translation in* PARADE *of an article by General Franco in* LA REVUE UNIVERSELLE.

Was his face Red !

Music Notes by Constant Lambert

Positively the Last on the Promenades.

SIR Thomas Beecham (or so I have been told) once announced his intention of giving a performance of Beethoven's 5th Symphony so bad that no one would ever want to hear the work again. A somewhat similar frame of mind has prompted my choice of subject. Had I called my article "The Proms in Retrospect" or even "The Proms in Perspective" my readers might well have felt only a baffled exasperation. But I like to think that in this instance their exasperation will be tempered with a genuine relief. In any case what do people expect music critics to write about between the end of one season and the beginning of the next? Perhaps they look on music critics much as they look on waiters. The music critic is expected to do his stuff just as the waiter is expected to do his stuff. But does anyone ever think how either feels when he goes home at night? Frankly, no.

If it wasn't for the Proms, the music critic during the summer months would either have to give up his livelihood or review books on Wagner by Ernest Newman. A delicate choice. As it is he can fill up one week by announcing the soloists, another week by announcing the new works, almost two months by reporting the actual concerts in a style of calculated drabness and finally he can write about the damned things in retrospect. And during the whole of this period he is spared the task of chasing round the smaller concert halls "covering" the innumerable recitalists who during the winter settle on London like a horde of rather ineffective locusts.

However bored he may be by the programmes, no critic in his heart of hearts has ever felt anything but gratitude for the Proms. The last time I went there my gratitude was tinged with the elegiac and autumnal feeling which seems to overtake so many of the contributors to this paper. Looking round the hall, I felt that the three levels, balcony, promenade and circle, symbolized in a slightly Strindbergian manner my own career as a concert-goer.

I started my career in the balcony. In those days I was at school and, surprising though it may seem, quite genuinely fond of music. The moment the summer holidays began I dashed to the Queen's Hall to get a copy of the programmes. I was invariably told they would not be ready for another week. Somehow I never quite believed this and would usually make two or three further and fruitless visits before the great day arrived. There then followed a period of acute mental stress during which I would count up my money and weigh the respective merits of the possible programmes. This was more difficult in those days, for the programmes were far less *en bloc* and, Russian music being my mania, I would spend harassed hours deciding whether I wanted to hear Rimsky's *Spanish Capriccio* more than Moussorgsky's *Night on the Bare Mountain*. When the chosen day came I would arrive ridiculously early and stay to the bitter end. For the sake of the final orchestral item I even sat through the appalling ballads which still carried on at that period. My Freudian censor has made me forget most of them, but I still have painful memories of a nursery song called *His Majesty's Mail* as being the only song ever written more embarrassing than *Tommy Lad.*

Even when not accompanied by my family, I always went to the balcony. Why I can't think. Perhaps it was considered more respectable. The days when the last tart was ejected from the

Promenade were before my time, but no doubt there were dangers of another kind.

My second and most genial phase as a concert-goer took place in the promenade when I was a student and after. Whether because the programmes were more varied and interesting or not I cannot say, but the Prom in those days was far less crowded and even lived up to its name. One could move about or even effect an exit during a boring work without being looked on as a howling cad. Those were the halcyon days of what is known as the "bar-item". One would go and listen to a little-known Haydn symphony or a new work by Bantok or Milhaud and then during some weatherbeaten concerto played by an even more weatherbeaten virtuoso one would retreat to the bar which had then the atmosphere of a pleasantly informal club. I never quite rivalled the record of the late Peter

Warlock who heard only 10 minutes of Schubert's C major Symphony (4 minutes of the first movement, 3 of the second, 2 of the third and 1 of the fourth), but I certainly took my pleasures more lightly than the present generation.

Now, in my third phase, I go in morose grandeur to the circle. And what is more I could go there every night if I wanted to. I suppose that when I was at school I would willingly have sold my soul for such a gift. It is melancholy to recall one's past enthusiasm. Now when the programmes arrive I open them more with apprehension than with any other feeling and wonder not how many I can afford to go to but how many I can afford to miss.

For one thing I find it increasingly difficult to sit through a whole concert, partly because I concentrate more and partly because I concentrate less. During the few works I like I concentrate

to such an extent that I am mentally exhausted at the end. During that large majority of works I dislike I find it almost impossible to concentrate at all. My eye roves vaguely round the hall and my mind pursues futile paths of a vaguely behaviourist and psychological nature. I wonder why the clergymen who like Wagner differ so sharply from the clergymen who like Brahms; I wonder what the connection is between Bach and hiking. The fact that I have not yet discovered what is precise the connection is the only thing that prevents me from writing a brochure about it. Of one thing, however, I am certain: my "bar-item" days at the Proms are over. For now that almost every programme is a one-man programme I either want to hear every note, however tiring it may be, or else the whole programme just becomes one continuous "bar-item" in which case the evening can more pleasantly and cheaply be spent elsewhere.

* * *

'Now do you see what I mean?'

AT THE THEATRE

Elizabeth Bowen

Measure for Measure

THIS play is full of magnificent false starts, great jets of rhetoric and lost tracks. It is, also, excellent melodrama. As a work of art it does not wholly come off. It seems likely that Shakespeare threw the sketch on the canvas, grouped the figures and began to touch in their ground of poetic darkness—then left a meaner hand to complete the work. For the last act, with its poppings-up and slapstick revenges, becomes a moral harlequinade. Every artist poses his own problems, and the greatest artist sometimes defeats himself. Where the rights and wrongs of sex are concerned, *Measure for Measure* gets down to brass tacks. Did the play—or rather its issues—defeat Shakespeare? At any rate, it was shelved—we have every reason to think so.

Its unfamiliarity, added to its directness, gives *Measure for Measure* immense force. It is seldom performed because schools still baulk at brass tacks, and school taste still governs Shakespeare performances. I once heard of a lady who said of a novel that it was not clever enough to justify its impropriety—and that probably goes for *Measure for Measure*. (For clever, read obscure, for impropriety, naturalness.) We are grateful to the Old Vic for giving this play now. The weathercock about morals has veered round since it was written: times have changed—but leaving us hardly more intelligent. Isabella is a great-hearted girl: nowadays great-hearted girls, at least in plays and fiction, are pretty free with their persons. For one or another admirable reason, they give themselves right and left. In fact, a new set of conventions now circulate. As much pious nonsense is nowadays

talked against chastity as used to be talked in its exaltation. It should be remembered that Isabella was a girl of her time, that Elizabethans were a good deal more genuinely lustful than we are, and that the obstinate virgin was, therefore, someone taking a stand of her own against pretty big odds: the liberty of the subject was involved.

At the outset of this play, Shakespeare raises some promising questions. The trouble is—there are rather too many of them. The Duke's enigmatic behaviour, for instance, would make a plot in itself. He disappeared and disguised himself, with the object of forming a view of his office from the outside. But his interfering nature makes this impossible—your interfering man will never make a philosopher. Then, Angelo—is he meant to be a plain monster, or the victim of his own complex appetites? As a fanatic with an inhibition, he is doomed from the start. But is his doom a tragedy?—for that matter, was Shylock's? We see a fine, if inhuman, will submerged. The Duke's choice of him as a deputy seems mischievous: he was the last man to operate the Vienna clean-up. And should Isabella be judged as a four-square character, or is she simply there as a factor in Angelo's doom? In fact, what is this play *about*? Like the story of Frankie and Johnnie, it seems to have no moral—and only a very arbitrary end.

Possibly it was a plea for natural living. But in that case, Isabella stays right out of the picture: she was content to let her brother die.

The obscure great play, the never-quite-realized great play, makes a first-rate opening for the producer, and Mr. Tyrone Guthrie takes full advantage of this. He gets away with the human unrealities and gives force to the few appallingly human situations by an at once stylized and furious production. The set (Mr. Frank Scarlett's work) —with its perspectives, depths, shad-

' Is there an actor in the house ?'

ows, that arcade, that upper gallery, the stairs inside the arch—helps Mr. Guthrie to pull the action together and overlap the scenes. Entrances, exits can take the value he wishes by being either leisurely or abrupt. The nuns, the monks and the crowd can either file in or gush in. The window is used effectively. The long step along the front of the stage allows gowns to deploy and makes for fine sprawling poses. . . . One must take off one's hat to Mr. Guthrie's production as a *tour de force*. Like any *tour de force*, perhaps it obtrudes a little. But Shakespeare should not have left him so much to get away with.

Mr. Emlyn Williams' virtuosity comes out well in his Angelo. What an actor this is. Here is no false naturalism, not a single slipshod or undirected movement. Mr. Williams' acting must constitute for every soul in the audience a hypnotic and terrible *tête à tête*. The black eyes rivet the vanishing-point of a hellish perspective; the gestures' volutions describe a circle of doom. Mr. Williams' great

subject is the *âme damnée* who cannot stop acting. One is constantly reminded that Night Must Fall. And how he enjoys his robes: he swishes round in them with the swirl of a peacock, turns his back on the top of the steps, is elongated to about fifteen foot of streaming height. *Is* his range limited? Is there, in every man's acting, a recurring decimal point, when the thing has to start over again? I am such a fan of Mr. Williams', I could watch him run twenty times his own diabolical gamut. I see that someone complains that as Angelo he looks too like Joan of Arc. I do not know whose fancy his make-up was.

The stylized production and Angelo's voluted and clawing gestures combine to make Miss Marie Ney's Isabella a little bunched and dim. This is unfair—Miss Ney's performance is reasoned, sensitive: in its own way, faultless. She has a fanatical glitter, too. But her gestures and attitudes are made to look sixth-form girlish. Her novice's habit is not well designed: it is undramatic and fussy. Purely in

terms of the part her figure plays in a group, she is a little too tall. She appears, alternately, not immobile enough and not abandoned enough. If she was to play her Isabella like this (and she plays her, in her own manner, excellently) the production should have been more adapted to her . . . There is a moment when Angelo, with his genius for attitude, twists her backwards into a vastly effective swoon.

Mr. Jay Laurier's Pompey got every possible bouquet. He gets away with his legitimate numbers, and is allowed to interpolate several more. I must confess to having found several Shakespeare clowns quite unspeakably dreary. Bottom and his friends have got me into a stupor, and I loathe the Gravedigger. Mr. Laurier's long lip, wondering eyes and confidential snigger would help out the most debilitated sense of humour. He is of every age—in fact, why doesn't he tap dance? The Policeman (for so he was dressed) was really too topical. I liked the shy verve of Froth, a Foolish Gentleman.

'And keep away from that crowd ; I don't like the look of them.'

MINUTES OF THE WEEK

Vicious Circle

As we shambled home yesterday, a little less numbed and jaded than usual owing to the crisp autumnal dusk, we fetched up opposite the brightly-lit window of the New South Wales Government offices in the Strand. Australia, we noted, was 150 years old; and the N.S.W. window-dresser

had had a stab at what it is nowadays horribly customary to call either a Panorama or a Cavalcade of Progress. It began at one end with a lot of brown antipodeans in loin-cloths; continued through a respectable succession of cravatted, Captain Cook-like pioneers, red-shirted bushwhackers, limber Anzacs and rugged, twinkling sheep-farmers; and ended (on the bathing beaches of 1937) with a lot of brown antipodeans in loin-cloths.

Time marches on.

★

Hangover From What?

The autumn air is charged, as far as we are concerned, with the spirit of reunion. In our social orbit, on our financial plane, the once familiar faces are becoming familiar once more. These faces belong to men connected with the Stock Exchange. A few weeks ago they were grumbling about the refrigerators on their yachts, the landing-speed of their aeroplanes, and the fact that you couldn't get a decent meal in London unless you ordered ahead. Now they are right back with us, riding in V8's and returning an unwonted, pseudo-truculent "No" to waiters who ask them if there will be anything further, sir. We're glad to see them again. We didn't compete for the winnings which they won on margin; and we welcome them back to the breadlines without permitting ourself a sneer, for they seemed well qualified to use the lucre only lately lost and always importuned us to take our whack of caviare and Krug.

But there is, look at it how you will, something obscurely funny about this slump. In comparison with 1929 its extent has so far been inconsiderable, and some of the old hands have got out unscathed. But the Great Crash was part of a general depression, whereas this one coincides with a still rising boom so widespread that Throgmorton Street cuts a most illogical figure as the latest recruit to the Distressed Areas. "All the factors of 1929 were missing," wail the stockbrokers as they close their accounts. It can't be the international situation because they've had that on their hands since 1931, and it can't all be due to the behaviour of American business indices and the heavy margin requirements under the New Deal regulations. Slingsby's theory, knowing little about money but a fair amount about those who juggle with stocks, is that the whole episode is purely Gadarene. When Izzy sells we all sell; only some of us don't get out in time and some of us go in again too soon. To be wise about a company's prospects or the economic situation in general is useless if the rest of the gang, individually sane and charming but collectively a drunken sailor, take the opposite view for no good reason. In short, as the proportion of speculators to investors increases, cause becomes ever more disconnected with effect. A dispassionate observer might almost bring himself to the point of arguing that there's something to be said for manual labour, such as writing these notes.

We keep a revolver in the top right-hand drawer for dispassionate observers.

★

Economy

We were chatting recently with an ex-convict, or perhaps in deference to Sir Samuel Hoare's aims we should say an ex-inmate of a detentive institution. He said it was curious how boastful people became when (as in prison) there was no handy means of checking their statements. "A postman, for instance," he said, "used to tell us that his wife came to visit him in a sixteen-cylinder Bugatti."

"Perhaps she really did," we suggested. "An oldish one." The lag wouldn't hear of this.

"I don't think she can have," he argued. "You see, this bloke also told us that she was economizing while he was in gaol by only running it on eight cylinders."

Slingsby

AS THE WORLD GOES ROUND
a spotlight on current affairs
by CHRISTOPHER HOLLIS

The Troubles of France

IN an article in the *Sunday Chronicle* a few weeks ago Mr. H. W. Seaman, contrasting Italian slavery with British freedom, recorded how an Italian complained to him that the Italian papers were not allowed to print the truth about the British abdication crisis. It was surely strange to select this as a point of contrast between England and Italy, for, if true, it was obvious that then the Italian and the British papers were in exactly the same boat. Even a Fascist dictatorship could not keep that news out of the Italian papers more successfully than it was kept out of the English. Notoriously our success in keeping the news out of the newspapers in this country, when it is "against the national interest" to print it, is the wonder and admiration of the world. No other nation has a technique remotely approaching ours. Only the other day some friends of mine and I were questioned by an American journalist. "How on earth do you do it?" he asked, and then added in tones of ringing admiration, "It is not as if you got away with it just once. But you do it again and again and again," and he mentioned about five instances from recent history, of which the abdication was the chief, where every other human being knew the story some months before it was known to the readers of English newspapers. There is certainly today a machinery for preventing people from knowing what is going on in the world such as no previous age could rival.

Take, for instance, the present situation in France. In conversation the facts are little disputed. The news is everywhere except in the newspapers. France is at the moment in a state almost of liquefaction. The present Government is despised; the past Government was despised, and the Government before that—the Right Government—was despised, too. All parties and all politicians are discredited in France today. A Frenchman's constant anxiety is for his savings, and that anxiety causes him, as the cantonal elections have shown, to retreat after a very short flirtation with Communism. On the other hand, the policy of the Right appeals to him no more than that of the Left. The Right has been disgracefully complacent towards the dictation of the Bank of France and has to pay the price for that. Nor are the Radical Socialists in the centre any better. Personally they are probably the most despised, if only because they are the best known, of all. They have talked the language of political liberalism and the defence of property, but the electorate has at

last discovered that what they really had in mind was a system of *laissez-faire*, under which the State agreed to do nothing to prevent the concentration of property in the hands of the capitalist. "He said that his constituents were behind him," Mr. Belloc once wrote of a French deputy, "and so they were, for when he went to address them, they chased him for miles until he fell into a horse-pond."

Dominating all in France is the fear of Germany. It was this fear which made the Stresa Front with Great Britain and Italy, and, because of it, it was a torture to M. Laval to have to choose between Great Britain and Italy at the time of the Abyssinian trouble. Then a Right-wing Government and a non-political Quai d'Orsay thought to repair the ravages of the Stresa Front by the Franco-Soviet Pact. It has proved a disastrous blunder. Militarily, Russia is, owing to her internal troubles, a worthless ally. The Russian alliance has lost France the support of Belgium and possibly of Rumania and Yugo-Slavia. It has been a cause of internal disturbance in France and has hampered French freedom to follow her own policy in Spain.

It is an open secret that the Quai d'Orsay is now working for the undoing of the Soviet Pact. But, with the Pact or without the Pact, the one hope for the French is at the moment in the British friendship. The intrinsic prestige of all their politicians is at zero, but among the zeros they will allow office to those whom the British nominate. Our policy is a subtle one. There is no sign as yet in

A*

France of a swing back to the Right, even if such a swing were desirable. On the other hand the Left deputies in the Chamber are so frightened that, if tactfully handled, there is a good chance of persuading them to support Right measures so long as they are proposed by ministers, nominally of the Left, who from time to time pay some lip-tribute to Left principles. That is what is happening. M. Chautemps is merely a smoke-screen. Behind him M. Bonnet and M. Daladier are pushing policy gradually and skilfully to the Right. The Cabinet, in which M. Blum sits, has been compelled to agree to the banning of the circulation of M. Blum's own paper among the troops. It is not magnificent, but at least it is not the war.

For we must be under no illusion how very real is the possibility that any day it may collapse into war. The Communists thought to use the formula of the Front Populaire to induce Radicals to vote for their measures. As long as M. Blum was in they had some success. Now the process is reversed. They are compelled to support a Right policy. There is always the chance that they will revolt against it and leave the Front Populaire. If so, no Government could be formed which did not include members frankly to the Right. But the Communists have arms, and few would be so confident as to prophesy that they would take that lying down. For, like most politicians, they can stand being fooled, but they cannot stand it being officially announced in the papers that they have been fooled. If they do not take it lying down, then there is fighting in the streets of Paris and probably a military dictatorship.

However do not imagine that the French are done for. The French nation does not die. It is a great nation, and the one certainty, amid so much that is uncertain, is that it will in the end emerge from its troubles as it has emerged from those of the past.

'*He's crazy about Gilbert and Sullivan, he booked all the seats.*'

Contentment Column

Reassuring and Inspiring Items from the Press, a Corrective to Scare Headlines and Private Worries.

ACTUARIAL

"The reason why *Rogue Herries* was the real turning-point of my writing life was because, when I ventured upon it, I took every risk in the world. . . ."—Sir Hugh Walpole.

TOWARDS A HIGHER BIRTH=RATE

" 'Where did you come from, Baby Dear?'—This question has roused an intense and burning interest. . . ."—Ruby Ferguson's Correspondence Column, *The British Weekly*.

FRIENDSHIP

"Mr. Neville Chamberlain held out the hand of friendship to Mussolini last night after receipt of a message from Lord Perth, our Ambassador in Rome, that the tone of the Italian reply to the Anglo-French note depended on the Prime Minister's speech to the Conservative Conference."—*The Daily Express*.

GENIUS

Frank Arthur Stanley, described in the press as " the prison poet ", is in the opinion of Sir John Squire " a poetic genius. That is why I pleaded for him at the Old Bailey ". We have pleasure in subjoining a specimen of Mr. Stanley's muse :

At even when I go to bed,
I see the stars shine overhead ;
I think they're little daisies—white,
That grow in meadows of the night.

TRY EVERYTHING ONCE

"WAR MINISTER IN ACTION The war minister, Mr. Hore-Belisha, spent a busy day in the interests of recruiting . . ."—*Evening Standard*.

GUIDANCE

"There is an obvious danger that inflated prices may be paid in these amalgamation schemes. While this may suit shareholders in the company being absorbed, it will be less satisfactory for those interested in the purchasing company."—Financial Page, *Sunday Express*.

PROSE POEM

"I like the taste and touch and sight and sound and smell that sing and dance round newspaper offices."—Viscount Castlerosse.

IN THE LIONS' DEN

BY DANIEL

5.—Architect Laureate

YEARS ago Edwin Landseer Lutyens was suspected of being the only man in England capable of taking architecture seriously and the suspicion has proved absolutely correct. He was born in March, 1869, which makes him 68 today. He is a rather big man with a phenomenally round, bald head fixed with wonderful precision on his shoulders. He has small, very blue, provocatively innocent eyes, curiously set; vaguely like portraits of Inigo Jones. He wears a steep butterfly collar and a neat, ordinary tie, and moves with a certain critical, half-humorous deliberation, by no means unimpressive. He smokes absurd little pipes, specially made for him, and lives in a large, quiet house behind Portland Place.

For years Lutyens has been "a figure". You never hear him mentioned without a chuckle and a comment. You rarely see him but in the company of a pack of fans, sniggering at his cracks and wondering what the great Lut. will say or do next. Bores all over the Empire hoard his doodles, do their damnedest to collect and recollect some encounter, some passage of wit, wherein they stood irradiated for a moment in the sunshine of authentic Genius. Architectural snobs assess and delimit his capacities with an off-hand gesture. And the man in the street tells stories about him at fifteenth hand.

Getting down to facts, Lutyens was the eleventh of the fourteen children of Charles Lutyens, an army officer turned artist. Landseer, the lion man, was a family friend: hence the architect's first names. He was educated "privately". At eighteen he designed a cottage. At nineteen, or thereabouts, he lost a job through being tactless. At

twenty-one he built a big house in Surrey, with grim white barge-boards and a Gothicky sort of porch. He had been apprenticed for a year to Ernest George and Peto who did that sort of thing well. Lutyens was soon doing it very much better. Before he was thirty he had built a dozen large houses and done a whole lot of alterations. He had spent the surplus profits of a good many influential people and they liked the way he did it.

By Diamond Jubilee year he had met two important women. One was Gertrude Jekyll, fifty-four-year-old gardening genius. He built a house for her, down in Surrey, very plain with steep gables; she made a garden round it, a marvellous woodland garden with an architectural rhythm running gently through it. Lutyens learnt a lot from that; Gertrude Jekyll had a lot to teach.

The other important woman was Lady Emily Lytton—granddaughter of the novelist, daughter of the Viceroy. Lutyens married her. An architect who marries well is always a success,

Sir Edwin Lutyens by Edmund Dulac

his grossest stupidity being forgiven, even approved, in the light of good connections. An alliance, therefore, of irresistible genius and vice-regal in-laws simply sweeps the board; which is, of course, what Lutyens has done.

Another early alliance must be recorded. In or about the year 1900, Lutyens met, at Gertrude Jekyll's, a certain Edward Hudson, ambitious newspaper-owner, connoisseur, lover of high life and fine houses. Hudson had bought a paper called *Racing Illustrated*, turned it inside out, rechristened it *Country Life Illustrated* and finally brought it to rest as *Country Life*. *Country Life* struck lucky with the idea of showing good photographs of the insides and outsides of people's houses, old and new, and in Lutyens the owner-editor spotted something worth following. The architect's houses, superbly photographed, appeared in the magazine. "A Lutyens house" began to mean something. The name, memorable and euphonious, passed from mouth to mouth, rarely perhaps without a reference to the family tree and a hint of the quaint, irrepressible, sometimes even rather embarrassing personality behind the exact and accomplished pencil.

"Huddy" of *Country Life* was nothing if not thorough. Once he was on to a good thing he followed it hard. Within a year of their meeting, Lutyens was building him a country house in Berkshire, the first in a string of commissions. Later, Lindisfarne Castle was transformed into a romantic playground for musical lions, and, after the war, Lindisfarne being sold, an old house in Sussex was elaborated in a setting of water-gardens. Hudson—*Country Life*—Lutyens: a nice little racket. ·All three prospered, which indeed is just what they deserved. And when *Country Life* built new offices in Covent Garden, London got its first Lutyens façade.

1890-1914—those were the days. Rising lawyers with political and dynastic aspirations planted themselves in the Surrey landscape. The cultivated and adventurous strata of Edwardian society—travellers, big-game hunters, literary garden-lovers — built their lodges, their retreats. And all this was very much in Lutyens's line. What charmed people was his unfailing invention. No two houses were even remotely alike; and you never knew what you were going to get. It might be something smooth and demure, with rows and rows of little plain casements. Or it might be a great tent-like mass with gables coming almost to the ground. You could never tell what would happen to your roof. It might start way up behind a parapet, then come sweeping down the flank of a chimney stack and dodge round the corner as an open porch. Everything was unexpected, fantastic—and, of course, enormously expensive, which merely added a welcome *cachet* to ownership of "a Lutyens house".

All styles, all materials were in the Lutyens repertory. Sometimes they came out one by one, sometimes several together. But the result was always brilliantly successful. There seemed to be no architectural feat this extraordinary young man couldn't perform, standing, as it were, on his head.

The country-house business was killed in the war. Lutyens, A.R.A. by then, was knighted at the end of it. Still under 50, and with the Whitehall Cenotaph to his credit, it was clear that he was on the verge of becoming Pontifex Maximus and Architect Laureate of the British Empire. Already he had one foot in India, being a member of the advisory committee on where to put New Delhi. Soon the other foot was in India too, and he settled down to one of the biggest tasks ever proposed to an English architect. In any other hands New Delhi would have been a ridiculous flop. It was a job for a Bernini or a Mansard. Even Wren could hardly have got away with a thing on that scale. But Lutyens, the country house man, architect of "Grey Walls", of "Chussex", of "The Pleasaunce", of "Heathcote", of "Folly Farm", succeeded.

He succeeded at Delhi for exactly the same reason that he succeeded in Surrey and Berkshire—because, as we said right at the beginning, he has the capacity, fantastically rare, for taking architecture seriously. The mind within that extraordinary round skull over the butterfly collar seeks and searches into every nook and cranny of an architectural situation. A building is a scheme of proportioned material and everything has a place and one place only. The most outrageous fantasy looks right once it has been got under this miraculous control. And Lutyens's fantasies are quite often outrageous. Who else could put fountains on a roof, or stick an Indian *tope* on top of a classic colonnade without making them look unspeakably foolish?

But Delhi was not all beer and skittles. The new Metropolis was far too big to be designed by one man and a collaborator had to be found. Lutyens chose Herbert Baker—and met (in his own phrase) his Bakerloo. Baker was an architect of the Vague School and the thesis of the Vague School is this: that if you are an artistic, cultivated, capable creature and know plenty about old buildings, traditional materials and so on and you get down to a drawing board, the result is liable to be all right. Well, sometimes it is. But it doesn't do for that sort of architect to be harnessed with the Lutyens sort. Especially when the Vague man develops strong views of his own, as Baker did in the Delhi business. It was all most distressing. Young Rob-

'Splice the mainbrace, Mr. Hardy.'

' I'd write—if only I had suffered.'

ert Byron went to India to see for himself, came back and published a devastating indictment which Baker has not yet lived down.

In England, meanwhile, the Lutyens office in Queen Anne's Gate was dealing with a heavy spate of war memorials. But in this line, the Cenotaph has been the architect's only palpable hit. Clearly there is something preposterous in the idea of purveying memorials in bulk—getting out a new combination of emblems for each building committee; Lutyens's later efforts prove it.

A stronger line, when things settled down after the war, was Banks and office buildings. The Persian Oil Company asked for a head office and Lutyens gave them that italianate fantasy in Moorgate Street called Britannic House. It is about as relevant to modern office design or to Persian oil as this article is to the Nicene Creed; but anybody with half an eye for architectural values knows that for invention and sheer ornamental eloquence it has never been surpassed. Then the Midland Bank came along with some fat commissions, including the little brick-and-stone box in Piccadilly which pokes perpetual fun at the dreary Wren Church alongside.

One of the few really dull things Lutyens has done is the Queen's Doll's House; and the checker-board flats in the Horseferry Road don't really come off; neither do the pavilions on the top of Grosvenor House—one wishes they did; and the bridge at Hampton Court is a rotten compromise with engineering; and, to go further afield, there's something wrong with the Washington Embassy building. In fact if you want to pull the idol off the pedestal there are plenty of handles within reach. But, as they say at Borstal, it's the system that's to blame. You can't get round the fact that Lutyens has the mental equipment for the very highest architectural adventure.

If surrealism wasn't so hopelessly *démodé* that would be the nearest pigeon-hole for a man like Lutyens. His view of life is imaginatively perverse from beginning to end. He always sees the backward logic of a situation. "What would you do with the Crystal Palace?" somebody asked him. "Put it in a glass case." And, as everybody knows, he wants to put gramophones in the bellies of the Trafalgar lions to make them roar. In the Roman Catholic Cathedral he is building at Liverpool the organ will

be sunk under the floor and there will be running water in the stoups.

Lutyens's public appearances are few. If he has to make a speech he reads it, very badly, in an undertone, like a sulky child made to play charades. But if a discussion intrigues him volleys of devastating wit come popping out all the time.

One of his more unexpected side-lines is being President of the Incorporated Association of Architects and Surveyors, a body founded in 1925, whose chief function is to annoy the Royal Institute of British Architects and to stop the Friba boys getting their registration bill through Parliament. Now that might appear strange, because Lutyens is himself a Royal Gold Medallist of the Institute. There is a story there. If you look in back numbers of the Institute *Calendar* you will find that Lutyens was once a Fellow: he was elected on the merit of his work in 1906. In 1923 he was invested with the Gold Medal, and the Institute's *Journal* will tell you that on that occasion he "appeared deeply overcome and expressed his inability to do more than utter his thanks for the great honour conferred upon him". So far so good. In 1926 the Institute's London Architecture Medal came his way and this time he "briefly and humorously thanked the Institute for the honour"; though what he really said nobody quite knows. Well, a few years after that something blew up; and now the only Lutyens in the Institute *Calendar* is Eadred John Tennant, Sir Edwin's nephew.

But all that is beside the point. Edwin Landseer Lutyens plays his own game and if it doesn't fit in with what the other boys are doing somebody may get hurt. And it won't be Lutyens. He is one of the very cleverest people alive and when another brain like his pops up out of the sands of mediocrity, architecture, as we know it, will probably have gone to its long and well-earned rest.

COCKT →

Felix Topolski

IN THE
FOYER

RESTAURANT ←

$F^E=$
$F^O=$
$F^I=$
FUM

LETTER FROM IRELAND

Elizabeth Bowen

CORK city has been very gay of late. Summer weather persisted, just lightly chilled, and on long gay glassy evenings the Lee estuary looked like the scene set for a regatta. Galway oysters reappeared at the Oyster Tavern, off Patrick Street: this is a long cavern of dusky mirrors with a grill fire (which grills really superbly) glittering at the end. The Opera House on the quayside reopened, and Jimmy O'Dea packed it for two weeks. Ireland's great little comedian is a tragi-comedian. He is a pool of temperament. There is a touch of Stan Laurel, a touch of Chaplin: any affinities he has belong to the screen, not the stage, because he has such a very *exposed* nature. He is ultimately and first of all himself. He is a Dublin man, but Cork thinks the world of him.

Cork left Cork for Killarney when the All Ireland Hurley Finals were played there. Tipperary won. This was a great day for the whole of the South of Ireland ; special trains were run and the roads for a hundred miles round streamed with cars and bicycles, most of them flying flags. The Tipperary contingent passed my way. Those who unluckily could not get to Killarney stood on banks for hours to watch the traffic. This is, in the literal sense, a very quiet country: the Troubles and civil war were fought out in an almost unbroken hush, punctuated by a few explosions or shots. Voices are seldom raised, and you can (so to speak) hear a dog bark or a milk-cart rattle or a funeral bell toll two counties away. But these great Sundays of sport galvanize everything; from the moment you wake you know that something is going on. This last year or two, the town of Killarney has begun to cash in on sport. Last year they had a Big Fight there. Hurley is the fastest game, short of ice hockey, that I have ever watched. It is a sort of high-speed overhead hockey, played with sticks with flat wooden blades, and it looks even more dangerous than it apparently is. Though a game that

would melt you in the Antarctic, it is, for some reason, played only in summer. I do not think nearly so much of Gaelic football. But I have only seen this game played in a sea mist, which, milkily shrouding goals and players, added to an effect of aimless mystery: there seemed to be effort but no fun, and sea birds—this was in the flats behind Waterville, County Kerry—circled rather drearily overhead.

Yes, certainly in early autumn the Cork social season is at its height. And English visitors constantly overlook this. English people apparently come to Ireland for reasons—such as scenery pure and simple—that would get me nowhere. (I except, of course, fishermen.) They disembark their cars from S.S. *Innisfallen* on to the Cork quay, and rattle at high speed, with minds set on the sublime, out of one of Europe's strangest and most beautiful cities. They go in droves to stay at boring hotels on lakes or bays. These hotels seem to me boring because they have no local life; they are built for strangers who want to look at scenery. Their lounges, though often lofty, are claustrophobic, and often smell of milk pudding. Their social atmosphere seems to be subnormal. I should add that these are very good hotels for those who like to stay in hotels of this kind. The surrounding scenery is handsome and undisappointing — if this were not so, the hotels would not be there.

But so much fun is to be had in the small towns. The small town hotels in Ireland are brightening up, and are now perfectly possible to stay in. They

have a great *va et vient*, and their saloons in the evening are full of excellent talk. In the town, there is nearly always something going on—a fair, a funeral or a politician's visit. Or if something is not going on while you are there, something has gone on just before you arrived, and everybody is willing to tell you all about it. All summer and autumn, circuses or strolling players are on the roads: these pitch their tents nightly and give their shows at the edge of one or another town. The remoter cinemas show where good films go when they die. South Irish small towns are beautiful in an abstract manner, with painted houses, wide streets, big dusty squares, knolls of bronze beeches and dark, quick rivers. They are full of shoe-shops, china shops and " medical halls". Dogs lie asleep in mid-street in the hub of the town, only dislodged now and then by big red Great Southern buses. When a bus pulls up in a town a surprising number of people come out of shops and pubs and stand round the bus in a ring, as though a whale had been landed. Anybody who gets into the bus or gets out does so in a glare of gratifying publicity. When the bus has been looked at for about twenty minutes it gets up, as it were, and dashes out of the town. To those who are set on scenery, and must have it, I would explain that most small towns in the coast-counties of Ireland are set in as much beauty as anybody could wish, that most streets have a backdrop of dark blue mountain, whether close or distant, and that on fine days they are drenched in dazzling light. The official grandeurs of Ireland are generally, too, within quite possible reach.

For two or three weeks after Horse Show, Dublin sits back and looks rather desultory. That gala week in August involves the whole south of the city, which becomes a sort of annexe of Ballsbridge. Dublin goes all out, and becomes very European. It seems such a pity that Horse Show should coincide with the height of the Salzburg Festival. When we become the United States of Europe, one may hope that something may be better arranged—though it will have to be

'*But, Henry, I said* chintz!'

★   ★   ★

made perfectly clear, from the outset, that nothing can alter the date of Horse Show. In September, Dublin stops being anti-climatic. Early autumn brightness polishes the façades of Georgian streets and squares; russet edges the trees in the park and along the canal. This autumn the city looks very brisk. One set of traffic-lights has been installed at a lower corner of Merrion Square: the tempo of progress is setting in. Car-parking regulations are being tightened: another sign of how prosperous we all are. There is a boom in civic pride—a fine exhibition of prints and maps, depicting the past of the city, has been opened and ought not to be missed. The Irish Academy of Letters has just elected three new members. The Abbey Theatre has started its winter season. The Grafton Street shops are full of the autumn modes. Trouble was caused at the trials before the motor races in Phœnix Park by a party of peacocks that escaped from the Zoo and, in the gloom of a very early morning, filed slowly across the racing track. This is said to have happened twice. But by the crucial Saturday, the surviving peacocks were under lock and key. Ireland becomes safer, though never obvious.

STERILIZATION

Carve delinquency away,
Said the great Professor Clay.

A surgical operation is just the thing
To make everybody as happy as a king.

But the great Dostoievsky the Epi-
    leptic
Turned on his side and looked rather
    sceptic.

And the homosexual Mr. Wilde
Sat in the sunshine and smiled and
    smiled.

And a similarly inclined older ghost in
    a ruff

Stopped reading his sonnets aloud and
    said " Stuff ! "

And the certainly eccentric Swift,
    Crashawe and Donne,
Silently shook hands and thanked God
    they had gone.

But the egregious Professor Clay
Called on Theopompous and won the
    day.

And soon all our minds will be flat as
    a pancake,
With no room for genius, exaltation or
    heartache.

And our children and theirs will preen,
    smirk and chatter,
With not even the sense to ask what is
    the matter.   STEVIE SMITH

★

Sitting at the bar I caught sight of
Peter Anstruther sitting with Peter An-
struther and Peter Anstruther, her sister.
—*The Perth Daily News.*

What was the beer like, ole boy ?

AN ART CRITIC IN PARIS

Holiday from Politics

IN this year of Our Lord, when the countries which have not yet suc-cumbed to one or other of the cultural movements symbolized by Magnetogorsk, the Nuremburg Stadium and the Great West Road can be counted on the fingers of one hand, one can still return from Paris with faith strengthened and sanity intact. Not that the Fascist, the Communist and the By-pass Baron have not been busy in the French capital, but the presence of other witnesses, living and dead, reduces these ideological manifestations to the level of pissoir doodles. By a reassertion of those classic ideals which have always been the foundation of French Art, even in its most flamboyantly romantic moments, the doctrinaire productions of totalitarian culture, together with the cheery sentimental bits of capitalist bric-a-brac that scored so heavily at Wembley and in Paris 1925, have been thrust into the background.

In no circumstances could those goitrous constipated groups of Teutonic youth and beauty, three times life-size cast in bronze, which guard the entrance to Herr Hitler's Valhalla, be considered as works of art; even by Slade standards the murals in the Italian pavilion (with the honourable exception of those map-like panels in the main corridor) achieve a new low; were one to come across that megalithic, aluminium-coloured Daphnis and Chloe of dialectical materialism waving their hammer and sickle in the courtyard of Burlington House instead of on top of the pavilion of the U.S.S.R., one would still be unable to suppress a gasp of shocked surprise;

but when these things are viewed almost alongside the greatest products of what is probably the soundest, most exacting and longest lived tradition in the whole of European art they cease to have any significance at all. Even Picasso's panel of the bombardment of Guernica sinks under these conditions to the level of a pot-house poster at a provincial election.

On entering the Palais des Arts one finds oneself back in the world of reality where the artistic triumphs of rival ideologies are but the half-remembered décor of a pipe dream. However knowledgeable one may be, one is astounded afresh at the staggering continuity of French Art. From Fouquet to Cézanne there is no break; classicism, romanticism, realism, impressionism, post-impressionism come and go; the vision changes but the fundamental integrity, the same austere sense of values, remains.

In such an exhibition one can survey the whole of the vast mountain range at once and pick out the highest peaks (for valleys there are none), whereas in the past one always had to assimilate the prospect by sections. Needless to say there are surprises. In my own case, and I fancy in a good many others, the overwhelming revelation of the exhibition is Poussin. One always knew he was a very great artist, but one tended to take his genius for granted and to pass on to other less austere masters. Now seeing him through the medium of this magnificent selection, and in the company of all his peers, one is instantly aware of the dizzy pinnacle of his achievement, soaring serenely in that rarified atmosphere where Ingres, Degas and, a little lower, Watteau are his only neighbours.

Next to the pleasure of being forced to reconsider one's previous ideas comes that of having one's judgments confirmed. No one with any previous knowledge can, I feel, leave the Palais des Arts without being strengthened in the opinion that the early death of Chasseriau was one of the greatest tragedies that ever befell French painting. Here is the man who, had he lived, would have succeeded in creating the ideal synthesis—bridging the gap

' Look, Bill, a denarius of Antoninus Pius !'

between Delacroix and Ingres to the immeasurable benefit of French painting. As it is he can hold his own with Delacroix in everything save the actual range and number of his achievements, and is always within hailing distance of Ingres.

There are many other painters whom this exhibition forces one to reconsider. Hubert Robert, for instance, has hitherto been regarded rather too much as a charming decorator, and not sufficiently as a highly accomplished landscape painter who at his best is not much inferior to Claude. Corot, magnificent paysagiste as he was, never perhaps attained such heights in his landscapes as in one or two of these figure paintings. And there remains the enigmatic and slightly sinister figure of Gericault—on no account miss his *Course des Chevaux Libres*,

one of the most extraordinary small-scale achievements in the whole exhibition.

As the impressionists and post-impressionists recede ever further into the distance one sees more clearly how superficial was the break they made with the immediate past and how truly, if unconsciously, they continued the great tradition. And now that all the surprise has vanished and one can consider them in relation not only to each other but to the whole procession of French artists, one is forced to allow a certain wholesome reshuffling of their order of precedence. Manet, despite *Déjeuner sur L'herbe* and similar miracles, seems now to be an artist who somewhere, somehow, missed the bus. Gauguin one is almost shocked to find in such exalted surroundings. But the towering genius of Degas emerges

more overwhelmingly than ever.

Coming out onto the Quai de Tokio one catches sight of the hammer and sickle thrusting up busily above the trees and one realizes what separates the artists in the Palais des Arts from so many of those outside: they knew that an artist, while he may comment —*vide* Daumier and Lautrec—must never preach. Only two French artists of undoubted genius ever transgressed this essential limitation—David and Courbet, the one openly the other implicitly. And of all the artists in this exhibition it is David, the Fascist painter *par excellence*, and Courbet, the iconoclast of the Vendôme Column and apostle of proletarian art, whose achievements, when seen alongside those of all their greatest countrymen, seem the most surely reduced.

OSBERT LANCASTER

A Tour by A. J. A. Symons

THE Spanish conflict has not, so far, affected the supply, price or popularity of sherry in England. Cadiz, which has been in General Franco's hands since the first days of the war, has continued its exports of wine without interruption, though not without difficulties. Agents in this country remit to Spain in sterling, which must be surrendered to the insurgent commander within a stated period in exchange for his brand of pesetas at the rate of 42 to the £. Quite lately General Franco has imposed a new tax of 24s. per butt, but as this is no more than a halfpenny a bottle, it will probably not be heard of by the ordinary drinker, though someone will have to pay it.

It is curious that sherry has almost completely changed its character since the days of Thackeray, when it had already changed its character from the days of Shakespeare. We drink sherry today as an appetizer, a habit which would have astonished Ruskin's father, who made £100,000 from the sherry trade. In his day good sherry was laid down like port, probably after a tossing journey to the equator; and, like port, it was drunk after dinner, or as a cordial against the cold, or with a biscuit at eleven. A fine sherry would remain under cork for perhaps forty or fifty years. During that time it would fine down the spirit with which it had been fortified, absorb its sugar, and acquire a commanding and delicious fumosity. It would become dry without harshness, the dryness of evolution, not manufacture. Such sherries have al-

most vanished from the world. Modern money-rates do not permit of maturition so slow and costly. Even in Spain old-bottled sherries are hardly to be found. Now and then, however, a few survivors turn up. A few weeks ago I asked the landlord of the Feathers (Ludlow, Shropshire) for some Madeira, and he brought up a webbed old veteran which, on tasting, proved not to be Madeira at all, but a fine old sherry. I believe a bottle still remains.

But those who wish to try for themselves a sherry of Thackerayan character need not travel as far as Ludlow. At either the Holborn Restaurant (Kingsway) or Frascati's (Oxford Street) there are to be found two sherries which have been in bottle for more than thirty years. These appear in the list as 209 Amontillado Waterloo 1815, and 209a Pemartin bottled in 1896; and they cost 20s. and 21s. respectively. These seem high prices, but actually they are very moderate. Modern champagne would cost more, and it is replaceable; these wines are not.

The sherries most in favour today have an entirely different excellence. They are not meant to be kept long in bottle, or to be drunk at the end of a meal; their function is to stimulate appetite, and they must be *cold* to be at their best—not frozen, but cold enough to be noticeable. My day-to-day favourites are the Macharnudo Fino of La Riva, the Tio Pepe of González Byass, Ivison's Montillado Fino, the El Cid of Duff Gordon, and the Isabelita of Ruiz. Most of these sherries can be tried by the glass at Emberson's Wine Lodge (Pelham Street, S.W.): the proprietor is an excellent judge of sherry, and glad to talk about it. Another good tasting ground is Shireff's (Ludgate Circus, E.C.). Further along the Strand is

El Vino's, and further still Short's, which is capped by Long's (Hanway Street, behind Frascati's).

Spanish food has also gained greatly in favour during recent years. Twenty years ago, London had no Spanish restaurant; today we have five. This is not a result of the civil war; the restaurateurs were here before, which makes the fact all the more surprising, for London has never had a large Spanish colony. Actually the first Spanish restaurant was run by M. Plano in Dean Street, but it has gone: Martinez, established in 1923, is much smarter and more ambitious. The white Valdepeñas here is a good example of its type, the service excellent, the decorations conventionally and pleasantly Spanish, the lighting sombre. Nearby is the Majorca (Brewer Street, W.), one of the most attractively decorated restaurants in London, and, like its manager, Señor Bonafont, very popular and competent. He keeps a special list of customers to be telephoned to when such delicacies as cuttle-fish arrive, and enjoys planning out-of-the-way menus for English gourmets. Both these restaurants are spacious, comfortable, and smart without being expensive. The Barcelona (Beak Street, W.) is smaller, and more humble, but has an excellent chef: for the moment it also has a monopoly (in London) of the Alicante and Jijona *turrones*, those attractive sweetmeats that resemble, respectively, nougat and marzipan, while surpassing both. Señor Carbonell laid in a liberal supply while they could still be got from Spain without difficulty. His inexpensive Habana panatellas are also good. The two remaining Spanish restaurants are the Cervantes (Old Compton Street, W.) and the España (Wardour Street, W.). The Cervantes can be recommended to those who want good Spanish fare at Soho prices—though none of these restaurants is expensive. Spanish cooking is economical. One misses the rich unctuous creaminess of fine French dishes and sauces; it is uncompromising rather than subtle, satisfying but farinaceous; too ornamental to be called the prose, it is not sufficiently inspired to be called the poetry, of gastronomic excellence.

THE FILMS BY GRAHAM GREENE

Wee Willie Winkie—The Life of Emile Zola

THE owners of a child star are like leaseholders—their property diminishes in value every year. Time's chariot is at their back; before them acres of anonymity. What is Jackie Coogan now but a matrimonial squabble? Miss Shirley Temple's case, though, has peculiar interest: infancy with her is a disguise, her appeal is more secret and more adult. Already two years ago she was a fancy little piece (real childhood, I think, went out after *The Littlest Rebel*). In *Captain January* she wore trousers with the mature suggestiveness of a Dietrich: her neat and well-developed rump twisted in the tap-dance: her eyes had a sidelong searching coquetry. Now in *Wee Willie Winkie*, wearing short kilts, she is a complete totsy. Watch her swaggering stride across the Indian barrack-square: hear the gasp of excited expectation from her antique audience when the sergeant's palm is raised: watch the way she measures a man with agile studio eyes, with dimpled depravity. Adult emotions of love and grief glissade across the mask of childhood, a childhood skin-deep.

It is clever, but it cannot last. Her admirers — middle-aged men and clergymen—respond to her dubious coquetry, to the sight of her well-shaped and desirable little body, packed with enormous vitality, only because the safety curtain of story and dialogue drops between their intelligence and their desire. "Why are you making my Mummy cry?"—what could be purer than that? And the scene when dressed in a white nightdress she begs grandpa to take Mummy to a dance—what could be more virginal? On those lines her new picture, made by John Ford, who directed *The Informer*, is horrifyingly competent. It isn't hard to stay to the last prattle and the last sob. The story—about an Afghan robber converted by Wee Willie Winkie to the British Raj—is a long way after Kipling. But we needn't be sour about that. Both stories are awful, but on the whole Hollywood's is the better.

It's better cinema anyway than *The Life of Emile Zola*. More pompous than *Pasteur* and far more false, this picture's theme is supposed to be truth—but truth to the film mind is the word you see on news posters. We begin in 1862 with Zola starving in a garret with Cézanne who keeps on popping up irrelevantly from then on. Zola meets Nana, and soon she is giving him her diaries and her letters, but not—what apparently Zola particularly wants—a baby's vest. ("Take all, all but this"). Then Cézanne pokes his head round the door, and Zola writes *Nana* which is an enormous success. (He had really, of course, been a successful writer for about eighteen years before he wrote *Nana*). Then suddenly—everything in this picture happens suddenly including Cézanne—comes war. Soldiers in the street; a woman says "Where are they all going?" and a man says "Haven't you heard? War's been declared." Zola says "Never did I think I should live to see France grovelling in the dust under the German heel." Cézanne pokes his head round the door—or doesn't he? Anyway the war's over. Zola's middle-aged at Meudon, though his wife's not changed at all. Cézanne looks round the door again. "The old struggling carefree days." He takes an ugly look at the majolica and starts away. "Paul, will you write?" "No, but I will remember." Then the Dreyfus case, and on the night before Dreyfus's rehabilitation Zola—he's an old man now—dies (it's more than un-studio, it's un-American to live another two years). Paul Muni acts Zola—quaintly, and lots of old friends turn up in fancy dress but quite themselves as the Governor of Paris, Clemenceau, Colonel Piquart, Count Esterhazy.

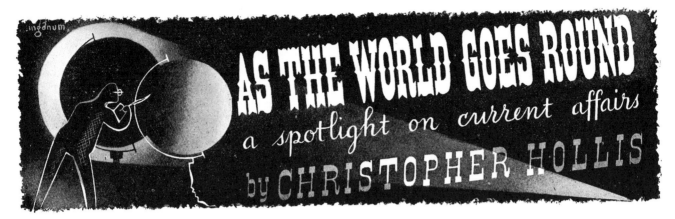

AS THE WORLD GOES ROUND
a spotlight on current affairs
by CHRISTOPHER HOLLIS

Germans in the East

IT is very easy to make game of Nazi racialist theories, and important from time to time to do so. But at other times it is equally important to perform the counter-service of trying to explain why such apparently lunatic doctrines are palatable to one alone among the civilized peoples of Europe. I went the other night to the Gate Theatre, where I saw a remarkable presentation of Mr. Gladstone by Mr. William Devlin, and it occurred to me, while watching Mr. Devlin act, that one of the main reasons why Mr. Gladstone was so right about Ireland was that he had the great wisdom never to go there. In the atmosphere of the nineteenth and earlier centuries it would have been impossible for a Protestant and English visitor to go to Ireland without being drawn insensibly into the landlord milieu. For the landlords talked a language which the Englishman could understand. The peasants talked a language which he could not understand. The Englishman's only chance of being right about Ireland was to keep away from it, knowing, like Socrates, that he knew nothing.

Now we made fuss enough about giving up Ireland, though it was only one little island. What would we have done if it had been the size of a continent and contained more than a hundred million people? Yet during the last six hundred years the Germans have played in Eastern Europe a part not unlike that of the English in Ireland. The Germans, the easternmost of the five great European nations, have been the guardians of Europe's gate against the Slavs of the East. Through the Hapsburgs they have held rule and given a kind of unity to the hotch-potch of the South-East. And further north, along the Baltic and elsewhere in Russia, German landlords and German settlers have established themselves far beyond any German political boundaries. It was race alone which differentiated those Germans from their neighbours, and it was at least arguable that the whole survival of Eastern Europe depended on the preservation of their racial purity. For the Germans were more efficient than their Slavonic neighbours. The most

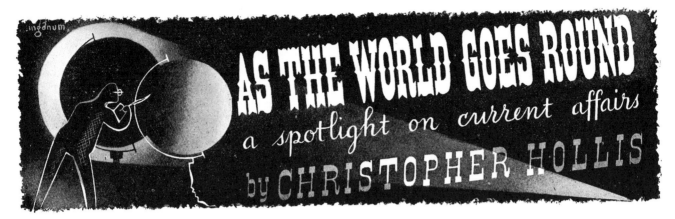

' Are you all right ? '
' Yes, I'm all right.'
' Good.   Then I've shot a bear.'

competent ruler who ever sat on the Russian throne, Katherine the Great, was a pure German. Germans always played a part, very much beyond their numbers, in the Czarist Empire, and it is not absurd to argue that it owed to its Germans what little efficiency it possessed. Now the great German racialists of today, like Rosenberg, come not from Germany but from the Baltic lands. They insist on the importance of race not as a new revolutionary doctrine but as the platitude of six hundred years through which alone they have survived. What is new today is not that they are saying such things but that there is no longer a Czarist Russia for them to say them in. The Versailles settlement shut Germany out from colonies and from the West and forced her to look east. The inevitable consequence of that was to increase the importance of the voice of the East German, and the consequence of that, equally inevitable, was racial theories. As with Mr. Gladstone and Ireland, Germany's relations with Eastern Europe can never be satisfactory until power in Germany is in the hands of Westerners who have never been there.

It is a platitude to confess that as a result of all this there are a hundred dangers and causes for anxiety in Eastern Europe and that the other races in their turn have many just grievances against the German. The grievances and counter-grievances create an atmosphere — an atmosphere in which no particular problem is discussed on its merits but everything is made to play its part in the great, all-embracing racial debate. Take the case of the Sudeten Deutsch in Czecho-Slovakia. When we think of the German problem in Czecho-Slovakia, we are apt to think of it, naturally enough, as a dangerously possible cause of a new European war, and the type of person who is, as a rule, most ready to proclaim the grievances of a suffering minority has but little to say of the grievances of the Sudeten Deutsch, because he is afraid that those grievances are being exploited by Herr Hitler and Herr Henlein (as indeed, of course, they are). It is a pity, for, leaving aside all controversial nationalist questions, it is certain that there has been and still is economic suffering in the German districts of Czecho-Slovakia of a quite appalling intensity. It is the curse of the ideological divisions of the modern world that a woman starving on a disputed frontier is no longer thought of as a woman starving but as an argument against some creed or alternatively as an invention of that creed's propaganda. How far the Czech Government is to blame is a far from simple question, but there is

no doubt at all about the fact that the unemployment in Czecho-Slovakia has been overwhelmingly concentrated in the German districts. There is happily a sign under Dr. Benes' Government of awakening to the desperate necessity of improving conditions.

Anyone who has been in Eastern Europe will agree on the uselessness of learned professors who tell the Germans that there is no such thing as purity of race. Maybe they are right in a pedantic sense, but it does not help. It is like telling the Jews that there is no Chosen People. If the Jews had not been the Chosen People (in some sense or other at any rate) they would not have survived at all throughout the ages. They would have perished like all the other races of two thousand years ago and mingled their blood to form the nations of to-day. So in Eastern Europe today it is only six hundred years of strong racial feeling that has prevented the Germans and the Slavs from joining together to form a new mongrel race. "The fact that we are", the Germans can argue, "is proof that we were destined to be." And the answer to them is: "Exactly. You are very like the Jews".

Contentment Column

Encouraging and Inspiring Items from the Press, a Corrective to Scare Headlines and Private Worries.

NUANCE

"You hear so much talk about the failure of the League, but it is not the League of Nations that has failed, but the nations of the League."—Admiral Drury-Lowe.

SHOCK TACTICS

"A cinema film depicting Miss Margaret Baker giving a lecture on 'Milk *versus* Beer' was made at the recent Temperance Summer School at Westhill, and copies are available for Temperance societies and other organisations possessing a projecting apparatus."—*The Christian World.*

NOBLESSE OBLIGE

"The 1,160 boys of Eton College are to be provided with gas-masks, and there are to be two gas-proof rooms in each house at the School These will ensure complete safety.... Mr. R. E. Marsden, one of the College masters, has been elected controller for the College, and Mr. R. Hartley, a tradesman, will act in a similar capacity for the town, in which a shelter will be provided."—*The Sunday Times.*

THE COMPLEMENT

From a testimonial to "Pelmanism—The Complement of All Education"—"In conclusion I state without any attempt of flattery whatever, that the sum paid for the course is the best money's worth which I have ever speculated, and that the value of the 'goods' is far and away the best, to my mind, in existence."

HIGH SERVICE, ETC.

A correspondent in the *News Chronicle* says that a hospital career has its rewards for girls with sufficient stamina. "My daughter left an office for hospital at 24 ; she is now 32. She has gained : (1) the consciousness of high service, (2) £200 a year, plus a furnished house, and a new car—all expenses paid."

ZEAL

According to the Dean of Durham, " it can do us no harm now and then to consider what good we are in fact accomplishing ".

H.K.

' We're the only girls here, Annie.'

Naturally, she is apt to begin her day at the shoe-cupboard. It's a luxury to allow

her eye to wander along its shelves — to debate possibilities and discuss altern-

atives. Finally, the one perfect inevitable pair . . . Natural complement of her new

dress . . . Shoes that might have been built for her alone: so subtly do they complete

the ensemble she has chosen—so cleverly do they underline its elegances

. . . such shoes only Rayne have the knack of creating.

Raynes

H. & M. RAYNE LTD., 152, REGENT STREET, W.I & 58, NEW BOND STREET, W.I

Freya Stark: Contrasts in Kuwait . . .

MISS FREYA STARK, whose knowledge of Arab life is unrivalled, describes the ancient city of Kuwait, betwixt the desert and the sea. Here the dignity and leisure of Arabia confront the hustle of air liners and the eagerness of oil prospectors; and here, when the price of pearls declines, the men who build ships for the pearl-fisheries tighten their belts.

Balkan Nomads on the March . . .

Who are the Vlachs? They call themselves Romans and their language is based on Latin; yet their life is primitive and they wander each year from summer to winter pastures with their sturdy horses, the fair-haired babies perched upon the household goods. Grown-up girls dye their hair, for Vlach gentlemen do *not* prefer blondes!

Pacifists who Fight Ghosts

So peaceful are the people of Koto-sho, one of Japan's remote island colonies, that they need no chiefs to rule them and regard violence with horror. Yet they always carry arms when they walk abroad —for fear of meeting ghosts! Japan, so ready to use force elsewhere, respects the pacifism of these simple folk.

Constable—Father of Modern Landscape Painting . . .

died in 1837. Professor W. G. Constable, the art historian, describes the great artist's connection with the country that, in his own words, ' made him a painter.'

ILLUSTRATED WITH 8 SUPERB STUDIES IN PHOTOGRAVURE

4 PLATES in FULL COLOUR of the 1400-Year-Old Cave Paintings at Ajanta, India

[208]

Life without a shoehorn
by James Murgatroyd

MY needs in life are simple—just the ordinary little conveniences—but among these I include a shoe-horn. Because, if my shoes don't fit, my socks wear out ; and if my socks wear out they are secreted by Amabel ; therefore my shoes do fit and I use a shoehorn to get my feet into them. But a shoehorn is neither simple to acquire nor easy to keep. To begin with, you don't buy a shoehorn. Like a corkscrew or a nutcracker, it is the sort of possession you expect to inherit ; or you might even get a chromium model for a wedding-present. Some of my best shoehorns I have just found, in an empty house or an hotel bedroom. And since I have lost as many as I have found (exactly) I don't hesitate to take what I find.

At one exalted period of my life I had no less than three. One was long and brindled, and might have been made out of the horn of a unicorn. Another was of celluloid, and suspected of being highly inflammable. The third was of painted tin, given away with a shoe-cleaning set. I was so proud of this horny affluence that I put three hooks in the wall, and hung them all in a row. It used to give me great pleasure every morning to hesitate for a moment in my choice. For a shoehorn is a pleasant shape to contemplate, and just as some men get a kick out of flint arrows or Chinese jades, so I find æsthetic satisfaction in the contemplation of shoehorns. Indeed, at one time I seriously thought of making a proper collection of them. Why not ? I know

a man with a unique collection of matchboxes ; another with five hundred custard-cups, all different ; and my aunt Elizabeth, who is a spinster, has fifty glass bells (but some of them have their clappers missing). When I broached the subject with Amabel, she made the usual objection —where would the things go, and who would dust them ?

But Amabel, I said, they would all go into the hall. What would you do if I had a collection of hundreds of wine-glasses, like Jim Eve ?

Throw a party, she replied, rather too promptly.

But I was not destined to keep a collection of even three shoehorns. One by one they disappeared. The celluloid one went first—it fell into a bucket of hot water, which quite changed its nature. It became as flabby as a leather tongue. I made the usual protest to Amabel, but there was nothing to be done about it.

The brindled beauty went next. I took it with me when I went to visit one of my wealthier friends. It was the kind of house where your bag is snatched from you as soon as you arrive ; where you find some of your things agonisingly displayed on your bed and the rest secreted in drawers. The first thing I looked for was my shoehorn : it had a place of honour on the dressing-table, so I felt reassured. When Monday came and I went down to breakfast knowing that my bag would be packed before I could return to the room, I was careful to leave my shoehorn in a prominent position. More I could not do—it would sound too silly to say to a servant : Please don't forget my shoehorn ! When I got home and vainly searched my bag, it seemed equally silly to send a wire about a shoehorn, and somehow when I came to write my bread-and-butter, I could not ask my wealthy and distinguished friend to instruct his superior footman to busy himself about such a seemingly trivial object. Besides, I had a strong suspicion he had stolen it, and I did not want to get the fellow into trouble.

So I fell back on the metal one. It was a very inferior article ; the black paint on it was chipping off, and it had

'I'm the Lord Privy one, you know.'

a rusty look about the edges. But it did the job all right and kept me happy for weeks. Then it too disappeared, most mysteriously. Amabel's brother came over to lunch one Sunday, and arrived with a flat tyre. After lunch he decided to investigate the trouble himself, took off the tyre, found and repaired a puncture and proceeded to put the tyre on again. But it proved a tiresome business and he was short of the right kind of tools. So he borrowed the shoehorn, and it is my conviction to this day that somehow or other the shoehorn slipped inside the tyre; and that now it is forever rolled round with rocks and stones and trees, like Lucy. A sublime end for such a simple object, you might think; anyhow, my brother-in-law laughingly refuses to remove his tyre for the sake of recovering a tin shoehorn.

Left without a shoehorn, I had recourse, as on previous occasions, to various miserable subterfuges. The first instinct is to try and get your shoes on without any instrumental aid. With an old and tempered pair of shoes it can be done by simply squashing the leather in, and then pulling it out by running your finger round the edge hookwise. But this soon causes the sewing to come out and the leather to disintegrate. Such brute force is not possible with a new pair of shoes. You may try to use a finger or two to ease the heel in, but it is a dangerous expedient and likely to give you a nasty nip. The simplest makeshift is an envelope, preferably with a letter inside it to give it substance, and with a glossy surface. It is a great mistake to use an unposted letter, for the letter has a habit of slipping down with the heel and becoming so firmly wedged that, when you attempt to pull it out, it tears in two. Weaker kinds of paper always behave like that; I have spent many a blissful day with a portion of the *Daily Mail* under my heel.

Other objects must be used with discretion. I have, on various occasions, broken an ivory paper-knife, a silver spoon, the membership card of a select club to which I belong, and the brass label on an hotel key. A clean handkerchief can be used if you know how, or even the end of a silk tie. On one occasion I made skilful use of a smooth penny.

I once voiced my troubles to my shoemaker. I suggested, facetiously, that instead of a seam the heel should be provided with a zip-fastener, but he only smiled and told me to undo my shoe-laces to the full extent I hotly resented the implication that I was making an unnecessary fuss. I undo them sufficiently to take my shoes off, I said; they must therefore be sufficiently undone to put my shoes on. It is the same mass and the same space, and the body is moving through the same path though in a reverse direction. The fellow obviously did not understand these simple technicalities, but did condescend to supply me with a new shoehorn. It is made of synthetic resin and has a deliciously smooth surface; but personally I would still prefer the kind made from the horn of an animal, for then you get that feeling of organic unity with all creation which is one of life's supreme thrills.

*

A few years ago a first novel called "Wanted, A Son" by Hazel Adair achieved considerable success. Later, Mrs. Addis, wife of Lieut.-Comdr. E. E. Addis, R.N. (retired), admitted to her husband that she was Hazel Adair, whose first novel was selling on every bookstall. —*Hutchinson's Book News.*

They weren't so blunt about it in Victorian days.

'*And I'm beginning to doubt if it ever was a lizard.*'

NEW BOOKS *reviewed by Evelyn Waugh*

All Memory Gone

A YOUNG English business man of normal upbringing—an orphan liberally adopted by a wealthy uncle, newly appointed chairman of an industrial company, fiancé of a pretty bore, a dull rather vulgar young man—has a unique experience. He runs into a gatepost in his motor-car and loses his memory completely. It is an absorbing theme and Mr. Beachcroft has made a very interesting book on it; he has failed in so far as he has found the possibilities of the situation too rich and diverting and seems never quite to have decided what aspect he wishes to make the determining one. For there are two or three themes here. There is the purely psychological problem—how would a sane healthy adult behave who was suddenly bereft of all knowledge and experience and habit? It is an enormous theme, and I think Mr. Beachcroft has made a mistake in tackling it at all. Within the limits of a novel any solution must be inadequate; he shirks what would in any case have been one of the most important—and was in his particular case *the* most important difficulty—how would the sex instinct manifest itself in a fully mature male who is so far removed from his habits that he does not know, until he is shown, that water will quench thirst? The difficulties of speech are touched on so lightly that they might have been omitted. But even in its rudimentary and, from a novelist's point of view, inartistic form, the subject stimulates speculation in the reader very agreeably. The second theme which Mr. Beachcroft has incorporated in his book is a familiar one—that of the inspired simpleton who by ignorance,

real or assumed, is able to baffle and disconcert the humbugs. Here, I think, was what should have been Mr. Beachcroft's subject; the title hints as much. The convincing narrative of the accident would have made an admirable introduction to a book of satire, where the hero could have questioned and rendered ludicrous the conventions which he had hitherto accepted. Once or twice Mr. Beachcroft seems disposed to tackle this job, but he is hindered by his own sense of probability; he is unwilling to let his hero become a mere dialectical abstraction, and so limits his inquiry that it stops at the point where it might have

---

The Man who Started Clean. T. O. Beachcroft. *Boriswood.* 7s. 6d.
Lords of the Equator. Patrick Balfour. *Hutchinson.* 12s. 6d.
The Complete Memoirs of George Sherston. Siegfried Sassoon. *Faber and Faber.* 8s. 6d.
The Fight for the Charta. Neil Stewart. *Chapman and Hall.* 6s.

---

begun to be interesting. "Edmund had raised a whole series of queries which nobody ever did raise." The whole trouble is that this is just what Edmund did not do. The queries he raised may be found any day in the correspondence column of the *Daily Express* and the conclusions he reaches—that it is nasty to eat meat, a bore to dress for dinner, a folly to wear a stock for fox-hunting; that Latin grammar is a tiresome study, that hiking about and gossiping to casual acquaintances (with a background of inherited capital) is a more agreeable form of life than sweating in an office are commonplaces to most people. Moreover the conventional types which Edmund flustered are so very fatuous as almost to be improbable. Mr. Beachcroft seems to suffer from a delusion that originality of mind is allied in some way to unconventional attire—a conclusion which, with the single, noble exception of Mr. Belloc,

seems to me utterly contrary to experience. There is a third theme. A Jekyll-and-Hyde-cum-Happy-Hypocrite love affair which is prettily handled. As a book *The Man who Started Clean* is a failure, but it is very much more interesting and promising than many successes.

Mr. Balfour is the ideal traveller—witty, topical and above all admirably sane. *Lords of the Equator* is a better book than *Grand Tour*. The latter, as its title suggests, was the journal of a trip undertaken for no other reason than the will to go places and see things. In his latest journey Mr. Balfour had a more serious object, to investigate conditions in the African mandated territories which, week by week, occupy a more prominent and threatening place in world politics. His account of them forms a more valuable document than many more laboriously compiled publications because his aim has been to give a first-hand impression of what life in these places is really like, what settlers and officials say about the situation when they are talking informally among themselves, not giving evidence across the table of a commission of inquiry. The more solid informative passages are very skilfully interposed with light and wholly delightful travel experiences of the kind one would expect from the author of *Grand Tour*. The illustrations are admirable; there is no indication who was the photographer; if, as seems likely, they are by the author, we must add Mr. Balfour's name to the small list of really good modern photographers.

The Complete Memoirs of George Sherston needs no commendation from me. It is already established as a classic. One welcomes its appearance in this compact and pleasant form.

The Fight for the Charta fills a gap in popular, mildly radical history. It is easily readable and should form a valuable book for students of economic history who want something lively on which to spend the last hour of the day before going to bed; the difficult hour in the month before examinations when the mind slips off the text-books and the conscience forbids a novel.

*

Literary Snack-Bar

MADE ON EARTH. A Panorama of Marriage, edited by Hugh Kingsmill. (*Hamish Hamilton*, 10s. 6d.) This admirable anthology opens with some general statements on matrimony from—among others—Milton, Bacon, Dryden, and the Earl of Rochester. The effect from a team like that—one bachelor, one divorcee and a couple of adulterers—is naturally a bit acid. We then move, as it were, closer in and watch Henry VIII, Pepys, Oliver Cromwell and again sourpuss Milton in action—the Duke of Marlborough too, though we miss Sarah's letter after she had visited the allied forces mentioning that her Lord had honoured her in his boots. The awe-inspiring panorama—bitter, tender and grotes-que—moves on right up to our own day with D. H. Lawrence smashing the crockery and Frieda telling him he's not a gentleman and Dorothy Brett tactfully pouring oil on the flames. The magnificent collection draws to a close on a high note with a section called *Attempted Matrimony* and a correspondent writing to *The Times* a year ago: "I for one will *never* acknowledge any other King while King Edward lives. I will recognize the woman he chooses for his wife as his Queen Consort." Up the rebel!

THE EPICURE'S COMPANION. Edward and Lorna Bunyard, and others. (*Dent*, 7s. 6d.) Even the slightly stuffed feeling which results from reading this book through from *Oysters* to *Index* cannot blind the re-viewer to the fact that it is a very good book indeed. One small criti-cism: Mr. Bunyard neglects the sound apple Granny Smith and by his silence envelops it in the contempt rightly conferred on the repulsive Jonathan—as thick-skinned, pulpy and Canadian as a Press Lord. There is an admirable section on Apple Pie: might one suggest grated *orange* as an occasional flavouring when Bramleys are insipid and to hell with cloves at all times?—and that the hard citron or orange-flavoured sugar on candied peel, which has in any case to be discarded for cake-making can be profitably used as an alternative to Barbadoes in the pie? The editors are to be thanked for the public-spirited attack on the "mess of apples crowning a slab of paste looking like an anæmic dog biscuit" which is offered as Apple Pie by cretins in wholesale restaurants. By deduction it is increasingly evident that Apple Pie will survive only in the homes of the professional classes in the provinces: in London and in whole-sale restaurants it is safer to avoid dis-appointment and order a confection of wet spongecake and egg-white called *Poudinge Jubilee à la Princesse*. Then at any rate you know what you'll get.

LIVES OF GREAT MEN ALL REMIND US...
Literary Pilgrimages by
H.K. and M.M.

1.—Samuel Butler's Needlewoman

HANDEL Street is in Bloomsbury, between Guilford street and Saint Pancras Station, and at its eastern end is a little row of late eighteenth-century houses. In one of these houses about fifty years ago lived a Frenchwoman, who used her mother's name of Dewattines. In earlier years she had used her father's name, Dumas, and it was as Lucie Dumas that she had made the acquaintance of Samuel Butler in 1872 close to the Angel, Islington.

We stood on the pavement in Handel Street, and fixed, rather arbitrarily, on one particular house as the house Lucie Dewattines had lived in. It was those steps which had been trodden by Butler once a week, not with hasty bounding strides, but with the sober measured tread of a man who is going to do what he has done many times before, and what he is prepared to do many times again. Lucie, Festing Jones tells us in his biography of Butler, had had predecessors in Butler's scheme of life, but she had no rivals. Butler, however, had a rival of sorts, in the person of Festing Jones himself, who shared Lucie's favours at Butler's own suggestion and expense, Butler paying a pound a head per visit. Butler visited her each week on Tuesdays, and Jones on Thursdays, an interval of one day for recoupment being adjudged advisable. This isosceles triangle lasted until the base collapsed with the death in 1892 of Lucie or, as her two cavaliers preferred to call her, "Madame". She was buried in Kensal Green Cemetery, and her coffin was followed by Butler and Jones, and Butler's confidential clerk, Alfred Cathie.

We discussed "Madame's" feelings when Butler asked her to oblige his young friend Jones. H.K. ventured the suggestion that she might have been hurt.

M.M.: Hurt? Why should she be?

H.K.: Well, Butler had been visiting her for years, presumably she had come to have a sort of wifely feeling for him, and then one day he suddenly dumps young Jones on her—tells her that Thursday suits Jones best, and that he'll stick to Tuesday as hitherto.

M.M.: Consider her situation. This near-homosexual-British-Museum-Reading-room habitué picks her up at the Angel, and gives her a pound a week for her Tuesday afternoons. I am not concerned to disparage Butler's person, but I draw your attention to Jones's picture of Butler unlacing his boots in front of "Madame's" fire, and being facetious about her cat as it ran in and out between his feet, and I suggest that someone who had gone through all this would hardly be hurt in her finer feelings when she was asked to duplicate this erotic calvary at the same figure.

H.K.: I had pictured her sitting in a darkening room, after Butler told her about Jones, and perhaps sighing— "Encore un rêve disparu". And then looking out of that window and down this street, along which henceforth two bearded lovers instead of one would hasten, though not together.

We, also, looked along the street, and wondered how long it was before young Jones's step became as sober as Butler's. Not very long, M.M. thought, having a low opinion of "Madame's" charm. The Angel, he said, was not the beat, nor was Butler

the man, to be chosen by a young and attractive woman. We pictured their first encounter, the flaring gas-jets outside the butchers' and fried-fish shops, the horse buses lumbering by, Butler reassured because he was away from his usual haunts—the Inner Temple, the British Museum—but still apprehensive, furtive, and "Madame", dark and large, glancing right and left, noticing Butler, finding him adequate, smiling. . . .

We thought how quiet and secure this respectable solid house in Handel Street must have seemed after the Angel. Two rooms on the second floor—it would not be hard to find the rent when Jones was added to Butler. And, according to Jones, there was also a small allowance from a Frenchman to whom she had borne a child. But was there really this small allowance? We agreed that Jones, who does not mention his own afternoons in Handel Street in the *Life*, had been at too great pains to present "Madame" as a woman whose association with Butler was rather from choice than necessity—her family engaged in the silk trade in Lyons, a devoted brother, herself a devout Catholic, absolutely trustworthy, an admirable woman with great natural intelligence and considerable knowledge of the world. If all this, we thought, why the Angel?

What, we speculated, was her attitude towards her two suitors, apart from her gratitude to Butler for having made possible her transference from the Angel to Handel Street? Was it black Thursday as well as black Tuesday? What did she feel when she heard their knock? Had she anything to say about the one to the other? "Votre Monsieur Jones n'est pas très fort" or "Monsieur Butler reste toujours jeune, n'est-ce-pas?" And they—what modification or enrichment of their friendship sprang from this common interest? Did Thursday wince on Tuesday? Did Tuesday fret on Thursday, listlessly turning over pages in the reading room of the British Museum near by?

We shook our heads, and turned down Handel Street towards Russell Square. Two pounds a week—it had been earned.

THE BALLET

As Miss Stein Says . . .

IT is not a question of talent—Diaghilev always said the English have as much talent for dancing as anyone—but Russians will be Russians, and if you go to Sadler's Wells to find "an English company fully up to the level of any foreign classical ballet troupe" you will be disappointed, disingenuous or simply distrait. Nevertheless you will spend an agreeable evening in a pretty theatre and see good dancing and you may soon form part of an audience so appreciative as to applaud even an announcement of a mistake in the order of the programme.

Checkmate.—Blood, Sand, Life and Death on the Chessboard. A new ballet, striking, picturesque, dramatic, muddling and well danced. Worth going to for Arthur Bliss's music alone. Costumes and décor by E. McKnight Kauffer and choreography by Miss de Valois. Both are effective, but one grows tired of being menaced by the Black Queen: too many *pas marchés sur les pointes* are vulgar, not stylish.

Wedding Bouquet. — Charming, charming, charming, to borrow three words from Miss Stein whose ballet this is. The music is by Lord Berners and I always like music by the aristocracy; he has also designed the entrancing décor and the adequate clothes. Ashton's choreography is entertaining, and except those that sing nicely all dance nicely, especially Miss Honer, Mr. Helpmann and Miss Fonteyn (is she always to be known as forlorn? There seems some danger). No need to take on so about Josephine getting drunk at the wedding.

The Rake's Progress.—Miss de Valois' greatest success. Story and scenery are by Gavin Gordon and Rex Whistler, respectively, after Hogarth, and music by Mr. Gordon, long after Hogarth. Mr. Helpmann makes an excellent progress from lucre to lunacy, Miss Miller displays "undying devotion in spite of everything" very prettily, Mr. Turner shows himself to be the most finished dancer at the Wells (no wisecrack) and the rest give vigorous performances. An old English atmosphere that would satisfy the most exacting American, but why are the programme notes in such horribly and falsely simple language?

Le Lac des Cygnes.—A thousand times no, or anyway five hundred. Too much team spirit and the chorus has arms like hockey sticks. Miss Fonteyn dances beautifully. The hunters appear preoccupied with an aeroplane in the dank Wagnerian grotto and not even the noble Mr. Helpmann and the statuesque Miss Argyle can reconcile us to curtailing the lovely duets into acrimonious arguments. Too difficult a work, but they can do better. Also I like the one-act version to prove fatal, not "bewildering".

Pomona.—The gods at it again. Vertumnus this time, disguised (you've guessed) as an old lady, but it's all right in the end. Very pretty when the dancers are posed in John Banting's costumes against John Banting's back-cloth. Mr. Helpmann is godlike with a funny interlude and Miss Argyle lovely and lifeless. She never holds her positions long enough. The choreography (Ashton) is gay, if confused, and Mr. Lambert's music is nicely tone-bordered, like the carpets in Tottenham Court Road.

Nocturne.—*Fade,* and belonging below stairs. Delius's music but not Delius's Paris. Of course there is *un bal* and some unvirtuous bustles (believe it or not one can have too much bustle-wagging) and a poor girl and a rich girl who lures away the poor girl's lover (a claret-coated moustachioed moth fascinated by the scandal), and *of course* there is a Spectator in a black cape silhouetted. He's certainly been drinking *absinthe* and will certainly again when he has done this job of mass-observation. Unexceptionable scenery, unremarkable choreography. Miss Fonteyn and Mr. Helpmann dance well, Miss Brae is sufficiently rich and Mr. Ashton looks on.

PERDITA STANLEY

'*Were you the stuffed neck?*'

THE FILMS BY GRAHAM GREENE

They Won't Forget—Nitchevo

OCCASIONALLY a film of truth and tragic value gets somehow out of Hollywood onto the screen. Nobody can explain it—perhaps a stage needs using, all the big executives are in conference over the latest Mamoulian "masterpiece"—Jehovah is asleep, and when he wakes he finds he's got a *Fury* on his hands, worse still *They Won't Forget*. Worse because Lang is a showman as well as a great director: he knows how to get his mixture down: he gives the melodramatic close, the happy ending, and the executives, after the first shock, discover a success. But I doubt whether *They Won't Forget* will have the same success—it hasn't in this country. It's a better, less comprising story than *Fury*—taken as a whole a better picture, though Mervyn Le Roy isn't in Lang's class.

It is the story of a murder trial run by an ambitious district attorney for political reasons (Mr. Claude Rains gives his finest performance to date). It takes place in the South and the South has banned the picture. A girl in a business college is found murdered on Commemoration Day—again the picture is uncompromising, she isn't a lay figure, the audience see enough of her before her death, young, quiet and vital, to feel the shock of her murder. The police at first settle on the negro janitor of the building, but the district attorney isn't satisfied. Beat a negro up enough and, innocent or guilty, he'll confess—it's too easy, it's unspectacular. The attorney's a stranger and he has the governorship in mind, and so a young teacher in the school—who has come down with his wife from the north—is charged. He was in the building, there is a spot of blood on the jacket he sent to the cleaners, the girl was in love with him—but above all, of course, he's a northerner. "Sell prejudice angle," the tape machines of the newspapers tap out continually: the trial becomes a sensational sporting event: a detective is sent by a northern newspaper and is beaten up by a

southern mob: a well-known New York counsel arrives and conducts the defence with cynical and heartless efficiency to get the spotlight on the prejudice and hang his client: the rival mothers are flung into the arena. The attorney, tie off, sweating in braces down the ranks of the jury while electric fans hum and the judge smokes a pipe and the audience applaud, wins all along the line; the man is—inevitably—found guilty; the Governor, an honest man, commutes the sentence to life imprisonment and ruins his career; a mob take the young man from the train which is carrying him to the state prison and lynch him; the attorney's well on his way to the Senate. In the last shot the attorney and the newsman who has supported him watch the widow go down the street—"I wonder if he was guilty." The doubt is valuable—we are not sold the usual story of the innocent man. The evidence was heavy against the teacher; the attorney was not completely unscrupulous—we are dealing with human beings. The direction of the picture is brilliant, the cameraman agilely snapping the wife as she falls in a faint at the news of her husband's arrest; the last scene of the lynching with the down-line express sweeping by and extinguishing the screams, snatching from the gallows-shaped erection by the line the small bundle of the mail bag. If it makes a little less impression than Lang's more melodramatic story it is because Lang has a finer talent for expressing human relationships; we are never so close to the married pair as we were to the garage man and his girl; relationships give the last twist to the agony—and we are spared that here.

Nitchevo has a bad story—and a very obscure one; it boils down in the end to the usual situation of French naval films—elderly officer with young wife; arrival of junior officer who once—platonically—served her in a sensational but not discreditable past; unreasonable mysti-

fications; arrival of gunrunner and blackmail; "bring me news of your husband's consent at the Pacha ball"; "your wife can at this moment be found at the house of Lieutenant —" But the picture is worth a visit for the final situation in a sunk submarine and for the acting of M. Harry Baur. Those features—of an old reptile which has learnt all the secrets the jungle can offer—can adapt themselves with perfect naturalness to any profession. A submarine commander, a police officer, a Kulak—M. Baur always seems about his proper unsensational business.

Night Climbing
THE ROOFS OF CAMBRIDGE
by Michael Roberts

WHAT has happened to the poet Austin Lee? I have heard nothing from him since I trod on his belly one nice dark summer's night in 1925, on my way from the Essex Building to Great Gate. Presumably he has graduated and become an Abominable Snow Man. What other profession can there be for people who scare the serious climber by sleeping like giant slugs in the hollows between roof and parapet?

My business that night was simple. As an official of a society called the Amalgamated Union of Presbyterians and Bodysnatchers of Great Britain and Ireland, with headquarters in Trinity, I was guiding a party who wanted to make a tour of the College. This is roof-hiking rather than roof-climbing, but it involves one or two pretty bits of work, and I am happy to learn from Whipplesnaith, author of *The Night Climbers of Cambridge* (Chatto & Windus, 7s. 6d.), that the crucial drainpipe is still as good as new, in spite of the anxiety expressed by the author of *The Roof-Climber's Guide to Trinity* over thirty years ago. *The Night Climbers of Cambridge* is not a guide book, but it is full of good reliable information, illuminating anecdotes and brilliant flashlight photographs. It does for Cambridge what Conway's *Alps from End to End* did for the Alps, and if Whipplesnaith had no Gurkhas in his retinue, he nevertheless picked up one or two men from Pembroke.

It is important to remember, however, that Cambridge differs in some respects from the Alps. Whipplesnaith quite rightly points out that there are no drainpipes in the Alps, whereas Cambridge without drainpipes is unthinkable. The relative scarcity of snow and ice in Cambridge is another important point of difference, and Whipplesnaith errs, I think, in not including a chapter on Winter Climbing. Good winter conditions are rare in Cambridge, and the snow is always liable to avalanche, but for those who enjoy the beauties of nature as well as the thrill of achievement there is no finer viewpoint than the roof of Trinity Library on a frosty night.

In general, however, it is true to say that the man who has mastered drainpipe technique, and can do a neat foot-and-back up and down a chimney, is equal to any problem that Cambridge can set him, provided that he knows the difference between good rock and bad. Whipplesnaith's experience of this matter is invaluable, but if I may revert to my home district for the moment, I would like to add something to his warnings and say that I know of nothing more treacherous than the stucco of New Court, except possibly the lower reaches of the Southern Aiguille d'Arves.

But Trinity, after all, is not the whole of Cambridge. To borrow a phrase from the poet Aiken, it is like "the vast ruin wherein Godhead dwells": it has some sensational climbs that are really quite easy; it has some first-rate stuff that is only perceptible to the experienced eye; it is a magnificent jungle; and it offers excellent facilities for escape from porters. But for good straightforward climbs it has little that can be compared with the Old Library, the Fitzwilliam Museum or the South Face of Caius. Whipplesnaith knows all this ground as well as a Chamonix guide knows the Grépon, but his deepest affection is for King's Chapel. It is interesting to note, from his account of the *Save Ethiopia* climb, that the old alliance between roof-climbing and extreme liberal sentiments still prevails at Cambridge.

It is seldom, however, that the serious climber allows ulterior motives to influence his action. He has no thirst for notoriety and no desire to enhance the reputation of his college or his political party by an act of exhibitionism. "Very quiet gentlemen, sir, they never disturb us if they can help it." The serious roof-climber eschews banners and jerries as the serious alpinist eschews pitons. These easy roads to notoriety are all very well in Oxford, and among German climbers, but they have no place in Cambridge. Whipplesnaith's moral principles—no damage to buildings, no unnecessary intrusion on residents, no personal violence to bobbies, or even to porters—show that the sport is developing on sound lines.

Whipplesnaith is, indeed, one of the finest products of Cambridge of recent years; he has just the right mixture of dash and prudence, he keeps off the drink at the right time, he has useful friends in the Force, and he is a man of wide interests. He keeps an eye on the things of general importance and his discovery that the dome of the Fitzwilliam is an iron dummy deserves some public recognition. His interest in folk-lore and anthropology of the country he explores is genuine and acute. He tells how, in the old heroic days, the Master of Pembroke was feeding with his fellows one day when the meat course was brought in. "With a resounding 'What, hash again!' the Master brought his spoon down heavily, causing the present breach in the walls." Of this college in general he says: "Its stone is good, its climbs legion, and we can thoroughly recommend any night climber to pay a few visits to it. Its hospitality is lavish and sincere, and it breeds those strong, silent Englishmen who suck pipes in the Malayan jungle but do not pass exams."

Finally, with admirable insight and good taste, Whipplesnaith makes his apology for the sport. He might have said that its moral value is incalculable; like Rugger, it does this, that and the other; it strengthens something and intensifies something else; it expresses the nature of the world, the struggle between disinterested moral virtue and the purely prudential values of society, etc., etc. But instead of this he merely talks about its use in giving a nervous man a job he can do and enjoy doing.

AS THE WORLD GOES ROUND

a spotlight on current affairs

by CHRISTOPHER HOLLIS

The Danger in France

I HAVE no wish to be an "ancestral voice prophesying war". Violence has not yet broken out in France, and every friend of France will trust that it may be avoided. The situation is far from hopeless. At the same time it is most dangerous. And, before the trouble comes, it can do nothing but good to make clear a few facts in order to avoid a repetition of the question-begging and time-wasting controversies with which the Spanish issue has been obscured.

In France today the parties of the extreme Right—the parties which by a legitimate metaphor might be called fascist ; the parties, that is to say, of M. Doriot, of Colonel de la Rocque or of the *Action Française*—have quite failed to capture popular imagination. At the recent cantonal elections they won next to no representation. It is true that the actual returns of those elections do not give a fair statistical measure of their strength, for many voters of conservative sympathies then voted radical-socialist as the best hope of keeping out communists or socialists. But the very recognition by conservative voters of the impossibility of electing conservative candidates is a sufficient proof of the weakness of the Right.

Both electoral returns and general judgment combine to agree that, unenthusiastic as are the French at the moment for any of their politicians, yet the radical-socialists have today more right to claim to speak for the people than any other group. Yet what does that mean? English newspaper correspondents who hailed radical-socialist victories at the cantonal elections as victories for the Popular Front were rather rushing in where even party bosses fear to tread. The truth is that a considerable proportion of the supporters of the radical-socialists would be glad to break with the Popular Front and, if conservatives are now voting radical-socialist, it is reasonable to believe that their proportion is increasing. The conservatives are teaching M. Dimitrov that two sides can use the Wooden Horse of Troy. But what proportion of radical-socialists are against the Popular Front nobody quite knows. On October 24 in the *Figaro* M. Roger Dardenne was making merry because at their conference the party-managers had decided to keep the discussion to agricultural questions rather than raise the issue in which everybody was interested.

There has been going on in the last weeks another French political congress, whose resolutions must be understood if we are to understand French politics—the congress of the Union of Syndicates at Vincennes. Neither the Socialists nor yet the Trades Unionists even claim to represent the opinion of the majority of Frenchmen. It is therefore a curiosity in democratic theory to read that M. Racamond, one of the Secretaries of the C.G.T., demanded that the Government "either satisfy the workers' demands, or else we will say to the Government 'The masses are strong enough to seize it for themselves'." The congress denounced what they called "the scandal" of the new non-intervention agreement and demanded that the French fleet be used in the Spanish war for the evacuation not only of civilians but also, explicitly, of "combatant units".

At the same time the communists have been celebrating the twentieth anniversary of the Russian revolution at the Velodrome d'Hiver, and, as so often happens with communist meetings, there has been an air of mystery both about what did happen and what did not happen. M. Marcel Cachin of course spoke, as he always does, but the chief advertised speaker was Señor Martinez Barrios, the President of the Spanish Cortes. He did not turn up. Why not? It is easy to think of reasons, but all Paris is wondering which is the true one. And all Paris is wondering whether it is true, as both French and Italian papers have reported, that M. Dimitrov was present in disguise, leaving his instructions to the faithful in France *en route* for Spain.

In these columns a few weeks ago the present writer showed that he had no wild hero-worship for radical-socialist politicians. Plenty of people despise them and there are plenty of good reasons for despising them. Yet in the present condition of France one cannot but tremble to think what would happen if they lost their strength. The conclusion of the report of the Union of Syndicates concludes with an unpleasant hint of what would be most likely to happen. "The meeting was without incident," ran the report. "Only a few anarchists . . . were beaten up by communists." If only idealists had the same ideals!

A*

NEWSPAPERMEN IN THE CIVIL WAR

Kate Mangan

THE Spanish Government is moving again ; with it must go the foreign journalists. What a move, and how will it be effected? Will each office with secretaries, files and other machinery be packed in lorries? And will the rest of us be labelled "correspondents, fragile, this side up"? I fear that, as the Spaniards say, "a formidable disorganization will ensue".

By now the newspapermen are accustomed to the diverse discomforts and inconveniences that Valencia has to offer and may well protest at the new and different problems presented by Barcelona.

As I remember them, the newspapermen in Valencia were extremely philosophical, extremely ill-assorted, but nevertheless just a happy family. They all resided in one hotel, because it was the one most patronized by visiting celebrities who could be buttonholed for interviews and was centrally located for the bombardments and the censor's office.

The place was a perfect Miltonic limbo. On the religious side there would be such combinations as the Dean of Canterbury, the Canon of Cordoba, and some visiting Quakers. There were endless delegations (representing international solidarity) and social service workers. There were men of letters ("Ernest Hemingway is back, so I suppose the season may be said to have reopened"). There was Stephen Spender; there was Dorothy Parker. There were movie actors from Hollywood. There were world-famous revolutionaries. There were fascists under arrest with their guards. People slept in the bathrooms and corridors. When I left it was still questionable whether two American congressmen and five Chinese generals might not all land up in the same dormitory.

The lounge of this hotel was darkly panelled and adorned with frightful oil-paintings of sunny Spain and had rather the atmosphere of an ocean-liner on which we were all bound on some interminable voyage. It was run by the most uncompromising and brutally tyrannical collective in town. The head-waiter was a little gangster who I always expected would produce a sub-machine-gun from under his white coat. The bells were relentlessly disconnected at 8 p.m., and if you were sick you were told that people with a fever should not eat—to avoid serving meals upstairs. One journalist, trying to buy an exorbitantly priced bottle of whisky, was told by a young page: "You can't have it, you have had quite

enough already"—which happened to be true. Drinking hours were more severely restricted than in England and you could not play the piano after dinner. "It's just F.A.I. (Anarchist) puritanism," complained the unfortunate clientèle.

Many were the times that I pleaded in Spanish for the journalists when they were late for meals and the waiters refused to serve them. I explained all the hardships of a reporter's life, how impossible it was for them to be on time, how they were always hanging on to the long distance telephone. On one occasion I waxed so eloquent that the waiter's response was "You are so good you ought to be on the radio."

The correspondents of Left newspapers employed a different technique. "It's all very well to treat us like this—we are comrades, we understand, we are working all day making propaganda for you—but think what a deplorable impression this makes on the bourgeois journalists!" This tactic usually produced cold cuts for comrades, but towards the representatives of capitalism they were implacable as ever.

One of the most trying features, inevitable with short rations, was that an invited guest was liable to be suddenly turned away from the table—terribly embarrassing for the host. Sometimes we had potato chips instead of bread, and sometimes we had tiny little glossy oval rolls, exactly like those artificial mice which are pulled along the floor on a string for the amusement of a young cat.

One correspondent, grey-haired and old-maidish, and very chivalrous with ladies, gave little coffee parties in his room and never could see the point of dirty stories. The old American military attaché, a Southern Gentleman, also gave coffee parties (there was no coffee in town and, if there had been, the hotel staff would have refused to make it) and read out extracts from a guide to Spain about the best seasons of the year to visit the different parts and the antiquities and objects of interest.

Whatever was the right season to visit Valencia, the summer months emphatically were not it. The weather was stickily warm; the journalists swore and cursed and mopped their brows, all the shutters were closed at sundown because of air-raids and after that hour one was gradually asphyxiated, as in an old-time speakeasy. The more Left a correspondent the more formal his attire—in fact a French communist correspondent, though rather stout and feeling the heat dreadfully, long refused even to remove his coat.

The shops in the Calle de la Paz (Rue de la Paix) presented limited possibilities, and there was no chance of new stock coming in, so, as what we stood up in wore out, I soon found myself in a suiting the identical twin to that of the air attaché. There was a certain pansyish quality about Valencia haberdashery, which was all artificial silk and came in pastel shades that gradually, to all superficial appearance, as one man after another was forced to appear in cute little numbers with pink spots or violet stripes, robbed the most virile journalists of their masculinity.

Without previous experience I could not say whether our lot were more exotic than most correspondents, but they were certainly exotic. There was the decadent young man, the son of a famous father, who kept a monkey and when the management protested said "What about all the other monkeys who live here?" and finally died, rather abruptly, of double pneumonia. There was the Greek, who had been imprisoned by the Italians in Abyssinia and finally reached jail and deportation here; there was the Oxford young man, who was very sensitive and a bit dilettante and who spoke in accents so cultivated that most of us could not understand what he said, though he was an excellent linguist. There was an elderly, disappointed intellectual who was always getting scooped, and a dopey young man who had been "covering" Mrs. Simpson before.

There were two keen rivals who rushed in looking in corners and under tables for news, like terriers looking for rats. They were nervous and jumpy and finally both collapsed almost simultaneously, and had to go for holidays. I never saw them without thinking of "a nose for news", as they both had long thin noses and sniffed with them. Scoops were always problematic, for the telephone was capricious and often enough an urgent call to Paris did not come through until hours after an ordinary one which had been asked for much later. Most of us developed a fatalistic despair about this phenomenon; only those two keen young men never became resigned to it, and I think it was their acute impatience that really wore them down in the end.

'He says he's a Lt.-Col. Fanshawe, and thinks there must have been a muddle about the tickets.'

The censor was what brought us all together. We were obliged to telephone from a kind of confessional box, with a censor, who more or less knew the language, listening in. Messages had to be written in duplicate and stamped beforehand and woe to the man who improvised. Questions from the London or Paris office produced an agonized silence, as one did not know whether or not it was permitted to answer them and could only pretend to be very stupid.

There were two under-censors, of some middle-European nation, who dealt with such languages as Polish and Czech, who ran in and out and made inopportune remarks rather like Rosencrantz and Guildernstern. On one occasion one of them was heard to say, over long distance, "This be London?" which also had a Shakespearean flavour.

But apart from our regular hacks, we had the distinguished visitors who sized up the situation in Spain in a few days. There was the man who owned a Yiddische typewriter which wrote backwards and who ordered a great many suits in Valencia, including a riding costume, because they were so cheap. There was the man who, on a tour of the front, while hiding in the fields and being strafed by Fiat planes, remarked "What a wealth of bright weeds! Cannot you tell me their names? If only I had my herbarium and botany book with me!" There was a venerable old man who had fought in the war of Greek independence—not the same one as Byron, but it must have been one just after.

During stirring times, such as the government crisis, or the meeting of the Cortes, all the newspapermen from Madrid flocked down and the whole crowd hung around like vultures. Then the rivals formed teams in which, as far as I recall, the Agence Havas always had a numerical superiority, being like the four Marx Brothers, and always able to station some of the members at strategic points from which they could telephone to one another. This plan was also very advantageous in the matter of waiting for telephone-calls: one man could, as

'What d'you mean, this is the story you were trying to remember last night!'

law-courts, where a judge unlocked a safe and produced the vessel in question, rather battered, with most of the enamel chipped off.

The censor would not let this story through. "But," protested the journalist, "it is the rebels' vulgarity, not yours." "Nevertheless, it is very vulgar, and very un-Spanish—I am sure it was thought of by a German, and I forbid you to send it."

The worst raid came one Sunday when a music-loving correspondent, who was at the symphony concert, wrote "The bombs are falling round me, Wagner's *Parsifal* is being played." The Norwegian Legation was wrecked on this occasion. The Norwegians did not know until they turned up at the office, next morning, and found it didn't exist any longer. The news went through to Oslo speedily, however, thanks to a keen newspaperman: "We have pleasure in informing you that your legation has been totally destroyed."

In one raid a bomb fell before the front door of the British Embassy. The Embassies moved—to their warships out at sea, to villas in the country; the Americans were rather bitter about having no warships there and cadged hard for invitations. The journalists had to stay in town to be near the censor, but they were not without malice and the diplomats were very sensitive about being accused of funk. "You will say, of course, that we are moving on account of the summer weather," begged one of a journalist, giving at the same time a few more packets of Luckys (unobtainable in town). "I shall say that on account of the hot weather, the day after the severe bombardment of Thursday night, you have decided to move."

★

The experienced medical practitioner always suspects "fatigue" when he is faced by a patient who shows the following general characteristics : he looks tired, his eyes are heavy, he yawns, his shoulders droop, he moves slowly, his complexion is pallid.—*From a British Association paper.*

And he says he is completely exhausted?

it were, keep the nest warm at the censor's while another went out for a bite.

Our first serious air bombardment was at about eight in the evening. Someone on the balcony saw a plane and we all heard the engine. It was immediately followed by an uncommonly loud and shaking crash. We put out the lights, closed the shutters and retired with a random collection of writing materials to an inner room, where the correspondents immediately began typing for dear life and squabbling about the number of bangs they heard. "What's the use? Interesting things always happen on a Saturday night. Why does the Government al-

ways have its victories on a Saturday night?" complained someone, while a timid Scandinavian cried "Où est la cave?" (there was no cellar). Anyway the interior darkness of the hotel seemed rather futile when we emerged into moonlight as bright as day.

In one bombardment the enemy dropped a chamberpot with insults written on it such as: "To Largo Canallero (implying 'dog' instead of 'gentleman')—greetings to the Reds." This fact was ferreted out by a rather crude individual who was in partnership with the Oxford young man and who sent the latter to examine this interesting object. He found it in the

The Shadow of Byron

ONE rainy Sunday a few weeks ago I revisited Horsley Towers. It gave me a shock to find it existed in the real world, the subject of an illustrated brochure in which it was described as a "stately mansion in first-rate order, of imposing appearance and soundly constructed". For, over a period of fifteen years, I had revisited the place so often in dreams it had become a kind of delusional obsession. I do not know how many nights I have spent floating down its wide shallow staircase, trudging up the spiral steps of the towers, losing myself in the cloisters and getting accidentally locked in the belfry.

But as soon as the estate agent's car deposited me at the flamboyant gatehouse with its walls of flint embedded in cement, its towers, its crossbow windows and its irresistible suggestion of a built-up set for a "historical" film, I was not surprised that it had for so long dominated my dreams.

For Horsley Towers is the production of a dominating character, a forceful Victorian with a mediæval imagination . . . that William, first Earl of Lovelace, who married Byron's daughter Ada. A self-taught architect and engineer, he worked out his curious fantasies in other elaborate houses besides "The Towers", such as Glen Damph in Scotland and Ashley Combe in Somerset. These I have not

seen, but I am told they have the same Castle of Otranto features of cloisters, tunnels, minarets and secret passages.

Passing under the gatehouse, you find yourself in a great stable yard with cottages in the same red and ochre neo-Gothic style. But of the "stately mansion" itself there is no sign. Instead, you are confronted with the dark yawning mouth of a huge tunnel. This tunnel has the peculiar property, for me at any rate, of never being twice in the same place. It is just as confusing in real life as in my dreams, and studying the plan makes it no easier because *there* it appears to lead direct to the back of the cloisters and I am convinced it does no such thing. In the days when Horsley belonged to T. O. M. Sopwith and I used to stay there, the mobility of that tunnel used to drive me nearly mad. It was like the house in Looking Glass Land, never there when you wanted it and always there when you didn't. I would steer by familiar landmarks which I knew were hundreds of yards away from it, only, on turning a corner, to find it gaping in front of me. I would comb the grounds for it and it would be entirely invisible. All that I can say is that there *is* a tunnel and that, a few Sundays ago, it was near the Bishop's Gate entrance.

Avoiding the tunnel and taking

care not to get lost in a series of walled gardens, greenhouses and buildings enough to make up a small village, you may at last, if you are lucky enough to slip through the right door in the wall and follow a twisting path through a dark shrubbery, come upon the house itself. It is a curious architectural jumble. The south front is sham Tudor; grey stone, high gables, mullioned windows and balconies looking over a terrace. The west begins as Tudor and suddenly breaks into an ecclesiastical-looking square tower of flint and cement with two round towers at the corners. In various parts of the house you will suddenly open an innocent-looking door and find yourself on the spiral stairs inside one of these towers. At the top of one is a dusty belfry with four great immobile bells.

Below the square tower the cloisters begin, bewildering cloisters paved and groined in cream stone and red and black tiling, with pointed Gothic windows and thick glass lights in the roof. There is nothing gloomy or sinister about them, and yet, after you have explored them a little, you will probably turn back and hope to goodness you have turned back in the right direction. For they are perpetually dividing, turning corners, offering little flights of steps which you climb only to find your way barred by a nail-studded door, luring you half-way up other towers, branching off into other cloisters which you follow only to be confronted by a locked door or to find yourself back where you started.

The front of the house combines mock-medieval and mock-Tudor with autocratic assurance. Round and square towers, and even an unexpected cupola, rear themselves above the steeply sloping roof and the mullioned stone front and gabled porch. Half-way up a wing, a bridge-like passage with Gothic windows suddenly emerges, leading to the largest, most aggressive tower of all, planted above a circular sweep of crenellated wall. One storey of the main tower is taken up with a chapel, and above, in the pointed spire, ringed with dormer windows, is a room from which the Lord of Horsley could survey every

part of the seventy-three acres of his domain. Rumour says that old Lord Lovelace spent much time in that tower room, watching with a merciless eye everything that went on, and bitterly resenting any interruption. I felt a guilty intruder myself as I unlocked a back door into the house and, after wandering through a series of monastic-looking pantries, found myself at last at the foot of the wide shallow oak staircase and, passing many familiar doors framed in moulded plaster garlands "in the regency style", stood once more in the great hall. The last time I had been there, a huge log fire had hissed in the carved fireplace, cheerful and frivolous people were having tea round it, someone was playing "You can't have the key to *my* cellar" on a grand piano, and Tom Sopwith was hopping from end to end of its stone floor on a pogo stick.

Now it was empty—silent and impressive in the early dusk—I could not imagine that anyone had ever dared to interrupt the Lovelace possession. The Lovelace crests and shields were inlaid in stained glass in the tall windows, in coloured tiles on the walls; family mottoes were gilded on the vaulted oak beams, so high you had to climb into the organ loft to decipher them.

The first and most significant that caught my eye was "Crede Byron". I remembered how Lady Caroline Lamb had had "Ne Crede Byron" engraved on her servants' buttons. Certainly the shadow of Byron scandals still lies across Horsley Towers. There must have been moments when the irascible Lord Lovelace cursed the day he had married Byron's daughter and when his sensitive and harassed son Ralph cursed the Byron blood in his veins. Lord Lovelace quarrelled violently not only with his wife's mother, but with his own three children of his first marriage. Ada's proficiency in mathematics led her to invent an "infallible" betting system by which she lost a great deal of money. Lady Byron paid her daughter's debts, but Lord Lovelace never spoke to his mother-in-law again. The elder son, Byron Noel King, Viscount Ockham, forced by his father to go back to sea after a first voyage which had disillusioned him, deserted his ship, arrived home ill and penniless, and died young, disowned by the old Earl. But it was on the younger, Ralph, that the Byron heredity weighed most heavily. He too seems to have been in disfavour with his autocratic father and he was brought up by his grandmother, Lady Byron. Fearing that Byron's wildness might reappear in his grandson, she had the boy educated in strict seclusion and under puritanical discipline. Two years after her death, Mrs. Beecher Stowe's revelation of Byron's relations with his half-sister, Augusta Leigh, caused one of the stormiest scandals of the nineteenth century. The second Lord Lovelace, torn between horror at the thought of the family secret being revealed to the public and desire to vindicate his grandmother whom her enemies accused of having maliciously fabricated the whole story, finally felt it his duty to publish evidence of the incest in a privately printed book *Astarte*. It was a painful duty and an ineffably wearisome one, involving much collecting and collating of documents, endless faulty bickerings and agonizing exposure for a man who had been brought up to avoid his kind and whose only real pleasure was climbing Alps.

What will become of Horsley Towers? Few people nowadays can afford to keep up its feudal state. Until recently, it was a girls' school. The only traces that it had ever passed out of the first Lord Lovelace's hands that I could find, were scraps torn from old exercise books, a few names pencilled in the belfry—and one other. Someone, optimistic or ironical, had rechristened three of the rooms "Sympathy", "Companionableness" and "Tolerance". ANTONIA WHITE

Horsley Towers

LIVES OF GREAT MEN ALL REMIND US...
Literary Pilgrimages by
H.K. and M.M.

2.—Monsieur Wortsworth's Great-Great-Granddaughter

MADAME BLANCHET lives in Paris near the Rue Wagram, in a commodious flat, twilit and sequestered. She is elderly, grey-haired and serene, and we thought we detected a suggestion of Wordsworth in her brow and eyes as we sat talking to her about him and Annette Vallon and their daughter Caroline, her great-grandmother.

Caroline, she said, was remembered long after her death for her gaiety and vivacity, in this taking more after her mother than her father. " He seems to have been sad even when he was young," she said, and showed us a pencil drawing of Wordsworth which he had given to Annette. The face was certainly neither gay nor vivacious.

Madame Blanchet had no portrait of Annette, but she had seen one, a miniature which had been lost. "She was not good-looking, but intelligent and so courageous," Madame Blanchet said, and we reflected that Annette needed all her courage and intelligence, left by the author of *The Excursion* to bring up their baby through the grim years of the French Revolution and the First Empire. "She was extremely devout," Madame Blanchet said, showing us Annette's prayer book, the fly-leaf covered with her firm irregular handwriting and inside a carefully cut-out picture of Louis XVI, on the back of which was written "Mort, Decembre 1793" —a relic of Annette's royalist sympathies and hatred of the Revolution.

We were also shown a copy of the *Lyrical Ballads*, sent to Annette by Wordsworth. "I've never read it myself," Madame Blanchet said, turn-ing over the pages. "I don't know any English. Some of his poems have been translated into French, but . . ." She shrugged her shoulders, and we hurriedly imagined a translation—

"Il y avait un temps quand les prés, les plantations, les ruisseaux, la terre et chaque spectacle vulgaire . . ."

"We often used to wonder why he left her," Madame Blanchet said, "when she loved him so devotedly; especially as it seems he had " un sens moral très developpé". We suggested rather diffidently that it was his passionate love of England which made him reluctant to marry a foreigner. "I think," Madame Blan-chet said gently but firmly, "that if he had asked her, Annette would have gone over to England with Caroline and made a home there."

"All the same," she went on, "there was no feeling of bitterness on Annette's part or Caroline's. Caroline was devoted to her father, and often spoke about him."

We remembered Wordsworth's visit to Calais with Dorothy to tell Annette that he was going to be married, and how he had walked by the sea with his nine year old daughter, now seen for the first time, and had commemorated this walk in a sonnet which made generous allowance for the fact that the child's moral sense was not yet as fully developed as the father's:

" Dear Child! dear Girl! that walkest with me here,
If thou appear untouched by solemn thought,
Thy nature is not therefore less divine . . ."

Madame Blanchet showed us a number of documents in which Word-sworth's name occurred—Caroline's marriage and birth certificate, a petition to Louis XVIII enumerating all Annette had done for the Royalist cause during Napoleon's reign. They treated Wordsworth's name and habitat in the carefree hit-or-miss French fashion where foreign names are con-cerned—Mr. Williams of Rydalmount near Kindal; W. Wortsworth; Wil-liams Wordsworth, propriétaire, Gras-ner Kendan, Duchy of Westermor-land; and M. Williams.

"It remains in a sense a mystery," said Madame Blanchet, reverting to Wordsworth's abandonment of Ann-ette, "but of course he was a poet." She said this tolerantly: we felt how enigmatic he must appear to a French lady, this Englishman with the wide choice of names, who wrote poetry and had a highly-developed moral sense.

As we walked away, our thoughts went back to Wordsworth and Annette sitting over a French grammar in Orleans a hundred and forty-five years ago; she four years older than he, spontaneous, romantic, not good-looking, and he shaken out of his native prudence by the new ideas of the Revolution and the ardour of a girl in a foreign land. He had loved her for a time, had been, in his own words, "a man too happy for morta-lity". But his love was not deep-rooted, she was alien to his life, he could not envisage her in "Les Lakes". Even the fact that she had never been able to realize that his name was William, not "Williams", must have seemed to him of ill augury. So, after a period of wretchedness and inde-cision, he had abandoned all thought of marrying her. But he had not the can-dour to cut his moral losses; the deserter became a prig, the deserted kept her kindliness and courage, married their child off to a good husband, enter-taining a hundred guests to the wedding breakfast, and in her last years worked in a public department in some small job. "In the year 1841, on the 10th January," the death register records, "died in Paris, Boulevard des Filles du Calvaire, Marie Anne Vallon, known as Williams, an employee, aged seventy-five years. Spinster."

MID NIGHT FOLLY

Round the London Cabarets

By Patrick Balfour

Supper-Class Fun

ONCE there was an upper class. Today it is a supper class. The upper class, on its lower evenings, used to go to the music-halls, where it got drunk at marble-topped tables in surroundings of gilded extravagance and witnessed, as an end in itself, a variety entertainment. The supper class decorously swallows its champagne and its *suprème de volaille* in surroundings of lalique and steel, with a periodic interruption from a distilled and abridged synthesis of the same entertainment, called cabaret. The latter is no longer an end in itself, but a diversion from the primary exercise of dancing. As such, however, it is still most successful when it is broadest and least sophisticated, when it most approximates to its parent music-hall. Its most popular items are still the legs of ladies, the low comedian (suitably Mayfairized), the acrobat, the knockabout clown and the conjuror who used to perform at children's parties.

Only the LONDON CASINO has done a wholesale adaptation of the music-hall principle to the cabaret medium. It provides a full-length music-hall spectacle through which you can eat a full-length dinner or a full-length supper and carry on, if you wish, a full-length conversation without anybody objecting. The show is a London version of the Folies Bergères and, if you dispense with opera-glasses, as nude. It combines the minimum of intellectual pretensions with the maximum of entertainment for the tired business man or the reader of *London Life*. No

expense has been spared, and the undress of the nudes embodies an appropriate profusion of fur, feather and fin. There is no nonsense about art in its décor, which is often extravagantly effective. The best scene is a Disneyish representation of the bottom of the sea, where the costumes are inspired by the aquarium at the Zoo, a lot of nudes swing across the stage in a giant fish-net, and a negro dancer, who is a friend of Mr. Geoffrey Gorer's, opens an oyster to reveal the nudest nude of all. The can-can is quite up to Bal Tabarin standards, there is a comedian who draws funny things on blackboards and acrobats who throw a member of the audience about the stage. In the intervals everyone dances. It is a pity that London's non-stop variety houses cannot combine their entertainment with similar facilities for eating, drinking and dancing in the audience.

The girls at the DORCHESTER provide a less showy but more accessible version of the same sort of entertainment, without the décor. Each one is as mouth-watering as anything in Fortnum and Mason's. The joints are of the very best quality. In one number they are dressed up like ostriches in red gloves. There is also a clown with a large valise and extensive changes of costume and a conjuror who borrows things from the audience.

GROSVENOR HOUSE provides a more elaborate and more cynical entertainment, in the form of a "Beauty Circus". A compère like a stage Lord Castlerosse introduces "the most expensive collection of beasts ever seen in Park Lane", and continues to mumble wisecracks at their expense. The

beasts are the Georgie Hale Glamour Girls, and the glamour shines white and firm between the suspenders. There is Pansy the Panther and Cissie the Seal and Tallula the Tiger and Baby Doll. The latter, and most intelligent, is a four-footed pony, in diamanté girths, which blows whistles, counts up to seven, shuts boxes, steals handkerchiefs, puts its tongue out, does addition sums in its head and finally goes to bed, alone, on the stage. There is a clown with a zip banana and an exploding guitar, and the whole entertainment provides plenty of value for hard provincial cash.

The MAYFAIR dishes up a more bucolic cup of tea—some Tyrolean yokels from Kitzbüchel. Their shirts are open at the neck, their sleeves are rolled above the elbow, their leather shorts are nice and short and nice and dirty (is it butter or motor grease?), their knees are knobbly and sunburnt and they have frank Nordic smiles. They sing hiking choruses and play cow-bell symphonies. They have brought along a couple of buxom Tyrolese barmaids with whom they do rather decorous dances. With each other their horseplay is more sophisticated—notably a spanking dance, when they get between each other's legs and spank each other on the shorts. Each yokel then selects a member of the English county families from the audience and dances a special sort of Tyrolese dance with her. It is all very jolly and uninhibiting, like the crew being allowed up into the first class on a gala night, and those members of the county families who were at Kitzbüchel for the ski-ing join knowingly and inexpertly in the dance, with each other.

The TRIANON has a comedian-about-town, in a white tie and tails. The point about him is that he can talk in so many different accents. "Creouch deown, sceouts, there's a ceow on the deown." "Oi dun it an' cut 'er up." He recites about a "retaired major at the seasaide", tells "quite the cleanest Little Audrey joke you've ever heard", and ends by misquoting a Ruthless Rhyme. It must in fairness be added that he keeps on explaining that his jokes are not really funny.

CINEMA

Another Lost Horizon

SNUG in the tame leopard-skin seats and gilded belly of the new Odeon cinema, as one watched Anthony Hope's perfect and improbable romance being flattened out on the screen, it was natural to wonder what lack of quality it is that makes this latest version of *The Prisoner of Zenda* so inferior to the original. It's a poor lavish film and, as always, blame for this falls—reading from bad to worst—on the acting, the studio script, and the direction.

Good acting will improve a film and may even save it as entertainment, but without all that is meant by good direction—itself a composite affair in this curiously conglomerate art of the cinema—a film is not worth a critic's time or the public's money. Here the director has shown respect but no feeling for a flamboyant minor classic. And by now the star of *The Lost Horizon* is well advanced in the third phase of his course: he began entirely in the dark as to how to act—when he was easier to watch than in his second stage of trying manfully hard; finally he has acquired a shining technique for appearing to undergo a whole galaxy of emotions: armed now with gestures, timing, tones and an expression against every heroic emergency. We were not surprised that, as Rupert of Hentzau, Douglas Fairbanks, Jr., who stood head and shoulders above the rest of a distinguished cast, should have taunted Rassendyll about his old school tie: often Mr. Colman's voice exactly echoed Herbert Marshall's. But the dumb pathos of the latter's playing is true at least to a true-blue type: Mr. Colman's Rassendyll, in this prize Ruritanian romance, was wholly false —the purest Westphalian ham.

The Prisoner of Zenda itself hasn't dated. Yet no doubt what's wrong with this Selznick International picture is that the escapism of its romance, despite its properly far-fetched form, is half-hearted. The story will do as a daydream still, as it served Hope's public, but the dialogue, to make it a more fashionable escape from the everyday, has been rendered synthetic in the usual style of inarticulate redundancy (" But you don't *understand*—he wants the *throne*"). The mirror which the films prefer to hold up not to nature but to our desires is brightest when it's a distorting mirror, and good and grotesque. Conventional romance, in its correct unconventional disguise, has become the fairly flexible backbone of the slapstick movies, like *Double Wedding*, which have pace and absurdity. For poetry in pictures there's hardly a hope outside the documentaries, just as the documentary directors always claim. They've cornered the romance of routine, and they make a fine thing of it. Strand Films, for instance, are celebrating the new Empire Air Mail rates with a swift and stirring little travel-film which takes you, with maps, commentary and music, from Southampton to Sydney, over the Mediterranean, the Persian Gulf, Bangkok, Bali. . . . Lighting gaspers in the desert, pilots refreshed by a nice cup of tea, sailing smoothly over dancers and jungles, carrying letters to sweethearts, maharajahs, and cattlemen—in its sights and its sound *The Future is in the Air* has meaning, beauty, interest. Another fine British documentary, better even than *Night Mail*.

Calling themselves Contemporary Historians—a good title to take— Joris Ivens and Ernest Hemingway have produced a very moving and noble documentary in *Spanish Earth*. Ivens made a first-class film of the damming of the Zuyder Zee: here his camera reports on the defence of Madrid against Franco's attack; shows life behind the lines—but on Madrid's only life-line—at Fuentedueña by the Valencia road; sees death in the streets, planes in the sky, tanks in the open, snipers in the ruins, work in the fields, slogans on the walls. Little has been cut from this film—so far as I can tell, only one unimportant shot, one important sequence, and one absurd remark: each concerning foreign intervention, on the Nationalist side. Intervention on the Government side is tacitly or openly illustrated in a dozen different shots. *Spanish Earth* is partisan certainly, but hardly propagandist. It's incomparably better than the Civil War films we've seen in London. Hemingway's commentary has genuine dramatic value and—equally good—is not obtrusive ; unlike the heroic accompaniment of bugles in the Jarama battle-scenes, which makes them so much less effective than the echoing shots in the shattered buildings of the University City. Most horrible of all: the jerking, begging hands of a woman in a bombed street. The Future and its suicide are in the air. . . . Every inch of this film, shot by shot, has of course its exact parallel on the Nationalist side.

JOHN MARKS

★

THE NEW ORDER

Clerks and typists end their toil
And don eccentric clothes to go
For coffee at the Café Royal
(Only ninepence each, you know),
And they romanticize their lives,
Weirdly garbed, in Soho dives,
Posing as Miss So-and-So,
A poetess from Pimlico,
Or, incognito, " Mr. J ",
An artist sent by *Night and Day*.
This faction in fantastic suits
With females smoking black cheroots
Is not, as you might think, the seamier
Side of London's gay Bohemia,
Nor dress reformists, ism cranks,
But honest city men from banks
And office girls, who hope to be
Described as Wits from Bloomsbury.
The bona-fide artists wear
Their fifty-shilling suits with care
And even budding poets dress
Aided by a trouser-press ;
For now that fast decreasing few,
Who once above this realm held sway,
Like Gusty John and Wyndy Lew,
Are seen no more ; gone with their
day !   DEREK NEAME

DIARY OF PERCY PROGRESS

By John Betjeman

4—THE BUSINESS MAN'S YULE

"MOVE with the times" is what I say and if you don't move with the times the times will move without you. I'd like to see that motto, suitably embellished, hanging in the office of every business man and woman throughout the world. There are certain things which are anachronistic like the Lord Mayor's Procession, the old churches and houses which still clutter up some of our towns, the lack of progress in the countryside, Saint's Days—these are all anachronistic. But the anachronisticest (if I may coin a word) thing of all is Christmas. In these days we cannot afford to waste time giving each other presents. Time is money; so are presents. I for one cannot afford it.

Of course, with my vast business connections, I have to give away a certain amount of Yuletide Gifts, but these I put down to the firm's account. Local surveyors, building and sanitary inspectors need a dozen of whiskey each, if I am to get round them during the coming year. For this purpose I go to a little man I know in Soho who dilutes whiskey and re-corks the diluted mixture in bottles bearing the labels of well-known firms. By this means I save 50 per cent. on the cost of real whiskey. Town-councillors and other amenable recipients need cigars and for this purpose I go to another little man who specializes in Business Men's Yuletide Gifts. He can fit up twopenny cigars with the bands of a good brand and pack them in the box of a high-class firm and let me have the whole outfit for 2s. 6d. Then there are little personal tokens it is necessary to give away to high-class clients or potential clients who appreciate a good thing, and who might suspect my whiskey and cigar gifts, not that they have any real cause for suspecting me. "It's the spirit of the gift that matters," I say, not the gift itself. Still these people are so touchy, it does not do to offend them.

This year I have hit on rather a novelty gift for my higher class clients I have had my head modelled in a substance obtained from condensed milk which comes out very cheap by the ton. The model was done from a photograph by the Nu-photosculpt Process and it stands about nine inches high. Owing to the shape of my head, it has been possible to make the scalp lift on a hinge to reveal an inkpot. The whole bust is washed over art bronze and I have had the following inscription written in my own handwriting on the base : "*In the hope that the cordial reciprocity of the past will redound to our mutual co-operation in the future.—Percy Progress.*"

You will understand that an art-novelty gift of this sort, an improvement to a desk in the most luxurious home, let alone office, costs at least 3s. per head and I do not wish to spend money unnecessarily on my office staff, who get reasonable wages anyhow.

Now this is why I dislike Christmas. It has unfortunately grown into a custom that we have a staff Christmas party, generally in the King Edward VII Rooms at the Hotel Caryatid, N.W.17, though we've

'*After all, Miss Peploe, it's a pleasure cruise.*'

now obtained a more reasonable quotation from the Chemical Catering Co. who supply a very decent room in Tudor style but a little less centrally situated.

In giving this advice on the Business Yule, I wish to repeat the story of a disaster which occurred last year at our staff party and lost us a valuable client. Perhaps I had better commence at the commencement, as the poet hath it.

The staff, of course, like the firm's Christmas party and look forward to it. You and I, who have had the advantages of a public school education—I'm an old Cag Bag (Carshaltonian) myself—  know how trivial these affairs are, compared with a spin down to Maidenhead cuddled up to a platinum cutie in the back seat or a binge in a roadhouse or any other of the really gay doings of the upper classes. Still it gives the members of our staff pleasure.

Unfortunately, when we made the subscription to the Firm's Christmas Party voluntary, not enough of the staff subscribed to make it an economical proposition. Now we levy a tax on their wages and far more turn up. I think it is useful in promoting office camaraderie and solidarity, if you know what I mean. With the money stopped out of wages we can generally make the Christmas Party pay, though we don't, of course, reckon to make a big profit. After all, it is, in a way, a Yuletide Gift. Indeed I go so far myself as to make a little present with my own personal compliments to every lady present. I generally reckon not to spend more than 3d. per head.

Well, last year through a pal I acquired some shares in a company for making imitation amber cigarette holders. These products are a high-class novelty article with all the appearance of real amber. They are made of a composition, discovered after careful tests in our laboratories,

consisting of egg powder and paraffin wax baked into a hard substance. The cost of each holder works out at $\frac{3}{4}d$. Carefully marketed, they yield up to 2,000 per cent. profit.

I obtained four dozen of these holders at cost price with a proviso that I could return any not wanted.

I was fortunate in obtaining as guest of honour to our party a lady Mayoress of my borough (Mutual Co-operative Reform) from whom I was expecting large concessions in my speculative building concerns. After making a speech in which I, as chairman, welcomed the staff and their lady friends or wives (laughter) on this auspicious occasion and regretted that this year it was impossible owing to the slump to give a bonus (applause) but hoped that their mutual co-operation in the coming year would promote the well being of the firm in the future (applause) by increasing that goodwill not only with outside hours but also among one another (laughter) especially on such a festive occasion as this when our hearts were lit by the Yule Log of Good Fellowship which we had great pleasure in extending to the kind lady (applause) who had done us the honour of being present at a banquet to which we all looked forward and if any of those present wanted drinks they would obtain them at a reasonable figure from any of the stewards and this reminded me of the story of the Englishman, the Scotchman, and the Irishman [I fear this is not printable in your esteemed columns; ask a pal on the Stock Exchange for it] and in conclusion I would like to present a little personal token of friendship and appreciation to every lady present and would those ladies who did not smoke do me the honour of returning the article to the steward at their table (applause).

The presents were then handed out.

The Assistant Accountant thereupon replied on behalf of the staff. Up till now everything had gone well and the cigarette holders were much appreciated, the Lady Mayoress receiving hers first. The Assistant Accountant's speech was long and there were several phrases in it to which I, personally, took exception,

but I need'nt mention them now.

Our honoured guest of the evening was then about to rise to speak. I noticed that her cigarette had burned low in the holder: she took a final puff before rising and her whole head became enveloped in what I can only call a sheet of flames. Owing to the inflammable nature of the paraffin used in the manufacture of these dainty presentation gifts, ignition had occurred from her allowing the cigarette to burn too low in the holder. When the flames subsided, the face of the lady Mayoress was revealed quite black. She is a queenly figure and, I regret to state, her fringe and eyebrows were totally burned off. I am glad to say she suffered no physical injury, but was naturally precluded from addressing us owing to her appearance after the accident. I am sorry to state that certain members of the staff had the bad taste to laugh.

Not only did this fiasco lead to the loss of the mutual goodwill of the lady Mayoress towards yours truly, but it involved the firm of manufacturers, in which, as I have stated, I am a shareholder, in considerable expense. We have been obliged to print a paper band to wrap round the article warning users of the holder not to allow cigarettes to burn low in the receptacle owing to the inflammable nature of the material of which it

is made. This may adversely affect the sales unless we can persuade retailers to remove the band before displaying for sale or unless retailers can persuade customers to do so before giving the holder away to friends.

That is one of the reasons why I have no time for Christmas.

7—The Children's Friend

A Brief Biography of Saint Nicholas

NICHOLAS was born at Smyrna in 265 A.D. His parents were not themselves in affluent circumstances, but the generous intervention of an important member of the growing Christian community in Smyrna opened a religious career to the youthful Nicholas who, at the early age of thirty-two, was appointed Bishop of Myra, in Syria. It has been alleged that he suffered in the so-called persecutions of Christians instituted by the Emperor Diocletian in the early years of the fourth century, but there is no truth in this allegation. His relations with the civil authorities were at that time, as they have since continued to be throughout the changes and chances of an unusually protracted career, entirely cordial. In actual fact Bishop Nicholas was very largely in sympathy with the Emperor's religious policy, which was characterized by severity only in respect of certain extreme sections of Christian opinion. After the death of Diocletian, Nicholas left Myra in response to an invitation to organize education in Alexandria, in which city, the most cultured at that date of all the cities of the Mediterranean littoral, he spent two happy centuries.

During the centuries which followed the break-up of the Roman Empire, Nicholas could not fail to note that the stories connected with his name were giving him a special status, and with that status a special opportunity. How he took pity on three homeless lads and, inviting them into his house, washed them with his own hands, and how on another occasion he saved three young girls from prostitution by a timely gift of money, were tales which by the beginning of the Middle Ages enjoyed a universal currency throughout Christendom. In due course the growing volume of opinion which regarded Nicholas as the guardian of the young and/or helpless was satisfied by the gesture which admitted him into the calendar of Catholic saints. His status in mediæval Europe may be inferred from two facts: in England alone four hundred churches were dedicated to him, and at the other extremity of the Continent he was adopted as the patron saint of Russia. (The narrative may be conveniently broken at this point to explain the attitude towards money early adopted and consistently held by Nicholas. To any and every offer of commissions, shares, or other pecuniary benefits, from building contractors, architects, furriers, manufacturers and vendors of votive offerings, children's toys, sleighs, buskins, etc. etc., he replies and has always replied with a blunt negative. On the other hand he welcomes donations towards his living and travelling expenses, while very properly refusing to regard such gifts as a matter of public interest. "I concern myself only with what I understand," he once said, "and I do not understand balance-sheets.")

At the time of the Reformation Nicholas found himself in a delicate position. The long dark nights of northern Europe had made the Eve of St. Nicholas in the first week of December a very special occasion. Even in the poorest cottages of Scandinavia and northern Germany there was the illuminated tree and some little gifts for the children. But in the sunny countries of southern Europe the giving of presents had never been associated with this feast. And so it had come about that Nicholas was more often to be found in the north of Europe than in the south. Was he now to sever his connection with the Reformed North? It was an anxious and painful time. He had enemies in Rome who did not fail to put an unattractive construction on his preference for northern latitudes, and to suggest that he

should apply for admission to the Lutheran calendar of saints, where he would find himself in congenial company. Hastening to Rome, Nicholas conciliated his most important enemies and was permitted, in consideration of the non-sectarian nature of his activities, to return to the north, on two conditions: the illuminated tree and the presents were to be transferred to Christmas Day, and his connection with this, as with all other heretic celebrations, was to be of a scrupulously unofficial kind.

It was not till the fifth decade of the nineteenth century that Nicholas paid his first visit to post-Reformation England. The time, he felt, was ripe to reconcile religious sentiment to Christmas Day, which since the Reformation, and indeed prior to it, had been little else than an occasion for pagan merriment and feasting, as Herrick's verses testify :

Come, bring with a noise,
My merry, merry boys,
The Christmas log to the firing,
While my good dame, she
Bids ye all be free,
And drink to your heart's desiring.

To a Christmas Day celebrated in this style Puritan opinion was, inevitably, deeply hostile. A writer during the Commonwealth stigmatized Christmas as "the Multitude's Idle Day, Satan's Working Day, and the True Christian's Fasting Day"; and while this attitude was modified after the political overthrow of the Puritans, Christmas Day was still regarded with mistrust by the sober and industrious middle classes until well into the nineteenth century. Meanwhile, in country districts it continued to be celebrated in the old style, though, owing to the increased virtue of the squirearchy, with a seemliness unknown to earlier centuries, as Washington Irving testifies in *Bracebridge Hall,* 1819, where he pictures a group of villagers entertained by the local squire—"The squire himself mingled among the rustics and was received with awkward demonstrations of deference and regard. The bashfulness of the guests soon gave way before good cheer and affability. There is something genuine and affectionate in the gaiety of the lower orders, when excited by the bounty and familiarity of those above them."

It was in the early forties of the nineteenth century, shortly after the marriage of Queen Victoria to Prince Albert, that Nicholas introduced the Christmas tree, with its attendant presents, to the English nation. "The German form of celebrating Christmas by an illuminated tree," he wrote in a pamphlet which had a wide circulation, "has long been well known to a few in England; especially to persons in any way connected with the old court. It now seems likely to become a naturalized plant. It is capable of adaptation to English national habits; and in less than a quarter of a century it will probably be familiar to all lovers of domestic observances, suggesting those feelings of 'peace and goodwill' among men, which it is the paramount duty of all to cultivate."

Never was a prophecy more amply fulfilled. The mingling of piety and festivity adumbrated in this pamphlet struck a chord which echoed throughout Victorian England, and within a few years the Christmas Tree, with its attendant presents, illuminated every home in the land, from the highest to the humblest. In estimating the influences which produced this happy result, the contribution of Charles Dickens cannot be overlooked. His *Christmas Books,* and notably *A Christmas Carol,* powerfully reinforced the mission undertaken by Nicholas. But they were only a reinforcement. In actual fact, Dickens was a continuator of the pagan tradition of Yule Tide, with, to quote from *A Christmas*

' I can't help feeling proud of our Djan, even though he is a Dictator.'

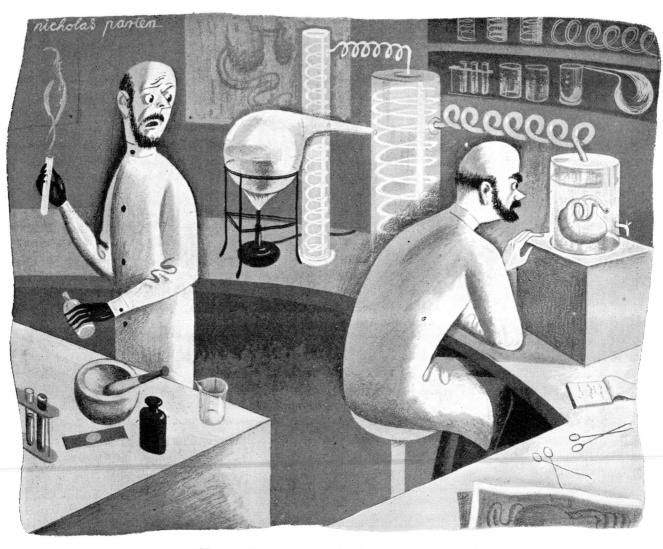

'That's all you ever think about—your stomach.'

*   *   *

Carol, its "holly, mistletoe, red berries, ivy, turkeys, geese, game, poultry, brawn, meat, pigs, sausages, oysters, pies, puddings, fruit, and punch". It is no disparagement to Dickens to say that the more refined and more spiritual note struck by Nicholas was outside his compass, and that his appeal was rather to the lower orders than to the more affluent section of the community which was the first to respond to the note sounded by Nicholas. It may be convenient at this point to state that, in spite of many irresponsible suggestions to the contrary, Nicholas has never had other than purely personal relations with those gifted writers who in the course of the last hundred years have specially devoted themselves to the celebration of childhood. He has been the honoured guest and friend of Charles Dickens and Victor Hugo. The author of *Peter Pan* had no more ardent admirer than Nicholas, and the letter which Nicholas wrote to Mr. A. A. Milne on a first reading of *Winnie the Pooh* is among Mr. Milne's most treasured possessions.

For America, where he is affectionately known as "Santa Claus", a name popularized in England towards the close of the nineteenth century, but now again yielding to the dearer appellation of "Father Christmas", Nicholas has a warm regard. But the place which England holds in his heart is unassailable by any other land. He is still a great traveller, and will wear a steel helmet in Berlin, a black shirt in Rome, or a bowler hat in Moscow with perfect address. But he is always happiest in England.

15.—CLAUS AND EFFECT

IN "Topsy Turvy Toy Town" at Selfridge's you will see, until December 24, some enormous white footprints leading you through a maze of crazy conceits, fantastic models of super- and sub-humans and an upside-down village. These footprints do not belong to The Abominable Snowman and they are inscribed, appropriately enough, "FOLLOW IN HIS FOOTSTEPS". You dare not turn back, for at the end of it all on his throne is Father Christmas presiding, as only Mr. Titman knows how, over the mass distribution of gifts from a series of pigeon-holes marked in order: BABIES. GIRLS UNDER 7. GIRLS OVER 7. BOYS UNDER 7. BOYS OVER 7.

Mr. Titman is not merely Father Christmas, he has been Santa Claus for sixty-one years. Since, in fact, the age of 17 when, while playing at the Opera House, Malta, he was persuaded by the humble Maltese equivalent of Selfridge's to assume the Yuletide scarlet. Since then he has been Father Christmas all over the world, in such places as Alexandria, Buenos Aires and Bombay, where apparently the Christmas spirit is less expansive than in Oxford Street. At Selfridge's he presides for two months, compared with the slight three weeks of his Indian winter. Mr. Titman has arrived at Selfridge's in considerable pomp and circumstance for the past four years, and the circumstances of his pompous arrival are of the utmost importance. Reindeer, of course, are completely démodés. Even last year Whiteley's Father Christmas appeared in the smartest of four-in-hands. And this year Mr. Titman, in his appropriate disguise, anticipated his less favoured rivals by landing at the end of October in an aeroplane. He says that he prefers air to sea travel, but really likes railways best.

It is not easy to be Father Christmas: some people appear to think that one only needs some gum, cotton wool and a red cassock to do the trick. They generally frighten children into hysterics and probably give them complexmas for the rest of their tender lives. No doubt that is the psychological reason why Chico, tearing up the contract, tells Groucho Marx: "There ain't no Sanity Clause." We learnt the basic requirements of a Father Christmas last year when somebody approached a Midland Employment Exchange for a dozen professional F.C.'s, stating that "a beaming countenance and a portly figure" were essential; also a pleasant voice and a genuine love of children. Mr. Titman, who is quite the most distinguished and highly paid member of this specialized profession, will tell you that even these exacting qualifications are not enough. No one, he says, is more passionately fond of children than he, but, above that, one must be capable of the greatest tact, of ready

conversation and humour and, most important of all, must be a genuine actor.

In the last respect Mr. Titman can claim the fullest experience, for he has been in theatre since he made his first stage appearance at the old Philharmonic, Islington, at the age of 7. He has been in public-house cabaret, fairground shows, circus, music-hall, the legitimate, and films. In what he calls his Pepper's Ghost days he earned his living on his back behind the phantascope. He can show you a telegram from Ivor Novello, commemorating his success as the Gipsy King in *Glamorous Night*. He has been the Dame in numerous pantomimes. But it is on celluloid that he has scored most of his recent successes. Do you remember him with Anna Neagle in *The Three Maxims*? Or as the Queen's coachman in *Victoria the Great*? He is an intense admirer of Anna Neagle ("the finest film actress we have") and, particularly of "dear old" Sybil Thorndike ("the dearest woman I've ever met on the stage").

With all this as his background, one can hardly doubt his success in the highly skilled rôle of Father Christmas. His work is arduous: an average of 12,000 children and parents pass through his "show" during each working day. On his throne punctually at 9 in the morning he maintains a one-man act until 2, starts again about 3.30 until 5.30, and, after about half-an-hour's tea interval, continues until 7. Lest his juvenile audiences should be disappointed he has an understudy who "doubles" in his absence. During the busy hours, which seem to include most of the day, he has to keep people moving and, in the benign way that we all expect from Father Christmas, disperse the insistent throngs that press in on him. Add to that the atmosphere, the heavy make-up, luxuriant beard and wig, amply furred cloak and hood, and you may not be surprised to know that he has to squeeze out his underclothes two or three times a day.

Yet he has some consolations. There is the fan mail: such a large fan mail that he has asked us not to give his private address. Just write c/o Selfridge's, he says, for he received 150 letters at his North London home one day—with 3d. to pay on each. There were a lot of requests for toys, and

most of them came from Scotland. "Any proposals?" we queried, but he shook his head and added "But I've had a lot of quiet hints." We then learnt that he is still a bachelor, "probably the only bachelor Father Christmas." And then there are the more precocious children who do a Lear Act on him, pulling at his beard and saying loudly: "That's not real. You are *not* Father Christmas." Or the anxious moment when in the middle of the pressing crowd his vision is suddenly blacked-out by the rather sticky face of a baby whose invisible mother is pleading: "Kiss Barbara." But most children fall for him right away and utter such charming whimsies as "Please, Santa Claus, will you bwing

me a bone for my doggie?"

On the other hand he is always liable to come up against less Barrie-esque little girls, like the one this year who brazenly produced a long shopping list of the things she required, beginning with a motor-car. He listened patiently, catechized her as to whether she was a good little girl, went to bed early, ate her dinner. The affirmatives came as convincingly and naively as from any divorce court witness-box. "Then," says Father Christmas, "you shall have all those lovely things, my dear." She turns on her incipient high heel and he hears her say to her parents (whom she's been playing up anyway)—"The flaming old liar."

Poor Mr. Titman.

'The guard, sir? Yes, sir, the man over there in the uniform.'

THE SHOCKER SHOCKED

WALTER DE LA MARE

The fire had fall'n to a drowsier heat ;
But cold lay body ; cold was its guest.
He wiped the knife on the tumbled
    sheet,
Rinsed off the blackening blood, and
    dressed.
He smashed the cheap watch beneath
    his feet ;
Flung out the clothes from the
    stained-deal chest ;
Stole letters, mock pearls from a key-
    less drawer—
Then listened, engrossed, while in
    the street
A constable passed on his midnight
    beat :
Paused, still to listen ; then opened
    the door ;
Drew off his gloves, prayed, wiped his
    face,
And stared at the moonshine, bleak
    and frore,
Curdling small snow now wanly at
    rest.

A wind from the east, as he turned
    west
Palsied his bones in a naked embrace ;
And an Imp—fallen mute for an hour
    and more—
Mocked : " Strange, is it not, that
    never before
Have we woven a plot on a similar
    case ! "

★

" A penny for your thoughts, Mr. Winn," a voice broke in. I came out of my reverie to discover that there was a girl standing a few feet away from me also leaning over the stone balustrade . . . " I hope you didn't mind my butting in, but I couldn't help recognizing you. Did you want to be alone ? "

I shook my head. " Not particularly."

Then, since that didn't sound very gracious, I went on quickly to tell her what had been in my thoughts, to tell her all about Sibelius, and how he is the only great modern composer whose talent has been nationally recognised so that he receives State protection.—*Godfrey Winn in the* DAILY MIRROR.

Oh well, it makes a change from the golf bore.

by Edward A. Bunyard.

The Christmas Dinner

EVERY human man and not a few psychologists have noted the surprising change that comes over our womenkind towards the end of November. Faces once wreathed in smiles are no longer so, care has engraved its harsh lines upon them. Conspiratorial meetings, purely female, take place at which papers, too large to be betting slips, pass from hand to hand.

Long have I pondered over this seasonal anxiety, what can it portend?

A married friend has solved the puzzle for me and like most puzzles the solution is humiliatingly simple. It seems that this is the time when Christmas puddings are engendered and confected. Raisin and currant growers have, for a year, been working to this end and every blare known to publicity merchants has been well and truly blared.

Our unfortunate women, strung to the brink of nervous breakdown, capitulate and succumb.

Do they want Christmas pudding? Of course not, no modern woman dares look a pudding in the face. And their husbands? Certainly not at such a price. " A piece of cheese, my dear, will do me very well." And the children? Well, it is quite time children were taught the rudiments of wise feeding and not initiated into the grosser manners of the Middle Ages.

Great occasions, from of old it is true, have been celebrated by great feasts, but we hear little of the indigestions of Merrie England. If great

occasions today were celebrated by *good* feeding, and if such feeding itself were regarded as a great occasion, our children would learn a useful lesson.

And if the pudding goes, what of the turkey?

Let it go too, it is an over-rated fowl, neither its risky and laborious upbringing or its mealy monotony are worthy of the extravagant price it demands. Who would not welcome the abolition of that awful aftermath of Christmas — cold turkey, with its gaunt architecture becoming more anatomical as day follows day ? A meal in the macabre museum of the Royal College of Surgeons would be as cheerful.

Away with them both, and let us reconsider Christmas in the light of our own day, not that of the twelfth century. The board which knows no groan can still be festive, and a joint or a bird we can discuss and dismiss from our thoughts removes the deadly apprehension of the days to come. Let us spread out our good will and our good food over a longer period and with a little practice (who knows?) we might finally stretch them over the whole year and escape that tornado of Christmas food and feeding which sweeps so many weaker vessels to destruction.

MANXMEN CAN'T SWEAR

There are no swear words in the Manx language, Admiral William Spencer Leveson Gower, Governor of the Isle of Man, was told yesterday when he was welcomed to the island in the Manx language by Mr. T. J. Reubens, Chairman of Ramsey Town Council.—*Daily Mirror.*

What sort of a welcome did he expect, anyway ?

LIVES OF GREAT MEN ALL REMIND US...
Literary Pilgrimages by
H.K. and M.M.

3.—Bert in the Davidson Road

WE found our way with some difficulty to the Davidson Road School from East Croydon Station, passing between rows of little houses, new fifty years ago but now already part of the past. The Davidson Road School serves this district. Put up at the beginning of the century, it is a red brick building with many windows and without the Victorian steeple, and has small classrooms and separate desks instead of long benches. D. H. Lawrence taught here from 1908 to 1913.

As we approached the school, we pictured Lawrence walking down Davidson Road just before nine, irritably quickening his pace when he heard the school bell ringing, arriving just in time for prayers and a hymn, leading his class into the classroom, starting off with scripture, and so on to arithmetic, geography, singing and the other subjects included in the curriculum laid down by the Board of Education. In the afternoon there would be drill in the asphalt playground marked out for basket-ball, Lawrence calling out "Knees bend! Arms upwards raise! Forward lunge!" No beard as yet, but already sandals.

M. M.: Did he hate these little houses, this red-brick school?

H. K.: Not more than he hated Cornwall, Sardinia, Mexico, Australia, Nottingham and Capri.

During his five years in Croydon Lawrence lodged with Mr. Jones, the School Attendance Officer. We called on Mr. Jones, now retired, and talked about Lawrence with him over tea. Lawrence, Mr. Jones said, was conscientious about his teaching, but hated it. The boys liked him, though; he

was good with children, and when Hilda, Mr. Jones's daughter, was six months old, Lawrence used to walk her up and down the passage exclaiming: "You *shall* walk! You *shall* walk!"

Mr. Robertson, the Inspector, an elderly Scotsman, and somewhat pompous, did not like Lawrence. When he came into Lawrence's classroom and all the children stood up, saying "Good morning, sir", Lawrence used to scowl and would not "sir" him.

He was strong enough physically, did his daily dozen in the bathroom each morning, but already had trouble with his chest. Most men considered him rather effeminate, but there was something about him which appealed to women. Some of them, his particular friends, used to call him Bert, but to men he was always Lawrence. He was devoted to his mother and became very morose after her death at the end of 1910, but had nothing good to say about his father. It was really horrible the way he spoke about him, Mr. Jones said.

Most evenings he wrote, sitting with a pad on his knee in front of the fire, and finished *Sons and Lovers* and *The White Peacock* while he was in Croydon. Occasionally he went out, and Mr. Jones particularly remembered one evening when they went together to the Greyhound after a visit to a billiard saloon which Lawrence cut short. At the Greyhound Lawrence asked for absinthe, and got into conversation with a French barmaid there, airing his French.

On Sunday mornings he and Mr. Jones used to paint together, copying from reproductions. One which Lawrence did was of the Greek god

Hermes with a young girl in a wood, some poppies lying about on the ground. Mr. Jones showed us one of Lawrence's paintings, a landscape in oils. Trying to get the clouds right, he had grown impatient and dabbed white paint on with his thumb. The thumb marks still showed clearly. Lawrence and Mr. Jones used to argue a lot, especially about religion, against which Lawrence was very bitter. He easily got worked up, and sometimes used to sit there with his mouth open, so excited he could not say a word.

He smoked very seldom, perhaps five cigarettes a week, and hardly drank at all in the ordinary way. If he did take a glass of Mr. Jones's beer, he insisted on providing a bottle in return. Once his brother, a miner, came on a visit, and Lawrence was patronizing with him. He had lately been taken up by some London writers, and when he came back from a weekend with them he used to speak with a different accent. On one of these occasions Mr. Jones interrupted him with "That's not your usual form of talk"—to which Lawrence haughtily replied: "I don't understand what you mean."

It was one of these weekends which led to his leaving the Davidson Road School. He arrived back on the Sunday evening all-in, apparently suffering from a frightful hang-over. On the Monday morning he tried to get up for school, but could not, developed double pneumonia and nearly died. He went to Bournemouth to convalesce and from there sent in his resignation. Some time later he wrote mysteriously that something had happened which he was not at liberty to divulge. "It was the German lady," Mr. Jones said.

As we walked away, we agreed that these five years, the period between mother and wife, were probably the best years he ever spent.

M. M.: And yet his numerous biographers hardly refer to them.

H. K.: Barren soil from their standpoint, and from his.

M. M.: With Lawrence it had to be either Debrett or the Dark Unconscious.

H. K.: High life or no life, but not the Davidson Road.

AT THE THEATRE

Elizabeth Bowen

Richard III

THIS horrific play about a handicapped person getting even with life—the furious spirit in the impeded body—is kept keyed up to the pitch Shakespeare must have wanted by Mr. Emlyn Williams' ecstatic villainy as Richard. Here is the real crook-artist: evil for evil's sake. In the Elizabethan world it was always ambition that made monsters of people—nowadays it is something more minor and puking: vanity. Thus it is always the villains who are engaged with life up to the hilt: the good characters have a touch of monkish detachment. The villain served the Elizabethan drama better—the good became useful only when they lost their detachment, when they threatened to fall. And we do still love to watch a villain in play.

The characters other than Richard in *Richard III*—except for Richmond (later Henry VII) who is abstract Nemesis—have just the one characteristic: they have no luck. They are unlucky in, however accidentally, coming Richard's way, in even chancing to catch his eye. The men he encounters (till Richmond comes along) put up about as good a show as roosters when the fox is around. The young or younger women are fascinated rabbits, the old women fateful ravens—croaking unheard. On this muddled and un-resisting mass of people, his brother Edward IV's entourage, Richard hurls, with extravagance, his malignant force. How should this make a play? But it does: the card-palace of one man's guilt topples to breathless height—then is sent crashing down. Richard comes to a bad end. But he has had a run for his money: we see him get it. . . . This play's Renaissance character is well kept at the Old Vic: some of the sub-villains—Buckingham, Catesby, Tyrrel—stand out as pretty pieces of actors' work. The production is up to Mr. Guthrie's standard: complex enough in design, but from the front effectively simple-seeming.

Ghosts

Ghosts at the Vaudeville is Miss Marie Ney's evening. She is Mrs. Alving. And it is Mrs. Alving—*her* mind, *her* memory, *her* sense of fate—that distils the horror that brims the Alving parlour—with its bright-

coloured charnel Scandinavian cosiness. That we magnetize our own doom, and then project it ahead of us, that we are stones that, however bravely rolling, are doomed to gather the most dreadful moss, appears to be the message of this Ibsen play. Mrs. Alving, with her cold courage, her deportment, her determination to outface life, is a figure of classic tragedy. Finally, beside her mad son's chair, we leave her whining like an animal run over by a car but not quite killed, as the sun rises on a universe of horror. Only when the last curtain is to drop does Mrs. Alving, or Miss Ney (for the two are fused) allow herself this: up to this, she has shown her strength by a terrific reticence.

The drama is lightened by some domestic, if not comic, relief. In the Vaudeville production, this lighter element is a little over-played. It was a bold idea, but not wholly successful, to make the specious Engstrand talk Cockney. And the girl Regina bounces about too much. Mr. Stephen Murray's Pastor Manders is excellent: he holds his own ground opposite Mrs. Alving. This is a new English version, or "adaptation", of *Ghosts*, and I am not sure that the loosening-up of the dialogue into so many colloquialisms is to the good: at the less high-pressure moments it sounds rather Dodie-Smithish.

Unless your nerves or heart really won't stand a racking evening, you would be exceedingly foolish to miss *Ghosts*. Miss Marie Ney (for less than three weeks, now) is giving us some of the finest acting in London.

It's in the Bag

This revue is the goods. It is quick, alert, intimate, unexpected and bold: it takes off with the rather clumsy precision of an air liner, but hums along loudly, all engines at full power, to its final port. Whoever packed the bag put in a lot of talent. A revue that exhilarates at a matinée

performance, after a sandwich lunch at a non-licensed snack bar (which was this critic's experience, owing to incompetence) can be backed to get across at the normal hour. There is a good deal of physical wit, and the people in it look at once *louche* and spontaneous, which is very winning. They look as though they had been routed out of bed to perform. They have got that kind of insolent self-possession that gets across so well. There is no room to name the artists without being invidious—enough to say that the dim have been excluded.

One or two of the show's æsthetic high points—I suppose no revue is complete without them—are rather chocolate-boxy and seem a pity. The up-to-the-footlights stuff, which needs nerve, is the best. I must commend the high speed at which everything

'Oh, hell! There's Santa Claus.'

happens. It will be interesting to watch the fate of *It's in the Bag* in London. In this our leading provincial city the damp squib goes on sizzling unaccountably long, while the good brisk show too often goes down with all colours flying. *It's in the Bag* deserves double stars as an evening out. If it disappears, it will be a pity. When I was there it showed every sign of prosperity. . . . It might do well to take the tail of one eye off New York —but it must do this without losing its excellent speed.

CINEMA

The Great and the Humble

"FIRST will I question with thee about Hell. . . ." Two films shown last Sunday by the Film Society were enough to shake anyone's complacency or self-pity: they followed each other in the programme with horrifying force: *Land Without Bread*, a five-year-old documentary study of the Hurdanos, a Spanish people inbred, diseased, forgotten, the adjective poor a mockery of their complete destitution, and *Personality Parade*, a deft little dramatisation of one day in the life of Mr. Godfrey Winn.

Land Without Bread is the picture of a pocket of misery in the mountains within a few miles of Burgos—life petering out in the stone crevices; images of awful inertia and more awful patience: a man shaking with fever: the goitred antique face of a woman of thirty-two: a child left in the road three days to die: the little edge of cultivation, a foot or two across, beside the river which will wash it out in the rains: the men trudging to Castile for work and returning without it, bony wrists and hollow chests, incredible rags: dwarf morons cackling at the camera, bobbing empty turnip faces above the rocks: the look of a mother whose baby has just died, shaken by human feeling into something you might take for the shadow of happiness after all those blank faces: the small body carried along stony tracks, up rocks from which we have seen even the goats tumble, pushed across a shallow river on its platter—like a tiny ferry-boat on an ignoble Lethe—until it reaches their only cemetery miles away—a few wood sticks stuck in long grass and weeds. At night between the stone cells, up a street like a crack in parched ground, an old woman walks clapping a death bell. An honest and hideous picture, it is free from propaganda, except for a single shot of a church interior—a couple of cheap statues and a little cheap carving—with some glib sentence about clerical wealth . . . Wealth! one smiles at the word in face of that twopenny interior and wonders whether five years of Republican politics have done so much for these people that one can afford to stop up this one hole they have to creep to for cleanness and comfort.

It's a grotesque world: the morons touching each other with private incommunicable meanings among the rocks, the dying child showing her throat to the cameraman ("We couldn't do anything about it. A few days later we heard she was dead"), and Mr. Winn waking prettily to order, kissing his dog upon the pillow —"the famous Mr. Sponge". "He really lives his page," the commentator remarks, and we watch him, at his country cottage, get into his car ("some flowers and a kiss from his mother"), start for the office. Next he is at work with his secretary, opening letters from readers. A mother writes: will he come and see her new-born baby? "Other things must wait. He will not disappoint her," the commentator tells us, and Mr. Winn kneels by the bed and the baby is introduced to "Uncle Godfrey". After that we are shown Mr. Winn entering a neo-gothic doorway ("He finds time from his engagements to pause at church"), and while the organ peals a voluntary we see in close-up Mr. Winn's adoring face lifted in prayer, sun falling through stained glass on the soft, unformed, first-communion features. Lunch at Quaglino's ("his genius for friendship"), a swim in the Serpentine, tea with a reader in Regent's Park, back to the office for his article, a game of tennis, behind the scenes at the ballet, and so home to mother—"sometimes after twelve o'clock". The commentator sums Mr. Winn up: "At ease with the great and happy with the humble". We have seen him with the great—with M. Quaglino and Mr. Nelson Keys—and we are tempted to imagine him for a moment with the humble. (After all his commentator describes him as a "traveller"—mother waving over the horizon and Mr. Sponge chaperoning him in his berth.) Suppose that among those rocks a correspondent should summon him to see *her* new-born, or new-dead, baby. "He will not disappoint her", and we picture him among those goitred and moron and hunger-tortured faces—the set boyishness, fifth-form diffidence and thinning hair. What message for these from "Uncle Godfrey"? and Mr. Winn's own voice recalls us to the actual screen: "Friendship is the one thing that matters in the end", and the eyes look out at us so innocently, so candidly, so doggily they might really be the eyes of "the famous Mr. Sponge".

GRAHAM GREENE

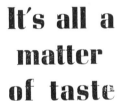

MINUTES OF THE WEEK

Sanctuary

Mr. Winston Churchill has been complaining bitterly about the candid cameraman's insensate urge to immortalize his and other prominent men's uvulæ in action. We string along with him on this (or would, if our gullet had any news value), but feel he might have let the world in on his solution. He was observed by our spies the other morning in one of the town's gilded *boîtes* chatting with a fellow-politician till 4 a.m. It seemed a trifle odd at the time that they should have chosen, for a tête-à-tête conversation, a joint where they were deafened by the band, stamped on by the clientèle, and choked by the atmosphere. But now we know. They were safe from the candid camera. We know that atmosphere. Even a candid camera with an

infra-red ray couldn't pierce the amalgam of smoke, breath, and phoney romance of which it is composed.

Lingua Franca

The chief of the German military advisers who have spoilt most of the old jokes about the Chinese Army is General von Falkenhausen. A distinguished soldier and a military theorist of weight and originality, he went to the Far East as chief of staff on von Seeckt's mission and stayed out there when von Seeckt came home. He naturally sees a good deal of Chiang Kai-shek, but neither can speak the other's language. They get round this by the somewhat incongruous expedient of talking Japanese, von F. having been military attaché in Tokyo and Chiang having been educated in Japan.

This just shows how small the world is, or something.

★

All Round Man

The national motto of Brazil (where we once spent a few laughable months) is *Ordem e Progresso*. When we read of the Fascist coup there—this is just to show you the whimsical way in which our mind works—we fell to working out a crack about *Auden e Progresso*. Our thought-processes soon came to resemble what Scotland Yard cynically calls a Police Division, and we were darned lucky to hit on the current issue of *New Verse*, which is entirely devoted to the poet Auden. "We salute in Auden," says *New Verse*, "the first English poet for many years who is a poet all the way round."

We are awfully glad to hear this about Auden. The vast majority of English poets are not, and have not been for some time, poets all the way round. They know it, too. It partly explains the way they dress. They can't face their tailor's mirrors. The only chance a man has of seeing himself all the way round is at his tailor's, when he is trying on a suit. The poor, incomplete poets have for years been shirking this acid test. They know they aren't poets all the way round. They daren't risk a glimpse of the hunting man's posterior, the strong, bullish, magnate's nape, which many of them involuntarily possess. That is why they dress the way they do. Auden, now, is different, and we hope to see his next slim volume chosen by *The Tailor and Cutter* as their book of the month.

Come to think of it, though, the only time we met him he was dressed like all the others are and asked us if we didn't think *Peter Pan* the most immoral play ever written. But that was a long time ago, and even then we thought him a nice chap. "As technically sufficient as any poet writing in English," says *New Verse*, and we agree.

Would to God we were as technically sufficient as something. The Brazilian navy would do, even. Anything would do.

★

Distinction

The B.B.C., when broadcasting the works of Shakespeare, substitute 'strumpet' for "whore" in all prose passages. In blank verse the dread monosyllable stands, on account of scansion.

Slingsby

LETTER FROM CHINA

W. Empson

WE are now at Kweilin, the capital of Kwangsi, and very nice it is. The scheme was to get through to Yunnan in the party of the Vice-Minister of Communications, who was travelling there on official business and very kindly offered to take us with him. Seven cars, two lorries, five revolvers. There are various other bona-fide travellers in the party, such as a Turk who teaches the dialect of Sinkiang at Nanking; apparently it is allied to Turkish. The point of the convoy is not so much brigands, though they are in question, as that nearly all cars and buses are needed by the military, so the trip takes a special arrangement. We started off from Changsha expecting to be either two days or two hours in Kweilin, and took a day off to walk up a sacred mountain, but the Minister is going to be kept here another week or two. We now plan to set off tomorrow for French Indo-China, but there is some doubt what certificates of inoculation for the prevalent cholera are going to be needed at the frontier, so it isn't a very reliable way to Yunnan. The usual haze of doubt hangs over all plans, and I might well be getting back to my job in Pekin.

The Minister is a jovial and imperturbable man, more the war lord than the mandarin. When one of his subordinates lit two of our cigarettes and then prepared to light his own— this, of course, was infringing a European superstition—the Minister dashed the match from his hand, and apologized for the subordinate. "He does not know the customs," he said, "but he is faithful."

There is hardly any spy-mania about, or heroics either. General Li has just set off to take up a command in the north, and you would have expected high speech-making at the farewell dinner, instead of the Chinese theatre performance that was provided. The only moral I could extract from the plays would be that women make better soldiers than men. Nor do you hear people pinning hopes on an economic boycott of Japan by other nations, though the war probably hangs on that. There is an extraordinary advisory council in Nanking with everything from communists to fascists on it. A very decent tone is taken about all this random bombing. In fact it is an impressive resistance. The muddle and disorder are of course very great, and it is annoying to be told every day that we are quite certain to move on tomorrow.

Kweilin is the capital of a kind of fascist state, which not long ago was quarrelling seriously with Nanking. The young of both sexes go about looking dapper in uniforms, and all officials except the very top ones wear little tabs on the chest stating their name and rank, like Rotarians. Students of course wear them too; their living arrangements are run by the army in the barrack style, and they have five hours' military training a week. There seemed nowhere for private reading in the university except the campus, which a few people were using for that. Bankers have to give instruction in banking and so forth. You do a forty-mile walk in a day at the end of your training to see if you are fit to enter the party. But the main objective of the new model education is, in theory, the adults in the country, not the young in the towns. I just put these bits of information down; I don't know what fascism amounts to here. The communist risings did not get so far south, and there is no feeling of repression, as in Germany, that I can smell out. It is not a manufacturing province, and rather poor because the land is mostly occupied by the hills.

The hills are another of those surprises which you keep getting if you suppose that good paintings are Pure Forms invented by painters. They are the hills that Chinese painters paint. A collection of ant-hills about two hundred feet high, or like the ruined brick stupas in Ceylon if you've seen them. Why the limestone should go like that all over this province and nowhere else seems quite unknown. I think it was Ruskin who said that Chinese landscape was no good because it never painted the bones of a hill, but these hills really haven't any bones. Still they don't

'*A Balaclava is always safe, sir*'.

look positively slimy to touch as they do in the paintings. There is one in the middle of the town, about twenty yards across and sixty high, popping out of a small flat park, and looking like a mountain. It makes the street distances very hard to gauge. You can walk up the steps, but the actual top is used for anti-aircraft and kept shut. It is rumoured to hold unbombable caves which could hold the entire Chinese Government and War Office.

• • •

Arriving in Tonkin from China on to the eastern branch of the French railway makes you feel rather like a Frenchman whose aeroplane has accidentally landed him in Dorsetshire. The inhabitants have heard about aeroplanes and France, and are well enough disposed; but they did not want him to come, they are not in the least interested in France, and nothing will induce them to take French money. The money problem drove us off by the Yunnan train next day, as much as anything else, though we had a little Hong Kong money still hanging about us. Chinese (and I daresay English) official maps will tell you that the eastern railway has got well across the frontier to Yung-ching, and a good deal of fuss and inquiry from hotel offices and the Minister's party did not succeed in telling us that this was only a hopeful gesture. In fact the road to Yungching takes you out of your way over a considerable range of hills, a queer place even for a "projected" railway line. On the morning that we set off brightly in our bus for this imaginary railhead the Vice-Minister was rumoured to have given up all plans in favour of return to Nanking, so it made a neat end to that section of the trip. The regular bus service was going over the frontier all right, and it was no frontier until you got to the genuine railway. There with the proper jerk was an entirely different population, the delicious smoky kitten-savage softness of Malaya and Burma, rich rustbrown gowns, scarlet and emerald scarves, a serious attention to Buddhism and, as the contribution of the ruling race, the intense and successful narrowness of provincial

'*Don't look so worried, Fothergill, you can get dozens from the agencies.*'

France. It was a great relief, or it would have been if they had taken Chinese money.

There was a problem story somewhere along the route, about a German doctor who was allowed a share of the executed prisoners of his province for dissection. He complained about the custom of beheading, because he was a throat specialist (very much needed in all that dust) and the throats always arrived in a mess. Not that hanging would have been any better. So next week eight communists roped together were marched into the dispensary, with a note from the Governor saying he could kill them any way he liked best. He drove them back to be killed elsewhere. You feel somehow that this was a natural step, but you can't say it was doing them a kindness. It is alarming when a doctor feels impelled to tell you that the operation is practically pain-

less and he never uses an anæsthetic—the thing is going to be pretty bad then; but he can kill you much less unpleasantly than any civilized state will. Of course this doctor may not have had enough morphia (or whatnot) to waste on eight killings, but they say the intravenal injection of one air-bubble is a quick tidy death for nothing. It is curious, if this is true, that the suicides haven't got onto it. And the doctor's consul might conceivably have made trouble, but he could at least have inquired. The attitude of the Governor was interesting. Naturally he was angry, seeing that this was a brusque refusal of a special kindness, but he also said it was typical of Europeans, whose minds run in fixed grooves, so that outside their grooves they are helpless. They cannot learn by experience; they cannot adapt themselves to circumstances.

NEW BOOKS reviewed by Evelyn Waugh

A Parnassian on Mount Zion

ONE of the characteristics of Mr. Betjeman's art is a galloping and highly contagious neurasthenia. It seems to have communicated itself even to the august firm of John Murray, armoured surely, if ever a firm was, by centuries of serene tradition against any form of literary eccentricity.

"The last fifteen poems in this book appeared in *Mount Zion*," Mr. Betjeman assures us in his preface; but the last poem (artfully nameless on its page, "Daily Express" in the table of contents) is not only new but topical. There are other peculiarities; three new poems, one without a title, are printed on an unnumbered sheet, inserted between pages 18 and 19; in the Table of Contents they are listed, complete with the missing title, as "pp. 22–23", further disturbing the author's plan by appearing between two old favourites. Well, there are plenty of books with correctly numbered pages and accurate indexes, and very few with the luxuriance of decoration which Messrs. Murray provide for 7s. 6d. The reader has no right to grumble; indeed I can only feel that Mr. Betjeman has agitated them out of all hope of profit unless they are confident of its being made the Religious Book of the Month.

Continual Dew contains all that was best in *Mount Zion*; "Death in Leamington" and "Hymn"—"The church's restoration"—are justly the most famous, but I have a particular relish for "Westgate-on-Sea" with its lapidary final couplet,

" Plimsolls, Plimsolls in the summer,
    Oh goloshes in the wet!"
and I am sorry to see the excruciating

little block which adorned this poem in its original form omitted from the new edition. But this is the only change. A minute scrutiny for "Variæ Lectiones" was unrewarded. (I was glad still to find the illiterate "h" of "oh" in the line quoted above.) Of the verses that have been omitted none were of the first quality, though I had a loyal affection for

". . . if you read a lie
    The gracious Lord will flutter down
    And peck away your eye"
from "Mother and I". I think "The Outer Suburbs" might have gone—if something had to.

The new poems bear somewhat the same relationship to *Mount Zion* as did *Last Poems* to *A Shropshire Lad*. The same limited range of mood and subject

---

Continual Dew.　*John Betjeman.*
　Murray.　7s. 6d.

---

matter finds rather more finished expression; since subject and mood are no longer arresting in their novelty, the reader can give his full attention to Mr. Betjeman's art. Its most remarkable characteristic is its haphazardness. No poem, except "Tunbridge Wells", comes within measurable distance of artistic finish; elsewhere lines of memorable force and beauty lie sandwiched between the clumsiest stuff. It has been Mr. Betjeman's fate to be mistaken for a satirist. Nothing could be further from him. He is an enthusiast who devotes his zeal to objects so singular that his stodgier readers diagnose affectation. Can anyone be inspired —literally "inspired", not merely goaded to literary expression—by *Art Nouveau*, Victorian gothic, gaslight, evergreens, the Irish Peerage, the contrasting liturgies of Protestantism? Yes, Mr. Betjeman can be and is, and his poetry springs from one shining pinnacle of feverish inspiration to another, leaving the intervening valleys to the moraine.

" When steam was on the window panes

And glory in my soul"
is as far from satire as anything that could be heard at the meeting house.

On one subject only does Mr. Betjeman allow himself to be satirical —the type whom he chooses to call "Wykehamist"—the donnish, cocoa-drinking amateur of Norman fonts. "A Hike on the Downs" carries on the tradition.

"Objectively, our Common Room
    Is like a small Athenian State—
    Except for Lewis: he's all right
    But do you think he's quite first
        rate?"
On the recurrent topic of lubricious business men Mr. Betjeman is divided between contempt of them as an inferior social class and genuine deep concern for the welfare of their souls. He really believes—at any rate in his poetic moments—in the existence and imminence of Hell fire and of supernatural exemplary dooms which the unwary and frivolous may provoke.

He loves the country—the country of Bewick (his new poem, "Dorset" has the lovely line: "Horny hands that hold the aces that this morning held the plough"), but mainly as a utopian contrast to the real world of brick gothic and lamplighters; as a background against which that material world must be seen if its grotesques and gargoyles are to be appreciated in their finest detail.

Mr. Betjeman's poetry is not meant to be read, but recited—and recited with almost epileptic animation; only thus can the apostrophic syntax, the black-bottom rhythms, the Delphic climaxes, the panting ineptitude of the transitions be seen in their true values. A final word must be said in praise of a slightly different poem—the last in the book, an epitome of the national uneasiness at the accession of Edward VIII, which flies away at the start, stumbles at the end of the fifth line, recovers, and finishes in a free and stylish gallop. Readers of NIGHT AND DAY should loyally applaud Mr. Lancaster's cover.

LIVES OF GREAT MEN ALL REMIND US...
Literary Pilgrimages by H. K. and M. M.

Whene'er He Came Where Ladies Were

WE walked one evening along the front at Hastings, and coming to the old town turned up a narrow street between low time-worn red-brick houses. The street widened out and we paused opposite a large mansion, standing well back from the road, with three storeys and a frontage of seven windows. It was here that Coventry Patmore had lived from 1875, when he was forty-two, until 1891.

We looked from the opposite side of the road at this mansion which had harboured the leading matrimonialist of the Victorian age. As we stood there, a hand drew down the blind in the only lighted room.

M. M. (shuddering): Gloomy!

H. K. : He lived here with Miss Byles.

M. M. : Miss Byles!

H. K. : His second wife, Marianne Caroline. Described as having "the pure effulgence of Catholic sanctity".

M. M. : What else did she have?

H. K. : Money—a great deal.

M. M. : What of the first wife?

H. K. : No money, but beauty. She inspired Patmore's *Angel in the House*, which states the case for marriage as affording refinements of sexual ecstasy unknown to libertines—

He worships her, the more to exalt
The profanation of a kiss.

M. M. : I get the idea.

H. K. : Another refinement is that the heroine is the daughter of a Dean. Over the port the hero, who is dining with the Dean, tremblingly asks for his consent to the marriage. He explains his financial position, which is excellent, and the Dean—how not?—is

amiable. Patmore makes one feel that a bridal night with a Dean's daughter is something for which Nero would have exchanged a dozen Roman Empires.

M. M. : And to think that he persecuted the Christians!

H. K. : Patmore was very wretched when his first wife died, became a Catholic and met Miss Byles. After they were engaged, he learnt that she was wealthy. It was a blow, but he rallied, and the marriage took place. They settled by Ashdown Forest, on a property of four hundred acres, which he managed so well that he was able to sell it at a profit of £8,500. Then they moved here, both of them by this time over fifty.

M. M. : Which was their bedroom, do you think?

H. K. : Who can say? During these years Coventry Patmore was concentrating on a poem to the Virgin Mary, which was to culminate in her marriage.

M. M. : Did he finish the poem?

H. K. : No, for his wife died, and he married a young girl, an intimate friend of his daughter, who had recently become a nun. His friends remarked that he aged very quickly after this marriage.

M. M. : Was this the end?

H. K. : No. When he was nearly seventy, he fell in love with Alice Meynell, who had praised his poetry as "the greatest thing in the world, the most harrowing and the sweetest". But Mrs. Meynell presently became more interested in George Meredith, and this caused Patmore great agony. He wrote to Mrs. Meynell's husband that he had been paralysed on finding

"from her own words and acts that my primacy in her friendship has been superseded". In another letter to Mr. Meynell he sent her his unalterable love. His health, he said, was bad, his heart pronounced dangerous. "One cannot live long without delight," he added, and a little later was dead.

We walked back down the road towards the sea, and went into a little Catholic church, Our Lady Star of the Sea. In a side chapel were two inscriptions—"Pray for the soul of Marianne Caroline Patmore in memory of whom her husband, Coventry Patmore, founded this church by a donation of five thousand pounds" and "The first Mass every Monday and Tuesday for ever is said for the intention of Coventry Patmore". Patmore was constantly at this church while it was being built, climbing the scaffolding to look at the distant sea, pottering 'round the foundations when the workmen had gone home in the evenings, quarrelling over plans and estimates.

As we emerged into the street, H. K. quoted—

Whene'er I come where ladies are
How sad soever I was before . . .
Then is my sadness banish'd far.

M. M. : So many ladies, the Angel in the House, Byles, the Virgin Mary, the nun daughter's friend, Alice Meynell, and so much sadness. Why?

H. K. : So Patmore must have wondered. In the last months of his life he could not sleep, and used to go for long walks, clinging to his son, and wrapped in a heavy overcoat. Once, as the two of them were hurrying along, he muttered "I am so cold, so cold." "But, father," gasped the son, who was sweating under his father's grip, "you've an overcoat on." "It's my heart that's cold" Patmore groaned.

★

" Counsel's opinion was taken as to the definition of a couple lying in bed. Lawyers finally propounded the theory that a couple were ' in bed ' when both pairs of feet were off the ground."— *Charles Graves on film censorship in the* SPHERE.

Is that on the level?

Music Notes by Constant Lambert

Toscanini and the B.B.C.

IT is curious how little attention has been paid by meteorologists to the influence exerted over the English climate by the visits of distinguished foreigners. Weather, like most other things in life, is subjective rather than objective. Distinguished foreigners expect a Bleak House type of fog, and what's more they get it. The inclement climatic conditions to which we were subjected at the beginning of the month were entirely due to the combined presence here of Toscanini and Nadia Boulanger.

It's a pity Paul Morand didn't come as well. Then we might have had a real pea-souper.

Of Toscanini there is as usual little to say. Either you think him the greatest conductor alive or else you don't, in which latter case you're wrong.

Newshawks did their pathetic best to vamp up a few stories about this most retiring of conductors and had to fall back on the old gag of Toscanini walking out of a rehearsal. I should have thought that by now these tough guys would have been told by their editors that, following the established principle of dog-bites-man, man-bites-dog, etc., when Toscanini walks out of a rehearsal it isn't news, when he stays to the end it is. They might have made more of a story out of the fact that even Toscanini proved his human fallibility by forgetting a bar in Beethoven No. 9. But then one could hardly expect newshawks to notice this, while as for the musical critics, whatever birds they remind one of, they don't remind one of hawks— I doubt if they remind one of birds at all. They are not so much feathered friends as denizens of the deep.

It seems a pity when a genius like Toscanini comes here so rarely that his programmes should be so con-stricted (presumably by that curious Edward Lear-like " They " who rule our musical destinies at the B.B.C.). When a man is the greatest living exponent of Italian music, why saddle us with the monumental mediocrity of the Brahms *Requiem* and *Tragic* Overture? It is true that Toscanini made them both sound better than one would have previously thought possible, but not even he could make the overture live up to its name or make the *Requiem* seem more than an impressive display of the trappings of woe, an undertaker's list expressed in terms of harmony.

I suppose one should not blame a man for his bad imitators, but it is difficult for anyone brought up under the shadow of the English tradition which centres round Brahms not to be irritated by the *Requiem*. It did far more harm to English music than either *The Messiah* or *Elijah*, and that is saying a great deal. It is typical Brahms in that it is monumental in conception and in conception alone. He had a talent for lyrical brooding on a small scale, and if his sycophantic admirers had not bolstered him up into trying to be a second Beethoven he might have pursued this talent (as of a slightly embittered Grieg) to the great advantage of all concerned.

While in the mood to attack the B.B.C. I should like to complain about the ever more frequent programme notes of Sir Donald Tovey, which seem to me to perform no useful function. They must be completely over the head of our dear old friend "the layman" and they must inevitably irritate nine musicians out of ten. Professor Tovey would have been thoroughly at home in the theological circles of the middle ages when he could have argued about the number of angels who can dance on a pinpoint to his heart's content. But I have yet to see that his laborious analyses show any appreciation of what goes on in a composer's mind.

He seems to think that Beethoven was chiefly worried by trying to get back to the flattened super-tonic in time, and he is quite capable of proving that Schubert's C major symphony is really not in C major at all but in B sharp or D double-flat. Even if one took his obsession about key relationships seriously, it would only apply to a very limited section of musical history. As for the whimsical donnish asides, the airy references to *The Frogs* or *Sentimental Tommie* . . . !

Nadia Boulanger's concert at the Phil. was a pleasant change from the usual routine of concert-going. She is not a great conductor and fails in the things that require hard-bitten technique, such as operatic recitatives or keeping brass and voices together. But in a work like the Fauré *Requiem*, which requires no virtuosity of technique, but the utmost sensibility and musical understanding, she produced exquisite results.

This *Requiem* is one of the finest things in French music and I can't imagine why it is not more often done in this country, particularly as it calls for very moderate forces. It is one of those works whose effect is out of all proportion to the means employed.

On paper one would hardly think that the *Pie Jesu* was one of the most moving things in all music. It has an inspired simplicity achieved only by the greatest masters. Perhaps after a few more performances the English public will realize at last that Fauré was one of the great masters. But it is more likely that he will remain "a musician's musician".

Nadia Boulanger's programme also contained three very interesting pieces of Monteverdi of which the best was the beautiful and little known *Lamento della Ninfa*.

The selection from Rameau's *Dardanos* which opened the programme was less successful. Partly because Rameau was a dull dog at times, partly because opera of this period simply won't go on the platform.

Apart from Mlle Gisèle Peyron who was outstanding the French soloists who came over were rather an undistinguished lot. The chorus trained by Kennedy Scott was excellent.

CINEMA
Dead End

THE slum street comes to a dead end on the river bank: luxury flats have gone up where the slum frontage has been cleared, so that two extremes of the social scale are within catcall: the judge's brother's son has breakfast with his governess on a balcony in sight of the juvenile gang on the waterside. For some reason the front entrance of the flats cannot be used and—too conveniently—the tenants must make their way by the service door past the children's ribald gibes. In this coincidence alone do we get a whiff of the cramped stage. Several plots interwind—a housepainter (Joel McCrea) has a transitory affair with a rich man's mistress from the flats; a girl (Sylvia Sidney) hides her kid brother from the police—he is the leader of the children's gang who beat up the judge's brother's son. And all the time, looking on at the game, is Baby-Faced Martin (Humphrey Bogart), a gangster on the run with eight deaths to his credit. He is the future as far as these children are concerned—they carry his baton in their pockets. He was brought up in the same dead end and like a friendly Old Boy he gives them tips—how to catch another gang unawares, how to fling a knife. Only the housepainter recognizes him and warns him off. I'm doubtful whether this interweaving of plots, which end in the kid brother giving himself up, in the housepainter realizing he loves the sister, in the gangster's death from the housepainter's bullet, is wise. It gives too melodramatic a tone to the dead end: some emotion of grief, fear, passion happens to everybody, when surely the truth is nothing ever really happens at all. It remains one of the best pictures of the year—but what we remember is the gangster, the man who in a sentimental moment returns to the old home. He wants to see his mother and his girl: sentiment is mixed with pride—he's travelled places; he shows his shirt sleeve—"Look—silk, 20 bucks." And in two memorable scenes sentimentality turns savage on him. His mother slaps his face ("Just stay away and leave us alone and die '), his girl is diseased and on the streets. This is the finest performance Bogart has ever given—the ruthless sentimentalist who has melodramatized himself from the start (the start is there before your eyes in the juvenile gangsters) up against the truth, and the fine flexible direction supplies a background of beetle-ridden staircases and mud and mist. He and the children drive virtue into a rather dim corner, and only Sylvia Sidney with her Brooklyn voice and her driven childish face is visible there.

GRAHAM GREENE

FOOTBALL

High Seriousness and Aston Villa

BIRMINGHAM and the Midlands are rejoicing. For though Aston Villa has dropped to third place in the Second Division table after being runner-up, Birmingham is betting that the club will be back in the First Division next season. If it is, it will not all be due to the excellence of its football, but partly to the fact that at the beginning of the season the directors provided the team with a debating society.

In any other professional football club a debating society would be presumption and a theme for low jokes. But not so in the Villa; and we who are fans see in the debating society, which, so say the directors, discusses international affairs as well as sporting matters, a welcome return to the High Seriousness which was once the hallmark of the Villa.

Even the club's origins were lofty. The Villa sprang from and took the name of the Aston Villa Wesleyan Chapel; though at this point the possibility of schism enters. The players were not all Methodists; some were members of the bible-class of the Great King Street Baptist Chapel. But the united front of Nonconformity produced the Villa.

That was in 1874. At first the players did nothing more than kick a ball about between themselves at Aston Park on Saturday afternoons. But one afternoon a young Scotsman named George Ramsay paused to watch. They asked him to join in; he gave them an exhibition of dribbling such as they had never seen before, became a member of the club, and later its captain and secretary.

Then they rented a field at Perry Barr, an undulating meadow with a hill near one goal and a pool just off the pitch. They played to two spectators, Ramsay's brother and William McGregor, founder of the Football League, who is commemorated in an unhygienic-looking drinking fountain in the centre of Aston.

The first time the club charged for admission the gate-money amounted to five shillings and threepence. At one time the club was so much in debt that the bailiff's men took possession of the field. Bankruptcy was averted by George Ramsay's dashing off to Glasgow to find a team that would play the Villa. Queen's Park was not available, but Ramsay and Johnny McDowell, the secretary of the Scottish F.A., toured Glasgow in a cab and collected eleven men who were christened the Scottish Crusaders on the way down to Birmingham. The Villa won, and the gate was a record.

When the Football League was founded in 1888 the Villa was one of the original twelve members. The year before the Villa had won the Cup. It has won it five times since; but the cup competed for today is not the original one. Somebody in Aston saw to that. It had been put on exhibition in a shop-window in Aston High Street, there was a smash-and-grab raid, and the cup disappeared for ever.

The Villa has also won the League championship six times. But the last time was in 1910; and for the past few years most Saturday nights have been gloomy in Aston. The Villa has been able to do nothing right, and the correspondence columns of the local papers have been filled regularly with letters of advice from disgruntled supporters. In pub smoke-rooms the usual suggestion was that the directors should bring "the Old Man" back into the team, "the Old Man" being a former captain, Billy Walker, who had retired some years before.

It is said the directors spent £40,000 in the season 1935-36 alone, buying new players. They might just as well have saved their money and recalled Mr. Walker, because the Villa went down into the Second Division just the same. But, in spite of everything, gates at Villa Park have not gone down and it is still a profitable thing to be a Villa shareholder. And the Villa's descent must have been welcomed by many a Second Division club on the verge of bankruptcy.

This year the Villa directors appointed a team manager for the first time in the club's history, and it was he who thought of the debating society. It was near-genius.

WALTER ALLEN

'I don't think you've met my husband.'

BIRTH OF A LOVE SONG
A Story By Gerald Kersh

"MIX me a Chartreuse with a brandy," says Blue, "and then put me in a tiny little spit of Absent. See? Then put me in a ginger ale, and swizzle me it round till it fizzes up—*pss-pss!*—see? Then throw me in a slice of orange, a bit of cucumber peel, and a lump of ice. See? Then a gin, Plymouth gin, see? Twice. Come on, brother, quick; quick, brother, mix 'em!" At this point, turning away from the barman, he seizes me by the lapels, and says : "Hey, did you get that? Eh? Did you get it? Is that a peach or is that a peach? ' I'll tell you. It's a peach. Oh boy, oh boy! Gimme bit paper."

"Eh? Did I get what? Is what a peach?"

"What I said. 'Quick, Brother, Mix 'Em.' *Da-da-da-doo, da-doo; da doo-doo-doo*: QUICK, BROTHER, MIX 'EM! Ain't that a great idea for a song? Eh? Can't you *feel* it? Don't it *get* you? *Ker-wick, ber-other,* MIX 'EM!" sings Blue, to the tune of *Yes, that's what you think.* "Oh boy! Lemme pencil."

He takes a pencil, and makes three wavy lines on an Income Tax envelope: "Listen—would you say *doo, da-doo,* or *doo-doo-*DOO?"

"They're both very nice."

"Congratulate me," says Blue. "I gotta smasher, a world-beater. Oh boy, can't you hear that plaintive refrain tootling through on the wop-sticks ? *Quick, brother . . . Oh, quick brother*—QUICK, BROTHER, MIX 'EM! Eh? Eh? Another hit from the pen of Blue!"

Who is Blue? He is a song-writer. He thinks that a Barcarolle is a kind of branded dog-biscuit, and once, when I said to him "I just heard Beethoven's Second", he replied: "I never back for a place. What race, anyway?" But for all that, he has music on the brain. He makes about £3,000 a year out of it. His soul wriggles in a perpetual jelly-roll. He rushes through life scooping up inspiration—tangos in trees, rumbas in railway trains, quicksteps in stones, and rhythm in every-

thing. He cannot buy a stamp without adding: "*Just a Letter to my Mother*—whaddaya know about that for a song? Eh?" He is to be seen running, hatless, in Charing Cross Road, crying "Wha-de-de-doo!" and beating the air with his fists. In quiet cinemas and peaceful restaurants people are startled by his deep-throated exclamations: "*Just the Screen, yes, the Screen of Life . . .*" or "Listen, waiter: *Pudden; de-da-de, de-da-de, Pudden*—tell me one thing and gimme a straight answer; is that a honey of an idea or is that a honey of an idea?"

He is always wise immediately after the event—so wise, and so immediately, that he has something of the air of a pioneer. When he first heard *The Music Goes Round*, he laughed, and said " Duff." Then, when everybody was singing it, he shouted with uproarious triumph: " Blue is always right! Whaddid I tell you?" And then he wrote, to a tune suspiciously reminiscent of *I Wonder Where My Baby is Tonight*, a song entitled " I'd Like to Shoot the Guy that Wrote ' The Music Goes Round and Around' ".

He says: "Boy, drink that drink. I invented it. Listen, whaddaya say I water it down and bottle it, and rush 'em seventeen-and-six a bol? Yes? Drink it right down to the dregs—did you get that? *Drink it right down to the dregs!*" He sings this to the tune of *It's Getting Around and About*— " Get it? D'ja get it? Is that a lulu or—tell me frankly—is that a lulu?"

" A lulu."

" My very words! Or listen. . .

' *If I find any more of this sort of thing, I'll make you play football on Saturday afternoons.*'

Haha, by God I got it this time! Yes, sir, inform the world that Blue has got it this time. Listen—*Quick, Brother, mix 'em; drink it right down to the dregs!* Eh? Eh? It goes like this . . ." And he sings these words to a tune subtly composed of a cross between *Land of My Fathers* and *Old Faithful.* "Yes? Nice, eh? Waiter, same again. Yes, waiter, let 'em mix me the same again."

Blue pauses. Then he scratches my hand and exclaims: "Now listen: philosophy. Deep stuff. That drink is a mixture, eh? Life is a mixture, see? Well, *life is like a cocktail! Drink it to the dregs.* By gosh! *Life is like a cocktail, drink it to the dregs.* 'Stormy Weather'! Fooey! 'Little Man You Had a Busy Day'? Bah! I got 'em groggy, I got 'em whipped. What rhymes with 'dregs'? Eh? Eggs?"

"Legs?"

"I said legs. *Life is like a Cocktail; Drink it to the Dregs; Life is just a Highball . . . dum-dum-dum-dum Legs.* World-beater!"

"You could say 'Don't let it knock you off your legs'."

"Well, of course! Why, certainly! Now. . . Inspiration is what we want . . . Now, let's see what comes

next. . . "

"Well, one could say something about a dash of bitters, a dash of——"

"I wish you wouldn't keep on interrupting! Now, where was I? Oh yes. . . *Don't let it knock you off your legs.* . . Now, *a dash of Bitters, a dash of Gin*—what rhymes with gin?"

"Pin? Sin? Tin?"

"Ssh! Be quiet just a second, just one second. Gin. Yes, *A dash of Bitters, a dash of Gin; a dash of Virtue a dash of Sin* — Boy, oh boy! Now all we have to do is just sort of round it off, kind of style. . . Dash of virtue, dash of sin. . . Oh, hell. Waiter! Waiter! Again, again! . . . What goes in cocktails? I know, olives! What rhymes with olives?"

The drinks seem to be filling my stomach with rainbows and sunlight. "Cherries?" I reply.

"Certainly cherries. What else?"

"Hey!" I exclaim, also inspired. "What about this? *But the Cherry that falls with a Splash from Above; is Love, you big palooka, sweet, sweet Love!*"

"Ssh!" Blue waves an angry hand. "I just had it on the tip of my tongue. Cherries, olives. . . Ah-ah! Gotcha! Ssh a minute! Now, listen: *But the sweet tender Cherry that Comes from Above— That's Love . . . Sweet Love!* Hoo! Aha! Nice work, eh? Nifty, I flatter myself? Oho, can't you hear that tune? Can't you *see* that tune? *Love, Sweet Love* —can't you imagine that being blown through an agony-pipe? Wow, can't you get that theme on a liquorice-stick, while all the cats let themselves go and beat out that refrain —*wha-wha-wha-wooo (pom, pom) just Sweeeet wha-whoo!*"

Blue smacks me in the face and gulps down his drink.

"Again!" he shouts.

I seem to be adrift in pink mist. Only two senses are left: hearing and taste. Taste is fading under a sticky blanket of Chartreuse, through which, like pinpricks, stab little memories of absinthe. Hearing is confused. I am beaten at by innumerable bars of half-remembered tunes. One last spark of consciousness, high up in the dome of my skull, throws a feeble light down upon the chaos, illuminating little bits of songs that I have known, which float up to the surface. . . And my ears piece these things together into a new tune . . .

I shake my head. Blue is singing.

"Life is like a cocktail,
Drink it to the dregs!
Life is just a highball—
Don't let it knock you off your legs!
A dash of bitters—a dash of gin,
A dash of virtue—a dash of sin;
But the sweet, tender cherry that comes from above,
That's love—sweet love . . .
Ain't it a wow? Eh? Ain't that something different? Eh?"

I reply: "Blue, that's not something dif-different. That's a mixture of *Sweetest Little Fellow* and *The Music Goes Round* and *Don't Let Your Love Go Wrong* and *That's What Harlem is to Me* and *It Ain't Gonna Rain No More* and—"

"Listen, boy," says Blue, "when you start insulting friends, that means to say you had enough to drink. Got me? So let's find your coat . . . "

The fresh air hits me in the face like an ice-pack.

"Take him home," says the voice of Blue.

A taxi-door slams.

The voice of Blue wafts back, singing: "*That's love (da-da-da-da-da)— sweet Lo-ho-hooove!*"

The uproar of the city blanks him out.

★

It is a great tragedy, but you have got to grit your teeth, grasp your mettle, and bear it like a man.—*Mr. Dummett, reported in* SUNDAY GRAPHIC.

That ought to put you on your nettle.

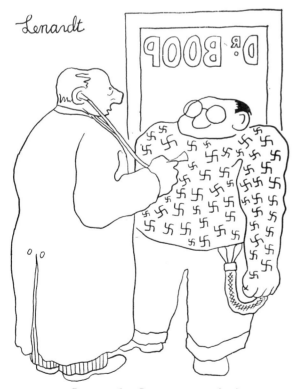

'*It must be German measles.*'

16.—RATS' BANE

ONE remembers the rat-catcher of fiction as a shabby, unshaven, rather sinister figure, wearing (somewhat optimistically) a deer-stalker. His pockets bulge with ferrets, his companion is a mongrel with tattered ears and scabs on the nozzle, and he is invariably a rogue of some magnitude. Mr. William Dalton, need we say, does not answer to this description in any particular. To begin with he is very jolly, wears a bowler hat, a butterfly collar, and the smartest of bow ties. He hates ferrets, and only uses them because the L.C.C. commands their services in the parks. Dogs, however intelligent, are also anathema to him, because they make one smell doggy to the rats who then of course "smell a rat".

Mr. Dalton can smell a rat anywhere; he has, indeed, smelt tens of thousands in his time, for at a ripe young sixty-six years of age he is the patriarch of Wm. Dalton & Sons, Expert Ratcatchers, Mouse, Cockroach and Beetle Destroyers. There are as many as sixteen "destroyers" in the firm, all related by blood or marriage. No stranger has been initiated into the family mysteries of the profession since about 1710, when an ancestor laid the foundations of that specialized knowledge which has been handed down from father to son until it seems to have become a hereditary sixth sense.

Today we find the results of over two centuries of extermination in an amazingly extensive business run on the most efficient lines. You can sense that, as soon as you enter the small but scrupulously tidy office in a little house in King James Street, off the Borough Road. What must once have been the front parlour contains a desk, telephone, typewriter, maps, files and a huge schedule of the month's activities. The only decoration is provided by some stuffed ferrets (one labelled " Old Joe ") and a glass case containing a huge and rather revolting stuffed rat.

"This," said Mr. Dalton, "is where we fix our executions." Mr. Dalton conducts the practical side of his business in premises on the other side of the street, where you will find a small fleet of bicycles, orderly rows of Gladstone bags, and perhaps some corpses—relics of the night's catch—

laid out ready for the enormous never-empty coffin which daily awaits the dustman. At the farthest end of this one-storied building are a number of cages containing very live specimens. These are reserved, Mr. Dalton explained, for the medical profession and divided into two groups, because (let the layman note once and for all) there are two species of rat. The large brown, or sewer, rat, sometimes called the Norway rat, is a handsome hardworking fellow who covers the waterfront or, more strictly, frequents sewers, drains, canals and other damp places. He is becoming increasingly scarce and is already outnumbered by nine to one by his more dangerous cousin, who received long overdue recognition from the nation last month during Rat Week. This is the ship, or black, rat, distinguished by his big eyes and big ears, Grandmamma, and a very long tail. "They are energy itself," said Mr. Dalton, playfully swinging one by the tail at us. "Sharp fellows and the greyhounds of the rat family," he added, as we sidestepped. He defies the most modern architect to design a building which could keep them out. They can climb anything, and are spreading rapidly in spite of the ceaseless war waged by Mr. Dalton and his family, who after all only have sixteen pairs of hands. As it is, the Daltons travel all over the British Isles in their crusade of extermination, cleaning up country houses, housing estates, hotels, snatching sleep when and where they can. Mr. Dalton has caught rats as far north as Skye and in various parts of Ireland, although he finds that the crossings disagree with him. Apart from their important contracts with public authorities like the City Corporation and the L.C.C., he "exterminates " for the Bank of England, the Stock Exchange, the "Big Five" of the banking world and a host of other important clients. He modestly places his status above that of a bank official, which is understandable when one realizes the enormous trust placed in Mr. Dalton when he is given, night after night, the keys and freedom of

' That's a fib.'

by just looking at it. But Mr. Dalton is more than their match and has brought things to such a fine art that he once actually caught a rat in the broad electric light of a city restaurant before a bewildered party of stockbrokers.

One of the less obvious reasons for bringing them back alive is that a number of his clients stipulate that there shall be no cruelty. All the rats are painlessly destroyed on the firm's premises, except selected specimens for the laboratory, such as the very attractive young albino that Mr. Dalton exhibited with pride. By way of variation the Daltons get after other game when they "have a moment to spare": pigeons, for instance, or bugs when they are in season, or mice. In fact we caught sight in the "works" of a dead mouse lying luxuriously in state on the expensive menu card of a West End restaurant that would certainly hate to have its name published. We didn't dare enquire how the mouse died.

Mr. Dalton says that there are more "bouncers" in his profession than in any other. Quite recently one of his sons was in Manchester inspecting a job, when he saw a theatrical-looking party carrying a piano-accordion. Mr. Dalton junior politely asked him for a tune and the gentleman, somewhat nettled, replied that he was the great ———, a rat-catcher; in proof of which he produced a card inscribed WITH OR WITHOUT MUSIC. He added that he charmed the rats away with his music and would be delighted to give a demonstration for a mere consideration. Asked where the rats went, he pointed dramatically to an adjacent canal. Mr. Dalton junior then produced his own card and the Pied Piper of Manchester was round the corner in a second. Mr. Dalton senior's opinion is that the music might actually have the same effect as poison. Mr. William Dalton always has the last laugh.

CHRISTOPHER SALTMARSHE

★

POLICE PERSUASION

If you are convicted, the court may require the licence to be produced to it. Failure to produce it is an offence and the licence is automatically suspended until fit is produced.—*Notice on police summons.*

premises containing stock worth (as in the Bank of England) a mint of money. Mr. Dalton justifies his classification tersely : "Bank officials sometimes go to prison—not us."

He doesn't go in for docks or ships much, and though the latter provide him with "plenty of fun and a good haul" the work is tiring, slightly dangerous and, we suspect, not so subtle and satisfying as the normal line of business.

For those who like statistics, his record is 1,600 rats at a sitting, while his largest victim measured 26 inches, weighed 1 lb. 6½ oz., and quite properly has a place of honour in the Natural History Museum at Cardiff.

Mr. Dalton's methods are necessarily a close family secret, but from what we have been able to glean they are as scientific as the results are successful. His slogan is "Bring 'em back alive"; his weapons are a torch, a pair of slippers, and a mysterious piece of delicate machinery, invented by his father, whose ingenious turn of mind

brought rat-catching up to date. Behind these apparently simple effects is a highly developed plan of campaign in which he pits his experience and knowledge against the rat's cunning. "No detective in Scotland Yard," he says, "goes to so much trouble." First of all there is a preliminary inspection by "Dad", who reports to his client on the probable numbers of the enemy and any structural complications in the building which may be aiding them. Then a family sit-down conference is held in the office, when individual deductions are exchanged and the final details of the night operations decided. After these preliminaries, in which even the minutest details are arranged, the work starts in earnest: it may mean waiting all night for one rat, or coming away with a bag of eight dozen after a couple of hours. Mr. Dalton aims at getting his rat " so that its pals don't know it's gone"—not so easy as it sounds, for the average rat has an intelligence only second to that of Mr. Dalton and can even detect a live wire

FE
= FO
= FI
= FU M

Feliks Topolski

IN

ST. JAMES'S ST.

5.—*Approved by the L.C.C.*

THE London County Council, we were informed at County Hall, has been affixing commemorative plaques since 1903 to houses where distinguished persons have lived. Altogether it has so far affixed one hundred and forty-seven, the first being to Lord Macaulay at Holly Lodge, Campden Hill. Since 1922 plaques have averaged between three and four annually, with two exceptional years—1933, when there were no plaques, and 1935 when there were seven, including one, at 41 Maitland Park Road, to Karl Marx. This plaque, however, rapidly became a focus of disorder and was, at the request of the owner of the property concerned, removed in the following year.

A plaque, we learnt, costs about £10 to buy and put up. In most cases the L.C.C. defrays this charge, though the Duke of Bedford pays for such plaques as are affixed to his properties. Suggestions for plaques, numbering about twenty each year, are carefully investigated; and the decision to affix a plaque is taken by the Parks Committee, and endorsed by the full council.

We were particularly interested in the plaque to Heinrich Heine, on 32 Craven Street, Strand, which we had examined on our way to the County Hall. The house is at present tenanted by a variety of occupants, including a tailor, an architect, and Mr. M. Morris, late manager of the Hairdressing Department of the National Liberal Club, and now operating independently. Heine lived here when he visited London in 1827. His banker uncle, Salomon Heine, a friend of the Rothschilds, had given him a draft for five hundred pounds, explaining that it was not to be cashed, but only to be shown in quarters where it might be expected to have a reassuring effect. Cashing it immediately on arrival, Heine used some of it to defray his German bills, and more on his own amusement. There was a Javanese girl with rooms off Regent Street; and a Kitty Clairmont, at 26 Osnaburgh Street, Regent's Park, who was the chief beneficiary from Salomon Heine's draft.

This did not seem to us the kind of record to impress the Parks Committee. Yet there was the plaque. It occurred to us that the proceedings when it was approved would make things clearer, so we looked them up:

"Mr. R. B. Marston has offered to defray the cost of affixing to 32 Craven Street, W.C., a tablet commemorative of the residence thereat of Heinrich Heine. We are of opinion that this offer should be accepted, although we should not have advised the Council itself to incur expenditure in the matter."

Looking through the list, we noticed that only four foreigners had plaques—Heine, Karl Marx, Madame Goldschmidt and Antonio Canal. Mozart, however, is shortly to be plaqued in Ebury Street. We were informed that the L.C.C. has no powers over plaque-posting by individuals acting on their own initiative, and at their own expense. The L.C.C. would not, for example, be empowered to veto the affixing of a plaque to commemorate Heine's visits to 26 Osnaburgh Street, if the owner raised no objection.

Leaning over Westminster Bridge, digesting all this information, H. K. asked M. M. whether Public Policy might not jib if the liberty of plaques were abused. For instance, a plaque on Boswell's favourite bordello.

M. M. : Or the restaurant where Swinburne bit Adah Mencken. Of course, there is the plaque to Verlaine in Howland Street. It was put up by some enthusiasts a few years ago. There was a little ceremony, and speeches. Verlaine lived there with Arthur Rimbaud in 1872.

H. K. : I see your point. But I believe the speeches were in French.

M. M. : No doubt the acid test of Public Policy's plaque-sensitivity would be a plaque to Wilde with speeches in English.

H. K. : That must be arranged.

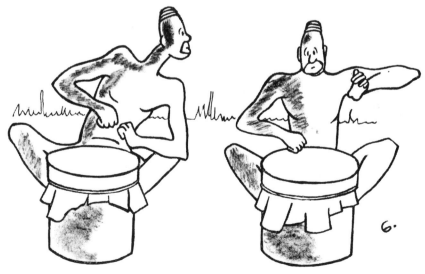

'What about the hyphen?'

ART IN THE HEADLINES

The Public Takes a Hand

UPON few subjects is there such formidable disagreement as on the nature of art. No generally acceptable answer has been provided, but we can at least say with some degree of certainty that it is not, except in certain circumstances, news.

Nevertheless, happily for art-dealers, critics and journalists, these circumstances are not altogether rare. Hardly a year passes without a Savanarola or James Douglas discovering that some picture, or more probably a piece of sculpture, is of a fantastic, though hitherto unsuspected, indecency; few exhibitions at Burlington House fail to include the work of a paralysed milkman from Muswell Hill or the five-year-old daughter of a Saffron Walden railway porter; and Mr. Epstein and Mr. Sickert are still remarkably industrious and, of course, automatically news. But in addition there are two other methods by which art may achieve the headlines, or at least the correspondence columns—the financial and the commemorative. If a painting changes hands for any sum in excess of five figures or if a statue is erected to any well-known and respected figure, art can be sure of obtaining at least half-a-column in the slack season, and if by any chance the slightest suspicion arises that the five-figure picture is considered by an expert not to be the work of the master, or if the statue of the great deceased includes a horse, then art temporarily attains the importance of a breach of promise case (rather a dull one) or a short story by Damon Runyon.

At the moment of writing, by a happy freak of fate, both these rare events have occurred almost simultaneously and moreover at a time when the perennial excitement aroused by one of Mr. Epstein's five-star religious masterpieces has hardly evaporated. Art, therefore, is more nearly news than it has been for years.

The first of these artistic sensations has a number of unusual features which make the subject one of exceptional interest. In the first place the party who it is politely maintained in certain quarters has been sold a pup is none other than the National Gallery, and as that institution is in part supported by the nation, it is the taxpayer's money that is in danger. And while no one cares two hoots if half a million or so is wasted on an unnecessary arterial road or several hundred thousand are devoted to the purchase of a Codex which nobody will read, if the capital of three hundred a year is paid for a picture which Giorgione may not have painted, then we all feel someone has let the country down. Secondly, it is a matter on which no more than half a dozen people at the most are qualified to express an opinion, and it is therefore naturally felt to be a matter for general and prolonged discussion and correspondence.

Briefly the facts are these. The authorities of the National Gallery purchased a set of four tempera panels with an oil glaze depicting arcadian scenes dating from some time at the end of the fifteenth century or the very beginning of the sixteenth, for the sum of £10,000. These, it was announced after acquisition, were the work of Giorgione: an artist who is not only one of the greatest and most mysterious figures in the whole history of art, but one whose acknowledged works can be counted on the fingers of one hand. If, indeed, they are the work of the master, then they are a very valuable acquisition at a reasonable price. But no sooner was their purchase announced than the still small voice of one of the greatest of living authorities on Italian painting of the Renaissance was heard blandly suggesting that they were the work not of Giorgione, but of Palma. While the offensive is still raging in the pages of the *Burlington*

Magazine it would be presumptuous to offer any opinion, but the sad fact remains that, if it is proved that they are the work of Palma, then £1,000 would be a stiff price. In passing it is interesting to note that Mr. Kenneth Clark now refers to the masterpieces as "Giorgionesque panels".

While this discussion is unhappily not one in which the general public can join with any degree of knowledge or satisfaction, the Haig statue provides the opportunity for a splendid free-for-all in which soldiers, sculptors, critics and horse copers can all with equal reason give us the benefit of their opinions. Curiously enough, for once in a way, a spirit of almost complete unanimity prevails and this heterogeneous collection of men-in-the-street find themselves in gratifying, if unaccustomed agreement. From the æsthetic standpoint the statue is completely negligible; and not even the persuasive tones of Sir Herbert Baker (speaking in the kindly, indulgent accents of Mr. Herbert Read explaining the beauty of one of Miss Hepworth's obscurer achievements), who tells us that the statue must not, of course, be regarded as a piece of representational art but rather as a three-dimensional embodiment of the sculptor's conception of military triumph, can persuade us to the contrary. From the purely equine point of view the statue is equally unsatisfactory. Is this curious charger of doubtful breeding walking forward, standing still or preparing to indulge in a capriole or one of the other decorative feats which have earned the Lilpizaner horses in Vienna such deserved commendation? Is the fact that its hind quarters appear to be stationary while its forelegs advance a subtle indication of the dual nature of the late Field-Marshal's command, or an unkind sculptural suggestion that his strategy suffered from divided counsels? These are questions which each man must decide for himself, but personally we can never feel that an equestrian statue is really equestrian if the steed is not rearing up in a dramatic manner with its stomach supported by a small iron rod and its rider's hand waving a baton.

OSBERT LANCASTER

More (Strictly Authentic)
PEN-PRICKS AND PRAISE
For NIGHT AND DAY

Dear Sir:

Night & Day is presumably an attempt to imitate that inimitable weekly masterpiece the New Yorker—or probably you'd prefer me to say that it was inspired by the N.Y.—or again you might prefer me not to say anything at all though you may not be even interested either way. But anyway, in lots of ways, it's not a bad attempt—in fact *any* attempt to introduce a first-class humorous magazine into this country is a good thing—even if it doesn't achieve first-classness at first. In the first place I can't quite make out who you are catering for—can you? It would appear that you're not out to attract the masses but rather to attract the type of people who are probably already whole or part time readers of the New Yorker. . . . But the New Yorker isn't all James Thurber. Not that a lot of people would mind very much if it was because J.T. *is* funny. As for Feliks Topolski—or whatever his name is—he may have come to England with a great reputation from Timbuktu or wherever he came from but—well I may know a lot of un-enlightened people—though a great many of them are connected one way or another with the arts and are in their twenties or thirties and inclined to consider themselves as—well—progressive shall I say—but honestly man —they all say—quite independently that he just doesn't mean a thing. . . . A sense of character isn't really enough in itself. As for ⊚ (I hope that doesn't constitute forgery), well he (or she) can't seem to make up his (or her) mind between Geo. Price, Thurber or Fougasse.
I know it's a damned site easier to criticise than create but my humble advice—for what it's worth—is don't make the same mistake as the English Newsmagazines did when they set out to produce English "TIME"s . . . they've tried to improve on the original.
K., London, S.W.

*

The drawings of Feliks Topolski are certainly the best in the magazine. He is a genius and he knows it.
There seems to be too many advertisements which somehow or the other make the magazine look like 'Punch'—which is a calamity because 'Night and Day' is so very intelligent.
A. L., London, S.E.6.

*

What has happened to your brilliant middle-page artist.—I spend more hours absorbing its back ground, down to the minutest detail, than I spend over all the rest of your paper.
H. R. M., Peebles.

*

Your latest issue is excellent. I was somewhat anxious for your longlivity after reading the first edition which seemed a mixture of the good and the "St. Olaf's Chronicle"—but you've improved with every issue, and as an old sourpuss weaned on the milk of Vanity Fair and the New Yorker I congratulate you most sincerely.
Your capture of Thurber was a triumph . . I expect you get lots of letters saying I think you're wonderful and the circulation stays down like a pirate submarine. Well, I've sent copies to America, Burma, Australia and the Argentine, so if your international demand zooms you might ask me to dine with you at Boulestin's.
Give my special thanks to Slingsby, John Crow, and your good selves.
D. M., London, S.W.1.

*

Le *N and D* nous semble joliment réussi. Nous sommes surtout en extase devant votre splendide dessinateur. Impression impeccable. Travail hors ligne! Et l'Humour! Un triomphe, je crois. L. F. C., Paris.

*

I wish you luck, and it will be well if you have it, for I think luck counts a good deal in any venture, but especially in publishing. Good luck and a lot of hard work.
H. W. R., New York.

*

Comment. *Covers:* good. *Entertainment Directory*—referring solely to *films*—should be fuller. *Dorchester Hotel* ad is messy. Shell ad. poor plates—poor large type-face —sort of ad. requiring distinctive face. Gill? *Minutes:* Night & Day can't afford to lean on anyone else, yet you invite the comparison. You will find your own character in time I suppose . . . . None of the other illustrated cracks are slick enough. They attempt to *be funny*. They won't come off until the intention is to poke less than gentle fun *at* contemporary life. Type-faces of titles and text too large, and the text carries too much leading. *The end-column fillers:* comment has to snap, most of these fizzle. The thing is to find a quote that invites the sharp snap comment. Topolski page is in right direction. *Reviews:* books — O.K. Fiction articles not read. VERY WELL-WISHER.

I have just made the acquaintance of your journal and it has made me very sad. I read a great deal and I know that the high standard you have set (Sept. 16th number) cannot possibly be maintained, so that I shall not be able to look forward to such excellent entertainment in the future as I have just enjoyed.
Only by some such miracle as has kept Punch going all these years can you maintain your standard—it will require something beyond mere human agency.
It would be your magazine on which the mantle of this Elijah should rightly fall . . . if only you could keep it up to this level of what I have just read.
Should you be able to organise your deliveries so that it arrives flat through the post count me as a permanent subscriber.
S. W., Kent.

*

Hoping to find something witty & snappy in a future edition if I am fool enough to buy another. Here's to your future, Yours hopefully. L. G. G., London, W.11.

*

There are two normal conversational gambits about "Night & Day": (i) Of course it will not last till Christmas . . . Poor Chatto's ruined, etc." (ii) "Such a pity that it's not funny." To these I have consistently opposed (i) "That is a malicious lie which was started before the first number was out. The circulation is leaping ahead." [I haven't the least evidence to support either of these loyal statements] and (ii) "Have you really read it? The later numbers have been as funny as can be, expecially the text . . ."
A. W., Isleworth.

*

How dare you insult the intelligence of the British Public by publishing such trash, it's a waste of ink, and absolutely rotten, there is not a sane passage from Cover to Cover, well may the men engaged to deliver them throw them over back walls in handfulls in disgust. You all want locking up. ANON.

*

Congratulations! Whether you had anything to do with the origin of the idea, or whether you were merely picked up and stuck in the editorial chair, I have no means of knowing: I do not, even, know your name, but I do wish you every success.
F. K. P., Manchester.

LION'S MOUTH
Theodora Benson

I HAVE it from an unimpeachable source that never a day passes without at least one person ringing up the Zoo and asking if he may speak to Mr. Lion. Sometimes several people ring up. On April 1 the Zoo is disconnected for incoming telephone-calls altogether, and can only be obtained after considerable parley and candour with the Post Office.

This is a fact told me without error or exaggeration, and I am charmed by it : every day people are perpetrating this same joke. It comes to them as a sudden inspiration. "That's a good one !" they think. "That'll knock them, that will. They *will* be surprised !" And each must feel elated by his neat originality : hundreds upon hundreds taken by storm by this same happy thought each year.

And they ask for Mr. Wolf. They ask for Mr. Fox. The cleverest of them ask, for instance : " Can I speak to Mr. C. Lion ? " or " Can I have a word with Mr. G. Raffe ? "

What is so pleasing about it all is the thought that there are so many happy people in the world. I do not think that this is the laughter of desperation. It seems to me essentially a jubilant gesture. I can imagine that if I got very happily and lovingly and triumphantly engaged to be married when I was right away in, let us say, the East Indies, I might have an overpowering desire to put a trunk call through to the Zoological Society of London. " Hold on— Sumatra wants you," the Post Office would say to them, and then would come my request, the most witty and ambitious of all the variations : " Hullo, is that the Zoo ? Can I speak to Mr. L. E. Phant ? "

Certainly I am not jeering at these recurring clowns. I think myself clever (well, let's face it, I do) and though thousands have independently thought of that joke and it looks as if thousands more are bound to think of it, I never did. I don't seem to be any good at inventing jokes. I had years and years to think it up in and somehow never got started.

The Zoo don't give one any kind of a rise for one's trouble. Because, of course, I've tried it. I'm no leader, but I'm fine way back in the middle of a crowd. At least—I haven't quite tried it myself, for as I reached for the telephone I was taken by uncontrollable laughter. Whenever I'd got myself damped down ready to begin, the drollery of it struck me afresh and everything slipped again. " Oh, go on, do it," said my sister. " No, you do it," said I, my voice shaking and trilling a little. " No, *you* do it," said she, giving me a nudge. " No, *you* do it," said I giving her a push, and she did. We had arranged not to start at the summit with Mr. L. E. Phant, but with the bottom rung of the ladder, as a novice should. " C-can I speak to Mr. Lion ? " said my sister. The Zoo young lady replied at once with great civility and hardly perceptible boredom : " I am sorry, but there is no one here of that name."

The only aspect of this game that disquiets me (and I know I ought to stop worrying, as it's only hypothetical, and get my mind on to something else) is that if Charles James Fox were alive today and devoted all his vigour and genius to getting a job to make good in at the Zoo, he wouldn't get it.

" Can I speak to Mr. Fox ? "

" Do you mean Mr. Charles James Fox ? "

" Yes."

Well, you see, even that's no good, because that, of its kind, is a joke too. In rather poor, informal hunting country I have heard a genial sportsman speak of the fox as Charles James twice in one afternoon. So the great man's Christian names wouldn't be any more help than if he had been baptized Sly Renard right away.

Even if he changed his surname to something distinct and distinctive like Jacksalson, I don't believe it would do. There would always be people who couldn't remember it ringing up and asking for him as Mr. Fox. The Zoo would have to be disconnected for incoming telephone-calls. And who wants to live in a permanent atmosphere of its being April 1 ?

'Fill her up !'

AT THE THEATRE

Elizabeth Bowen

Macbeth

THIS *Macbeth*, at the Old Vic, is shot through with Celtic darkness and fire. The pre-Elizabethan element, the savage element, is strongly brought out. The actors' built-up foreheads (giving them all the look of terrible, fateful hammers), the shadow-contorted depths of the back stage, that looming Y-shaped monolith, the murky torch-yellow lighting of the indoor scenes—all date back the passion behind the language to what must have been in Shakespeare its unconscious source: some inherited intuition of the past. Major emotions, whether good or evil, have their common denominators, in all the ages, in any setting. But there is more to *Macbeth* than the timeless element—there is definite time and place colour.

Is it because M. Michel St. Denis is not English that he has been able to make this direct, this intuitive approach to *Macbeth*? Clearly the play has never been blurred for him. He has escaped being the prey of conventions: at the same time one does not feel him self-consciously keeping clear of them. It is true there are moments when his production overreaches itself, moments in which it is far from being inspired or happy. His fancy sometimes goes beyond his (as it might beyond any producer's) powers. The witches are not, to my mind at least, a success: they are inchoate; they have a curdled appearance—and then, their genteel little fluting stagey voices come oddly out of their monstrous masks. Can nothing be done to these voices? Could they not, perhaps, speak *through* something? The procession of spirits, later, is also more grotesque than impressive: these look like carnival figures. My wish is to see a stage ghost towed on hidden wheels along a concealed groove: this would do away

with the bumpiness of the human walk. The diagonal descent of the spirits is good in conception, and ought to be more impressive. But, alas, they bump. . . . Banquo's Ghost, on the other hand, is excellent.

Mr. Laurence Olivier and Miss Judith Anderson are magnificent as the Macbeths. "The Macbeths" they very much are. Played as it is played at the Old Vic, *Macbeth* might be called, first of all, a play about a marriage: the instinctive complicity of these two people, their powerful natural tie, the hypnosis they exercise over one another is palpable the whole time. Too often, in other productions, Macbeth and Lady Macbeth have been simply a pair of fine actors playing opposite each other. . . . Miss Anderson's Lady Macbeth would be comprehensible even in dumb show: every spoken line seems to come through the whole of her fluid, controlled body. She commands—more, she generates—gestures of which every one tells. As for Mr. Olivier, he has that gift, above price for a Shakespeare actor, of speaking every majestic, well-known line as though it sprang, only now, direct from his own heart. As somebody sitting just behind me said, "You would hardly think there was a quotation in the play".

Thank You, Mr. Pepys

If this bonhomous little play lasts, it will be the very thing for the Christmas holidays. The boys and girls will love it—and they are no fools. In this not propitious age for merry monarchs, *the* Merry Monarch is as popular as ever, and Mr. Barry K. Barnes gets him across well. Here is plenty of dash and gusto, a homely mixture of idiom, and some slimy crooks, who are routed to applause. Here, also, we see the chatty side of rearmament. Mr. Edmund Gwenn's Mr. Pepys is vigorous (how could he not be vigorous, being Mr. Gwenn?) and exceedingly, almost ex-

cessively sympathetic. Miss Margery Mars' Nell Gwynn is as strapping and as upright a Girl Guide as you could wish: the hoydens of yesterday are the Guides of today. The costumes and décor are well up to Christmas Annual standard, and cheer the jaded heart.

Distant Point

A Soviet general's Pullman gets wheel trouble, has to be unhooked from a Moscow-bound express at a diminutive station called Distant Point, on a main line across Far Eastern Siberia, and is held up for about twenty-four hours while local ingenuity tinkers with the wheel. Then the coach is rehooked to another express, and the general rushes on to Moscow and his more than probable death from cancer of the lungs. But during the forced pause at Distant Point the general, his wife and his A.D.C., have emerged from the Pullman and mingled with the inhabitants. When they depart again, they leave ideals heightened, errant emotions centralized. I seem to remember a song sung by a Tchehov character called "When Comes the Day when the Russian Peasant will not Lament?" Apparently it is coming. The Distant Point inhabitants still tend to lament, but a slogan stops them at once, and sends them off into ecstasy. Only Vlas Fillipovich, ex-deacon, remains a recalcitrant, a romantic defeatist—he has never filled the vacuum left when religion went. (Mr. George Benson's playing of this part should be starred.)

This play from Soviet Russia is excellent: the Gate has done well to put it on. Given the tiny stage, the settings are romantic and atmospheric. The casting (which is important) is inspired: Miss Judith Furse gives the amazon, Liubov Seminova, the native vigour of Perranporth; while Miss Christine Roberts and Miss June Grimble, appearing for the first time on the professional stage, bring to their two young parts a quivering earnestness, an unspoilt mixture of physical grace and energy which are attractive and heighten the play's effect. The Distant Point community seems to be dominated by odious but deeply affecting Communist little girls.

THE FILMS BY GRAHAM GREENE

Un Carnet de Bal— Underworld

A RICH widow looks back on her first ball with melancholy nostalgia; she wonders what fate has done to the men who said they loved her when she was sixteen. Their names are there on an old dance programme. . . . The mood is meant to be autumnal—memories dance through empty salons, woo her at her bedside. But Duvivier is not the director for so intangible a mood (we remember what Kirsanov did ten years ago in *Brumes d'Automne* with a few dripping boughs). A great director— *Pepé le Moko* his masterpiece—his mood is realistic, violent, belongs to the underside of the stone. This widow's nostalgia is too corseted; some other device than her prosaic ringing of doorbells and presenting of cards was needed to introduce the story of the men's lives—the provincial mayor marrying his cook, the mad mother pretending her son had never killed himself, the night-club keeper and gang leader quoting Verlaine with deft sentiment as the detectives arrive at 4 a.m., the middle-aged monk teaching choirboys to sing. Each episode is beautifully acted and directed, whether comic, melodramatic, sentimental, but whenever the widow appears upon the scene illusion rocks like stage scenery under her heavy and soprano tread. Nevertheless it is a film which must be seen—Harry Baur, Françoise Rosay, Raimu, Fernandel, it contains the finest French acting, and in one episode we have Duvivier's real greatness—the seedy doctor at Marseilles so used to furtive visitors and illegal operations that he doesn't wait for questions before he lights the spirit flame: the dreadful cataracted eye: the ingrained dirt upon his hands: the shrewish wife picked up in God knows what low music-hall railing behind bead curtains: the continuous shriek and grind of winch and crane. Nostalgia, sentiment, regret: the padded and opulent emotions wither before the evil detail: the camera shoots at a slant so that the dingy flat rears like a sinking ship. You have to struggle to the door, but you can run down hill to the medical couch and the bead curtains. There has been nothing to equal this episode on the screen since *Pepé*. It makes Renoir's *Underworld*, a slow agreeable undistinguished picture based on Gorki's novel, about a thief and a bankrupt baron and a dosshouse keeper and innocent love, oddly stagey and unconvincing. The dosshouse squalor is laid Dickensianly on, but you never believe in its aspiring thief, its poetic madman, its old philosopher, its virginal affection. This isn't what poverty does—tatter the clothes and leave the mind unimpaired. The genuine poverty is in Duvivier's Marseilles flat—the tin surgical basin, the antiseptic soap, the mechanical illegality and the complete degradation.

6.—Dawn in Wimpole Street

TENNYSON was at Somersby, his Lincolnshire home, when he heard of Arthur Hallam's death in Vienna. Earlier in that year, 1833, he had spent a week or so with Hallam at 67 Wimpole Street, where Hallam lived with his father. They had visited the Zoo, the Tower and the British Museum together, and Hallam had cheered Tennyson up, helping him to make light for the moment of Lockhart's savage attack on his second volume of poems. The gloom into which Tennyson was thrown back by Hallam's death lasted for many years, and sometimes when he was in London he used to leave his room in Norfolk Street before anyone was astir, stride blankly towards Wimpole Street, and stand there staring at No. 67.

Preparatory to seeing Wimpole Street at dawn, we spent the night at a Turkish Bath.

As an attendant took off our shoes, M. M. said: "What was Hallam like to look at? Is there any portrait?"

H. K. : The portrait is rather disappointing, I believe. Chubby. One would have said a good life.

We walked to our couches across a dim hall, water gurgling in the distance, a faded red carpet, here and there tables and red plush chairs, a marble swimming pool at the far end—the total effect rather West-of-Suez.

Undressing, M. M. said: "If not beautiful, clever perhaps?"

H. K. : Brilliant at Eton, brilliant at Cambridge, and wrote poems and essays.

M. M. : What are they like?

H. K. : Not brilliant.

As we walked in our loin-cloths towards the hot rooms, through an antechamber where one or two lolled reading evening papers, M. M. said: "Why did Tennyson love him so?"

H. K. : He was everything Tennyson wasn't—bubbling, knew everyone, marked out for a triumphant career, popular, and of course brilliant.

In great heat we sat upon a stone slab. On another slab close by an enormous body was spread out like a derelict whale, occasionally convulsed and emitting groans.

H. K. quoted:

He is not here; but far away
    The noise of life begins again,
    And ghastly thro' the drizzling rain
On the bald street breaks the blank
        day.

Stretched out under the masseur's hands, kneaded, thumped, soaped and sluiced, M. M. called out: "Had he a wife?" and H. K. called back: "He was engaged to Tennyson's sister." M. M. : "Why?"

Wrapped in warm towels and laid out for the night, we continued our conversation.

H. K. : Extraordinary, Hallam's fascination. Gladstone was as fond of him as Tennyson.

M. M. : The two great Victorian spell-binders, both spell-bound by Hallam. How to explain it?

H. K. : I suppose it was just because Hallam wasn't a spell-binder, and they were two desperate egotists, with all the weight of their future struggle on them.

M. M. : You still haven't told me where Tennyson's sister comes in.

H. K. : It rounded it off.

M. M. : Rounded what off?

It was dark in the streets at six-thirty, but the clouds were turning a dull grey. We passed the British Museum, where a yellow light shone through tall windows, as though some secret trial were in progress. The darkness thinned away in Oxford Street, and in Wimpole Street it was already day.

After the carefree variety of architecture in Wigmore Street, Wimpole Street was narrow and monotonous, and obviously hardly changed at all in the hundred years since Tennyson stood there at that same hour. Already milk bottles had been left at the doors. There were the doctors' name-plates. Up above, a light here and there in a servant's bedroom, but no one stirring in No. 67.

M. M. : What a place to see as a deserted shrine! What desolation!

H. K. :—

Dark house, by which once more I
        stand
    Here in the long unlovely street,
    Doors, where my heart was used to
        beat
So quickly, waiting for a hand. . . .

M. M. : How he must have loved him to face the dawn in Wimpole Street! These rich houses, this ghastly mausoleum of affluence!

H. K. :—

. . . And like a guilty thing I creep
    At earliest morning to the door.

We pictured him striding in from Wigmore Street, tall, sallow and unshaved, not a man, we thought, that anyone would ask the way of, his eyes fixed on No. 67.

H. K. : I wonder whether it would have made any difference if Hallam had lived.

M. M.: I can't see why. If, instead of dying in Vienna, he had survived in Downing Street, Tennyson would still have watched by that dark door, and groaned as the blank day broke on bald Wimpole Street.

H. K. : I suppose so.

M. M. : A doubly barren love.

Smoot's Shaving Cream

for beardless brilliance

"I'm sorry, dear, but I couldn't find my Smoot's"

In jars and tubes, 5/6, 3/9 and 1/3

If you have any difficulty in obtaining Smoot's, please write to Dept. S/C, 40 Chandos Street, W.C.2

AS THE WORLD GOES ROUND
a spotlight on current affairs
by GEORGE MARTELLI

Africa or Europe?

ONE of the more melancholy pastimes of those who dabble in international affairs is re-reading Hitler's *Mein Kampf*. It procures them the same kind of masochistic satisfaction as would a perusal of the back numbers of Old Moore's Almanack. With all due respect to Old Moore, however, it must be conceded that Hitler is the better prophet. Not all the disasters predicted in the Almanack occurred. Every major European crisis during the last five years was clearly foreshadowed by *Mein Kampf*.

To anybody who has not read that portentous work, either in the German, English, Hindustani, original, or expurgated editions, I would strongly recommend it. In particular it contains a good deal about colonies which is worth looking up at the present juncture. No doubt Lord Halifax marked the relevant pages before his interview with the author. It would help him to keep the conversation to the point, from which Hitler, if hearsay speaks true, is prone to stray.

Well, the first thing to note in this curious document—half profession of faith, half political programme—is its complete repudiation of German colonial policy. Colonies, according to Hitler writing in 1924, had been the cause of all Germany's troubles. They had deflected her from her real destiny, which was to conquer Eastern Europe, and brought her into fatal collision with the British Empire. There-

fore no more colonies, but friendship with Great Britain, and a free hand for expansion eastwards.

In the light of his most recent declarations, especially the statement which followed the visit of Lord Halifax, it might appear that for once Hitler had departed from the programme laid down in *Mein Kampf*. And to a certain extent this may be the case. In 1924 he could not foresee that a British Government might be prepared to consider a colonial redistribution. I do not say that the present British Government does consider it. But there is clearly, in the open way the question is discussed in this country, enough to encourage Germany to stake a claim, which she would otherwise, perhaps, have abandoned.

That need not mean that Hitler has reversed his fundamental conception. On the contrary everything suggests that expansion in Europe is still the main objective of German policy. If the colonies can be recovered without compromising that policy, so much the better. It would help to have access to raw materials, which could be exploited with German capital and German management, paid for in German currency or with German goods. It would also be good for prestige.

On the other hand, if these things are not to be, the demand for colonies still retains a nuisance-value. It is calculated, as one of the knowing ones put it, to fill the mind of the British Government with inexpressible tedium. Something that is always with

us, as the poor or the Irish used to be. In this state concessions are sometimes made from sheer mental exhaustion. Not the concession ostensibly asked for, of course; that would look too obvious. But others, which can possibly be dressed up so as not to appear concessions at all.

Naturally I am not suggesting that the British Government are contemplating any such dubious arrangement. They have said, and I'm sure they mean it, that the German demand could only be discussed as part of a general constructive settlement, giving a serious guarantee of peace. They were thinking presumably that Germany must first return to the League of Nations (which she would have to do theoretically to qualify for a colonial Mandate), and also subscribe to various pacts guarding her neighbours from attack. This would certainly look very well.

There are, however, a number of difficulties about it and they explain why in well-informed circles (read the Foreign Office) heads were shaken over the Halifax visit, while in other but not-so-well-informed quarters (read Fleet Street: journalists and politicians below Cabinet rank are quarters; ministers, diplomats, and civil servants, circles) there were rumours of Mr. Eden's resignation.

One of the difficulties is British public opinion. Even in six years' time it is not easy to see our Liberals and Socialists transferring the government of coloured people to the Nazi exponents of racial superiority. The Conservatives are officially against restoration, but their evolution is so

'My God, there's a face at the window!'

much more rapid than that of the other two parties, and their adaptation to a changing world so much more agile, that it is extremely difficult to predict their future attitude. Led by the diehards one would not exclude them from the rôle of pioneers in a general reshuffle of possessions. After all, we may be Sahibs and of course the nigger likes us, but you can't get away from the fact that Jerry ran the country very well.

But a graver objection than public opinion is that there is no conceivable guarantee which Germany could give that the return of her colonies would secure us peace in Europe. If we hand them over it will be as a present and we must not expect anything in return. And that goes for a lot of other things too.

DIARY OF PERCY PROGRESS
By John Betjeman
5—ADVERTISING DE LUXE

CHEERIHO, chaps! Bung-ho! And a thousand times bung-ho! I've been taking a bit of time off, but here I am back in the frolicsome columns of NIGHT AND DAY and, looking round me, I think I'm just about the wittiest, chirpiest fellow that e'er wielded the goose's quill to invoke the epistolary muse. From this you may gather that P.P. is feeling on the top of the world. That's just about it, boys. He *is*. That is to say, I am.

Fact is I've been in on a new racket. Like to hear about it? Sure. Here goes, then. Gather round, my chick-a-biddies. Pal of mine, Sam Tab, good sport, wife and a coupla kids down at Claygate, old Cag Bag. Occupation not much. Now he's got a craze for gadgets. Give him a gadget and he's like a youngster. He's invented a wizard dodge. It's a loudspeaker that can be heard three miles off against a thirty-mile-an-hour breeze—that is to say, given normal weather conditions said gadget can enter anyone's aural orifice for a radius of ten miles round our balmy English countryside.

"Now look here, Sam," I said. "You've got to let me handle this thing for you. It's big," I said. "I'll pay you a good sum down for the said gadget or, if you like, you can enter into a contract with me on a percentage basis. I mean we were at the old place (Carshalton) together," I said, "and we must stick together on this. Not that there's anything in it," I said, for these gadget merchants often want to collar the dibs that rightly belong to their financial backers, "but I'll do my best to help you with it. First let's give it a trial."

I'm a bit of a hand at mechanics myself, but I won't bother you with a technical description of the dodge. Suffice it, as Shakespeare hath it, the aforementioned egg is a good egg. It's a simple attachment that may be affixed to the radio, radiogram or gramophone in a very few moments by a technical engineer.

Well, I popped Sam and his blessed gadget into the dicky of my little bus and whisked 'em off to a quiet haven I wot of in the Wiltshire Downs far from the madding crowd and any nosey-parkers that might want to nibble the invention and make Sam a better offer than necessary.

We brought a gramophone and a couple of cuties to help the party go. Sam isn't exactly a ladies' man so I managed to have both cuties to myself. 'Nuff said. We called ourselves "The Noise Gang". I took some records—Bing Crosby crooning, and some experimental ones of gear-changing on a cheap car, realizing that these are the two chief noises you hear nowadays.

We drove across some fields and then over the grass of some downs. It was a fine day with the lark singing and whatnot. I plumped Sam and his instrument and the grammy on the grass in a lonely spot. "Right, Sam," I said, "set her going in a quarter of an hour's time, by which jiffy we should

be in a village somewhere on the ten-mile radius and will note the effect. Keep her going till we come back."

The cuties and I roared into a one-eyed place with a lot of gaping yokels and some thatched cottages and trees and a church, in fact the usual sort of rot the guide-books yap about. By that time Sam's loudspeaker was crooning out Bing Crosby full swing. I must say it was lovely. You couldn't hear yourself speak. The usual dullness of this one-eyed wonky place was quite gone. "It's lovely," said my extra-special as she snuggled up. To give you some idea of the volume of sound, let me tell you this—you couldn't even hear the engine of my car when I revved her up full throttle.

Laugh! Did I laugh? A peppery old fool came running out of the old manor house, outside which we were, yammering and gesticulating. Of course we couldn't hear what he said. Then the padre came along. We couldn't hear him either. Thinking they might be interested in the scheme I gave them each my card:

> *Mr. Percy Progress*
>
> **Business Efficiency Expert**

and wrote on the cards "To introduce the Progress Patent Loudspeaker". Then we buzzed off to some other places and noticed people going about with their fingers in their ears—well, if people don't like good music, they must lump it. Then we went out of earshot of the thing and had a damn good lunch. I told the cuties to bring their own sandwiches, which they ate in my little bus outside the hotel.

I suppose Sam must have been keeping the thing going for three or four hours. I noticed cattle in the fields all round careering about, a couple of sheep had killed themselves against a hedge, horses had gone crazy. It was a wonderful show. As we drove up to Sam, we put cotton-wool in our ears and I motioned to him to turn the thing off.

"Not bad, Sam," I said. I didn't want to appear enthusiastic for reasons already mentioned. I had already told the cuties where to step off.

Well, a few days later letters started appearing in *The Times* :

LOUD SPEAKER MENACE

SIR,—A gentleman calling himself Progress recently disturbed this quiet village with so-called music from a loudspeaker in a position I was unable to locate. As a result of protests from farmers whose loss in cattle is irreparable, from invalids whose recovery has been retarded, and from others like myself who resent still further the intrusion into our privacy by the resources of so called "civilization", I write to protest. Could not the Country authorities take steps to see that these public nuisances are abated? I have no quarrel with advertisements provided they are in their proper place, which is on the pages of such periodicals as your own.

Yours, etc.,

HUGH DE L. YOCKMINSTER,
Yockminster Manor,
Yockminster, Wilts.

Gee, boys, did I have a think! (Pardon your old pal using American expressions.) I should think I did think. Our friend de Courcy de Montmorency de Higginbottom put me on to an idea. Of course—use the gadget as an ad. Make forty or fifty of 'em, set 'em going at once advertising some of our products, with crooning in between the announcements, and yours truly could cover the whole of England, introduce the names of Amalgamated Spare Parts Ltd., Automatic Stone Toadstools, Chemical Vegetables Co., etc., into every home, hospital, church, loony-bin and pigsty throughout the country.

First thing then was to settle Sam Tab with a fair price. Some more protests appeared in *The Times*. I must thank de Vere de Vere, etc., for their help. "Now look, ole boy," says I, "the papers are getting onto this. People don't like it, see? They may legislate." And I showed him the letters of protest. "This is hard luck on you, ole chap. I still think your gadget's a good wheeze, ole man, and I feel I may have raised false hopes, ole chum. Anyhow I've given you a lot of trouble."

"Not at all," says Sam.

"Well, I'll tell you what I'll do," I said. "What did the gadget cost you to make?"

"About £5 in material—that doesn't include my own time."

"Well, I'll offer you double that, 'ole man, for the exclusive rights. Of course I won't be able to use the thing, but I'd like to show you I appreciate what you've done. I said we must stick together."

"Oh, I couldn't let you pay all that for something that isn't worth anything."

"Well, let's say seven-ten then and split the difference, ole man." So the thing was settled and I got the rights.

Well, I tinkled up a big bill-posting firm I know. "Hullo—Publicity Progress here. I've got a wheeze. Care to see it?" Upshot was, yours truly (who's not been in the blackmail business for nothing) demonstrated Sam's loudspeaker. Bill-posting firm twigged Percy's idea. This sort of advertising would cut out hoardings. "Well, what do you want for it?"

"£750,000," I said.

"Too much," said the manager. "For that sum we could supply the public with free ear-plugs and thus cut you out."

We finally compromised on £500,000. I don't think the bill-posting people will use my loudspeaker yet. They'll probably sell it to the government for propaganda purposes.

That's the way to do business, boys. Cheer-bye.

'*I don't know how to thank you.*'

A Tour by A. J. A. Symons

ONE of the obscurest yet most interesting restaurants in London is that of Mr. O. Bartholdi (No. 4 Charlotte Street, W.1, at the corner by Percy Street and Rathbone Place). At first sight it hardly seems to be a restaurant at all; the window proclaims delicatessen. But within, behind the small shop, are half a dozen not very comfortable tables. Not very comfortable; yet one might on occasion have seen the late Mr. Walter, manager of the Ritz, enjoying a meal here. For Mr. Walter was a Swiss, and Mr. Bartholdi is the best Swiss sausage maker in England; and he or his cook still retains the art of making the dishes of his country. So, unless you arrive in very good time, you will find every seat patriotically and substantially occupied.

But it is not so much his Swiss cuisine as his sausages that make Mr. Bartholdi worth visiting. First, the Bundenfleisch. Actually this is not a sausage, but dried raw beef—akin to the biltong or pemmican of childhood's Wild West stories—which has been dried in the sun for six months till it becomes a solid block almost as hard as stone. From that block, however, delicious shavings come, full of flavour, just the thing to embellish or create an appetite. It costs 12s. a pound. You purchase it in wafer thin slices, which are to be eaten, like the tapas of Spain, which include raw ham, as an accompaniment to sherry before the meal. Once cut, however, it soon shrivels.

If you are adventurous, try the Landjäger. This is a raw sausage, the thickness of two thumbs, made of beef and pork, flavoured with carraway seed, and alternately pressed and smoked for a month. It is last-minute fare; you can keep it hanging three or four weeks before hoicking it down to surprise a guest. But be sure to skin it.

Mr. Bartholdi offers fifteen different sorts of veal and pork sausage, all made from English meat on his own premises. Mettwurst is a mousee-like minced meat sausage which can be spread on sandwiches for picnics. Bratwurst is a lightly seasoned standby, of milk and veal, admirable at breakfast or for an occasion. Lasschinken should be tried; a delicious form of smoked ham. The Bundnerli is a beef and pork sausage made with Veltliner wine, and the Bundnerschinke is an attractive form of uncooked lean ham. Fleischkase, too, is attractive—chopped veal with liver and fried in the oven—if you have a taste for charcouterie; and who, save the least adventurous, has not?

There is more than this. Mr. Bartholdi keeps the real Gruyère. Most of what passes for Gruyère in this country comes from nearby Emmenthal. It can be distinguished by its larger holes, yellowish colour, and full, soft flavour. The true Gruyère has much smaller holes (about sixpenny size), whiter colour, and sharper taste than Emmenthal.

I found the true Gruyère, also, at Horcher's recently (Old Burlington Street, W.1). This is the newest, the smartest, the best and the most expensive of the German restaurants now open in London. Its long ground floor room is pleasantly decorated; it has an ample and excellent wine list, in which all the German growths are properly distinguished by districts; and a very good chef. The Paté St. Hubert can be recommended for those who like strong game flavours. It is bracketed on the menu with Cumberland sauce, but an alternative is served which I found preferable—a rich cream sauce with a distant lobster basis, which lacks the sweetness of the Cumberland. I have found the plat du jour invariably excellent.

Kempinski (Swallow Street, W.) is, like Horcher, a newcomer to London who was already famous in Berlin. His restaurant is below ground, but dexterous lighting and good ventilation save it from stuffiness. Two out-of-the-way dishes which I have enjoyed several times are filleted herrings in sour-cream sauce, an hors d'œuvre which I particularly recommend — one that serves the true purpose of the hors d'œuvre by stimulating the gastric juices—and saddle of hare with red cabbage and cranberry sauce. These sweet German sauces go well with the iced German white wines, and it is best to abandon the classic association of Burgundy with game in their presence. It is important to have the saddle of hare under- rather than overdone. The difference is remarkable.

Schmidt's, in Charlotte Street (opposite Mr. Bartholdi), was the pioneer among German restaurants in London. Less elegant than his two later-arrived compatriots, he is less expensive though not less successful. All three have a pleasantly germanic conception of the human appetite.

AT THE THEATRE

Elizabeth Bowen

Oh! You Letty

MUSICAL comedies are such fun—unless you are so unhappy as to dislike them—because they are so solid. You could almost eat one. Electric sunlight floods the lettuce-green leafage of a perpetual spring; the dresses are confections in the sugary sense. A revue is dowdy if it does not hit the exact topical mark, but the musical comedy is timeless—and does therefore (if it comes off) create a complete, jolly illusion. It can be, and ought to be, a hundred per cent theatre. It attempts to represent nothing, and therefore misrepresents nothing. The extreme surface propriety gives value to the run of frisky *doubles entendres*—these evoke snorts of cosmic laughter that run under the house and seem to come from nowhere and everywhere. (How rightly one talks about "the pink of propriety".) The thump of the orchestra, and the bounding choruses, impose such a fine feeling of sheer *muscle* that one knows there must be hope for the race. There is no aspiration to pure (or intellectual) nonsense: the silliness is sterling, a variation of equally sterling common-sense. If a musical comedy does happen to fall flat, that is, of course, awful: then there occurs a vacuum that all the despairs of life rush in to fill.

Oh! You Letty, presented by Mr. Jack Waller at the Palace, is quite up to the mark. Mr. Sydney Howard, largely, carries it—like a seal playing Atlas with a world on his nose. The scenes are pleasantly set in the plutocratic quarter of Fairfield Garden City, among loggias, rock gardens, festive marquees and lounges in the Hollywood-Spanish manner. The superb Miss Bertha Belmore, with her "presence", her pince-nez and her unexpectedly high kick (which brings the house down) plays, as Mrs. "Hattie" Simmons, the suburban châtelaine. Miss Patricia Leonard and Miss Phyllis Stanley are prettily adequate—but this is their elders' evening. Except for a threatening droop in the second act, the fun keeps a steady pace and is reasonably furious. There are several promising song-hits. Intervals at the Palace, with its warm red foyers, mirrors and bustling bars, are far less deadly than intervals in most theatres, with their genteel gloom.

Aristocrats

Aristocrats, at the Unity, is a remarkable play: both its technique and its subject are arresting. It is founded on fact—written by Nikolai Pogodin for the Realistic Theatre of Okhlopov, and based on a book compiled by Maxim Gorky, called *The White Sea Canal*. There is some resemblance to that film *The Road to Life*: only, the film dealt with juvenile delinquents, and these are adult convicts of both sexes, living in a prison camp and engaged in construction work on the canal. Some are plain criminals, some are reactionaries—recalcitrant intellectuals. The theme of *Aristocrats* is the building up, in these people, of a new morale, and the breaking down of that individualistic spirit that makes a man Man's enemy. Here " aristocrat" is used ironically for the self-exalting person who will not co-operate. One great virtue of this play is that it is not priggish; it is, rather, informed with an early Christian simplicity. *Aristocrats* opens with the arrival at the camp of a new batch of prisoners: two engineers, who have been convicted of sabotage, are full of bitter pride; Kostya the Captain (a grand brigand) meets an old acquaintance, or love, Sonya, the drug-fiend, and the two look likely to make an ugly combination. But the regeneration of these people, and others, keeps pace with the work on the canal.

The play consists of a succession of interleaved, very short, very vital scenes: there is a suggestion of clever cutting (in the cinema sense). There is nothing flatly or clumsily "episodic" about the construction: this method gathers emotion, instead of dispersing it. The Unity's theatrecraft and production are quite first rate; the lighting and grouping are *tours de force*. The crowd work (an important element here) is excellent. The acting is above the set professional level; it shows a touch of human genius unspoilt by the conventions but at the same time closely disciplined. *Aristocrats* has qualities in common with the great Russian films ; all the same it is essentially theatre, and opens a wide (and cheering) view of the theatre's possibilities. If you believe in the theatre, and still have hopes for it, do not miss *Aristocrats*. And humanly speaking,

do not miss it either. This is an important study of reform. Our own prison system does not do us credit: let us see how the problem is being coped with elsewhere.

Out of the Picture

The Group Theatre has presented Mr. Macneice's play for two successive Sundays at the Westminster. *Out of the Picture* is interesting, vivid, effective, but it appears to have a significance that one cannot wholly digest. Is it not simple enough? The little quick scenes that compose the first act are like revue scenes and, purely as entertainment, come off quite excellently: the people are attractively unabstract, the dialogue is full of vigour and snap. But this play is, clearly, more than an entertainment; it is an indictment, a charge levelled at most of us; it sets out to disturb—and does, though the disturbance it sets up is hard to analyse. Most ivory towers, by now, have been pretty badly chipped. Some of Mr. Macneice's shots are well placed, but some go rather wide. This play shows a certain waste of poetic energy. As drama it grips. But it was hard to determine how much of the very genuine tension felt in the audience during the last act was due (as it should have been) to spiritual crisis, how much to elementary, essentially unheroic warfears being played upon. It is not only concience, these days, that makes cowards of us.

Mr. Rupert Doone's production of *Out of the Picture* seemed to me excellent—economical, telling and not involved. The Group Theatre offers no play that is not important; it is doing very valuable work, to which support and interest are essential—essential to us, the public, as well as to the Group Theatre, for here is something we cannot afford to lose. We grumble at the fatuities of the commercial theatre, and leave the non-commercial theatre to fight heavy odds. It is very much to be desired that the Group Theatre should soon have a theatre and offices of its own. We need plays that cut ice, plays that get somewhere, plays that are of our time: we are badly behind most other countries in this.

CINEMA

Monica and Martin
Mademoiselle Docteur
Eastern Valley

AN artist who doesn't trouble about money, who isn't interested in selling his pictures, who lives in domestic bliss with his wife (she is his model too)—it's the old Bohemian fairy tale which once, I suppose, represented a nostalgic dream of the successful bourgeois making money to satiety in the industrial age. But it was already a bit unconvincing by the time of du Maurier, and *Monica and Martin* has the added disadvantage of being Teutonic—Germans are congenitally unfitted for irrational behaviour. We sigh with relief when the plot emerges from the garret (Monica sells Martin's pictures as her own and complications arise when she is commissioned to paint a mural in a new sports stadium and is awarded the Cranach Prize), away from the playful hunger and the humorous poverty which is like a cruel insult to genuine destitution. There *is* one point of interest: Consul Brenckow, a stupid self-important would-be patron, insulted, mocked, led up the garden. That absurd poster dignity and preposterous moustache: where have we seen them before? We are haunted by the memory of an upraised arm and a fast car and lines of Storm Troops facing inwards with hands on their revolvers towards a loyal populace.

Mr. Ford Madox Ford has divided fiction into novels and nuvvels. So one may divide films into movie and cinema. *Monica and Martin* is movie: so, too, I'm afraid, is Mr. Edmond Greville's spy film *Mademoiselle Docteur*. Mr. Greville has an impeccable cinematic eye, but he has been badly

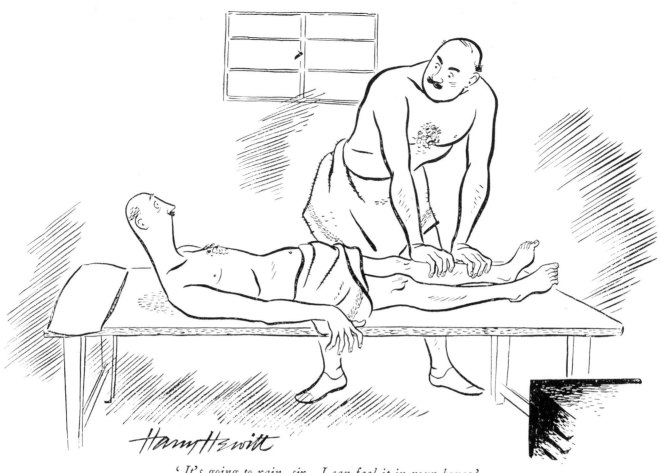

' It's going to rain, sir—I can feel it in your bones.'

served by a really shocking script, with childish continuity. Even a thriller cannot thrill unless the characters are established in our imaginations, and the packed plot of this film allows them no chance. Things are happening all the time: there's no opportunity to establish anything. Once the ghost of a theme did seem about to emerge when the medical student turned spy (played by Miss Dita Parlo with a charming spherical vacancy) protests to her employer "My ambition was to save lives". But the idea is never developed: it is swept away on a torrent of secret plans, villainous agents, dancing girls, passwords. As for the dialogue, it ambles flatly along, like conversation between strangers at the beginning of a cocktail party before anyone's had a drink. The general idea seems to be that people must talk all the time even if they've got nothing relevant to say. Eric von Stroheim makes his come-back in this film— one recognizes the uniform and the monocle. The uniform is as tight but a good deal less shapely than it used to be in the old silent days of *Foolish Wives.* "The man you will love to hate"—so they used to advertise him (climbing a ladder in his skin-tight Prussian breeches towards an innocent bed). No one will hate him now. Inclined to stoutness, with a rough friendly American accent, he looks dressed up for a party. I shall prefer to remember him as the great realistic director of *Greed* (1923)—the dentist's chair, the hideous servant's bedroom, the lovers walking in the rain down the long grey breakwater.

Finally one example of cinema. *Eastern Valley* has been made by the Strand Film Company to describe the activity of a society called the "order of friends" in a distressed Welsh area. The older men have been given a chance to work on the land without losing their unemployment pay. The object is a psychological one–they receive no pay; but the whole community of unemployed families benefit by the cheaper goods. The film has been directed by a newcomer, Donald Alexander. He has learnt from Anstey the value of direct reporting: the appalling cottages held up by struts from falling, dwarfed by the slagheaps: the trout stream turned into a drain, one empty fag packet floating down between the old tins: the direct interview with the wife of an unemployed man; but he has learnt too from Basil Wright how to express poetically a moral judgment. Life as it once was before industry scarred and mutilated the valley; life as it is; life as it should be.

GRAHAM GREENE

★

REALISM

NONSENSE ABOUT IBSEN
By
James Agate.
—SUNDAY TIMES *poster.*

EUPHEMISM

" Price of Ignorance " (Regal). Herbert Marshall, Barbara Stanwyck, Eric Blore and Glenda Farrell, in an attempt to cash in on the vogue for crazy comedy. But I doubt if the public is as crazy as all that.—*Daily Telegraph.*

MINUTES OF THE WEEK

All Our Own Work

From time to time people have asked us whether we, Slingsby, are personally responsible for the drawings which do so much to improve the appearance of this page. Hitherto we have had to reply that it was not us, but another chap; an artist—"a very decent feller," we have usually been prompt to add, in our broad-minded way, although we have never actually met him.

Well, this week, as you can see for yourselves, there has been a hitch. We have let down the long-haired fraternity by failing to write these notes on time. As a result, the artist has been unable to illustrate them. In order, therefore, to give the block-maker a chance of thinking over the question of hari-kiri in a cooler, more detached frame of mind, we dashed off the drawings ourself.

"Dashed" is perhaps the wrong word. To be frank, it's a long time since we had a stab at creative art, and early Slingsbies in any case suffer, as more than one connoisseur has pointed out, from the artist's inability to remember whether it is blue and yellow that

make green, or green and yellow that make blue. Still, we have done our level best, and we do not think that we are presumptuous in claiming that the result — "Business Man Obsessed by Yaks" — is something rather out of the ordinary, even in these days. As for the functional, the representative value of this picture, all we can say is (a) that more business men than you might imagine are troubled and haunted by yaks, and (b) that a yak is one of the few quadrupeds who are so providentially overgrown that you don't have to draw their legs.

In an adjacent column you will see a later, an almost unfinished work. It is entitled "Marks and Spencer: or Faute de Mieux". The birds were put in as an extra, free of charge; and the letters A and B, though done entirely by hand, mean absolutely nothing at all.

Tantamount to a Rebuff

NIGHT AND DAY is forever getting into trouble with the Giants of Fleet Street. First Mr. Peter ("In Spite of Everything") Howard, who found us ever so Macchiavellian in his *Sunday Express* column; and now Mr. Godfrey Winn of the *Daily Mirror* (the only gossip-writer we know who is *definitely* dew-drenched) accuses this periodical of bad taste. He didn't mention NIGHT AND DAY by name; and in preferring his dread charge he was as circumlocutory as a games-mistress adumbrating the Facts of Life. All

the same, we stand condemned. And not for the first time, as far as poor old Slingsby is concerned. Mr. Winn recently exhumed, and lyrically refuted, a crack we made some time ago about débutantes. Old fogey that we are, we went so far as to say that the average débutante of our day could be summed up as two hot hands and a heavy silence. Mr. Winn wrote that the débutantes he knew were a jolly sight better than this, thus making us feel a bully and a tease.

We were told the other day—and cannot, for the sake of those acquainted with the *Daily Mirror*, forbear retailing—a typical and probably untrue story about Mr. Winn, who is said to take his standing as a journalist seriously. He was playing tennis (at which he is extremely good) at a house in Oxfordshire. He brought off a very dashing drive to win a set and was heard, when leaving the court, to say: "I wish my readers had been here to see me do that."

"If they had," was an unfeeling and quite uncalled-for comment, "we should have beheld the largest concourse of domestic servants ever assembled in these islands."

All the same, journalistically Mr. Winn is a wow. Winnie the Wow. We take off our hat to him.

Slingsby

WITH DIZ AT

THE LOCAL

A

MERRY

CHRISTMAS

PURSUITS & VERDICTS

Herbert Read

Blood Wet and Dry

WHY does a new Agatha Christie still seem so acceptable? We know before we open it that there will still be the same old Poirot, an ageless eunuch, immune from the vicissitudes of life; that the plot will be ingenious to the point of improbability; but we also know that we shall be kept guessing to the end; and though in a few months *Death on the Nile* will blend with *Murder in Mesopotamia* or any other title on the growing list of "Books by the same Author", we do not mind. And we suspect it is because she is true to pattern that we are true to her; for it is the pattern that makes the interest, and the only rule in this trade is: find a pattern and pursue it. If authors write true to form, publishers will—or should—do the rest. For the rest is the nasty business of publicity, but before that business can get going, two things must be guaranteed: a standard article and a continuous supply of it. Efficient and cynical publishers (the one quality implies the other) do not want their authors to change or "develop"; they pray that the next book will be like the last; that all the characters and all the plots will only shift within the mechanical limits of a kaleidoscope.

Within those limits, the pattern can be original. I do not know any-one who has, in such a supreme degree, what I would call Mrs. Christie's despatch. She wields her humane-killer with a butcher-like indifference to life; her murders are clean, explicit, feline. "But above the ear was a tiny hole with an incrustation of dried blood round it." That is the typical Christie sentence for such occasions. It is almost Websterian. Her pistols

seem poetic toys, the knives are surgical instruments; there is a house-wifely neatness in the slaughterhouse. The very style is cut to pattern. She does not "intimate" and "terminate" like Mr. Gask; she is not judicious like Mr. Wade, nor facetious like Mr. Jepson. She is neither too short nor too long, too tough nor too tender ; she is energetic, decisive, and slightly catty where women are concerned.

It is only necessary to add that in the present case she brings about twenty characters from the four corners of the

---

Death on the Nile. Agatha Christie. Collins. 7s. 6d.

The Night of the Storm. Arthur Gask. Jenkins. 7s. 6d.

The High Sheriff. Henry Wade. Constable. 7s. 6d.

---

earth, puts them all on a pleasure-steamer going down the Nile, has three of them murdered under the unblinking eyes of Hercule Poirot, and finishes it all off with a suicide pact. And since he had a soft spot in his heart for the guilty couple, Poirot merely nodded.

The Night of the Storm is the first thriller by Arthur Gask that I have read, but he is an old hand with fifteen or more to his credit. As I have already hinted, his style is rather stilted, and he handles the passions with a crude and elemental vigour:

" '. . . . You overheard him black-mailing your sister, and if you were listening when he made his vile demands, then—'

'I was,' she interrupted fiercely, 'but I didn't kill him for that only. I—I—' Her voice choked, and then with a sudden movement she drew herself up and slipped off the shoulder-strap of her dress. 'Look, look! I killed him for that. He had been drinking and he bit me there!'—and she fell back limply into the chair."

The moral is that such cannibalistic he-men deserve to be shot, and a

gentlemanly detective must bamboozle the police and bury the secret in the depths of his sentimental heart. But it is a very readable story, and the usual butler is unusually good.

Mr. Henry Wade (actually Sir Henry Aubrey Fletcher, Bart., D.S.O., M.V.O., Eton and Oxford and some-time a High Sheriff himself), on the basis of a dozen detective stories, has built up a very respectable reputation. The story he tells in *The High Sheriff* is a good story, but I do not think it is a particularly good thriller. There is far too much "business"—country life business, gentleman's honour business, father and son business. "Hunting was part of the life of the countryside, an important component in the struc-ture of agriculture." "In January, the cock pheasant is the most wily of birds, a worthy adversary against whom to pit both brains and skill." "It gave him some satisfaction to see the man where he was"—in the dock —"one of those opinionated, socialist fellows that the teaching profession threw up from time to time." "I thought I'd disgraced the name of D'Arcy." "His secret fear of a strain of cowardice engendered by himself . . ." Such phrases are all very well as indications of character, but there should only be enough character in a thriller to "motivate" the crime. In this book the characterization runs away with the story and the crime is only incidental. It is possible that the hunting and shooting fraternity will like it—and I suspect that country houses order their thrillers in hampers —but the hard-bitten reviewer, faced with his pigeon-holes, can only place it among the misfits.

★

"Stick 'em up," he called out, then said they had better be going. The boys moved away, but shortly afterwards they were fired at.

One of the boys was hit on the hand, the knee and the arm ; another on the ear and shoulder; the third on the temple.

"You might have blinded the boys," said the chairman, placing him on pro-bation.—*Daily Mirror.*

Good heavens, yes, you might have scared the life out of them !

THE FILMS BY GRAHAM GREENE

Marie Walewska—True Confession

SHE is, of course, the finest filly of them all. . . . And yet a dreadful inertia always falls on me before a new Garbo film. It is rather like reading *Sartor Resartus*—Carlyle's a great writer, but need one—now—this week . . . he's waited half a century: he can afford to wait a little longer: he'll still be on the public library shelves when one is old. And so too, I expect, will Garbo be: she will figure like Duse and Rachel in the reminiscences of bores; that magnificent mare's head of hers will puzzle our descendants, seeking a more obvious beauty, as it stares dumbly from the printed page, caught in a still in Napoleon's embrace, in Armand's embrace, in—the fictional names fail us—Fredric March's embrace, John Gilbert's embrace. A great actress—oh, undoubtedly, one wearily assents, but what dull pompous films they make for her, hardly movies at all so retarded are they by her haggard equine renunciations, the slow consummation of her noble adulteries. She is a Houyhnhnm in a world of Yahoos, but, being Yahoos ourselves, we sometimes yearn for less exalted passions, for people who sin for recognizable reasons, because it's pleasurable. "It is a bawdy planet."

She has been badly served, of course, by writers and producers. They seem to feel uneasily that the films are unworthy of so superb an actress, and in compensation they treat her with deathly reverence: she is like a Tudor mansion set up again brick by numbered brick near Philadelphia. *She Married Her Boss, True Confession*, films like these—contemporary, carefree—are good enough for Claudette Colbert, Carole Lombard, but for Garbo you've got to have Great Scenarios (supplied lavishly and rotundly to order by S. N. Behrmann). So we are given *Queen Christina*, *Marie Walewska*: fake history, masquerades in fancy dress, dialogue written in the conventional rhetoric of the middlebrow historical novelist. But there's no satisfactory half-way house between poetic and realistic drama: if you can't give Garbo poetry to speak, you ought to give her prose. "I kiss the hand which refused to sign away our country's independence"—that isn't prose.

Marie Walewska is one of the dullest films of the year. O, it has its moments when the Frenchman Boyer and the Swede Garbo are together alone, but the awful ocean of American vulgarity and good taste (they are the same thing) laps them round—soon Marie's brother will bounce in like a great Buchmanite Blue troubled about sex, or her husband (Henry Stephenson) will slip through the lath and plaster, honeyed and Harvard and humane, behaving as America thinks the Polish aristocracy behaved—with new-world courtesy. There are moments too of unconscious comedy—when Prince Poniatowski (one of our old gangster friends, uneasy, speechless and pouter-breasted in his hussar uniform) and one or two unidentifiable Polish leaders call on Marie Walewska and in her aged husband's presence suggest gently and avuncularly that she sleep with Napoleon for the sake of her country. An awkward situation for romantic drama, and one which attains a fine height of crazy comedy when they embrace Count Walewska—"Goodbye, old friend"—and retire reverently on tiptoe from the awkward domestic impasse they have created. There is another scene too which is dangerously close to laughter when Napoleon's bastard child prays by the bed in Elba—"Bless my father whom I have never seen and help him to be good"—and Napoleon lurks and listens round the night-nursery door. There's "Old Stephan," too, the faithful retainer; a revolutionary whom you recognize at once by his tousled straw-coloured wig, who cries "Liberty" in front of a firing squad; and printed captions—"Two Months Later. The Castle of Finkenstein." And all the while the great fake emotions booming out—Love, Country, Ambition—like a *Times* leader-writer taking a serious view of the Abdication crisis.

You aren't like me—you don't *have* to see Garbo. Go to *True Confession* instead—this is that rare thing, cinema, and the best comedy of the year. Do not be put off by the stock phrase—"crazy comedy": this picture is constructed firmly and satisfactorily on human nature. It is—more or less—about the murder of a lecherous business man who goes in for private secretaries; the heroine—an inveterate and charming liar played by Carole Lombard—pleads guilty to a murder she didn't commit because it seems easier to get off that way; the trial scene is a magnificent parody of all American trial scenes, and the picture succeeds in being funny from beginning to end—never more funny than when the corpse is disclosed under the carpet, or the heroine is warned that she will "fry". If it appears crazy it is only because we are not accustomed on the screen to people behaving naturally and logically. An inexperienced young barrister defends his wife on the charge of murder: we expect heroics and we get comic incompetence: that isn't crazy—it's an old melodramatic situation presented for once in terms of how people really behave. This is one of those comedies—Capra made them before he read James Hilton—in which the small parts are perfectly cast and played. I advise a quick visit: the public, I think, found it oddly shocking, for the middlebrow screen is more and more dictating how people ought to behave—even at a deathbed. I remember lying in bed a few years ago in a public ward listening with fascinated horror to a mother crying over her child who had died suddenly and unexpectedly after a minor operation. You couldn't question the appalling grief, but the words she used . . . they were the cheapest, the most improbable, the most untrue . . . one had heard them on a dozen British screens. Even the father felt embarrassment standing there beside her in the open ward, avoiding every eye.

APPENDIX

The first piece in this Appendix, Evelyn Waugh's review of *Eyeless in Gaza*, was printed in the dummy issue of *Night and Day* that was produced for publicity before the magazine's launch. The other three pieces – two by Waugh and one by Osbert Lancaster – were intended for the issues of 30 December and 6 January, but owing to the closure of the magazine, they were never published.

★

Eyeless in Gaza. Aldous Huxley.
  Chatto & Windus. 10s. 6d.

For many years now the increasing facility with which library subscribers get through their books has been a threat to the novelist's income. The three-hundred-odd pages that were designed to occupy a weekend now barely survive a journey in the Underground; the faster books circulate, the fewer copies are needed. To meet this danger it has become customary either to write at greater length or with more confusion of manner. In his new book, *Eyeless in Gaza*, Mr. Huxley has resorted to both expedients. It is not difficult for him to be diffuse, as he has shown before, but his clear mind does not naturally express itself obscurely; his vocabulary is so wide and precise that he has no need to experiment with speech-forms; his thoughts tend to follow one another in classical sequence. Thus, in order to delay the middlebrow, he has left things to the binder, and has been content, unambitiously, to sew up the chapters in their wrong order. The result is a novel of conventional plan – four long episodes in single life, like suits in a pack of cards – arbitrarily shuffled and redealt. An attempt made in the blurb to justify this to the middlebrows with the magic word "counterpoint" need not occupy the serious reader. Once or twice there is a discernible association between the contiguous incidents – but only once or twice, and then with singularly little profit. There is, however, another, perhaps a primary, motive in the arrangement. The book describes the formative events in the life of a completely intolerable cad, bore and crank; in order to expose, ruthlessly, the depth of boredom and crankiness to which the hero finally descends, Mr. Huxley has permitted us to look over his shoulder and watch him writing his private notebook; pages from this journal constitute a formidable part of the book; taken in lump they would be unreadable; I believe that, more than avarice, guile was the motive for administering the emetic dose in small pills concealed in the doughy but sometimes pungent dish.

It should be an irrelevant criticism of a novel that its characters, in real life, would be unwelcome guests. A first-class artist like Mr. P. G. Wodehouse can keep one endlessly amused by a group of people who would drive one lunatic in five minutes. I think it is a grave defect of Mr. Huxley's art that his hero should affect one with an antipathy so strong that reading about him becomes inordinately painful (and not only the hero but, with two exceptions, every character in the book). Anthony Beavis is, at the present date, a man of early middle age. He is middleclass – and this again is a defect of Mr. Huxley's art that it makes the least snobbish reader violently classconscious; it is not that Beavis is of modest means and undistinguished family; there is something radically second-rate about him so that one can hear the undertones of his genteel accent in every sentence of his journal. He and most of the characters are bourgeois and squeamish; the heroines belong to an order of society in which the girls go out to do the day's household marketing: nothing wrong with that; the trouble is that Mr. Huxley's young ladies feel sick in the butcher's shop. Beavis is himself intensely class-conscious. When in youth he meets proletarian children he has to run away and spit for fear of microbes; when, at the University, he was asked to dinner by a gentleman his reflections are these: "Why *did* he go about with Gerry? For of course he didn't like the man... Mere snobbery... it pleased him to associate with Gerry and his friends. To be the intimate of these young aristocrats and plutocrats, and at the same time know himself their superior in intelligence, taste, judgment, in all the things that *really* mattered, was satisfying to his vanity... He was their intimate, yes; but as Voltaire was the intimate of Frederick the Great." An unamiable state of mind in which to go out to dinner. And his behaviour there was very odd. His method of entertaining his tipsy host was to discourse about Plotinus. "Science is reason and reason is multitudinous." Frederick the Great got better value for his wine.

Beavis had little chance in life. His father was an inhuman prig; his mother died while he was young. (At her funeral his only thought was of the microbes he might be breathing in the musty air of the church.) He was sent to a private school of preternaturally prurient little boys, many of whom he was unable to shake off in after life. Of his public school we know little; at Oxford he was already set in the pathetic little path he followed to the end. At the beginning of the war he had a moment of generous enthusiasm, joined the army, was wounded while still in training, and expensively nursed back to health at the public charge without having done anything to the public benefit. This is how he regards the ignominious incident: "What unlikely forms the grace of God assumes sometimes! A half-witted bumpkin with a hand grenade. But for him I should have been shipped out to France and slaughtered... He saved my life. My freedom, too."

For, unlike many pacifists, Beavis is a coward. As a little boy he was servile to the school bully and disloyal to his only friend. Threatened with a pistol in Mexico, he nearly expires with fright. At the close of the story we see him, in a mood of exaltation and self-esteem, going to a political meeting at which there is a chance of rowdyism. That is certainly an experience more common for Conservatives than Radicals, but it is symptomatic of the seedy tone of the book that such a supremely commonplace achievement should be represented as a high spiritual triumph.

Beavis has many cold-blooded love affairs, mostly with the wives or fiancées of his friends. Mr. Huxley's treatment of women is always greatly superior to that of his men. The men represent ideas – and the softest, shoddiest ideas – but the women represent matter and sometimes come to life. Helen, because she is unintellectual and has a sense of humour, her mother because she is at least a whole-hearted debauchee, are both real people. It is in the pages where they appear that Beavis's inadequacy is most painful. It did not need a dog from the air to show up the drabness of his affair with Helen.

The male characters of the book, almost without exception, suffer from obscure pathological derangements. A chapter that promised adventure – when Beavis goes off to Mexico on an exciting mission – finds its climax in the appearance of Doctor Miller – the apotheosis of Huxleyan boredom and crankiness – and the recommendation of colonic irrigation. That, perhaps, is the solution of all the problems in the book. Beavis suffered all the time from a queasy stomach and a hypersensitive nose; there is not a chapter in which he does not feel sick, scarcely a page in which he does not encounter an unpleasant smell. Indeed, one is reminded less of Samson than of blind Gloucester smelling his way to Dover. That is the odd part of the book. Is it just the desire to puzzle the middlebrows and send them to their Milton, or can it be possible that in some monstrous haze Mr. Huxley does really see his sub-human hero as the counterpart of the blinded and betrayed giant? Can it be possible?

EVELYN WAUGH

A. E. H. Laurence Housman.
  Cape. *10s. 6d.*

As literary executor to his brother, Mr. Laurence Housman has been charged with a responsibility requiring great discretion and sense of duty. There must inevitably be some critics who will think that, in a case of this kind, the requirements of the public should be secured first. We are naturally inquisitive about the private affairs of men whose public work interests us; we like too to look behind the scenes of his art, and to learn about the perfect product from the discarded fragments and failures. It was Professor Housman's wish unequivocally expressed, that, in death, he should be allowed the aloofness which he fostered when alive. He trusted in his younger brother to fulfil his wish loyally and the trust was well placed. There can be little doubt that, as a case of conscience, Mr. Laurence Housman has acted rightly, but the result of his self-denial is, unavoidably, a book that has the mark of poverty and inadequacy.

The present little volume – rather excessively priced at 10s. 6d. – contains a personal memoir, some letters, some poems and – heaven knows why – a horoscope. The poems will excite the keenest anticipation and, here, Mr. Housman has allowed himself some legitimate laxity. Professor Housman's instructions were that none of his poetry found after his death should be published which his brother considered inferior in quality to anything whose publication he had himself authorised. Mr. Laurence Housman considered one of the published poems – he leaves us speculating which – inferior to the others, and he has very sensibly taken this poem as the test of what could be saved from destruction. The result is eighteen poems, all of which, if not comparable to the best of *Last Poems*, are certainly well worth saving. There are also some light verses whose main function is to prove that the Professor did have the lighter side which was, sometimes, one thought, rather dubiously, claimed for him. The lightness, it is true, has some of the quality of jokes on the scaffold; sudden and painful death is the subject of much of the whimsey; it is the sort of humour which children, at their safe distance from the grave, particularly relish, and the Professor was able to play with it in ingenious forms.

The letters are far the most valuable and revealing section of the book. Here both the poet and the don combine to give a splendid pungency to every utterance. In particular the series addressed to a Mr. Houston Martin are models of how such correspondence should be treated. Mr. Martin was an adolescent American who pressed his attentions upon Professor Housman during the last years of his life. No one was more quick than the Professor to detect and resent an impertinence, but the importunities of Mr. Martin were of such a staggering order that he found himself captivated as though by the gambolings of a kitten and he replied to them in a unique measure of charity and humour.

"Such infatuation as yours," he wrote, "is quite intimidating", and from one of the earlier letters in which he wrote, "it is now a great many years since I began to refuse requests for poems written out in my own hand, and therefore you must not mind if you receive the same answer as many others"... he was, in a little over a year, saying . . . "you are an engaging madman and write more agreeably than many sane persons".

Ten months later he writes, "I suppose it would be impossible for me to explain to you, perhaps to any American, the impropriety of your conduct in writing, as you seem to have done, to ask famous people their opinion of me. I hope that some of them, at any rate, have ignored your letters."

But a year later again: "Your questions, though frivolous, are not indecent . . ." and it is quite clear that the old man got considerable pleasure from the correspondence.

Mr. Housman's "personal memoir", which fills nearly half the book, is disappointing. It was not to be expected or desired that all the secrets of the Professor's heart should be revealed. It is highly doubtful whether Mr. Laurence Housman or any living man understood them. There are hints from which it is possible to build a story, which, very likely, is far from the truth. How far the events which formed that sombre and enigmatic character were purely interior, how far they were occurences in the objective world, we do not know and it is not our business to enquire; but Mr. Housman fails us in many respects, in the information which should be general knowledge. Perhaps he has already dealt with many of the topics in his own autobiography and is reluctant to repeat himself, but those of us who have not read that book may reasonably ask for further details of the subject's upbringing. We are given no hint of the character of his father or even of his occupation and position in life; we are told practically nothing of the other occupants of the nursery. It is probable that with two brothers so remarkable, the other members of the family deserve some description. The details of his undergraduate life are of the most meagre and one particular omission is conspicuous. Professor Housman failed completely in Greats and was obliged to take a pass school in order to get his degree at all. He then crammed for the civil service and for some years occupied an unimportant post there, from which he was suddenly elevated to the Chair of Latin at London University. It seems inconceivable that he could have earned this honour purely on the strength of his Mods papers, however brilliant they may have been. There must, surely, have been a highly interesting period of reconstruction, when, after his failure, Professor Housman renewed his self-confidence, re-established his scholastic connections, consolidated his reputation by research and publications.

Mr. Housman's narrative is enlivened by many anecdotes illustrating his brother's biting and lapidary wit; many of these are already familiar as part of the old tradition which surrounded him. It is interesting how many of them, repeated appreciatively from senior common-room to senior common-room, grew and were polished in the telling, and now that they are printed in their original forms, seem sadly bald and even bookish.

I have been re-reading Mr. Betjeman's poems and notice with pain that there *is* a change in an old favourite. The second line of the third verse of the Restoration Hymn now reads "Sing art and crafty praise". The change no doubt was prompted by the wish to calm the wounded susceptibilities of a well-known firm of ecclesiastical decorators, but it is one that all true lovers of Mr. Betjeman's art will deplore. Art-and-craftiness is the last complaint which can be made against the finished and intransigently prosaic ornaments of 1883.

EVELYN WAUGH

[See Bevis Hillier, *John Betjeman: A Life in Pictures*, John Murray, 1984, p. 63]

VOICE FROM VALHALLA

Alan Parsons' Book
  Heinemann 10s. 6d.

Alan Parsons' Book is a selection, made by his widow and a friend, from the Commonplace Book which he kept, with intermittent application, throughout almost the whole of his adult life.

The keeping of such a book is a delectable literary pursuit – very rare nowadays – which requires many high gifts if it is to be worthwhile. Alan Parsons fulfilled all the conditions. He was a man of large reading and, what is more important, large love of reading. His book was wholly personal; there was no qualification for the entries included other than that they moved him or tickled his fancy. There were numerous quotations from Pepys, Johnson, Shakespeare, Webster, Lamb and other classics; there were extracts from the newspapers and from private correspondence; 'My favourite misspellings'; extracts from poets as fashionable as Gerard Hopkins and as unfashionable as Walt Whitman. It was a completely unsnobbish book; nothing was included because it *ought* to be. He had no self-consciousness about mixing the hackneyed and even the banal with the recondite. The guests were all there for the delight of the host – because he loved them or because they amused him. Purely as an anthology it is one which countless readers who, like myself, never knew Alan Parsons will wish to keep permanently by them. But it is much more than this. It is the portrait and memorial of its compiler and it is with this avowed purpose that the editors now make public what was originally intended as a private recreation. When Alan Parsons died, at the beginning of 1933, he left a reputation that was somewhat nebulous to all except his immediate circle. With every gift except that of physical health he left little of positive, concrete achievement. He had written one book and some lyrics – good but not of the first order. He had been an accomplished scholar, a civil servant, a genial dramatic critic. The charm, wit and culture for which he was loved are qualities which seldom outlive the memories of friends; in this series of extracts and in her felicitous biographical notes, Mrs. Parsons has found a way of perpetuating them with a large part of their colour and fragrance. And she has done more; she has sketched the portrait of his generation.

"Alan," in death, she tells us, "did not look peaceful, he looked – as his mother said, almost amused – smiling, at what? Release? Forgiveness? Triumph to know at last that he was loved? Or – even more, that which it takes enormous faith even to hope for – a going back to youth – the Valhalla of Julian, Billy, Charles, Denys, Denny, Eric, Edwin, Mona, Pat?"

Alan Parsons' Book is a voice from this Valhalla; that shadow world, inhabited, in heroic proportions, by the generation that lay between the 'Souls' and the 'Bright Young People'. The characteristics of that generation, as one enumerates them, strike a contrast with their successors; their virtues were chivalry, romance, gentleness of mind, loyalty, tolerance, mutual appreciation, and, above all a zest for human and natural beauty. Their limitations are implicit in this list. They were most of them, though by no means all – Alan Parsons himself was an example to the contrary – born in circumstances of financial certainty, which gave a taint of amateurishness to their contact with the arts. They mostly wrote verse, which was melodious and elegant enough, but, with few exceptions, soft and immature; in their very gusto of enjoyment which they squandered on everything that seemed to them beautiful, they abdicated their rights as a critical society. The function of a cultured class should be to maintain and impose right standards of taste, not to lower them by imitating the professionals. They lived in an age of tumultuous aesthetic heresies; most of them seem to have been quite unaware of the influences abundantly apparent on the Continent that were preparing the disintegration of what they understood by Art. For all their classical prowess they were not classicists.

Many of them had a hereditary and active connection with politics – mostly with Liberal politics – but they seem to have known little of the underlying economic problems of their time. The war, which tragically scattered them, came to most as a complete surprise. They enjoyed England so hugely that few of them troubled to travel much or to discover what was going on in the world outside.

While they pursued conventionally successful careers at the Bar and in government service, they looked longingly at the drab professions of acting and journalism. They seem to have held few intellectual opinions and to have felt no need for logical formularies. Ease, exuberance, warmth were what made them enviable; they were poles apart from the rapacious, pompous and macabre heroes of the Elizabethan age to whom they are so frequently compared.

All this is vividly reflected in *Alan Parsons' Book*. The Commonplace books of an earlier age are full of maxims and moral precepts; nothing here seems to owe its place to content except the jokes. It is all style and charm.

It is significant that, nowadays, to say that a writer is 'personal' has come to imply either that he is conceited or malicious. Alan Parsons seems to have read all literature for its personal implications, seeking precedents and expressions for his own moods and more particularly epithets that could be gracefully turned to the adornment of his friends; and his lack of conceit illumines the book through and through.

EVELYN WAUGH

AT BURLINGTON HOUSE

Art of the Seventeenth Century

It is a matter for congratulation that the Royal Academy have decided that this winter's exhibition at Burlington House shall be bounded by temporal instead of the usual national limitations. It is perhaps more enjoyable and certainly more profitable in these days of nationalism run mad to be able to study a collection of masterpieces by artists of a dozen nationalities who all paid allegiance to a common European tradition – who all contributed to a common European culture. The French frequently maintain that Poussin displays a typical French mastery of formal design, the Flemings that Rubens was the supreme product of Flemish vitality, and there may still be certain Col. Blimps who like to imagine that Van Dyck is the finest artistic example of English restraint (presumably on the grounds that even a brief residence in our country is sufficient to endow a well-behaved visitor with our virtues). But the fact remains one is justified in supposing that none of these masters regarded themselves as the apostles of their country's culture; Poussin most likely looked on himself as a Roman in artistic matters, while both Rubens and Van Dyck undoubtedly prided themselves on their cosmopolitanism.

Apart from this healthy internationalism there's another reason why the coming exhibition should be of particular interest at the present time. Futile and misleading as are the majority of analogies which we like to draw between two periods of history, there does exist a certain similarity between the intellectual and spiritual conditions prevailing in the seventeenth century and in the twentieth. The Thirty-Years' War is the only conflict that can compare with the late war in ferocity and destruction and the total collapse which it produced in Central Europe; then and now the world was divided into two ideological camps; the fanaticism and organising ability of Loyola find their counterpart in Hitler, and the world has produced no gloomier hero than Calvin until the appearance of Lenin. From this similarity, at first sight so dismal, there arises one supremely comforting fact; in few periods of history was so much really great art produced as during this time of conflict and collapse. If the analogy holds good there's hope for us yet.

While at first sight the masterpieces at Burlington

House may seem to have little enough in common with the works of our modern masters, in many cases the difference is one of technique and content rather than of inspiration and achievement. M. Helion has recently drawn a most interesting comparison between Poussin and Seurat, and though the latter has long been dead he belongs to our generation rather than his own (a fact one is perfectly prepared to accept even if one cannot follow M. Helion in his contention that it is Seurat rather than Cézanne who must be regarded as the real father of modern painting). In the work of the Italian painters of the time, of the schools of Naples and Bologna and in certain of the followers of Salvator Rosa one may detect a foreshadowing of the Surrealists and catch an echo of those tossing waves that beat on Signor Chirico's horse-infested shores.

However, it is always foolish to push such comparisons too far and in this case it is also to be guilty of an unjustified complacency. For not only have we so far failed to produce any artists of the stature of Rubens, to name but one, but we have also lost something which the seventeenth century for all its *Sturm und Drang* retained – that international tradition of which mention has already been made. Although their spirits had been troubled by cracks and crumbling in the old foundations of the Catholic faith and their minds confused by a new curiosity as to natural phenomena the artists of the seventeenth century still enjoyed the benefits of an unbroken tradition which provided them with the necessary scaffolding from which to make their experiments. There are new tendencies and novel modifications but no visible break; the High Renaissance merges into the Baroque which later gives way to Roccoco. National differences exist, in England the Baroque gains no foothold and the school of Palladio achieves its greatest if belated masterpieces, but they are differences of degree not of kind; the provincial dialects of a common language. Today in an age which is as far removed from the classic serenity of the eighteenth century and the cosy certainty of the nineteenth as was the age of Bernini and Inigo Jones, of Poussin and Rembrandt, we suffer aesthetically from the curse of Babel. We have no generally accepted criteria and until we discover them our art will never be truly comparable to that of the great periods of the past.

OSBERT LANCASTER

INDEX OF CONTRIBUTORS

(Pseudonymous contributors are listed here as they appeared; the introduction contains certain revelations.)